Also by
JENNIFER ROBERSON

__THE SWORD-DANCER SAGA__
SWORD-DANCER
SWORD-SINGER
SWORD-MAKER
SWORD-BREAKER
SWORD-BORN
SWORD-SWORN

__CHRONICLES OF THE CHEYSULI__
Omnibus Editions
SHAPECHANGER'S SONG
LEGACY OF THE WOLF
CHILDREN OF THE LION
THE LION THRONE

THE GOLDEN KEY
(with Melanie Rawn and Kate Elliott)

__ANTHOLOGIES__
(as editor)
RETURN TO AVALON
HIGHWAYMEN: ROBBERS AND ROGUES

And coming in hardcover in April 2006:
KARAVANS
A new series from Jennifer Roberson

JENNIFER ROBERSON

The Novels of Tiger and Del
Volume One

DAW BOOKS, INC.

DONALD A. WOLLHEIM, FOUNDER
375 Hudson Street, New York, NY 10014
ELIZABETH R. WOLLHEIM
SHEILA E. GILBERT
PUBLISHERS
http://www.dawbooks.com

First Trade Paperback Printing, February 2006

2   3   4   5   6   7   8   9

DAW TRADEMARK REGISTERED
U.S. PAT. OFF AND FOREIGN COUNTRIES
—MARCA REGISTRADA
HECHO EN U.S.A.

PRINTED IN THE U.S.A.

Sword-Dancer

*For Russ Galen of the
Scott Meredith Literary Agency,
because too often authors forget
to acknowledge their agents.*

Chapter 1

*I*n my line of work, I've seen all kinds of women. Some beautiful. Some ugly. Some just plain in-between. And—being neither senile nor a man with aspirations to sainthood—whenever the opportunity presented itself (with or without my encouragement), I bedded the beautiful ones (although sometimes they bedded *me*), passed on the ugly ones altogether (not being a greedy man), but allowed myself discourse with the in-betweeners on a fairly regular basis, not being one to look the other way when such things as discourse and other entertainments are freely offered. So the in-betweeners made out all right, too.

But when *she* walked into the hot, dusty cantina and slipped the hood of her white burnous, I knew nothing I'd ever seen could touch her. Certainly Ruth and Numa couldn't, though they were the best the cantina had to offer. I was so impressed with the new girl I tried to swallow my aqivi the wrong way and wound up choking so badly Ruth got off my left knee and Numa slid off my right. Ruth commenced pounding on my back awhile and Numa—well-meaning as ever—poured more aqivi and tried to tip it down a throat already afire from the stuff.

By the time I managed to extricate myself from both of them (no mean feat), the vision in the white burnous had looked away from me and was searching through the rest of the cantina with eyes as blue as Northern lakes.

Now it so happens I haven't ever *seen* any Northern lakes, being a Southroner myself, but I knew perfectly well those two pools she used for eyes matched the tales I'd heard of the natural wonders of the North.

The slipping of the hood bared a headful of thick, long hair yellow as the sun and a face pale as snow. Now I haven't seen snow either, being as the South has the monopoly on sand, but it was the only way to describe the complexion of a woman who was so obviously not a native Southroner. I am, and *my* skin is burned dark as a copper piece. Oh, I suppose once upon a time I might have been lighter—must've been, actually, judging by the paler portions of my anatomy not exposed to daylight—but my work keeps me outdoors in the sun and the heat and the sandstorms, so somewhere along the way my skin got dark and tough and—in all the necessary places—callused.

Oddly enough, the stuffiness of the cantina faded. It almost seemed cooler, more comfortable. But then it might have had more to do with shock than anything else. Gods of valhail, gods of hoolies, but what a breath of fresh air the woman was!

What she was *doing* in this little dragtail cantina I have no idea, but I didn't question the benevolent, generous fate that brought her within range. I simply blessed it and decided then and there that no matter who it was she was looking for, I'd take his place.

I watched in appreciation (sighing just a bit) as she turned to look over the room. So did every other male in the place. It isn't often you get to look on beauty so fresh and unspoiled, not when you're stuck in a dragtail town like . . . *Hoolies,* I couldn't even remember its name.

Ruth and Numa watched her too, but their appreciation was tempered by another emotion entirely—called jealousy.

Numa tapped me on one side of the face, trying to get my attention. At first I shook her off, still watching the blonde, but when Numa started to dig in her nails, I gave her my second-best sandtiger glare. It usually works and saves me the trouble of using my *best* sandtiger glare, which I save for special (generally deadly) occasions. I learned very early in my career that my green eyes—the same color as those in a sandtiger's head—often intimidate those of a weaker constitution. No man scoffs at a weapon so close to hand; *I* certainly don't. And so I refined the technique until I had it perfected, and I usually got a kick out of the reactions to it.

Numa whimpered a little; Ruth smiled. Basically, the two girls are the best of enemies. Being the only women in the cantina, quite often they fight over new blood—dusty and dirty and stinking of the Punja, more often than not, but still *new*. That was unique enough in the stuffy adobe cantina whose walls had once boasted murals of crimson, carnelian, and lime. The colors—like the girls—had faded after years of abuse and nightly coatings of spewed or spilled wine, ale, aqivi . . . and all the other poisons.

My blood was the newest in town (newly bathed, too), but rather than sentence them to a catfight I'd taken on both of them. They seemed content enough with sharing me, and this way I kept peace in a very tiny cantina. A man does not make enemies of any woman when he is stuck in a boring, suffocating town that has nothing to offer except two cantina girls who nightly (and daily) sell their virtue. Hoolies, there isn't anything *else* to do. For them *or* me.

Having put Numa in her place (and wondering if I could still keep the peace between the two of them), I became aware of the presence newly arrived at my table. I glanced up and found those two blue eyes fixed on me in a direct, attentive stare that convinced me instantly I should change the errors of my ways, whatever they might be. I'd even make some up, just so I could change them. (Hoolies, what man *wouldn't* with *her* looking at him?)

Even as she halted at my table, some of the men in the cantina murmured suggestions (hardly questions) as to the status of her virtue. I wasn't much surprised, since she lacked a modesty veil and the sweet-faced reticence of most of the Southron women (unless, of course, they were cantina girls, like Ruth and Numa, or free-wives, who married outlanders and gave up Southron customs.)

This one didn't strike me as a cantina girl. She didn't strike me as a free-wife either, being a bit too independent even for one of them. She didn't strike me as much of anything except a beautiful woman. But she sure seemed bent on something, and that something was more than a simple assignation.

"Sandtiger?" Her voice was husky, low-pitched; the accent was definitely Northern. (And oh-so-cool in the stuffy warmth of the cantina.) "Are you Tiger?"

Hoolies, she *was* looking for me!

After losing a moment to inward astonishment and wonder, I bared my teeth at her in a friendly, lazy smile. It wouldn't do to show her how much she impressed me, not when it was my place to impress *her.* "At your service, bascha."

A faint line appeared between winged blond brows and I realized she didn't understand the compliment. In Southron lingo, the word means *lovely.*

But the line smoothed out as she looked at Ruth and Numa, and I saw a slight glint of humor enter those glacial eyes. I perceived the faintest of twitches at the left corner of her mouth. "I have business, if you please."

I pleased. I accommodated her business immediately by tipping both girls off my knees (giving them pats of mutual and measured fondness on firm, round rumps), and promised them substantial tips if they lost themselves for a while. They glared at me in return, then glared at her. But they left.

I kicked a stool from under the table and toed it in the blonde's general direction. She looked at it without comment a long moment, then sat down. The burnous gaped open at her throat and I stared at it, longing for it to fall open entirely. If the rest of her matched her face and hair, it was well worth alienating *all* the Ruths and Numas in the world.

"Business." The tone was slightly clipped, as if to forestall any familiarity in our discussion.

"Aqivi?" I poured myself a cup. A shake of her head stirred the hair like a silken curtain, and my mouth went dry. "Do you mind if *I* drink?"

"Why not?" She shrugged a little, rippling white silk. "You have already begun."

Her face and voice were perfectly bland, but the glint in her eyes remained. The temperature took a decidedly downward dip. I considered not drinking at all, then decided it was stupid to play games and swallowed a hefty dose of aqivi. This one went down a lot smoother than the last one.

Over the rim of my cup, I looked at her. Not much more than twenty, I thought; younger than I'd judged on first sighting. Too young for the South; the desert would suck the fluids from her fresh, pale body and leave behind a dried out, powdery husk.

But gods, she was lovely. There wasn't much of softness in her. Just the hint of a proud, firm body beneath the white burnous and a proud, firm jaw beneath the Northern skin. And eyes. Blue eyes, fixed on me levelly; waiting quietly, without seductiveness or innuendo.

Business indeed, but then there are degrees in all business confrontations.

Instinctively, I straightened on my stool. Past dealings with women had made me aware how easily impressed they are by my big shoulders and broad chest. (And my smile, but I'm sparing with that at first. It helps build up the mystique).

Unfortunately, this one didn't appear to be impressed much one way or another, mystique or no. She just looked at me squarely, without coyness or coquetry. "I was told you know Osmoon the Trader," she said in her husky Northern voice.

"Old Moon?" I didn't bother to hide my surprise, wondering what this beauty wanted with an old relic like him. "What do you want with an old relic like him?"

Her cool eyes were hooded. "Business."

She had all the looks, but she wasn't great shakes at conversation. I shifted on my stool and let my own burnous fall open at the throat, intending the string of claws I wear around my neck to remind her I was a man of some consequence. (I don't know what *kind* of consequence, exactly, but at least I had some.)

"Moon doesn't talk to strangers." I suggested. "He only talks to his friends."

"I've heard *you* are his friend."

After a moment, I nodded consideringly. "Moon and I go back a ways."

For only an instant she smiled. "And are you a slaver, too?"

I was glad I'd already swallowed the aqivi. If this lady knew Moon was involved in the slave trade, she knew a lot more than most Northerners.

I looked at her more sharply, though I didn't give away my attentiveness. She waited. Calmly, collectedly, as if she had done this many times, and all the while her youth and sex disclaimed the possibility.

I shivered. Suddenly, all the smoky interior candlelight and exterior sunlight didn't seem quite enough to ward off an uncommon frosty chill. Almost as if the Northern girl had brought the North wind with her.

But of course, *that* wasn't possible. There may be magic in the world, but what's there is made for simpletons and fools who need a crutch.

I scowled a little. "I'm a sword-dancer. I deal in wars, rescues, escort duty, skirmishes, a little healthy hired revenge now and then . . . anything that concerns making a living with a sword." I tapped the gold hilt of Singlestroke, poking up behind my left shoulder in easy reach. "I'm a sword-dancer. Not a slaver."

"But you know Osmoon." Bland, guileless eyes, eloquently innocent.

"A lot of people know Osmoon," I pointed out. "*You* know Osmoon."

"I know *of* him." Delicate distinction. "But I would like to meet him."

I appraised her openly, letting her see clearly what I did. It brought a rosy flush to her fair face and her eyes glittered angrily. But before she could open her mouth to protest, I leaned across the table. "You'll get worse than *that* if you go near Old Moon. He'd give his gold teeth for a bascha like you, and you'd never see the light of day again. You'd be sold off to some tanzeer's harem so fast you couldn't even wish him to hoolies."

She stared at me. I thought maybe I'd shocked her with my bluntness. I meant to. But I saw no comprehension in her eyes. "Tanzeer?" she asked blankly. "Hoolies?"

So much for scaring her off with the facts of Southron life. I sighed. "A Northerner might say prince instead of tanzeer. I have no idea what the translation is for hoolies. It's the place the priests say most of us are bound for, once we leave this life. Mothers like to threaten their children with it when they misbehave." Mine hadn't, because as far as I know she died right after dropping me into some hole in the desert.

Or simply walked away.

"Oh." She considered it. "Is there no way I could see the trader *neutrally?*"

The white burnous opened a little wider. I was lost. Prevarication fell out of my mind entirely. "No." I didn't bother to explain that if Moon got his hands on her, I'd do my best to buy her for myself.

"I have gold," she suggested.

All that and money too. A genuine windfall. Benignly, I nodded. "And if you go flashing any of it out here in the desert, my naive little Northern bascha, you'll be robbed *and* kidnapped." I swallowed down more aqivi, keeping my tone idle. "What do you want to see Moon for?"

Her face closed up at once. "Business; I have said."

I scowled and cursed into my cup and saw she didn't understand that either. Just as well. Sometimes I get surly and my language isn't the best. Not much opportunity to learn refinement in my line of work. "Look bascha—I'm willing to take you to Moon and make sure he doesn't fiddle with the goods, but you'll have to tell me what you want to see him for. I don't work in the dark."

One fingernail tapped against the scarred wood of the liquor-stained table. The nail was filed short, as if it—and the others—weren't meant to be a facet of feminine vanity. No. Not in this woman. "I have no wish to hire a sword-dancer," she said coolly. "I just want you to tell me where I can find Osmoon the Trader."

I glared at her in exasperation. "I just *told* you what will happen if you see him alone."

The nail tapped again. There was the faintest trace of a smile, as if she knew something I didn't. "I'll take the chance."

What the hoolies, if that's the way she wanted it. I told her where to find him, and how, and what she should say to him when she did.

She stared at me, blonde brows running together as she frowned. "I should tell him 'the Sandtiger plays for keeps'?"

"That's it." I smiled and lifted my cup.

She nodded after a moment, slowly, but her eyes narrowed in consideration. "Why?"

"Suspicious?" I smiled my lazy smile. "Old Moon owes me one. That's all."

She stared at me a moment longer, studying me. Then she rose. Her hands, pressed against the table, were long-fingered and slender, but lacked delicacy. Sinews moved beneath the fair skin. Strong hands. Strong fingers. For a woman, very strong.

"I'll tell him," she agreed.

She turned and walked away, heading for the curtained doorway of the cantina. My mouth watered as I stared at all that yellow hair spilling down the folds of the white burnous.

Hoolies, what a woman!

But she was gone, along with the illusion of coolness, and fantasizing about a woman never does much good besides stirring up desires that can't always be gratified (at least, not right away), so I ordered another jug of aqivi, called for Ruth and Numa to come back, and passed the evening in convivial discourse with two desert girls who were not part of any man's fantasy, perhaps, but were warm, willing, and generous nonetheless.

That'll do nicely, thank you.

Chapter 2

Osmoon the Trader was not happy to see me. He glared at me from his little black pig-eyes and didn't even offer me a drink, which told me precisely how angry he was. I waved away the smoke of sandalwood incense drifting between us (wishing he'd widen the vent in the poled top of his saffron-colored hyort), and outwaited him.

Breath hissed between his gold teeth. "You send me a bascha like that, Tiger, and then say to keep her for *you?* Why did you bother to send her to me in the first place if you wanted her for yourself?"

I smiled at him placatingly. It doesn't do to rile past and potential allies, even if you are the Sandtiger. "This one requires special handling."

He swore to the god of slavers; an improbable series of names for a deity I'd never had the necessity of calling on, myself. Frankly, I think Old Moon made it up. "Special handling!" he spat out. "Special *taming,* you mean. Do you know what she did?"

Since there was no way I could know, short of having him tell me, I waited again. And he told me.

"She nearly sliced off what remains of the manhood of my best eunuch!" Moon's affronted stare invited abject apologies; I merely continued waiting, promising nothing. "The poor thing ran screaming out of the hyort and I couldn't pry him from the neck of his boy-lover until I promised to beat the girl."

That deserved a response. I glared at him. "You *beat* her?"

Moon stared at me in some alarm and smiled weakly, showing the wealth of gold shining in his mouth. I realized my hand had crept to the knife at my belt. I decided to leave it there, if only for effect.

"I didn't beat her." Moon eyed my knife. He knows how deadly I can be with it, and how fast, even though it isn't my best weapon. That sort of reputation comes in handy. "I couldn't—I mean, she's a Northerner. You know what those women are. Those—those *Northern women.*"

I ignored the latter part of the explanation. "What *did* you do to her?" I looked at him sharply. "You *do* still have her—"

"Yes!" His teeth glinted. "Ai, Tiger, do you think I am a forget-ful man, to lose such things?" Offended again, he scowled. "Yes, I have her. I had to tie her up like a sacrificial goat, but I have her. You may take her off my hands, Tiger. The sooner the better."

I was mildly concerned by his willingness to lose so valuable a commodity. "Is she hurt? Is that why you don't want her?" I glared at him. "I know you, Moon. You'd try a doublecross if the stakes were high enough. Even on *me.*" I glared harder. "What have you done to her?"

He waved be-ringed hands in denial. "Nothing! Nothing! Ai, Tiger, the woman is unblemished." The hands stopped waving and the voice altered. "Wellll . . . *almost* unblemished. I had to knock her on the head. It was the only way I could keep her from slicing *my* manhood off—or casting some spell at me."

"Who was stupid enough to let her get her hands on a knife?" I was unimpressed by Moon's avowals of her witchcraft *or* the pic-ture of the slaver losing the portion of his anatomy he so willingly ordered removed from his property, to improve temperament and price. "And anyway, a knife in the hands of a woman shouldn't pose much of a threat to Osmoon the Trader."

"Knife!" he cried, enraged. "*Knife?* The woman had a sword as long as yours!"

That stopped me cold. *"Sword?"*

"Sword." Moon glared back at me. "It's very sharp, Tiger, and it's bewitched . . . and she knows how to use it."

I sighed. "Where is it?"

Moon grumbled to himself and got up, shuffling across layered rugs to a wooden chest bound with brass. He lives well but not ostentatiously, not wishing to call excess attention to himself. The local tanzeers know all about his business, and because they get a healthy cut of the profits, they don't bother him much. But then they don't know just how healthy the business is. If they knew, undoubtedly they'd all demand a bigger cut. Possibly even his head.

Moon lifted back the lid of his chest and stood over it, hands on hips. He stared down into the contents, but didn't reach down to pick anything out. He just stared, and then I saw how his hands rubbed themselves on the the fabric of his burnous, brown palms against heavy yellow silk, until I got impatient and told him to hurry it up.

He turned to face me. "It's—it's in here."

I waited.

He gestured. "Here. Do you want it?"

"I said I did."

One plump hand waved fingers at the chest. "Well—here it is. You can come get it."

"Moon . . . hoolies, man, will you bring me the woman's sword? What's so hard about that?"

He was decidedly unhappy. But after a moment he muttered a prayer to some other unpronounceable god and plunged his hands into the chest.

He came up with a scabbarded sword. Quickly he turned and rushed back across the hyort, then dumped the sheathed sword down in front of me as if relieved to let go of it. I stared up at him in surprise. And again, brown palms rubbed against yellow silk.

"There," he said breathlessly, *"there."*

I frowned. Moon is a sharp, shrewd man, born of the South and all of its ways. His "trading" network reaches into all portions of the Punja, and I'd never known him to exhibit anything akin to fear . . . unless, of course, circumstances warranted a performance including the emotion. But this was no act. This was insecurity and apprehension and nervousness, all tied up into one big ball of blatant fear.

"What's your problem?" I inquired mildly.

Moon opened his mouth, closed it, and opened it again. "She's a *Northerner,*" he muttered. "So's *that* thing."

He pointed to the scabbarded sword, and at last I understood. "Ah. You think the sword's been bewitched. Northern witch, Northern sorcery." I nodded benignly. "Moon—*how* many times have I told you magic is something used by tricksters who want to con other people? Half the time I don't think there *is* any magic—but what there is, is little more than a game for gullible fools."

His clenched jaw challenged me. On this subject, Moon was never an ally.

"Trickery," I told him. "Nonsense. Mostly illusion, Moon. And those things you've heard about Northern sorcery and witches are just a bunch of tales made up by Southron mothers to tell their children at bedtime. Do you *really* think this woman is a witch?"

He was patently convinced she was. "Call me a fool, Tiger. But I say *you* are one for being so blind to the truth." One hand stabbed out to indicate the sword he'd dumped in my lap. "Look at *that,* Tiger. Touch *it,* Tiger. Look at those runes and shapes, and *tell* me it isn't the weapon of a witch."

I scowled at him, but for once he was neither intimidated or impressed. He just went back to his carpet on the other side of the incense brazier and settled his rump upon it, lower lip pushed out in indignation. Moon was offended: I doubted him. Only an apology would restore his good will. (Except I don't see much sense in offering an apology for something that *makes* no sense.)

I touched the sheath, running appreciative fingers over the hard leather. Plain, unadorned leather, similar to my own; a harness, not a swordbelt, which surprised me a little. But then, hearing Moon name this sword the girl's weapon surprised me even more.

The hilt was silver, chased by skilled hands into twisted knotwork and bizarre, fluid shapes. Staring at those shapes, I tried to make them out; tried to make sense of the design. But it all melted together into a single twisted line that tangled the eyes and turned them inward upon themselves.

I blinked, squinting a little, and put my hand on the hilt to slide the blade free of the sheath—

—and felt the cold, burning tingle run across my palms to settle into my wrists.

I let go of the hilt at once.

Moon's grunt, eloquent in its simplicity, was one of smug satisfaction.

I scowled at him, then at the sword. And this time when I put my hand on the hilt, I did it quickly, gritting my teeth. I jerked the blade from the sheath.

My right hand, curled around the silver hilt, spasmed. Almost convulsively, it closed more tightly on the hilt. I thought for a moment my flesh had fused itself to the metal, was made one with the twisting shapes, but almost immediately my skin leaped back. As my fingers unlocked and jerked away from the hilt, I felt the old, cold breath of death put a finger on my soul.

Tap. Tap. Nail against soul. *Tiger, are you there?*

Hoolies, *yes!* I was there. And intended to remain there, alive and well, regardless of that touch; that imperious, questioning tone.

But almost at once I let go of the hilt altogether, and the sword—now free—fell across my lap.

Cold, cold blade, searing the flesh of my thighs.

I pushed it out of my lap to the rug at once. I wanted to scramble away from it entirely, leaping up to put even more room between the sword and my flesh—

And then I thought about how stupid it would be—*am I not a sword-dancer, who deals with death every time I enter the circlet*—and didn't. I just sat there, defying the unexpected response of my own body and glaring down at the sword. I felt the coldness of its flesh as if it still touched mine. Ignored it, when I could.

A Northern sword. And the North is a place of snow and ice.

The first shock had worn off. My skin, acclimated to the nearness of the alien metal, no longer shrank upon my bones. I took a deep breath to settle the galloping in my guts, then took a closer look at the sword. But I didn't touch it.

The blade was a pale, pearly salmon-pink with a tinge of blued steel—except it didn't look much like steel. Iridescent runes spilled down from the gnarled crosspiece. Runes I couldn't read.

I resorted to my profession in order to restore my equilibrium. I jerked a dark brown hair from my head and dragged it across the edge. The hair separated without a snag. The edge of the odd-colored blade was at least as sharp as Singlestroke's plain blued-steel, which didn't please me much.

I gave myself no time for considereation. Gritting my teeth, I plucked the sword off the rug and slid it back into its scabbard with numb, tingling hands—and felt the coldness melt away.

For a moment, I just stared at the sword. Sheathed, it was a sword. Just—a sword.

After a moment. I looked at Moon. "How good is she?"

The question surprised him a little; it surprised me a lot. Her skill might have impressed Moon (who is more accustomed to women throwing themselves at his chubby feet and begging for release, rather than trying to slice into his fat flesh), but I know better than to think of a sword in a woman's hands. Women don't use swords in the South; as far as I know, they don't use them in the North, either. The sword is a man's weapon.

Moon scowled at me sourly. "Good enough to give *you* a second thought. She unleashed that thing in here and it was all I could do to get a rope on her."

"How *did* you catch her, then?" I asked suspiciously.

He picked briefly at gold teeth with a red-lacquered fingernail and shrugged. "I hit her on the head." Sighed as I scowled at him. "I waited until she was busy trying to eviscerate the eunuch. But even *then*, she nearly stuck me through the belly." One spread hand guarded a portion of the soft belly swathed in silk. "I was lucky she didn't kill me."

I grunted absently and rose, holding the Northern sword by its plain leather scabbard. "Which hyort is she in?"

"The red one," he said immediately. My, but he *did* want to get rid of her, which suited me just fine. "And you ought to thank me for keeping her, Tiger. Someone else came looking for her."

I stopped short of the doorflap. "Someone *else?*"

He picked at his teeth again. "A man. He didn't give his name. Tall, dark-haired—very much like you. Sounded like a Northerner, but he spoke good Desert." Moon shrugged. "He said he was hunting a Northern girl . . . one who wore a sword."

I frowned. "You didn't give her away—?"

Offended again, Moon drew himself up. "You sent her with your words, and I honored those words."

"Sorry." Absently, I scowled at the slaver. "He went on?"

"He spent a night and rode on. He never saw the girl."

I grunted. Then I went out of the hyort.

Moon was right: he'd trussed her up like a sacrificial goat, wrists tied to ankles so that she bowed in half, but at least he'd made certain her back bent the proper way. He doesn't, always.

She was conscious. I didn't exactly approve of Moon's methods (or his business, when it came down to it), but at least he still had her. He might have given her over to whoever it was who was hunting her.

"The Sandtiger plays for keeps," I said lightly, and she twisted her head so she could look at me.

All her glorious hair was spread about her shoulders and the blue rug on which she lay. Osmoon had stripped the white burnous from her (wanting to see what he wouldn't get, I suppose) but hadn't removed the thigh-length, belted leather tunic she wore under it. It left her arms and most of her legs bare, and I saw that every inch of her was smoothly and tautly muscled. Sinews slid and twisted beneath that pale skin as she shifted on the rug, and I realized the sword probably *did* belong to her after all, improbable as it seemed. She had the body and the hands for it.

"Is it because of *you* I'm being held like this?" she demanded.

Sunlight burned its way through the crimson fabric of the hyort. It bathed her in an eerie carnelian glow and purpled the blue rug into the color of darkest wine; the color of ancient blood.

"It's because of me you're being held like this," I agreed, "because otherwise Moon would've sold you off by now." I bent down, sliding my knife free, and sliced her bonds. She winced as stiffened muscles protested, so I set down her sword and massaged the long, firm calves and shoulders subtly corded with toughened muscle.

"You have my sword!" In her surprise, she ignored my hands altogether.

I thought about allowing those hands to drift a little southward of her shoulders, then decided against it. She might be stiff after a few days of captivity, but if she had the reflexes I thought she did, I'd be asking for trouble. No sense pushing my luck so soon.

"If it *is* your sword," I said.

"It's mine." She pushed my hands away and rose, stifling a groan. The leather tunic hit her mid-thigh and I saw the odd runic glyphs stitching a border around the hem and neck in blue thread that matched her eyes. "Did you unsheathe it?" she demanded, and there was something in her tone that gave me pause.

"No." I said, after a moment of heavy silence.

Visibly, she relaxed. Her hand caressed the odd silver hilt without showing any indication she felt the same icy numbness I'd experienced. She almost touched it as a lover welcoming back a long-missed sweetheart.

"Who are you?" I asked suddenly, assailed by a rather odd sensation. Runes on the sword blade, runes on the tunic. Those twisted, dizzying shapes worked into the hilt. The sensation of death when I touched it. What if she were some sort of familiar sent by the gods to determine if my time had come, and whether I was worthy of valhail or hoolies for a place of eternal rest—or torment?

And then I felt disgustingly ludicrous, which was just as well, because I'd never thought much about my end before. Sword-dancers simply fight until someone kills them; we don't spend our time worrying over trivial details like our ultimate destination. *I* certainly don't.

She wore sandals like mine, cross-gartered to her knees. The laces were gold-colored and only emphasized the length of her legs,

which almost put her on a level with me. I stared at her in astonishment as she rose, for her head came to my chin, and very few
men reach that high.

She frowned a little. "I thought Southroners were short."

"Most are. I'm not. But then—I'm not your average Southroner."
Blandly, I smiled.

She raised pale brows. "And do *average* Southroners send
women into a trap?"

"To keep you out of a greater one, I sent you into a small one."
I grinned. "It was a trick, I agree, and maybe a trifle uncomfortable,
but it kept you out of the clutches of a lustful tanzeer, didn't it?
When you told Moon 'the Sandtiger plays for keeps,' he knew
enough to hang onto you until I got here, instead of selling you to
the highest bidder. Since you were so insistent on seeing him without my personal assistance, I had to do something."

A momentary glint in her eyes. Appraisal. "Then it was for
my—*protection.*"

"In a backhanded sort of way."

She slanted a sharp, considering glance at me, then smiled a little. She got busy slipping her arms into the sword harness, buck-
ling it and arranging it so the hilt reared over the top of her left
shoulder, just as Singlestroke rode mine. Her movements were
quick and lithe, and I didn't doubt for a moment she *could* nearly
emasculate a eunuch who had very little left to lose anyway.

My palms tingled as I recalled the visceral response of my body
to the touch of the Northern sword. "Why don't you tell me what
business it is you have with Old Moon, and maybe I can help," I
said abruptly, wanting to banish the sensation and recollection.

"You can't help." One hand tucked hair behind an ear as she
settled the leather harness.

"Why not?"

"You just can't." She swung out of the hyort and marched
across the sand to Moon's tent.

I caught up. But before I could stop her she had drawn the
silver-hilted sword and sliced the doorflap clear off his hyort. Then
she was inside, and as I jumped in behind her I saw her put the

deadly tip of the shining blade into the hollow of Moon's brown throat.

"In my land I could kill you for what you did to me." But she said it coolly, without heat; an impartial observation, lacking passion, and yet somehow it made her threat a lot more real. "In my land, if I didn't kill you, I'd be named coward. Not *an-ishtoya*, or even a plain *ishtoya*. But I'm a stranger here and without knowledge of your customs, so I'll let you live." A trickle of blood crept from beneath the tip pressing into Moon's flesh. "You are a foolish little man. It's hard to believe you had a part in disposing of my brother."

Poor old Moon. His pig-eyes popped and he sweated so much I was surprised the sword didn't slide from his neck. "Your brother?" he squeaked.

Cornsilk hair hung over her shoulders. "Five years ago my brother was stolen from across the Northern border. He was ten, slaver . . . *ten years old*." A hint of emotion crept into her tone. "But we know how much you prize our yellow hair and blue eyes and pale skin, slaver. In a land of dark-skinned, dark-haired men it could be no other way." The tip dug in a little deeper. "You stole my brother, slaver, and *I want him back*."

"*I* stole him!" Outraged, Moon gulped against the bite of the sword. "I don't deal in boys, bascha, I deal in women!"

"Liar." She was very calm. For a woman holding a sword against a man, very calm indeed. "I know what perversions there are in the South. I know how high a price a Northern boy goes for on the slaveblock. I've had five years to learn the trade, *trader,* so don't lie to me." Her sandalled foot stretched out to prod his abundant belly. "A yellow-haired, blue-eyed, pale-skinned boy, slaver. A lot like me."

Moon's eyes flicked to me quickly, begging silently. On the one hand, he wanted me to do something; on the other, he knew a movement on my part might trip her into plunging the blade into his throat. So I did the smart thing, and waited.

"Five years ago?" He sweated through his burnous, patching the yellow silk with ocher-brown. "Bascha, I know nothing. Five years is a long time. Northern children are indeed popular, and I see them all the time. How can I know if he was your brother?"

She said nothing aloud, but I saw her mouth move. It formed a word. And then, though the sword bit into Moon's throat no deeper, the bright blood turned raisin-black and glittered against his throat.

Moon exhaled in shock. His breath hissed in the air, and I saw it form a puff of cloudy frost. Instantly he answered. "There—was a boy. Perhaps it was five years ago, perhaps more. It was in the Punja, as I traveled through." A shrug. "I saw a small boy on the block in Julah, but I can't say if he was your brother. There are many Northern boys in Julah."

"Julah," she echoed. "Where is that?"

"South of here," I told her. "Dangerous country."

"Danger is irrelevant." She prodded Moon's belly once more. "Give me a name, slaver."

"Omar," he said miserably. "My brother."

"Slaver, too?"

Osmoon shut his eyes. "It's a family business."

She pulled the sword away and slid it home without feeling for the scabbard. That takes practice. Then she brushed by me without a word, leaving me to face the shaking, sweating, moaning Moon.

He put trembling fingers to the sword slit in his neck. "Cold," he said. "So—*cold.*"

"So are a lot of women." I went after the Northern girl.

Chapter 3

I caught up with her at the horses. She already had one saddled and packed with waterskins, a little dun-colored gelding tied not far from my own bay stud. The white burnous had
disappeared somewhere in one of Moon's hyorts, so she was bare
except for her suede tunic. It left a lot of pale skin exposed to the
sunlight, and I knew she'd be bright red and in serious discomfort
before nightfall.

She ignored me, although I knew she knew I was there. I
leaned a shoulder against the rough bark of a palm tree and
watched as she threw the tassled amber reins over the dun's head,
looping one arm through as she tended the saddle. The silver hilt
of her sword flashed in the sunlight and her hair burned yellow-
white as it fell down her tunicked back.

My mouth got dry again. "You headed to Julah?"

She slanted me a glance as she tightened the buckles of the
girth. "*You* heard the slaver."

I shrugged the shoulder that wasn't pressed against the tree.
"Ever been there?"

"No." Girth snugged, she hooked fingers in the cropped, spiky
mane and swung up easily, throwing a long leg over the shallow
saddle covered with a coarse woven blanket. Vermilion, ocher and
brown, bled into one another by the sun. As she hooked her feet

into the leather-wrapped brass stirrups, the tunic rucked up against her thighs.

I swallowed, then managed a casual tone. "You might need some help getting to Julah."

Those blue eyes were guileless. "I might."

I waited. So did she. Inwardly, I grimaced; conversation wasn't her strong point. But then, conversation in a woman is not necessarily a virtue.

We stared at one another: she on a fidgety dun gelding layered with a coating of saffron dust and me on foot (layered with identical dust, since I'd come straight from the cantina), leaning nonchalantly against a palm tree. Dry, frazzled fronds offered little shade; I squinted up at the woman atop the horse. Waiting still.

She smiled. It was an intensely personal smile, but not particularly meant for me—as if she laughed inwardly. "Is that an offer, Sandtiger?"

I shrugged again. "You've got to cross the Punja to reach Julah. Ever been *there* before?"

She shook back her hair. "I've never been South at all before . . . but I got this far all right." The subsequent pause was significant. "By myself."

I grunted and scratched idly at the scars creasing my right cheek. "You got to that dragtail cantina all right. *I* got you *this* far."

The little dun pawed, raising dust that floated briefly in the warm air, then fell back to mingle once again with the sand. Her hands on the braided horsehair-and-cotton reins were eloquently competent; her wrists showed subtlety and strength as she controlled the horse easily. He wasn't placid with a rider on his back. But she hardly seemed to notice his bad behavior. "I said it before—I don't need to hire a sword-dancer."

"The Punja is my country," I pointed out pleasantly. "I've spent most of my life there. And if you don't know the wells or the oases, you'll never make it." I thrust out a hand to indicate the south. Heat waves shimmered. "See that?"

She looked. The miles and the desert stretched on forever. And we weren't even to the Punja yet.

I thought she might turn me down again. After all, she was a woman; sometimes their pride gets all tangled up with stupidity when they want to prove they're able to get along on their own.

She stared out at the desert. Even the skies were bleached at the horizon, offering only a rim of brassy blue merging with dusty gray-beige.

She shivered. She *shivered,* as if she were cold.

"Who made it this way?" she asked abruptly. "What mad god turned good land into useless desert?"

I shrugged. "There's a legend that says once the South was cool and green and fruitful. And then two sorcerers—brothers—went to war to decide who would lay claim to all the world." She turned her head to look down at me, and I saw the clear, direct gaze. "Supposedly they killed one another. But not before they halved the world perfectly: North and South, and both about as different as man and woman." I smiled in a beguiling fashion. "Wouldn't you agree?"

She settled herself more comfortably in the saddle. "I don't need you, sword-dancer. I don't need *you*—I don't need your sword."

I knew, looking at her, she was not referring to Singlestroke. A woman alone in the world, beautiful or not, learns quickly what most men want. I was no different. But I hadn't expected such forthrightness from her.

I shrugged again. "Just trying to lend a hand, bascha." But I'd lend a sword—*both* swords—if she gave me half a chance.

I saw the twitch at the corner of her mouth. "Are you broke? Is that why a sword-dancer of your reputation would offer his services as a *guide?*"

The assumption stung my pride. I scowled. "I visit Julah at least once a year. Time I went again."

"How much do you want?"

My eyes drifted the length of a well-shaped leg. So pale; too pale. I opened my mouth to answer, but she forestalled what I was more than prepared to name as my price by saying, distinctly, "In *gold.*"

I laughed at her, buoyed by her awareness of her value to me as a woman. It makes the game a little more enjoyable. "Why don't we decide that when we get to Julah?" I suggested. "I always set a fair price based on the degree of difficulty and danger. If I save your life more than once, the price goes up accordingly."

I didn't mention I knew a man was hunting her. If she knew him and *wanted* to be found, she'd say so. Her behavior said she didn't. And if that was so, the price just might go up sooner than she thought.

Her mouth twisted but I saw the glint in her eyes. "Do you conduct *all* your business this way?"

"Depends." I went over to my own horse and dug through my leather pouches. Finally I tossed a bright scarlet burnous at her. "Here. Wear it, or you'll be fried by noon."

The burnous is a little gaudy. I hate to wear it, but every now and then it comes in handy. Like when one of the local tanzeers desires my company at a meal to discuss business. A few gold tassels depended here and there from sleeves and hood. I'd cut a slit in the left shoulder seam so Singlestroke's hilt poked through unimpeded; ease of unsheathing is exceedingly important when you're in a business like mine.

She held up the burnous. "A little too subtle for you." She dragged it on over her head, arranged the folds so her own sword hilt was freed, and shoved the hood back. It was much too big for her, falling into shadowed ripples and folds that only hinted at her shape, but she wore it better than I do. "How soon can we reach Julah?"

I untied the stud, patted his left shoulder once warningly, then jumped up into my blanketed saddle. "Depends. We might make it in three weeks . . . might take us three months."

"Three months!"

"There's the Punja to cross," I shook the bleached tassels of my vermilion reins into place. Out here, nothing retains its original color for long. Eventually, brown swallows everything. In all its shades and variations.

She frowned a little. "Then let's not waste any more time."

I watched as she wheeled the little dun gelding around and headed south. At least she knew her directions.

The burnous rippled in her wind like a crimson banner of a desert tanzeer. The hilt of her Northern sword was a silver beacon, flashing in the sunlight. And all that hair, so soft and silky yellow . . . well, she'd be easy to keep track of. I clucked to my stud and rode after her.

We rode neck and neck for a while at a reasonable pace. My bay stud wasn't too thrilled to match gaits with the little dun gelding, preferring a faster, more dramatic gait (often enough, that's a full gallop spiced with intermittent attempts to remove me from his back), but after a brief "discussion," we decided on a compromise. I'd do the directing and he'd do the walking.

Until he saw another chance.

She watched me handle the stud's brief mutiny, but I couldn't tell if she appreciated my skill or not. The stud is one nobody else willingly climbs aboard, being a sullen, snuffy sort, and I've won wagers on him when betting men thought he might be the winner of the regular morning hostilities. But he and I have worked out a deal whereby he provides all the fireworks and I make it look good; whenever I come out ahead with a few coins jingling in my belt-pouch, he gets an extra ration of grain. It works out pretty well.

She didn't say a word when the stud finally settled down, snorting dust from his nostrils, but I caught her watching me with that blue-eyed sideways appraisal.

"That's not a Northern horse you're riding," I pointed out conversationally. "He's a Southron, like me. What kind of horses do you have up North?"

"Bigger ones."

I waited. She didn't add anything more. I tried again. "Fast?"

"Fast enough."

I scowled. "Look, it's a long journey. We might as well make it shorter with good conversation." I paused. "Even bad conversation."

She smiled. She tried to hide it behind that curtain of hair, but

I saw it. "I thought sword-dancers were generally a surly lot," she said idly, "living only for the blood they can spill."

I slapped one spread hand against my chest. "Me? No. I'm a peaceful man, at heart."

"Ah." With all the wisdom of the world contained in the single syllable.

I sighed. "Have you got a name? Or will *Blondie* do?"

She didn't answer. I waited, picking sandburs out of the clipped mane of my stud.

"Delilah," she said finally, mouth twisted a bit. "Call me Del."

"Del." It didn't suit her, somehow, being too harsh and abrupt—and too masculine—for a young woman of her grace and beauty. "Are you really chasing your brother?"

She slanted me a glance. "Do you think I made up that story I told to the slaver?"

"Maybe." I shrugged. "My job is not to pass moral judgment on my employer, just to get her to Julah."

She nearly smiled. "I'm *looking* for my brother. That's not chasing."

True. "Do you really have any idea where he might be or what might have happened to him?"

Her fingers combed the dun's upstanding mane. "Like I told the slaver, he was stolen five years ago. I've traced him here—now to Julah." She looked at me directly. "Any more questions?"

"Yes." I smiled blandly. "What in hoolies is a girl like you doing chasing down a lost brother? Why isn't your father handling this?"

"He's dead."

"Uncle?"

"He's dead."

"*Other* brothers?"

"They're *all* dead, sword-dancer."

I looked at her. Her tone was even, but I've learned to listen to what people *don't* say more than what they do. "What happened?"

Her shoulders moved under the scarlet burnous. "Raiders. They came north about the same time we headed south, into the border-lands. They crossed over and attacked our caravan."

"Stealing your brother—" I didn't wait for her to answer "—and killing all the rest."

"Everyone but me."

I pulled up and reached over to grab her tasseled reins. Ocher tassels, and orange, no longer bright. "How in hoolies," I demanded, "did the raiders miss *you?*"

For a moment the blue eyes were shuttered behind lowered lids. Then she looked at me straight on. "I didn't say they did."

I said nothing at all for a minute. Through my mind flashed a vision of Southron raiders with their hands on a lovely Northern girl, and there was nothing pleasant about it. But the lovely Northern girl looked right back at me as if she knew precisely what I was thinking and had come to terms with it completely, neither humiliated nor embarrassed by my knowledge. It was merely a fact of life.

I wondered, briefly, if the man Moon had mentioned tracking her was one of the raiders. But—she'd said five years. Too long for a man to chase a woman.

But not for a woman to hunt a brother.

I let go of her reins. "So now you've come south on some lengthy cumfa hunt, searching for a brother who could very well be dead."

"He wasn't dead five years ago," she said coolly. "He wasn't dead when Osmoon saw him."

"*If* he saw him," I pointed out. "Do you think he'd tell you the truth while you held a sword at his throat? He told you exactly what you wanted to hear." I scowled. "Five years makes it nearly impossible, bascha. If you're so determined to find your brother, what took you so long to begin?"

She didn't smile or otherwise indicate my irritation bothered her. "There was a matter of learning a trade," she told me calmly. "A matter of altering tradition."

I looked at the silver hilt rearing above her shoulder. A woman bearing a sword—yes, that would definitely alter tradition. North *or* South. But my suspicions about the trade she referred to couldn't possibly be right.

I grunted. "Waste of time, bascha. After so long in the South—I'm sure he's probably dead."

"Perhaps," she agreed. "But I'll know for sure when I get to Julah."

"Ah, hoolies," I said in disgust. "I've got nothing better to do." I glared at her crimson back as she proceeded on ahead of me. Then I tapped heels against the stud's slick sides and fell in next to her again.

We camped out under the stars and made a meal of dried cumfa meat. It isn't what you'd call a delicacy, but it is filling. The best thing about it is it isn't prepared with salt as a preservative. In the Punja, the *last* thing you want is salted meat, except for a trace of it to keep yourself alive. Cumfa is rather bland and tasteless, but it's dressed with an oil that softens and makes it palatable, and it's the best thing for a desert crossing. A little goes a long way, and it's light, so it doesn't weigh down the horses. I've become quite accustomed to it.

Del, however, wasn't too certain she thought much of it, though she was too polite to mention her dislike. She gnawed on it like a dog with a slightly distasteful bone; not liking it, but knowing it was expected of her. I smiled to myself and chewed on my own ration, washing it down with a few swallows of water.

"No cumfa up North?" I inquired when she'd finally choked down the last strip.

She put one hand over her mouth. "No."

"Takes some getting used to."

"Ummm."

I held out the leather bota. "Here. This will help."

She gulped noisily, then replugged the bota and handed it back. She looked a little green around the edges.

I busied myself with rewrapping the meat I'd unpacked. "Know what cumfa is?"

Her glance was eloquent.

"Reptile," I told her. "Comes out of the Punja. Mean. The adults can grow to twenty feet and they're tough as old boot leather—

about this big around." I held up my circled hands, thumbs and fingers not quite touching. "But catch and dress out a youngster and you've got a meal on your hands. I've got two pouches full of it, and that ought to more than get us across the Punja."

"Is this *all* you have to eat?"

I shrugged. "There are caravans we can trade with. And we can stop at a couple of settlements. But this will be our main diet." I smiled. "Doesn't spoil."

"Ummm."

"You'll get used to it." I stretched luxuriously and leaned back against my saddle, content. Here I was, alone in the desert with a beautiful woman. I had a full belly and the sunset promised a cool night. The stars made it ideal. Once we reached the Punja things would change, but for now I was happy enough. Some good aqivi would make it better, but when I'd left the cantina to go after Del, I hadn't had the coin to buy a bota of it.

"How far to the Punja?" she asked.

I glanced at her and saw her twisting her hair into a single braid. Seemed a shame to bind up all that glorious hair, but I could see where it might be a bit of a bother on the sand. "We'll reach it tomorrow." I shifted against my saddle. "Well, now that we're comfortable, how about you telling me how it was you knew to ask for me in the cantina?"

She tied off the braid with a strip of leather. "At Harquhal I learned Osmoon the Trader was the likeliest source of information. But finding Osmoon promised to be difficult, so I asked for the next best thing: someone who knew him." She shrugged. "Three different people said some big sword-dancer calling himself Tiger knew him, and I should look for *him* instead of Osmoon."

Harquhal is a town near the border. It's a rough place, and if she'd gotten such information out of people I knew to be close-mouthed without the right encouragement, she was better than I thought.

I eyed her assessively. She didn't look all that tough, but something in her eyes made a man take notice of more than just her body.

"So you came into the cantina looking for me." I fingered the scars on my jaw. "Guess I'm easy to find, sometimes."

She shrugged. "They described you. They said you were tough as old cumfa meat, only then I didn't know what they meant." She grimaced. "And they mentioned the scars on your face."

I knew she wanted to ask about them. Everybody does, especially the women. The scars are a part of the legend, and I don't mind talking about them.

"Sandtiger," I told her, and saw her blank look. "Like the cumfa, they live in the Punja. Vicious, deadly beasts, who don't mind the taste of people if they're accommodating enough to walk into a sandtiger's lair."

"You were?"

I laughed. "I walked into the lair purposely. I went in to kill a big male who was terrorizing the encampment. He took a few chunks out of my hide and raked me a good one across the face— as you see—but I beat him." I tapped the string of claws hanging around my neck on black cord. The claws are black, too, and wickedly curved; my face bears good testament to that. "These are all that's left of him; the hide went to my hyort." That blank look again. "Tent."

"So now they call you the Tiger."

"Sandtiger—Tiger for short." I shrugged. "One name is as good as another." I watched her a moment and decided it wouldn't hurt my reputation—or my chances—to let her in on the story. "I remember very clearly the day it happened," I said expansively, settling in for the tale. "That sandtiger had been stealing children who wandered too far from the wagons. No one had been able to track it down and put it out of business. Two of the men were killed outright. The shukar tried his magic spells, but they failed—as magic often will. So then he said we'd angered the gods somehow, and this was our punishment, but that the man who could kill the beast would reap the rewards of the tribe's gratitude." I shrugged. "So I took my knife and went into the lair, and when I came out, I was alive and the sandtiger was dead."

"And did you reap the rewards of your tribe's gratitude?"

I grinned at her. "They were *so* grateful, all the young, marriageable women fell on their faces and begged me to take them as wives—one at a time, of course. And the men feasted me and gave me all sorts of things to mark my greatness. For the Salset, that's reward enough."

"How many wives did you take?" she asked gravely.

I scratched at the scars on my face. "Actually—I didn't settle on any of them. I just made myself available from time to time." I shrugged. "I wasn't ready for *one* wife then, let alone several. Still not."

"What made you leave the tribe?"

I closed one eye and squinted up at the brightest star. "I just got restless. Even a nomadic tribe like the Salset can get confining. So I went off on my own and apprenticed to a sword-dancer, until I achieved the seventh level and became one myself."

"Does it pay well in the South?"

"I'm a very rich man, Del."

She smiled. "I see."

"And I'll be even richer when we're done with this chase."

She tightened the strip of leather that bound her hair into its shining braid. "But you don't really think we'll find him, do you?"

I sighed. "Five years is a long time, Del. Anything might've happened to him. Especially if he wound up with slavers."

"I have no intention of giving up," she said clearly.

"No. I didn't figure you did."

She tugged the burnous over her head and then carefully folded it, settling it next to her saddle. She'd been shrouded in it all day; suddenly seeing all that pale, smooth flesh again reminded me—vociferously—how much I wanted her. And for an ecstatic moment my hopes surged up as she glanced at me.

Her face was perfectly blank. I waited for the invitation, but she said nothing. She merely slid her sword free of its sheath and set it down in the sand next to her. With a rather long, enigmatic look at me, she lay down and turned her back on me, one hip thrust skyward.

The blade gleamed salmon-silver in the starlight; the runes were iridescent.

Chilled, I shivered. And for the first time in many a night I didn't strip off my burnous. Instead, I flattened myself on my rug and stared at the stars while I willed myself to go to sleep.

Hoolies, what a way to spend a night—

Chapter 4

To the inexperienced eye, the border between the desert and its older, deadlier brother is almost invisible. But to someone like me, who has spent thirty-odd years riding the shifting sands, the border between the desert and the Punja is plain as day and twice as bright.

Del reined in as I did and glanced around at me curiously. Her braid hung over her left shoulder, the end just tickling the mound of her breast beneath the crimson silk. Her nose was pink with sunburn, and I knew the rest of her face would follow soon enough if she didn't pull up the hood of the burnous.

I did so with my own, though needing it less; after a moment she followed my lead. I pointed. "That, my Northern bascha, is the Punja."

She stared out across the distances. The horizon merged with the dunes into a single mass of dusty beige. Out here even the sky is sucked dry of all color. It is a smudge of pale taupe, paler topaz; a trace of blued-steel, met by the blade of the horizon. To the south, east and west there was nothing, miles and miles of nothing. Hoolies, we sometimes call the place.

Del glanced back the way we had come. It was dry and dusty also, yet there is a promise in the land, telling you it will end. The Punja promises too, but it sings a song of death.

Her face was puzzled. "It looks no different."

I pointed down at the sand in front of the horse's hooves. "The sand. Look at the sand. See the difference?"

"Sand is sand." But before I could reprimand her for such a stupid statement, she dropped off the dusty dun gelding and knelt. One hand scooped up a fistful of sand.

She let it run through her fingers until her hand was empty, except for the glitter of translucent silver crystals. They are the deadly secret of the Punja: the crystals catch and keep the sun's heat, reinforcing it, reflecting it, multiplying its brightness and heat one thousandfold, until everything on the sand burns up.

Del's fingers curled up against her palm. "I see the difference." She rose and stared out at the endless Punja. "How many miles?"

"Who can say? The Punja is an untamed beast, bascha, it knows no fences, no picket ropes, no boundaries. It goes where it will, with the wind, freer than any nomad." I shrugged. "One day it might be miles from a settlement; within two days it may swallow down every last goat and baby. It's why a guide is so necessary. If you haven't crossed it before, you don't know the markers. You don't know the waterholes." I waved a hand southward. "Out there, bascha, death is the overlord." I saw her twisted mouth. "I'm not being overly dramatic. I'm not exaggerating. The Punja allows neither."

"But it *can* be crossed." She looked at me and wiped her hand free of dust against the crimson, tasseled burnous. "You've crossed it."

"I've crossed it," I agreed. "But before you step over the invisible border onto the silver sands, you'd best be aware of the dangers."

The little dun nosed at her, asking for attention. Del put one hand on his muzzle, the other beneath his wide, rounded jaw, scratching the firm layers of muscle. But her eyes and her attention were on me. "Then you'd better say what they are."

She wasn't afraid. I thought she might be dissembling so I wouldn't think her a weak, silly woman trying to behave like a man, but she wasn't. She *was* strong. And, more importantly, she was ready to listen.

The stud snorted, clearing dust from his nostrils. In the still, warm air I heard the clatter of bit and shanks; the rattle of weighted tassels against brass ornamentations. An insect whined by, making for one tufted, twitching bay ear. The stud shook his head violently, ridding himself of the pest, and stomped in the sand. It raised dust, more dust, and he snorted again. In the desert, everything is a cycle. A wheel, endlessly turning in the soft harshness of the environment.

"Mirages," I told Del. "Deadly mirages. You think you see an oasis at last, yet when you reach it, you discover it's been swallowed up by sand and sky, blurring in the air. Do it one time too many and you've left yourself too far from a real oasis, a real well. You are dead."

Silently, she waited, still scratching her little dun horse.

"There are simooms," I said, "siroccos. Sandstorms, you might call them. And the sandstorms of the Punja will wail and screech and howl while they strip the flesh from your bones. And there are cumfa. And there are sandtigers."

"But sandtigers can be overcome." She said it blandly, so blandly, while I scowled at her and tried to discern if she were serious or merely teasing me about my name and reputation.

"There are borjuni," I went on finally. "Thieves who are little better than scavengers of the desert. They prey on unwary travelers and caravans. They steal everything, including the burnous right off your back, and then they kill you."

"And?" she said, as I paused.

I sighed. With her, when was enough, enough? "There are always the tribes. Some of them are friendly, like the Salset and the Tularain, but many of them aren't. The Hanjii and Vashni are good examples. Both of them are warrior tribes who believe in human sacrifice. But their rituals differ." I paused. "The Vashni believe in vivisection. The Hanjii are cannibals."

After a moment, she nodded once. "Anything else?"

"Isn't that enough?"

"Maybe it is," she said at last. "Maybe it's more than enough. But maybe you're not telling me everything."

"What do you want to hear?" I asked curtly. "Or do you think I'm telling tall tales to occupy a child?"

"No." She shaded her eyes with one hand and stared southward, across the shimmering sands. "But you mention nothing of sorcery."

For a moment I looked at her sharply. Then I snorted inelegantly. "All the magic *I* need is that which resides in the circle."

The sunlight beat off the bright crimson of her hood and set the gold tassels to glowing. "Sword-dancer," she said softly, "you would do better not to belittle that which holds such power."

I swore. "Hoolies, bascha, you sound like a shukar, trying to make me think you're full of mystery and magic. Look, I won't say magic doesn't exist, because it does. But it's what you make of it, and so far about all I've ever seen are fools tricked out of their money or their water. It's mostly a con game, bascha. Until it's proved otherwise."

Del looked at me squarely a moment, as if she judged. And then she nodded a little. "A skeptic," she observed. "Maybe even a fool. But then—it's your choice. And I'm not a priest to try and convince you otherwise." She turned and walked away.

Automatically, I reached out and caught the reins of the little dun gelding as he tried to follow her. "Where in hoolies are you going?"

She stopped. She stood on the invisible border. She didn't answer me. She merely drew her gleaming sword and drove it into the sand as if she spitted a man, and then she let go of the hilt. It stood up from the sand, rune-scribed blade half buried. And then she sat down, cross-legged, and closed her eyes. Her hands hung loosely in her lap.

The heat beat at me. Moving, it isn't so bad. I can forget about it and concentrate on where I'm going. But sitting still on horseback with the deadly sands but a dismount away, I could feel only the heat . . . and a strange wonder, stirred by the woman's actions.

Eyes closed. Head bent. Silent. A shape in scarlet silk, cross-legged on the sand. And the Northern sword, made of alien steel (or something), hilt thrust against the fabric of the air.

I felt the sweat spring up. It rose on brow, on belly, in the pockets of flesh beneath my arms. The silk of my burnous melted against my skin and stuck there. I could smell an acrid tang.

I looked at the sword. I thought I saw the shapes twist in the metal. But that would take magic, a powerful personal magic, and there is so little in the world.

Except in the sword-dancer's circle.

Del rose at last, jerking the sword free of the sand. She slid it home over her shoulder and walked back to the dun, slipped tasseled reins over his flicking ears.

I scowled. "What was that all about?"

She mounted quickly. "I asked permission to continue. It's customary in the North, when undertaking a dangerous journey."

"Asked *who?*" I scowled. "The sword?"

"The gods," she said seriously. "But then, if you don't much believe in magic, you won't much belive in gods."

I smiled. "Bang on the head, bascha. Now, if the gods—or that sword—have given you permission, we may as well continue." I gestured. "Southward, bascha. Just ride south."

The Southron sun is hard on anyone. It hangs in the sky like a baleful god of hoolies, staring down with a single cyclopean eye. A burnous is good for protecting the flesh, but it doesn't dissipate the heat entirely. The fabric of the silk, over-heated, produces heat itself, burning against the skin until you shift within the folds, seeking cooler areas.

After a while, your eyes ache from squinting against the brightness and, if you shut them, all you see are crimson lids as the sun bakes through. The sands of the Punja glitter blindingly; at first it seems a lovely sort of taupe-and-amber velvet stretching across the miles, crusted with colorless gemstones. But the gemstones burn and the velvet has no softness.

There is the silence, so oppressive, save for the sloughing of hooves threshing through the sand and the occasional creak of saddle leather beneath the muffling blanket. Southron horses are bred for the heat and brightness; long forelocks guard their eyes and form a sort of insulation against the heat, and their hides are slick as silk without excess hair. Many times I'd wished *I* was as adaptable as a good desert pony, and as uncomplaining.

The air shimmers. You look out across the sand and you see the flat horizon, flat sky, flat color. You can feel it sucking the life from you, leaching your skin of moisture until you feel like a dry husk ready to blow into millions of particles on the first desert breeze. But the breeze never comes, and you pray it doesn't; if it does, it brings with it the wind, and the simoom, and the deadly sand sharp as cumfa teeth as it slices into your flesh.

I looked at Del and recalled the freshness of her pale skin and knew I didn't ever want to see it burned or scarred or shredded.

We drank sparingly, but the water levels in my botas went down amazingly fast. After a while you find yourself hyperaware of the liquid, even though you ration it carefully. Knowing you have it within reach is almost worse than knowing you have none. Having it, you want it, knowing you can have it instantly. It's a true test of willpower and a lot of people discover they don't have that in their psychological makeup. Del did. But the water still went down.

"There's a well," I said at last. "Ahead."

She turned her head as I caught up to her. "Where?"

I pointed. "See that dark line? That's a ridge of rocks marking the cistern. The water isn't the best—it's a little brackish—but it's wet. It'll do."

"I still have water in my botas."

"So do I, but out here you don't ever pass up a well. There's no such thing as an embarrassment of riches in the Punja. Even if you've just filled up your botas, you stop. Sometimes a swim can make all the difference in the world." I paused. "How's your nose?"

She touched it and made a rueful face. "Sore."

"If we find an alla plant, I'll mix a salve. It'll leach some of the pain, and the paste keeps the sun off delicate extremities." I grinned. "No use in denying it, bascha—your tender Northern flesh just isn't up to the heat of the Punja."

A twist of her mouth. "And yours is."

I laughed. "Mine's tough as cumfa leather, remember? The

Punja is my home, Del . . . as much as any place is." I stared out across the blazing sands. "If there is such a thing as home when you're a sword-dancer."

I don't know why I said it. Least of all to her. Women sometimes use such things as weapons, fighting with words instead of blades.

But Del had a sword. And it seemed she never spoke a frivolous word.

"There is," she said softly. "Oh, there is. There is always a home in the circle."

I looked at her sharply. "What do *you* know about circles, bascha?"

Del smiled slowly. "Do you think I carry a sword for mere effect?"

Well, it *was* successful. Even if she couldn't use the thing. "I saw you terrorize Old Moon with it," I admitted grudgingly. "Yes, you're handy with it. But in the circle?" I shook my head. "Bascha, I don't think you understand what a circle really is."

Her smile didn't diminish. But neither did her silence.

The bay stud picked his way down through dark umber-colored stone. After the cushioning of the sand it sounded odd to hear hoof on stone again. Del's dun followed me down and both horses picked up the pace as they smelled water.

I swung off the bay and turned him loose, knowing he wouldn't wander with water so close at hand. Del dropped off the dun, waiting silently as I searched for the proper spot. Finally I found my bearings in the huddled rocks, paced out the distance, then knelt and dug out the iron handle. It was twisted and corroded, but my hand slid into it easily enough. I gritted my teeth and yanked, grunting with effort as I dragged the heavy iron lid from the cistern.

Del came forward with alacrity, tugging the dun behind her. That's what gave me the first clue; that, and when the bay refused to drink. Del spoke to her horse, coaxing him softly in her Northern dialect, then sent me a puzzled glance. I scooped up some water, smelled it, then touched the tip of my tongue to the liquid in my palm.

I spat it out. "Fouled."

"But—" She stopped herself. There was nothing left to say.

I shoved the lid back over the cistern and dug a hunk of charred wood out of one of my pouches. Del watched silently as I drew a black X on the metal. The sand would cover it soon enough, scouring the mark away, but at least I'd done what I could to warn other travelers. Not everyone would be as we were; I've known men who drank bad water because they couldn't help themselves, even knowing it was fouled. It's a painful, ugly death.

I took one of my botas and poured good water into my cupped hand, holding it to the bay's muzzle. He slurped at it, not getting much, but enough to dampen his throat. After a moment Del did the same for the dun, using water from her last bota. We hadn't ridden hard, taking our time without pushing the horses, but now they'd have a long spell before they could water properly.

I tossed Del my last bota as the dun emptied hers. "Swallow some."

"I'm all right."

"You're burning up." I smiled at her. "It's all right. It has nothing to do with you being a woman. It's that Northern skin. A disadvantage out here, much as I admire it." I paused, noting the downward twisting of her mouth. "Drink, bascha."

Finally she did, and I could see the difference it made. There hadn't been a single complaint out of her or even a question as to how far to the next water. I appreciated that kind of fortitude, especially in a woman.

She tossed the bota back. "You?"

I started to tell her I was tough and could handle the extra miles with no water; I didn't, because she deserved better. So I drank a couple of swallows and hung the bota onto my saddle again.

I gestured, south as always. "We have enough water to reach an oasis I know. We'll fill up there. Then we'll head directly for the next well, but if that one's fouled too, we'll have to turn back."

"Turn *back*." She jerked her head around to look at me. "You mean—not go on to Julah?"

"That's what I mean."

She shook her head. "I won't turn back."

"You'll have to," I told her flatly. "If you go much farther into the Punja without knowing precisely where your next water is, you'll never make it." I shook my head. "I'll guide you to the oasis, bascha. Then we'll decide."

"*You* decide nothing." Color stood in her cheeks.

"Del—"

"I *can't* turn back," she said. "Don't you understand? I have to find my brother."

I sighed, trying to keep the exasperation out of my voice. "Bascha, if you go in without water, you'll be as dead as the rest of your family and of no use to your brother."

Loosened strands of hair framed her face. Her nose was red, and her cheeks; her eyes, so blue, were intent upon my face. She studied me so intensely I felt like a horse under inspection by a potential buyer not certain of my wind, my legs, my heart. She studied me like a sword-dancer seeking weaknesses in my defense, so as to cut me down an instant later.

Briefly, a muscle ticked in her jaw. "You don't have a family. Or else—you don't care a whit about them." There was no room for inquiry in her tone. She was utterly convinced.

"No family." I agreed, divulging nothing more.

Contempt flickered at the edges of her tone. Not quite pronounced enough to offer insult, but plain enough to me. "Maybe if you did, you'd understand." It was tightly said, clipped off; she turned and swung up into her saddle and settled the reins into place. "Don't judge—don't *devalue*—what you can't understand, Sandtiger. A sword-dancer should know better."

My hand shot out and caught one of her reins, holding the dun in place. "Bascha, I *do* know better. And I know better than to devalue *you*." That much, I gave her. "But I also know when a woman's being a fool to give herself over to emotionalism when she would do better to rely on a man's proven experience."

"*Would* I?" she demanded. Both hands clenched on the reins. For just a moment I thought she might swear at me some vile

Northern oath, but she didn't. She simply withdrew into silence long enough to collect her thoughts, and then she sighed a little. "In the North, kinship ties are the strongest in existence. Those ties are power and strength and continuation, like the birth of sons and daughters to each man and woman. It's bad enough when a single life is lost—boy or girl, ancient one or infant—because it means the line is broken. Each life is precious to us, and we grieve. But also we rebuild, replant, replace." The dun shook his head violently, rattling bit and shanks. Automatically she soothed him with a hand against his neck. "My whole family was killed, Tiger. Only my brother and I survived, and Jamail they took. I am a daughter of the North and of my family, and I will do what I must to return my brother home." Her eyes were steady; her tone more so, even in its quietness. "I will go on regardless."

I looked up at her, so magnificent in her pride and femininity. And yet there was more than femininity. There was also strength of will and a perfect comprehension of what she intended to do.

"Then let's go," I said curtly. "We're wasting time standing out here in the heat jawing about it."

Del smiled a little, but she knew better than to rub it in.

Besides, it was only a battle. Not the entire war.

Chapter 5

*L*ook!" Del cried. "Trees!"

I looked beyond her pointing arm and saw the trees she indicated. Tall, spindly palms with droopy lime-colored fronds and spiky cinnamon trunks.

"Water," I said in satisfaction. "See how the fronds are green and upright? When they're brown and burned and sagging, you know there isn't any."

"Did you doubt it?" Her tone was startled. "You brought me here, knowing there might not be any water?"

She didn't sound angry, just amazed. I didn't smile. "In the Punja, water is never guaranteed. And yes, I brought you here knowing there might not be any water, because you took care to impress upon me how dedicated you are to finding your brother."

Del nodded. "You think I'm a fool. A silly, witless woman." Not really a challenge. A statement.

I didn't look away. "Does it really matter what I think?"

After a moment, she smiled. "No. No more than it matters what I think of *you*." And she rode onward toward the oasis.

This time the water was clear and sweet. We watered the horses after testing it, then filled all the botas. Del expressed surprise at finding such luxury in the Punja: the trees offered some shade and there was grass, thick Punja-grass; hummocky, pale green, linked together by a network of tangled junctions. The sand was finer here, and cool; as always, I marveled at the many faces of the Punja. Such a strange place. It beckons you. It sucks you in and fools you with its countless chameleon qualities. And then it kills you.

The oasis was big, ringed by a low manmade rock wall built to provide shelter against simooms. Palm trees paraded across the latticework of grass. The oasis was big enough to support a couple of small tribes and maybe a caravan or two for a couple of weeks at at a time, provided the animals weren't given free rein to overgraze. Overgrazing can destroy an oasis entirely, and in the Punja not many people are willing to cut off another supply of food and water, even for their animals. What happens generally is that the nomads pitch camp for a week or two, then move on across the sands toward another oasis. That way the oasis recovers itself in time to succor other travelers, although occasionally one is destroyed by thoughtless caravans.

The cistern wasn't really a cistern, more like a waterhole. It was formed by an underground spring, bubbling up from a deep cleft in the ground. A second manmade ring of stones formed a deep pool more than a man-length across from lip to lip; a larger gods-made ring of craggy, tumbled stone jutted out of the sand like a wedge-shaped wall forming a haphazard semi-circle. It was within this larger ring the best grazing grew, tough, fibrous grass, lacking the sweet juice of mountain grass, but nourishing nonetheless.

Some seasons I've seen the spring merely a trickle, hardly filling the pool to the lip of the ring of stones. And during those seasons I approach it with sword drawn, because occasionally other travelers grow incredibly attached to the oasis, desiring no others to intrude upon it. There have been times I've had to fight just to get a swallow. Once I killed a man, so I could water my horse.

This time of year the spring runs high and fills the pool, lapping against the greenish rocks. And so Del and I, having unsaddled and watered our horses, shed our burnouses and sat in the thin shade of palms and rock ring and relaxed, enjoying the needed respite.

She tipped back her head, baring her face to the sunlight. Eyes closed. "The South is so different from the North. It's like you said—they're as different in appearance and temperament as a man and woman." She smiled. "I love the North, with its snow and ice and blizzards. But the South has its own crude beauty."

I grunted. "Most people never see it."

Del shrugged. "My father taught his children to look at all places—and at all people—with openness and compassion, and willingness to understand another's ways. You should not judge by appearances, he said, until you understand what lies beneath the clothing *or* the skin. And even, perhaps, the sex of the individual." A trace of wry humor threaded her tone. "That one's more difficult, I think, judging by Southron customs. Anyway, I don't pretend to understand the South yet, but I can appreciate its appearance."

I slapped at an insect attempting to burrow its way beneath the flesh of my thigh now bared by the absence of the burnous. I was mostly naked, clad only in the suede dhoti most sword-dancers wear; physical freedom is important in the circle. "Most people don't call the Punja a *pretty* place."

Del shook her head, and the blonde braid snaked against her shoulder as a lizard ran across the rocks behind her. "It *isn't* a pretty place. It's desolate and dangerous and angry, like the snow lions in the mountains of the North. And, like them, it walks alone, trusting to its confidence and strength. The snow lion kills without compunction, but that doesn't make it less alive." She sighed, eyes still shuttered behind her lids with their pale yellow lashes. "Its ferocity is a part of it. Without it, a lion wouldn't be a lion."

A good description of the Punja. I looked at her—head tipped back to worship the blazing sun—and wondered how so young a girl could already have such wisdom. That sort of knowledge take years of experience.

And then, looking at her, I didn't think about wisdom anymore. Just her.

I got up. I walked over to her. She didn't open her eyes, so I bent and scooped her up, carried her to the pool and dumped her in.

She came up sputtering, spitting water, startled and angry. Wet fingers gripped the rock circle and hung on as she glared at me, hair slicked back against her head.

I waited. And after a moment I saw the lines of tension wash from her face and the rigidity from her shoulders. She sighed and closed her eyes, reveling in the water.

"Soak it up," I told her. "You need to saturate the skin before we start on the next part of the journey."

She answered me by sliding under the water entirely. I watched the bubbles a moment, then turned away to my saddle to dig some cumfa meat out of my pouches.

I heard the growl before I saw the beast. When it had come out of its lair in the rocks I have no idea, but it crouched against the grass and sand with all its black claws bared and stub tail barely twitching. Long fangs curved down from the roof of its mouth and embraced the powerful lower jaw. Green eyes glowed in its wedge-shaped, sand-colored head.

A male. Full-fleshed and muscled. Sandtigers don't grow to mammoth sizes; they don't need to. They are, quite simply, small bundles of menace: short-legged, stub-tailed, practically earless. Their eyes are large and oddly unfocused before an attack, as if their minds are somewhere else entirely. But they never are. And the disarmingly weak glare—a prelude to the razor-sharp attack stare—can prove deadly, if you fall victim to it. Sandtigers, regardless of size, pack more power in hindquarters and haunches than a full-grown horse, and their jaws can break a man's arm in a single bite.

Seeing the tiger evoked enough memories to drown a man. Images flashed inside my skull. Another cat. Another male. Prepared to rake my guts from my abdomen. Or tear the flesh from my throat.

It had been a long, long time since I had seen a sandtiger. They aren't as common anymore. It's one of the reasons my name is perfect for my profession—a sandtiger is considered by some to be a mythical beast, a figment of stories and imagination. But there's nothing mythical about a tiger. There was nothing mythical about this one.

Only about me.

Singlestroke lay in harness, dumped on the ground with my

saddle. I cursed my own stupidity in being so concerned about water I neglected personal protection. Carelessness such as that could prove deadly.

I stood my ground, knowing that to move now merely invited attack. The tiger would attack regardless, no matter what I did, but I didn't want to encourage it.

Hoolies, but I didn't want that. Not again.

My hand slipped to my knife, closing around the hilt. Sweat made it slippery. I felt the knot tying itself in my belly.

Gods, not *now*.

The slitted green eyes stared with the telltale dreamy, unfocused cast. But I saw the stare begin to change.

I heard the slop of water behind me. "Stay in the water, Del."

She called something back in a questioning tone, but the tiger leaped, and I never did hear what she asked me.

The knife was out of my sheath in an instant, jabbing toward the cat, but he was smarter than I expected. Instead of leaping for my throat, coming down on my shoulders and chest with all his compact weight, this one landed on my gut and expelled all my air.

I felt the hind legs bunch up, claws spreading and opening as I went down under the impact. My knife dug in through toughened fur and hide, and I heard the tiger's unnerving scream of pain and rage.

My left hand was at the cat's throat, straining to push its gaping mouth away from my vulnerable belly. My knife hand was slippery with feline blood. I smelled the stench of dead, rotted meat on the tiger's breath and heard his snarls and tiny screams as he fought to sink elongated fangs into me. I fought just as hard to sink my knife deeper, into something vital.

One of the powerful hind legs kicked out, raking claws along my thigh. It scared me. But it also made me angrier. I already have enough sandtiger scars to show. I don't need any more.

Then I heard the cry of a female and realized Del and I had stumbled onto a cub-lair. A sandtiger is dangerous enough on its own, but a male with a mate is worse, and a female with cubs is the worst of all.

And there was Del—

I managed to roll over, forcing myself on top of the male. The position was unnatural to him and made him fight harder, but I plunged the knife in deeper and heard the horrible scream of a cat in mortal agony. It gave me no pleasure; it never does, but I had no time for recriminations. I thrust myself to my feet and turned to go after the female—

—but Del already stood there, Northern sword gripped in both hands.

Light ran down the rune-kissed blade. She stood poised before the female like a living sculpture, water running down arms and legs, hair slicked back, teeth bared in a challenge as feral as the cat's. Had I not seen the rise and fall of her breasts to indicate she breathed, I might have thought she was a statue.

Then I quit admiring her and moved.

"No!" Del shouted. "This one is mine!"

"Don't be a fool!" I snapped. "A female is far more deadly than a male."

"Yes," she agreed, and after a moment—looking at her—I understood the meaning of her smile.

The female, in slow fits and starts, crept out of the black hole in the dark-green rocks. She was smaller than her mate but much more desperate. Somewhere back in the rocks were her cubs, and she would go to any lengths to keep them safe. Del would go down before her like a piece of fluff in the blast of a simoom.

The cat pushed off the sand and leaped straight up, hind legs coiling to rake out at Del. I didn't waste a second wondering if I could do it, I just did it. I launched myself as quickly as the cat and thrust a shoulder into her ribcage as we met in midair.

I heard Del's curse and knew she'd had to hold her sword-stroke, that or risk lopping off my head. The cat went down with a cough and a grunt, the wind knocked out of her, then grunted again as I came down on top of her. I pushed my left forearm beneath her jaw, dragging her head up from the sand, and severed her throat with one stroke of my knife.

My thigh hurt. I glanced down at it as I sat hunched over the dead female and realized the male had striped me good. More scars. Then I glanced up at Del and saw her blazing more brightly than any sun.

"She was *mine!*" she cried. "Mine!"

I sighed, shoving a forearm across my sweaty forehead. "Let's not argue about it. She's dead. That's what counts."

"But you killed her and she was *mine*. You stole my kill."

I stared at her. She was white with anger, sword still gripped in rigid fingers. For a moment I had the odd impression she might bring down that deadly blade in a vicious killing swipe. *"Del—"*

She let out a string of Northern words I didn't understand, but didn't need to. The girl had mastered the most foul-sounding oaths I'd ever heard, and I'm rather good at it myself. I heard her out, letting her vent her anger, then pushed to my feet and faced her. The tip of the sword rested against my chest.

Almost at once I shivered. The blade was cold, *cold*, even in the blazing heat of the Southron sunlight. It put that finger into my soul and tapped.

Tapping: *Tiger, are you there?*

I took a single lurching step away. "That cat might have killed you." I said it curtly, more out of reaction to the sword than anger at her behavior. "Don't act like a fool, Del."

"Fool?" she blurted. *"You* are the fool, sword-dancer! Does a man steal another man's kill? Does a man forbid another man to kill? Does a man protect another man when he's perfectly prepared *and* willing to handle the situation himself?"

"Aren't you forgetting something?" I threw back. "You're not a man, Del. Quit trying to act like one."

"I'm just *me!*" she shouted. "Just Del! Don't interfere simply because of my sex!"

"Hoolies, woman, don't act like you've got sand in your head." I walked past her to the water.

"You're the one, sword-dancer," she said bitterly. *"You* are the fool if you think I'm helpless and soft and unable."

I ignored her. My thigh was afire, and reaction to the attack was setting in. I was also hungry, and anger never solves any confrontation, even in the circle. *Especially* in the circle. So I stripped off my sandals and stepped over the ring of stones into the water, blowing bubbles as I sank beneath the surface.

When I came up again, hanging onto the rocks, I saw Del twisting her way into the sandtiger lair. That got me out of the water instantly. I went dripping across the sand to her, roaring a question, but by the time I got there she was backing out again. When she was free of the crags, she shook back her damp braid and looked up at me. Clutched in her arms were two sandtiger cubs.

They squalled and bit at her, paws batting at her hands, but the claws of sandtiger cubs don't break through a membranous bud until they're three months old. It's what makes the parents so protective and vicious; cubs have no natural defenses for far longer than most animals of the Punja. These still had their milkteeth, which meant they were only half-weaned.

I swore, dripping all over the sand. "You plan on keeping them?"

"They'll die without help."

"They'll die *with* help." I squatted down, ignoring the pain in my clawed thigh, and put out my hand to one of the cubs. I couldn't deny it—at two months they were cute as could be. And about as cuddly as a cumfa. "They'll be better off if I kill them now."

Del jerked back. "Don't you dare!"

"Bascha, they're helpless," I told her. "They're *sandtiger* cubs, for valhail's sake! We don't need any more of them inhabiting this oasis, or we'll start losing people."

"People can look after themselves. These cubs can't."

I sighed again, letting the cub grab onto a finger. "Right now they have no defenses. Their teeth are blunt and their nails are budded. But in a month they'll have fangs and claws, and they'll kill anything that moves."

The cub gnawed at my hand. It was painless. The purring growl was only the merest shadow of the angry scream I'd heard coming from his father.

Del thrust the cub into my arms and cradled the other one. "They're just babies, Tiger. They deserve a chance to live."

I scowled at her, but the cub kept gnawing on my finger until it fell asleep in my arms. She was right. I couldn't do it. Tough old Tiger, professional sword-dancer.

I lugged the cub over to my burnous, put it down, watched it sleep, and swore. "What the hoolies do you want to *do* with them?"

Del was dangling her braid at her cub's nose. It batted at the hair, grizzling deep in its throat. "We'll take them with us."

"Across the Punja?" I asked incredulously. "Hoolies, bascha, I know it's a woman's prerogative to want to mother something, but we'll be lucky to get *ourselves* across. We don't need to be saddled by a pair of sandtiger cubs."

"We have no choice." She met my eyes steadily. "You killed their parents. You cut off the line. Now you owe them a debt."

"Hoolies!" I swore. "Trust me to pick up a crazy Northern woman with crazy Northern notions. And anyway—the last I heard *you* wanted to kill the female. Don't make me the villain."

Her eyes were incredibly blue beneath pale, sun-bleached brows. "You are what you are, sword-dancer."

I sighed, giving it up. "Look, I have to get some sleep. We'll talk about it when I wake up."

She quit dangling the braid at once. "I thought you wanted to go on once we'd watered and rested."

"I do. But I can't, not until I get some sleep." I saw the puzzled frown on her face. "Bascha, the claws of sandtigers are poisoned. If they claw you badly enough, they paralyze you—so they can enjoy a leisurely meal." I gestured toward my thigh. The water had washed the blood away initially, but more crawled sluggishly down my leg. "This isn't much, but it's best if I get some sleep. So, if you don't mind . . ." I stifled my grunt of effort and dropped down on my burnous, next to the sleeping cub. It—*he*—slept on, and in a moment I joined him in oblivion.

Chapter 6

The circle. A simple shape drawn in sand. Dark against light; the shallowness of the circle a chasm in the silk of the glittering sand. And yet, even in silence, the circle was loud with the promise of blood. Its scent was a tangible thing.

Mutely, I slipped out of my burnous and let it fall from my flesh. Soft silk, its slide a sibilant whisper; billowing briefly, then settling in a bright-brown puddle against the sand. Umber-bronze against ivory-taupe.

I unlaced my sandals and slipped free of them, kicking them aside. Deftly, I unbuckled my harness and let it fall atop my sandals: a pile of oiled leather, stained sienna by my sweat. But even as it fell, I slid the sword from the sheath.

Singlestroke, whose name was legendary. Blued blade, gold hilt. Blinding in the sunlight.

I walked to the edge of the circle. I waited. Against my feet the sand was hot, yet from its heat I took my strength; desert-born and bred, the Southron sun was, to me, an energizing force.

My opponent faced me. Like me, she had shed sandals and burnous, clad only in a suede tunic bordered with blue runic glyphs. And the sword. The salmon-silver sword with the shapes upon it; alien, angry shapes, squirming in the metal.

I looked at it. It touched me not, for we had yet to enter the circle, and

*still I felt the breath of death. Cold. So cold. Reaching out to touch my soul.
In the heat of the day, I shivered.*

And Del sang. She sang her Northern song.

I jerked into wakefulness and realized I *had* shivered, because
Del's hand was on my brow and it was cool, cool and smooth,
against the heat of my flesh.

Her face loomed over me. So fair, so young, so grim. Almost
flawless in its beauty, and yet there was an edge beneath the softness. The bite of cold, hard steel.

"Your fever's gone," she said, and took her hand away.

After a moment, I rolled over and hitched myself up on one
elbow. "How long?"

She had moved away, kneeling by the wall of rock behind us.
Her hands rested on her thighs. "Through the night. You talked a
little. I cleaned the wound."

I looked into those guileless eyes and saw again the level gaze
of a dedicated opponent about to enter the circle. Behind her left
shoulder rode the Northern sword, sheathed, settled quietly in its
harness, the glint of rune-worked silver almost white in the rain of
sunlight. I thought of the dream and wondered what I'd said.

But somehow I couldn't ask her.

She wore the crimson burnous again. Her hair had been re-
braided. The skin of her nose was redder than before, almost ready
to burst and peel. That blonde, blonde hair and those blue, blue
eyes pointed up the differences between North and South blatantly
enough, yet I knew it didn't have to do only with physicalities, but
culture. Environment. Quite simply: we thought differently.

And it was bound to come between us.

I assessed the tiny camp. Del knew what she was doing. Both
horses were saddled and packed, waiting silently in the heat. Heads
hung loosely at the end of lowered necks, eyes were half-shut
against the sunlight, patches of flesh quivering as stud and gelding
tried to rid themselves of bothersome insects.

I looked at Del, prepared to make a comment, and she handed
me a chunk of roasted meat. But I knew it wasn't cumfa.

Tentatively, I tongued it. "Sandtiger," she said. "I thought the male might be too tough, so I cooked the female."

The first bite was in my mouth, but I didn't swallow. It sat there in my teeth, filling up my mouth even though it wasn't that big a bite; the *idea* of eating the animal I'd been named for struck me as something close to cannibalism.

Del didn't smile. "In the Punja, one eats what meat one can find." But there was a glint in her eyes.

I scowled. Chewed. Didn't answer.

"Besides, I fed the cubs on cumfa meat mixed with milk, so I had to replace it with something."

"*Milk?*"

"They're only half-weaned," she explained. "There was still milk in the female, so I put the cubs on her. No sense in wasting what was left."

"They suckled from their dead mother?"

Del shrugged a little; I got the feeling she knew how odd it sounded. "She was still warm. I knew the milk wouldn't turn for an hour or so, so I thought it was worth the try."

To give her credit, I'd never have thought of it. But then, *I* wouldn't be so concerned with cubs bound to turn vicious in a month. Trust a woman . . . "What do you intend to do with them?"

"They're packed on your horse," she told me. "I made room in your pouches because there wasn't any in mine. They'll be no trouble."

"Sandtiger cubs on *my horse!*"

"*He* didn't seem to mind," she retorted. "Why should you?"

Ah, hoolies, some women you just can't talk sense to. So I didn't even bother. I finished the roasted tiger, which wasn't too bad, tugged the burnous over my head and stood up. My thigh still stung, but the poison had worked its way out of my system. The claw marks stretched from the edge of my dhoti to mid-thigh, but they weren't terribly deep. They'd slow me down for a couple of days, but I heal fast.

"You ready to ride?" I took a final drink and headed for the stud.

"Since dawn."

There was, I thought, the slightest hint of a reprimand in her tone. And I didn't like it. I glared at her as she mounted her little dun, and then I recalled the reason. "You're still angry about me killing the female!"

Del hooked her feet into the stirrups and settled her reins. "She was mine. You took her away from me. You had no right."

"I was trying to save your *life*," I pointed out. "Doesn't that count for anything?"

She sat atop the gelding, the crimson silk of the burnous almost shimmering in the sunlight. "It counts," she agreed. "Oh, it does, Tiger. An honorableness on your part." Her Northern accent twisted the words. "But in adding luster to your honor, you tarnished mine."

"Right," I agreed. "Next time I let you die." I turned my back on her. It's useless arguing with a woman when she has her back up, or her mind set on something. I've been in this kind of situation before, and there's *never* a simple resolution. (And while I'm the first to admit I've never embroiled myself in a conflict involving the right to kill a *sandtiger* before, for valhail's sake, the principle's the same.)

The stud sidled a little as I swung up, which made it difficult to hook my feet into my stirrups. I heard the hissing whip of his tail as he slashed it in eloquent protest of my temper. He swung his head low and brass ornamentation clashed. I heard a muted questioning mewl from one of the pouches and realized all over again I was packing two sandtiger cubs. Here I'd gotten my name from killing one, had just killed two more, and now I was hauling cubs across the desert like a besotted fool.

Or a soft-hearted woman.

"I'll take them on my horse," Del offered.

She'd already said her pouches were too full. The offer made no sense, unless it was a peace offering. Or, more likely, an implication I couldn't handle my horse.

I scowled at her, kicked the stud into a trot and headed out across the sand. The spine beneath my saddle twisted alarmingly a

moment—the stud, when he protests, is fairly dramatic about it—
and I waited for the bobbing head and whipping tail that signaled
a blowup. It'd be just like him to wait until I had a pouch full of
sandtigers, a wounded leg, and a gut full of irritation before he
bucked me off. Then I'd have a craw full of crow.

But he didn't buck. He settled, a bit hump-backed to remind
me of his mood, and walked quietly enough, for him. Del came up
beside me on her undramatic dun and kept an eye on the pouches.
But I heard no more protests out of the cubs and figured they'd
gone to sleep. If they had any sense, they'd hibernate permanently.
I wasn't looking forward to unpacking them.

"Well?" I asked. "What's the decision? Plan on raising them
as pets?"

She shook her head. With the hood up I couldn't see her hair;
her face, even shadowed by the bright silk, was pale as cream. Except for her sunburned nose. "They're wild things. I know what
you say is true: in a month they'll be deadly. But—I want to give
them that month. Why let them starve to death because their
mother's dead? In a couple of weeks they'll be weaned, and then
we can turn them loose."

A couple of weeks. She was downright crazy. "And what do
you plan on feeding them in place of milk?"

"We only have cumfa meat. It'll have to do." Her mouth
quirked a little and I saw a glint in her eyes. "Surely if a human
mouth can swallow it, sandtiger mouths can."

"It's not *that* bad."

"It's horrible."

Well, it is. No getting around it. But it's the best thing for crossing the Punja, where edible game is scarce and almost uniformly
smarter than you are.

I squinted as the sunlight flashed off the silver hilt of her sword.
So incongruous, harnessed to a woman. "Do you really know how
to use one of these?" I tapped Singlestroke's hilt, rising above my
shoulder. "Or is it mostly to scare off men you'd rather not deal
with?"

"It didn't scare *you* off."

I didn't dignify that with an answer.

After a moment, she smiled. "Asking me that question makes as much sense as me asking it of *you*."

"Implying, I take it, a vigorous yes."

"Vigorous," she agreed. "Yes."

I squinted at her dubiously. "It's not a woman's weapon."

"*Usually* not. But that doesn't mean it *can't* be."

"Down South it does." I scowled at her. "Be serious, bascha— you know as well as I do that very few women can handle a *knife* well, let alone a sword."

"Perhaps because too often the men won't let us." She shook her head. "You judge too quickly. You deny me my skill, but expect me to honor yours."

I thrust out my arm, flexing the fingers of my hand. "Because you only have to look at me—and my size—to know no woman could go against me and win."

She looked at my fingers; my hand. And then she looked at me. "You are bigger, much bigger, it's true. And no doubt more experienced than I. But don't disregard me so easily. How do you know I haven't entered the circle myself?"

I let my hand slap down against my thigh. To laugh outright at her would be uncharitable and unnecessarily rude, but I couldn't quite hide the tail end of the sound that turned into a snort of amusement.

"Do you wish it proven?" she asked.

"How—by going aginst me? Bascha . . . no *man* has gone against me and won, or I wouldn't be here."

"Not to the death. In mock-battle."

I smiled. "No."

Her mouth twisted. "No, of course not. It would be unbearable for you if you discovered I'm as good as I say I am."

"A good sword-dancer *never* says how good he is. He doesn't have to."

"*You* do. By implication."

"I don't think so." I grinned. "I wouldn't say my reputation comes by *implication*. It wouldn't be fair to Singlestroke." I hunched my left shoulder and joggled the hilt a little.

Del's mouth fell open in eloquent shock. *"You named your sword."*

I frowned at her. "Every sword has a name. Doesn't yours?"

"But—you gave it to *me*." She reined in the gelding and stared at me. "You told me the name of your sword."

"Singlestroke," I agreed. "Yes. Why?"

Her left hand rose as if to touch her own sword hilt protectively, then she stopped the motion. But her face was pale. "What did your *kaidin* teach you?" She asked it almost rhetorically, as if she couldn't believe the thoughts forming in her head. "Didn't he teach you that to make your sword's name known is to give its power to another?" I didn't answer, and she shook her head slowly. "To *share* a magic that is personal, meant only for one, is sacrilege. It goes against all teachings." Pale brows drew down. "Do you place so little trust in magic, Tiger, that you deny your own measure of it?"

"If *kaidin* is a Northern word for shodo—sword-master—then I'd have to say he taught me respect for an honorable blade," I said. "But—a sword is still a sword, Del. It takes a man to give it life. Not magic."

"No," she said. "No. That's blasphemy. In the North, the *kaidin* teach us differently."

The stud stomped in the sand as I frowned at her. "Are you maintaining you learned from a sword-master?"

She didn't appear interested in answering my questions, only in asking me hers. "If you don't believe in magic, then how did you come by your sword?" she demanded. "In whom did you quench it? What power does it claim?" Her eyes were on Singlestroke's golden hilt. "If you can tell me its name, you can tell me all of this."

"Wait," I said, "wait a minute. First of all, how I came by Singlestroke is personal. And I never said I didn't believe in magic, just doubted the quality—or *sense*—in it. But what I want to know is why you sound like you've been apprenticed."

A little of her color came back. "Because I was. I learned a little from my father and uncles and brothers, but—later, there was more. I was *ishtoya*." Her lips tightened. "Student to my swordmaster."

"A woman." I couldn't hide the flat note of disbelief in my tone.

Surprisingly, she smiled. "Girl, not woman, when my father first put a sword into my hands."

"*That* sword?" A jerk of my head indicated the weapon riding her shoulder.

"This?—no. No, of course not. This is my blooding-blade. My *jivatma*." Again, her eyes were on Singlestroke. "But—aren't you afraid your sword might turn on you now that you've told me its name?"

"No. Why should it? Singlestroke and I go way back. We look after one another." I shrugged. "It doesn't matter to me who knows his name."

She shivered a little. "The South is so—different. Different than the North."

"True," I agreed, thinking it an understatement. "And if that's your way of telling me you're a sword-dancer, it's not very convincing."

A glint came into her eyes. "I'll let my dance speak for itself if we ever meet in the circle."

I looked at her sharply, thinking of my dream; at the shrouded, hooded figure of a woman fit for a tanzeer, sharp as a blade and twice as deadly.

Sword-dancer? I doubted it. I doubted it because I had to.

Del frowned. "Tiger—is that a breeze I feel?" She pushed back her hood. "Tiger—"

We had been standing on horseback abreast of one another, facing south. I twisted in the saddle, looking back the way we had come, and saw how the sky had turned black and silver, which meant the sand was already flying.

The storm hung in the air, swallowing everything in its path. Even the heat. It's an immensely peculiar sensation, to feel the heat sucked out of the air. Your hair stands on end and your skin prick-

les and your mouth goes very, very dry. When the desert turns
cold, so does your blood, but it's from fear, no matter how brave
you are.

"Tiger—?"

"Simoom," I said harshly, wheeling around and tightening my
reins as the stud began to fret. "We're only a couple of miles from
the oasis. There's shelter back in the rocks. Del—*run for it!*"

She did. I caught a glimpse of the dun as Del shot by me. The
gelding's ears were pinned back and his eyes were half-closed, anticipating the storm. No horse likes to face into the wind, particularly a desert-bred horse, so it spoke volumes for Del's
horsemanship that she managed to outdistance the stud, even for
a moment. Our tracks showed plainly in the sand and Del followed
them easily, ignoring the rising wind.

It's frightening to ride *into* a deadly simoom. All your instincts
scream at you to turn tail and flee in the opposite direction, so you
won't have to face it. I'd never turned into the face of a simoom before and intensely disliked the feeling; it left me sweating and
slightly sickened. And I wasn't the only one: a line of sweat broke
out on the stud's neck and I heard his raspy breathing. He
crowhopped a bit, then lined out and overtook Del's dun almost
instantly.

"Faster!" I shouted at her.

She was hunched low in the saddle, hands thrusting the reins
forward on the gelding's neck. The scarlet hood flapped behind her
as my own flapped behind me, tassels glinting in the strange
amber-green light. Everything else turned gray-brown, hanging
over our heads like an executioner's sword. Only, when it dropped,
it would fall so quickly we'd never see the blow.

A cold wind blew. It filled my eyes with tears and my mouth
with grit, chapping and tearing at my lips. The stud faltered, snorting his alarm, fighting his own demons in the wind. I heard Del
shouting and turned in my saddle in time to see her little dun rear
and plunge, totally panicked. She tried to ride it out but the gelding was terrified. And the delay was costing us.

I yanked the stud around and raced back to Del. By the time I reached her she was standing on the ground, fighting the dun from there because riding him had become impossible. But now she was in danger of being trampled, and I yelled at her to let the horse go.

She shouted something back, and then the world was brown and green and gray and my eyes were filled with pain.

"Del! *Del!*"

"I can't see you!" Her shout was twisted by the storm, ripped away from her mouth and hurled into the wailing of the wind. "Tiger—I can't see *anything!*"

I dropped off the stud, slapped him on the left shoulder and felt him go down, folding up and rolling onto his side, as he'd been trained. He lay quietly, eyes closed and head tucked back into his neck, waiting for my signal to rise. I hung onto the reins and knelt next to him, shouting for Del.

"Where are you?" she called.

"Just follow my voice!" I kept yelling until she reached me. I saw a faint shape loom up before me, one hand thrust out in front of her. I grabbed the hand and pulled her to me, shoving her down by the stud. His body would shelter us against the worst of the storm, but even so we'd be buffeted and blasted senseless if the simoom lasted long.

Del's breath rasped. "I lost my horse," she panted. "Tiger—"

"Never mind." My hand was on her head, urging her down. "Just stay down. Curl up and stay next to the stud. Better yet, stay next to me." I pulled her closer and wrapped an arm around her, glad of a legitimate excuse to touch her. Finally.

"I have knife and sword," came her muffled voice. "If you'd like to keep your hands, put them where they belong."

I laughed at her and got a mouthful of sand for my trouble. Then the simoom was on us in all its fury, and I had surviving on my mind instead of seducing Del.

Well, time for that later.

Chapter 7

You don't count the minutes during a simoom, or even the hours. You can't. You simple lie huddled against your horse and hope and pray the storm will blow itself out before it strips your bones of flesh and spills your brains into the sand.

Your world is filled with the raging banshee howl of the wind; the scouring caress of gritty, stinging sand; the unremitting drying up of flesh and eyes and mouth until you don't dare even *think* about water, because to think about it is torture of the most exquisite kind.

The stud lay so still I thought, for a moment, he might be dead. And the thought filled me with a brief, overwhelming uprush of fear because in the Punja a man on foot is prey to many predators. Sand. Sun. Animals. Humans. And all can be equally deadly.

But it was only a brief moment of fear—not because I am incapable of the emotion (though, admittedly, I don't usually admit to it) —because I couldn't risk trying to find out; I was alive myself at the moment and worrying too much about the stud might effectively get me killed, which more or less goes against my personal philosophy.

Del was curled in a lump of twined limbs, face tucked down against her knees as she lay on her side. I'd pulled her against my chest, fitting my body around hers as an additional shield; it left some of *me* bare to the wind and sand, but I was more concerned about her Northern skin than my Southron hide, which was—as she'd said—tough as old cumfa leather. So Del lay cradled between the stud's back and my chest, blocked from most of the storm by us both.

Much of my burnous had already shredded, which left me mostly naked except for my dhoti. I felt the relentless buffeting of the wind and sand as it scoured my flesh. After a while it merged into one unending blast, which I blocked out fairly well in my mind. But at least Del didn't have to deal with it much; I had the feeling that if she lost *her* burnous, she'd wind up shedding more than crimson silk. Probably most of her skin.

Her back was against my chest, rump snugged up against my loins. Since I have never been the stalwart sort when it comes to denying myself the pleasures of the flesh—or, occasionally, the mind—it made things a little rough for me in more ways than one. But the circumstances certainly didn't encourage any intimate notions, so I restrained myself and concentrated mostly on simply breathing.

Breathing seems easy, most of the time. But it isn't when you're swallowing sand with every inhalation. I sucked air shallowly, trying to regulate my breathing, but it's not a simple thing when you want to suck in great gulps. My nose and mouth were masked with a portion of my hood, but it wasn't the most efficient filtering system. I cupped my hand over my face, stretching fingers to shield my eyes, and waited it out as patiently as I could.

But after a while, I sort of slid off the edge of the world into a cottony blankness with only the faintest of textured edges.

I woke up when the stud lunged to his feet and shook himself so hard he sent a shower of sand and dust flying in all directions. I tried to move and discovered I was so stiff and cramped I hurt in every fiber of my body. Muscle and sinew protested vociferously as I slowly straightened everything out. Stifling the groan I longed to make (it doesn't do to shake the foundations of a legend), I slowly pushed myself into a sitting position.

I spat. There was no saliva left in my mouth, but I expelled grit nonethelss. My teeth grated. I couldn't swallow. My eyes were rimmed with caked sand. Carefully I peeled the layers away, de-gumming my lashes, until I could open both eyes at once without fear of sand contamination.

I squinted. Grimaced. Nothing makes a man feel filthier inside *and* out than surviving a simoom.

On the other hand, I much prefer filth to death.

Slowly I reached out and grasped Del's shoulder. Shook it. "Bascha, it's over." Nothing much came out of my throat except a husky croak. I tried again. "Del—come on."

The stud shook again, clattering brass ornaments. A tremendous snort cleared most of the dust from clotted nostrils. I saw eyelids and lashes as gummed as my own, even beneath the brown forelock. And then he yawned prodigiously.

I pushed myself up, stretching to crack knotted sinews. Then I looked around, slowly, and felt the familiar grue slide down my spine.

The aftermath of a simoom is so quiet it is oppressive. Nothing is the same; everything *looks* the same. The sky is flat and beige and empty; the sand is flat and beige and empty. So is a man's soul. He has survived the savage sandstorm, but even the knowledge of survival is not as exciting as it might be. In the face of such strength and mindless fury—and the awesome power of an elemental force no man may hope to master—all you sense is your own mortality. Your transience. And an overwhelming fragility.

I moved to the stud and used the remains of my shredded burnous to finish clearing his nose. He snorted again, but I didn't curse him for the blast of damp sand and mucus that splattered me. His head drooped dispiritedly; horses fear what they can't understand, trusting to the rider to keep them safe. In a simoom, only luck keeps you safe.

I patted him on his dusty bay face and carefully de-gummed his eyes. By the time I was done, Del was up.

She was in better shape than the stud, but not by much. Her lips were cracked, gray-white, even when she spat out sand. Her face and body were one uniform color, the color of sand; only her eyes had any true hue, and they were made bluer by the raw, red rims.

She hawked and spat again, then looked at me. "Well, we're alive."

"For the moment." I unsaddled the stud and set the pouches on the sand, pulling my burnous off all the way to wipe him down. His fear had caused him to sweat and sand was caked on him, altering his color from dark bay to taupe-gray. Carefully I began scrubbing it off, hoping his flesh wasn't so abraded he'd refuse to carry us.

Del walked over to the the pouches stiffly, hissing as she discovered how much she hurt. She knelt and unlaced one of the big pouches and pulled forth the two sandtiger cubs.

I'd forgotten about them entirely. And I had put the stud down on his side without even considering the results if he'd gone down on top of the pouch they rode in. Crushed cubs.

Del, realizing it about the same time I did, sent me an accusatory glare. Then she winced and sat down all the way, cradling the cubs in her lap.

From all appearances they were unharmed and equally unsanded. Protected by the pouch, they'd slept through the entire simoom. Now they rediscovered one another and attacked, rolling around in her lap like kittens.

Except they weren't.

Already their green eyes had the unfocused menace of adult sandtigers. Their tiny stub tails stuck straight up in the air as they crouched and attacked. Watching, I thanked valhail their claws were budded and their fangs immature. Otherwise Del would have been clawed, poisoned, paralyzed, and wide awake as they consumed her flesh.

Eventually, I unplugged one of the botas and handed it to her. Del took it in shaking hands, ignoring the cubs as they rolled and tumbled and sank buds into her legs. Some of the water trickled out of her mouth, channeling dark lines in the dusted face; she cupped a hand beneath her chin in an attempt to catch the precious drops.

Her throat moved as she swallowed. Again. Again. Then she stopped herself and handed the bota back, staring at one dampened hand. The moisture was sucked into her flesh almost instantly.

"I didn't know it would be *this* dry." She squinted through gummed lashes. "It was hot before, when I crossed over from the North. But this is—worse."

I sucked down a substantial swallow of water and plugged the bota again, tucking it into the pouch. "We can turn back."

Del stared at me, eyes unfocused like those of the cubs still scrabbling about in her lap. She was—somewhere else. And then I realized she was dealing with the experience in her own way, acknowledging her fear and therefore dissipating its power over her. I could see it move through her body, knotting her sinews until they stood up beneath her dusty skin; unknotting, passing through her body like a ripple of cumfa track in the sand.

She sighed a little. "We'll go on."

I licked at my cracked lips, wincing inwardly at the pain. "We risk another simoom, bascha. There's rarely one when there can be two. Or even three."

"We survived this one."

I looked at the set of her jaw: locked into place, it was a blade beneath her flesh, sharp-edged and honed. "Your brother means *that* much to you, even though it's possible you might die trying to find him?"

She looked back at me. In that moment her eyes mirrored her soul, and what I saw made me ashamed of my question; of myself. Of my tactless, unthinking assumption that she valued her life more than her brother's.

But I was alone in the world, as I have always been, and the realization of such familial loyalty is not very easy to deal with.

Such binding, *powerful* kinship, as alien to me as the sword she bore. And the woman herself.

Del rose, cradling the cubs by fat, tight bellies as she pushed them back into the pouch. She ignored their mewling, muted protests as she laced the leather closed. Her spine was incredibly rigid. I had offended her deeply with my question.

I resaddled silently. Done, I swung up and held my hand down to Del, who used my stiffened foot as a stirrup as she climbed up behind me.

"Half-rations," I told her. "Water and food both. And that goes for the cubs, too."

"I know."

I tapped the stud's dusty sides with my heels, hooking toes into the stirrups. I fully expected him to protest the added weight—he's more than strong enough to carry a heavier second load than Del; he just likes to make a fuss—but he didn't. I felt a hitch-and-a-half in his first step out, then something very like a shrug of surrender. He walked.

We headed south again.

Surviving a simoom sucks the strength and heart out of you. I knew we couldn't go on much longer. The stud was stumbling and weaving; I swayed in the saddle like a wine-drowned man and Del slumped against my back. The cubs were probably the most comfortable of us all. I almost envied them.

The fouled well had also fouled our course. Because we had gone to the oasis, we now no longer followed the shortest way to Julah. It meant we had to go even farther before we reached water again. I knew it. Del, I had the feeling, also knew it. But the stud didn't.

A horse can't acknowledge the need for rationing. He simply wants. *Needs.* In the Punja, with the sun burning down on a blazing carpet of crystal sand, water becomes a commodity more precious than gold, gems, food. And I have known times when I was more than willing to trade a year of my life in exchange for a drink of cold, sweet water.

Even *warm* water.

The sand had scoured us dry, leaching our flesh of moisture. Slowly, we died of thirst from the outside in. The stud wobbled and wavered and drifted in a ragged journey across the bright sands. I didn't do much better, though at least I could ride instead of walk.

I roused Del twice when I slid to the ground to pour a little water into my cupped hand for the stud, but she refused her own ration. So did I. A taste can become a gulp, a gulp a sustained swallowing, and that consumes the resource so fast you only hasten your own death.

And so the water became the stud's property, and we his parasites.

I felt her hand on my bare back. "What are these marks?"

Her voice was raspy from dryness; I almost cautioned her not to talk, but at least speaking kept us from sliding all the way into a stupor.

I shrugged, enjoying the sensation of Northern flesh against Southron. "I've been a sword-dancer more than ten years. It takes its toll."

"Then why do it?"

Another shrug. "It's a living."

"Then you would do something else, given the chance?"

I smiled, though she couldn't see it. "Sword-dancing *was* my chance."

"But you might have stayed with—who? The Salset?—and avoided swordwork altogether."

"About as much as you could turn your back on your brother."

She removed her hand from my spine.

"You claim *you're* a sword-dancer," I said. "What's the story behind that? It's not exactly the sort of life every woman carves out for herself."

I thought she wouldn't answer. Then, "A pact," she said, "with the gods, involving a woman, a sword, and all the magic in a man."

I snorted. "Of course."

"A contract," she said. "Surely you understand that much, Tiger . . . or do you not have such here in the South?"

"With the gods?" I laughed, though not—*quite*—unkindly. "*Gods.* What a crutch. And the weak, who can't rely on themselves, sure know how to use it." I shook my head. "Look, I don't want to debate religion with you—it's never accomplished anything. You believe whatever you want. You're a woman; maybe you need it."

"You don't believe in much of anything, do you?" she asked. "*Is there anything, for you?*"

"Yes," I answered readily. "A warm, willing woman . . . a sharp, clean sword . . . and a sword-dance in the circle."

Del sighed. "How profound . . . and how utterly predictable."

"Maybe," I agreed, though the jibe hurt my pride a bit. "But what about you? You claim yourself a sword-dancer, so you know what the circle involves. You know about commitment. You know about predictability."

"In the circle?" I heard a measure of surprise in her tone. "The circle is never predictable."

"Neither is a woman." I laughed. "Maybe you and the circle are well-matched after all."

"No less than a woman and a man."

I thought maybe she smiled. But I didn't turn my head to find out.

Later, Del told me the stud was tired. As he'd been stumbling and trembling for quite some time, I agreed.

"We should rest him, then," she said. "We should walk." She didn't wait for my answer. She simply slid off his dusty rump.

And landed in a tangle of arms and legs.

I reined in the stud and looked down on her, admiring the clean lines of her long legs since the burnous was caught around her hips. For a moment, only a moment, my fog evaporated, and I smiled.

Del glared up at me wearily. "You're heavier than I am. Get off."

I leaned forward in the shallow saddle and joggled my right foot enough to free it of the stirrup. Then, sloppily, I dragged the leg across the stud's rump and saddle and slithered down, scraping my bare abdomen against the left stirrup. And not caring.

Discovering a desire in my legs to collapse upon themselves, I clung to the saddle until I could lock my knees. Del remained sprawled in the sand, although she had decorously rearranged the burnous.

"Neither of us is in any shape to walk anywhere," I informed her. But I bent and caught a muscled wrist, pulling her to her feet. "Hang onto me, if you want."

We staggered across the desert in a bizarre living chain: me leading the stud and Del latched onto the harness holding Singlestroke. Though he was two legs up on us, the stud didn't do much better; he had that many more legs to coordinate. He stumbled, kicking sand against my ankles. It added to the layers already there. And even though my hide is accustomed to the heat and sunlight, I could still feel the exposed portions of my body, which was everything but the areas covered by my dhoti and harness, broiling in the blistering glare. But at least I could take it better than Del, still wrapped in scarlet silk. There were rents in the fabric and most of the gold tassels were gone, but I didn't miss such questionable majesty. At least what remained protected her somewhat.

We walked. Always southward. Horse and man and woman.

And the two sandtiger cubs, oblivious of it all.

The stud sensed it first. He stopped short, head swinging clumsily eastward, nearly knocking me over. His nostrils expanded as he blew loudly, and I saw his ears twitch forward rigidly. Eastward. Telling me precisely the direction from which the threat came.

I squinted. Stared. Shaded my eyes with one hand. And eventually made out what came riding from the east.

"Hoolies," I said flatly.

Del stood next to me, mimicking my posture with one pale hand. But her puzzlement was manifest, as was her consternation. Her Northern eyes couldn't see it. I could. Clearly.

Across the horizon rose a shadow, an ocher smudge against bleached blue sky. A fine veil of sand, floating, floating, prefacing an arrival. And when the veil dissolved into the undulating vanguard of a line of riders, Del touched my arm.

"Maybe they'll share water with us," she said.

"I don't think so." It was all I could do not to snap at her.

"But the courtesy of the traveler—"

"In the Punja there is no such thing. Out here there's one simple philosophy: fend for yourself. No one will do it for you." I

didn't take my eyes off the advancing line of riders. "Del—stay behind me."

I heard the hissing whine of a sword withdrawn.

I glanced at her sharply over a shoulder and saw grim determination in her face. "Put it away!" I snapped. "Don't *ever* bare blade
in the Punja unless you understand desert customs. Bascha—
sheathe it!"

Del looked past me to the approaching riders a long moment. I
knew she was tempted to disobey me; it was in every line of her
posture. But she did as I had asked. Slowly. And when I glanced
back myself and saw the rippling black line shimmering in the heat
like a wavering mirage, I sucked in a deep, deep breath.

"Del, *do not* say a word. Let me do the talking."

"I can speak for myself." Coolly, not defiantly; a simple declaration.

I swung around and trapped her head between my hands. Our
faces were only inches apart. "Do as I say! A mouth flapping when
it shouldn't can lose us our lives. Understand?"

Her eyes, looking past me, widened suddenly. "Who *are* those
men?"

I let her go and turned around. The line of riders drew up before us, spreading out in a precise semicircle that effectively cut off
our escape in three directions. The fourth lay open behind us in obscene invitation: we'd be dead before we mounted, if we were foolish enough to try it.

Like me, they were half naked. Like me, they were burned dark
by the sun, but their arms were striped with spiraling scars dyed a
permanent blue. Bare chests bore blue sunburst designs of differing
complexities; each boy, upon reaching puberty, competes with his
peers at designing the sunburst his mother—or closest female relative—incises into his skin in a painful scarification ritual. But there
was one uniformity in all the sunbursts: each was offset by a yellow eye set in the exact center. Black hair was greased, clubbed
back, laced with cords of various colors. Black eyes dwelled avidly
on Del and me.

"Their *noses*—" she said in horror.

Well, they had them. But each nose was pierced by a flat enameled ring. The color of the rings, along with the cords in their hair, denote rank; colors are changed if they move upward or downward in the caste system. In this tribe, nothing is immutable except ferocity.

"Hanjii," I said briefly.

Del's indrawn breath of alarm was audible. "The *cannibals!*"

"They'll give us a bath," I told her. "Makes us taste better."

I ignored her muttered comment and turned my attention to the warrior who wore a gold ring in his nose, signifying highest rank and equivalent authority. I used the Desert dialect as I spoke to him; it passes as a universal language in the Punja.

I told him the truth. I left out nothing, except that Del had hired me to lead her across the Punja. And with good reason: to the Hanjii, women are slaves. Non-people. If I indicated that Del claimed any amount of authority over me, even in something so simple as an employer-employee relationship, I'd be considered a non-man and therefore perfectly acceptable for their cannibalistic rites. Since I didn't want to wind up in their cookfires, I took care to depreciate Del's value as an individual. No doubt it would earn me her enmity, if she knew, but then I didn't intend to tell her.

Unless, of course, I had to.

I finished my story, grandly embellished Hanjii-fashion, and waited, hoping Del would keep her mouth shut.

Gold Ring conferred with the others. They all spoke Hanjii with a few scattered slang terms in Desert, so I was able to follow well enough. The gist of the discussion was they hadn't had a feast for a while and wondered if our bones might appease their rather voracious gods. I swore inwardly and hoped my apprehension wouldn't transmit itself to Del.

Finally the Hanjii stopped discussing matters altogether and simply stared at us intently. Which was worse. And then Gold Ring rode forward to face us from a distance more conducive to intimidation.

Except I wasn't intimidated. Just tense. There's a difference.

Gold Ring had four knives stuck in his braided belt above the short leather kilt he wore. The others all carried two and three, which meant he held very high rank indeed.

He gestured toward the stud. "Now."

That needed no interpretation. I turned to Del. "We've been invited home for supper."

"Tiger—"

I shut her up with a hand pressed aginst her mouth. "Poor joke. They haven't decided anything yet. We're supposed to mount up and go with them." I sighed and patted the stud's dusty shoulder. "Sorry, old man."

Mustering what energy I had left (the Hanjii are merciless when it comes to tormenting those they believe are weak), I sprang up into the blanketed saddle and leaned down to offer a hand to Del. It took all I had not to fall out of the saddle as she swung up behind me.

Her hands, clasping my waist, were ice-cold.

For that matter, so were mine.

Chapter 8

*H*anjii women, like Hanjii men, believe scarification enhances beauty. I've seen the results before and therefore
can afford to be a bit blasé about them; Del, who hadn't, reacted
much as I'd expected: in horror and disgust. But, thank valhail, also
in utter silence.

The women go barebreasted to show off the designs spiraling
around their breasts, each line dyed bright crimson. Like the men,
they wear rings in their noses, but plain silver ones; women don't
earn the colors of rank through the same system. Their rank is
earned through marriage or concubinage, and it's only after
they've achieved one or the other that they undergo the scarification ritual.

You can always tell a Hanjii woman who's still a virgin because
her dark skin is smooth and unmarred, her nose free of silver. For
a man like me, who prefers unblemished women, it's easy to overlook the older women with their scars and dye and nose-rings and
look instead to the younger ones. But there is a problem: the Hanjii believe no woman should remain a virgin past the age of ten,
which leaves the unblemished girls very young indeed.

And I've never thought much of bedding babies.

"I feel overdressed." Del's whisper crept over my shoulder to
my ear, and I grinned. She *was*. Hanjii women wear only a brief

linen kilt; Del's tunic and my borrowed burnous covered almost all of her.

Which I *preferred,* in the middle of a Hanjii camp.

"Keep your hood up," I advised, and was pleasantly surprised to hear silence in return. The girl was catching on.

We were escorted by all forty members of the warrior party through the flock of dusty sheep (sheep being the tribe's primary source of food; the second being people) to a yellow hyort at the very center of the circular encampment. The Hanjii don't call them hyorts, but I couldn't think of the proper term. There we were told to dismount, which Del and I did with alacrity.

Gold Ring hopped off his horse and disappeared inside the hyort. When he came back out he was flanked by a man whose hide was liberally scarred and dyed with colors of every desert shade: vermilion, ocher, amber, verdigris, carnelian, sienna, and many more. His nose-ring was a flat plate of gold flopping down against his upper lip; difficult to eat, drink or talk, I thought, but then you don't argue with a Hanjii who thinks he's beautiful.

Besides, this man was the shoka himself.

Before anyone could say anything, I jerked Singlestroke from the sheath and knelt, pressing callused knees against hot sand, and carefully set my sword in front of the shoka. The sunlight flashing off the blade was blinding. I squinted. But didn't move again.

A dozen or so knives came out of the closest belts, but no one moved to strike. Properly obeisant, I waited, head bowed, then— judging the homage time sufficent—I rose and walked around to the right side of the stud, unlacing the largest pouch.

I pulled the two squalling sandtiger cubs from it, carried them back to the shoka, and bent to dump them at his sandaled feet.

"A gift." I spoke in Desert. "For the shoka of the Hanjii, may the Sun shine on his head."

I heard Del suck in a shocked and outraged breath—they were *her* pets, after all—but she wisely kept her mouth shut. I stood before the chieftain of the Hanjii and hoped her Northern gods thought highly of her, since she spoke to them so often. The whole enterprise was a risk. I'd heard others had managed to buy their way out of a festival fire with gifts, but no one could predict what might catch the eye—and therefore the clemency—of a Hanjii shoka.

The cubs rediscovered one another and began rolling around in the sand, growling and shrieking and generally doing a first-rate job of sounding fierce—if a trifle ineffective. The shoka stared down at them a long moment, as did everyone else. I watched his face instead of the cubs, holding my breath.

He was an older man, most likely an *old* man; it was impossible to gauge his age with certainty. In the Punja the youth gets baked out of a face very quickly, and I've seen thirty-year-olds who looked fifty. (Or older.) This warrior had a good thirty or forty years on me, I thought, which meant he was especially dangerous. You don't live to the age of sixty or seventy here without learning a few nasty tricks. Especially among the Hanjii.

He glared down at the cubs, dark forehead furrowed so that graying black brows knitted together over his blade of a nose. The Hanjii are not a pretty race, with all their scars and dyes and nose-rings, but they are impressive. And I was dutifully impressed.

Abruptly the shoka bent and scooped up one of the cubs, ignoring its outraged grunts and shrieks of protest. He peeled back the dark lips to examine its—*his*—forming fangs, then carefully spread each paw and felt the buds on each of the immature claws. Black eyes went to the string of claws around my neck, then to the scars on my face.

He grunted. "The shoka has heard of a dancer called the Sandtiger." Unaccented Desert, though he used the Hanjii habit of referring to himself as a third person. "Only the Sandtiger would ride in the desert with cubs in a pouch on his horse."

High praise, from a Hanjii. Grudging respect. (Grudging because the Hanjii consider themselves the toughest tribe in the desert; while they admire courage in others, they hate to admit others possess the attribute). I was surprised he recognized me, but said nothing about it. Instead, I looked back at him gravely. "He is indeed the Sandtiger."

"The Sandtiger has given the Hanjii a great gift."

"The gift is deserved." Careful intonation: enough negligence to emphasize the reputation of the Hanjii; enough conviction to win his approval. "The Sandtiger has heard of the ferocity of the Hanjii and wished only to add to the legend. Who but the shoka of the Hanjii would keep sandtigers in his camp?"

Who but the shoka of the Hanjii would *want* to? The cubs would prove very violent pets, but if any tribe was a match for them the Hanjii were. I'd let the shoka worry about it, although most likely he'd be delighted with their ferocity.

The old man smiled, showing resin-blackened teeth. "The shoka will share aqivi with the Sandtiger." He shoved the cub at Gold Ring and disappeared within the hyort.

"Reprieve," I muttered to Del; it wouldn't do to let the others see me speaking to her, since a woman is beneath general conversation. "Come on."

Silently, she followed me into the hyort.

The shoka turned out to be a very civil sort, generous with aqivi and compliments. By the time we finished the first bota we were good friends, telling one another what marvelous warriors we were and how no man could possibly beat us. Of course it happened to be *true;* had anyone ever beaten the shoka he'd have gone into the cooking pot, on his journey to the Sun. As for myself, had anyone beaten *me,* I wouldn't be sharing a Hanjii hyort with a rainbow-scarred shoka and a blond-haired Northern woman who was smart enough to keep her mouth shut.

By the time we finished the second bota, we were done with trying to impress one another with our battle exploits, and the talk turned to women. This necessitated the embellishment of how many conquests we had made over the years; when we had first lost our virginity—he claimed at eight, I went him better and claimed six, until I remembered I was in *his* hyort and 'admitted' I was wrong—and methods. All this made me very conscious of Del sitting so silently by my side.

After a while I tried to turn the talk to another subject, but the shoka was perfectly content to ramble on for hours about all of his wives and concubines and how tiring it was keeping so many women satisfied, yet how fortunate he was that the Sun had blessed him with endless vigor and a magnificent tool.

For a horrible moment I thought he might propose we compare, but he downed another squirt of aqivi and seemed to forget all about the subject. I breathed a deep sigh of relief that stopped short when I heard Del's muffled snicker.

It also caught the shoka's attention.

He peered at her out of black eyes that suddenly reminded me of Osmoon's: small, deep-set, piggy, and full of clever guile. He reached out and flipped back the hood, revealing bright hair, pale face, and blue, blue eyes.

It was his turn to suck in a breath. "The Sandtiger rides with a woman of the Sun!"

The sun—or Sun—is their major deity. So long as he considered Del so blessed, our safety was more or less assured. I shot her a sharp glance and saw the limpid expression in her eyes and the faint polite smile curving her lips.

"The shoka wishes to see her better."

I looked back quickly at the old man as I heard the belligerent note in his voice and saw how avidly his eyes traveled over the burnous-shrouded form.

"What do I do?" she muttered between her lips.

"He wants to see you. I think it's safe; he believes you've been blessed by the Sun. Go ahead, Del—take the burnous off."

She rose and pulled the crimson burnous over her head, dropping it at her feet in a bright pile of silk and gold tassels. She was dusty and droopy with exhaustion, but none of it hid her flawless beauty and magnificent pride.

The shoka stood up suddenly and reached out, spinning Del around before she could say a word. I was on my feet instantly, but all he did was look at the sword strapped to her shoulder.

I saw what he saw: how the alien shapes in the hilt seemed almost alive, squirming in the silver. A basket of serpents, tangled in living knots—a dragon's mouth belching flame that became the draperies of a woman; the kilt of a fighting warrior—Northern knotwork with no beginning, no middle, no end—countless, nameless things, all set into the metal.

Inwardly I shivered, recalling the touch of that sword, and how *cold*, how cold the steel felt. How it tapped at my soul, seeking something I could neither give nor comprehend.

I saw how the shoka looked at the sword and then at Del. After a moment, he looked at me. "The woman wears a sword." All friendliness was gone.

I cursed myself for forgetting to take the sword and harness from her, claiming both as my own. Routing custom in the Punja can be deadly.

I sucked in a careful breath. "The Sun shines also in the North beyond the Punja," I said clearly. "The Sun that shines on the shoka's head also shines on hers."

"Why does she wear a sword?" he demanded.

"Because in the North, where the Sun also shines, customs are different from those of the shoka and the Sandtiger."

He grunted. I could feel tension radiating from Del. We stood almost shoulder to shoulder, but even two against one would result in our deaths. Killing a shoka would simply buy us a more painful, lingering death in the Hanjii stewpots.

He looked at her again. All of her. He chewed on the tip of his tongue. "The shoka has never painted a woman of pale skin."

The thought of Del's fairness marred with scars and dye made me sick. But I kept it from him. I actually managed to smile at him. "The woman belongs to the Sandtiger."

His brows shot up. "Does the Sandtiger wish to fight the shoka of the Hanjii?"

Hoolies, he was asking for her. The Hanjii have an elaborate courtesy that circles around and around the issue until it finally comes close enough for you to figure out what they really mean. Inviting me to fight him for Del was his way of telling me he fully expected me to hand her over without argument, for no man willingly goes against a Hanjii warrior.

"He wants you to fight." Del had just discovered it. And very calm she was, too, considering the fight would be to the death.

"Looks like he might just get it, too. I mean—part of the deal we struck is to make sure you get to Julah, not into an old man's bed." I grinned. "Ever had two men fight over you before?"

"Yes," she said grimly, surprising me; but not surprising me at all, once I thought about it. "Tiger—tell him no."

"If I tell him I won't fight, it means I'm giving in to him," I pointed out. "It means I'm making a gift of you to him."

Del squared her shoulders and looked the shoka in the eye. Not a wise thing for a woman to do. And it got worse when she totally circumvented custom and spoke to him directly. "If the shoka wishes to fight over the Northern woman, he will have to fight the woman first."

Plainly put, the shoka was flabbergasted. So was I, to be honest. Not only had she ignored the rules of common Hanjii courtesy, but she also challenged him personally.

His nose-ring quivered against his lip. Every sinew in his body stood up beneath his sun-darkened skin. "Warriors do not fight *women*."

"I'm not a *woman*," she said dryly, "I'm a sword-dancer, as is the Sandtiger. And I will fight you to prove it."

"Del," I said.

"Be quiet." She'd given up on politeness altogether. "You're not stealing *this* fight from me."

"By all the gods of valhail," I hissed, "don't be such a fool!"

"Stop calling me a fool, you stupid sand-ape!"

The shoka grunted. "Perhaps it would be better if the woman fought the Sandtiger."

Del didn't see the humor in that, especially when I laughed aloud. "I will fight," she said clearly, "anyone."

A gleam crept into the shoka's black eyes. He smiled. That effectively banished my momentary good humor and Del's irritation, and we exchanged frowning glances of consternation.

"Good," he said. "The Sandtiger and the woman will fight. If the Sandtiger wins, the woman is his . . . and then he will fight the shoka of the Hanjii to see which of us may keep her." His eyes drifted from my face to Del's. "If the woman wins—" his tone expressed eloquent disbelief as well as elaborate courtesy "—she is obligated to no man, and given her freedom."

"I have that already," Del muttered, and I waved a hand to shut her up.

Hoolies, the shoka was smart. He knew I would win, thereby obliging his wish to fight me for Del. There was no way he believed Del capable of fighting me on a warrior's terms, so he was certain of winning her in the end because the shoka would be fresh while I was not—*and* after I'd let him see my habits in the circle, which is an advantage every man likes to have. It would make his victory all the sweeter.

I looked at Del and saw the realization in her eyes. Then I saw a tightening of her face and defiant determination—and felt the first brush of fear.

I couldn't throw the fight. To do so would damage my reputation; while I was certain I could survive the damage ordinarily, the shoka would be so insulted he might forget all about letting us live. We'd undoubtedly become dinner.

Besides, there is no way I'd deliberately lose to a woman. There's such a thing as pride.

Del smiled. "See you in the circle."

"Ah, hoolies," I said in disgust.

Within a matter of minutes the news made the rounds of the camp. Everyone knew the Northern woman and the Sandtiger would meet in a circle for the sword-dancer. The Hanjii don't have swords, but they do appreciate a good dance. And they're masters with the knife. Once I'd defeated Del, I'd have to give up Singlestroke and fight the shoka with my knife, which isn't my strongest weapon. I'm deadly enough with it, but the sword is my magic and I've always felt incredibly at ease with Singlestroke resting so comfortably in my hands.

Del hadn't bothered to put the burnous back on. We stood outside the hyort in full view of the camp, and her fair coloring and unblemished skin were causing a lot of comment. Me they ignored altogether.

"I can't throw the dance," I told her quietly. "You know that. It has to be real."

She slanted me an enigmatic glance. "I admire your modesty."

"Del—"

"I dance to win," she said evenly. "You need have no fear of damaging your name or your pride by matching a woman who will go down with the first stroke. The Hanjii won't be disappointed."

"Del, I don't want to hurt you. But if I hold back too much, they'll know it."

"So don't hold back," she suggested.

"I just want to apologize in advance for any cuts and bruises."

"*Ah.*"

I scowled at her. "Del, come on—be serious about this."

"I *am* serious. I don't think *you* are."

"Of course I'm serious!"

She faced me squarely. "If you were truly serious, you'd stop talking and simply judge me as a dancer instead of as a woman."

She had a point, much as I hated to admit it. Never before had I *apologized* for any injuries I might administer to an opponent. The whole thing suddenly struck me as ludicrous, so I ignored her altogether and stared grimly out at the gathering Hanjii.

Del started singing softly under her breath.

We were both tired and sunburned and sand-scoured and uncertain of the dance facing us. Del's face was unreadable, but I could see it in her eyes. For all her proud talk, I doubted she'd ever gone against a man before.

As for me, I felt helpless and exasperated. I knew she'd fight me with all her strength and skill—expecting me to do the same—yet knowing I'd be hampered by the knowledge of her sex. It was an advantage for her. And I wasn't about to give in to it.

She was still singing softly as the Hanjii warrior with the gold nose-ring led us to the circle drawn in the sand. Del unlaced her sandals and tossed them aside; I did the same. Both of us were unharnessed, having shed them in the shoka's hyort along with our burnouses. And then she unsheathed her sword.

I heard startled exclamations, indrawn breaths, astonished mutters. Well, I couldn't really blame the Hanjii. Cold, clean steel can startle anyone not accustomed to it. But then, Del's sword was not precisely clean *steel.*

But cold? Yes. Unequivocally. She unsheathed that thing in the bright sunlight of the Punja, and the day immediately altered. It wasn't just that she was a stranger from the North or a woman with a sword. It was as if the black cloud of a summer storm had shut away the face of the sun, banishing the heat.

Hot? Yes. Still was. But I felt the flesh tighten and rise on my bones, and shivered.

She stood just outside the circle. Barefoot, bare-legged, bare-armed. Waiting. With that unearthly sword held lightly in one hand.

I glanced briefly at Singlestroke. Blue-steel, glinting in the sunlight. Honed and polished and prepared, as Singlestroke always was. But—there was a difference. For all he was a formidable sword, he didn't alter the tenor of the day.

Together we stepped into the circle and walked to the center, to the blood-red rug spread precisely in the middle of the circle. We set our weapons down carefully.

Singlestroke was inches longer and certainly heavier than her nameless Northern sword. No, not nameless—just unnamed to me. I thought the weapons as unevenly matched as we were.

Perhaps that's what got the Hanjii so excited. They crowded around the circle like men wagering on a dog fight.

Del and I walked to opposite sides of the circle and stepped outside facing one another. It would be a foot race to the swords in the center, then the sword-dance proper, full of feints and slashes, footwork and flashing blades.

Her lips still moved in the song. And as I looked at her I was revisited by my dream: a Northern woman singing a Northern sword-song facing me across the circle.

I felt an unearthly tremor slide down my spine. Shook it away with effort. "Luck, Del," I called to her. She tilted her head, considering it. She smiled, laughed—

—and then she was racing for her sword.

Chapter 9

el's sword was in her hands and slashing at my face before I got my hands on Singlestroke. I felt the breeze—oddly, in this heat, a *cool* one—as the Northern blade whipped over my head in a bizarre salute. By then Singlestroke was up and facing her, and she backed off. But the first blow had been struck, and it was hers.

I did not return it immediately. I moved away, slipping through the sand to the edge of the circle, and watched her. I watched how she held her sword, judging her grip; watched how her thighs flexed, muscles rolling; watched how she watched me.

And I watched the sword.

It was silver-hilted, the blade a pale, subtle pink; not the pink of flowers or women, but the pink of watered blood. There was an edge to it. Hard, honed, prepared, just as Singlestroke was. But my blade was plain. Runes like water ran down Del's blade from the twisted, elegant crosspiece to the tip. In the sunlight, they glittered like diamonds. Like ice. Hard, cold, ice.

And for just a moment, as I looked at the blade, I could have sworn it was still sheathed; not in leather, but ice. Ice-warded against the heat of the Southron sun.

And the skill of a Southron sword-dancer.

Del waited. Across the circle, she simply waited. There was no tension in her body, no energy wasted in anticipation. Patiently, unperturbedly, she waited, assessing me as I assessed her; judging my skill with the eye of a student taught the rituals of the dance by a shodo. Or, in her language, a *kaidin*.

Silver. White, blinding metal tinged with salmon-pink, intensified by the sunlight. And as she swept the sword up to salute the beginnings of the dance, a salmon-silver line seemed to follow the motion of the blade like a shooting star trailing smoke and flame.

Hoolies, what *was* that sword?

But the dance was begun, and I had no more time for questions or imagery.

Del moved around the circle in a blaze of yellow hair, feinting and laughing and calling out encouragement in her Northern tongue. The muscles in her calves and forearms flexed, sinews standing up in ridges whenever she shifted her stance. I let her do most of the dancing while I judged her technique.

No doubt my performance disappointed the Hanjii for its lack of fire, but I was too busy trying to discover a weak spot in Del's defense to give it a thought.

Like her, I stayed up on the balls of my feet, weight shifted forward, evenly distributed. I moved through the sand smoothly, but I don't rely on the supple quickness that appeared to be her particular strength. My dance is one of strength and endurance and strategy. I'm too heavy for suppleness, too muscled for that light quickness, though far from being slow. But Del's upright posture and amazingly precise blade patterns made me look like a lumbering behemoth.

Still, we were poorly matched. It wasn't a proper sword-dance, because neither of us particularly wanted to dance against the other. At least, *I* didn't want to dance against Del. She looked fairly well pleased by it, herself.

Singlestroke beat back her every advance with ease. I had a longer reach, longer sword; she was quicker but couldn't get in close enough, so her advantage didn't tip the odds in her favor. On the other hand, I was clearly hampered by not wishing to hurt her. I didn't employ my strength and experience to overcome her utterly. We danced like a coy, teasing mare and a determined, frustrated stud; neither winning, neither losing, and both of us getting wearier by the moment.

Some sword-dance. The simoom had sapped us of energy, no matter what the demands for greater exertion under these bizarre circumstances. Pride notwithstanding, neither of us had the endurance to make a proper showing. We simply followed the rituals perfunctorily, without exhibiting the skills and techniques a shodo-trained sword-dancer ordinarily exhibits.

But then Del wasn't really a sword-dancer, even if she did claim to be *kaidin*-trained. Southroner I am, but I'm also a professional sword-dancer; one of the responsibilities of the profession is keeping up to date on all sword-related customs.

And women weren't part of them, even in the North.

But she was good. Incredibly good. Even slowed by fatigue and heat, even pressed as she was, her skill was obvious. Her blade work was limited to a small area generally, pointing up the unexpected strength in her wrists and the differences in our styles. Tall as I am, my reach is much longer than that of most opponents. Singlestroke is correspondingly longer and heavier, therefore. Which gives me an advantage over many men. But not much of one over Del.

Rarely did she employ scything sweeps or thrusts that might overextend her balance; never did she exhibit the frustration that often leads men to attempt foolhardy patterns that do little more than tire them or leave them open to counterthrust. I used a few of my ploys, trying to force her into my style of fighting (which would, of course, jar her out of her own and make my victory easier), but she didn't fall for my 'suggestions'. She just danced.

Coolly, so coolly, she danced. Blocked, feinted, riposted. Parried. Thrust, tightly and with incredible forearm/wrist control. Caught my own blade again and again, twisting it aside. Smoothly, so smoothly, she danced.

Hoolies, but how the woman could dance!

Nonetheless, fatigue began to take its toll. Del's face slowly flushed an alarming shade of red. It was already burned from the sun, and the rising color only confirmed she was on the edge of imminent collapse. The combination of sun and heat and sand would overcome her long before I could.

Especially as I was just as worn out as *she* was, and more than ready to call a halt to this farce.

Again and again Del dipped her head to scrub her brow against an arm, wiping away the sweat that threatened her vision. I was covered by it myself, aware of it trickling down my belly, my back, my brow. But I am more accustomed to it, and accustomed to ignoring it, and I didn't allow it to distract me.

I worried about her. I worried so much I forgot about the object of the sword-dance, which is victory. Del's blade twisted out from under mine and came up to nick the underside of my left forearm, spilling blood so fast it stained the taupe-gray sand vermilion.

For a moment I hesitated (which was stupid), then leveled my sword in renewed defense.

Del's teeth were gritted so hard the muscles of her jaw stood up, sculpting her face into a mask of delicate marble; silk and satin and infinitely seductive. As well as determinedly dangerous. "Fight me—" she gasped. "Don't just throw up a guard—*fight* me!"

So I did. I stepped forward, feinting a stroke that I quickly turned against her. I slapped the flat of my blade against her upper arm, smacking it hard enough to raise a welt instantly. Had I used the edge, it would have sheared off her arm at the shoulder.

The Hanjii were a blur. Part of me heard their voices muttering and mumbling, but most of me was focused on the dance, and my opponent. Breathing came hard and painful because I was hot and tired and dehydrated, yet somehow I had to conserve my strength for the second fight. If I allowed Del to tire me too much, I'd go down far too easily beneath the shoka's knife.

"I dance to *win*—" Del lunged at me across the circle.

I'll admit it, she caught me by surprise. Her sword slid easily under my guard, nicked the heel of my hand and continued along the line of my ribs.

Angrily I slapped the flat of her blade aside with my bare hand (not generally recommended, but she'd stabbed my pride with the move), caught her wrist and squeezed hard enough to drop the sword from her hand. Her red face went white with pain. Ignoring it, I hooked an ankle around her feet and jerked.

(Not precisely a move approved by the shodos, either, but then this had gone past being a ritualized dance).

Del went down. Hard. She bit her lip, which bled immediately, and sprawled so awkwardly I almost felt sorry for her. She had blooded me twice, but in a single move I'd disarmed and tripped her onto her back, leaving her throat bare to my blade. I had only to rest the tip against her neck and ask for her to yield, and the dance was done.

But not for Del. Her sword was out of reach, but not the rug. I'd forgotten about it. She hadn't. She tore it from the sand, threw it around Singlestroke to foul the blade, then scooped a handful of sand into my face.

To hoolies with the sword and the dance! I dumped it and lunged for Del, blind but not helpless. Both hands went around a slim ankle. I heard her cry out and felt her struggle, twisting, but I dragged her to me, inch by inch. Through the sand clogging my vision I saw her hand clawing out for the nearest sword—my own—but both were out of reach.

"*I* don't need the sword to win," I jeered, trying not to gasp aloud. "*I* can kill you with my bare hands. How do you want it, bascha?" I put my hands around her throat and hung over her, knees on either side of her hips. "I can strangle you, or break your neck, or just plain *sit* on you until you suffocate." I paused. "You can't do anything to me—you can't even *move*—so why don't we just end this little farce? Do you yield?"

Blood from her bitten lip was smeared across her face, mingling with the dusting of sand. Her breasts quivered as she struggled to breathe, which only made me want to forget all about winning and smother her in another fashion, with my mouth on hers.

Del twisted her hips and jammed a knee up between my spread thighs. Hard.

Once I finished making a thoroughly disgusting and humiliating spectacle of myself by throwing up into the sand, I realized the dance was decidedly over. So I just lay there trying to recover my breath and composure while over a hundred Hanjii warriors and double the number of wives and concubines looked on in silence. And astonishment.

But I thought the women looked suspiciously satisfied.

Del stood over me with her rune-worked sword grasped in one hand. "I have to ask you to yield," she pointed out. "Are you all right?"

"Are you happy now?" I croaked, refusing to give into the urge to cradle the portion of my anatomy she'd nearly destroyed. "You practically turned me into a eunuch without even using a knife."

Del's expression was suitably apologetic, but I saw something lurking in the corners of her eyes. "I'm sorry," she said. "It was a trick. It wasn't fair."

At least she *admitted* it. I just lay there on my side and stared up at her, wishing I had the strength to jerk her down into the sand again. But I knew any sort of violent—or even nonviolent—movement would renew the pain, and so I didn't. "Hoolies, woman, why do you even bother with a sword? You can beat a man with a *knee!*"

"I have to ask you to yield," she reminded me. "Or do you wish to continue the sword-dance?"

"That wasn't a dance," I retorted. "Not a *proper* one. And I don't think I can continue anything right now." I scowled up at her. "All right, bascha . . . I yield. *This* time. And I think even the shoka will be satisfied that the woman beat the Sandtiger."

She pushed loose hair back with one hand. "You're right, it wasn't proper. My *kaidin* would be outraged. But—it's a trick my brothers taught me. A woman's trick."

I sat up and wished I hadn't. "Your brothers taught you *that?*"

"They said that I needed an advantage."

"Advantage!" I said in disgust. "Hoolies, Del—you almost ruined me for life. How would you like *that* on your conscience?"

She looked at me for a long moment, shrugged a little, and turned her back on me as she marched across the circle to the shoka. By the time I was on my feet (trying to act as if I felt fine) and had Singlestroke in harness again, strapped on, the shoka himself had buckled the harness on her, though he studiously avoided touching the sword. A mark of high respect, since ordinarily the Hanjii shun anything to do with swords. (And women, too, much of the time.)

He looked at me as I joined them. "The dance was good. The woman was good. The Sandtiger was not so good."

Privately I agreed with him, but I didn't say it aloud. Somehow my pride wouldn't quite let me.

Especially in front of Del.

"The Hanjii have need of strong warriors," the shoka announced. "Hanjii women do not always breed enough. The shoka will take the Northern woman as his wife and will improve the blood of the Hanjii."

I stared at him. Del, not understanding the dialect, glanced at me sharply. "What does he say?"

I smiled. "He wants to marry you."

"*Marry* me!"

"You impressed him." I shrugged, enjoying the look of horror on her face. "He wants to get children on you—Hanjii warriors." I nodded a little. "See what you get for resorting to dirty tricks?"

"I *can't* marry him," she squeezed out between gritted teeth. "Tell him, Tiger."

"*You* tell him. You're the one who impressed him so much."

Del glared at me, looked at the shoka a minute, then back at me again. Still glaring. But also, apparently, at a loss for words.

I wasn't, but neither could I figure out a diplomatic way of refusing the man. Finally I cleared my throat and tried the only thing that came to mind: "The woman is more than the Sandtiger's woman, shoka. She is his wife, blessed by the Sun."

He stared at me out of malignant black eyes. "The Sandtiger did not tell the shoka that before."

"The shoka didn't ask."

Del frowned, watching us both.

The shoka and the Sandtiger spent endless minutes staring at one another, then at last the old man grunted, relinquishing his claim. "It was agreed: if the woman won, she was free to choose. The woman will choose."

I breathed a sigh of relief. "Pick one of us, bascha."

Del looked at me a long, silent moment, blandly weighing us both. I knew it was all for my benefit, but I couldn't say anything or risk being accused of manipulating her decision.

And she knew it.

Finally, she nodded. "The woman has a husband, shoka. The woman chooses him."

I translated.

If nothing else, the Hanjii are an honorable sort of people. The shoka had said she could choose; she had chosen. He couldn't go back on his word, or he'd lose face in front of all his people. I felt a whole lot better.

Then the shoka looked at me with hostility in his eyes, which is a whole lot worse than malignancy. Hostility he might *do* something about.

He did. "The shoka promised nothing to the Sandtiger. He has his fate to suffer. Since the woman has freely chosen him, she will suffer it also."

"Uh, oh," I muttered.

"What?" Del whispered.

"We're free," I told her, "in a manner of speaking."

Del opened her mouth to ask me something, but she shut it again as the shoka gestured. A moment later Gold Ring arrived on horseback along with his thirty-nine fellow warriors. He led two horses: Del's dun gelding—no longer lost—and my bay stud.

"You go," the shoka said, and made the sign of the blessing of the Sun. A rather definitive blessing.

I sighed. "I was afraid of that."

"What?" Del demanded.

"It's the Sun Sacrifice. They won't kill us or cook us—they'll just let the sun do it for us."

"Tiger—"

"Mount up, bascha. Time to go." I swung up on the stud. After a moment, she climbed up on the little dun gelding.

Gold Ring led us into the desert. We rode in circles all over for an hour or two before he motioned us to dismount, and even then

I don't think Del quite understood. At least, not until two other warriors gathered the reins to our horses.

I patted the stud as he was led away. "Luck, old man. Remember all your tricks." I grinned, recalling them myself. Some I'd taught him; most he'd been born knowing, as horses sometimes are.

Del watched as her dun was taken away. And then she understood.

Neither of us said anything. We just watched the Hanjii ride out of sight into the line of the horizon, an undulating line of black against the brown. The sun beat down on our heads, reminding us of its presence, and I wished it *was* a god.

Because then we might reason with it.

Del turned to face me squarely. She waited.

I sighed. "We walk." I answered her unasked question, "and hope we're found by a caravan."

"What if we followed the Hanjii? At least we know where they are."

"We've been dedicated to the Sun," I told her. "If we go back, they'll cook us for certain."

"We'll cook out here, anyway," she said in disgust.

"That *is* the general idea."

We stared at one another. Del's pride and defiance warred with realization in her sunburned face, but the acceptance portion won. She looked at me in irritated acknowledgment. "We could die out here."

"We're not dead yet. And I'm tough as old cumfa leather, remember?"

"You're wounded." Consternation overrode the dry displeasure in her tone. "I cut you."

The cut wasn't deep, mostly just a shallow slice along my ribs. It had bled quite a bit but was dry now, starting to crust, and it wouldn't bother me much.

Recalling the rather painful trick she'd played on me in the circle, I was tempted to let her think the sword cut was worse than it really was. But I decided it would be utterly stupid in light of the situation.

"It's nothing," I told her. "Hardly more than a scratch. See for yourself."

She touched the wound with gentle fingers and saw I spoke the truth. Her mouth twisted. "I thought I cut deeper than that."

"Not dancing against *me*," I retorted. "You're lucky you got close enough even for a little cut like this."

"That wasn't a real dance. That was a travesty. And you weren't so tough," she threw back. "You went down quickly enough when I kneed you. Howled like a baby, too."

I scowled at her. "Enough, woman. Do you know how hard it was for me to ride a horse out here?"

She laughed, which didn't do much to settle my ruffled feathers. Then she recalled our circumstances and the laughter went away. "Why did they leave us our weapons?"

"We're a Sun Sacrifice. It would be blasphemy if we went to the god incomplete, and the Hanjii believe a man without his weapons is incomplete. It would lessen the sacrifice. As for *you* . . . well, I guess you proved yourself worthy in the circle."

"For whatever good it did me." She scowled. "Maybe if I'd *lost*, we wouldn't be here."

"We wouldn't," I agreed. "If you'd lost, I'd have had to fight the shoka. And if *I'd* lost, you'd have become his wife—all scarred and dyed. And that's something I wouldn't stand for."

She looked at me expressionlessly a moment. Then she walked away from me and drew her sword. Again I saw the blade plunged into the sand and her cross-legged posture on the hot sand. The hilt stood rigidly upright, a locus for the sunlight. The shapes twisted in the metal.

I shivered. Frowned. Wanted to accuse her of carrying an ensorcelled sword, which took her right out of the realm of fairness when it came to a proper sword-dance.

But Del was talking to her gods again, and this time I did some talking to my own.

Chapter 10

Within two hours, Del was bright red all over. The sun sought out all the portions of her skin that the burnous had hidden, and now she was on the verge of blistering. Never had I seen such color in a sunburn; such angry red flesh. Against the blonde hair and brows and blue eyes, the burn looked twice as bad.

There was nothing I could do. The skin would swell until something had to give, and the skin itself would give, forming blistered pockets of fluids that would burst, spilling badly needed moisture over other blisters. And then she would burn again as the flesh—lacking moisture—shriveled on her bones, until she was nothing more than a cracking hide stretched incredibly taut over brittle bones.

Hoolies, I hated the idea. And yet I was helpless to prevent it.

We walked. To stop would only intensify the heat, the pain, the futility of our situation. Movement gave the impression of a breeze, though nothing moved at all. I almost wished for a simoom; was glad there was none, for the wind and sand would scour the burned flesh from our bones.

For the first time in my life, I wanted to see what snow was like; to learn firsthand if it was as cool and soft and wet as people claimed. I thought of asking Del if it were true—but didn't. Why speak of something you can't have? Especially when you need it.

The Punja is filled with mystery, including the mystery of its own sands; one moment you walk on hardpack, the next you stumble into a pocket of loose, deep softness that drags at your feet, slowing you, making the effort of continuing that much harder. Poor Del was having a more difficult time than I because she didn't know and couldn't tell the subtle differences in the sand's appearance. Finally I told her to step where I did, and she fell in behind me like a lost, bewildered puppy.

When darkness fell, she threw herself down on the sand and flattened herself against it, trying to soak up the sudden, unexpected coolness. This is yet another danger of the Punja: the days are hot and blistering, yet by night—if you are unprotected—you can shiver and shake with cold. When the sun drops below the horizon, you draw in a sigh of relief: release from the heat; and then the Punja turns cold and you freeze.

Well, cold is relative. But after the blistering heat of the days, the nights seem incredibly cold.

"Worse," Del muttered. "Worse than I thought. So much *heat.*" She sat on the sand with the sword unsheathed, resting across red thighs. Recalling the cold bite of the alien metal, almost I wanted to take it from her and touch my flesh with its own.

Except I recalled also the numbing tingle I'd experienced, the bone-deep pain that was unlike any pain I'd ever felt. And I didn't want to experience that again.

I saw how her hands caressed the metal. The hilt: tracing out the shapes. The blade: gently touching the runes as if they might bring her surcease. Such odd runes, worked into the metal. Iridescent in the twilight. They lighted the blade with a rosy, shimmering lambence.

"What is it?" I asked. "What is it *really?*"

Del's fingers caressed the shining sword. "My *jivatma.*"

"That doesn't tell me anything, bascha."

She didn't look at me. Just stared out across the blackening desert. "A blooding-blade. A *named* blade. Full of the courage and strength and skill of an honorable fighter, and all the power of his soul."

"If it's so powerful, why doesn't it get us out of here?" I was feeling a trifle surly.

"I asked." Still she didn't look at me. "But—there is so much heat . . . so much sun. In the North, there would be no question. But *here* . . . I think its strength is diluted even as my own is." She shivered. "Cool now, but it's wrong. It's just—*contrast.* Not an honest coolness."

And yet with her skin burned so badly and her physical defenses down, Del was twice as chilled. She sheathed the sword and drew herself up into a ball of huddled misery. I shared my own measure of the discomfort: your skin is so burned it feels incredibly hot, even when the night is cool. And so you burn and freeze all at once.

I wanted to touch her, to hold her close and give her some of the fiery heat of my own burned flesh, to warm her, but she cried out at my touch, and I realized it hurt too much. The sun had seared her Northern skin, while my Southron hide was barely darkened.

We slept side by side in fits and starts, dozing and waking, only just losing ourselves in the blissful release of sleep before we would wake again, and the cycle would begin once more.

By midday the sun is so hot it burns the soles of your feet and you walk with funny, mincing steps, trying to avoid keeping each foot on the sand for very long. Your toes curl, arching back over your foot until they cramp, and then you find yourself hopping on one burning foot while you rub the cramp out of the other. When the heat is too bad and the cramp is worse, you sit down until you can stand again, and then you walk some more.

If you have tough soles, like mine, the foot stays on the sand longer and the toes do less curling; the stops are less frequent, and you keep your rump off the sand. But if your soles are like Del's—softer, thinner, whiter—each step is agony, no matter how quickly you hop onto the other foot. After a while you stumble, and then you fall, and then you do your best not to cry because your feet are burning, your skin is afire, and your eyes are so hot you can hardly see. But you don't cry. To cry means using moisture, and by now you have none left.

Del stumbled. Nearly fell. Stopped.

"Bascha—?"

Her hair was white against the livid redness of her skin, which had formed blisters and spilled now-caking fluids down her flesh. I saw how she trembled from pain and exhaustion.

"Tiger . . ." It was little more than a breath of sound. "This is not a good way to die."

I looked down and saw how her toes curled up away from the sand; how she shifted her weight continually: foot to foot, hip to hip, until she fell into a rhythm she could focus on. I'd seen it before. Some people, with the sun beating on their brains, lose touch with their physical coordination. Del didn't look that far gone yet, but close. Too close.

I reached out and pushed some hair from her face. "*Is* there a good way to die?"

She nodded a little. "In battle, honorably. Bearing a child who will be better, stronger. When the heart and soul and body weaken after years and years of life. In the circle, following all the rituals. Those are good ways. But this—" an outthrust hand, trembling, encompassed all we could see of the Punja, "—*this* is like burning a perfectly good candle until it's all gone, leaving you with nothing . . ." Her breath rasped in her throat. "Waste—*waste*—"

I stroked her hair. "Bascha, don't rail at it so. It sucks the heart out of you."

She looked at me angrily. "I don't want to die like this!"

"Del—we're a long way from dying."

Unfortunately, we were.

In the desert, without water, your lips crack until they bleed, and you lick at the moisture with a swollen tongue. But blood tastes like salt and it makes you thirsty, and you curse the sun and the heat and the sand and the helplessness and the absolute futility of it all.

But you go on, you go on.

When you see the oasis, you don't believe in it, knowing it's a mirage; wondering if it's real. This is the edge of torture, honed sword-sharp; it slides in painlessly and then, as you stare in surprise, it opens you from guts to gullet, and what's left of your spirit spills out into the sand.

The oasis will be the saving of you; it will be the killing of you.

It moves as you move, shifting on the burning sands: first near, then far, then but inches from your feet.

Finally you cry out, and then you fall onto your blistered, weeping knees when the vision fades and leaves you with a mouthful of hot sand that clogs your throat and makes you sick.

But being sick is an impossibility because there is nothing in your belly to bring up.

Nothing.

Not even bile.

When I went down, I pulled Del down with me. But she got up again almost immediately and staggered onward. I watched her go. On hands and knees, half-delirious, I watched the Northern girl go on stumbling through the sand.

Southward. Unerringly.

"Del," I croaked. "Bascha—*wait*—"

But she didn't. And that got me up on my feet again.

"Del!"

She didn't even glance around. I felt a flicker of disbelief that she could leave me behind so easily (a man likes to think he inspires at least a *little* loyalty), but it was replaced with the hollowness of fear. It punched me full in the gut and drove me into a staggering run.

"Del!"

Still she stumbled on: bobbing, weaving, nearly falling, but continually moving southward. Toward Julah. Toward whatever news she could learn of her brother; poor, pretty boy (if he was anything like his sister), whose probable fate was the ugliest of all.

Better to die, I thought grimly.

But I wasn't about to tell his sister that.

I caught up to her easily enough; for all I was near delirium from the heat and the sand and the sun, I wasn't as bad off as Del. Not nearly as bad off.

And when she swung around to face me, I knew she was worse than that.

Del's face was swollen, crusty, seared so badly she could hardly see. Her eyelids were giant, puckered blisters, stretching the skin out of shape until they broke, sealed over, broke again, until she wept without shedding tears.

But it was what lay behind the lids that chilled my soul: the first touch of coldness I'd felt since daybreak. Her eyes, so blue, so bright an alien hue, were filled with emptiness.

"Hoolies," I croaked in despair, "you're sandsick."

She stared at me blindly. Maybe she didn't even recognize me. But as I put out a hand to touch her arm, meaning to urge her down onto the sand before she ran amok from all the pain and delirium, she tried to jerk her sword from its sheath.

There was no grace in her movement, no flexibility. Just an awkward, ragged motion as she tried to drag the sword from her harness.

I caught her left arm. "Bascha—no."

The other arm continued to move. I saw the futile cross-reaching of her right hand, clawing at the silver hilt that stood up behind her left shoulder. As always, the sunlight flashing off the blade nearly blinded me. But squinting hurt too much.

I caught her other arm. I felt her instant withdrawal: my touch, lighter than normal, was still too much for her blistered flesh. Her indrawn breath of pain hissed in the stillness of the desert.

"Del—"

"Sword." There was no shape to the word; no recognizable tone with inflections. Just—noise. A ragged, whispered word.

A plea. "Bascha—"

"Sword." Her eyes were out of focus, like the stare of a sandtiger cub. It was eerie, and for a moment I nearly let her go.

I sighed. "No, bascha, no sword. Sandsickness makes you crazy—no telling what you'd do. Probably cut out my heart." I tried to smile, but the motion cracked my lips and made them bleed again.

"*Sword.*" Pitifully.

"No," I told her gently, and she began to cry.

"*Kaidin* said—*an-kaidin* said—" She could hardly speak in her incoherence. "*An-kaidin* said—*sword*—"

I caught the difference at once. *An-kaidin,* not *kaidin.* "No sword." Gently, I overrode her. "*Tiger* says no."

Tears welled up into her eyes again; the right one spilled its weight of moisture in a single drop that rolled down her cheek. But the tear didn't reach her chin. Her skin sucked it up immediately.

"Bascha," I said unevenly, "you have to listen to me. You're sandsick, and you'll have to do as I tell you."

"*Sword,*" she said, and jerked both wrists from my grasp.

Seared flesh broke, leaking fluid mixed with blood. But her hands were on the hilt of her sword, closing, jerking it up and then over when she forced it to extension; a travesty of her normally supple unsheathing. But however awkward the motion, the fact remained that Del had a sword in her hands.

I'm no fool: I fell back a step. Men say I'm fearless in the circle; let them. It helps the reputation. But I wasn't in the circle now; what I faced was a woman full of sandsickness with a glittering sword in her hands.

Her grip shifted. The blade pointed downward, parallel to her body. Both hands gripped the hilt by the curving crosspiece; she lifted the sword slowly toward her face, and then she pressed the pommel against her cracked, blistered lips.

"*Sulhaya,*" she whispered, and shut her eyes.

I watched her warily. I wanted to take the weapon from her, but she was too unpredictable. What skill she claimed made her doubly dangerous: no man risks himself against a blade *and* a sandsick woman. Not even against a woman without any sword-skill at all.

She whispered something to the sword. I frowned, disturbed by the note in her voice; I've seen sandsickness before, and I know how it can strip a man—or woman—of a mind, leaving nothing behind but madness. Generally it's fatal, because about the only time people *get* it is when they're stuck in the desert without water or shelter or any hope of rescue.

Just like Del and me.

"Bascha—" I began again.

She turned away from me. Awkwardly, she lowered herself and the sword to the ground, kneeling: angry red flesh against sepia sand. The suede tunic she wore was taut against her body—a sheath around a blade—and yet for once I didn't consider what the supple body could do for my own. I just watched her, feeling despair rise up within me, as the girl gave in to the imbecility of the sandsick.

Hoolies, what a waste.

She knelt, but did not crouch. Her spine was straight. Carefully she put the tip of the blade into the sand and pushed downward on the hilt, trying to seat it firmly. But she was too weak, the sand too firm; it was me, finally, who leaned on the pommel and pushed it into the ground so that the sword stood upright like a standard.

But not before I felt the pain that seared my palm. It ran up my arm to the shoulder, thrumming so hard I shook with it, and it was only as I wrenched my hand away that the eerie sensation abated.

"*Del,*" I said sharply, shaking my tingling hand. "Bascha—what in hoolies *is* this sword—?"

I felt a bit of a fool for asking—a sword, after all, is a sword—but the remembered explosion of pain in my hand confirmed that, indeed, the Northern blade was more than merely a piece of steel coaxed into the shape of a lethal weapon. My palm itched; I looked at it suspiciously, rubbed it violently with my other hand, and glared at Del.

Simple tricks and nonsense, designed for gullible people. But I'm not a gullible man.

And, though I'm quick enough to scoff, I know the smell of real magic when it clogs the air I breathe.

Like now.

Del didn't answer me; I wasn't certain she had heard me. Her eyes were fixed on the hilt that was level with her face. She said something—a sentence in her Northern tongue—repeating it four times. She waited: nothing (or so it appeared to me); she repeated the sentence again.

"Del, this is ridiculous. Knock it off." I reached out to yank the sword from the sand. Didn't. My hand stopped several inches away as I recalled the sickening feeling of numb weakness, the irritating, painful *itch* that had run through my veins like ice.

Some sort of spell?

Possibly. But that would make Del a *witch* . . . or something like.

Still, I couldn't touch the hilt. I couldn't *make* myself, though nothing was preventing me. Nothing, that is, except an extreme unwillingness to experience the weirding again.

Del bent, curling her body downward toward the sand. Her hands pressed flat, fingers spread. Her brow touched the sand three times. A glance at the sword. Then the homage was repeated.

The blonde braid, now bleached white, slapped against the sand. I saw the grains adhering to the blistered flesh across her forehead; to her nose, her lips. And as she bent again in obscene obeisance to the sword, I saw how her raspy exhalations stirred the dust beneath her face.

Puff . . . puff . . . puff—

Dust drifted: ivory-umber.

I said nothing. She was beyond any words from a human mouth.

She knelt in complete obeisance. And then, awkwardly, she stretched out until she lay prostrate on the sand. She wrapped her hands around the shining blade just above the level of the sand. I saw how the blistered knuckles, burned red, turned white from the tension in her hands.

"*Kaidin, kaidin,* I beg you—" Half the words were in Southron, the other half in Northern. So the sense of things was lost. "*An-kaidin, an-kaidin,* I beg you—"

Her eyes were closed. Her lashes were gummed by leakage and sand. It crusted on her face, where the swelling rawness obliterated the lovely lines of her flawless bones. And I felt such a rage build up in me that I bent down, pulled her hands from the sword, and—steeling myself for the weirding—jerked the blade from its makeshift altar in the sand.

Pain ran up my arm and into my chest. Ice-cold. Sharp as a dagger though nothing cut into my skin. It was just cold, *so cold*, as if it would freeze my blood, my bones, my flesh.

I shuddered. My hand seemed fixed upon the hilt, even as I tried to let go the sword. Light filled up my head, coruscating light, all purple and blue and red. Blinded, I stared into the desert and saw nothing but the light.

I shouted something. Don't ask me what. But as I shouted it, I hurled away the sword with all the strength I had left. Which, at the moment, wasn't very much.

My hand, thank valhail, came unstuck. Several layers of flesh were peeled away in ridges, still adhering to the hilt. In my hand remained the pattern of the hilt, the twisted, alien shapes of Northern beasts and runes. Beads of moisture sprang up into the patterns seared into my hand. Dried. Cracked. Sloughed away with an additional layer of skin.

I was shaking. I gripped my right wrist with my other hand, trying to hold it still; trying to dull the ringing pain. Hot metal burned. Seared. I'd seen cautery before. But this—*this* was something different. Something more. This was *sorcery.* Ice-cold sorcery. The North personified.

"Hoolies, woman!" I shouted. "What kind of sorceress *are* you?"

Still prostrate, Del stared up at me. I saw the complete incomprehension in her eyes. Utter bewilderment. Her mouth hung open. Elbows shifted, rising; she pressed herself up from the ground, though she very nearly didn't make it. She knelt on one knee, bracing herself with a shaking hand thrust against the sand.

"The magic," she said in despair, "the magic wouldn't come . . ."

"*Magic!*" I was disgusted. "What power does that—that *thing* hold? Can it make the day cooler? Can it soothe our blistered flesh? Can it turn the sun's face from us and give us shade instead?"

"All those, yes. In the North." She swallowed and I saw the blistered flesh of her throat crack. "*Kaidin* said—"

"I don't care what your sword-master told you!" I shouted. "It's just a sword. A weapon. A blade. Meant for cutting through flesh and bone, shearing arms and legs and necks—to take the life from a man." And yet even as I denied the power I'd felt, I looked at my hand again. Branded with the devices of the North. Ice-marked by the magic.

Del wavered. I saw the trembling in her arm. For a moment there was sense in her eyes. And bitterness. "How could a *Southroner* know what power lies in a sword—"

I reached up and caught Singlestroke's heated hilt with one broad hand, ignoring the twinge in my newly-scarred hand, and jerked him free of his sheath. I presented the tip of the blade to her just inches from her nose. "The power in a sword lies in the skill of the man who wields it," I said distinctly. "There isn't anything else."

"Oh yes," she said, "there is. But I doubt you will ever know it."

And then her eyes rolled back in their sockets and she crumpled bonelessly to the sand.

"Hoolies," I said in disgust, and put Singlestroke away.

I heard the horses first. Snorts. The squeak of leather. Clattering bits and shanks. The creak of wood, and voices.

Voices!

Del and I lay sprawled on the sand like cloth dolls, too weak to go on; too strong to die. We lay an arm's-length apart. When I turned my head and looked at her, I saw the curve of hip and the spill of her sun-bleached braid; long, firm, blistered legs, with white striations across the knees.

And sand, crusted on her sun-crisped flesh.

When I could manage it, I turned my head the other way. I saw a dark-faced woman wrapped in a blue burnous, and I knew her.

"Sula." It came out on a croak that died on my swollen tongue.

I saw her black eyes widen. Her wide face expressed utter astonishment. And then it shifted to urgency.

She turned, shouting, and a moment later other wagons pulled up. People gathered around us. I heard the surprised exclamations as I was identified. My name was passed around from man to woman, woman to woman, woman to children.

My *old* name, which isn't a name at all.

Nomads like the Salset understand the desert. With very few words of instruction necessary, they wrapped Del and me in cool, wet cloths and brought the wagons closer to throw some shade upon us. Camp was established immediately. The Salset are good at that: a hyort here, one there, until there's a huddled bunch of them packed onto a tiny stretch of desert. And they call it home.

I couldn't speak, though I wanted to tell Sula and the other women to tend Del first. My tongue was too thick and heavy in my dehydrated mouth, and when I breathed it took great effort. Finally, after Sula kept shushing me, I gave in to silence and let them do the work.

When the cloths dried on my scorched body, Sula dampened them again from the wooden barrels of water lashed to the wagons. After the fifth application of wet linen, she called for alla paste and I sank into blissful numbness as the cool salve soaked crusted tissue and leached away the pain. And Sula, thank the gods of valhail, lifted my head and gave me my first drink of water in two days.

My last coherent thought was for Del, recalling how oddly she had behaved. As if the sword was more than merely a sword. As if she expected the sword to get us out of our predicament.

Singlestroke, much as I respect and admire him, is only a sword. Not a god. Not a man. Not a magical being.

A sword.

But also my deliverance.

I've always healed fast, but even so it took me days before I felt like a living being again. My skin was peeling off in clumps and layers that left me feeling like a cumfa in molt, but regular applications of alla paste kept the new skin underneath moist and soft until it could toughen normally. The Sandtiger, who had always been dark as a copper piece, emerged looking like some unfortunate woman had birthed a full-grown baby; I was splotchy and pink all over, except where the dhoti had covered me.

And since that's a part of my body I'm rather attached to, in more ways than one, I was significantly grateful.

Del, however, was very ill. She lay in Sula's little orange-ocher hyort, lost in sandsickness delirium and the black world of the infusion Sula poured into her several times daily. Even the alla paste couldn't entirely assuage her pain.

I stood just inside the door-slit, staring down at the shape beneath the saffron-dyed cotton coverlet. All I could see was her face. Still burned. Still blistered. Still peeling.

"She won't talk to you." Sula spoke with the Salset intonations I hadn't heard in so long. "She has no mind. The mindless don't talk."

"It'll *pass*." More wishful thinking than anything else; sandsickness is a serious thing.

"Maybe." Sula's wide face didn't give me the benefit of the doubt.

"But she's getting good care now," I reminded her. "She has water again and that stuff you're giving her. The sandsickness will go away."

Sula shrugged. "She won't talk to you."

I looked again at Del. She moaned and cried in her drugged stupor, whispering in her Northern tongue. I heard *kaidin*, over and over, but if she spoke of the sword I didn't know the word.

Resigned, I shook my head. "Foolish little bascha. You should have stayed in the North."

I wanted to sleep in the hyort at nights, but Sula—cognizant of Salset proprieties—wouldn't allow it. I was an unmarried male and she an unmarried woman, who tended yet another. And so I slept outside curled up in a rug that smelled of goat and dog, evoking memories of many years before. Memories I preferred to forget, but couldn't.

Each day I exercised, trying to work the stiffness out of my muscles and stretch the tender new skin until it fit me better. I practiced with Singlestroke for hours, amused when all the children gathered to watch with their cunning black eyes stretched wide in astonishment, and yet I sensed a restlessness within me. Apprehension. I couldn't shake it, either. And when I walked among the hyorts and wagons, recalling my childhood with the tribe, I felt oppressed and sick and scared; *scared:* the Sandtiger. I wanted to get away—*needed* to get away—but I couldn't go. Not without Del.

I mean, I'd made a deal with her to do a job. I had to finish it or tarnish my reputation.

The shukar came and looked at me once, studied the sandtiger scars on my face and the claws hanging around my neck and went away again, saying nothing. But not before I saw the bitterness in his eyes: his recollection of the past, the present, the future. Crafty old man. Cunning old shukar. He went away from me, but not before I saw the ugly set to his mouth.

Gods, the man hated me.

But no more than I hated him.

The men refused to speak to me, which wasn't particularly surprising. They remembered, too. The matrons ignored me utterly: Salset custom doesn't allow a married woman to speak to or indicate interest in another man except for traditional courtesy; I especially was not deserving of that. At least, not from those women old enough to remember me from before.

But the young women didn't remember me at all, and the young *unmarried* women—having more freedom than their sisters—watched me with avid, shining eyes. And yet instead of making me feel tall and tough and strong, it made me feel small. And weak. And wary.

The Salset are an attractive race. They aren't as dark as the Hanjii with their spiraled, dyed flesh; the Salset are golden-brown and smooth-skinned. Hair and eyes are uniformly black. They are, for the most part, short and slender, though many of the older women—like Sula—run to fat. They are supple and quick, like Del, but they aren't a warrior race.

They are nomads. They wander. They live for each day, from dawn to dusk, and they blow with the sand; coming, going, staying. They have a tremendous sense of freedom, strong traditions, and a great love for one another that makes an outsider feel ashamed he cannot share it.

They made *me* feel ashamed, as they intended to, because I am not a Salset, though once I lived with them. I couldn't be a Salset then, or now. Not with my height, my bulk, my color; my green eyes and brown hair; my strength and natural sword-skill.

I was alien to them; then, now, forever. And for the first sixteen years of my life they had tried to beat it out of me.

Chapter 11

*S*andsickness is a frightening thing. It makes a sieve of your mind: spilling some memories, retaining others; those it loses are replaced by dreams and visions that are so real, so *very* real, you have to believe them, until someone tells you no.

I told Del no, but she wasn't listening. She lay on a rug in Sula's orange-ocher hyort and slowly healed physically, but I wasn't certain about what she was inside her head. Her skin was lathered generously in alla paste. Sula had wrapped her in damp linen to keep the peeling skin moist. She resembled not so much a living person as a dead one, sloughing a ruined shell. But at least she breathed.

And dreamed.

I settled into a daily routine: food, general exercises, food, sword practice, companionship to Del. I sat by her for hours each afternoon, talking as if she could hear me, trying to let her know someone was with her. I don't know if she heard me. She whispered and moaned and talked, but it was only rarely that I understood her. I don't speak her Northern tongue.

Sometimes, neither of us spoke at all. We shared long private silences—Sula had tribal chores—while Del slept and I stared at the woven walls of the hyort, trying (mostly unsuccessfully) to reconcile my presence once again among the Salset. It had been more than sixteen years since I'd left the tribe, thinking (hoping) never to see the Salset again. But not much had changed in the intervening years. Sula was a middle-aged widow instead of the young woman I recalled. The children all had grown to adulthood, reflecting the traditional biases and beliefs of the tribe, rearing their children as they themselves had been reared. The old shukar also was the same, oddly unchanged in his strange, ageless fashion: fierce, austere, bitter—tight as a wineskin filled to bursting with an impotent anger whenever he looked at me.

But I recalled the years it hadn't been impotent.

Sitting in Sula's hyort, I thought about how time changed all things except the Punja and everything which lived in it. How time had changed *me*.

Time, and a relentless desperation.

Sula entered silently. I paid no attention to her, accustomed to her quiet comings and goings, but this time she dropped a leather-wrapped bundle into my lap and I glanced at her in surprise.

She was swaddled in rich, cobalt-blue; the blue of a starless Punja night. Black hair, greased back from her face, held a tracery of silver. "I kept them for you," she said. "I knew I'd see you again before I died."

I looked into her golden face and saw the sunlines clustered around her eyes, the sag at her jowls, the heaviness of hips, breasts, shoulders. But most of all, I saw the calmness in her black Salset eyes and realized Sula had accepted me for what I had made of myself and not what I had been.

Slowly, I unwrapped the bundle and freed both items. The short spear, blunted at one end and pointed at the other, painstakingly sharpened by a piece of broken stone and hands too big for the boy who used them. Now the spear was about the length of my arm; once it had been half my height.

The wood was darker than I recalled, until I realized it still bore bloodstains, blackened by the years. The lopsided, unbalanced point was scarred with claw and bite marks. Holding it in my hands again, sensing the ambiance of memory recalled, I felt all over again the emotions I'd experienced so many years before.

Wonder. Determination. Desperation. Fear, of course. And pain.

But mostly the blind, fierce defiance that had so nearly killed me.

The other item was exactly as I recalled it. A piece of bone, carved in the shape of a beast. A sandtiger, to be precise. Four stumpy legs, a nub of a tail, snarling mouth agape to show the tiny fangs. Time had weathered the bone to a creamy yellow-brown, almost the color of a real sandtiger. The incised eyes and nose were worn down almost to smoothness. But I could still see traces of the features.

My hands were bigger now. The bone tiger fit into the palm of my right hand easily. I could close my fingers over the toy and hide it from sight. But sixteen or so years before, I couldn't. And so I had stroked it every night, whispering the magical words into the tiny bone ears as the wizard had told me to do, and dreaming of a wicked beast come to eat my enemies.

Oh yes, I believe in magic. I know better than to doubt it. Although much of it is little more than tricks and sleight of hand practiced by charlatans, there are genuine magicians in the world. And genuine magic with such power as to completely alter a life in dire need of it.

But that kind of power carries its own cost.

I shut the toy in my right hand, pressing the smooth yellowed bone against the palm that bore the ice-brand of the Northern sword, and looked at Sula.

I saw the compassion in her eyes; a complete comprehension of the emotions the spear and toy recalled. And I put them both back into her hands. "Keep them for me . . . to recall the good nights we shared."

She accepted them, but her mouth tightened. "I'm surprised you can say there were good nights, after the bad days—"

I cut her off. "I choose to put away the days. I'm the Sandtiger now. The days before are forgotten."

She was unsmiling. "The days before are *not* forgotten. They can't be. Shouldn't be. Not by the shukar, not by me, not by the tribe . . . not by you. The days before are what *made* you the Sandtiger."

I made the sharp gesture of negation. "A shodo made me the Sandtiger. Not the Salset." Inwardly, I knew better. And chose to deny it. "No one here tells me what to remember, to think, to speak . . . to wish for." I scowled at her fiercely. *"Not— any—more."*

Untroubled by exaggerated distinctness, Sula smiled. In her face was the serenity I had always associated with her. But in her eyes was a bittersweet knowledge. "The Sandtiger no longer walks alone?"

She meant Del. I looked at the linen-draped, sunburned Northern girl and opened my mouth to tell Sula the Sandtiger—human or animal—*always* walks alone (being an exceedingly solitary beast); then I recalled, oddly, how I had killed a male sandtiger attempting to protect his mate, his cubs.

I smiled. *"This* one only temporarily walks with the Northern woman."

Sula, kneeling, wrapped spear and bone in the leather binding again. She tilted her head assessively as she studied Del. "She's very ill. But she's also strong; others less burned and not so ill have died, while she hasn't. I think she'll recover." Sula glanced at me. "You had sand in your head to bring a Northern woman into the Punja."

"Her decision." I shrugged. "She offered me gold to lead her across to Julah. A sword-dancer never says no to gold—especially when he's been out of work for a while."

"Neither does a chula say no to gold—*or* to a dangerous, tragic endeavor—if it buys him the freedom he craves." Sula rose and ducked out of the hyort before I could summon an answer.

I felt the faintest breath of a touch on my leg and glanced down in surprise to find Del's eyes open and locked on my face. "What does she mean?"

"Bascha! Del—don't talk—"

"My voice isn't burned." She formed the words carefully, a little awkwardly; her lips were still blistered, still cracked. No smile— she couldn't manage it—but I saw it in her eyes.

Blue eyes, bluer than I recalled; lashes and hair bleached whiter by the sun. New skin, vividly pink, showed in the rents of peeling flesh.

I scowled. "Concentrate on resting. Not talking."

"I *will* survive, Tiger—even if it means you have sand in your head for bringing me into the Punja."

"You heard Sula." Accusation.

"I heard it all," she answered. "I haven't been asleep the *whole* time." And suddenly there were tears in her eyes; embarrassed, she tried to hide them from me.

"It's all right," I told her. "I don't think you're weak—at least, not *weak* weak. Just tired from your bout with sandsickness."

Her throat moved as she swallowed heavily. Old skin cracked. "Even when I was lost and wandering, I knew you were here. And—something told me you'd be here even when I found myself again."

I shrugged, discomfited. "Yes, well . . . I owed you that much. I mean, you're paying me to get you to Julah. I can hardly go off and leave you; it plays hoolies with the reputation."

"And a sword-dancer never says no to gold." Irony; a little.

I grinned at her, feeling better than I had in days. "You realize I'll have to raise my price, don't you? I told you I charge based on how many times I have to save your life."

"This is only once."

"*Three* times."

"Three!"

I ticked them off on my fingers. "Sandtiger. Hanjii. Now this rescue."

She glared as much as she was able to. "You got us lost in the *first* place."

"That was the Hanjii. Not my fault."

"You had nothing to do with the Salset finding us," she pointed out. "That was the will of the gods." She paused. "*Mine.*"

I scowled. "We'll argue about it when we reach Julah. And besides, I may have to save you a few more times—in which case my price climbs even higher."

"Aren't you forgetting something? The Hanjii took all my gold." Her eyes glinted. "I can't pay you any more."

"Well then, we'll just have to work out another arrangement." I gave her a slow, suggestive smile.

She hissed something at me in her unintelligible Northern tongue. Then, weakly, she laughed. "Perhaps we *will* have to make another arrangement. Some day."

Anticipating it, I nodded consideringly. Smiling.

Del sighed. "Northern, Southron—you're all alike."

"Who is?"

"Men."

"That's sandsickness talking."

"That's *experience* talking," she retorted. Then, more softly, "Will you tell me about it?"

"Tell you about what?"

Her eyes didn't move from my face. "Your life with the Salset."

I felt like I'd been kicked in the gut. Talking with Sula about my past was one thing—she'd been a part of it—but telling it to a stranger was something I had no intention of doing. Even Sula skirted the edges of the topic, knowing how delicate it was. But with Del's blue eyes fixed on me in calm expectation (and knowing she'd just lived through her own sort of hoolies), I thought perhaps I *should* tell her.

I opened my mouth. I shut it almost immediately.

"Personal," I muttered.

"She said the past had made you what you are. I *know* what you are. I want to know what you *were.*"

Tension gripped my body. Muscles knotted. Belly churned. Sweat broke out on my new skin. "I *can't.*"

Her eyes drifted closed, lids too heavy to keep raised. "I've trusted my life to you. You've honored that trust. I *know* what you want from me, Tiger—what you're hoping for—because you mask your face but not your eyes. Most men don't even bother." The corners of her mouth moved a little, as if she wanted to smile wryly. "Tell me who you were so I can know who you are."

"Hoolies, Del—it's not the sort of thing that makes for polite conversation."

"Whoever said you were polite?" A definite smile, though somewhat tentative. "These are your people, Tiger. Aren't you happy to see them again?"

I recalled how close Northern kinship circles were. It's what had brought her here, against odds most would never face, man *or* woman. "I'm not a Salset," I told her flatly, figuring I owed her that much. "Nobody knows *what* I am."

"Well—the Salset raised you. Doesn't that matter?"

"It matters. *It matters.*" It spilled out of my mouth unexpectedly, a flood of virulent bitterness. "Yes, the Salset raised me . . . *in hoolies,* Del. As a chula." I wanted to spit out the word so I'd never know its foul taste again. "It means slave, Del. *I didn't even have a name.*"

Her eyes snapped open. *"Slave!"*

I looked at her shocked, pitiful face and saw a horror as eloquent as my own. But not disgust (in the Punja slavery is a stigma you escape only in death). Empathy, instead; honest, open empathy, as well as astonishment.

Maybe in the north they don't believe in slavery (or else they don't consider it a horrible fate), but slavery in the South—especially the Punja—guarantees a lifetime of utter misery. Complete humiliation. A slave is unclean. Tainted. Locked into a life that is less than a life. In the South, a slave is a pack-animal. A slave is a beast of burden forced to withstand beatings, curses, degradation. It is a bondage of the spirit as well as the body. A slave is not a person. A slave is not a man. He is less than a dog. Less than a horse. Less than a goat.

A slave develops self-hatred.

In the South, a slave is a simply a *thing.*

A pile of dung upon the ground.

Which is where I had learned to sleep, when I could sleep at all.

I heard the indrawn hissing of Del's sucked-in breath and realized I had said the words aloud. And I wanted to take them back, grinding them up between my teeth and swallowing them back down my throat where they could remain hidden away, not vomited out like foul, malodorous bile.

But it was too late. I'd said them. They couldn't be unsaid.

I shut my eyes and felt the stark desolation fill up my soul again, as it had so often in childhood. And the anger. Frustration. The rage. All the insane fear that gave a boy the courage to face a full-grown male sandtiger with only a crude wooden spear.

No. Not courage. Desperation. Because that boy knew he could win his freedom if he killed the beast.

Or if he let the beast kill him.

"And so you killed it."

I looked at Del. "I did more than kill it, bascha . . . I *conjured* the tiger."

Del's lips parted. I saw her start to form a question, and then she didn't. As if she had begun to comprehend.

I drew in a deep breath. And for the first time in my life, I told a woman the story of how I had won my freedom.

"There was a man. A wizard. And the Salset honored him, as they honored anyone with power." I shrugged a little. "For me, he was more than that. He was a god come to life before me because he promised me absolute freedom." I recalled his voice very well: calm, smooth, soothing—telling me I could be free. "He said a man always knows his freedom in what he can make for himself, in how he conjures dreams and turns them into reality; that if I believed in myself hard enough, I could become anything I desired; that magic such as his was known only to a few, but the kind *I* needed was available to anyone." I drew in a deep breath, remembering all he had told me. "And so when I took to following him around, even though I was beaten for it, he knew my misery, and did what he could to ease it. He gave me a toy."

"A toy?"

"A sandtiger carved out of bone." I shrugged. "A trinket. He said a toy can give a child freedom in mind, and freedom in mind is freedom in body. The next day he was gone."

Del said nothing. Silently, she waited.

I looked down at the palm that bore the brand of the Northern sword. And I thought it likely Del could comprehend the magnitude of the power I had summoned, having her own measure of it.

"I took the toy, and I talked to it. I named it. I gave it a history. I gave it a family. And I gave it a great and terrible hunger." I recalled the echoes of my whispers again, hissing into the ivory ears. "I begged for deliverance in such a way as to convince even the shukar I deserved my freedom. I asked for the tiger to come to me so I could kill it."

Del waited, locked in silence.

I recalled the smooth satin finish of the bone beneath my fingers. How I had stroked it, whispering; how I had shut out the stink of dung and goat, the pain of a whip-laced back, the emotional anguish of a boy reduced to a beast of burden when he needed to be a man.

How I had shut out everything, dreaming of my tiger, and the freedom he would bring.

"He came," I said. "The tiger came to the Salset. At first word I rejoiced: *I would win my freedom*—but then I saw what the cost of that freedom would be." I felt the familiar sickened twisting of my gut. "My tiger came because I conjured him. A live sandtiger, big and fierce as I could wish for, filled with a great and terrible hunger. And to diminish that hunger, he began to eat whatever prey he could catch." I didn't look away from Del's direct gaze. "Children, bascha. He began to eat the children."

A soft, quiet breath of comprehension issued from her lips.

I swallowed heavily, cold in the warmth of the hyort. "The Salset have no understanding of weapons and killing, being a tribe who raises goats for food, and trading. When the sandtiger began stealing children, the elders had no idea of how to stalk and kill it. They *tried*—two men tracked it to its lair and tried to kill it with knives, but it killed them. And so the shukar—after all his magic failed—told us it was a punishment for unknown transgressions, and that to break the beast's power would make its killer permanently blessed by all the tribal gods." I remembered his speech so clearly; the old, angry man, who had never thought a *chula* might be responsible for the beast. "It was mine to do. And so I made my spear in secret because the tribe would never countenance a chula considering such a thing; and when I could, I went after the tiger myself."

Her hand was on my clenched fist. "Your face—"

I grimaced, scraping a broken fingernail across the marks. "Part of the price. You've seen sandtigers, Del. You know how quick, how deadly they are. I went after my conjured tiger with only my spear—somehow I hadn't provided for genuine ferocity while I did my conjuring. I'm lucky these scars are all he gave me." I sighed. "Still, he'd eaten four children and killed three men. It was more than worth the risk, after what I'd done."

Something blazed up in her eyes. "You don't *know* you conjured it! It might have been coincidence. That old wizard told you what *anyone* could tell you: believe in something hard enough and often you will get it. Sandtigers are common in the Punja—you told me so yourself. Don't blame yourself for something you may have had nothing to do with."

After a moment, I smiled. "You're a sorceress, bascha. You know how sorcery works. It's twisted. It's edged. It gives you what you want if you request it properly and then it demands its price."

Her jaw tightened. "What makes you say I'm a sorceress?"

"That sword, bascha. That uncanny, weirding sword with all the rune-signs in the metal." I lifted my hand and displayed the ice-marked palm to her for the first time. "I've felt its kiss, Del . . . I've felt a measure of its power. Don't try to deny the truth to a man who knows sorcery when he smells it . . . or when he *feels* it. That sword *stinks* of Northern sorcery."

Del turned her head from me and stared steadfastly at the woven wall of the hyort. I saw the gulping of her throat. "It stinks of more than that," she said unevenly. "It stinks of guilt and blood-debt, as much as *I* do. And I too will pay the price." But even as I opened my mouth to question her, she was telling me to finish what I had begun.

I sighed. "I crawled into the lair in the heat of the day, when the tiger slept. He was full of the child he had eaten earlier. I took him in the throat with the spear and pinned him against the wall, but when—thinking he was dead—I crawled closer to admire my handiwork, he came to life again and caught me here." I touched the scars again; the badges of my freedom. "But my poison was stronger than his because he died and I didn't."

Del smiled a little. "And so you won your conjured freedom."

I looked at her grimly, remembering. "There was no freedom. I crawled away from the lair—sick from the cat's poison—and nearly died in the rocks. I was there for three days: half-dead, too weak to call for help . . . and when the shukar and the elders came hunting the cat and discovered it dead—with no one claiming the kill—the old man said his magic had worked at last." It hurt to swallow. My throat was filled up with bitterness and remembered pain. "I didn't come back. They assumed I'd been eaten, too."

"But—*someone* must have found you."

"Yes." I smiled a little. "She was young then, and beautiful. And unmarried." The smile faded. I masked my face to Del. "Not everyone treated me as a chula. I was big for my age—at sixteen, the size of a man—and some of the women took advantage of that. A chula can't refuse. But—I didn't want to. It was the only kindness I knew . . . in the women's tents . . . at night."

"Sula?" she asked softly.

"Sula. She took me into her hyort and healed me, and then she called the shukar to me and told him he couldn't hope to deny that I had killed the tiger. Not with the marks on my face. My *proof*." I shook my head, remembering. "Before the entire tribe he had to name me a man. He had to give me the gift of freedom. And when the words were said, Sula—who had cut off the sandtiger's claws—gave this necklace to me." I tangled my fingers in the cord. "I've worn them ever since."

"The death of the boy, the birth of the man." She seemed to understand.

"I walked away from the tribe the day I put on the claws. I never saw the Salset again—until the day they found us."

"The cat who walks alone." Del smiled a little. "Are you so certain you're tough enough for that?"

"The Sandtiger is tough enough for *anything*."

Her eyes challenged me briefly, then closed. "Poor Tiger. I have your secret. Now I should tell you mine."

But she didn't.

Chapter 12

Del healed slowly. She was, she claimed, like an old woman: crippled, stiffened, withered. First she shed linen wrappings, then alla paste, but Sula frequently applied an oil also made out of the alla plant so the new skin wouldn't tear and crack from unaccustomed movement. Finally some of the vivid pinkness faded and she looked more like the Del who had walked into the cantina in search of a sword-dancer called the Sandtiger.

With my long-buried feelings about the Salset dredged up and vocalized, I felt a little as if the hounds of hoolies had been exorcised from my soul. Though undoubtedly I remained alien to most of the tribe, *I* didn't consider myself an outsider anymore. I was still different, but differences are tolerable. No longer was I the nameless boy whose only past, present and future was that which faced a chula.

Now, when the young women looked at me, I looked back.

And when the shukar, in passing one day, muttered an insult beneath his breath, I stepped into his path and confronted him.

"The chula is gone," I told him. "There is only the Sandtiger now—a shodo-trained, seventh-level sword-dancer—and such a man is due common Salset courtesy."

Sixteen years with the Salset had embedded certain behavior codes within me. Sixteen years *away* from the Salset hadn't quite erased them, I discovered. Even as I challenged him, I felt the old feelings of insignificance and futility rousing themselves from the corners of my being. It was difficult to look him in the face; to meet his eyes, because for too many years I had been permitted only to look at his feet.

A shukar must always be respected, revered. He is different from everyone else; more than a man. He has magic. He is sacred. Touched by the gods; the touch was evidenced by the deep, wine-red splotch on the old man's sallow face, stretching from chin to left ear. The Salset have no kings, no chiefs, no war-leaders. They rely on the voice of the gods (shukar means *voice*, in Salset speech), and the voice tells them what to do and where to go. He is the pattern of the days, forever, until the gods choose another.

To confront this old man before the rest of the tribe was my first genuine act of freedom and independence. Even as a newly freed chula, I'd been unable to face the man. I had simply walked away from him; from the others; from the memory of my conjured tiger.

Age had swallowed the golden pigmentation of his skin. He wore a saffron-colored burnous freighted with copper stitching around the hem. His hair, once black, was now completely gray. I smelled the acrid tang of the oil he used to slick it back from his face, meaning for all the world to see the wine-purple mark of the gods on his face; showing the mark, he showed his rank. His authority. And his black eyes, fixed on my face, hadn't lost one degree of their hatred for me.

Deliberately, he drew back lips from teeth like a dog showing his dominance and spat on the ground next to my right foot. "I have no courtesy for you."

Well, I hadn't really expected any different. But the denial of common courtesy (the highest order of insult in Salset customs) still rankled.

"Shukar, you are the voice of the gods," I said. "Surely they have told you the Sandtiger walks where he wills—*regardless* of what the cub once was." I had his attention now; he glared back as I met his eyes directly. "You gave me no courtesy when I killed that cat so many years ago," I pointed out, reminding him of his failure to conduct himself as a proper shukar. "I'm claiming it now, before the entire tribe. Will you shirk your duty? Will you bring disgrace upon the Salset?"

I left him no choice. In front of so many people (many of whom knew me *only* as the Sandtiger), even a bitter old man knows how to bow to necessity. I hadn't claimed the courtesy due me when I killed the sandtiger, thereby releasing the shukar from a very distasteful duty; now I claimed it with every right and justification. He had to honor the request.

"Two horses," I said. "Water and food for two weeks. When I ask for them."

His mouth worked. I saw how yellowed his teeth had become from chewing beza nut, a mild narcotic. A common habit in the Punja; supposedly it enhances magic, provided one has it already. "We have given you life again," he said curtly. "We reclaimed you and the woman from the sand."

I folded my arms. "Yes. But that's something the Salset must do for anyone. The tribe has my gratitude for the reclaiming, but *you* must honor my request for courtesy." Idly I ran a finger along the black cord around my neck, rattling the claws. Reminding him how I had won my freedom.

Reminding him he had absolutely no choice.

"When you ask for them," he said bitterly, and turned his back on me.

I watched him walk away. I knew satisfaction in the victory, but it wasn't as sweet as I'd expected. When a man is grudgingly given what he is due anyway, there is no pleasure in it.

Del was on her feet before I expected it, moving slowly with the aid of a staff. At first I protested until she rattled off something in her Northern tongue that sounded angry, frustrated and impatient, all at once, and I *knew* she was almost back to normal.

I breathed a sigh of relief. We had shared a brief, odd closeness in the hyort as she lay trapped in sandsickness. While it had been special, it also proved discomfiting for me. Staying with the Salset upset the hardwon equilibrium I'd so carefully built in the years since I'd left. It left me vulnerable to things, feelings I'd left behind. The Sandtiger had lowered his guard, even if only briefly, and it was something I simply couldn't afford. I was a professional sword-dancer, earning my living by doing dangerous, demanding work few others were willing to tackle. There was no time, no room for sentimentality or emotions other than those necessary to survival, if I were to continue.

Del came out as I lounged in the shade of an awning outside Sula's hyort. She had put on her belted tunic once again (Sula had cleaned and brushed it), and the blue runic embroidery glowed brightly against the brown suede. Most of the pink new flesh had toughened, weathering to a more normal color (though a little darker); she was a smooth, pale gold all over. Sunbleached hair was tied back with blue cord, sharpening the lines of her jaw and cheekbones. She was thinner, slower, but she still moved with the grace and poise I admired.

I admired it so much I felt my mouth dry up. If I hadn't been so sure she was still weak and easily tired, I might have pulled her down beside me to investigate the possibility of payment in something other than gold coin.

Then I realized she was in harness and carried that sword in her hand.

"Del—"

"Dance with me, Tiger."

"Bascha—you know better."

"I have to." There was no room for argument. "I'll be no good if I don't dance. *You* know that."

Still sprawled nonchalantly, I glared up at her. But there was nothing nonchalant about my tone of voice. "Hoolies, woman, you almost died. You still might, if I join you in a circle." I looked at her bared sword, scowling, and saw how the patterns of the designs seemed to move in the metal, confusing my eyes. I blinked.

"You're not *that* good."

I quit looking at the sword and looked instead at her. "I am," I explained with dignity, "the best sword-dancer in the Punja. *Possi-*

bly even the South." (I thought it likely I *was* the best sword-dancer in the South, but a man has to maintain some sense of modesty.)

"No," she said. "We haven't tested each other properly."

I sighed. "You're good with a sword—I saw that when we danced before the Hanjii—but you're no sword-dancer, bascha. Not a *proper* one."

"I apprenticed," she said, "very much as you did. Before that, my father, uncles and brothers taught me."

"*You* apprenticed?" I asked. "*Formally?*"

"With all attendant ritual."

I studied her. I could grant that she had trained with father, brothers and uncles, because she *was* good—for a woman—but formal apprenticeship? Even in the North, I doubted a woman would be admitted into the sort of relationship I had known with my shodo.

"Formal, huh?" I asked. "Well—you *are* quick. You're supple. You're better than I expected. But you haven't got the strength, the endurance or the coldness."

Del smiled a little. "I am a Northerner—a *sorceress*, he claims—and he says I am not cold."

I raised an eyebrow. "You know what I mean. The *edge.*"

"Edge," she echoed, exploring the word.

"A sword-dancer is more than just a master of the blade, bascha," I explained. "More than someone who understands the rituals of the dance. A sword-dancer is also a killer. Someone who kills without compunction, when he has to. I don't mean I kill without good reason, just for the hoolies of it—I'm not a borjuni—but if the coin and the circumstances are right, I'll unsheathe Singlestroke and plant him in the nearest belly requiring it."

Del looked down on me; I hadn't bothered to get up. "Try to plant him in mine," she suggested.

"Hoolies, woman, you've got sand in your head," I said in disgust.

She glared at me as I made no movement to rise. After a moment the expression altered. She smiled. I knew enough to be wary of her, now. "I'll make a deal with you, Tiger."

I grunted.

"Dance with me," she said. "Dance with me—and when we catch up to my brother, I'll pay you in something other than gold. Something—*better*."

I won't say it was easy to show no change of expression. "We may never *find* your brother; what kind of a deal is that?"

"We'll find him." The flesh of her face was taut. "Dance with me now, Tiger. I need it. And if we get to Julah and can't find any traces of him, none at all . . . I'll still honor the deal." She shrugged a little. "I don't have any gold. I don't even have any copper."

I looked at her. I didn't let my eyes roam over her body; I'm not *entirely* insensitive. Besides, I already knew what she had to offer.

"Deal, bascha."

The sword glittered in the sunlight. "Dance with me, Tiger."

I looked at her weapon. "Against *that?* No. Against another sword."

The flesh of her face stiffened. *"This* is my sword."

Slowly I shook my head. "No more secrets, bascha. That sword is more than a sword, and you have someone hunting you."

She went white, so white I thought she might faint. But she didn't. She recovered her composure. I saw only the briefest clenching of her jaw. "That is private business."

"You didn't even know," I accused. "What's private about something *I* have to tell you?"

"I have expected it," she said briefly. "It comes as no surprise. It is—blood-debt. I owe many *ishtoya*. If this is one, I will accept the responsibility." She stood rigidly before me. "But this has nothing to do with what I ask *you* to do."

"You've invited me into the circle," I said blandly. "And you ask me to dance against an ensorcelled sword."

"It's not—ensorcelled," she said flatly. "Not exactly. I don't deny there is power in this sword . . . but it must be *summoned*—much as your tiger had to be conjured." Indirectly, she challenged me. "In this circle, against the Sandtiger, my sword will be a sword."

I looked down at my palm. Closed it to shut away the brand. But it didn't shut away the memory of the pain or the power I had felt.

My harness was at my right side. I pulled Singlestroke free of the sheath and pushed myself to my feet. "The circle will be small," I said flatly. "The dance will be short and slow. I will not contribute to your death."

Del showed her teeth in a feral little smile. "*Kaidin* Sandtiger, you honor your *ishtoya*."

"No, I don't," I assured her blandly, "I'm just *humoring* her."

Within weeks she was sleek and supple again, swift as a cat, though not swift as *this* cat. I held back in the circle, teasing her along because I didn't want to overextend her; she knew it, I knew it, but there was little she could do about it. A couple of times she tried to push me, dancing faster, darting the shining sword at me in a barrage of intricate patterns and parries, but I beat her back with the strategies I had learned long ago. It wasn't difficult. It would take time for her to regain her rhythm and strength.

Our styles were incredibly different. It was to be expected of a man and woman, matched, but Del's blade patterns were quicker and shorter, confined in a much smaller space. It took great strength and flexibility in the wrists themselves, as well as the arms and shoulders, and it proved she had indeed been properly trained. But by a shodo—or, in her tongue, *kaidin?* I doubted it. For one, she employed no ritual in her practice dance. She simply moved, moving well, except I could see no formal patterns. No signature. Nothing that indicated a formal apprenticeship. Nothing that exhibited the hallmark of a true *master*, no signature pattern that identified a sword-dancer as a former student of this shodo or that one.

Still, with her yellow-white hair darkened by sweat and her long, supple limbs moving so smoothly in the circle, it was easy to imagine she had been taught by *someone*. And someone very good.

But not good enough to dance against the Sandtiger.

For real, that is.

After a few short weeks spent walking, running, dancing, Del's quickness and strength were restored. Sula's alla oil kept her skin from tearing; natural health and vitality did the rest. Five weeks after our rescue from the sands, Del and I mounted the horses I claimed from the shukar and rode away from the Salset.

As we headed south, Del studied me in blandness and unsettling candor. "The woman cares for you."

"Sula? She's a good woman. Better than the rest."

"She must have loved you very much when you were with the tribe."

I shrugged. "Sula looked after me. She taught me a lot." I recalled some of the lessons in the darkness and privacy of her hyort. Thinking of the heavy, aging woman now made me wonder how I could have desired her, but the flicker of disbelief faded quickly into comprehension. Even had Sula not been young and beautiful when I killed the sandtiger, her kindness and warmth would have made her special. And she had made me a man, in more ways than one.

"I had nothing to give her," Del said. "To thank her."

"Sula didn't do it for *thanks*." But then I saw the genuine regret in Del's face, and subsequently regretted my curtness.

"I feel wrong," she said quietly. "She was deserving of a guest-gift. Something to acknowledge her kindness and generosity." She sighed. "In the North, I would be considered a rude, thoughtless person, unworthy of courtesy."

"You're in the South. You're not rude, thoughtless *or* unworthy," I pointed out. Then I grinned. "When do you plan on thanking *me*?"

Del looked at me consideringly. "I think I liked you better when you thought I might die of sandsickness. You were nicer."

"I'm never nice."

She reconsidered. "No. Probably not."

I brought my horse up next to hers so we rode side by side. I'd been pleasantly surprised by the choice the shukar had made for us: both geldings were good ones, small, desert-bred ponies. I had a buckskin with a clipped black mane and tail; Del rode a very dark sorrel marked by a strip of white running from ears to muzzle. The vermilion blankets over our shallow saddles were a bit threadbare; the quality of the animals *under* the saddles and blankets was more important. But someone had cut the tassels off the braided yellow reins.

"What do you plan on doing when we get to Julah?" I asked. "It's been five years since your brother was stolen. That's a long time, down here."

Del pulled at the azure burnous Sula had given her, settling it around her harness. Sula had given me one also, cream-colored silk edged with brown stitching. Both Del and I had immediately cut slits in the shoulders for our swords. "Osmoon said his brother Omar was the trader who'd be able to tell me about Jamail going on the slaveblock."

"How do you know Omar is still in Julah?" I asked. "Slavers move around a lot. And how do you know he'll be willing to tell you anything even if he *is* still in Julah?"

Del shook her head. "I *can't* know . . . not until we get there. But I have planned for certain instances."

My buckskin reached out to nibble on the cropped, upstanding mane of Del's sorrel. I kicked free my right foot from the stirrup, stretched my leg between the horses, and banged a heel against the buckskin's nose. He quit nibbling. "I don't think you'll make much progress, bascha."

"Why not?" She popped her reins a bit and rattled shanks against bit rings, suggesting to her sorrel he not seek redress from the buckskin.

I sighed. "Isn't it obvious—even to *you?* It's true that here Northern boys are prized by tanzeers and wealthy merchants who have a taste for such things. But that isn't the rule. Usually it's Northern *girls* who are so highly prized." I looked at her steadily. "How in hoolies do you think you'll find anything out when every slave trader in Julah is going to be trying to steal *you?*"

I saw the realization move through her face and eyes, tightening her skin minutely. A muscle ticked in her jaw. Then she shrugged. "I'll dye my hair dark. Stain my skin. Walk with a limp."

"Are you going to be mute, too?" I grinned. "Your accent is Northern, bascha."

She glared at me. "I suppose you've already worked out a solution."

"As a matter of fact . . ." I shrugged. "Let *me* do the looking. It'll be safer and probably quicker."

"You don't know Jamail."

"Tell me what to look for. Besides, there can't be that many Northern boys in Julah who are—what, fifteen? I don't think it'll be hard to track him down, provided he's still alive."

"He's alive." Her conviction was absolute.

For her sake, I hoped he was.

"Dust," Del said sharply, pointing eastward. "Is it another simoom?"

I saw the billows of sand rising in the east. "No. Looks like a caravan." I woke up my buckskin with heels planted into his flanks; his bobbing head indicated he was half-asleep. Hoolies, but I missed the stud. "Let's go take a look."

"Isn't that asking for trouble? After the Hanjii—"

"Those aren't Hanjii. Come on, bascha."

When we got within clear sight of the caravan, we discovered it *was* under attack, as Del had feared. But the attackers weren't Hanjii, they were borjuni; although the desert bandits are extremely dangerous, they're also generally very slow about killing their prey. They like to play with you first.

I glanced at Del. "Stay here."

"You're going in?"

"We need gold if we're to buy information in Julah. One way of getting it is to aid a caravan under attack; the leader is always incredibly grateful and usually very generous."

"Only if you're alive to collect the reward." Del arranged her reins in one hand—her left. "I'm going in with you."

"Have you got sand in your head?" I demanded. "Don't be such a fool—"

She drew her sword with her right hand. "I really wish you'd stop calling me a fool, Tiger." Then she slapped her Salset horse with the flat of the rune-worked blade and galloped straight toward the shouting borjuni.

"God of hoolies, *why* did you saddle me with this woman?" And I went after her.

Originally the caravan had been guarded by outriders. Most of these were dead or wounded, although a few of them still tried to put up a defense. The borjuni weren't incredibly numerous, but then they don't need to be. They ride quick, knee-trained horses that allow them to strike, wheel and leap away, wheeling back to finish what they have started. Never do borjuni stand and fight when they can slash and ride.

I let loose with a bloodcurdling yell and rode smack into the middle of everything, counting on catching the borjuni off-guard. I did, but unfortunately the caravan outriders *also* were caught off-guard; instead of attacking while the borjuni were momentarily surprised, they stood and stared.

Then Del shouted from the other side of the wagons and the melee broke out afresh. I caught glimpses of her streaking by on the sorrel horse, burnous snapping and rippling, sword blade flashing silver-white until it turned red and wet. For a moment I was astonished by her willingness to shed blood. The next moment I was too busy to worry about it.

I wounded two, killed three, then came face to face with the borjuni leader. He wore shiny silver earrings and a string of human finger bones around his neck. His sword was the curved blade of the Vashni. It's unusual to find a Vashni out of his tribe; they are fiercely loyal to one another, but occasionally a warrior leaves to make his own way.

Unless, of course, he's been exiled, which makes him doubly dangerous. He has something to prove to the world.

The Vashni's teeth were white and bared in a red-brown face as he came at me on his little Punja horse, curved blade slung behind his shoulder so he could unleash a sweeping slash at my neck, thereby severing skull from shoulders instantly. I ducked, but heard the whistling hiss as the blade swept over my head. Singlestroke was there when the Vashni swung back around to try again, and the warrior tumbled slowly from his horse in a tangle of arms and legs. Minus *his* head.

I looked around for my next opponent and discovered there were none; the ones who remained were all dead, or nearly so. And then I saw Del, still engaging her final opponent.

She was off her Salset horse. The sword was bloody in her hands as she stood her ground and waited. I saw the mounted borjuni come running, right hand filled with sword, left hand filled with knife. One way or another, he'd kill the woman on the ground.

Except Del was unmoved by his ululating cry or the steadiness of his horse. She waited, and as he flashed by and lowered the sword in a scything sweep, she ducked it. Ducking, she cut at the horse's legs and severed connective tendons.

The horse fell out from under the borjuni. But the man was on his feet before he hit the ground, knife flying from his hand in Del's direction. I saw her sword flash up, strike, knock the knife aside. And as he came at her, running on foot, the sword flashed up again.

Borjuni steel and Northern blade never engaged one another. Calmly, Del dropped flat below his thrust, allowed him to overextend, rolled, came up with her blade at an angle and took him through the belly.

It was only after the body fell that I knew I'd been holding my breath. I sucked air, then slowly rode over to Del. She wiped her sword on the clothing of the borjuni who lay dead in the sand and slid the blade home in its sheath.

"You've done this before," I observed.

"This? No. I've never rescued a caravan."

"I mean: you've fought and killed men before."

She tucked loosened hair behind her ears. "Yes," she agreed evenly.

I sighed and nodded. "Seems like I've underestimated you all the way around . . . sorceress."

She shook her head. "No sorcery. Just simple sword-work."

The *hoolies* it was! But I let it go at that because a voice was shouting for our attention. "We're being summoned. Shall we go?"

"You go. I need to catch my horse. I'll join you in a moment."

I rode over to the lead wagon and saluted a fat, high-voiced eunuch clad in jewels and silken robes.

"Sword-dancer!" he cried. "By all the gods of valhail, a *sword-dancer!*"

I dropped off the buckskin and wiped Singlestroke's bloodied blade on the nearest corpse. I slid the sword home over my shoulder and said a brief word of greeting in Desert.

"I am Sabo," the eunuch explained, after exchanging customary courtesies. "I serve the tanzeer Hashi, may the Sun shine on him long and well."

"May it be so," I agreed gravely. I glanced around and saw how many of his outriders the borjuni had killed. Of ten, only two were still alive, and they were wounded. Then I frowned. "Are you *all* eunuchs?"

He looked away at once, avoiding my eyes; an acknowledgment of stupidity. "Yes, sword-dancer. Escort for my lady Elamain."

I stared at him in astonishment as Del rode up and dropped off her sorrel. "You're escorting a lady across the Punja with only a bunch of *eunuchs?*"

Sabo was shame-faced. Still he looked away from me. A gesture indicated a guilt willingly assumed; he would be held responsible, even if it hadn't been his idea. "My lord Hashi insisted. The lady is to be his bride, and he—he—" Sabo's eyes flicked briefly to my face, then away again. He shrugged. "*You* understand."

I sighed. "Yes. I think I do. He didn't want the lady's virtue compromised. Instead, he compromises her safety." I shook my head. "It's not your fault, Sabo, but you should have known better."

He nodded, triple chins wobbling against the high, gem-crusted collar standing up beneath his wine-colored robes. He was dark-skinned and black-haired, but his eyes were a pale brown. "Yes. Of course. But what's done is done." He smiled ingeniously, dismissing the shame at once. "And now that *you're* here to help us, we need fear no longer."

Del's smile was ironic. I ignored it. Sabo was playing right into my hands. "I imagine the tanzeer would be—*pleased*—to recover his intended bride."

Sabo understood. And he had a flair for dramatics. "But of *course!*" His pale brown eyes opened wide. "My lord Hashi is a generous lord. He will reward you well for this generous service. And I'm sure the lady herself will be just as grateful."

"The lady *is* grateful," said the lady's voice.

I glanced around. She stepped out of a fabric-draped wagon, fastidiously avoiding the bodies scattered on the sand as she approached. She pulled her own draperies out of the way as she moved, and I saw small blue, gold-tasseled slippers on her feet.

Following the dictates of desert custom, she wore a modesty veil over her face. It fell from the black braids piled on top of her head pinned with enameled ornaments. But the veil was colorless as water and twice as sheer; she looked at me out of a flawless, dusky face and liquid, golden eyes.

She dropped to the sand in a single practiced, graceful movement and kissed my foot, which was dusty and sweaty and no doubt incredibly rank.

"Lady—" Startled, I pulled the foot away.

She kissed the other one, then gazed up at me in an attitude of grateful worship. "How can this poor woman thank you? How can I say in words what I am feeling, to be rescued by the Sandtiger?"

By valhail, she *knew* me!

Sabo gasped in astonishment. "The Sandtiger! Gods of valhail, is it true?"

"Of course it's true," the lady snapped, but softened it with a smile. "I've heard of the sword-dancer with the scars on his face, who wears the claws that scarred him."

I raised her with a blood-stained hand. I felt dirty and smelly and unfit for such elegant duty.

"My, *my*," said Del.

I glanced at her suspiciously, scowled, then turned back to the lady and smiled. "I *am* the Sandtiger," I admitted modestly, "and I will be more than happy to escort you to the tanzeer whose good fortune it is to be engaged to a lady as lovely as you."

Del looked pretty amazed I'd managed to get my tongue around such eloquent words; so was I. But it had a nice effect on the blushing bride, for she blushed even more and turned her head away in appealing embarrassment.

"The lady Elamain," Sabo announced. "Betrothed to Lord Hashi of Sasqaat."

"Who?" asked Del, as I asked, "Where?"

"Lord Hashi," he replied patiently. "Of Sasqaat." Sabo waved a be-ringed hand. "That way." He looked at Del a moment. "Who are you?"

"Del," she said. "Just Del."

The eunuch looked a little disconcerted, perhaps expecting a little more out of a woman who rode with the Sandtiger, but she didn't say anything else and didn't appear to want to. Her eyes, I thought, looked suspiciously amused; I had the distinct impression she found all this gratitude rather funny.

Elamain put a soft, cool hand on my wrist, which had borjuni blood on it. She didn't seem to mind. "I wish you to ride with me to Sasqaat in my wagon. It will honor me."

Del's brows rose. "Difficult to protect the caravan if he's *in* the wagon, instead of outside guarding it."

Elamain flashed her a quick look of irritation out of those wide golden eyes. Next to her dark desert beauty, Del's fairness made her look washed out. White-blonde hair straggled down her back, wisping into her eyes; dust and blood streaked her face. Her burnous was torn, stained. The two of them, standing so close, looked about as much alike as queen and lowliest kitchen maid—especially to a man who had been around unwilling women far too long.

Elamain smiled at me. "Come, Tiger. Join me in my wagon."

Determined that Del wouldn't have the last word (or that anything she might say could have the slightest effect on my decision and subsequent behavior), I shot her a bland look and smiled at the lady. "I would be honored, princess."

Elamain led me to her wagon.

Chapter 13

The lady was properly grateful. In the privacy of her very private wagon, as it bumped gently across the sand, Hashi's intended showed me she was no modest virgin, but an experienced woman who saw what she wanted and went after it. For the moment it happened to be me, which was very satisfactory all the way around.

Riding with Del hadn't been easy. I'd wanted her from the moment she'd walked into the cantina, but I knew she'd likely stick her knife into me for any unexpected—and unencouraged—intimacy. The night she'd put her naked sword between us had pretty well informed me how she felt about the matter, and I've never been one to insist when all it requires is a little patience. *Then*, of course, we'd gotten picked up by the Hanjii, and all thoughts of making love to Del had rather quickly gone out of my head.

Especially after she kneed me.

Del's suggestion as to what could be considered "payment" for my services once we reached Julah had set my mind racing with anticipation and made the rest of me hot with impatience, but—once again—*patience* was what was required. Well, it runs out after awhile. Del wasn't available yet, but Elamain was.

Young, sweet, tempting, hungry Elamain. Only a fool or a saint ignores a gorgeous, grateful woman when she's feeling amorous.

And, as I've said before, I'm neither.

We had to be quiet, of course. Hashi's bride was supposed to ar-rive unflawed and untouched. How she intended explaining to a new husband why she was no longer a virgin wasn't my problem, and I didn't allow it to linger in my mind very long. I had other things to think about.

A lot of women rather enjoy making the Sandtiger growl. I suppose it has to do with having the name in the first place. Occa-sionally, when the time and the woman are right, I don't mind, be-cause I really can't help myself. But I told Elamain it was stupid to expect me to stay discreetly quiet and then do everything she could to make me growl like a big, tame cat.

She just smiled and bit me on the shoulder. So I bit her back.

Where Del was—or what she did—during all this, I have no idea. If she had any sense at all, she'd be making friends with Sabo, who could probably be very persuasive when it came to suggesting to his master that generous thanks might be in order. But I hadn't known Del long enough; although I thought she was probably pretty sensible, she was also a woman, and therefore unpre-dictable. And, probably, prone to behavior that is occasionally not so sensible.

"Who is she?" asked Elamain as we lay sweating gently into the cushions and silks.

I thought about asking who, then didn't. I didn't think Elamain was stupid, either. "She's a woman I'm guiding to Julah."

"Why?"

"She hired me to."

"Hired." Elamain looked at me. "No woman *hires* the Sandtiger. Not with gold." The tip of her tongue showed. "Does she do this for you?" And she did something very creative with her hand.

After I recovered myself, I told her no, Del didn't; I did not tell her I had no way of knowing if Del *could*.

"What about this?"

"Elamain," I groaned, "if you want this pleasant little tryst to *re-main* a secret, I think you'd better stop."

She laughed deep in her throat. "They're eunuchs," she said.

"Who cares what they know? They're only wishing *they* could do it to me."

Probably. Nevertheless, I have *some* sense of decency, and I told her so.

Elamain ignored my comment. "I like you, Tiger. You're the best."

She probably said it to every man, but it still made me feel good. It always does.

"I want you to come with me, Tiger."

"I'm *going* with you—as far as Sasqaat."

"I want you to *stay* with me."

I looked at her in surprise. "In Sasqaat? But you're getting married, Elamain—"

"Marriage need not stop anything," she said testily. "It's an inconvenience, to be sure, but I have no intention of stopping just for *that*." Her smile came back, along with the invitation in her golden eyes. "Don't you want more, Tiger?"

"That question is unworthy of you."

She giggled and slid over on top of me again. "*I* want more, Tiger. I want *all* of you. I want to *keep* you."

This kind of talk makes any man nervous. Especially me. I kissed her, as she wanted, and did everything else she wanted as well, but deep in my gut I had the sickening feeling of apprehension.

"*Elamain has the Sandtiger . . .*" she whispered gleefully, licking at my ear.

For the moment, she certainly did.

When the lowering sun set the horizon aglow with magenta and amethyst fire, I circled the perimeter of the tiny camp on my buckskin Salset gelding. Altogether there were eight wagons: Elamain's personal transport and those carrying her maids and possessions. The drivers were all eunuchs, the maids all women, and I the only normal male for miles. If Elamain hadn't been so accommodating, I might have been distracted by all the ladies. As it was, I didn't have the time—or the energy—for anyone else.

At one juncture I stopped and stared off across the purpled

desert, lost in contemplation of Elamain's unexpected—and unde-
niable—skill, when Del came riding up. Her hair was freshly
braided and tied back. She had washed the dust of the desert from
her face, but I was too full of Elamain to notice the exquisitely
bland expression.

"Sabo says we'll get to Sasqaat without the slightest difficulty,
now that the Sandtiger leads the caravan," she said.

"We probably will."

Del snickered. "She keeping you happy, Tiger? Or—should I
say—are you keeping *her* happy?"

I glared at her. "Mind your own business."

Her pale brows slid up in mock surprise. "Oh no, have I offended you? Should I get down and kiss your feet?"

"Enough, Del."

"The whole caravan knows," she said. "I hope you realize this
Lord Hashi of Sasqaat is considered a rather short-tempered man.
Sabo says he kills anyone who crosses him." She looked out across
the darkening desert even as I did, exuding neutrality. "What's he
going to say when he finds out you've been dallying with his
bride?"

"He can't blame me," I declared. "She's not giving away anything she hasn't given away before."

Del laughed outright. "Then the *lady* is no lady. Well, I don't
feel sorry for Hashi. I suppose he'll get what he's paid for."

I looked at her sharply. "What do you mean?"

"Sabo told me Elamain's father was more than happy to marry
his daughter off. Apparently she's been—indiscreet with her affec-
tions. He was so thrilled to have Hashi offer for her that he reduced
the bride-price. Hashi's getting a discount." She shrugged. "Used
goods, after all."

"You're *jealous*." Belatedly, it dawned on me.

Del grinned. "I'm not jealous. Why should I be?"

We stared at one another: Del genuinely amused and me generally disgruntled.

"Why should Sabo tell *you* all this?" I demanded. "Hashi's his
lord. How could he know so much about Elamain?"

Del shrugged. "He said everyone knows. The lady has a terrible reputation."

I frowned, shifting in the shallow saddle. "But if *Hashi* doesn't know . . ." I considered it.

"It seems likely he would," Del pointed out. "But I suppose there's no telling what a desert prince will do—I've been told often enough how acquisitive they are; how jealous and possessive. How poorly they treat their women—although that seems to be the generally accepted custom in the South." She cast me a bland glance. "How do you treat *your* women, Tiger?"

"Keep this up and *you'll* never find out."

She laughed. I rode away to circle back in the other direction, and Del laughed.

I didn't think it was funny at all.

Before long, Elamain gave up all pretense of being a circumspect, virtuous woman and openly declared her current passion by keeping herself as close to me as possible, even when I rode at the head of the caravan on the lookout for borjuni. She made one of the wounded eunuchs ride in her wagon on these occasions, taking his horse for herself. Underneath all the flowing draperies she wore the silken jodhpurs of desert tanzeers and rode astride with aplomb. Outside of the wagon she also wore the transparent veil, but everyone knew it was nothing more than hypocrisy. In all truth, Elamain had no right to wear the veil signifying virtuous womanhood, but no one had the courage to tell her what she undoubtedly knew anyway.

To my surprise, Elamain made some effort to get to know Del better, even to the point of asking Del into her wagon on more than one occasion. What they discussed I have no idea; women's talk doesn't interest me in the least. I wondered, uneasily, if Elamain wanted to discuss something she and Del had in common—me—but neither of them ever said.

I also wondered what Del's answer would be if I *were* the topic. She could do irreparable harm to my reputation if she told Elamain we hadn't been intimate; then again, Del was Del, and I couldn't expect her to lie. And, knowing Elamain, I doubted she'd believe Del even if she *did* deny that intimacy. Altogether it was very confusing, and I decided the better part of valor was to simply ignore the whole thing.

Still, I couldn't help wondering what Del thought of it all. The situation between us was odd. On one hand, she knew I wanted her. She also knew she'd promised to sleep with me when the journey to Julah was finished, so there was no need for coyness or games.

On the other hand, the businesslike demeanor of the entire situation dissipated all the anticipation, reducing it to a mere contract. I'd get her to Julah, she'd pay up. Before, when just Del and I were together, I was happy enough with the anticipation. Now, with Elamain so close at hand (and so *active*), I discovered my feelings for Del were ambivalent. There was no doubt I still wanted that fair-skinned, silk-smooth body, but the anticipation had altered from eagerness to acceptance.

It didn't occur to me that it was *because* Elamain was so demanding that I didn't have anything left over for Del.

The woman was insatiable. We gave up all pretense of a business relationship; I stayed with her in her wagon at night, and occasionally during the day we'd retire for a while. Her maids—well-trained—never said a word. The eunuchs also kept quiet. Only Sabo looked worried, but he said nothing to me or Elamain.

As for Del, she no longer even joked about it. I thought it was a bit of jealousy turning her fair skin green, but I wasn't too certain. Del didn't seem the jealous type, and all the jealous women I've known aren't capable of behaving so—*normally*. I wasn't even aware of any daggered glances when my back was turned.

Did she think so little of me, then, that an affair with another woman meant nothing? Or was it simply that she figured I wasn't worth the trouble?

I didn't like that idea. I decided it was because she thought she wasn't up to the competition. Which was stupid, because Del was up to anything. Clean *or* dirty.

Finally Sabo approached me. We rode at the head of the caravan, and in the distance lay the formless, sand-colored shape of Sasqaat, Hashi's city.

"Lord," he began.

I waved off the honorific. "Tiger will do."

He stared at me from his eloquent pale brown eyes. "Lord Tiger, may I have permission to speak? It's a situation of some delicacy."

Naturally. I'd been expecting it. "Go ahead, Sabo. You can speak freely to me."

He fiddled with braided scarlet reins, chubby fingers glittering with rings. "Lord Tiger, I must warn you that my lord is not a calm man. Neither is he precisely *cruel*, but he is jealous. He ages, and with each added year he fears to lose his manhood. Already some of his vigor fades, so he tries to hide it by keeping the largest harem in the Punja, so everyone will think he is still young and strong and vigorous." The eyes, couched in dark, fleshy folds, peered at me worriedly. "I speak of personal things, Lord Sandtiger, because I must. They also concern the lady Elamain."

"And therefore me."

"And therefore you." He moved plump shoulders in a shrug of discomfort, setting the gold stitching of his white burnous to glow in the sunlight. "It's not my place to interfere between my betters, but I must. I must warn you that my lord Hashi may be very angry that his bride is no longer virgin."

"She wasn't a virgin *before* me, Sabo."

"I know that." He made certain of the fit of each of his rings. "I'm certain my lord Hashi knows it, too . . . but he'll never admit it. Never."

"Then all he has to do is ignore the fact his bride is a little more experienced than he expected." I smiled. "He really shouldn't complain. If anyone can restore Hashi's lost vigor, *she* can."

"But—if she can't?" Sabo was openly fearful. "If she can't, and he fails with her, he will be angry. Violently angry. He will blame the lady, not himself, and he'll look for a way to punish her. But— because she is a lady of some repute, with a wealthy father—he can't kill her. So he'll search for another person on which to vent his anger and frustration, and I find it very likely he will look to the man responsible for the most recent 'deflowering' of his bride." His voice was apologetic. "Everyone in Sasqaat, I think, knows the lady's reputation. But *no one* will say so, because he is the tanzeer. He'll punish *you*, probably kill *you*, and no one will try to stop it."

I smiled, hunching my left shoulder so the sword moved a little. "Singlestroke and I have an agreement. He looks out for me, I look out for him."

"You can't bear arms into the presence of the tanzeer."

"So I won't see the tanzeer." I looked at him blandly. "Surely his faithful servant can tell him how helpful I've been, and suggest a fitting reward be given to me through *his* offices."

Sabo was astonished. "You would trust *me* to give you your reward?"

"Of course. You're an honorable man, Sabo."

His brown face lost color until he resembled a sallow, sickly child. I thought he was having some sort of seizure. "No one—" he began, stopped, began again. "*No one* has ever said that. It's Sabo *this*, Sabo *that*; run so fast your fat wobbles, eunuch. I am not a man to them. Not even to my lord Hashi, who is not really so bad a person. But the others—" He broke off, shutting up his mouth.

"They can be cruel," I said quietly. "I know. I may not be a eunuch, Sabo, but I understand. I've experienced my own sort of hoolies."

He gazed at me. "But—whatever it was—you left it. You must have left it. The Sandtiger walks freely . . . and whole."

"But the Sandtiger also remembers when he didn't walk freely." I smiled and slapped him on his flabby shoulder. "Sabo, hoolies is what you make of it. For some of us, it's to be endured because it makes us better people."

He sighed. His brows hooked together. "Perhaps. I should not complain. I have some small wealth, for my lord Hashi is generous with me." He waved his ring-weighted fingers. "I eat, I drink, I buy girls to try and rouse what manhood I have left. They are kind. They know it wasn't my choice—what was done to me as a boy. But it's not the same as freedom." He looked at me. "The freedom to take a woman like Elamain, as you do, or the yellow-haired Northern girl."

"The yellow-haired Northern girl is my employer," I declared at once. "No more than that."

He looked at me in utter disbelief; I couldn't really blame him. And then I got irritated all over again that I hadn't at least *tried* to get closer to Del. A sword on the sand never stopped the Sandtiger before!

But then it had never been a sword like Del's sword, wrought of hard, cold ice and alien runes that promised a painful death.

Still, it wasn't really the sword at all. It was Del herself, and that odd integrity and pride. Maybe it wouldn't stop another man, but it sure stopped me.

I sighed with deep disgust.

Sabo smiled. "Sometimes, a man does not have to be a eunuch," he said obliquely. I understood him well enough.

I glanced around, searching for Del, and saw her riding at the tail of the caravan. The sun burned brightly on her hair. She was smiling faintly, but the smile was directed inwardly and not at any person. Certainly not at me.

Chapter 14

*E*lamain was properly demonstrative during our final assignation in her wagon. We bumped closer to Sasqaat and to the end of our affair with each moment; she said she didn't want to miss anything I had to offer. By this time I wasn't certain I had anything *left* to offer—but I certainly tried.

"Growl for me, Sandtiger."

"Elamain."

"*I* don't care who knows. Everyone *does* know. Do you care? Growl for me, Tiger."

So I growled. But very softly.

Afterward, she sighed and slung one arm around my neck, snuggling her chin against one shoulder. "Tiger, I don't want to lose you."

"You're getting married, Elamain, and I'm going on to Julah."

"With *her*."

"Of course, with her. She hired me to take her there." I wondered how much Del had told her of our purpose, or if that had even come up during their discussions.

"Can't you stay a while in Sasqaat, Tiger?"

"Your husband might not like it."

"Oh, *he* won't care. I'll have him so exhausted he'll be glad to let me spend some time with someone else. Besides, why should you let a husband interfere with our pleasure?"

"He'll have a little more right to your favors than I will, Elamain. I think that's the way marriage works."

She sighed and snuggled closer. Black hair tickled my nose.
"Stay with me a while. Or stay in Sasqaat, and then I'll have you
called to the palace. For your reward." She giggled. "Haven't *I* rewarded you enough?"

"*More* than enough." It was heartfelt.

"Well, I want more for you. I'll introduce you to Hashi—
respectfully, of course, and properly—and I'll tell him how wonderful you were when you saved the caravan. How you struck
down all those horrible borjuni single-handedly, and personally
rescued me from their clutches."

"It *wasn't* singlehandedly and you weren't *in* their clutches. Not
yet, anyway."

She made a moue of dismissal. "So I'll lie a little. It will only
win you greater reward. Don't you want a reward, Tiger?"

"I'm fond of rewards," I admitted. "I've never yet turned one
down."

She laughed deep in her throat. "What if I said I'd get you a reward far greater than you can imagine?"

I looked at her consideringly, but couldn't see much more than
silky black hair and a smooth, dusky brow. Still, I had learned not
to underestimate the lady. "What did you have in mind?"

"That's *my* secret. But I promise you—you won't regret it."

I traced the line of her nose. "Are you sure of that?"

"You won't regret it," she whispered. "Oh Tiger . . . *you won't.*"

Which meant, of course, I would.

Del and I had to wait in one of the outer rooms when we reached
Hashi's palace in Sasqaat. Sabo flamboyantly escorted Elamain into
the main part of the palace, leaving us cooling our heels, but promised he'd send word as soon as he could. He did, too; within an
hour a swarm of servants descended upon us and ushered us into
separate rooms. For baths, they said.

I needed no urging to climb into the huge sunken bath filled
with hot water and sweet-scented oil. I jumped in before anyone

could suggest it—although I did take off sandals, burnous, dhoti and harness. The dusty, sweat-stained garments disappeared at once, replaced by rich silks and soft leather slippers. My servants were all female, which didn't bother me in the least; I did wonder, however, if they gave Del women as well, or at least eunuchs.

Two of the servants came into the bath with me and proceeded to wash my hair and the rest of me as well. This led to giggling and half-serious suggestions of another way to enjoy a bath, so it took a little longer than I expected. By the time I climbed out, I was clean and drowsy and very, very relaxed. All I needed was a good meal.

I munched on fresh fruit as I got dressed. The grapes were marvelous, and the oranges; the melons were cool and juicy and delicious. The accompanying wine was light but slightly too sweet to provide a good complement to the fruit; it was also quietly powerful. By the time I'd put on the fresh dhoti and deep blue burnous freighted with genuine gold embroidery, my head felt muzzy and heavy.

One of the palace eunuchs came and escorted me to the huge audience hall. It was decked with silken and tasseled draperies of every color so that it almost resembled a giant hyort. The floor was tiled in dizzying patterns of mosaics that repeated themselves all the way up to the dais, on which rested a golden throne. Empty.

Additional eunuchs stood around the throne and dais, all dressed in magnificent clothing and all bearing great curving swords strapped to their chubby waists. Almost unconsciously, I hunched my left shoulder in the automatic gesture that told me Singlestroke rested safely in the scabbard.

Except that he didn't. I'd left Singlestroke in the bath chamber.

Hoolies, I'd left my sword!

I started to swing around and march back out of the chamber, but one of the eunuchs stepped into my path. "Lord Hashi comes soon. You must wait."

"I left my weapons behind. I'm going back for them." Inwardly I chafed in disgust that I could be so stupid.

"A man doesn't go armed in the presence of the tanzeer."

I glared at him. "I never go *unarmed*."

"You do now," said Del from behind me. I swung around and she shrugged. "They took mine, too."

"You let them have *that* sword?"

She looked at me oddly, and I realized how I'd placed the emphasis. I saw a strange expression in her eyes a moment, a combination of possessiveness, apprehension, and acknowledgment. "Sheathed," Del answered. "But if they *un*sheathe it—" She stopped. Shrugged a little. "I can't be held accountable."

"For *what?*" I demanded. "What happens if anyone but you unsheathes that sword?"

Del smiled a little. "*You* have unsheathed it. *You* have put your hand upon the hilt. You are better able to explain what happens than I."

Instantly I recalled the searing pain in my hand, my arm, my shoulder, flooding through bones and flesh and blood. Hot and cold, all at once. I sweated. I shivered. Felt sick. No, she need have no fear that sword would fall into another man's hands. No one could use it, I knew. No one at all, save Del.

After a moment, I shook my head. "No. No, I can explain nothing. That—that *thing* is different from anything I know."

"So am I." And she smiled.

I glared. "If you were, I'd think you'd be a match for this man." I indicated the tanzeer's empty throne.

She shrugged. "Perhaps."

Then I forgot all about discussing magical swords and witchcraft and old men, because I saw what they'd done to Del. Gone was the loose-limbed Northern girl who claimed herself a sword-dancer; in her place was a woman swathed desert-fashion in translucent rose-colored silks that only served to make her fair body more tantalizing than ever. Each time she moved the veils parted, displaying more veils, or else showing a brief flash of long, pale leg. Her bright hair shone with washing and was twisted on top of her head, pinned with golden clips set with turquoise stones. But the servants had left off the modesty veil, perhaps assuming she wasn't a true lady if she rode across the Punja with a sword-dancer called the Sandtiger.

"Don't laugh at me," she said crossly. "*I* wanted to stay in my tunic, but they wouldn't let me."

"Who's laughing? I'm too busy staring."

"Don't stare." She scowled at me. "Didn't your mother teach you better manners?" Then she clapped a hand over her mouth, recalling I *had* no mother.

"Forget it," I told her. "Let's just try to brace ourselves for whatever's coming."

She frowned a little. "Why? What do you think is coming?"

I thought about what Elamain had said, *when* she had said it, and how she had phrased it. "Never mind. You wouldn't understand."

Her mouth twisted wryly. "Wouldn't I?"

But I didn't answer because I was too busy staring at the withered old man who was making his way onto the dais from a side door, with Sabo's assistance.

He was ancient. He was stooped and wrinkled and shaking with palsy, but his black eyes glittered fiercely as he took his seat on the throne. I gestured to Del and she turned also, automatically falling in beside me as we slowly approached.

"My lord Hashi, tanzeer of Sasqaat!" Sabo announced. "May the sun shine on him long and well!"

The sun had certainly shone on him *long*. He had to be close to ninety.

"Approach the throne!" Sabo shouted.

Since Del and I were engaged in doing precisely that, we simply continued.

"My lord Hashi wishes it known he is grateful for the service you have done him in rescuing his bride from certain death and bringing her safely to him. You will be rewarded." Sabo's expression held the faintest of secret smiles.

Del and I stopped before the dais. I made the traditional desert gesture of respect: spread-fingered hand placed over the heart while I inclined my head. Del said and did nothing, apparently having been warned that a woman never speaks to a tanzeer until he acknowledges her and invites conversation.

Hashi waved Sabo away. The eunuch moved five paces behind

the throne and waited silently, his face perfectly blank. Then the old tanzeer leaned forward in his throne. "You are the sword-dancer they call the Sandtiger?"

"I am the Sandtiger."

"And the woman travels with you."

"I'm guiding her to Julah."

"Julah is not so nice as Sasqaat," Hashi said harshly, in the quick irritation of the elderly.

I didn't smile. Old men are unpredictable; old tanzeers are unpredictable and dangerous.

"The tanzeer in Julah is too young for his place," Hashi continued. "He knows nothing. He lets his servants run wild with no discipline, and he traffics in slaves. It's no wonder the city is a pisspot of common thieves, borjuni, sword-dancers, crooked merchants and slavers, as well as other foolhardy people." His beady black eyes were fastened on my face. "Sasqaat is a peaceful place, and much safer."

"But I need to go to Julah," Del said calmly, and I winced.

Hashi stared at her. His scrawny hands grasped the armrests of his throne. The veins stood out like bruises, crawling across his mottled skin. The healthy dark tan he once had known had grayed with age, leaving him ash-pale and sickly looking. It was no wonder he couldn't perform in bed anymore; I only wondered how Elamain had reacted to him.

"Elamain, you may enter," Hashi called.

I glanced around in surprise, saw a small side door open, and a moment later Elamain came into the hall. She was dressed similarly to Del, although her colors were subtle yellows and browns instead of the pale pinks and roses Del wore.

She came in smiling sweetly, black hair hanging loose past her rounded rump to her knees. I'd never seen it completely unbound before and I almost swallowed my tongue. Her smile grew a little as she looked at me, and instantly I looked at Hashi to see if he had noticed.

He had. His eyes glittered. "My lady Elamain has told me how kind you have been to her, and how thoughtful. How carefully you guarded her virtue." He smiled. "Although it is well-known Elamain has none."

Her smile froze. Her flawless face went very still and her eyes turned from gold to black as they dilated. I wasn't feeling so well myself.

"But I'll have her anyway," Hashi went on conversationally in his grating little voice. "I'm an old man, well past my prime, and I have nothing else left me in this life. It will bring me some pleasure to take the most beautiful woman in the Punja as my wife—and make certain she never lies with a man again." His smile was malicious, creeping out of the dark shadows of his soul. "Elamain has made a career out of bedding men. So many men, her father feared never to wed her properly. Well, I said I'd take her off his hands. I'll take her to wife. And I'll make certain she discovers *precisely* what it is to want someone so badly, knowing she'll never be able to have him."

Elamain was so pale I thought she might drop dead. But she didn't. She lowered herself to her knees on the tiled floor in front of the dais. *"My lord—"*

"Silence! This sword-dancer has delivered you to me, for which I am grateful, and I fully intend to reward him as you requested." He ignored her and looked at me. "Do you know what my bride suggested? Artfully, I must admit—she was magnificent." He grinned; he had lost most of his teeth. "She said it is customary for a husband and wife to exchange wedding gifts, gifts so special they become highly personal and therefore that much more prized. I agreed. I offered her whatever she would have, within my power to give." He nodded. "She said she would have *you.*"

"Me?"

"You." His eyes bored into mine. "You must be good, to have Elamain require you for more than only a few nights. She never has before."

"My lord Hashi—" I attempted.

"Silence, sword-dancer. I'm not finished." He looked at Elamain. "She said I should give her the Sandtiger as a wedding gift because she had one equally magnificent for me." That almost-toothless grin again. "She said if I gave her the Sandtiger, she would give me a white-skinned, white-haired, blue-eyed Northern woman. For my own."

My hand flashed to my left shoulder and came up empty. Singlestroke was gone. So was my knife. I saw Del make the same futile gestures, and then she stood very still. She did not look at me.

"She *is* magnificent." Hashi stared at Del. "And I think I will take her."

I became aware that a cluster of tall, heavy eunuchs were at my back and sides. The wicked, curving swords were naked in their hands.

I sucked in a breath. "We are free people," I told Hashi. "We are not chula, to be traded at your whim." I didn't tell him he couldn't get away with it, because he probably could.

"I'm not trading anything," Hashi said. "Elamain gives me a gift, which I accept." He smiled. "But I'm afraid I can't make her the same gesture. You, Sandtiger, have already had your pleasure on Elamain, and that's something no man will have again." He nodded; the cords of his thin neck trembled. "But I'll keep you here so she can see you, and be reminded of her foolishness. And lest you consider cuckolding me again, I will have it made impossible." He laughed. "I will have you made a eunuch."

That's the last thing I heard because I leaped for his stringy little throat and went down beneath a dozen guardsmen.

Chapter 15

Hashi had drugged the wine. I realized that after I woke up because I'd gone down with hardly a fight, and that's not like me at all. The odds had, of course, heavily outweighed me (and I'm not stupid); I knew the eunuchs would overpower me quickly.

But not so *easily.*

Hashi's generosity had ended dramatically. I still had my own room, but this time I wasn't in a bath chamber. I was in a tiny little cell somewhere in the bowels of the palace. And I wore iron jewelry.

I sat with my back against a cool, hard wall. My head ached dully from the aftermath of drugged wine and the thumping I'd received in the hall. My wrists were cuffed in iron and bolted to the wall sans chain, which limited movement considerably. Same with my ankles. My legs were stretched out in front of me, ankles cuffed and bolted to the floor. As long as I sat there quietly, I was fine. But I've never been real good at sitting quietly.

I shut my eyes against the pain in my head a moment, then opened them and looked at the damage done to my body. The scuffle had stripped me of the burnous so I could see the bruises rising on my skin, above and below the suede dhoti. My slippers also were missing, and I noticed that the little toe on my right foot stuck out to the side in a rather bizarre salute to the others. The rest of me, however, seemed to be in one piece, although that one piece was pretty sore. No one had used a sword or knife on me, so I had only bruises to show for my efforts, no cuts or slashes. I was grateful for that much.

The cell was a dark, close place, fouled with the stink of urine and defecation. Not my own; I wasn't that desperate yet. But it was obvious to me the former occupant(s) had been held for quite a while. You don't dissipate the stench of close confinement too quickly, even if you sluice the place from top to bottom. And no one had.

My neck was stiff. I had a pretty good idea I'd been in the cell for a while. And, from the way my belly felt, probably overnight. I was starving. I was also incredibly thirsty, but that might have more to do with the drugged wine than any natural factors. I tested my iron bonds and found them solid. No escaping them, unless someone unlocked them for me. And that didn't seem likely. The only one who'd unlock them was Del, and she was as much a prisoner as I—if in a different way.

Elamain wouldn't be any help, either; she was probably too busy trying to talk the old man around. Sabo?—I doubted it. He was the old man's servant. So—I was stuck.

And scared, because no man wants to think about losing his manhood.

Sickness knotted my belly until I wanted to spew it out into the cell, adding to the stench. I could *see* the sharp blade, *hear* Hashi's maniacal laughter, *feel* the pain as they started to cut. I clamped my teeth closed and screwed up my face as I tried to ignore the picture, shuddering so hard the cold bumps rose up on my skin. Better *death* than emasculation!

The door to the dungeon opened quietly, but I heard it. I'd have heard *anything* that heralded an approach. Why would Hashi want it done so soon? Or was it Elamain, come to beg forgiveness?

Well, no, she wouldn't do that. Not Elamain.

But it wasn't Elamain, or even Hashi and his eunuch-servants. The door to my cell clanked and creaked open, and it was Del.

I stared at her in the dimness, rigidly prepared to fight to the death the moment I was out of the iron cuffs. But now I wouldn't need to. It was *Del.*

She paused in the tiny doorway, ducking down to move into the cell. Her white-blond hair was tumbled around her silk-draped shoulders and over her breasts like she'd been in a man's bed.

Hashi's? The thought made me sick, sick and angry and— maybe—more than a little jealous.

"Are you all right?" Her whispered question hissed in the dimness.

"How did you get down here?" I demanded in astonishment, "How in *hoolies* did you manage it?"

She waited as I babbled all my half-incoherent inquiries, then displayed the large iron key dangling from her hand. Eloquent answer to all my questions.

"Hurry up!" I hissed. "Before they come after me!"

Del smiled. "That old tanzeer's got you scared silly, hasn't he? The Sandtiger, sword-dancer of the Punja, scared pissless of a little old man."

"You would be *too*, if you were a man and in my place." I rattled my cuffs. "Come *on*, Del. Don't dither."

She snickered and came into the cell, kneeling to unlock my ankles. I couldn't help myself—the moment my legs were free, I dragged them up to protect the part of my anatomy Hashi wanted to rearrange.

"How'd you get the key?" I demanded. The most obvious answer popped into my mind at once. "I suppose you let Hashi bed you in exchange for it."

Del paused momentarily as she reached to unlock my wrists. "And would it matter to you if I had?"

Her loose hair hung across my bare chest and face. "Hoolies *yes*, woman! What do you *think*?"

"What do I think?" She unlocked my right wrist. "I think you jump to conclusions pretty quickly, Tiger."

My impression was she was a tad angry. Maybe a little bitter. I don't know why; it wasn't *Del* stuck down here in a cell awaiting castration.

I peered at her face, trying to judge her expression. "You *did* sleep with that little Punja-mite."

She unlocked my left wrist. "I got you free, didn't I?"

I scrambled to my knees and grabbed her by the shoulders, imprisoning her in my big hands. "If you think I'm willing to keep my manhood in exchange for that kind of sacrifice and *not care*, you've got sand in your head."

"But you *would*," she said. "Any man would. As for caring? I don't know. Do you?"

"Care? Hoolies *yes*, Del. I don't want you to think I don't appreciate what you did for me."

Her smile wasn't really a smile, just a twisting of her mouth. "Tiger, a woman only loses her virtue once—right? She survives—right? . . . and learns what it is to pleasure a man. But that man—maybe a man like the *Sandtiger*—losing his manhood, might *not* survive. Right?"

Before I could answer, she twisted out of my hands and ducked out of the cell. I followed, cursing up a storm beneath my breath.

I hated the thought of Del in Hashi's bed. I hated the thought of her doing it for me, even if she *had* learned how to pleasure a man years before. But most of all I hated myself, because deep inside I was relieved. *Relieved* she had done it and saved me from the life of a eunuch, which was surely far worse and degrading than the life of a Salset chula.

But being relieved isn't the same as being *glad*.

I wasn't glad at all.

At the top of the narrow dungeon stairs waited Sabo. He threw me a dark-blue burnous and a leather pouch filled with coin. "Payment," he said. "For rescuing the lady and myself. Maybe Hashi isn't grateful, but *I* am." He smiled. "You treated me like a man, Sandtiger. The least I can do is make certain *you* remain one."

I saw Del hand him the iron key. "*You* gave her the key!"

Sabo nodded. "Yes. I drugged Hashi's wine, and when he fell asleep, I took Del from her room and brought her here."

I looked at her. "Then you *didn't*—"

"No," she agreed. "But you were certainly willing to believe I *had*." She brushed by me, by Sabo, and disappeared.

I looked at the eunuch. "I've made a horrible mistake. And a fool of myself."

Sabo smiled, creasing plump cheeks. "Everyone makes mistakes and every man is a fool at least once in his life. You, at least, have it out of the way." He touched my arm briefly. "Come this way. I have horses waiting for you."

"Singlestroke," I said, "and my knife."

"With the horses. Now, come."

Del waited in the darkness of a shadowed corridor. She had exchanged the diaphanous pink and rose veils for a simple burnous of apricot silk trimmed with white embroidery. The neck of the burnous gaped open and I saw her leather tunic underneath; like me, she lacked sword and knife.

I thought of her sword, and wondered if Sabo had experienced the same sort of sickening feeling I had known when touching the hilt. But I recalled Del's comment: sheathed, the sword was harmless.

Harmless. No. Not quite.

"Where?" she whispered to Sabo.

"Straight ahead. There is a door that opens into the back courtyard of the palace, where the stables are. I have seen to it that horses await you, and your weapons."

I reached out and grabbed his arm. "I give you heartfelt thanks, Sabo."

He smiled. "I know. But there was nothing else I *could* do."

Del leaned forward and slung her arms around his neck, kissing him soundly on one plump brown cheek. "*Sulhaya*, Sabo," she whispered. "That's Northern for 'thank you,' and anything else you want to make it."

"Go," he said. "Go. Before I wish to come with you."

"You could," I agreed. "Come with us, Sabo."

His pale brown eyes were dark in the dim corridor. "No. My place is here. I know you think little of my lord Hashi, but once he was an honorable man—I choose to remember him so. You go, and

I will remain." He jerked his head toward the door. "Go now, before the stable servants grow uneasy and take away the horses."

Del and I left. But we did it with the knowledge that it was Sabo who had gotten us free, and not any of the skills we claimed.

We hastened out of the palace into the stableyard, glad of the darkness. I judged the hour somewhere around midnight. There was little moon to speak of. We found the horses and untied them immediately, swinging up without delay. I felt Singlestroke's familiar harness hanging over the short pommel, along with a knife tied to it. Gratefully I slid the harness over my head and buckled it around my ribs, then dragged on my burnous.

Del had arranged her own harness. The silver hilt of her sorcerous sword poked up behind her shoulder. "Come on, Tiger," she whispered urgently, and we went out of the gate Sabo had paid one of the guards to open.

We clattered through the narrow streets of Sasqaat, heading south. I did not consider staying the night in the city. It might be clever to find a place beneath the very nose of Hashi, but a tanzeer is *absolute* authority in a desert city-state, and he could easily order Sasqaat shut up and searched house by house. Better to get free of the place once and for all.

"Water?" Del asked.

"Saddle pouches," I said. "Sabo thought of everything."

We rode on through the streets, anticipating alarms from the palace. But no tocsin sounded. And it was as we rode out of the city gates and passed the clustered hovels forming the outer edge of Hashi's domain that we finally began to relax. For the first time in my life I was glad to see the Punja.

"How far to Julah?" Del asked.

"At least a week. More likely two. I've never gone by way of Sasqaat; I think it's a little out of our way."

"So what's our next water-stop?"

"Rusali," I said. "Bigger than Sasqaat; at least, from what I saw of Sasqaat."

"Too much," she said fervently.

Whole-heartedly, I agreed.

* * *

We rode through half the night and into the early hours of false dawn, not daring to stop in case the tanzeer sent men out after us. I doubted he'd do it; Hashi hadn't really lost anything. There was Del, but for a man like old Hashi it would be no trouble buying half a dozen girls, or more. Admittedly, none of them would be *Del*, but then he didn't know her, so he wouldn't know what he'd be missing.

As for me . . . well, he could make a eunuch out of someone else. Not me.

At true dawn we finally stopped to rest. Del slithered off her sorrel and hung onto the stirrup a moment, then set about untacking the horse. I watched her a moment, concerned about her welfare, then dismounted and unsaddled my own horse. Sabo had even managed to give us our own Salset mounts. I still missed the stud, but the buckskin was at least a little familiar.

I hobbled the gelding, gave him a ration of the grain Sabo had thoughtfully included in our pouches, then spread a rug and dropped onto it. My ankles and wrists ached from the iron cuffs. The rest of me was pretty tired, too.

Del slung a bota into my lap. "Here."

I unplugged it and drank gratefully. I felt a little more human as I replugged it and set it aside. I stretched out on my back and proceeded to stretch my arms and legs carefully, popping knotted sinews as I worked all the kinks out.

I very nearly drifted off. But I snapped back when I saw Del, sitting on her own spread blanket, unsheathe her sword and examine the rune-worked blade.

I rolled over onto my right hip, propping my head up on a bent elbow. I watched as she tilted the blade, turning it this way and that, studying the steel for marks or blemishes in the plum-bright light of the sunrise. I saw how that light ran down the blade: mauve and madder-violet, orchid-rose and ocher-gold. And through it all shone the white light of Northern steel.

Or whatever metal it was.

"All right," I said, "time for a real explanation. Just what *is* that sword?"

Del tucked sun-bleached hair behind her left ear. All I could see was her profile; the smooth curve of a flawless, angular face. "A sword."

"Don't go tight-lipped on me now," I warned. "You've spent the last few weeks dropping hints about your training as a sword-dancer, and I know from personal experience that sword has some form of magical properties. All right, I'll bite. What *is* it?"

Still she didn't look at me, continuing to examine every inch of the sword. "It's a *jivatma*. My blooding-blade. Surely you know what that is."

"No."

At last, she looked at me. "No?"

"No." I shrugged. "It's not a Southron term."

She shrugged a little, hunching one shoulder. "It's—a sword. A true sword. A named sword. One that has been—introduced." Her frown told me she couldn't find the Southron words that would express what she meant to say. "Two strangers, introduced, are no longer strangers. They *know* one another. And, if they get to know one another *well*—they become more, even, than friends. Companions. Swordmates. Bedmates. Just—more." Her frown deepened. "A *jivatma* is paired with an *ishtoya* upon attainment of highest rank. I—*feed* my sword . . . my sword feeds me." She shook her head a little in surrender. "There are no Southron words."

I thought of Singlestroke. I'd told Del often enough he was just a sword, a weapon, a blade; he wasn't. What he *was* I couldn't articulate, any more than she could explain what her sword was. Singlestroke was power and pride and deliverance. Singlestroke was my freedom.

But I felt hers was more.

I looked at the runes on the blade. The shapes on the hilt. In the colors of the sunrise, the sword was everchanging.

"Cold," I said. "Ice. That thing is made of ice."

Del's right hand was set around the hilt. "Warm," she said. "Like flesh . . . as much as I am flesh."

The grue ran down my spine. "Don't make riddles."

"I don't." She wasn't smiling. "It isn't—alive. Not as you and I are. But neither is it—*dead*."

"Blooding-blade," I said. "I assume it has drunk its fill?"

Del looked down at the blade. The sunrise turned the salmon-silver carmine in the rubescence of the dawn. "No," she said at last. "Not until I have drunk *my* fill."

The grue returned with a vengeance. I lay back down on my rug and stared up at the break of day, wondering if I had gotten myself mixed up in something a little more serious than simple guiding duty.

I shut my eyes. I draped one arm across my lids to shut out the blinding sun. And I heard her singing a soft little song, as if she soothed the sword.

Chapter 16

Rusali is your typical desert town, crawling with people of all tribes and races. Rich and poor, clean and dirty, sick and ill, legal and crooked. (Actually, Rusali pretty well fits the description Hashi had given Julah.)

Del didn't bother to put up her hood as we rode into the narrow, sandy streets and she drew plenty of attention. Men stopped dead in the street to stare at her, and the women who were for sale muttered loudly among themselves about Northerners trying to steal their business.

I realized then I'd made a mistake. I should have come in the front way, like any man with gold hanging on his hip. Instead, I'd come in as I usually do, seeking out the back streets and alleys like a thief myself. I've never *been* a thief, but sometimes a sword-dancer finds business better in the seamier parts of town.

"Just ignore them, Del."

"It isn't the first time, Tiger."

Well, it was the first time while riding with *me*. And I didn't like the way the men stared at her. Lewd, lascivious fools, practically drooling in the streets.

"We'll need to get rid of the horses," I said, to change the subject.

Del frowned at me. "Why? Don't we need them to get to Julah?"

"Just in case old Hashi *does* decide to send people after us, we should switch mounts. Maybe it'll confuse the pursuit a bit."

"Hashi won't come." She shook her head. "He's got Elamain to keep him busy."

"Elamain'll *kill* him!" I couldn't help it. *Imagining* the old man in her bed was enough to make me laugh.

Del gave me a sidelong glance. "Yes, well . . . then he won't be our problem any more."

I smiled, thinking about it. "We'll switch horses anyway. I'll sell these, then go elsewhere to buy others. That way no one'll get suspicious." I glanced around the street. "There—an inn. We can get something to eat and drink. Hoolies, but I'm thirsty for some aqivi." I dropped off my buckskin and tied one of the reins to the ring in the buff-colored wall.

The place was dark and stuffy with smoke from huva weed. It formed a wispy, greenish layer up near the rooting beam work of the adobe inn. There were no windows to speak of, just a couple of holes knocked in the mud bricks. I nearly spun around and marched back out, Del in tow.

Only she wasn't near enough to grab. She sat down on a stool at an empty table. After a moment spent scowling at her, I joined her.

"This isn't the place for you," I informed her.

Her brows rose a little. "Why not?"

"It—just isn't." I made certain Singlestroke was loose in his sheath. "You deserve better."

Del stared at me a long moment. I couldn't read the expression on her face. But I thought I saw a hint of consideration in her eyes, and more than a trace of surprise.

Then she smiled. "I take that as a compliment."

"I don't care *how* you take it. It's a fact." Irritably, I looked around for the wine-girl and shouted for aqivi.

But I stopped looking when I heard Del's indrawn hiss of shock.

And then I looked at the tall, lanky, blond-haired Northerner as he walked into the inn, and I knew why she stared.

Almost instantly, Del was on her feet. She called out to him in Northern, catching his attention.

It occurred to me the man might be her brother. But no, I knew better almost instantly. The big Northerner looked thirty. Not fifteen.

It occurred to me *then* the man might be the one who hunted her, one of the *ishtoya* she claimed she owed. And it was quite obvious that had occurred to Del as well, for she had drawn the Northern sword.

Conversation in the inn broke up almost at once as one by one the patrons became aware of the confrontation. And then, bit by bit, I heard the voices start up again. And all the comments had to do with the fact that one of the Northerners was a woman, and a woman with a sword.

My right hand itched. At first I thought it was the ice-brand in the palm, then realized it had nothing to do with that. What it had to do with was my desire to draw my *own* sword in defense of Del.

Except she didn't look like she needed any.

The inn was close, stuffy, cramped. What light there was came from the open door and the holes serving as windows. The scent of huva weed was cloying, almost stifling. The atmosphere was so thick you could cut it with a knife.

Or a sword.

Del waited. Her back was to me so she faced the open door; the Northerner, silhouetted, lacked clear features. But I could see his harness. I could see the bone-handled hilt of his own sword, poking up behind one shoulder. Conspicuously, his hands were empty.

Del asked him a question. His answer was accompanied by a shake of the head that told me he voiced a denial. Del spoke again for several minutes, rolling the strange-sounding syllables around on her tongue smoothly.

Again the Northerner shook his head. His hands remained empty. But I did understand a couple of words. One was *ishtoya*. The other was *kaidin*.

After a moment, Del nodded. I couldn't see her face. But she shot her sword home in its sheath, and I knew she was satisfied.

The Northerner's expression was speculative, then his eyes took on the warm, interested glow most males' eyes assume when they light on Del, and I saw his smile of appreciation.

He strolled over to the table and sat down as Del gestured to the remaining stool. The aqivi arrived with two cups; Del filled one and handed it to the Northerner, the other she took for herself. So I grabbed the jug and drank out of that.

The only thing I got out of their conversation was the word Alric, which I took to be his name. Alric was tall. Alric was strong. Alric looked powerful enough to knock down trees.

In contrast, his white-blond hair curled with a gentle softness around broad shoulders. He wore a burnous striped in desert tones—amber, honey and russet—and carried a big sword. A curved sword. A *Southron* sword, not a Northern one like Del's. And I recognized its origins: Vashni. A *Northerner* with a Vashni sword; tantamount to sacrilege, as far as I was concerned. Worse, he had also acquired a Southron tan. It wasn't nearly as dark as mine, but it would do in a pinch.

I drank from my jug of aqivi and discovered a predilection within myself to glower at Del's new friend.

I heard the name Jamail and realized she was telling Alric about her missing brother. He listened closely, frowning, and spat out a violent comment between his white teeth. Probably something about the Southron slave trade. I'm not exactly proud of the practice, myself, but nothing gave *him* the right to criticize my desert.

Del glanced at me. "Alric says there are slavers who deal *specifically* in Northerners."

"They make more money that way," I agreed.

Del turned back at once to Alric, chattering away so fast I doubted I'd be able to understand it even if I *did* speak her dialect.

After a while I got bored. "Del." I waited a moment. "Del, I'm going to get rid of the horses." I waited again, but she didn't seem to hear me. Finally, I cleared my throat noisily. *"Del."*

She looked at me, startled. "What is it?"

"I'm going to sell the horses."

She nodded and turned immediately back to Alric.

I rose, scraping my stool against the adobe floor, and glared at them both a moment. Then I walked out of the inn, wishing the big lunk had never shown his face south of the border.

Outside, I untied the horses, mounted my buckskin and led Del's sorrel down the cobbled street. It was late in the afternoon, going on evening, and I was beginning to get downright hungry. But Alric the Northerner had left a bad taste in my mouth.

Why was Del so interested in him? Wasn't *I* getting her to Julah? What made her think *he* might be able to tell her anything?

She'd sure latched onto him in a hurry. Like I wasn't even there. And I hadn't missed the glow in his blue eyes as he looked at her, or the hungry expression on his face. Del has that effect on men.

Still, there was little I could do about it. She was a free Northern woman, and I already had the idea Northern women enjoyed a whole different order of freedom than Southron ones. Which left Del in a dangerous position here, because any woman with the freedom to come and go as she chooses is believed by one and all to be readily available.

I cursed as I rode down the street, threading my way through people afoot. I couldn't very well go back to the inn and tell the Northerner to get lost. After all, Del had a legitimate reason for talking to him. Two of them, as a matter of fact. Alric just might know something about her brother, although it was unlikely; he was also from her homeland. That could be enough of a link for her to forget all about me and take up with him. The curving sword he carried pretty well established him as a fighter. He might even be a sword-dancer.

In which case Del could *un*hire me and hire him instead.

By the time I found a local horse trader, I was angry and irritable and snappish. I sold the horses, pocketed the money, and went away without buying replacements after all. I could do it in the morning. So I went back to the inn to extricate Del from Alric's big, Northern hands.

She wasn't there. Our table was filled with four Southron men; Del wasn't anywhere to be seen. Neither was Alric.

I got a sick feeling in the pit of my belly. Then I got angry.

I approached the girl who'd brought the aqivi to the table. "Where'd she go?"

The girl was dark-haired, dark-eyed and flirtatious. Another time I might have appreciated it; right now I had other concerns on my mind.

"What do you want *her* for?" She smiled winsomely. "You got me."

"I don't want *you*," I told her rudely. "I'm looking for *her*."

The girl lost her smile. She tossed her head, sending dark ringlets tumbling around abundant breasts. "Then I guess she doesn't want *you*, because she left here with the Northerner. What do you want with a Northern girl anyway, beylo? You're a Southroner."

"Which direction did they go?"

She pouted, then jerked her head west. "That way. But I don't think she'll want you to find her. She looked real happy to go with him."

I muttered sullen thanks, flipped her a copper piece from the pouch Sabo had given me, and left.

I made my way down the crowded street, stopping every so often to ask vendors if anyone had seen a tall Northern girl with a tall Northern man dressed Southron. All of them had. (Who could forget Del?) Of course they all claimed they weren't *certain* it was her—until I jogged their memories with more of Sabo's reward. At this rate it wouldn't last long, but Rusali was little more than a sprawling rabbit warren; if I didn't buy the information, I might spend weeks combing the alleys and dead ends and dwellings.

I got hungrier as I searched, which didn't improve my temper at all. I was also tired, which wasn't surprising. When I stopped to think about it, I realized I had been through the mill in the past two months, thanks to Del. Clawed by a sandtiger, engulfed by a simoom, "hosted" by the Hanjii, left for dead in the Punja (and baked to a dry husk), taken prisoner by Hashi of Sasqaat. (And Ela-main, of course). All in a day's work, I might say, except the day was getting to be far too long and this worker was getting weary.

The shadows deepened as the sun went down, gilding the alleys and streets dark-umber and tawny-topaz. I walked more warily, anticipating almost anything. Rusali, like most desert cities, is a place of varied moods and inclinations, including desperate ones. I hated the thought of Del being in it unchaperoned.

Of course, with Alric, she wasn't precisely unchaperoned. He looked capable of protecting her, but for all *I* knew, he was a slaver himself. And Del, dropping into his hands like ripe fruit, would be too tempting. Even now she might be bound, gagged, and imprisoned in some smelly room, awaiting transportation to a wealthy tanzeer.

Or (possibly worse to my mind at the moment), would the big Northerner keep her for himself?

My teeth ground at the thought. I could just see it: two blond heads; pale arms, pale legs; supple, sleek bodies tangled together in the slack-limbed embrace of satisfaction.

(I could see Del giving to him what she wouldn't give to me, and all because he was Northern, not Southron, and therefore more entitled).

And I could see him laughing at Del's stories of our travels, ridiculing the big, dumb Southroner who called himself the Sandtiger because he had no real name, being born and deserted all at once, and raised a slave instead of a man.

By the time the dinner-plate moon rose and most of the shopkeepers latched their doors and shutters, I was ready to kill anything that *resembled* Alric the Northerner.

Which is why I beheaded a yellow melon as it rolled from its pile in front of a vendor's wagon.

I stood there feeling foolish and stupid and embarrassed as the sliced halves rolled neatly to the ground. Singlestroke dripped juice and pith.

Furtively, I glanced around. No one, *thank valhail,* had witnessed my foolishness. (Or else they weren't mentioning it). The vendor wasn't around, so I scooped up the cleanest half of the melon, wiped it off, and took it with me.

I was hungry, and it was delicious.

The thieves came out of the shadows like rats and surrounded me in the alley. Six of them, which meant they had to be very busy thieves because the cut for each of them would be correspondingly smaller. Instinctively, I sought the best footing in the sand-packed alley, braced myself, and waited.

They converged at once, not unexpectedly. I tossed the rind of my melon into one face, drew Singlestroke and spun around to attack the thieves at my back, who were expecting me to attack the thieves at my *front;* subsequently, they were somewhat surprised when I removed one head, sliced through the throat of a second man, lopped off the weaponed hand of a third—and swung around to defend myself against the first three.

The one with melon drippings in his face shouted something at the other two, ordering them to take me down; they were having nothing of it. Not now that the odds had rearranged themselves so suddenly.

The three sidled around me warily, armed with knives and Southron stickers, but they did not attack.

I waved my sword gently. Encouragingly. "Come on, men. Singlestroke is hungry."

Three pairs of eyes looked at the sword. Saw how my hands were locked around the hilt. Saw the smile on my face.

They backed off. "Sword-dancer," one of them muttered.

I smiled more widely. There are times the title comes in handy. In the South, a sword-dancer is considered the very highest level of expertise in the weapon-trade, be it common thievery, the life of a borjuni, or even a soldier. Sword-dancing is comprised of many different levels even within its own school, too numerous for me to detail. Suffice it to say that in the argot of the thieves, calling someone a sword-dancer meant, basically, he was off-limits. Untouchable.

Of course, there was another explanation. Thieves don't generally like to attack sword-dancers for three basic reasons: first, sword-dancers either have lots of money or none at all; why risk your life when your prey may be more broke than you? Second, sword-dancers are weapon-kin, relatively speaking, and you don't attack your own kind.

Third (and most importantly,) sword-dancers are invariably

much better at killing than common, ordinary thieves because that's how we make our living.

I smiled. "Want to join me in a circle?"

They all turned me down (rather politely, I thought), explaining they had pressing business elsewhere. They excused themselves and disappeared into the darkness. I bid them good-night and turned to find the nearest corpse on which to clean Singlestroke—

—and discovered I had made a very costly mistake.

There were two corpses instead of three. The third man, missing his right hand, was still very much alive—in addition to being a bit perturbed because I had deprived him of a hand.

But it was the left hand that held the knife. As I swung around, he thrust himself against me and brought the knife down into my right shoulder, tearing through flesh and muscle until it caught on the leather harness and grated against bone.

He was too close for Singlestroke to prove effective. I grasped my own knife left-handed as I kneed him in the crotch. I sent swift thanks to Del for giving me the idea, then flipped the knife to my right hand and threw it, cursing the pain in my shoulder. Nonetheless, I was pleased to see the weapon fly home into his heart. He tumbled to the ground. This time he stayed there.

I staggered to the closest wall and leaned against it, cursing again as I tried to regain my shaken senses. Singlestroke lay in the alley where I'd dropped him, dulled by blood. It was no place to leave a good sword, but I was a trifle indisposed at the moment.

The ragged hole in my shoulder wasn't a mortal wound, but it bled frightfully. Also, it hurt like hoolies. I wadded handfuls of my burnous into the wound, clamping my left hand against the fabric to stop the bleeding. When I could stand it, I retrieved knife and sword. Bending over nearly finished me, but I wobbled back onto my feet, steadied myself, then departed the alley as fast as I could. Thieves might respect a sword-dancer when he's in good health, but stick a knife in him and he's fair game for anyone.

I knew if I behaved in any way like I'd been seriously wounded, I'd be asking for trouble. So I let the arm hang naturally as I walked, although I could feel the blood running freely beneath my burnous. I had no choice. I had to go back to the inn to patch myself up before I continued the hunt for Del.

My black-eyed hussy was there, and those eyes opened wide as I walked into the place. (Well—staggered). I guess I wasn't doing too well by then. She plopped me into the nearest chair, poured me a hefty portion of aqivi and guided it to my mouth. Without her help I'd have spilled it all over everything, because my right hand was useless and my left one was pretty shaky.

"I told you you'd do better with me than her," she reproved.

"Maybe so." The room was beginning to move in very odd patterns.

"Come with me to my room." She hitched her right shoulder under my left arm and lifted.

I grinned at her woozily. "I don't think you'll get much out of me tonight, bascha."

She smiled back saucily. "You don't know that, beylo. Marika knows many things that will restore a man, even one who's a little short on blood." She grunted a little. "Come on, beylo. I'll help."

She did. She got me through the beaded doorway and into a tiny closet of a room, but it had a bed. (Naturally). Probably a busy one.

I sat down on the edge, stared at her through foggy eyes and tried to summon a properly imperative tone. "I'll sleep here tonight. But in the morning I must be on my way to Julah, so don't allow me to sleep late. The tanzeer expects me."

Marika put her hands on her hips and laughed at me. "If that's your way of warning me to keep my fingers out of your coin-pouch, save your breath. I'll look after you *and* your money. I know enough not to mess with the Sandtiger."

I peered at her blearily. "Do I know you?"

"I know *you*." She grinned. "*Everyone* knows you, beylo. You and that sword, and the claws around your neck." She bent down, displaying some of her charms, and ran a gentle hand across the right side of my face, caressing my scars. "And these," she whispered. "Nobody else has these."

I mumbled something and sort of faded back onto the bed.

Aqivi on an empty belly has that effect. (Not to mention a knife wound accompanied by substantial blood loss.) If Marika expected the Sandtiger to perform with his legendary prowess, she was going to have to wait.

The last thing I recall is Marika removing my sandals, murmuring something about cleaning my wound, and examining my bent toe. Something else for the legend, I thought hazily, and fell asleep.

Chapter 17

I woke up to find two pairs of eyes staring at me fixedly. Waiting. Both of them were very blue. But one pair belonged to Del.

I sat up sharply, uttered one pained exclamation, and fell back against the cushions.

Del's hand felt my brow. "Stupid," she remarked. "Don't move around so much."

I opened my eyes again when my head stopped reeling and the pain faded down into a manageable level of intensity. Del appeared to be perfectly safe and healthy, no different than she had been the day before. She still wore the apricot-colored burnous, which gilded the tan she'd acquired to a warm, tawny-gold. Pale hair was confined in a single thick braid, falling over one shoulder.

"How'd you find out?" I asked.

She was hunched forward on the stool, elbows on knees, chin in hands. "Alric brought me back here to wait for you. You never showed. We hung around a couple of days, and finally Marika told us where you were."

I looked past Del to the big Northerner, who lounged against the wall like a huge, dangerous bear. "What did you do with her?"

The bear showed his teeth briefly. "I took her home, Southron. Isn't that what you expect me to say?"

I tried to sit up, but Del's hands pressed me back and I was too weak to protest. I called Alric a rather impolite name in Southron dialect; he answered with an equally offensive term in the same tongue, unaccented. Stalemated for the moment, we glared at one another.

Del sighed. "Stop it. This is neither the time nor the place."

"What did he do to you?" I asked her, ignoring the darkening of the bear's looming face.

"*Nothing*," she declared, enunciating distinctly. "Do you think *every* man wants to get me in his bed?"

"Every man who's not dead already—or gelded."

Del laughed. "I suppose I should thank you for the compliment, backhanded or otherwise. But right now I'm more concerned about you." She felt my brow again and critically examined my bandaged shoulder. "What happened?"

"I was looking for *you*."

She let that sit a moment. "Ah," she said at last. "I see. It's *my* fault."

I shrugged, then wished I hadn't. "If you'd stayed where I'd left you, I wouldn't be flat on my back with a knife wound in my shoulder." I glared briefly at Alric. "You trusted him too easily, bascha. What if *he* had been a slaver?"

"*Alric?*" Del gaped. "He's a Northerner!"

"Right," I agreed, "and we both know someone's looking for you. For that debt you owe." I scowled at her. "You know as well as *I* do you thought that's who Alric was when you first saw him. Well—he still might be."

Del shook her head. "No. That was settled. There are rituals involved in the collection of a blood-debt. If Alric were an *ishtoya* hunting me, we'd have settled it in the circle."

Alric said something to her in their twisty Northern tongue, which left me out and made me more sullen than ever. I've never much liked feeling weak and sick; my temper suffers for it. Of course, having Alric around didn't help that much, either.

Alric said something to Del that brought her up short. She said something very briefly, very clipped, but filled with a myriad of tones: disbelief, astonishment, denial and something I couldn't identify. Something like—discovery. And she looked at me sharply.

Alric repeated his sentence. Del shook her head. I opened my mouth to ask her what in hoolies they were wrangling about, but she clamped a hand over my mouth.

"You be quiet," she ordered. "You've already lost enough blood . . . complaining won't help any. So Alric and I are going to put a stop to it."

"Put a stop to *what?*—complaining or bleeding?" I asked when she removed her hand.

"Probably both," Alric remarked, and smiled contentedly.

"How?" I asked suspiciously.

His grin broadened. "With fire, of course. How else?"

"*Wait* a minute—"

"Be quiet," Del said sternly. "He's right. Marika bound up the wound but it's still bleeding. We have to do something, so we'll try Alric's suggestion."

"*His* suggestion, was it?" I shook my head. "Bascha, he'd sooner see me dead. Then he'd have you to himself."

"He doesn't *want* me!" Del glared. "He's already got a wife and two little babies."

"This is the South," I reminded her. "Men are entitled to more than one wife."

"*Entitled!*" she inquired distinctly. "Or is it they just *take* them?"

"Del—"

"He's a Northerner," she reminded me, somewhat unnecessarily. "He doesn't believe in multiple wives."

Alric grinned bearishly. "Del might persuade me to consider adopting the practice, though."

I glared at him, which only served to amuse him further. He was big and strong and undeniably good-looking, as well as undoubtedly sure of himself.

I hate men like that.

"What are you going to do?" I demanded.

Alric gestured to a brazier on the floor. I saw a bone-hilted knife was in it already, blade heating. "*That's* what we're going to do."

I chewed on the inside of my mouth. "There isn't another way?"

"No." Del said it so promptly I began to suspect she was looking forward to it.

"Where's Marika?" I thought maybe the wine-girl would give me a little needed support.

"Marika is out plying her trade," Del said briskly. "Her *other* trade—the one you interrupted by taking over her bed."

"The knife is ready," Alric announced, in a tone that sounded amazingly like undisguised glee.

I looked at Del. "*You* do it. I don't trust him."

"I'd planned to," she agreed serenely. "Alric's going to hold you down."

"Hold me down?"

She bent and wrapped a cloth around the knife handle. "I think even the Sandtiger might find this a painful experience. He will probably yell a great deal."

"I don't yell."

Del's raised brows expressed eloquent doubt. Then Alric's big paws came down on my shoulders. His right hand was perilously close to the wound, which didn't make me any fonder of him. "Watch it, Northerner."

His face hung over mine. "I could *sit* on you—"

"Never mind."

Del handed me a cup of aqivi. "Drink."

"I don't need a drink. Just do it."

She smiled crookedly. "Foolish Tiger." Then she set the red-hot blade against the bleeding wound and I didn't care what Alric thought of me anymore (or even Del), I yelled loudly enough to bring down the whole building. I attempted one leaping lunge off the bed, but the Northerner leaned on me and I didn't go anywhere. I just lay there and cursed and sweated and felt sick, and smelled the stink of my burning flesh.

"You're enjoying this," I accused Del weakly through gritted teeth.

"No," she said. "No."

She might have said something more, but I didn't hear her. I just sort of went somewhere else for a while.

*   *   *

I woke up in a strange room in a strange place and in a very strange frame of mind. I felt floaty and detached, oddly numb, but I realized I wasn't in Marika's little room anymore.

"Del?" I croaked.

A woman came into the room, but she wasn't Del. She was black-haired and black-eyed, like Marika, but she wasn't her, either. She was also heavily pregnant. "Del is with the children." Her accent wasn't one at all, being familiarly Southron. She smiled. "I'm Lena. Alric's wife."

"Then—he really *is* married?"

"With two babies, and another on the way." She patted her swollen belly. "Northern men are lusty devils, aren't they?"

I scowled at her, wondering how she could be so blithely unconcerned with Del in the house providing all manner of distraction for a man she *herself* described as lusty. (Which wasn't anything I hadn't already suspected). "How am I?" I asked glumly.

Lena smiled. "Much better. Alric and Del brought you here a couple of days ago. You've slept since then, but you look much better. If the Sandtiger is the man I've heard he is, you should be up and around in no time."

The Sandtiger was feeling a little green around the edges. But he didn't tell her that.

"I'll get Del." Lena disappeared.

Del came in a moment later. There was an odd wariness in her eyes, and I asked her why.

"Because you're going to start in on Alric again, aren't you?"

"Shouldn't I?"

She glared. "You're being very stupid about this, you know. Alric offered us the hospitality of his house, which is hardly big enough for him, Lena and the babies. *You're* in the only bedroom! The rest of us share the front room."

Almost at once I felt pretty uncomfortable, which is precisely what she intended. "Then tell him we'll be on our way just as soon as I'm able."

"He knows that." Del hooked a three-legged stool over near the bed. "What happened to you, Tiger? Marika couldn't tell us."

I felt at the bandage over my right shoulder, wondering what the cauterized wound looked like. "Thieves. One of them got lucky." I paused. "Briefly."

"I'm sorry," Del said contritely, "I *should* have stayed at the inn; you wouldn't have gotten hurt. But Alric wanted to take me home to his wife and babies. He's very proud of them." She shrugged. "I'm a Northerner, and he hasn't seen anyone from his homeland for a long time."

"What's he *doing* here?"

She smiled a little. "Hunting dreams. Like everyone. He came South several years ago, hiring out his sword. Then he met Lena, and stayed."

"He could have taken her North."

"He could have. But he loves the South." She scowled a little. "You don't *have* to be born here to like the South, you know."

I sat up experimentally. For the moment I was all right. I shifted around so I could lean against the wall, settling my sore arm across my ribs. "He doesn't want to add to his collection of wives?"

The scowl disappeared as she smiled. "He only has *one*—and I think she might object. Tiger . . . there's no reason to be jealous of Alric."

"I'm not jealous. Just—protective. That's what you hired me for."

"I see." Del rose. "I'll get you some food. You look hungry."

I was. I didn't protest when she brought it. I munched away at bread and meat and goat's cheese. No aqivi, so I settled for water. (Tame stuff). Del waited as I ate, making certain the patient was doing well, and as she hunched on the stool Alric's babies came tumbling in. I stopped chewing and stared in amazement as both of them tried to climb simultaneously into Del's lap.

Both were girls, black-haired and dark-skinned like their mother, but claiming their father's blue eyes. An attractive combination. They couldn't be much older than two and three, both wobbly and clumsy, but—like puppies—all the cuter for it.

I watched Del with the girls. She had an easy way with them, showing affection without strangling them with it. An offhanded sort of manner, but obviously satisfactory. The girls looked serenely content.

So, for that matter, did Del. She smiled absently, smoothing curly black hair into place and, for a moment, hardly seemed aware of me in the room.

Abruptly, I broke the moment. "You'll go back North, then, when your business here is finished? Look for someone like Alric and start having Northern babies?"

"I—don't know. I mean—I haven't thought about it. I haven't really thought much at all past finding Jamail."

"What happens if you don't find him?"

"I told you once before: I haven't considered that possibility. I *will* find him."

"But if you *don't*," I persisted. "Del—be realistic. It's all well and good to go charging off on a quest of rescue and revenge . . . but you've got to consider all the angles. Jamail *might be dead* . . . and then you'll have to take a look at your priorities."

"I'll look at them *then*."

"Del—"

"I don't know!" Astonished, I saw tears in her eyes.

I just stared in amazement at what I'd started with my question.

Del sucked in an unsteady breath. "You keep hammering at me, Tiger. You keep telling me I won't find him, that I can't *possibly* find my brother. Because a woman doesn't stand a chance of tracking down a boy stolen five years ago. But you're wrong. Don't you see?" Her eyes were fastened on my face. "My sex doesn't matter. It's the task. That's all. It's what needs to be done. And I can do it. I *have* to do it."

"Del, I didn't mean—"

"Yes you did. They all do; all the men who look at me and see a woman with a sword. Laughing inwardly—*and* outwardly—at the games of a silly woman. And humoring me. *Humoring* me because they want me in their beds, and they'll put up with just about any silliness to get me there." She shook back her braid. "Only it isn't silliness, Tiger. It's a need. A duty. I *have* to find Jamail. I *have* to spend days, weeks, even years searching for him, because if I don't—" She stopped abruptly, as if all the emotions that had propelled her through her declaration spilled out at once, leaving behind an empty shell.

But she went on regardless. "Because if I don't, I have failed my brother, myself, my kin, my *kaidin* . . . and my sword."

The food was forgotten. One after the other, the girls climbed out of Del's lap and went away, frightened by the anger and grief in her voice. Tears spilled down her face unchecked and she didn't wipe them away.

I inhaled a careful breath. "There is only so much a person can do, Del. Man or woman."

"I can do it. I have to."

"Don't let it become an obsession."

"Obsession!" She stared at me. "What would *you* do? What would *you* do if you saw all but one of your family killed right in front of you?" She shook her head. "All I could do was *watch*. I couldn't help them, couldn't run, *couldn't even look*—until one of the raiders held me around my neck and made me watch them kill the men and rape the women, my sisters, my *mother,* and laughed while I cried and screamed and swore I'd castrate every one of them." She shut her eyes a moment, then opened them again. There were no tears now, only a quiet determination. "It made me what I am as much as the Salset made the Sandtiger."

I set the plate down beside me. "I thought you said you'd escaped the raiders."

"No." Her mouth was a flat, grim line.

"Then—" I didn't finish.

"They were going to sell us both, Jamail and I. Everyone else was dead." She hunched a shoulder. Her left one, naked of the sword. "But—I got away. *After* they were done with me. And—I left Jamail behind."

After a moment, I released a long, heavy breath. "Oh, bascha, I'm sorry. I've done you an injustice."

"You didn't take me *or* my mission seriously."

"No."

Del nodded. "I know. Well, it didn't matter. I was just using you to get me across the Punja." She shrugged. "I made a pact with the gods. With my sword. I don't really need anyone else."

"That secret you mentioned once," I said, "is it what you've just told me?"

"Part of it," she agreed. "The other part is—private." And she rose and walked out of the room.

I faced my opponent across the circle. I saw pale blond hair, tawny-gold suntan, sinews beneath firm flesh. And a sword, in supple hands.

"Good," observed the familiar voice, and I snapped out of the momentary daydream.

I scowled. Alric faced me across the haphazard circle he'd drawn in the dust of the alley behind his house. The curved Vashni sword was in his hands, but he had dropped the posture of preparedness. "What's good?" I asked.

"You," he answered. "You heal quickly." He shrugged. "No more need for this."

We had practiced for three days. My shoulder hurt like hoolies, but a sword-dancer learns to ignore pain and, eventually, overcome it entirely. Often, you don't get a chance to heal properly. You fight, you heal, you fight again. Whenever it's necessary.

Alric flicked a tuft of spore from his wickedly curved blade. One bare foot obliterated a portion of the circle; finished with practice, there was no more need for circles drawn in dust.

I glanced over at the girls. They sat quietly against the shaded wall, eyes wide and mouths covered with small fists. Alric had given them permission to watch, but only if they kept silent in the watching. They had. At two and three, they behaved themselves better than most adults.

"We're finished," he told them, giving them their release; both girls got up and headed for the front of the adobe house at a run.

I bent and scooped up my discarded harness, sliding Single-stroke into the sheath. Sand gritted against the soles of my bare feet. Bending over hurt, but not as much as participating in a dance, practice or no.

I hooked the harness over my arms. Did up the buckles. "Why a Vashni sword?" I nodded at Alric's blade. "Why not a Northern sword—one like Del's?"

"Like Del's?" Alric's pale brows jerked up beneath ragged bangs. "I *never* had a sword like Del's."

I frowned, haphazardly erasing the circle with one sweeping foot. "You're a Northerner. And a sword-dancer—more or less."

Unoffended by my gibe, Alric nodded. "Sword-dancer, Northerner, yes. But not of Del's caliber."

"A woman—?"

"Oh, it's true *that's* unusual," he agreed, going over to the bota he'd left sitting in the shade of a buff-colored wall. "But then *Del's* unusual to begin with." He unplugged the bota, sucked down a couple of swallows, then held it out in silent invitation.

I quit erasing the circle and went over to accept the bota. We sat down and leaned companionably against the wall, which was faintly warm even thought it lay deep in shade. In the South, shade is not necessarily cool.

I sucked down my own share of aqivi. "No. I'd never say Del was anything *but* unusual. But that doesn't tell me why you use a Vashni sword."

Alric shrugged. "A fight," he said. "Me against a Vashni. Nasty fellow, too. He managed to break my Northern sword." He raised a silence hand as I opened my mouth to protest. "No—it wasn't a sword like hers. It was—just a sword. And it broke. About the time I was looking up the curving edge of the Vashni's blade, I decided I didn't need *my* sword to kill him. So I grabbed his right out of his hands . . . and killed him with it." He smiled as he looked fondly at the shining blade. The hilt was made of a human thighbone. "I kept it for my own."

"Del calls hers a *jivatma*—a blooding-blade—" Alric nodded. "What's that mean?"

He shrugged and drank more aqivi as I handed him the bota. "What it sounds like. A blade made specifically for drawing blood. For killing. Oh, I know—you can say *any* sword suits that purpose—but in the North, it's different. At least—it is if you're a sword-dancer." He gave me back the bota. "The rituals are different in the North, Tiger. That's why you and I aren't a good match—our styles differ too much. And I imagine even Del and I would have trouble performing the proper rituals."

"Why?"

"Because her style and mine would be similar. *Too* similar, to offer a superior match. Blade patterns, maneuvers, footwork—" he shrugged "—even though we learned from different *kaidin*, all Northerners know many of the same tricks and rituals within the circle. And so it would be an impossible dance."

"But not if the dance were to the death."

Alric looked at me. "Even if I were an enemy, I'd never dance with her."

My brows ran up into my hair. "A woman—?"

"Doesn't matter." He frowned thoughtfully, watching his right foot as he scuffed it in the dirt. "In the South, sword-dancing is made up of levels. A student works his way through the levels as far as he can. You, I've heard, are seventh-level." As I nodded, he went on. "Here, I'd be considered third-level. In the North I'm better than that, but the comparisons don't really apply. It's like comparing a man and a woman—you just can't." Blue eyes flicked up to meet my green ones. "I guess what I'm saying is that the highest level of training in the North has no corresponding level in the South. It isn't a matter of *skill*—at least, not exclusively. It's more a matter of total, absolute dedication and determination, a complete surrendering of your will to the rituals of the dance." He shook his head. "Hard for me to say, Tiger. I guess the best way is just to say that Del—if she's telling me the truth—was *ishtoya* to the *an-kaidin*. And all I can say about that is what I know, which isn't much. I never stood so high." He drank again. "She must be telling the truth. Otherwise she stole that Northern sword . . . and a named blade can't be stolen."

Named blade. There it was again. A deliberate distinction. "My sword has a name."

"And a legend." Alric smiled and smacked the bota against my hand. "I know all about Singlestroke. Most sword-dancers do.

But—well, it's not the same. A *jivatma* is a little more than that. Only *an-kaidin* bestow them on selected *an-ishtoya*, those students who have proven their worthiness."

"Why is it *you* don't have one?"

"I don't have one because I never stood high enough in the ritual rankings to be awarded one." He said it easily enough, as if the pain of the knowledge had faded years before. Alric, I thought, was content with his lot. "As for what one *is*—it's hard to explain. More than a sword. Less than a person. It doesn't really *live*, although some might say it does." He shrugged. "A *jivatma* has particular attributes. Like you or me. In that respect, the sword has a life of its own. But only when matched with the *an-ishtoya* who has earned his—" he paused significantly a moment "—or *her* right to it, who knows the sword's name, and who knows how to sing the song." He shrugged. "*Ishtoya* who achieve the highest ranking from the *an-kaidin* are no longer *ishtoya*. They are *an-ishtoya*. And then *kaidin* themselves, if they choose to be. Or sword-dancers."

"*Kaidin—an-kaidin.*" I frowned, mulling over the nuances in the tones. "Del always called her sword-master *kaidin*, without the prefix."

After a moment, Alric nodded. "The prefix is an honorific. *Kaidin—you* would say shodo—means sword-master. Teacher. Highly skilled, but a teacher. *Kaidin* is someone all *ishtoya* know. But—*an-kaidin* is more. *An-kaidin* is the highest of the high. I think she drops the prefix as a way of trying to deny what has happened."

I frowned. "What has happened?"

Alric shoved hair out of his face with a forearm. "There is— *was*—only one *an-kaidin* of the old school left in all the North. Newer schools have replaced the old, but many *ishtoya* preferred to follow the old ways instead of the new."

"Was?" I asked sharply.

"He was killed a year ago, I heard. In ritual combat against an *an-ishtoya.*"

It happens. Even to the best of us. It isn't always easy to avoid bloodshed in the circle, even if it's nothing more than an exhibition.

The big Northerner with the curving Vashni sword looked at

Singlestroke. "Swords are—*different* here in the South. But in the North, there are swords and swords. A named blade, a *jivatma*, is made of steel that is more than steel. The *an-kaidin* makes them for the special students, the *an-ishtoya* who will someday take the *an-kaidin's* place. Being *ishtoya* only, I never had the chance to learn more about the blooding-blades. But—it is precisely that: a sword quenched in blood. And the first blood is always carefully selected, because the sword assumes all the skill of the life that is taken."

Selected. I looked at him sharply. "Then—you're saying it wasn't an accident that killed the *an-kaidin.* That someone desired to assume the skills of the *an-kaidin.*"

Alric's face was taut. "I heard it was purposely done."

I thought of the Northern sword. I recalled the alien shapes in the metal; the sensation of ice and death. As if the sword lived. As if the sword knew me. As if it meant to kill *me* as it had killed the *an-kaidin.*

Alric fingered the hilt of his Vashni sword. I wondered, absently, if *it* had a name. "Killing an *an-kaidin,* as you might imagine, is punishable by execution," he said quietly. "Blood-guilt isn't a thing anyone carries lightly."

"No," I agreed.

He met my eyes squarely. "In the North, there is a thing called blood-debt. The debt is owed to the kin of a man—or woman— whose death was undeserved. One person, or two, or even more than twenty, may swear to collect the debt."

I nodded after a moment, thinking about the man who followed Del. Sworn to collect the blood-debt? "*How* is the debt collected?"

"In the circle," Alric answered. "The dance is to the death."

I nodded again. I wasn't particularly surprised. I didn't doubt the dance *was* justified by the crime that had been committed. A man killed; a teacher slain by his student. Because the student had needed the skill that was *in* the man, and not merely what he had taught.

I blew breath out of stiff lips. I thought of how desperately Del wanted to avenge the massacre of her kin; the enslavement of her brother; the humiliation she must have suffered at the cruel hands of Southron raiders. It was, I thought, a blood-debt owed to her. One she was more than due, regardless of the cost.

I knew full well Del was capable of doing anything she wanted to do.

Anything at all.

No matter what the cost.

Chapter 18

Alric handed me the bota. But before I could unplug it and suck down a swallow, the two little girls came running around the side of the house.

They went straight to Alric, tugged on both arms, and babbled at him in an almost unintelligible mixture of Northern and Southron. I wasn't sure how much of the unintelligibility had to do with their age, how much of it with their binguality.

Alric sighed and got up. "We're to go inside. Lena sent them to fetch us both." Then he said something in Northern to the little girls, and both went scurrying off again.

"Well-trained," I remarked.

"For girls." He grinned. "Del would skin me if she heard me say that. Well, she'd have the right. In the North, women know more freedom."

"I noticed." I rounded the corner of the adobe dwelling and ducked inside the door that was decidedly too short for Northerners, or Southroners like me.

And stopped.

Alric's house is small. Two rooms. A bedroom, which I had willingly turned back over to Alric and his family once I was feeling better, and a front room, which doubled as sleeping quarters at night for Del and me. There was no question that with four adults and two children, the house was very crowded.

Except now it claimed one more adult, and the room got smaller still.

Del sat cross-legged on a pelt-rug of curly saffron goathair. She watched Alric and I enter, but said nothing. Locked in silence, she sat with her sword across her thighs.

Unsheathed.

I stepped aside so Alric could slip in. Lena stood in the shadows of the room. Her daughters flanked her, one on each side. No one said a word.

I looked at the stranger. He wore a mouse-gray burnous. The hood was pushed back from his head. Brown-haired, like me. Tall, like me. Very nearly as heavy. Other factors I couldn't determine because of the burnous. But I saw the sword-hilt riding his left shoulder, and I knew the hunter had finally run down his prey.

The stranger smiled. The seam of an old scar diagonally bisected his chin. His face had been lived in. There was gray in his hair. I thought he had a good ten years on me, which put him a couple of years past forty. His eyes were as blue as Del's and Alric's, but mostly he looked like me.

He made me the desert gesture of greeting: spread-fingered hand placed over his heart, brief bow. "She says you are the Sandtiger." A cool, smooth voice, tinged with the Northern accent.

"I am."

"Then I am truly pleased to meet the legend at last."

I listened for the bite of sarcasm, the tracery of scorn. There was none. No impoliteness I could discern. But it didn't make me like him any better.

"His name is Theron." Del, finally. "He has been the shadow who was not a shadow."

Theron nodded a little. "I came down from the North seeking the *an-ishtoya*, but circumstances have conspired to delay me time and time again. Now, at last, they are in my favor."

Beside me, Alric let out a breath. "How many of you are there?"

"Only me." So quietly. So assured. "That is how I requested it."

"So," I said sharply. "If Del kills you, no one else will take up the hunt."

"For the space of a year," Theron agreed. "A Northern custom bound by agreements and the rituals of the circle. Since you are a sword-dancer—Southron or no—I assume you understand."

"Explain it to me anyway."

Briefly, Theron's cool smile fell away. But then he took it back. "She owes blood-debt to many people in the North. *Ishtoya, kaidin, an-ishtoya, an-kaidin.* Many desire her death, but only one may claim it in the circle—for the space of a year. When that year is done, another—or more—may seek her out again."

"There is more to it than that," Alric said sharply.

Theron's smile widened. "Yes. In all fairness, Southron, I must also say there is a choice for the *an-ishtoya* to make. Although I have been given permission to challenge her to a dance, I must also offer the *an-ishtoya* the chance to gain full pardon."

"How?" I demanded.

"By going home," Del said. "I can go home and face judgment by all the *kaidin* and *ishtoya.*"

"Sounds more sensible than facing him in a circle," I told her flatly.

Del shrugged. "I would almost certainly be judged guilty of premeditated murder. That is blood-guilt; why the debt is owed. Acknowledgment of an undeserved—and unnecessary—death."

"Then you don't deny you killed the *an-kaidin.*"

"No," Del said in surprise. "Never. I killed him. In the circle." Her hands tightened on the sword. "It was for the blade, Tiger. To blood my blade. Because I needed more sword-magic than what the *an-kaidin* had taught me."

"Why?" I asked quietly. "Why did you need it *so much?* I've seen you dance, bascha, even if it wasn't for real. I can't believe you lacked so much skill as to need the *an-kaidin's* more."

She smiled a little. "For that, I thank you. But yes—I needed the *an-kaidin's* skill. I *required* it . . . and so I took it." For a moment she looked down at her bared sword, caressing the gleaming metal. "There were more than twenty raiders, Tiger. More than twenty men. Alone, would even the *Sandtiger* approach so many men intending to kill them all?"

"Not alone," I answered. "I'm still alive because only rarely am I a fool, and *never* when it comes to figuring the odds."

Del nodded. Her face was unmarred by frown or anxiety. Except for the continual movement of fingers against blade, she appeared more than composed enough. "It was owed me, Tiger. The blood-debt of more than twenty men. There was no one to collect it but me. There was no one I *wished* to collect it *for* me. My duty. My desire. My determination." The hint of a smile at the corners of her mouth. "I am not so foolish as to claim a woman, alone, could kill more than twenty men. And so I took the *an-kaidin* into my sword, and no longer was I a woman alone."

I felt the faintest chill. "Figuratively speaking."

"No," Del said. "That is the quenching, Tiger. A named blade, unquenched, is merely a sword. Better than good. But cold metal, lacking life and spirit and courage. To get it, to bring a *jivatma* to life, it is quenched in the body of a strong man, as strong as you can find. The *an-ishtoya*, to become *kaidin*, seeks out a respected enemy, and sheathes the sword in his soul. The sword assumes the will of the man." She shrugged a little. "I had need of much skill and power in order to collect the debt the raiders owed me. And so I took it." She didn't look at Theron. She looked at me. "The *an-kaidin* knew. He could have refused to join me in the circle—"

"*No,*" Theron said sharply. "He would never have refused. He was an honorable man. He could not, in all conscience, deny his *an-ishtoya* the chance to prove herself."

Now she looked at him. "Let it be known: the *an-kaidin* joined the *an-ishtoya* in the circle, and the blooding-blade was quenched."

I released a slow breath. "As she says, it's done. And—I think maybe she had reason for what she did."

Theron's face tightened. "It's possible the *kaidin* and *ishtoya* would agree her need justified the death. It's also possible they would unanimously convict her of premeditated murder and order her execution."

"Depriving you of your bounty."

Theron shook his head. "If she chooses to go home for judgment, I will be paid my price. If she is sentenced to death, I will be paid my price." He laughed aloud. "There's no way I can lose."

I had conceived a distinct dislike for Theron. "Unless she chooses the circle."

Theron's smile came back. "I do hope she does."

"He's a sword-dancer," Del said lightly. "He was trained by the *an-kaidin* who trained me. Theron was one of the few *an-ishtoya* who were given a choice upon completion of his schooling: would he be sword-dancer or *an-kaidin?*" Her face was very calm as she looked at me. "Do you understand, Tiger? He was *an-ishtoya.* The best of the best. Only *an-ishtoya* are given the choice between teaching or doing." She sighed a little. "Theron chose to be a sword-dancer instead of *kaidin,* and so the dwindling ranks of the *an-kaidin* were denied the younger, stronger man they needed. A man who could have trained promising *ishtoya* to achieve the highest rank."

"*An-ishtoya.*" I said. "The best of the best."

"You have heard," Theron said flatly. "You have heard how it was the old *an-kaidin*—the master who taught *me!*—offered the choice to his female *an-ishtoya,* and how she repudiated him. How she invited him into the circle so she could quench the thirst of her blade before it tasted the blood of another." The grave politeness was banished from his tone. "You have heard *her* choice!"

"This is blood-feud," Del said quietly. "Sword-dancer against sword-dancer. *An-ishtoya* against *an-ishtoya.*" She smiled. "And, as Theron would also have it, man against woman. So he can prove he is superior."

Theron said something in Northern. The tone was almost a singsong, and it didn't take much for me to recognize a formal challenge. I've given and received my own share over the years.

When he was done, Del nodded once. Said something quietly, also in Northern. And then she got up and walked out of the shadowed house into the light of the day.

Theron turned to follow. But when he reached me, he smiled. "You are welcome to watch, sword-dancer. There should always be a witness to the collection of a blood-debt."

I waited until he was gone from the house. I looked at Alric. "I don't think I much like that son of a Salset goat."

Solemn-faced, Alric nodded. He said something to Lena and the girls—requesting they remain inside—and followed me outside.

The circle Alric and I had used was nearly obliterated. Here and there I saw a trace of the curving line, but we'd obscured much of it with bare and sandaled feet. Now it begged to be drawn again.

I looked at Theron. Quietly he stripped himself of sandals, belt, harness. Of everything save his dhoti. In his hands he held his naked sword, and I saw the alien runes.

For a brief moment we faced one another: Northerner to Southron. Judging. It wasn't our dance, but we judged. Because he knew as well as I did that if he overcame Del, the next opponent in the circle would be a sword-dancer called the Sandtiger.

Deftly, Del stripped out of her burnous. Unlaced sandals and set them aside. Unbuckled harness and put it with the sandals. Tunicked, with the *jivatma* in her hands, she turned to look at Theron. "I would ask the Sandtiger to draw the circle."

Theron didn't smile. "Agreed: he will draw the circle. But he may not act as arbiter. The Sandtiger would hardly be impartial to the woman in whom he sheaths his *other* sword."

I thought Del would immediately deny it. But she let him think what he would.

It was *me* who wanted to speak; to split open his Northern face.

"I will be arbiter." Alric, next to me. Like me, he looked at Theron.

The older man dipped his head in a gesture of acceptance. "It might be as well. As a Northerner, you will have some better idea of the rituals required." Another subtle gibe at me. Or was it aimed at Del? Hard to tell, though it was possible Theron intended to put her in poor temper.

But I had never seen Del angry, not *really* angry, and I doubted this would do it.

"Tiger," she said. "It would please me if you set the circle in the sand."

For a dance, the ground was treacherous. For a practice circle, it had done well enough because we had no better. The alley between this row of dwellings and that row of dwellings was not particularly wide, although there was more room at the junction of this alley and another running at a right angle from it. The ground was hardpacked, yet veiled in a layer of sand and soft dirt. Alric and I had spent much of our time unintentionally sliding around the circle, trying to keep our feet beneath our bodies. For practice it was all well and good. For a genuine sword-dance, the footing would be deadly.

Del and Theron waited. I saw by the grim set to Alric's mouth he knew as well as I did the implications of a genuine dance conducted here. But the thing was settled. Del and Theron had settled it.

I unsheathed Singlestroke and began to draw the circle.

When it was done, I put my sword away and looked at both of the dancers. "Prepare."

Theron and Del stepped into the circle, placed swords in the precise center, and stepped outside again.

I looked at the weapons on the ground. Del's I knew; at least, as much as I *could* know. Theron's was strange to me. Cold, alien steel, steel that was not steel, as Alric had described it. Del's was the now-familiar salmon-silver. Theron's was palest purple.

They faced one another across the circle. To me, preparation meant positioning oneself outside the circle. Taking up a posture that lends itself to speed, strength, strategy. A moment for introspection and self-evaluation, before the mind tells the muscles what to do. And it was what I expected out of them.

I had, however, reckoned without the Northern rituals. I'd forgotten just how different all the similarities could be. Del and Theron stood quietly on either side of the circle, and they sang.

Softly. So softly I could hardly hear it.

Confidence. Serenity. Exultation, exhortation. All of these, and more.

Deathsong? No. A lifesong. The promise of victory.

Alric took his place. As arbiter, it was his word that claimed the dance was won or lost. Even if it was obvious one of the dancers was dead, the ritual required a declaration.

I moved away. My task was done. Theron was right; there was no way I could possibly be impartial. But not because Del and I had shared a bed.

Because I *wanted* to.

But also because I'd come to know the woman as more than just a woman.

I smiled a little. Wryly. Shook my head. Alric frowned across the circle at me, not understanding, but I didn't bother to explain. Such things are just too personal.

"Dance," Alric said. It was all either of them required.

Together they reached their swords. I saw Del's hands flash down, flash up; saw Theron's flash down, flash up.

And then I stopped looking at their hands. I stopped listening to their songs. Because the swords had come alive.

Del had told me, once, a named blade *wasn't* alive. But she'd *also* said, neither was it dead. And as I watched, astounded, I perceived the paradox in the explanation. The paradox in the swords themselves.

Salmon-silver, flashing in the sunlight. And Theron's: pale purple. And yet, they changed. The colors shifted, running from hilt to tip, until I saw rainbows in the sunlight. Not the sort that comes after a rainstorm, but rainbows of darkness and light. Pale-rose, raisin-purple, a tint of madder-violet. All the colors of the night. All the colors of a sunset, but showing their darker side. No pastels. No water-washed tints. Lurid luminescence. Raw color stripped down to nakedness.

Both blades were a blur. From wrists too subtle for me to follow sprang patterns I'd never seen. And I *could* see them, clearly, because each blade as it moved traced the pattern in the air. It etched a ribbon of purest color, a streak of livid light, like the afterglow of a torch carried away too quickly.

As if the blades severed the air itself like a knife will cut into flesh.

They danced. How they danced. Spinning, gliding, feinting, sliding, ripping apart the day to leave eerie incandescence in its place: cobalt-blue, livid purple; viridescent, lurid rose.

When I could, I stopped watching the swords. Instead I watched the dancers, to learn what I could learn. To soak up the gift they offered: the gift of the Northern style.

It was, as I have said, far different from my own. With my height, strength and reach, my best strategy is endurance. I can swing steel with the best of them. I can hack and slash and sweep, thrust and counter and riposte. I wear down my opponents. I can stand toe to toe and hew them down, blocking and stopping their blows. Or I can dance with the fastest man because, for all my size, I am quick. Just not as quick as Del.

Theron, nearly my physical duplicate, might have done better to mimic my style. But he hadn't been trained that way. Like Del, he employed the subtle strength in wrists and forearms, using quick, slashing patterns. Much like a stiletto against an ax, if you were to compare his style to mine. He might have stood there and banged on her sword, but it wasn't Theron's way. And I could tell it wouldn't beat her.

Quite frankly, I'd done the lady a disservice. In all my arrogance and pride in my own reputation (warranted, of course), I'd neglected to acknowledge her own tremendous ability. I'd scoffed, supremely confident a woman could never face a man in the circle and win. Not even against a less than competent dancer. But I'd been too quick to underestimate her talent. Now I saw it plainly, and realized my mistake.

So did Theron. I could see it in his eyes. The grudge-match now was more than a simple determination of guilt or innocence. It had gone past collection of a blood-debt. It had slipped under the guard of his masculine pride and pricked him in the gut, just as her sword tip pricked him in the knuckles.

Del was better than good. Del was better than Theron.

Alien steel clashed, twisted, screeched. Blade on blade in the cacophony of the dance. Slide, slide, step. The belling of the steel. The hiss of bare feet against the grit of sand on top of hardpack.

A latticework of ribbons glowing in the sunlight. Pattern here, pattern there; a tracery of flame. Salmon-silver, palest-purple, and all the colors in between.

Sweat ran down their bodies. It lent a sheen to the pale apricot of Del's tanned skin. Bare arms, bare legs, bared face with white-blonde hair tied back. I saw grim determination in her face. Total loss of awareness except for the dance she danced against a good opponent.

Quite clearly, Theron fought to kill. In the circle, death is not mandatory. Victory is the thing. If a man is overcome and yields at the asking, a winner is declared. Often enough, the dance is little more than an exhibition, or a testing of sheer skill. I've danced for the joy of it before, against good and bad opponents. I've danced to kill as well, though the deaths have never pleased me. What pleases me is surviving.

Del, I thought, would survive. Theron, I thought, might not.

A breeze kicked up. It ruffled the thin layer of saffron sand. Increased to a wind. Lifted the sand and blew it into my eyes. Impatiently, I brushed the grit away.

But the wind remained. Intensified. Ran around the circle like a child's spinning toy. And then I saw how it centered itself as a whirlwind inside the circle: a dust-demon licking at feet. Licking, licking, growing, until even Theron and Del fell away from one another because the demon made them do it.

Spinning, spinning, spinning, so fast the eye couldn't follow. *Mind* couldn't, no matter how hard I stared. And then the dust exploded in a shower of grit and film, and in the dust-demon's place was a man.

Sort of. Not really a—*man*. Rather, a being. Small. Neither ugly nor attractive. Just—a sort of formless shape with the barest suggestion of human features. It hung in the air between Del and Theron, floating in the circle.

"I am Afreet," it announced. "My master wants a sword."

Four of us merely gaped.

"I am Afreet," it repeated, a trifle impatiently. "My master wants a sword."

"You said that already." The thing didn't seem particularly dangerous, just a trifle odd. So I decided conversation wouldn't do us any harm.

Tiny features solidified in a tiny misshapen face. It frowned. It stared, much as we did.

I saw hands form. Feet. Ears appeared, and a nose. But the thing was naked. Quite clearly, the thing was male. And abruptly, I knew what it was.

"*An* afreet," I said. "That isn't a proper name, it's a description of what it *is*."

"Then what *is* it?" Del asked in some distaste.

"I am Afreet," the afreet announced. "My master wants a sword."

Simultaneously, Theron and Del each took a single step back from the tiny floating being. I almost expected them to put their swords behind their backs, as if to hide them from view.

Apparently the afteet did, too. It—*he*—laughed.

And if you've ever heard an afreet laugh, you don't much like the sound.

"I am Afreet," it began. "My master—"

"We know, we know," I interrupted. "Change your tune, little—" —pause—"—*man*. Who is your master, and why does he want a sword?"

"My master is Lahamu, and Lahamu desires a sword of power."

"So he sent you out to get one." I sighed. "Little afreet, you don't frighten me. You're only a manifestation of his power, not a measure of it. Go home. Go back to Lahamu. Tell him he can get his sword another way."

"Tiger," Del said uneasily. "*You're* not the one standing so close to him."

"He can't hurt you," I told her. "Oh, I suppose he could kick sand in your face or pull your hair, but that's about the extent of it. He's just an afreet. A busybody. Not a genuine demon."

"But this Lahamu *is?*" she demanded. "Not so wise to treat his servant badly."

"Lahamu isn't a demon." Alric, from the other side of the circle. "He's a tanzeer. Rusali is his domain."

"A tanzeer with an *afreet!*" That sounded odd even to me. "How'd *that* come about?"

"Lahamu dabbles in magic." Alric shrugged. "He's not the brightest man in the South, Tiger. He inherited the title, which means he doesn't necessarily deserve it." Alric eyed the afreet. "I've heard some odd stories about him, but I don't think I'll repeat them where little ears can hear them. Let's just say he's not known for his—judgment."

"Ah." I scowled at the little afreet. "That means he's after a *magical* sword."

The afreet laughed again. "A magical Northern sword, with magical properties. Power. *Better* than Southron swords only good in the hands of a dancer, or so my master says."

I nodded. "Lahamu fancies himself a sword-dancer *too*, does he?"

"Told you." That from Alric. "Maybe he wants to steal a little of your glory, Tiger."

The afreet glared at him. "Lahamu is *many* things."

This time *I* laughed. "Sorry, little afreet. No time for this right now. We're a bit busy at the moment."

The tiny face glared. "My master wants a sword. My master will *get* a sword."

"How?" I asked gently. "Does he want you to steal one?"

"Steal the dancer, steal the sword." An afreetish grin showed pointed teeth. "But not the woman; *the man*."

Theron never had a chance. I saw his blade whip up as if to halve the afreet, but the whirlwind swallowed him whole. And with him his Northern sword.

A thin veil of dust settled back to the ground. Alric and I blinked at one another across the circle. It was empty except for Del, who glared at me. "I thought you said that little—thing— couldn't *do* anything."

"Guess I was wrong."

"Tell him to bring Theron back! Tell him I wasn't finished with him." Del frowned. "Besides, if Lahamu wanted a Northern sword so much, why take only one when he could have had two?"

"I *think* I know the answer, but I don't think you'll like it much."

Her glance was level. "Why not?"

"Because, being Southron, Lahamu probably doesn't think much of women." I shrugged. "Theron had more status."

Del scowled. Then she swore. Softly, beneath her breath.

"Does it matter?" I asked, exasperated. "At least Theron's out of your hair. You should be grateful to Lahamu for sending out the afreet."

"Grateful? For stealing my fight?" She scowled at me. "*I* wanted to take Theron—*I* wanted to beat him—"

"Beat him? Or kill him?"

Her chin rose. "You think I'm not capable of either?"

"I think you're capable of both."

Del stared at me a long moment. I saw the subtleties of changing expressions in her face. But then she turned away to step outside the circle, and I knew the dance was finished.

But only the one against Theron.

Chapter 19

Alric bought two horses and gear with the money I gave him, and three days later Del and I took our leave. I thanked the big Northerner and his wife for their hospitality, apologized for putting them out of their bedroom, hugged each of the little girls, and left it at that.

Del's farewell was a little more involved than mine, at least when it came to the girls. She picked each one up, whispered something in her ear, hugged her, kissed her, then set her down again. It was an odd dichotomy, I thought: woman with child; woman with sword.

I mounted my blue roan gelding and waited for Del to climb aboard the gray mare Alric had purchased. The mare was little, almost dainty-looking, and yet I took note of the deceptively wide, deep chest and long shoulders that marked endurance and good wind. My own blue roan was larger and rangier, almost clumsy-looking with his jug-head, gaunt flanks and big hips, but nothing really set him apart from other horses, at least in class distinctions. (If anything, he came out of a *lower* class entirely). Another horse had gnawed on his slate-gray tail, leaving it short and very ragged; not much of a flyswatter, now.

I glanced at Alric and gave him a grimace that was half-scowl, half amusement. He knew what I meant. I'd given him enough money for excellent mounts, but he'd purposely chosen horses of unexceptional quality. The better to blend in with other people in Julah.

Sighing, I recalled the bay stud. It would take me years to find another horse like him.

The respite (if you could call it that) in Rusali had made the Punja pale in our minds. Out upon the sands again we quickly remembered the harsh reality; how lucky we were that the Salset had found us while we were still alive. Del pulled up her apricot hood and hunched her shoulders against the heat of the sun; I rubbed at my sore shoulder and wondered how soon it would be before I could use it without pain. A right-handed sword-dancer can't afford to be disabled very long, or he loses more than just a sword-dance.

"How far to Julah?" Del asked.

"Not far. Two or three days."

She twisted in the blanketed saddle. "That close?"

I stood up in the stirrups a moment, trying to urge the roan out of a jagged, rambling trot into a more comfortable long-walk. At this rate, he'd rattle my mouth completely clean of teeth. "As I recall, Rusali is a bit northwest of Julah. Of course it all depends on the mood of the Punja, but we should be within a couple of days' ride." I gritted my teeth and stood up again, removing my backside from the pounding of the shallow saddle. "Fool horse—"

Del slowed her gray mare. No longer competing, my roan dropped into a more comfortable walk beside her. "Better?" Del asked calmly.

"I'm trading in this sandtiger-bait as soon as we get to Julah." I saw the dark-tipped ears twitch toward me. "Yes, *you*." I looked at Del. "Well, have you decided what your plans are once we reach our destination?"

"You asked me that once before."

"And you never really told me."

"No," she agreed, "and I don't know as if I feel like telling you now, anymore than I did *then*."

"Because you don't know."

She slanted me a gloomy scowl. "I suppose *you* have a plan."

"Matter of fact . . ." I grinned.

Del sighed and tucked a wisp of sunbleached hair behind her right ear. The silver hilt of her Northern sword—her *jivatma*—shone in the sunlight. "I should have known . . . all right—what is it?"

"I'm going to become a slave trader," I explained. "One who just happens to have a gorgeous Northern bascha in his possession." I nodded. "This trader is no dummy. He realizes full well what a big market there is for Northern boys and girls. And—since it isn't always easy to steal them—he's decided to breed them."

"*Breed* them!"

"Yes. So, since he's got a prime breeder on his hands, he needs to match her with a Northern male."

Pale brows knitted over her nose. "Tiger—"

"He can't be too old, because *she's* not," I pointed out. "He should be young and strong and virile and as good-looking as she is. That way the children are more likely to be attractive. What I *need* is a duplicate of her, except a male." I waited expectantly.

Del stared at me. "You intend to use me as bait, to flush my brother into the open."

"Bang on the head, bascha. I'll offer a deal to the man who has him: pick of the litter, so to speak. He can have the first child of the mating in addition to my gold, so he can start his own kennel of Northern slaves."

Del stared down at her braided gentian reins. Fingers picked at the cotton.

"Del—?"

"It might work." Her tone was subdued.

"Of course it will work . . . so long as you go along with my suggestions."

"Which are?" A pair of direct blue eyes fastened themselves on my face.

I took a careful, delaying breath. But there wasn't anything for it but honesty and baldness. "You'll have to be my slave. A genuine slave. That means wearing the collar and serving me as a docile slave, submissive and silent."

After a moment, her mouth twisted. "I don't think I'd be very good at that."

"Probably not," I agreed drily, "but it's the only chance we have. You willing to *take* that chance?"

She looked away from me, pushing rigid fingers through the dark-gray stubble of the mare's roached mane. The apricot hood spilled from Del's head and lay tumbled against her shoulders. The once butter-yellow tint of her hair had been almost completely swallowed by the platinum-white of sunbleaching, but it was still glossy as cornsilk in its single braid.

"Del?"

She looked back at me steadily, taking fingers from the shaven mane. "What would happen if we simply went in looking for a Northern boy of fifteen?"

I shook my head. "For one thing, they'd want to know why I wanted to buy him specifically. For another, if they found out about *you,* they'd make me an offer. If they learned you're a free Northern woman, they'd simply *steal* you." I didn't smile; it wasn't amusing. "But—if you're a slave already, they'll simply try to talk me into selling you. And I, naturally, will refuse every offer."

"You like money," she pointed out. "You like money a *lot.*"

"But I wouldn't *dream* of selling you," I retorted. "At least, not until you've paid me in the manner to which we've agreed."

"You don't get *that* until we find my brother."

"And we won't be able to *do* that unless we give this a try."

Del sighed, teeth gritted so hard the muscles in her jaw stood up. "You'd take my knife away from me, then . . . and my sword."

I thought about that sword in my hands again. I thought about what Alric had told me about quenching its thirst in the blood of an enemy.

Or the blood of an honored *an-kaidin.*

"Yes," I told her. "Slaves don't generally carry knives and swords."

"And you'll put a collar around my neck."

"It's customary."

She swore. At least, I *think* she swore. I needed Alric to translate. "All right," she agreed at last. "But—I think I'm going to regret this."

"Not with *me* as your owner."

"That's *why*."

The first blacksmith we found in the outskirts of Julah was more than happy to make a collar for Del. I already had her sword—harnessed and sheathed—strapped to my saddle and her knife stuck in my belt; she resembled a rather recalcitrant slave as she sat on the sand and waited to have her neck put into iron.

I watched the blacksmith at his anvil, hammering the circlet into shape with speed and skill. He'd taken one look at Del and said he'd waste no time: a bascha like her would surely be worth considerable money: I didn't want to risk losing her. Del, only half-understanding his rough dialect and vulgar Southron slang, glared at him balefully as I told him to hurry it up.

His teeth were stained yellow from beza nut. He spat out a stream of acrid juice and saliva. "Why'nt you collar her before?"

"I bought her off a man who believed slaves had a right to dignity."

He snorted, spat again; hit the beetle he'd been aiming for. "Stupid," he told me. "No slave's got a right to dignity." He hammered a bit more. "Better have a chain, too; from the looks've *her*, I'd say she'd try'n hightail it out've here first chance."

"Fine." My teeth were tightly shut.

"Then tell her to get her rump over here."

I gestured. Del came, slowly. The blacksmith took a good, long look at her and said something that would have earned him her knife in his gut, if she'd understood him. But the tone got through to her. She went red, then white, and her eyes turned dark with anger.

There was nothing I could do. Slaves are less than nothing in the South, and therefore open to insults of all kinds. Del would be a target for nearly any manner of abuse; so long as the blacksmith didn't actually hurt her, there was little I could do.

"You saying that for *her* benefit, or mine?" I asked lightly.

He glanced at me, dull red seeping into his broad, forge-flushed face. "She don't speak Southron?"

"Some. Not the filth you're spewing."

He got ugly. So did I. He reevaluated my size, weapons and the sandtiger claws hanging around my neck.

"Tell her to kneel." He spat again. The dead beetle was flipped over onto its back, legs splayed.

I put my hand on Del's right shoulder and pressed. She knelt after a momentary hesitation.

"Hair." He spat.

Del knelt in the sand, apricot burnous billowing in the wind of the bellows. Her head was bowed submissively, but I could tell from the tension in her body she didn't like the posture one bit. Well, neither did I.

After a moment I swallowed, knelt on one knee and lifted the braid out of the way, sliding callused fingers over smooth skin. I could feel her trembling. Her eyes lifted briefly to mine, and I saw bleakness and fear and darkness in them.

It came to me to wonder, more strongly than ever before, just what the raiders had done to her.

The blacksmith slipped around her neck the hinged iron collar with its length of chain. The lock was fitted through loops, then closed. He handed the key to me.

Del: collared and chained like a dog. At least with the Salset, I hadn't known *that* humiliation.

"Better be careful," observed the blacksmith. "She finds out you care that much, she'll stick a knife in you first chance she gets."

I forgot Del was on a short chain. I stood up so fast I jerked her up with me. "How much?" I asked, when I could speak clearly again.

He named his price. Inflated, but I was too anxious to leave his forge to haggle. I paid him and turned immediately toward the horses, hardly noticing that Del trailed after me like a dog on a rope. I was angry, angry and sickened, because I'd been a slave and here I was making *her* behave like one, when she was the freest thing I'd ever seen.

"I can't mount," Del said quietly, as I put my foot in the roan's stirrup.

I turned back, frowning, and realized belatedly I'd removed from her even the capacity to make the simplest movements. But, under the eyes of the watchful blacksmith, I couldn't give her her own chain. So I mounted my horse more carefully, led Del—on foot—over to the mare, and watched her climb up. Her face was pale and tight and strained, and I had the feeling mine was, too.

"Ought to make her walk," the blacksmith said. "She'll get up-pity, otherwise."

Del said nothing. Neither did I. I just kept my hand away from Singlestroke with all the resolution in my body, and clicked my tongue at the roan.

Because of the chain, Del and I had to stay close. Because of the chain, I was so angry I saw red. I'd locked myself into the role of a slave trader as securely as I'd locked Del into iron; I couldn't give her her freedom on the streets of Julah if we were to pull off our subterfuge. Thoughtlessly, I'd declared this was what we would do; now we did it, and I think it made both of us sick.

I sucked in a deep breath. "I'm sorry, bascha."

She didn't answer.

I looked at her in profile. "Del—"

"Is this how you like your women?" No bitterness, none at all; somehow, it made the question worse. As if she believed I did.

"I'd trade places with you if I could." And knew I meant it.

Del smiled a little. "Wouldn't work, Tiger. Besides—haven't you been here already?"

"In a manner of speaking," I agreed grimly, and that ended the conversation.

Julah is a rich city. It skirts the Punja on one side and flirts with the Southron Mountains on the other. It celebrates the wealth of the tanzeers who own the gold mines in the mountains and the slavers who speculate in human flesh instead of ore. Nearness to the mountains means Julah has plenty of water, but for anyone bound north across the Punja, it is the last bastion of safety and comfort. It seemed hard to believe Del and I had come so far.

We found Omar's house easily enough, once pointed in the right direction. It was painted a pale orchid-blue, tiled in yellow-ocher, shrouded by palms and foliage that shielded it from the street, sun and prying eyes. The turbaned gateman took one look at Del, knew what business I had with Omar, and let us through. One servant took our horses and another escorted us into the house, leading us into a cool, private foyer. I sat down; when Del started to, I told her no.

Omar was incredibly polite. Instead of making us wait (we didn't have an appointment), he came in almost at once. He waited until a third servant had served gritty effang tea, then seated himself upon a saffron cushion.

Like his brother Osmoon, he was chubby. Black-eyed. But his teeth were his, lacking the flashiness of Osmoon's gold dentures. He wore a pale-pink turban and darker robes, with pearls strung around his neck. His fingers were ringed. The slave trade in Julah appeared to be more profitable than the desert business his brother ran.

"Osmoon wishes you well." I sipped effang and completed the welcoming rituals, which eat up a lot of time even as they betray a visitor's true feelings. But I'm on to them, and know how to speak blandly about meaningless topics all day long.

Omar knew it. He gave me welcome, then waved a hand to dismiss the rituals. "Your business?"

"Yours," I said smoothly. "I am told you know if there are Northern males to be had."

His face betrayed nothing but polite interest. "Who is asking?"

I considered lying. False names have their uses, just like false trades. But too many people know the Sandtiger; Omar might not know me on sight, but my reputation does generally precede me. That's what reputations are for. "I'm known as the Sandtiger. Sword-dancer. And sometime slave trader."

His black brows moved as he plucked a pale-green grape from a bowl set upon the low laquered table between us. "I know of a

man called the Sandtiger. Like you, he is scarred and wears the
claws. He is truly a friend of my brother. But he has never, to my
knowledge, traded in slaves before."

"No," I agreed, "but after a while one grows tired of seeing the
wealth of others engaged in business similar to your own. *My* poor
wealth is won only by force of arms."

Omar had studiously avoided looking at Del. As a slave, she
had no stake in our discussion. But now he let his eyes drift to her,
and over her apricot-shrouded form. "You wish to sell?"

"I wish to *buy.*" I said it very distinctly. "A Northern male to put
with my Northern female."

His black eyes jerked back to me. "You intend to *breed* them?"

"Provided I find the proper mate for her."

He spat out grape pips. "How much are you willing to spend?"

"As much as I have to. But I will also give the first child to
the trader who sells me the right boy." Actually, we didn't have
much money left from Sabo's reward. I had thoughts of finding
her brother, haggling over the price, withdrawing to consider it.
Then I'd turn Del loose, rearm her, and we'd settle on a plan
then.

"I'll buy *her,*" Omar said, "but I can sell you no Northern boys.
I have none."

"None?"

"None." He clamped fleshy lips together.

"Who does?"

No answer.

I sighed. "Look, I'll find what I want *with* your help or without
it. If someone's got a monopoly on Northerners here in Julah you
don't stand to lose anything by telling me anyway."

Omar prevaricated a while, not wishing to lose a potential customer, but in the end he agreed there was a monopoly and told me
who had it. "Aladar. But he is the tanzeer; you must see his agent
if you wish to buy or sell."

"Who's his agent?"

Omar nodded. "I'll tell you, of course, friend of my brother . . .
for a price worthy of the Sandtiger."

Sometimes reputations can hurt business dealings. But in the end, I got the name I wanted and he got his price.

"Honat," Omar said.

"Where?"

"At Aladar's palace, of course."

So Del and I went to Aladar's palace. Of course.

Chapter 20

Aladar's palace was quite impressive, even coming in the back entrance as we did. The adobe walls were lime-washed white. Elegant tiled archways were patterned with repeating mosaic designs in tangerine, pale-lime, canary-yellow. Even in the stableyard, cream- and copper-colored gravel crunched beneath our sandaled feet. Palm and citrus trees gave the impression of cool spaciousness.

And all of it, I thought, had been paid for by Aladar's slave trade.

I thought briefly about leaving Del with the horses, for fear Honat the agent might take a liking to her and complicate matters considerably. Then I decided she'd be safer with me, in the long run, because it would be a lot easier for them to snatch her *without* me than if she sat—or stood—right next to me.

Honat was an oily little man with a surprisingly deep voice. His fingers were very short and his palms quite wide, reminding me of a toad. His eyes were toadlike, too (peat-green and bulging), which didn't make me feel any better.

He wore a pale-green turban fastened with a glittering emerald. Rather ostentatious, I thought, for a tanzeer's agent. His robes were gold tissue and he wore little gold slippers on his fat, splayed feet. I towered over him; so did Del, but that didn't seem to bother him in the least. He picked thoughtfully at his receding chin a moment (staring at her from baleful toadlike eyes), then gestured for me to sit down on a fat crimson cushion. I did so, doling out enough chain so Del—standing—wouldn't choke.

Honat looked at her again. "The woman may sit."

Well, progress. But she had to sit on the woven rugs because there were no more cushions, which weren't for slaves anyway. By this time Del was getting good at keeping her head bowed submissively. I had no idea what thoughts were running through her mind, but at least Honat didn't either.

He asked my business and I went through the whole story again, making certain he understood I had no intentions of selling, only buying. When I discussed the breeding program, his eyes lighted. I wasn't sure if the response was good or bad.

Honat glanced sharply at Del again, commanded her to lift her head; after I repeated the order in Southron she could understand, she did so.

The agent smiled his oily little smile. "Children from this woman would be beautiful indeed. I see why you wish a match with her."

"Do you have one?"

He waved a hand, curiously naked of rings or ornamentation. "We have several. It's only a matter of selecting the most appropriate one."

True. I didn't know Jamail at all on sight and couldn't look to Del for direction, because a slave has no say over the purchase of a fellow slave. But Del would *have* to see him, because I wouldn't be able to recognize him otherwise. Del's description of him wouldn't do me much good. After five years, Jamail most likely no longer resembled the ten-year-old Del remembered.

"I'm looking for a young one," I explained. "Perhaps fifteen, sixteen . . . no older. Young enough to make certain he has many years left to him, for—as you know—a male will have more time in which to breed than a female. Even *this* one will use up nearly a year carrying but a single child."

Honat, still staring at Del, nodded understanding. "We have

two young Northern boys. I can't say precisely how old they are—they were *acquired* as children, you understand, and sometimes children aren't certain of their ages." Blandly, he waited for my answer.

"I'd like to see them." No more would he get from me.

"All in good time," Honat promised smoothly. "First I must discuss this with my master. It is his decision to buy or sell." Toad-eyes flicked in Del's direction again. "I think it likely he would be more interested in acquiring *this* one, rather man selling another."

"*This* one is not for sale." Equally bland. "I paid a fortune for her. I expect to earn an even greater one when I sell her children."

Honat studied me. His face was perfectly blank, although in his eyes I saw the merest trace of distaste. "You are cold, Sandtiger. Even *I* don't speak so blithely of selling children in front of the woman who will bear them."

Inwardly I cursed myself. Was I being *too* cold, *too* unfeeling for a slave trader? I'd believed them less than human. (Or was I simply careless because I knew none of the story was true?)

I shrugged off-handedly. "The Sandtiger's work has taught him to be cold. Hasn't Honat's?"

His eyes narrowed a bit. "Is she virgin?"

I scowled. "We are not discussing this woman, Honat. And if you persist in it, I'll take my business elsewhere." I made as if to rise, certain the agent would talk me into staying.

He did. He didn't want to lose the potential profit, for as Aladar's agent he was entitled to a commission on the sale of any property.

Honat smiled. "If you will excuse me, Sandtiger, I will see if my master is willing to have the slaves shown to you." He rose, balancing carefully on his wide toad feet. "Please refresh yourself. There is cooled wine." A naked hand fluttered in the direction of the decanter sitting on the table. He left.

I looked at Del. "Well? Think he went for it?"

"Two Northern boys," she said grimly. "But neither of them may be Jamail."

"I'll take you with me to make sure of a proper match." I

poured a cup of wine and held it out to her. "Here. This nonsense has gone on long enough. I don't *care* if Honat comes back and discovers me treating you like a person instead of a thing."

She smiled a little and thanked me, accepting the wine in hands showing the white knuckles of tension. I realized she was deeply apprehensive, for herself *and* her brother. Here within the palace she was a slave. She would be treated as one. No one would listen to her claim that she was a free woman, and if she came face to face with Jamail, he might give away the game. And it would be all over for all of us.

Del gave me back the emptied wine cup. And Honat came into the room, followed by two blond boys. I sat there staring at them both as Honat sat down on the cushion opposite my own. Then I looked at Del.

Color had spilled out of her face. Her breath was ragged and harsh as she stared at the two boys; I saw her teeth close over her bottom lip. She was angered by what she saw, and sickened, but I saw no recognition in her eyes. Only disappointment.

Honat smiled. "Both of these slaves are young and strong and— as you undoubtedly see—whole. Fit for breeding."

Both were naked. They stood before Del and me silently, staring over our heads with frozen faces, frozen eyes, avoiding my own as if not seeing me would keep me from seeing them, thereby diminishing their humiliation. My hand on Del's chain clenched so hard it hurt; I longed to shout at the boys that I *wasn't* a slaver, that I had come hoping to free one of them. I knew the overwhelming temptation to free them both, regardless of their identity. Simply to let them be the men they were originally intended to be.

I felt Del's eyes on me and looked at her slowly, seeing understanding and empathy in her face. Before she had only sympathized with my past. Now she understood it fully.

More than anything I wanted to find her brother for her.

"Well?" Honat asked, and I realized I'd have to continue the farce.

"I don't know," I said. "They look young."

"You said you *wanted* them young." Honat frowned. "They will grow. They're Northern. Northerners grow tall and heavy, like yourself." Peat-green eyes briefly assessed my own height and weight; the conditioning sword-dancing brought. "More wine?"

"No," I answered absently, setting Del's cup on the table. I got up and dropped her chain, walking up to the boys. I had to make it look good. So I walked around them slowly, consideringly, not touching them as one would a horse because I couldn't bring myself to, but I did everything else I could think of. "How do I know either of them is potent?" I demanded stiffly. Slavery can castrate a man even without the blade. I'd known it myself, before Sula gave me back my manhood.

"Both of them have gotten palace slave girls with child."

"Uh huh." I rested hands on hips. "How do I know it was *these* two?"

Honat smiled. "You are a shrewd man, Sandtiger. I can nearly believe you were born to the trade."

I suppose he meant it as a compliment. It made me feel sick, even as I smiled back at him. "I won't be conned by any man, Honat. Not even the tanzeer's agent."

He spread his wide, naked hands. "I'm an honest man. If I were not, word would soon get out and no one would deal with me. My master would dismiss me. I assure you, both of these boys are ideal for your purposes. Which one do you want?"

"Neither," I said shortly. "I'll keep looking."

Honat's dark brows shot up into a forehead furrowed by surprise. "But we are the only ones who deal specifically in Northerners, my master and I. You must do your business with us."

"I do business with whomever I choose."

Honat stared at me. I got the impression he was judging me, waiting for something. Then he smiled and clapped his hands, dismissing the boys. They turned and filed out of the room. "Of course you may deal with whomever you choose," Honat agreed readily, as if placating a stubborn child. He picked up the heavy decanter as I sat down again. "Did you like the wine? It is from my master's own vines."

"I didn't have any wine," I told him irritably. "I prefer aqivi."

"*Ah.*" It was a blurt of discovery, and then Honat threw the decanter at me while he shouted for assistance.

By the time I was on my feet with Singlestroke free of his sheath, the room was filled with burly palace guards. They were neither eunuchs nor young boys, and each had a sword in his hands.

The wine dripped from my face and burnous. I'd knocked the decanter out of the way, but it had cost me valuable time. Fast as I am, Honat had used the delaying tactic to get out of my reach. "Honest man, are you?" I snarled.

"Honat does what I tell him to." The quiet, calm voice issued from the wall. "It's what I pay him for." From a secret door stepped the man who could only be Aladar.

He was a tanzeer, all right; he wore the rich silks and jewels that branded him a desert prince. His pale-brown face was smooth and youthful, framed in a carefully trimmed black beard and moustache. He was a trifle hawk-nosed, and it gave him the look of a predator. Mahogany eyes were very, very cunning. Also genuinely amused.

"The Sandtiger, is it?" One hand stroked his beard, which glistened with scented oil. Aladar was an attractive man, if you like them smooth as honey. "I've always wondered what his growl would sound like."

"Come a little closer. You'll be able to hear his growl *and* feel his claws."

Aladar laughed. His voice was a warm, clear baritone. "I don't think so. I'm many things, but not stupid. I'll keep my distance, thank you, until the Sandtiger is safely netted and declawed." His eyes were on Singlestroke. "I am grateful you have made an offering of yourself. It saves me some little trouble."

"Me?" I scowled at him. "I'm offering you nothing, slaver."

"Well, then I'm *taking.*" Aladar seemed untroubled by the change of phraseology. "You'll serve my purposes very well, I think. As for the woman—" he looked at Del a moment "—you said you wouldn't sell her, so the only way to get her is to steal her from you. But then—slaves can't own property, can they? Certainly not other slaves."

Not counting Aladar and Honat (neither of whom resembled the fighting type), there were six men. Not bad odds, when you consider I had Del beside me. Her neck was in iron, but not her hands.

"Do you wonder why I want you?" Aladar stroked his beard again. Gems glittered on his fingers, reflecting in his eyes. "I'm a very rich man who intends to become richer. I own gold mines and slaves, and I deal in both regularly. Both are equally important to me. How else does one find labor to work those mines?" He smiled. "With those arms and shoulders, friend sword-dancer, you could do the work of three men."

I felt my mouth go dry. The *thought* of going back into slavery scared me so much I felt the blade of panic cut through my concentration. But something else made me more frightened.

"She's not a slave," I told him clearly. "She's a free Northern woman."

Aladar's brows rose up to his bronze-colored turban with its winking garnet eye. "Then why is she collared, and why do you come to me as a slave trader?"

I wet my lips. "Too long a story. But you're making a mistake if you think you can take her for yourself, because she isn't a slave."

"She is now." He smiled. "So are you."

I pulled Del's knife out of my belt and tossed it to her. Then I invited Aladar's men to take us both.

"Both?" Aladar inquired. "Look at the woman again, sword-dancer . . . she drank the wine meant for you."

I looked. Del wavered on her feet. The knife fell out of useless hands. "Tiger—"

She was unconscious before she hit the ground. I caught her in one arm, easing her down. Then I spun around, letting Single-stroke tickle the throat of the nearest man.

"Surely you can't take all *six*," Aladar remarked.

"Call in a few more," I suggested. "Might as well make it a real challenge."

Aladar tapped one fingernail, long and buffed, against a tooth. "I *have* always desired to see your sword-dance."

"Pick up a sword yourself," I invited. "Dance with me, Aladar."

"Oh, I'm afraid not." He sounded sincerely regretful. "I have other matters to attend to, and I dislike the sight of my own blood." He signaled dismissal to Honat. "It will be a sorry thing to see the Sandtiger's teeth and claws pulled, but I can't tolerate a slave who spends valuable time thinking of rebellion. But you mustn't worry. I'll be watching from my secret closet, which is where I watch all of Honat's transactions."

He was gone. So was Honat. And I was alone with an unconscious Del and six armed, fanatically loyal men.

"Come on." I said it with a bravado I didn't entirely feel. "Dance with the Sandtiger."

At first, they did. One by one. It was a contest of quickness and strength, skill and strategy, and each of Aladar's men fought fairly. Then, as two of them went down beneath Singlestroke, they realized I was killing them. Not just testing them. *Killing* them. And it made them angry. I heard Aladar's outraged shout from somewhere deep in the walls, and then the remaining four were on me.

I moved immediately against the wall so no one could come at my back. It left me open on three sides, but Singlestroke and I are very fast; I slashed through the fence of steel that came at me again and again. I nicked a couple of arms and moved on, reaching for others. The problem was, they weren't out to kill *me*. All they wanted was to wear me down.

It's very frustrating when you want to kill a few enemies, and all *they* want to do is capture you.

My shoulder ached. Still I kept Singlestroke flying, slashing out to catch blades, arms, and ribs, but the four men concentrated on me en masse, which made it hard to focus on one enemy when I had three others to worry about. I wanted to swear at them all, but you don't waste your breath on such things when your life (or your freedom) is at stake.

The wall scraped against my back. I felt a tapestry behind me, flapping against my waist. Then the tapestry was whipped aside and an arm came out of the wall to encircle my throat.

Aladar. Aladar in his infernal secret closet.

One-handed, I kept Singlestroke in the fray. With the other hand I reached for the remaining knife tucked in my belt. Aladar's arm was locked tight around my throat; his men fell back. Why should they fight when he'd do it for them?

A red mist rose up before my eyes, distorting my vision. I saw four pairs of watching eyes and, beyond them, Del's slack body on the rugs. I jerked the knife free and tried to stab it behind my back, but one of Aladar's men woke up to the threat to his master and sliced me across the knuckles with his sword.

The knife clattered to the floor. So did Singlestroke. I reached behind me, trying to hook both hands around Aladar's head. All I got was an armful of turban, which came off and tumbled to the floor in tangled strips of rich cloth.

Unfortunately, Aladar's arm did not fall with it.

One of his men got bored. Maybe he saw his master wasn't making as much progress as he hoped. Whatever the reason, he doubled up a big fist and slammed it beneath my ribs, which effectively expelled what little breath I had left.

After that it didn't take long for Aladar to choke me down, and as I faded into darkness I heard him cursing.

"Double-weight!" he gasped. "I don't want any chance of him getting loose on the way to the mine."

And that, as they say, was that.

Chapter 21

Double-weight meant chains around my neck, waist, wrists, ankles. It meant iron so heavy it dragged with every step, but the steps didn't last long because the guards threw me into a wagon and headed it toward the mountains.

I lay sprawled in the wagon (or as sprawled as you can get while wearing iron). It rattled against the floorboards as the wagon trundled across the ruts in the road. I was bruised, cut, battered and aching, and my throat hurt like hoolies.

But mostly I was scared.

People have called me a brave man. A fearless man. The man who will face anything and everything without flinching or blinking an eye. (None of it is true, of course, but you can't muck around with a legend when that legend is what gets you work.) So I'd gone on about my business without much bothering to acknowledge that yes, even the Sandtiger can be frightened, and now—as I faced slavery once again—I realized I'd been a bit seduced by my own reputation. I *knew* I wasn't any braver than any other man. You sort of come face to face with your own shortcomings when the thing you dread most becomes your immediate future.

I had been stripped of everything but suede dhoti and sandtiger claws. That meant no burnous, no belt, no sandals, no harness.

Certainly no Singlestroke, but that didn't surprise me. What did surprise me was being allowed to keep the claws.

Unless, of course, it was some bizarre form of retribution on Aladar's part. How better to get under the Sandtiger's hide than by announcing his identity to the slaves he would work with day in and day out?

Possibly. Aladar struck me as the type of man to enjoy inflicting psychological torture as well as physical hardship. He might be intending to use me as a form of control, saying, in effect: *The Sandtiger is a strong, brave, independent man. See how he is caught? See how he is humbled? See how he does what he is told?*

Hoolies.

I dragged myself up, hearing the cacophony of iron links and cuffs, and knelt on the floor of the wagon. I was escorted by a full contingent of palace guards: twenty men. A compliment, in a way; twenty men for one, and a man who was so heavily chained he could hardly breathe, let alone move.

Of course, it was also practical. Aladar probably *knew* I had every intention of getting free. He probably knew I intended to make my way back to the palace to find and free Del. *Undoubtedly* he knew I wanted to open him up from guts to gullet with any weapon I could find.

I'd do it, too. Once I got free.

I planned my escape all the way to the mine. It took my mind off the journey. It took my mind off imagining what it would be like to be a chula again.

Only when I got to the mine, I realized Aladar didn't really have anything to worry about. I'd be lucky if I *survived.*

The guards took me into the runnels. They led me deep into the guts of the mountain: twisting, turning, ascending, descending, turning, turning, *turning* . . . until I lost all track of direction and knew myself truly lost.

The tunnels were filled with men; a gut stuffed to bursting on the helplessness and futility of men who were no longer men, but effluvia. *Chula.* Arms and legs. Each man wore iron as I did, but the waist chain was about ten feet long and locked to yet another chain. This one ran along the wall, bolted into bedrock at every other man. The men were stationed some fifteen feet apart. It left each of them with a limited area in which to work. In which to live. I could tell, from the stench of the tunnel, that no one was ever unlocked from the wall. Not even to relieve himself.

In the harsh, stark torchlight, I saw the dead man. He lay on the rock floor: a limp, sprawled body devoid of life. He stank, as dead men do. And I was his replacement.

The body was unlocked. I heard the iron dropping away, ringing against bedrock. Then a guard prodded me in one kidney, and I took a single step forward.

Then backward. Rigidly. Spasmodically. I *could not* make myself take up the dead man's place.

In the end, the guards did it for me. I felt the tug of iron at neck, wrists, waist, ankles as they locked me to the wall and made certain the links were strong. I heard the metallic clangor. I heard the voice of one guard; bored, he droned the information. No inflection. No nuances. Just—noise.

I was to hammer at the wall with mallet and chisel, breaking away chunks of the reef to free the ore, which was hauled out of the mine in wooden wagons. Any man discovered trying to chisel himself free of the chains or the bolts free of the wall would be taken outside, flogged, and left to hang on the post for three days. Without food and water.

If I worked well, the guard droned on, I'd be fed twice a day: morning and night. I was to sleep on the tunnel floor at my station. Water was brought around three times a day, no more, no less. I was expected to work from dawn until dusk, with breaks at morning and evening meals.

This, he said, was my life. For the *rest* of my life. He dropped the mallet and chisel at my feet and walked away with the other guards, taking the light with him.

I stood facing the wall. Everything was black, black and livid purple; torch brackets were infrequently set into the walls and only half of them were lighted. My eyes would adjust, I knew, because the body makes shift where it can . . . but I wasn't sure I *wanted* to see what I was doing.

I felt the sweat break out on my skin. My flesh rose up on my bones as shudder after shudder wracked me. My belly tied itself into knots until I thought my bowels would burst. Iron rattled. I couldn't stop it from rattling. I couldn't stop myself from shaking.

The stink of the tunnel engulfed me: Urine. Defecation. Fear. Helplessness. Death. The knowledge of futility.

I closed my eyes and set my forehead against the ribs of the wall, digging fingers into the stone. I was in darkness of mind, of body, of spirit. All I could see was madness. It filled up all my senses until I was small again, so small, *so small.*

Even among the Salset I hadn't felt so helpless, so frightened, *so small.*

I forced myself to look at the others. They squatted, all hunched against the wall, staring at me blankly; chained I was, as they were chained, and equally hopeless. I looked at their broken, callused hands; their overdeveloped shoulders; their empty, staring eyes, and realized they had been here months. Maybe years.

Not one of them seemed to have the slightest trace of sanity left. And I realized, staring at them even as they stared at me, that I looked into my own face.

The sun went down and sucked more light out of the tunnel, leaving me in the mosaic of patchwork darkness: madder-violet, gentian-blue, raisin-black. And a splash of brilliant fuchsia whenever I closed my eyes. The evening meal had been served before my arrival; now the men slept. I heard their snores, their groans, their cries, their yips. Heard the continuous rattle of iron.

Heard the wheeze of my own breath as it rasped in and out of a throat constricted by a symphony of fear.

My appetite, after disappearing, eventually returned. It increased with the heavy work of breaking free the reef and ore and loading it into carts pulled by slaves chained to them, but the food ration didn't. I went to sleep hungry and empty and woke up an hour or two later with cramping belly, cramping muscles. When morning came I was dulled from a sleep that didn't refresh me. The water was tepid and foul and often caused dysentery, but I drank it because there was nothing else. I slept in the dirt of the tunnel floor, accustomed to restricted movements and the necessity of relieving myself in my own corner, like a wounded animal. I knew myself degraded, humiliated, sickened; I knew myself a chula. And the knowledge swept away the years I'd spent as a free sword-dancer.

The nightmares came again. This time there was no Sula to make them go away. This time I lived in the lowest level of hoolies. Dwelling on vanished days of transitory freedom was to dwell on madness, and so I didn't think of them at all.

The circle was drawn in the sand. The swords lay in the center. A two-handed Southron sword, with gold hilt and blued-steel blade. A two-handed Northern sword: silver-hilted, rune-bladed, singing its siren song of ice and death.

A woman, standing near the circle. Waiting. White hair shining. Blue eyes calm. Gilded limbs relaxed. Waiting.

A man: sunbronzed, dark-haired, green-eyed. Tall. Powerfully built. Except that even as he stood there, waiting to start the dance, his body changed. Lost weight. Substance. Strength. It melted off him until he was a skeleton with a bit of brown hide stretched over the bones.

He put out a hand toward the woman. The woman who sang his deathsong.

Day became night, night became day.

—*daynightdaynightdaynight*—

—until there was no day or night or even *daynight*—just a man in a mine and the mine in the mind of the man—

He squatted. Spine against wall. Hardened rump barely brushing the floor. Forearms across knees. Hands dangling. Forehead against forearms.

Until a foot rattled his iron, and eventually he looked up.

The tanzeer was richly dressed in cloth-of-gold and crimson

embroidery. He was a clean man, well-groomed; he was a man who took pride in appearances. In his right hand he carried a slim ivory wand, an ornamental baton, carved and knurled. A nacreous pearly-white.

A brief gesture with the wand. The guard hooked a foot into iron chain and rattled it, until the chained man looked up.

A second brief gesture with the wand. A torch was brought closer. Sulfurous yellow light spilled out of the flame to illuminate the face of the man looking at the tanzeer; the tanzeer saw a beast, not a man. A filthy, befouled, stinking beast, clad in a ragged suede dhoti. Worn down to nothing but skin and ropy sinew, stretched over a frame that might once have claimed a powerful, impressive grace. The face was mostly hidden in dusty hair and tangled, matted beard. But out of the face peered a pair of green eyes, squinting against the blinding torchlight.

"Stand him up," the tanzeer ordered, and the guard jerked his head in such a way as the man knew well.

Rising, the chained man was tall, much taller than the tanzeer. But he didn't stand in the attitude of a tall man comfortable with his height. He stood with shoulders hunched, as if it was difficult to bear their weight.

The tanzeer frowned. "It *is* the sword-dancer, isn't it?" he asked the guard, who shrugged and said as far as *he* knew, it was the same man who had been brought in three months before.

The tanzeer hooked the tip of his wand under the clotted cord around the chained man's neck. He rattled the clots and saw that yes, indeed, the clots—beneath their dirt—were really claws.

Satisified, he let the cord drop back against the man's throat and nodded. "Take him off the wall. Double-weight him and put him in the wagon. It's time I hosted him in the palace once again."

Before the woman, unguarded, the tanzeer showed off the man he had brought from the mine. He told the woman what had happened to the man in the mine; he watched her face, her eyes, her posture. He saw what he had always seen: dignity, strength, quiet pride and absolute insularity. In three months, he had not broken her.

But he had broken the man, and he thought it might be enough to break the woman.

He turned from her and faced the man who stank of his own excrescence. "To your knees," and pointed to the floor with his ivory baton.

Slowly the man got down on knees that had been bruised so often they were permanently discolored. Blue-black, against faded copper skin mottled with dirt and chisel cuts; pocked with bits of ore and reef trapped beneath the top layer of his skin. The chains rang against one another and the tessellated floor, spilling around his knees like the entrails of an iron serpent.

The tanzeer looked at the woman. "He will do whatever told. *Whatever* he is told."

The woman looked straight back at the tanzeer. Her disbelief was blatant.

The tanzeer gestured with his wand. "Down," he said. "Face down."

The kneeling man, once young, moved as an old man moves. Bent forward. Placed palms flat against the patterned stone. Sinews stood up beneath encrusted flesh.

He prostrated himself on the floor.

The tanzeer extended one slippered foot. "Kiss it. Kiss it— chula."

And at last, the woman broke. With an inarticulate cry of rage she sprang at the tanzeer like a female sandtiger, one hand clawing for his face. The other one came down on his ornamental knife and jerked it free—

—jerking it as the man on the floor tore himself from the stone and twisted loops of iron chain around the tanzeer's throat.

Lips drew back from his teeth. But instead of growling he spoke one word. A husky, broken word: *"Keys."*

"Where?" the woman demanded of the tanzeer. And when he told her she dug them out of the jewelled pouch hanging from his jewelled belt.

She ignored the iron collar around her own throat. Instead, un-locked the cuffs from his ankles, waist, neck—and finally as he twisted the loops more tightly around the tanzeer's throat, she unlocked the cuffs from his wrists.

He shed them all. Sloughed off the serpent's coils as if he sloughed his skin. And all the iron rang down on the floor and cracked the careful patterns.

With the iron he shed his captivity, as much as he could, and she saw in the beast's place a trace of the man she had known. Only a trace, but a trace was better than nothing. Tentatively, she smiled. "Tiger?"

I shoved Aladar up against the nearest wall and took the knife from Del as she offered it. Placed the tip against his flat, tissue-clad belly and bared my teeth at him. "One claw left, tanzeer. Care to feel it?"

He stared back at me, saffron-colored from shock, but he didn't give in. He had too much pride for it.

I flicked a glance at Del. I didn't have much voice left—three months of silence, except for occasional outcries in my sleep, had leached me of the faculty—but she seemed to comprehend my abbreviated speech well enough. "Swords and knives. Clothes. Anything. I'll wait."

She ran, leaving me with Aladar.

I was shaking. Reaction had set in. I could almost hear my chains rattling, except I didn't wear them anymore. But I heard them. I hear them still.

I sucked in a deep breath. Bared my teeth again at Aladar. "Ten-year-old boy, five years ago. Northerner. Omar's slaveblock. Jamail. Looks like her." It was all I could manage. I didn't dare let him see how shaky I was; it wouldn't be difficult for him to break free. The mine had stolen strength, flexibility, speed. All I had left was hatred.

A wild, killing rage.

"Do you expect me to know what happens to every slave in Julah?" he demanded.

He had a point. But so did I, and it was pressing against his gut. "What happened to *this* one?"

"He was a *chula!*" Aladar hissed. "I buy them, I sell them . . . I can't keep track of every one!"

The little knife wasn't worth much as a real weapon, but its steel was very sharp. It sliced through the cloth easily enough; I had the feeling it would slice through flesh equally so. "I'm going to cut you, tanzeer, and spill your guts out onto the floor like ropes, so you can trip over them."

Apparently he believed me. Just as well; I meant it. "I had such a boy," he admitted. "I let him go three years ago."

"*Where?*"

"Vashni." Clearly, Aladar knew what he was saying. His pallor deepened. "I gave him as a gift to the chief."

Hoolies. "You have trade with the Vashni?" No one else did. I wondered if he lied.

Aladar swallowed heavily. "I needed it. With this particular clan. I needed access to the mountains, to the mine, for the gold. With—with the Vashni settled there, I stood no chance. So—I sent all manner of things, including chula. One of them was a Northern boy. He was twelve."

The age fit. "Where?" I asked grimly.

Aladar's brown eyes were black with fear and hatred. "Just ride due south, into the foothills. The Vashni find you even when you don't want them to."

That was undoubtedly true. "The boy's name?"

"I don't know!" Aladar shouted. "Do you expect me to know the name of a *chula?*"

"Tiger," Del said.

I turned my head and saw she wore her tunic again, complete with sword harness. The silver hilt stood up above her left shoulder. She carried a black burnous, sandals and Singlestroke, along with knife and harness. A white burnous was draped over her other arm.

She dropped everything into a pile as she reached up to draw her sword. "Get dressed," she said calmly. "I'll watch Aladar."

I stepped away from him. Del saw my face as I turned my back on the tanzeer; something in hers told me I wasn't maintaining as well as I'd hoped. The ornamental knife was slippery in my hand. From sweat. The sweat of tension and emotion.

I let Del go past me to Aladar. Carefully, I bent and picked up the black burnous, concentrating on cutting a slit in the shoulder seam for Singlestroke's hilt. My hands shook. The seam split. The tip of the knife nicked a finger. I didn't feel it. My hands were too callused.

I shrugged into my harness, dismayed to discover I didn't need to undo the buckles. No. I needed to punch new holes. To make the harness smaller. But that would have to wait.

The sandals were hard to lace up. Eventually, I knotted them. Pulled the burnous over my head, glad to cover most of my stinking, scarred hide. Felt a wave of weakness break over my head and threaten to suck me down.

I turned. Del watched me. I felt sluggish heat rise into my face. Sweat stung my armpits. Singlestroke was in my hands, but I didn't raise him. I didn't sheathe him. I looked at Del, and I saw her turn back to Aladar and spit him on her rune-worked blade.

"*No—*" But the shout was little more than a tearing in my throat. "By hoolies, woman, *that death was mine!*"

Del didn't answer.

"Bascha—*mine—*"

Still she didn't answer.

My mouth opened. Closed. I said nothing. I watched as she pulled the blade free. The body, sagging against the wall, slowly slid toward the floor. It bled gently through cloth-of-gold and crimson embroidery.

Del turned, and at last she answered me. "That was for you." The soft voice was incredibly intimate. "For what he did to you."

She was unreadable. I saw the stark harshness of the bones beneath pale flesh and realized she'd lost her tan. She was a Northern bascha again, as I'd seen her originally.

And an incredibly dangerous woman.

There wasn't much room in my throat for my voice. "Del—I do *my own* killing."

She looked directly back at me. "Not this time, Tiger. No."

Something jumped deep in my chest. A cramp. Something spasmodic. "Is that how you killed the *an-kaidin?* Is that how you blooded that blade?"

I saw her twitch of shock. Her face was paler still; had I shocked her that much with my question? Del was aware I knew what had happened to her sword-master, and how. Just not all the reasons for it.

Or was it the *tone* of my accusation that had drawn the reaction from her?

"This was for *you*," she said at last.

"Was it?" I croaked. "Or was it for Del?"

She looked down at her sword. Blood ran from the blade. It filled up the runes, then dripped raggedly from the steel to puddle on the tessellated floor.

Her mouth twitched a moment, but it wasn't an expression of humor. It was Del dealing with an emotion I couldn't name. "For us both." But she said it so quietly I wasn't certain what words were said.

Three months apart. We owed each other nothing. Not now. The thing had gone past employer and employee. Del and I were free to go our separate ways.

"Jamail is with the Vashni," I told her. "A mountain clan."

"I heard him."

"You're going?"

Her jaw was a blade beneath taut flesh. "I'm going."

After a moment, I nodded. I was incapable of anything else.

Del picked up the white burnous. She slid the sword home in the sheath behind her shoulder—she'd clean it later, I knew—and went out of the room.

But not before she relieved Aladar's body of his jewelled pouch.

I love a practical woman.

Chapter 22

Del bought our way into a disreputable inn on the disreputable side of Julah. We made an odd pair; I wasn't much surprised at the odd looks we got as we climbed the narrow adobe staircase to the second floor and the tiny room Del had rented for us. She ordered a bath with lots of hot water, and when the serving girl muttered about the extra work, Del cracked her across the face with the flat of her hand. With the mark still blazing red on the girl's tawny skin, Del promised her gold if she hurried. The girl hurried.

I sat on the edge of the threadbare, rumpled cot. I stared blankly at Del, recalling how easily she had slipped the sword blade into Aladar's belly. For me, she had said. But I've long been accustomed to doing my own killing when it needed doing; I couldn't imagine why she would do it for me. Or what it was in me that had triggered her lethal response.

No. More likely it had been for her brother and for the treatment she had known at Aladar's hands.

"You'll feel better when you're clean again," Del said.

The burnous covered most of me. But I could see my sandaled feet, callused hands. Finger and toenails were split, broken, missing, peeled back, blackened. Nicks and ingrained ore dust discolored faded copper flesh. Across the back of my left hand was a jagged scar, healed over: a chisel had slipped once, in the shaking hands of a dying man chained next to me.

I turned my hands over and looked at the palms. Once they had been callused from years of sword-dancing. It had only been months since they had known the seductive flesh of Singlestroke's hilt, and yet I knew it was too long.

The door crashed open. Del swung around, hands on sword hilt; she didn't unsheathe the Northern blade because it was the serving girl and a fat man. He rolled a wooden cask into the room, dumped it on end, left. The girl began lugging buckets of hot water in one by one, pouring them into the cask.

Del waited until the cask was filled. Then she gestured dismissal to the girl, who took one hard look at me and did as Del suggested. She left. And after a moment, so did Del.

I picked at the knots in my laces. Untied them, stripped off the leather. Dropped burnous and dhoti. Lastly, shed harness and sword. And climbed into the hot water, not even caring that all the cuts and nicks and scrapes clamored protest at the heat.

I slid down into the cask until the water lapped at my chest. Carefully, I leaned my skull against the edge of the cask, giving myself over to the heat. I didn't even bother with the soap. I just soaked. And then I slept.

—*the rattle of iron . . . the chink of mallet against chisel, chisel against stone . . . the yips and cries of sleeping men . . . the sobs of dying men*—

I woke up with a jerk. Disoriented, I was aware of flaxen light in the room, slanting through the slatted window . . . a *room*, not a tunnel! No more torchlight. No more darkness. No more *iron*.

A hand, against my back. Scrubbing soap into the flesh, until I was coated with yellow-brown lather. Del's hand pressed down on my head as I began to rise. "No. I'll do it. Be easy."

But I couldn't. I sat stiffly in the cask as she scrubbed, working the brown soap into the filthy skin. Her fingers were strong, very strong; she kneaded at the tension knotting shoulders, neck, spine.

"Be easy," she said softly.

But I couldn't. "What did that bastard do to you?"

I could feel her shrug. "It doesn't matter. He's dead."

"Bascha." I reached and caught one of her hands. "Tell me."

"Will you tell me?"

At once I was back in the mine, swallowed up by darkness and despair. I felt the emptiness teasing the edges of my mind. *"No."* It was all I could do to form the word, to expel a sound from my mouth. I couldn't. I couldn't tell her.

"Shave?" she asked. "You need a haircut, too."

I nodded. Washed hair and beard. Nodded again.

Considerate of my modesty, Del turned away while I heaved myself up in the cask, washed the parts of me which Del hadn't, rinsed, and dripped across the floor to the rough sacking on the cot. There was also a fresh dhoti and brown burnous. I dried myself, pulled the dhoti on, told her she could turn around.

She did. I saw momentary pity in her eyes, "You're too thin."

"So are you." I sat down. "Rid me of this rat's-nest, bascha. Make me a man again."

Carefully, she cut my hair. Carefully, she stripped the beard away. I watched her face as she tended mine. The flesh was drawn tight over her bones. Aladar had kept her indoors for three months; the honey-tan had faded. Except for the sun-frost in her hair, she looked so very much like the Northern woman I'd met in the little cantina in the nameless town on the edge of the Punja.

Except I knew what she was, now. Not a witch. Not a sorceress, though some might name her that because of the *jivatma* and all its power. No. Del was just a woman bent on doing whatever it was she had to do. No matter what the odds.

Finally she smiled. I felt gentle fingers briefly touch the claw marks on my face. "Sandtiger." It was all she said. All she needed to say.

"Hungry?" When she nodded, I pulled on the burnous and Single-stroke, and we went down to the common room.

The food was spicy and tangy; not the best, not the worst. Certainly better than what I'd known in the mine. And I learned I couldn't eat much more than I'd eaten for the last three months. My belly rebelled. And so I turned to aqivi instead.

Finally, Del reached out and put a hand over the rim of my cup. "No more." Gently said, but firmly.

"I'll drink what I want."

"Tiger—" She hesitated. "Too much will make you sick."

"It'll make me *drunk*," I corrected. "Right about now, drunk is precisely what I'd like to be."

Her eyes were very direct. "Why?"

I thought she probably knew why. But I said it anyway. "It'll help me forget."

"You can't forget that, Tiger. No more than you could forget your days with the Salset." She shook her head a little. "There are things about *my* life I'd like to forget; I can't, so I live with them. I think them through, deal with them, put them in their place. So they don't affect the other things I must do."

"Have you forgotten the blood-guilt, then?" I couldn't help myself; the aqivi made me hostile. I looked at her whitening face. "How did you deal with *that*, bascha?"

"What do you know of blood-guilt, Sandtiger?"

I shrugged beneath brown silk. "A little. I recall how the chula felt when he realized his conjuring—his *wishful thinking*—had made a dream come true, at the cost of innocent lives." I sighed. "And another story about an *ishtoya* who killed an *an-kaidin*. Because of a blooding-blade." I looked at the hilt standing up behind her shoulder. "It had to be quenched in the blood of a skillful man, so the *ishtoya* could seek revenge."

"There are needs in this world that supersede the importance of other things." Flat, unwavering tone.

"Selfish." I swallowed more liquor. "I saw what you did to Aladar, and I know you're capable of killing for the sake of revenge. *Of need.*" I paused. "Obsession, bascha. Wouldn't you agree?"

Del smiled a little. "Maybe." And the word had an edge, like the blade of her Northern sword.

I put down my brimming cup. "I'm going to bed."

Del let me go. She didn't say a word.

*　　*　　*

A shadowed figure approached from the end of the tunnel. The light was stark behind it, throwing it into sharp relief: a silhouette without features. Without shape. Simply a form in a black burnous. And in its hands was a sword, a Northern sword, silver-hilted and worked with alien runes.

The figure approached the first slave slowly. He was chained five men down from me. The sword flashed briefly in the muted light. I saw two hands lift it, rest the tip against the man's upstanding ribs, push. The blade slid in silently, killing without a sound. The man sagged against his chains. Only the rattling of the iron told me he was dead.

Withdrawn. Blood shone on the blade, but in the strange light from beyond the tunnel it shone black, not red.

The figure came closer. The next man died, silently as the first. The next. Blood dripped from the blade. I saw, as the figure approached, that it was hooded, and the black burnous wasn't black at all, but white.

Two more men died and the figure stood before me: Del. I looked into her hooded face and saw blue, blue eyes, pale, fair skin, and a mouth. A mouth filled with blood as if she had drunk that which spilled from each man she had killed.

"Bascha," I whispered.

She lifted the sword and placed the tip against my chest. Her eyes did not waver from my face.

The Northern sword pierced my flesh and sank into my heart. Soundlessly, but for the rattle of the chains, I sank against the wall.

I died.

I woke up with a hand on my shoulder. I thrust myself into a sitting position, reaching for Singlestroke; realized it was Del. Realized I had, in my drunken stupor, gone to sleep on the floor, as if I were still in the mine. And I realized it was my own fear I smelled, filling up the darkness.

I heard my breath rasping raggedly in the silence of the room, and I couldn't stop the sound.

"Tiger." Del knelt at my side. "You were dreaming."

I shoved an arm across my face and knew I'd been doing more than that. I'd been crying. The realization, and the instant humiliation, was horrible.

"No," she said softly, and I knew she'd seen it.

I was shaking. I couldn't help it. I was cold and scared and sick on too much aqivi; lost on the borderland of illusion and reality. Aqivi rolled in my belly, threatening to spew out of my mouth; it didn't only because I put my head down on my upthrust knees. Trembling, I swore softly, repeatedly, until Del's arms slid around my neck from behind and hugged me like a child.

"It's all right," she whispered into the shadows. *"It's all right."*

I threw off her arms and lurched to my feet, staring at her. The candle was gone but the moonlight crept between the slats covering the window. It slanted across her pale face and striped it: dark—light—dark—light. Her eyes were hidden in shadow.

"It was *you.*" The shaking renewed itself. "You."

She knelt on the floor and stared up at me. "You dreamed about me?"

I tried to speak evenly. "One by one, you killed them. With your sword. You spitted them. And then you came to me." I saw the hooded face before me. "Hoolies, woman, *you stuck that sword into me as easily as you stuck it into Aladar!*"

Silence. The echoes of my accusation died away.

"I saw it." Her voice was little more than a whisper, but I detected the faintest trace of despair. "I saw it. In that moment, when I turned away from Aladar, I saw the hatred in your eyes. For *me.*"

"No." It was expelled all at once. "No, Del. I hated *me. Myself.* Because I've done it so often, and with less compunction—less *reason*—than you did." I began to move, unable to stand still. I paced. Like a caged cat. "I saw myself when I watched you kill Aladar. And it's never easy to look at yourself and acknowledge, at long last, exactly what you are."

"Sword-dancer," she said. "Both of us. We are neither of us better or worse than the other. We are what we have made of ourselves, because we had reason. Justification. Because of obsession." She smiled a little. "Chula: freed by his own courage. Free to take up a sword. Woman: freed by rape and murder. Free to take up a sword."

"Del—"

"You said once I wasn't cold enough. That I lacked the edge."
She shook her head. The braid moved against her right shoulder.
"You were wrong. I *am* cold, Tiger; too cold. My edge is honed too
sharp." She didn't smile. "I've killed more men than I can count,
and I will go on killing them when I have to—because of murdered
kin . . . a stolen brother . . . violated virginity." The moonlight set
her pale hair shining. "Your dream was right, Tiger. I would kill a
hundred Aladars . . . and never look back while the bodies fall."

I looked at her. I looked at the proud sword-dancer who knelt
on the hard wooden floor of a dingy Southron inn and knew I
looked at someone worth all the sacrifice in the world because she
had made and accepted her own.

"What have you done?" I asked hoarsely. "What have you
done to yourself?"

Del looked up at me. "If I were a man, would you ask that?"

I stared at her. "What?"

"If I were a man, would you ask that?"

But she already knew the answer.

Chapter 23

Del and I did not leave Julah immediately. For two reasons, actually: Aladar's murderer was sought by palace guards, and I wasn't in any shape to leave as yet. Three months in the mines had taken their toll. I needed food, rest, exercise. Mostly I needed time.

But time was a commodity we didn't have. Now that we were so close to Jamail (both Del and I were pretty sure Aladar had told us the truth about giving Jamail as a gift), she was understandably anxious to track down the Vashni. But she waited. With more patience than I've ever seen in anyone, let alone myself.

We didn't speak again about past experiences or reasons for what we had become. We spoke instead about plans for shaking Jamail loose from the Vashni. I'd never had much experience with the tribe, but I'd learned some over the years. Unlike the Hanjii, they weren't overtly hostile to strangers. But they were dangerous. And so we had to plan accordingly.

"No more slave and slave trader scam," I told Del on the third day of our freedom. "It got us into too much trouble the last time. If this Vashni chieftain has acquired a taste for Northern slaves, we don't want to risk losing you as well."

"I thought you might eventually come to that conclusion." Del's head was bent as she wiped the blade of her sword with soft chamois. "Do you have another idea?"

I squatted on the floor, hunched against the wall. The posture had become habitual, though now there were no chains. "Not really. Maybe it would be the best if we just rode in and checked out the lay of the land."

"We'll have to have something the chieftain wants," Del reminded me. "Otherwise, what would tempt him to give up Jamail?"

I scratched at the scars on my face. "We've still got most of the money that was in Aladar's pouch. And the pouch itself, which is worth a small fortune because of all the gems." Absently, I shrugged my left shoulder. "When it comes right down to it, he may want to *reward* us for ridding him of Aladar. Seems to me it cancels the trade alliance."

The Northern blade shone. Del glanced over at me. Unbound, her hair was like platinum silk in the saffron sunlight. "I hired you to guide me across the Punja; to Julah. I didn't hire you to risk your life for my brother."

"In other words, you don't think I'm ready for sword-work—if it comes to that."

"Are you?" she asked calmly.

We both knew the answer. Three days out of the mine; three months in. "I said I'd go."

"Then we'll go." She put the tip of the sword against the lip of the leather sheath and slid the blade home. A sibilant song: steel against fleece-lined leather.

In the morning, we went.

We rode into the foothills of the Southron Mountains on yet another pair of horses. Del's was a white gelding generously speckled with black from nose to rump. He had odd, watchful eyes, almost *human*, and a frazzled motley mane and tail. My own mount was also a gelding, but less colorful than Del's; he was a plain, unremarkable brown horse. Not bay, not like my old stud; he lacked black points, black mane and tail. Just—brown. Like his personality.

We rode out of sand into the saltpan hardpack of the border between desert and foothills. With each step the earth changed, chameleonlike; first sand, then hummocky patches of dry, wispy grass, then footing akin to something more like a natural topsoil.

I watched Del's gelding. He had a funny way of stepping out. He appeared almost to *mince,* womanlike; I'd have mentioned it to Del, except I couldn't think of any time at all when *she* had minced.

At any rate, the speckled gelding was full of *something.* He minced, sashayed, whiffled through flaring nostrils, slanting my gelding coy glances out of eerily human eyes.

"I think I know why he was gelded," I said finally. "As a stallion, I think he'd be a washout."

Del's brows shot up. "Why? He's a perfectly good horse. A little skittish, maybe—but there's nothing wrong with him."

"*It,*" I reminded her. "There isn't any *him* left in him. But I'm willing to bet there wasn't any *him* in him when he was *whole.*"

Del chose not to answer my charge. Well, he—*it*—was her horse. Maybe she felt some loyalty.

We left behind the saltpan, the dry, hummocky grass, the webbing of healthier growth. Horse shoes clinked against slate-colored shale, gray-green granite. We climbed, though the elevation was debatable; the Southron Mountains, even at their summit, are not tremendously tall. From the sloping shoulders, spotted with scrubby trees and catclawed brush, steel-blue shalefalls dribbled toward the desert.

Del was shaking her head. "Not like the North. Not like the North at all."

I leaned forward, half-standing in my stirrups as the brown gelding negotiated a jagged shale escarpment. "No snow."

"Not just that." Del tapped her speckled horse with sandaled heels, urging him to follow me. "The trees, the rocks, the soil . . . even the *smell* is different."

"Should be," I agreed, "seeing as it's Vashni you're smelling, not mountains."

I stopped my horse. The warrior sat on his own sorrel mount about twenty paces away. Around his bare brown neck hung an ivory necklace of human finger bones.

Del stopped next to me. "So it is."

We waited. So did the warrior.

He was young. Probably about seventeen. But the first thing a Vashni male knows in this life is a sword; a Vashni woman, giving birth, cuts the cord with her husband's sword. And then the male child is circumcised with it.

No, you don't underestimate a Vashni warrior. Not even the young ones.

This one was mostly naked, clad only in leather kilt and belt. Even his feet were bare. His bronzed flesh was oiled to a feral sleekness. He wore his black hair long, longer than Del's; like her, he braided it. But the single braid was wrapped in furred hide. From his ears depended earrings of carved bone. What part of the human body *they* came from, I couldn't say.

He made certain he had our full attention. Then he turned and headed south. Across his back, naked except for the thin harness, was strapped a traditional Vashni sword. Unsheathed, the wickedly curved blade gleamed. The hilt was a human thighbone.

"Come on," I told Del. "I think we're expected."

The young warrior led us into the Vashni encampment: a clustering of striped hyorts staked out almost cheek-by-jowl against the sloping mountainsides. We rode through a tribal reception party: two parallel lines of Vashni, winding like a serpent through the encampment. Warriors, women, children. All were silent. All watched. And all wore as finery the bone remains of men, women, children.

"They're *worse* than the Hanjii," Del breathed to me.

"Not really. The Vashni don't believe in live sacrifice, like the Hanjii. The trophies you see are honorable ones, won in honorable battle." I paused. "Taken from *dead* people."

Our guide escorted us to the largest hyort, dropped off his horse and gestured us to dismount as well. Then he signaled me forward. But as Del stepped forward also, he shook his head sharply.

I looked at Del and saw the conflict in her face. She wanted so much to argue with the warrior; she knew better, and didn't. Instead, she moved back to her speckled horse. But not before I saw the desperation in her eyes.

"Do you speak Vashni?" she asked.

"A couple of words. But they speak Desert. Most people in the South do. Bascha—" I didn't touch her, though I wanted to. "—Del, I'll be careful what I say. I know what this means to you."

She let out a ragged breath. "I know. I—know. But—" She shook her head. "I guess I'm just afraid he won't be here after all. That he'll have been traded or sold off to someone else, and we'll have to search some more."

There was nothing more I could say. So I left her with the horses, as most would do with a woman. I turned my back on her and stepped inside the chieftain's hyort, and I came face to face with her brother.

I stopped short. The flap fell down behind my back; Del would not be able to see in. She wouldn't be able to see her brother as I saw him: braided, like a Vashni. Kilted, like a Vashni. Mostly naked, like a Vashni. But blond. Blue-eyed. Fair-skinned. Like Del. And lacking sword and fingerbone necklet.

Which meant he wasn't—quite—a Vashni.

He was nearly Del's height. But not quite. He was nearly Del's weight. But not quite. And never would be. Because I knew, looking at him, that his physical growth had been impaired by castration.

I've seen it before. It's in the eyes, if nowhere else. Not all of them grow fat, like Sabo. Not all of them grow effeminate. Not all of them look that much different from a normal male.

Except in the eyes. Except in the odd, almost eerie physical immaturity. A permanent immaturity.

In no way did I betray I knew who he was. In no way did I betray I knew *what* he was. I simply stood there silently, waiting, and trying to deal, in my own way, with the horror and shock and grief.

For Del's sake, because she would need me to be strong.

Jamail stepped aside; I saw the old man seated on a rug on the floor of the hyort. The chieftain of all the fierce Vashni: white-haired, wrinkled, palsied. And half-blind; his right eye was filmed completely over. His left showed signs of the same disability, although not as advanced. And yet he sat rigidly upright on his rug and waited for Jamail to return to his side.

When the boy did, the old man took hold of a soft, fair-skinned arm and did not let it go again.

Hoolies. How in the name of valhail do I deal with *this?*

But I knew. And when the old chieftain asked me my business with the Vashni, no doubt expecting a wish for trade expressed, I told him. Everything. And I told him the absolute truth.

When I was done, I looked at Jamail. He looked back out of Del's blue eyes. Not once had he said a word or made a sound of disbelief, grief, relief. Another man might have said the boy was afraid to indicate his feelings, out of fear for retribution. But I knew better. I saw how the old man clung to his Northern eunuch; how the old man depended on his Northern eunuch, and knew the Vashni chieftain would never hurt him. He wouldn't so much as speak a harsh word to him.

But he spoke to me. In Desert, the old man gave me Jamail's side of the story; as much as he knew of it. It was true Aladar had offered a Northern slave-boy as part of a trade treaty. It was true Jamail had been accepted as chattel. But it was not true he had remained such. It was not true he had been treated as chula. It was not true the Vashni had castrated him. It was not true the Vashni had cut out his tongue.

And so I knew why Jamail said nothing. Mute, he couldn't. Castrated, he might not want to.

"Aladar," I said only.

The old man nodded once. I saw the trembling in his chin. The tears forming in his failing eyes. The brittle strength in his palsied hands as he held Jamail's arm. His mouth twitched as he formed the words of his question: "Will the Northern woman want a man who is not a man?"

I looked at Jamail. Trapped forever in physical immaturity, he looked more like Del than he should. But I knew better than to think for one moment that what her brother had suffered would alter her intentions.

Still, I couldn't speak for her. "I think the woman will have to say."

After a moment, the old man nodded again. He gestured permission; I rose, gathered what courage I could muster, and went out to tell Jamail's sister.

Del listened in rigid silence. She said nothing when I finished speaking. She went in.

It wasn't my place to follow. But Del didn't speak Desert, and Jamail couldn't translate her words to the chieftain. So I ducked back into the hyort.

Jamail was crying. So was Del. So was the old man. But all of them did it in silence.

Del didn't look at me. "Ask the chieftain if he will let Jamail go."

I asked. The old man, crying, said yes.

She swallowed. "Ask Jamail if he will come."

I asked. Jamail, at length, nodded. Once. But I saw a fair-skinned hand creep out to touch the old man's liver-spotted one and cling in a dependence all too evident.

Del was dry-eyed now. "Tiger—will you tell the chieftain thank you? Tell him—*sulhaya*."

I told him. And then Jamail, because the chieftain told him to, got up to go out of the tent with his sister.

Del stopped him with a hand pressed lightly against his chest. She spoke in soft Northern, with tears in her eyes, and when she was done speaking, she hugged the brother she had sought for five long years and gave up her claim on him.

After a moment, I followed her out of the tent.

Chapter 24

Stark-faced, Del had said nothing on the journey from the foothills to the oasis on the border of the Punja. And now, as she sat in the muted shade of six palms with her back against the cistern's rock wall, I saw the beginnings of shocked comprehension coming into her eyes.

A goal achieved often brings no joy. Only a fleeting sense of satisfaction in the knowledge that the thing is done, but also the first taste of anti-climax. In this case, that taste was fouled by the additional knowledge that what she had done was for nothing.

Well, not entirely for *nothing*. But it seemed that way to her.

"They were kind to him," I told her. "For two years he lived in hoolies with Aladar. The Vashni gave him welcome. They gave him dignity."

"I'm *empty*," was all she said.

I heard the anguish in her tone as I sat down next to her. She'd built a little fire near one of the palms as the sun went down, using the kindling we carried in our pouches as well as a couple of dead palm fronds. We'd sat on spread rugs, chewed dinner, drunk wine, thought silent, private thoughts, and watched the sun go down across the desert. Now, except for the wind-whipped fire and snorts from hobbled horses, there was no noise at all.

Del turned her face to me and I saw the pain in every line. "Why am I so *empty?*"

"Because what you wanted most has been taken from you by circumstances you can't begin to change." I smiled a little. "There's no circle for this, bascha. No dance. No *kaidin* or *an-kaidin* to show you how to overcome it with skill and training. Not even a magicked sword can help, Northern- or Southron-forged."

"It hurts," she said. "It hurts *so much.*"

"For a long time to come."

We sat shoulder to shoulder against the cistern wall. I could feel the warmth of her skin through the thin silk of my burnous; the thin silk of her own. Neither of us were in harness, having shed our swords not long after dismounting. But both weapons lay in easy reach; neither of us is a fool.

I thought of how maybe once I might have asserted a certain degree of somewhat forceful masculine interest in the woman at my side. How maybe once I might have pressed physical attentions when she wasn't desirous of them, knowing so many women wanted to be teased and hugged and kissed into capitulation. But Del was not most women. Del was Del, sword-dancer first, and I respected her for that.

But not to the extent that I could ignore the fact I wanted her more than ever.

It became apparent her thoughts were much the same as mine. I saw the softening of her mouth; a slight smile widening slowly. Her glance was sidelong. Eloquent in its directness. "There was a deal, sword-dancer," she said. "A bargain we struck, because you wouldn't enter the circle with me otherwise. Payment for a sword-dancer's services, because I had no other coin."

I shrugged my left shoulder, naked of Singlestroke's weight. "We split Aladar's purse. Payment enough, bascha."

"Is that a *no?*" she asked in astonishment. Amusement, as well; she was not affronted by the idea I might not want her after all. But neither did she seem particularly relieved. "After waiting so patiently?"

I smiled. "Patience is as it must be, or some such thing. No, bascha, it isn't exactly a *no*. Just—an equivocal yes." I reached out and tucked a sunbleached strand of hair behind her ear. "I don't want you on the basis of a bargain. I don't want you if you feel it's obligatory. Or even a form of thanks." The calluses on my fingers caught and snagged the silk of her burnous. "Neither do I want it if you're simply feeling lonely and unfulfilled because your search is at an end."

"No?" Pale brows rose a little. "Not the Sandtiger *Elamain* knew, is it?"

I laughed out loud. "No, thank valhail. No."

Del's fingers—callused as my own—were cool on my silk-clad arm. "That's not why, Tiger. But if we *each* of us took, gave, shared—on an equal basis . . . regardless of the reasons?"

"Equal basis?" In the South, a man in bed with a woman knows so little of equality, being taught from childhood he is unquestionably superior.

Unless, of course, he grows up a chula.

Del laughed softly. "Think of it as a sword-dance."

I thought at once of my dreams. Del and I, in a circle. Facing one another. The image made me smile. The circle she offered now had nothing to do with dreams. At least, not *those* dreams; another sort entirely.

"Freely offered, freely taken." I thought it over. "Interesting idea, bascha."

"Not so different from Elamain." Del didn't smile, but I saw the twitch at the corner of her mouth.

"You're on." I rolled on one shoulder and caught her in my arms—

—Just as the stranger's voice came out of the deepening twilight—

—but not a stranger's at all.

The voice was clearly Theron's, challenging Del to a dance.

Theron's voice?

Del and I were on our feet instantly, swords bared. In the light of a full moon I saw the man approaching from the other side of the cistern. He walked. But beyond him, in the distance, stood a horse. A very familiar horse.

My stud—

I broke off the thought at once. Theron had purposely—and cleverly—dismounted, approaching on foot so our own mounts would not give warning.

And in our mutual lust (or love—call it what you will), we hadn't heard him. We hadn't heard him at all.

He wore the mouse-gray burnous. The hood was pushed back from his head. Still brown-haired, like me, with a trace of gray. Still tall, like me. But heavier now, because the mine had stripped too much weight from me.

Theron looked at Del. "We have a dance to finish."

"*Wait* a minute," I said "The afreet *took* you."

"But I'm here now, and this is none of your concern, Southron."

"I think maybe it *is*," I declared. "How did you get away? What exactly are you doing here?"

"It should be obvious. There is a bit of business remaining between the woman and me." He looked straight at Del, ignoring me entirely "I came here to finish a dance."

"Maybe you did." Butting in had never bothered me in the least. "But before you two continue your unfinished business, I want some answers."

Theron didn't smile. "As for the afreet, he lacks a master. As Rusali lacks a tanzeer."

Well, I wasn't really surprised. Alric had said Lahamu wasn't terribly bright. And Theron was clearly a dangerous man to cross.

I looked at the dangerous man. Quietly he stripped himself of sandals, burnous, harness. Of everything save his dhoti. In his hands he held his naked sword, and I saw again the alien runes, iridescent against the steel of palest-purple that wasn't—really—steel.

Again, we faced one another. Again, I saw the man who wanted to kill her, and I thought of killing him myself.

But it was Del's dance. Not mine.

Del stripped out of burnous, sandals, harness. Set them aside. With the naked sword in her hands, she turned to look at me. "Tiger," she said calmly.

I walked away from the rugs and the cistern, closer to the fire. I set Singlestroke's tip into the sand and began to draw the circle. There was moonlight, more than enough to see by. There was firelight. More than enough to die by.

The circle was drawn. Singlestroke was sheathed. I indicated they were to place their swords in the center of the circle. Silently, they did so, and stepped outside again.

They faced one another across the circle. In the argent moonlight it was a shallow ring of darkness; a thin black line in the ash-gray sand. But the line wavered. It moved on the sand like a side winding serpent. Because, though it had no beginning and lacked an end, the wind-whipped flames of the freshening fire lent the line a measure of life. An aspect of independence.

"Prepare."

I heard the soft songs begin. I looked at the swords in the center of the circle. Both silver-hilted. Both rune-bladed. Both alien to my eyes.

Slowly I walked to the cistern wall. I sat down. The stone was hard against my buttocks. But not as hard as the word I spoke.

"Dance," I said; that only.

They met in the center, snatching up swords, circling in the perpetual dance of death and life. I saw how Theron measured her more closely now, as if he recalled all too well how very good she was. No more male supremacy; he took her seriously.

Barefoot, they slipped through soft sand made softer by fire-cast shadows. The curving line of the circle wavered in the light. Such a thin, blade-thin line. For *me* to say if a dancer stepped outside the circle.

I saw the flash of silver as both swords met and sang. And all the colors poured out, shredding the darkness into a lace of luminescence. Ripples, curves, spirals, angles sharp as the edge of a knife, slicing across the shadows. I began to see the patterns clearly, as if Del and Theron wove of a purpose. A dip here, curlicue there, the whipstitch of a sudden feint.

Thrust, counter, thrust. Parry and riposte. The darkness was filled with light; my ears knew deafness from the crash of ensorcelled steel.

Thighs bunched, sinews rolled. Wrists held firm as they unleashed lurid luminescence. Del's face was stark in the wavering light, planed down in concentration. But I saw Theron begin to smile.

The shift was so subtle I nearly missed it altogether. I was aware mostly that the sound changed, the clash and hiss of rune-worked blades. Then I saw how the patterns began to change as well; how the intricate latticework became a slash here, slash there, bold and aggressive, until the slashes began to resemble my own.

Theron stood in the center of the circle and rained Northern steel on Northern steel, but the style was distinctly Southron.

No longer did I sit atop the cistern wall. I was at the edge of the circle, frowning at the man who began to dance against Del in a style she didn't, *couldn't* know.

But neither, I thought, could Theron. Or he would have used it in the first dance *before* the afreet arrived.

He broke her pattern. Once. Twice. A third and final time. He knocked the sword from her hands.

"*Del*—" But she didn't need my warning. She leaped up and over his blade, then dropped and rolled. Her hands were bare of blade, but she avoided his as well.

More closely, I watched him. I saw the light in his blue eyes and the satisfaction in the curving lines of his mouth. He was not a man who fought fairly, was Theron; not now. Maybe once. Maybe when he had faced her before. But now there was an *edge* to the look of the man. As if he had somehow acquired a style he had lacked before.

"*Del*—" This time I didn't wait. Not even for Theron. I simply dived over the curving line, caught Del in my arms and carried her out of the circle.

The *jivatma* lay outside as well. Del, cursing me angrily,

pressed herself into an upright postion. *"What are you doing, you fool—?"*

"Saving your life," I said grimly, pressing her down again. "If you'll give me a chance, I can explain."

"Explain *what?* How you lost this dance for me?" Del was vividly, impressively angry. And even as she struggled to shout curses into my face, she lost her Southron entirely.

Theron walked across the circle. With the song silenced, the sword was quiescent in his hand. The darkness was dark again, except for the argent moon.

"Forfeit," he said, "or yield. That is the only choice I will give you."

"Neither," Del answered. "This sword-dance isn't finished."

"You have left the circle."

Even in the South, the custom is the same. Out of the circle: out of the dance. She had no choice but to yield or forfeit.

"Not my choosing!" she cried. *"You* saw what he did!"

"He forfeited the dance *for* you." Theron smiled. "What's done is done, *ishtoya.*" He paused. "Pardon. Your rank is *an-ishtoya.*"

"I'm a sword-dancer," she threw back. "No rank. Just the dance." She struggled briefly. "Tiger—let me *up*—"

"No." I pinned her down again. "Couldn't you sense the change? Couldn't you feel the difference?" I looked over my shoulder at Theron. "He isn't the man you faced in the circle in Rusali. He's someone else entirely."

"Not quite," Theron said. He stood near the perimeter of the circle. The silver hilt of his blooding-blade was grasped lightly in his hand. "I'm the same man, Sandtiger. Only the *sword* is different."

Del frowned. "It's the same sword. It's *your* sword."

"What did you do?" I asked sharply. "What *exactly* did you do to Lahamu?"

"I killed him." Theron shrugged. "The tanzeer was foolish enough to take up my *jivatma.* Even you must know that isn't a thing for anyone but me to do. But I was wise enough to let him do it." He smiled as he looked at Del. "A lesson from you, *an-ishtoya.* When you are in need of a special skill, you acquire it however you may."

"You requenched." Del stiffened into absolute rigidity in my arms. "You *requenched your jivatma*—"

"*You* summon up the wind and storm and ice with that one of yours," Theron told her. "*You* suck down all the power of a banshee-storm with that sword! I know *that* much—so does every student who has learned the history of the *jivatmas*—even if I don't know the proper name for that butcher's blade." He bared white teeth in a smile of feral intensity. "And how do you defeat Delilah's famous Northern *jivatma*? With heat. With fire. With all the power of the *South*, invested in this blade."

"Theron—requenching is *forbidden*—" But her protest wasn't heeded. I wasn't sure he *heard* it.

One big hand caressed the glowing runes. "You felt it, didn't you? A weakness. A warmth. A sapping of your strength. Otherwise, I'd never have ripped that hilt from your hands." He smiled. "I know it, *an-ishtoya*. So do you. But it's important for me to win. I'll use what methods I can. So—yes, I requenched. I used the forbidden spell."

Del's lips were pressed flat, pale against her face. "The *an-kaidin* would be dishonored by his *an-ishtoya*."

"That I don't doubt," Theron agreed. "But the *an-kaidin* is also dead."

Del wasn't making an effort to go anywhere now. So I let go and sat up slowly, brushing sand from my hands. "If requenching means what I think it does, you've gained more than Southron heat. You've also gained the Southron style." And he was big enough to do damage.

"Yes," Theron agreed. "The tanzeer was hardly as good as you are—perhaps third level, instead of seventh—but he knew the rituals. Matched with my natural skill, the style isn't hard to use effectively."

"Probably not," I agreed. "Of course, against *another* Southron sword-dancer, the odds are decidedly different." I shed harness, burnous and sandals and dropped them all to the sand. "My turn, bascha."

"It's *my fight*—" she said. "Tiger—you can't—you're not fit for the circle yet."

She was right. But the choice had been taken from us. "You need to go home," I told her flatly. "You can't enter the circle again—you're too honorable to cheat. But I can. I can take your place."

"Is this to pay me back for killing Aladar?"

I laughed. "Not even close. I just want to *beat* this son of a Salset goat." I grinned at her. "Go home. Face your accusers. You have a chance with them. More than you have with Theron, who intends to cut you to pieces." I shook my head. "Del—he's countermanded the rituals of the dance. He's sought means he shouldn't have. There isn't a choice with him." I took Singlestroke into the circle.

Theron barely raised his brows. "And does the woman forfeit? Does the woman yield?"

"The *an-ishtoya* bows to necessity," I answered. "Will you accept a seventh-level *ishtoya* in her place?"

The sword-dancer smiled. "But who will arbitrate? Who will start the dance?"

I walked past him and placed Singlestroke in the center of the circle. "In the South, we do a lot of things on our own."

He accepted the challenge calmly. Stepping to the center, he set the requenched sword next to Singlestroke. Both weapons were of a like size. Probably of a like weight. Theron and I were evenly matched in height and reach, but now I lacked the weight. Maybe the speed and power. Because most of what skill I claimed had been left in Aladar's mine.

"Tell me something before we begin?" I asked.

Theron, frowning, nodded.

"Where'd you get that stud?"

It was obviously not the question he expected. He scowled at me blackly a moment, then sighed a little and shrugged; tolerance is not his virtue. "Found him in the desert, at an oasis. He was standing over a Hanjii warrior. A very *dead* Hanjii warrior."

I smiled. I suggested we begin.

Theron sang. I just danced.

*   *   *

Noise: the clangor of blade against blade; the sloughing of feet in sand; the inhalations of harsh, hurried breaths; grunts and half-curses expelled against our wills. The screeching hiss of Southron steel against an alien blade forged in the North and quenched in the blood of an enemy . . . requenched in the flesh and blood of a Southron tanzeer.

Color: from Theron's blade, not mine, pouring out of the black night sky filled up with the light of the moon, the stars, the fire, and all transfixed upon the Northern blade as it slashed out of the shadows to blind me with its light, that all-encompassing Northern light.

So much noise . . . So much color . . .

So much—

—*fire* . . .

So much—

—*heat* . . .

So much—

—*light*—

But all I knew was pain.

"Tiger—*no*—"

In shock, I came back to myself. I saw the lurid lights before me, with Theron in their midst. And felt the unsettling lack of balance in my sword.

Singlestroke.

I glanced down. Saw the broken blade. Heard the shriek of Theron's sword as it slashed down through the darkness and lit up the sky beyond.

"Tiger—*no*—"

Del's voice. I threw myself aside. Felt the icy blast of the winter wind; the scorch of a Punja summer. Heard Theron's contented laugh.

"*No sword*, Theron!" Del's voice shouted. "You dishonor your *an-kaidin!*"

The lights died. The winter/summer went away. I found myself kneeling in the sand with a broken sword in my hand, while Theron scowled down at me.

Singlestroke.

Blankly, I looked at the broken blade. A blemish? No. Blued-steel, shodo-blessed, doesn't ever break. Not of normal means.

I looked at the requenched weapon Theron held in his hand. At the alien shapes in the hilt; the alien runes in the blade. And I hated that sword. Hated the power that made it more than just a sword. Singlestroke's destruction.

Bewitched. Ensorcelled. Magicked. Cheater's blade; no better.

Singlestroke.

"Yield," he said, "or forfeit. For the woman and yourself."

"No." In my anger, in my shock, one word was all I could manage. But I thought it might be enough.

Theron sighed. "You have no sword. Do you mean to fight with your hands?"

"No." From Del this time, as she came up to the edge of the circle.

"Bascha." But she had the sword in her hand—

—and she put it into mine.

"Take her," she said softly, so only I could hear. "Use her. Her name is Boreal."

Theron shouted something. Something about breaking oaths. Something to do with the sword. The name of the sword, divulged. But by then it didn't matter. By then the sword was mine.

Boreal: *cold winter wind*, screaming out of the Northern Mountains. Cold banshee-storm blast, freezing flesh to the ice-cold hilt. And yet I gloried in the ice. I gloried in the wind. I gloried in the pain. Because I needed it all to win.

Boreal: *a sword*. A sword of alien metal. The North personified. Empowered by all the strength of Del herself. And the skill of a dead *an-kaidin*.

The Northern sword-dancer didn't stand a chance against the Southron one.

How we danced, Theron and I. How we did our best to carve the guts from one another; to cut the heart from one another. No finesse. No intricate, glowing patterns. No delicate tracery. Simple power, unleashed within the circle. An elemental fury.

Cut, slash, hack. Catch a blade and try to break it. Thrust, engage, riposte. Try to scythe the head from shoulders.

The requenched sword made him good. The requenched sword made him better. But no better than Del's made me.

—*fire*—

—*light*—

—*pain*—

And a wailing winter wind . . .

"Tiger?"

I woke up: silence. Opened my eyes: morning. Prepared myself for pain: nothing happened. "Del?"

No immediate answer. I was flat on my back; rolled over onto my belly. I lay sprawled within the circle. I vaguely recalled collapsing after sheathing Del's sword in Theron's belly.

I turned to look over my shoulder. Yes—still dead. Had to be, with all his blood and guts spilled into the sand.

I turned back. "Del?"

I saw her then. She knelt outside the circle, still not profaning it with her presence. For her, regardless of what had happened, the rituals were still in force.

Hoolies. Got up slowly. Felt earth and sky trade places a moment. Waited. Scrubbed a hand across gritty, burning eyes. "That's some sword, bascha." Anything else would be overkill.

"Can I have her back?"

I glanced behind me and saw the sword lying in the circle. I wasn't sure she'd let me touch her.

Del smiled. "She won't bite, Tiger. Not anymore. You know her name."

I retrieved the sword and gave her to Del outside of the circle. "That's the key, then? Her name?"

"Part of it. Not all. The rest is—personal." Pale brows knitted. "I can't say. You're Southron, not Northern—I don't have the language. And it takes years to comprehend. An *an-kaidin* to teach you the rituals involved."

"You're an *an-kaidin*."

"No." She looked past me to Theron's body. "No more than *he* was. *An-kaidins* never kill."

I looked back at the body. "Do you bury your dead, up north?"

"Yes."

So I buried him under a palm, beneath the Southron sun.

From atop her speckled horse, Del looked down on me. "It's a sword," she said, "that's all. Theron's dead. No one but Theron knew the blade's true name, so it will never be to you what it was to him. But—it's still a sword. A *sword* sword—nothing magical. Not a *jivatma*. But it'll work."

"I know it'll work." The hilt was a hilt in my hand. No eerie, discomfiting cold. Nothing but alien shapes. Runes unknown to me. And if Del knew, she wasn't saying. "But—it's not Single-stroke."

"No," she agreed. "I'm sorry, Tiger. I know what he was to you."

I sighed, feeling the now-familiar pinch of sorrow in my gut. *No more Singlestroke*— "Yes, well, the aqivi's spilled. Nothing I can do."

"No." She glanced northward a moment. "Now that I've decided, I guess I should get started. It's a long ride across the Punja."

"You remember all the markers, like I told you?"

"Yes."

I nodded. Turned to the stud and swung up into the shallow, blanketed saddle after I sheathed my Northern sword. Waited for him to settle. "Go on, Del. You're not getting any younger."

"No." She smiled a little. "But I'm not so very old."

No. She certainly wasn't. Too young for the South. Too young for a man like the Sandtiger.

On the other hand . . . "My offer stands," I said. "You've got a whole year before they can send anyone else out after you. And it's pretty obvious you'd beat any sword-dancer in the circle." I grinned, knowing she expected me to add *except for the Sandtiger*.

"It's freedom, Del, for a while. Ride with me, and we'll hire *both* swords out."

"No." The sun was bright on her white-blonde hair. "Better to have it settled for once and for all. If there's a way the blood-debt can be pardoned . . ." She frowned a little. "I make no apologies. Even to those who grieve for the death I gave the *an-kaidin*. But— I'd sooner be free to face them all, to know the final decision—instead of forever running."

I smiled. "Good. No sense in running when you can walk." I *suggested* the stud turn his head in the direction of Rusali; for a change, he acquiesced. "I'll tell Alric what you're doing. I think he'd like to know."

Del nodded. "Goodbye, Tiger. *Sulhaya.*"

"No thanks necessary." I reached out and slapped her horse on his speckled rump. "Go home, Del. No sense wasting time."

She clapped heels to the gelding and went away from me at a run.

I reined in the stud as he crowhopped, complaining about the gelding's departure. He wanted to run as well; to catch up and forge ahead. To compete. To prove he was unquestionably the *best*.

I grinned. "A lot like me, old son." I patted his heavy bay neck. "Glad to have me back?"

Horselike, he didn't answer. And so I reined him in—ignoring his disgruntled protests—and turned him toward the east.

But I didn't let him run. It's hard to think when a horse like the stud is going on, because you never know when he'll take a notion to drop a shoulder, duck his head and catapult you from the saddle. It's not particularly enjoyable. And one day it might even prove fatal.

So I made him walk, to preserve my life and because I could ruminate a little, turning things over inside my head.

—can't go to Julah. Not with Aladar dead. So I'll bypass it entirely and head for Rusali another way—

Pulled up. Held the stud in check, even though he stomped and sidled, snorting his displeasure, indicating he wished I'd make up my mind.

I ignored him and stared fixedly after Del. Glared.

In the distance, I could see the veil of saffron-colored dust raised by the northbound horse. Could see the white blot of her silken burnous—

"Ah, hoolies, horse, we've got nothing better to do—"

—so I turned the stud loose and went north.

Sword-Singer

For Barry Malzberg:
Who discovered me in the Scott Meredith slush pile and
helped my dream come true (while warning me it might);
and Mark O'Green: Who made me write it again and again,
(and again), until I got it right.

Chapter 1

"Flea-bitten . . . jug-headed . . . lop-eared—" I sucked in a deeper breath, "—thrice-cursed son of a Salset *goat!*"

Or similar sentiments. Trouble was, I was mostly incoherent, being somewhere on the delicate edge of discomfort and disaster.

He didn't answer. At least, not verbally. Physically, yes, and fervently; he humped and hopped and squealed, then buried his nose in the sand. Since he simultaneously elevated eloquent hindquarters with a powerful precision, I didn't stand much of a chance.

My saddle does not, thank valhail, have much of a pommel on it, being little more than a hummock of rigid leather shaped to fit the stud's back and my rump. I'd bought it thinking mostly of comfort for the long, hot hours spent crossing the Punja on one job or another. But now I blessed myself for picking it; a man in imminent danger of taking a nosedive off a horse—headfirst, belly-down, scraping over the shoulders and neck—doesn't much want to leave the best part of himself hung up on the front of a saddle while the rest of him sprawls in the sand.

Of course, I did have other worries. Like where my sword might end up. Even the most active sword-dancer doesn't generally entertain his opponent *upside down* in the circle; this meant there existed the possibility my borrowed sword might end up out of its sheath and in something else entirely, possibly even me.

Or—*(just give me half a chance)*—in the stud himself.

Face-first, I slid over the sloping front of my saddle (sucking up belly and everything else I could) and proceeded to dangle, however briefly, in the vicinity of his head.

To which the stud took an immediate dislike, not being an animal who much cares to have a large, cursing man shrouding his head like a glop of half-cooked egg.

The hindquarters came back down. It was the head's turn to elevate itself. Because I knew what was likely to happen if I didn't take immediate action, I wrapped arms and legs around whatever equine parts I could grab, and hugged.

Hard.

I'm big. I'm strong. It might have worked.

Unfortunately, the stud had the benefit of panic.

A horse's head is harder than a man's belly. A horse is stronger than a man. But I discovered just *how* hard and how *strong* as he tossed me aside like a wad of soiled silk.

—*airborn*—

Ah, hoolies.

I landed mostly on a tucked right shoulder, but also on the side of my face and the business end of my sword, sheathed and slung diagonally across my back in harness. Which meant that while it didn't dig too deeply into the sand, the blade *did* provide just enough leverage, as I rolled purposefully toward my shoulder blades, to tip me back over onto face and belly.

I sucked up enough sand to seed a new desert and proceeded to cough up my lungs all over the border between my land, the South, and Del's, the North.

Del. Some help *she* was. While I hacked and gagged and retched and discovered I had a bitten, bloody lip, she dismounted (in the normal fashion) and went off to fetch back the stud, who was wandering in a northwesterly direction for no discernible reason.

"—*flea*-bitten—" I spat out sand. "—*jug*-headed—" More sand. "—*lop*-eared—" Blood, this time. I touched my lip with a tentative finger, felt the sting of salt and sand in the wound. "—thrice-cursed son of a Salset *goat!*"

I sat up. Scowled horrifically at Del as she brought back the stud. Her expression was bland, noncommittal; innocence personified. (She is very good at that.) Certainly she appeared neither amused *nor* particularly concerned or sympathetic. But a closer look at guileless blue eyes told me she only bided her time.

I tongued my lip. "Ought to leave him staked out for the cumfa." I had to pick my way with words gingerly around the swelling lip, but the intent was clear enough.

"Long ride on a single horse." *So* bland. So infuriatingly casual.

I glared. Del began examining the stud for injury.

"*He's* fine." I paused. "He's *fine.*"

"Just checking."

I glared at her some more, absently admiring the clean lines of her face, so intent on the stud's condition. Couldn't see much more of her, as she was swathed in a white silk burnous that pretty well hid arms and legs and all of her womanly curves, spectacular as they were. In the South, that's the point of a burnous on a woman: to hide the lady from masculine eyes that might otherwise become inflamed with lust at the sight of a shapely ankle.

Trouble was, the custom *caused* difficulties, rather than avoiding them; a shapely ankle, promising other related anatomical niceties, becomes little more than an invitation to fantisize about the rest of the woman.

Of course with *Del,* it took a lot less than an ankle. One glance out of those blue, blue eyes, and I was . . . well . . .

Ah, hoolies. Me and every *other* male.

Deftly, gently, she ran hands down forelegs, briefly examined tendons, led him forward a few steps to observe his action, then proceeded to strip off the saddle, pouches and blankets to look at his back. He was wet where the gear had been, but that was to be expected.

"He does this," I told her. "You know that. You've seen him do it before."

She pursed lips, raised pale brows. "Bit more violent this time."

"So am I." I got up, winced, rolled my head from side to side. "Del—"

"The stud's all right." She turned. "How are you, Tiger?"

Now she asks. "Fine." Flexed wrists, fingers, wriggled shoulders up and down. Then I unsheathed the sword to make sure all was well with my weapon, as any sword-dancer will do, and as often as necessary.

Hoolies. This thrice-cursed Northern butcher's blade.

It is not mine. Not really, although I use it when I have to. It is borrowed, taken from a dead man who had no further use for it. I hated him, dead as he was; hated *it*, although the latter emotion was more than a little silly. But looking at the sword, touching it, wearing it, using it in my profession, reminded me time and again that my own shodo-blessed, blued-steel blade was dead as the man I'd killed in the circle beneath the moon.

Singlestroke.

Well, no sense crying when the aqivi's been spilled.

But I hated the thing. No sense, either, in denying it. Or in denying it frightened me in some weird, indefinable way.

The sword was Northern. Not Southron, as Singlestroke had been; as *I* am. Northern-forged, Northern-blooded; a *jivatma*, what Del called a blooding-blade, because the man who had made it his own had sought out a respected enemy in order to quench the blade, to blood it, in some unknown Northern ritual. Here in the South, it's different.

Sunlight ran down the blade. Alien runes worked into equally alien metal took life in the light and writhed, though it was only an illusion . . . or so I've always maintained. For me, there is no magic; I am not Theron, who quenched the blade, and I don't know its name or the key to bring the sword to life.

But *he* had, in the circle before I killed him. *He* had, and I'd seen all the brilliant lights of what Del called the palette of the gods: purples, violets, magentas, all lurid luminescence. Each sword had a soul (for lack of a better word) as well as a name, and that soul marked its passing in a glowing tracery of light, a delicate lattice of visible color. Generally only when keyed, but a little of it showed in the blade even when quiescent: Del's was salmon-silver, Theron's palest purple.

Or had been, before he died.

It had been a magnificent dance, while it lasted; a test of skill, strength, training and, on one side, treachery. How we danced, did Theron and I, in the name of a Northern woman.

A sword-dancer called Delilah.

Mouth grim-set, I sighed, expelling the air through my nose. The twisted hilt was cool in the heat of the day. Too cool; not even when we'd been riding in the blazing Southron sun for hours on end did the unprotected metal grow warm. An odd, eerie silver, ice-white/blue-white, like the snowstorms Del had described. But snow and snowstorms, like the sword, are alien to me. Born of the Southron sun, knowing heat and sand and simooms, I couldn't begin to comprehend (or even envision) the things she told me existed in her cold, Northern land.

All I know is the circle.

"One day," she said, "you will have to make your peace with Theron's sword."

I shook my head. "Once we can spare the time for me to seek out the shodo who trained me—or one of his apprentices—I'm trading this thing in on a real sword, a *Southron* sword, something I can trust."

"Trust *that* one," she told me calmly. "Never doubt it, or yourself; in your hands, it knows no magic. With Theron dead, it's only a sword. You know that. I've told you."

Told me, yes, because she knew how I felt about it. About the loss of Singlestroke. To a sword-dancer, a man who makes his living with the sword, a good blade is more than just a piece of steel. It's an extension of himself, as much a part of him as hand or foot, though decidedly deadlier. Your weapon lives, breathes, takes precedence over so much, because without it you are nothing.

For me, it was *less* than nothing; Singlestroke had given me freedom.

Theron's sword, I knew, was not precisely dead, but neither did it live. Not as Del's blade did. But there was something about it, something *odd;* when I put my hands upon the twisted hilt, I always felt a stranger, a usurper, little better than a thief. And I always felt a funny little twitch in the hilt, a recoiling, as if the sword, too, was startled by my touch. As if it expected another's flesh touching its own in that odd intercourse of man and sword. More than once I'd wanted to mention it to Del, but I never had. Something kept me from it. Pride, maybe. Or maybe just an unwillingness to admit I felt *anything;* I am not a man who puts much stock in magic, and the last one to admit I sensed such power in a sword. Even if it was mostly dissipated. For one, she might tell me I was imagining things.

For another, she might tell me I *wasn't.*

Del understands swords. Like me, she is a sword-dancer, improbable as it sounds. (Hoolies, it had taken *me* long enough to admit it; even now I still flinch a little when she steps into the circle to spar with me. I'm just not used to facing a *woman*—at least, not in the circle.) Our customs are so different, *too* different here in the South, where the sun and sand hold dominance. Del had done her best to alter my perceptions (and continues to alter them on a daily basis), but parts of me still view her as a woman, not a sword-dancer.

Of course just about the *last* thing a man might want of Del is a sword-dance. Dancing, yes, but not in the circle. Not with a *steel* blade . . . or whatever other kind of metal the *jivatma* was.

In the South, a woman has nothing to do with weapons of any kind. She tends the house, the hyort, the wagon; tends the children, the chickens, the goats; tends the man who calls her his.

But Del is Northern, not Southron. Del has no house or hyort or wagon, no children, chickens or goats. And she does not, most emphatically, have a man who calls her his, because Del belongs solely to Delilah.

Of course, *I* know better than to try.

I know better. But I try.

I looked at Del, knowing better than most what lay under the burnous; beneath the sleeveless, thigh-length, rune-stitched leather tunic hidden by glossy silk.

She is tall. Slender, but sinewy. Narrow-waisted, but wide-shouldered. Tough. Fit. Far stronger than an ordinary woman.

There is nothing at all of fragility about Del, though she is all female, and all the pieces are quite distinctly in the proper places.

Blue-eyed, fair-haired, fair-skinned bascha, although after a few years under the Southron sun the hair is nearly white and the skin a tawny, creamy gold.

We are so different, Delilah and I. I am a true son of the desert: skin burned dark as a copper piece, dark brown hair bleached on top a streaky bronze, green eyes couched in a fan of sun-baked creases that, when spread, display the color I was at birth, thirty-some-odd years ago. Paler then, though darker still than a Northerner's creamy color.

I am tall, broad, heavy, but considerably quicker than I look. Sword-dancing teaches even the slowest man how to move—or it teaches him how to die.

I looked at Del, because Del is good to look at. But I also looked at the sword hilt that rode her left shoulder. I know it well now. Better than I prefer, because I had been forced to learn. All the months of watching Del wield it with uncanny skill and grace, knowing it more than simply a sword, I had had time to learn to respect it, even to *fear* it, because it was more than just a sword. In her hands, it was *alive,* and a thing of awesome power.

Boreal: born of Northern banshee-storms, blooded in the body of one of the finest sword-masters of the North. *Her* sword-master—her *an-kaidin*—a man she honored and respected, who had taken a determined fifteen-year-old girl bent on a highly personal revenge and honed her into a weapon nearly as lethal as the one she'd eventually sheathed in him.

Boreal. Who had, in my hands (however briefly loaned) come to life at the sound of her name, saving me, saving Del, destroying the man who meant to kill us.

But Boreal was Del's. I had no part of her. No more than I did of Theron's blade, which now replaced Singlestroke even if only temporarily.

Necessity is often distasteful.

I sheathed the sword and ignored it, accustomed to its weight across my shoulders. Then I took the stud's reins from Del's hand and led him a few steps away.

"Look, old son," I began, "you and I have to come to an understanding. That sort of blowup is acceptable when we're in a village or a town or an encampment and there's money riding on the outcome, but not when it's just you and me and Del, and that sandsick horse of hers." I patted his neck. "Understand? You could get one of us hurt out here in the desert, and that's not such a good idea."

He blew noisily through brown nostrils and flicked a tufted ear. Then he bared his teeth in a sideways attempt to bite.

"Affectionate as ever." I thumbed the prehensile lip and he twisted his head away, rolling an eloquent eye.

Del caught up the reins of her own mount—a gutless, washed-out speckledy gray-white gelding with a frazzled tail and the temperament of an aging woman who considers herself still skilled at being coy—and looked at me. "How long before we reach Harquhal?"

"Should be by nightfall." I shielded my eyes and squinted up at the Southron sky that seemed to shimmer in the warmth. "Of course, we're losing time with this idiot horse."

"Then saddle him and let's go."

"In a hurry, are we?" I took the stud back to where his gear lay and bent to gather up the bits and pieces. "The North will still be there, Del . . . has been for years."

She mounted, swinging free of her billowy white silk burnous one long leg and slender foot with its Southron sandal cross-gartered to her knee. "And it's been six since *I* was there."

"Not *quite* six," I corrected. "You've been with me, not counting respective captivities, for at least nine months." I grinned as she shot me a scowl beneath sun-bleached blonde brows. "Even if it took us five and a half *more* years, bascha, it'd still be there."

"You forget yourself, Sandtiger." Her tone was suddenly cool. I stopped saddling the stud and turned to look directly at her. "Only two months remain before Theron's agreed-upon year is done . . . and then they will be sending another sword-dancer to collect the blood-debt I owe."

Not a laughing matter, with Del or with anyone else. What she faced was serious. If, in the specified months, Del refused to go North to face trial for that blood-debt, the task of killing her would then belong to any man, or multiples thereof. Northern, Southron, sword-dancer, soldier, bandit; it simply didn't matter. Her killer would be rewarded for discharging the blood-debt owed for the murder of her *an-kaidin*.

Del was guilty. She *had* killed the *an-kaidin*. She carried blood-guilt freely, and did not deny responsibility. It made the sentence just in the eyes of the Northern *an-kaidin* and all their students, the *ishtoya* and *an-ishtoya*.

Hoolies, in a weird sort of way even *I* understood the reason for it.

But anyone who wanted her would have to go through me.

Chapter 2

*I*n the desert, the sunsets are glorious. I've never been a man for painting pictures with words, but often, at day's end, watching, I wished I was. There is something oddly tranquil and satisfying in watching the sun slide down beyond the bright blade of the horizon, setting the ocher and umber desert ablaze with the brilliance of richer colors: copper, canary, saffron and cinnabar. The desert is transfigured into a paradise of pigments, a collection of colors on the palette of gods different from those Del knew, or created with Boreal.

Sunset. There is something that speaks in quiet inner places about the ordering of the world, today and tomorrow, then and now, and all of the yesterdays.

I sat my bay stud and stared westward, watching the sun go down, and knew contentment in the company I kept. Del was mute, watching as I watched; feeling, I knew, some of the same feelings, sharing the quietude. There were many things unknown between us, many things unspoken, because we had both been shaped by circumstances far beyond ken or control. We were an odd amalgam, the woman and I; sword-dancers both; dangerous, deadly, dedicated, as loyal to the rituals of the circle as to one another. And yet denying, in our own independently stubborn ways, any loyalties to one another at all; preferring, for countless ridiculous reasons, to claim ourselves invulnerable to the normal course of human wants, needs, desires.

And knowing, perfectly well, we needed one another as much as we needed the dance.

The sunset gilded Del's face. She had pushed the hood off her head so the silk settled on her shoulders, baring hair and features. She was all aglow: old gold, ivory, ice-white. In profile, she was flawless; full-face, even better. Inwardly, I smiled, thinking of the bed we would share in Harquhal. A *bed* bed, not a blanket spread upon the sand, or the naked sand itself. We had not, yet, ever shared a proper bed, being confined for so long to the Punja.

But now we left the deadly Punja far behind, passing out of dunes and flatlands into the scrubby, hilly high desert that presaged the borderlands. Already it was cooler than the scorching days spent on blinding sands, hiding vulnerable eyes amidst the shade of burnous hoods.

Here there were tough, fibrous red-throated grasses, warring with other groundcover; the tangle and tang of jade-hued creosote, haphazard in its growth; vast armies of thorny trees with feathery silver-gray leaves. Even the bloom of fragile flowers, unexpectedly tenacious, climbing out of the fretwork of webby groundcover and the tassles of taller, duller grasses to wave fluted gaudy petals, like pennons, in whatever breeze they could find.

Here there was water. Here there was game. Here there was the promise of a survival less difficult than in the arid sea of sand known as the Punja.

Harquhal. It rises out of the desert like a blocky pile of mud, girded by sloping hills and taupe-gray abode walls to hide its many faces from the threat of capricious simooms blowing northward out of the Punja. It is a characteristic of the South that towns, villages, semipermanent habitations, as well as the countless oases, are warded with man-made walls or hills or natural rock formations so that the deadly sandstorms, called simooms, cannot sweep away what men, women and children have labored so hard to build. In the Punja, it is necessity; the sands, never sated, swallow towns and cities whole if not properly maintained, disdaining the curses of powerful tanzeers and the wretched poor alike.

I have seen walls, left to crumble by lazy inhabitants, swept away in a matter of hours, and the dwellings within destroyed by abrasive, voracious wind. I have seen cisterns and natural springs filled permanently by choking sand, though we have none to spare, in the South, in the Punja. I have seen scoured skeletons eaten clean of even a shred of flesh; by no beast but the wind, the sand, the heat. Horse, dog, goat. Man. Woman. Child.

There is no mercy in the South, from humans, beasts, elements. There is only the way things are, and will be forever; ceaseless, unchanging, moved by no pleas for leniency or forgiveness.

If there are gods who hear those pleas, they pass the time with fingers planted firmly in useless ears.

Del sighed. "I thought, when I went home again, my brother would be with me."

So much said with so little. Del hoarded thoughts and feelings like a merchant coin, dispensing each with grave deliberation and at unpredictable moments. She had said nothing of Jamail for weeks, locking away in tenacious silence all the pain born of a futile search.

For five years she had meticulously prepared herself to track down and free the younger brother stolen by raiders for profitable commerce with Southron slavers who knew the true value of blue-eyed, blond-haired Northern boys in a land of dark-faced people. For five years she had apprenticed herself to a shodo—in Northern lingo, *an-kaidin*—to learn the requirements of sword-dancing, fashioning herself into a human weapon with the sole purpose of rescuing Jamail. Knowing it was not perceived a woman's task; knowing also there was no one else to do it. No one even to care; the raiders had robbed her of kin as well as innocence.

Futile. No, not exactly. She *had* found Jamail, but there was little left to rescue.

Tongueless, castrated, shaped in mind and body by years of Southron slavery, Jamail was not the ten-year-old brother she had adored. Only a boy-man who could now, never, be a *man*, no matter how hard he wished it; no matter how hard *she* did. Jamail, Delilah's beloved brother, desired to stay in the South with the savage tribe he had grown to love.

I wanted to touch her, but our horses stood too distant from one another. Instead, I nodded. And after a moment, intending to lighten the mood, I smiled and shrugged. "Well, you do have *me.*"

At length, she slanted me an eloquent glance from the corners of her eyes without even turning her head. "That is something, I suppose."

"Something," I agreed blandly, choosing to ignore Del's tone altogether. "I *am* the Sandtiger, after all."

"After all." She twisted her head to look north. "There is food in Harquhal. *Real* food; something other than dried cumfa and dates."

I nodded, brightening. "And aqivi as well."

"We don't have the coin to spend on spirits."

"Do you expect me to drink *goat's milk?*"

She contemplated me a moment. "They both smell about the same. What difference would it make?"

"About as much difference as you swapping Boreal for Theron's sword." I stopped short as I saw how shock turned her to stone. And then I realized what I'd done. "Del—Del, I'm sorry—" Wondering: *Oh, hoolies, how could I have been so stupid?* "Del—I'm *sorry*—"

She was white-faced with anger as she reined her speckledy gelding next to the stud. She didn't seem to notice as the stud laid back ears and bared teeth stained yellow by Southron grasses and grains.

But I noticed. I noticed also the rigid hand that reached out to catch my wrist. And closed. More tightly than was pleasant.

"Never," she said distinctly, "speak her name aloud again."

No. No, of course not. I knew better. I *knew* better. "Del—"

"Never," she said again, and took her hand away from my wrist.

There were marks upon it. They faded even as I watched, but the sensation didn't. Certainly the memory wouldn't. Ever.

I flexed my hand to see if all the fingers worked. They did; Del isn't *that* strong. But strong enough; I felt guilty as well as resentful that she could command me so easily.

"I'm sorry," I repeated, wishing there was something more I could say.

Del's mouth was a flat line. Its grimness ruined the symmetry of her features, but also impressed upon me the depth of her displeasure. "Her name is sacred." It was so taut a tone as to lack definition, and yet I heard the undercurrent of shock, fear, despair.

"Del—"

"*Sacred*, Tiger." Del released an unsteady breath and I saw some of the tension leave her body, replaced with outright anguish. "It's all a part of the power, the magic . . . if you divulge her name to others, all the rituals are undone—" She stopped short, searching for comprehension in my face. "All the time, all the years, all the dedication . . . the sacrifice is as nothing—"

"Del, I know—*I know*. You've told me. It was a slip, nothing more." I shrugged, keenly uncomfortable, knowing I devalued her feelings even as I tried to assuage my guilt. "I promise, I won't ever say her name again."

"If another heard it—another Northerner trained as I was trained, knowing how to tap the magic, how to destroy the *jivatma*—" Again she broke off, then scrubbed a hand against her face and swept fallen pale hair out of blue eyes. "I am in trouble enough because of the blood-debt. A man sent to fetch me back, to kill me, could take my skills, my strength, my blade—all with a single word."

"But *I* know her name. You told me."

"I told you." The tone, now, was lifeless. "I had no choice. But you are a *Southroner*, lacking the magic, the power, the knowledge; you know nothing of the *jivatma*, and what it means. And yet you saw how it served you, how *she* served you, answering your need."

"But not as she serves you."

"No. No, of course not." Distracted, frowning, she shook her head, and the curtain of hair rippled. She had not braided it lately, leaving it loose to fall over shoulders and down her back. "There are rituals—personal, private rituals . . . no one else may know them. Only me, when I make the sword my own." Her eyes were on the hilt poking above my left shoulder, freed by the slit cut so deliberately in the seam of my russet burnous so that nothing would hinder me if I required it. Theron's *jivatma* made powerless by his death. "Had *Theron* known her name, he would have killed you. Killed *me*—"

"—and killed the sword." I nodded. "I understand, Del."

"No," she said, "you don't. But I cannot expect it of you. Not now. Not *yet*. Not until—" And abruptly she shrugged, clearly choosing not to finish what she had begun, as if I was not prepared to hear it. "It doesn't matter. Not the understanding; not yet. What *does* matter is that you never again say her name, not aloud, to anyone."

"No."

"*No*, Tiger."

I nodded. "No."

Her stare was so direct I wanted to look away, but I didn't. I saw her seek some answer in my face, some expression she could trust, assurances unspoken but as binding, if not more so, than the words. There had been many things between us— death, life, survival; more than mere affection, more than simple lust—that counted for very much, but I knew, looking at her now, that nothing counted to her so much as a man who kept his word.

After a moment she turned her gelding north, toward Harquhal. She said nothing more of the sword or my commitment to permanent silence, but I knew the slip was not forgotten. Nor ever would be.

Hoolies, I hadn't meant it. But an apology wasn't enough, no matter how sincere. In the circle, it means nothing to a dead man to hear his killer's apology.

*   *   *

Harquhal is representative of most towns in the South. Adobe walls ward it against the wind, showing handprints and other geometric patterns laid in at construction. Cracks are plugged with fresh gobs of claylike mud, meticulously fingered into place, denying the wind and sand even subtle means of entry. But walls, like intentions, are transitory; tents and stalls and wagons clustered haphazardly around the perimeter of the walls like chicks around a hen, ignoring the possibilities of such things as simooms and smaller sister storms.

Harquhal is also representative of most border towns. Serving Northerners and Southroners alike, it has no nationality, and fewer loyalties. Ostensibly Southron, Harquhal pays only hapahazard allegiance to the land I call my home. Here, wealth holds dominance.

Del and I had little. In the weeks since we had left Jamail with the Vashni in the mountains near Julah, we had survived on wagers won and a few odd jobs here and there; collections for a Punja-mite of a greedy merchant who then tried to cheat us out of our commission; effecting the rescue of the kidnapped son of a powerful tanzeer who embraced the Hamidaa religion, which proseletyzed the uncleanliness of women, while all the time the kidnapped "son" was in reality a daughter; escort duty for a caravan bound from one domain to another; other assorted employments.

Nothing, certainly, requiring remarkable ability with sword or guile. Nothing that added to the reputation of the Sandtiger, the legendary Southron sword-dancer, whose skill in the circle was matched by no man.

Unfortunately, now there was a woman. And she *had* displayed remarkable abilities with a sword, relieving a renegade sword-dancer of his life. As for guile, Del had little; she was blunt-spoken, straightforward, intolerant of Southron word courtesies that often did little more than waste time. And time was her enemy.

The worst part of our journey was done. The Punja lay behind us. What we faced now, once free of Harquhal, was the North.

Hoolies. I was a *Southroner*—what did I want with the North?

Nothing. Except Del, who had more than casual ties with the land of snow and banshee-storms.

More than casual ties with powerful Northern magic.

Glumly, I swung down off the stud in front of a lopsided adobe cantina roofed with a lattice of woven boughs, and tied tassled reins to a knobby post set crookedly in the ground. I heard the sounds of laughter and merriment inside, male and female; smelled the pungent stink of huva weed, the aroma of roasting mutton, the tang of wine and aqivi.

Also the sweet-sour smell of urine; the stud was relieving himself.

Swearing, I skipped back and nearly stumbled over my own sandaled feet, not wanting my burnous splattered. The stud rolled an eye in my direction and wrinkled a pale-brown muzzle forested with whiskers. I began again my endless litany of unflattering equine appellations.

Del avoided the steaming puddle as she dismounted and tied her gelding to another post. Absently she hooked a left hand up to the exposed hilt of her sword, snicked it twice against the lip of the hidden sheath to check ease of movement, nodded once. I'd seen her do it before, many times. It is a habit, though varied in execution, all sword-dancers develop.

We all have idiosyncracies. Some of them keep us alive.

"I take it you want to leave at first light." I waited for her to fall into step beside me.

She shrugged. "There are things we much purchase first. Food, clothing—"

"Clothing!" I frowned. "I admit we could use cleaner apparel, but why spend good coin on things we already have?"

She pulled aside the threadbare vermilion curtain at the door. "If you wish to go north with nothing more to wear than a dhoti and burnous and freeze your *gehetties* off, you may. But *I* have no intention of freezing to death." And she ducked in, forgetting, as usual, that I require more room than she does in entrances built for shorter men.

I jerked the curtain off my face and scowled after her as I followed. Then I coughed; huva smoke packed the exposed rafters of the cantina, drifting in slow, eddying, malodorous ocher-green wreaths. The vice is one I abhor since a sword-dancer needs all his faculties in the circle. Of course Del had taken my opinion as somewhat tainted by the fact I drink aqivi with great abandon, pointing out that a man with a gut full of aqivi is no less likely to die than a man with a head full of huva dreams.

(Well, Del and I don't always agree on everything. Sometimes we don't agree on anything.)

She squinted and waved a hand in front of her face, peering irritatedly through the smoke as she sought an open table. And, as is common when Del walks into a cantina (or any place, for that matter), desultory conversation devolved into a muddle of hissed comments, muttered questions, unsubtle speculation.

I sighed. Wished I had Singlestroke. Bared my teeth in a lazy, friendly grin at the two dozen or so men who looked from Del to me, to see if I was capable of protecting the Northern bascha.

I don't consider myself a vain man. What I am is fact: big, strong, quick. There is a certain dangerous edge in my face, my posture, my eyes, shaped by the demands of my profession. And there are times I am perfectly willing to flaunt whatever advantages this affords me; I fight when I must, and with gusto, but only when there is no other way around it.

Idly I assessed the room, letting them see what I did. Just as idly I scratched the scars on my face. Deep scars, old scars; four clearly defined claw stripes curving from right cheek to jaw, unmistakably from a beast some men labled mythical: the lethal Punja sandtiger from which I'd taken my name.

My badge of honor, in a manner of speaking. For men who knew of sword-dancers, it identified me at once.

(Not everyone carries the mark of his profession and expertise on his face; I rather like it. Saves time.)

"No trouble," Del muttered under her breath. Half suggestion, half command.

I slapped a spread hand over my heart. "Need you even say it?"

She grunted. Waved away more smoke. Strode across the floor

through crowded aisles to a tiny table in a corner at the very back of the cantina.

Still smiling, I followed, watching everyone else watch her, even the cantina girls, who scowled, chewed bottom lips, nibbled thoughtfully on thumbnails. And who, if they were quick enough, realized they had better beguile their chosen partners immediately, if they were to recapture clearly divided attention.

One of the girls, perched on the thigh of a lean young man sprawled casually at a table, got up at once and made her way to me, blocking my view of Del. Black-haired, dark-skinned, brown-eyed. A typical Southron girl: lush-figured, bold of features; at six-teen or seventeen, in full bloom. But it would fade too quickly, I knew; the desert sucks women dry before they are thirty.

"Beylo." She smiled, showing crooked teeth and a curiously at-tractive overbite. "Beylo, will you share your wine with Jemina?" Her hands were on my arms, caressing me through the thin fabric of my burnous. "I can bring you huva and many, many dreams."

"Of that I have no doubt." I glanced past her to the young man she had deserted, marking black hair, blue eyes, the smudge of a new mustache, a rueful expression. He was not angry, and did not appear moved to protest her defection. He seemed amused by the performance, which was at least a welcome change from bruised male pride, which always demands reparation. (Generally in blood.) "But you are partnered already, bascha, and so am I."

Jemina shrugged a dusky naked shoulder, ignoring the loose neckline that slid lower still, exposing most of one plump breast. "He's a *boy*, beylo . . . you are a man."

Well, yes, last time I looked. "Bascha, another time," I set her out of my way and saw Del seated at the little table, clearly amused.

Ah, well, too much to hope she might be *jealous*.

I hooked out a stool and sat down, scowling as the uneven legs rocked me back and forth, threatening to tip me over entirely. I wedged the stool against the wall, settled substantial weight gin-gerly, looked up again to see the wry twist of Del's mouth. And then she looked past me, and up, to watch the wine-girl who eyed her so assessively.

Back again. I sighed. "Bascha—"

"Wine?" she asked. "Aqivi?" She tossed black curls behind a shoulder. "I *work* for my living, beylo. I am not a common whore."

Unless, of course, the price was right. I sighed again and fingered my shriveled coin pouch. A few coppers clinked; hardly enough to buy a full meal and all the aqivi I wanted.

My eyes strayed hopefully to Del. She tapped slender fingers on the scarred, sticky tabletop, sighed, waved a hand at the girl. "Stew," she said, "and the cheapest wine you've got."

"Wine!" Aggrievedly, I stared. "A few coppers more will turn up a jug of aqivi."

"Wine," Del said coolly, and the girl turned away with a flounce of layered skirts that clearly signaled my reduction in her esteem.

I leaned forward, resting my weight on one planted forearm. "Just how do you propose to buy *clothing* if we haven't enough coin for a proper meal?"

"I propose to buy clothing by forgoing unnecessary expenditures on unnecessary things." She paused, sweeping back a fall of hair. "Like aqivi."

A tendril of huva smoke drifted down from the beamwork. I waved it away. "Aqivi is hardly *unnecessary* when I've spent the last three or four weeks sucking water on our way across the Punja."

Jemina returned and plunked down two wooden bowls of mutton stew, a half-risen loaf of brown bread, a sloshing stoneware bottle, and a pair of battered wooden cups bound by greenish copper.

Del smiled sweetly. "Suck wine."

I might have answered, but I was too busy sniffing the stew in my bowl. Mutton is not one of my favorite dishes, although I'm accustomed to it. It's better than dog. Certainly better than roasted sandtiger, which Del had ignobly served me once.

After a moment I drew my knife and hacked off a chunk of hard bread, lifted the bowl and prepared to scoop watery stew into my mouth.

Prepared. I never got any farther. Not when I saw the expression on Del's face as she stared, transfixed, across the crowded cantina.

Shock. Anger. Suspicion. And a cold, rising rage that glittered like ice in her eyes.

By all the nameless gods of valhail, I swear I have never seen a look like that. On man *or* woman.

Not even on a sword-dancer.

Chapter 3

She rose slowly, so slowly, until the tabletop hit her midthigh. Shrouded in the burnous, most of her was hidden. But I knew her. I knew how she moved, how she tensed, how she waited. I knew how to judge her intentions simply by reading her eyes.

"Del—"

She did not even glance at me.

I wrenched my head around and stared across the cantina, trying to see what she saw. Trying to see what had set her on edge; what had stripped her of the woman I knew, reducing her to little more than an animal on the stalk.

I saw nothing. Well, not *nothing*. I saw men. Just men. Bent over tables, hunched on stools, trading stories, jokes, insults. And wine-girls, plying their trades. And smoke and lamplight and shadows.

"Del—" I turned back, frowning, and saw the color slowly fade from her face. There isn't much to begin with, what with her Northern complexion, but now there was a decided difference. Now she looked like a woman dead three days.

Slowly, she sank back onto her stool. Her hands still braced her balance against the table, fingers spread, rigid, and trembling. *Trembling;* I'd never seen Del shake.

"Could I be wrong?" she asked herself in an odd, toneless voice. Then again, more forcefully, and yet still curiously toneless. "Could I be *wrong?*"

I wrenched my head around yet again to seek out what had affected her so dramatically. And again, I saw men. I saw one of them rise from his stool and turn away, moving purposefully toward the door. He ducked through the curtain, was gone; I heard Del release a slow, noisy breath.

"What in hoolies—" An upthrust hand cut me off. I waited, still concerned to see the minute trembling of her fingers, and eventually her eyes lost their opaque, blind expression and Del looked at me. This time, I think, she saw me.

"Private," she said only, and scooped up a cup of wine.

Del doesn't drink much. It isn't like her to gulp wine, but now I saw how she held the cup against her mouth as if the liquor might restore her strength. I watched her throat move as she swallowed repeatedly, sucking wine like a man trying to chase away demons.

Or a woman, with her own.

"Privacy's one thing." I caught the cup in one hand, took it away from her, set it firmly on the table. "This is another. Maybe what you need is to talk about it."

"*Maybe* what I need is a jug of aqivi to shut you up," she said sharply. And then, tight-jawed, she apologized for her tone.

But not for the words. I smiled. "Effective bribery. Shall I call Jemina back?"

"No." Del stared at the cooling mutton stew. "No; we need to save the coin."

"Then let's treat the wine as it should be treated." I refilled her cup. "With slow and deliberate appreciation."

"It's sour."

Her color was returning along with her mettlesome mood. "Yes, it's sour," I said blandly. "So, at the moment, are you."

"But you don't know—" She stopped herself.

"No," I agreed, "I don't. Unless you tell me."

"It's private," Del repeated.

I stirred congealing stew with a piece of bread, making islands out of the meat and channeling the gravy. Mildly, I said: "You know more about me than anyone else alive."

Her glance was sharp, startled; she considered it, then withdrew abruptly, shaking her head. "I can't. Not now."

"That man—"

"*Not now.*"

There are times, with Del, when silence is the best strategy. Accordingly, I turned my attention to sour wine and mutton stew, while Jemina made eyes at me from across the smoky cantina.

In the morning Del rousted me out of bed with a fist snugged none too gently against my short ribs. When, aggrievedly, I protested such bad manners, she merely threw me my dhoti, harness and burnous and suggested I put them on as soon as possible, as she had plans for us this morning.

"Plans?" I dressed, slipped into harness, tested the weight of the borrowed blade. "What *sort* of plans?"

"Supplies," she said succinctly, and yanked aside the curtain.

The motion proved too much for the threadbare cloth that separated our tiny inn room from the corridor outside. Fabric parted and Del was left standing with a handful of faded green cloth. With a tongue-click of irritation she tossed it aside.

"Out of sorts this morning, are we?" I picked up saddle pouches and preceded her out of the musty, low-roofed room. "Maybe if you'd spent more of last night *sleeping* instead of thinking—"

"You snored."

Ah. My fault, then; I should have known. Accordingly, I possessed myself of silence and went down into the common room to order breakfast.

Del was off her feed, as well; she was too well disciplined to ignore food when it was offered, not knowing when we might have another meal, but clearly she did not enjoy it. Impatiently she chewed hard bread, spooned down spiced kheshi, swallowed pungent goat's milk. And then told me to hurry up as I considered a second bowl of kheshi.

I cast her an exasperated scowl. "Hoolies, Del, we don't need to *run* across the border."

"We don't need to dawdle here, either. Tiger, you know there is a time limit."

"Time limit, shmime limit," I said testily. "A man's got to eat, Del. Or he won't be any help at all, should you need it."

It shut her up, as I thought it might. She recalled I accompanied her only through personal whim; I could leave any time I felt like it. And by reminding Del I intended to render her aid as best I could, I deflated all her righteous indignation.

It's hard to be angry with someone who's lending you a hand. Also bad manners.

I looked at Del's expression. And then, quietly, I sent the girl away with the second bowl of kheshi and stood up, gathering saddle pouches once more. Silently, I indicated the door.

Del turned on her heel and marched out.

It was clear Del recalled more of Harquhal than I did, though it had been nearly a year since she had been here. She led me directly to a small shop tucked into the shadows along the wall, and proceeded to spend an untold amount of time examining what appeared to be piles of furry pelts, supple leather, and a heavy, dyed fabric. Weary of following along like a bearer waiting attendance on a Southron lady, I dumped the pouches by the door and began to do my own examining.

The shop reeked of tanned leather and pungent fur, as well as other smells I could not begin to name. Accustomed to desert silks and gauzes, I could not comprehend what a man would want with so much weight and bulk. But Del apparently did; eventually she chose the things she wanted and gave the shopkeeper very nearly all of our coin.

"*Sulhaya,*" she said, as he rolled the pelts around soft leather into long, flexible bundles and tied them.

He answered back in Del's indecipherable Northern tongue; I looked at him more sharply. He was old, and therefore white-haired, and the South had baked his flesh, but his eyes were blue as Del's. No Southroner, this; he was clearly a Northerner, which meant Del apparently knew what she was doing. Some consolation, I guess, considering *I* didn't.

The old man's eyes were on her sword hilt, poking above Del's left shoulder. Boreal's hilt is fashioned in such a way as to fool the eye, to bewitch the beholder into something like a trance if you stare at the hilt too long. The silver is everchanging, one shape melting into another, then another, until you forget about time entirely, thinking only of the moving forms within the metal. Trying to follow, to name at least *one*, before the blade assumes the aspect of the hilt and dispatches you entirely.

"An-ishtoya?" the old man asked, and Del stopped short.

Her face was frozen, sculpted into a flawless display of rigid beauty. But hard as stone, and equally inflexible.

An-ishtoya. The highest rank a Northerner can know, as student, apprentice, in the circle. The rank is bestowed by the *an-kaidin,* the sword-master, higher than the teachers themselves, the *kaidin;* highest of the high. She had been *ishtoya*—student—and then *an-ishtoya*—the paramount—proclaimed so by the *an-kaidin* himself.

But Del had turned her back on it, naming herself, instead, a sword-dancer, as she was free to do, and bound by no rituals other than those determined by the circle.

The old man had clearly trespassed upon her rigidly guarded privacy. But she did not react as she so often did with me. Perhaps because of his age. Perhaps because he was a Northerner. Perhaps also because he knew better what the word meant, and all its accompanying weight.

"No," she said after a moment. "Sword-dancer."

Something moved briefly in his eyes. But his face—a webbing of lines and creases deeply incised in flesh lighter than my own—did not change. He looked again at Boreal, and then he nodded. Once. "Sing well," he said, in Southron, and turned away to tend another customer.

I shouldered saddle pouches, took on one of the rolled bundles, stepped out of the shop just ahead of Del. As she exited I paused to fall into step beside her.

"Sing well," I said, puzzled. "Didn't he mean 'dance'?"

Del had hitched her sausage of hides under one arm. Her face was expressionless. "No," she said. "He didn't."

So much for expecting an answer *or* further explanation. Knowing better, however, than to hound her for it, I let the subject drop.

We tacked and loaded the horses with care, knowing Harquhal was our last settlement before the border. And once out of the dun-colored walls and heading north, I would become a stranger to my environs; Del would be guide, while I was left to do as she suggested in all matters of conduct, not knowing Northern ways.

Our roles would be reversed, and I wasn't certain I liked it.

Though Del undoubtedly would.

She was still locked in silence as we led her coy gelding and my snuffy stud out of the lath-built stable behind the inn. Across broad rumps our mounts now carried the sausage rolls of fur and leather, jutting up and out. The stud wasn't yet certain he approved of such measures; he walked with his massive hindquarters curiously elevated, as if on tiptoe. The frequent and noisy swishing of his tail told me quite eloquently he was considering making comment, as only a horse can.

He snorted, banged my right shoulder—purposely—with his nose, nibbled.

"Knock it off," I suggested, fully aware of the fore-hooves tromping so closely to my own heels.

He did not, and so I thrust a doubled fist noseward as he reached for my shoulder again. Fist and nose connected. He jerked backward instantly, nodding and bobbing his head at the end of braided, blue-dyed reins while one eye rolled in innocent, baffled amazement. But the eye also shrewdly judged; I smiled, wagged a warning finger, saw the tip-tilted ears flick up. Instantly he pinned them back again, but he'd given himself away; he wasn't angry so much as disgruntled that I'd caught him at his tricks, and disgruntlement I could deal with.

Del shook her head. "I don't know why you keep him. He's more trouble than he's worth."

"That depends," I said, recalling the stud had, by all accounts, killed one of my enemies. Unfortunately, I hadn't been present to witness it. "As for why, I guess it's mostly habit. Like a man who keeps a nagging wife year after year after year."

She cast me a level glance, refusing to enter the debate. "One of these days he's liable to kill you."

"Oh, I don't think so. He might dump me on my head every now and again, but in the long run I think he's rather fond of me." I patted the firm, plate-shaped jaw. "We're a lot alike."

"Thickheaded," Del agreed, and then looked past me to the cantina where we had spent most of the former evening.

I looked with her and saw nothing. But, looking back at her, I saw she *did.*

And knew she would have to finish it before we left Harquhal.

I sighed. Nodded. Stopped. "Go on," I told her. "Get it over with."

She snapped her head around. "You *know?"*

"I know you'll never let it rest," I said calmly. "Go, bascha. See if he's there. If not, we can ride out of here knowing at least you looked. If he is, well . . ." I shrugged. "Up to you, bascha."

"But—you don't know *why*—" She broke it off, shook her head a little. Silk-bright hair, unbraided, slid across silk-clad shoulders. "You can't."

"Thickheaded I may be, but I am not entirely stupid," I told her bluntly. "You saw a man last night, and until you see him again and satisfy whatever craving kept you awake last night—in a *real bed,* I might add—you'll be moody as a breeding woman."

She opened her mouth promptly to protest the last part of my comments. Del dislikes me to make fun of women, or otherwise discount them because of their gender. Now, mostly, I do it out of a desire to bait her, hoping for verbal combat; once I did it because, in the South, women count for little. Del had changed much of my attitude, but so had slavery. A man raised a slave suffers his own humiliation, and quickly learns not to judge others as he is judged.

But Del, after a moment, did not rise to the bait at all. She merely clamped her mouth closed. Her expression was grim. "It is a thing I have to do."

"I know that. I just *said* that."

"I will be fair," Del told me. "It will be a sword-dance."

I nearly laughed; trimmed it to a smile when I saw that however I responded would matter greatly to her. "If he's a sword-dancer, it'll be fair," I agreed. "If he's not, it'll be a joke."

Pale brows knitted. "Tiger—" But she stopped short, locking away whatever words she had meant to say, and left me looking into the face of torment.

"Go," I said gently. "I'll be there, bascha."

We tied the horses and left them, pulling aside the same vermilion curtain we had pulled aside the night before. Huva stink clung to the cantina, but the smoke was barely visible. It was early yet for the place to fill with men seeking dreams in liquor, smoke, women.

But not too early for the man Del sought.

At last he saw her coming. I knew him only by that; by the surprise in his eyes, the admiration; the slow flame of desire. He was clearly Southron, dark of hair and skin, with deep-set, pale brown eyes. The age I could not say, save to mark that he had spent his years in the desert, for the sun had taken its toll. His teeth flashed white against the swarthiness of his face.

Del ignored the others at his table. She merely stepped to the edge, leaned forward a little, to make certain he heard her words, and invited him into the circle.

And the man was clearly astonished. "Circle?" he echoed blankly, in patent disbelief. And then he recovered himself, and laughed. "Bascha, I will gladly meet you in *bed*, but never in a circle." He waited out the snickers and laughter, smiling blandly, but I saw the faintest line of puzzled consternation mar the flesh between dark brows.

Fluidly, Del pulled Boreal free of her sheath in a brief, hissing slide, then brought the sword down to rest crosswise in front of her breasts, hilt at waist, wrists cocked; the tip reached at least five inches above Del's head. It was a diagonal slash of steel that focused every eye upon blade and woman. The move was flawlessly executed, obviously well-practiced; the posture—and its intent—was dramatically dominant, and eloquently underscored by Del's gender. Not a man in the cantina was blind to the implications.

One might say it is no great thing to draw a sword from its sheath. But Del, as I, went in harness, with the sheath strapped diagonally across her back. It is far more comfortable when seeking an even distribution of weight, far more balanced than dangling heavy steel to bang against one leg, but the ease of sheathing or unsheathing is reduced immeasurably. It is a mark of pride (or vanity—call it what you will) that a true sword-dancer, thoroughly trained in the art of the dance, always goes in harness.

But it was a sword, and this was the South, and Del was clearly a *woman*.

He laughed, the Southroner. And then stopped, as the others stopped, abruptly, in shock, as she set the salmon-silver tip against the flesh of his throat.

Easily, in silence, she parted the fabric of his burnous. I saw something move in her face, something almost indefinable, except I had seen the expression once before. When Del had first seen Jamail—and what had been done to him—five years after his disappearance.

She nodded once, but I thought it was mostly to herself. As if it signaled a hardening of her resolve. "Step into the circle."

I nearly mouthed them with her, so familiar were the words. The eternal challenge of a sword-dancer, to spar, to fight, to *dance*. For the fun or to the death.

Desire was augmented by irritation. The Southroner's nostrils pinched. "Woman," he said, "go home. Go home and tend your man."

Del's tone was very calm. "*You* are my man," she told him. "I will tend you in the circle."

He had been dicing with companions. Now supple hands scattered dice and coin and cups, as, in anger, he swept the table clean.

Boreal nicked his throat.

He cursed. Del smiled, but only a little. "Dance with me," she invited, in the siren song of the circle.

Chapter 4

I saw the blood at his throat. A few drops only, crimson against browned flesh. Fresh blood, and free of ice; Del had not keyed the sword.

He spat onto the blade. "I do not fight *women.*"

The tip shifted. Rose. Pressed the underside of his chin, lifting, lifting, so that to escape the promised cut he had to tip the back of his skull against his shoulders.

"No?" Del asked. "But you fought *me,* nearly six years ago." Her eyes narrowed. "Fight me again, Southron. Now that I know *how.*"

His friends muttered angrily, obviously unimpressed by Del's attitude. To forestall any efforts on their parts, I moved closer to Del and deliberately fixed them with the stare I knew was disconcerting, for it mimicked the feral stare of a stalking sandtiger, green eyes and all. I made it very plain, if silently, that the fight was to remain between the woman and the man; otherwise, they personally, each of them, would have *me* to contend with. Now, or later; their choice.

It worked. It works often. I practiced it carefully, when the similarity had first been pointed out to me, knowing better than to ignore an advantage, in or out of the circle.

Del's opponent glared past her at me, made aware that there would be no rescue, none at all. That he was not a sword-dancer, I knew. We are often strangers to one another, but there are ways a man can tell. Certainly with him it was easy; his sword was sheathed at his side.

So, it *was* to be a joke. Not a sword-dancer. Not Northern. But clearly an enemy. And one she had claimed for nearly six years, which meant he was undoubtedly one of the raiders who had destroyed her family.

I blew out a slow breath of comprehension and compassion. Revenge I understand.

Pale brown eyes flicked from side to side, judging the intent of his companions, the tenor of the room. No one laughed now. No one smiled. Neither did anyone look away.

A Southroner myself, I knew what he was feeling. And I knew avoiding the fight would do as much damage to his pride as the thing itself. Del was a *woman.*

His lips writhed against his teeth. "Yes," he said, *"yes."*

"Outside," Del said coolly, and turned her back on him to exit the cantina.

In any city or settlement, it takes little time for word of a sword-dance to pass through the populace. In a border town like Harquhal, full to bursting with cutthroats, thieves, raiders and the like, word spills through even faster. And so as the Southroner prepared to face the Northern woman, the others came to watch. From shops and shade and gambling games like sandslugs from under a stone.

Calmly, Del slipped out of her burnous. She dropped the silk to the sand, ignoring the ribald comments. Bare-armed, bare-legged, she was naked in their eyes.

Hardly that, to me. But I've grown accustomed to the soft leather tunic snugged so firmly about her waist. Fitted so tautly at breasts and shoulders because of the harness straps. But seeing her through their eyes I saw merely the woman again. Not Del. Not the sword-dancer. Only the Northern bascha.

And in that moment, for only a moment, I forgot all the truths we had shared and thought only of myself.

But very briefly. And then Del was *Del* again.

She unhooked her harness, set it atop the silk, slanted me an enigmatic glance. "Sandtiger, will you draw the circle?"

A nice way of letting all the observers know who I was; plainly, they recognized the name, most of them. Certainly those I was most interested in. The Southroner's friends looked at me sharply, muttered among themselves, observed the sword hilt poking above my shoulder *and* the scars on my face. And did not look very happy.

I smiled a little and made a slight gesture with my head, acknowledging their unintended tribute. But mostly, I singled them out: one, two, three, four. Perhaps raiders, perhaps not: perhaps merely men who had fallen in with Del's opponent for the dicing in the cantina. But it did not matter. I marked them out. Then I turned my attention back to Del's request.

In the code of the true dance, the invitation was an honor. But this was little more than a travesty.

I put my hand on the hilt of the Northern sword and heard an echo of eerie laughter. Theron's, maybe. Maybe even the soul of the man in whom he had quenched the blade so long ago.

The sword hissed free of the sheath and gleamed in the sunlight. A second hiss followed on its heels: indrawn breaths from everyone gathered to watch the sword-dance. I set tip against earth and saw the umber-hued sand curl away as if I divided flesh. Another hiss, and murmurs of sorcery. Well, maybe so. The circle was made of itself; I was only the instrument.

Del stepped into the circle and waited.

Ordinarily, there are rituals to be observed. Requirements of the dance to satisfy the honor of the teachings handed down. It didn't matter that she was Northern-born and trained, and he a Southroner; the learning is much the same, with similar rituals. But this was no true sword-dance. The chosen opponent knew little, if anything, of the dance itself, knowing only that he had to fight a woman to salve pride and to save his life.

Reason enough, I knew, to make him dangerous.

He swore a vile Southron oath and stripped out of his burnous. Beneath it he wore the thin baggy jodhpurs and silk-sashed tunic of a desert man, not the brief chamois dhoti of a dancer. Raider he might be, but there was nothing in clothing or appearance that proclaimed him one, unlike a professional sword-dancer.

Del waited. He unbelted his sword, unsheathed it, threw the leather down on top of his burnous. He said something quietly to his four companions; immediately they looked at me, giving themselves away, and I knew he had told them to kill the woman—and me—if he died. Although it was plain he did not expect to die.

He stepped into the circle—

—and *lunged.*

She is so quick, so very *fast,* is Del. Feet sluffed through the warm sand with the soft, seductive sibilance of bare flesh against fine-grained dust. Wisps rose, drifted; layered our bodies in dull, gritty shrouds: pale umber, ocher-bronze, taupe-gray.

But the shrouds, I thought, were applicable; the woman could kill us all.

I watched her move. I watched the others watch her move. All men. No women, here, at this moment, under such circumstances; never.

Except for Del.

I watched her move: detached appreciation. Admiration, as always. And pride. Two-edged pride. One: that the woman brought honor to the ritual of the dance within the circle, and two: that she was my right hand, my left hand; companion, swordmate, bed-mate.

Edged? Of course. Pride is always a two-edged blade. With Del, the second edge is the sharpest of all, for *me*, because for the Sandtiger to speak of pride in Del is to speak also of possessiveness. She'd told me once that a man proud of a woman is too often prouder of his possession *of* her, and not of the woman for being herself.

I saw her point, but . . . well, Del and I don't always agree. But then if we did, life would be truly boring.

I watched Del and the men who watched her as a matter of course, but I also watched the man she faced in the circle. I saw the untutored pattern of his sword flashing in the sunlight: dip here, feint there, slash, lunge, cut, thrust . . . and always trying to throw the flashes and glints of sunlight into her eyes. He knew enough to know *that;* ordinarily, a shrewd ploy. Another opponent might have winced or squinted against the blinding light, giving over the advantage; Del didn't. But then, Del was accustomed to conjuring her own light with Boreal; the Southron sword the man used was hardly a match for her own.

I knew she would kill him. But *he* didn't. He hadn't realized it yet.

Few men do realize it when they enter the circle with Del. They only see *her,* and hardly notice the sword in her hands. Instead, they smile. They feel tolerant and magnanimous because they must face a woman, and a beautiful woman. But because she is beautiful, they will give her anything, if only to share a moment of her time, and so they give her their lives.

She danced. Long legs, long arms, bared to the Southron sun. *Step. Step. Slide. Skip.* Miniscule shifting of balance from one hip to the other. Sinews sliding beneath the firm flesh of her arms as she parried and riposted. All in the wrists, with Del. A delicate tracery of blade tip against the brassy afternoon sky, blocking her opponent's weapon with a latticework of steel.

Del never set out to be a killer. Even now she isn't, quite; she's a sword-dancer, like me. But in this line of work, more often than not, the dance—a ritualized exhibition of highly-trained sword-skill—becomes serious, and people die.

I sighed a little, watching her. She didn't *play* with him, precisely, being too well-trained for such arrogance within the circle, but I could see she had judged and acknowledged her opponent's skill as less than her own. It wouldn't make her smile; not Del. It wouldn't make her careless. But it *would* make

her examine the limits of his talent with the unlimited reper-
toire of her own, and show him what it meant to step into the
circle with someone of her caliber.

Regardless of her gender.

And I watched the man. The Southron fighter who had so care-
lessly undervalued the Northern woman. I saw the slack wetness of
sweat-soaked black hair hanging lankly against his neck, no longer
moving as he moved. I watched the telltale flush of frustration
commingled with futile effort darken his features. And I saw the
negligent arrogance of the man alter itself in brown eyes into be-
lated acknowledgment; he knew. At last, he knew; knew also there
was nothing he could do.

Except die.

Del stripped the blade from him instantly with a subtle flick of
her own, slicing fingers before he could blink, and then, as he
sucked in a breath to bellow, cut open the naked palms that no
longer grasped a sword. In shock, he gaped at her.

She balanced lightly on both feet, clearly poised to strike again.
But she did not, at once. She watched him only, and I saw the odd
glint in her eyes. "Have you stolen so many Northern women that
you cannot remember this one?" Her tone was deceptively mild.
"So many *Northern baschas?*"

"Afreet!" he cried. "Jinni!"

"Human," she mocked, "and woman. Or does that foolish masculine pride forbid you from acknowledging the truth?"

"Del," I said quietly, "that is not the issue."

I saw the subtle start of surprise, the realization in her eyes. No,
it was *not* the issue. Color touched her face; the line of her mouth
hardened. "I want Ajani," she said.

Brown eyes widened in patent astonishment, then narrowed as
he frowned. "Ajani," he echoed. "Why?"

"For much the same reason," she told him. "I intend to kill
him."

He laughed harshly. "*Men* have tried that, bascha. And still
Ajani thrives."

"Temporarily." She flicked her sword and the blade sliced air, neatly nicking the tip of his nose. "Ajani," she said softly.

He stepped out of the circle at once. But this was not a sword-dance; Del followed smoothly. He halted against the confines of the larger, human circle, was pressed back against his friends, who sought to hold him up—and knew the fight was lost. "North," he said sullenly.

"But you are *here*, Southron."

He spat to the side. "I no longer ride with Ajani."

"No?" Pale brows rose. "Did it begin to pall at last, this wealth earned by stealing children?"

Nostrils flared. "And did I steal *you?*"

I thought she might kill him then. But her control was firmly in place. "You tried, Southron. But luck and the gods preserved me."

"Then why hound me now?" He spread bleeding hands. "You are free, bascha. What sense is there in this?"

"None at all," she said gently. "This is merely collection of a blood-debt I am owed."

It was Del's fight, not mine. But I wished she would finish it.

"Blood-debt—"

"Ajani," she said, "and you go free."

Hope flared, was extinguished almost at once. I knew what he was thinking. His life was precious, but so was his pride, especially before friends; spared by a woman, he kept the former and lost the latter. "I am a loyal man."

Del lifted an eloquent shoulder. "Loyal men die as easily as others." She gestured with a jerk of her head. "Step back into the circle. Pick up the sword. I will give you *that* much; more than you and the others gave me."

Clearly, he wanted to refuse. But he was bound by his own pride and the silence of the others; slowly, he stepped back into the circle and retrieved the sword with bleeding hands. He turned to face the woman, clearly unafraid. If anything, he was angry. Not that he would lose his life, but that a woman would be the instrument of it.

Del smiled. I saw her lips stretch thin, then part, and then the thread of a sound issued forth. Only a little song, but enough to enrage the man.

Enough. No excess. Just the Northern woman stepping to the flaccid curtain of steel, who parted it effortlessly to slide three feet of salmon-silver blade into sweaty, heaving flesh.

They deny it, each and every one of them, even as their blood flows from their bodies to stain the Southron sand. Even when they cannot speak, they mouth the words, denying her the victory as their bodies tell them differently. Bloodied, bitten lips, wet faces powdered with sand, widened eyes full of wonder, dismay, despair.

And always the denial.

She turned away from the sprawled body and looked at me. The Northern sword, blood-painted, hung loosely in her hand. Alien blade, with equally alien runes, dripped a string of wet rubies into umber sand, drop by drop by drop, until the delicate, deadly necklet lost its shape and became nothing more than a puddle of blood sucked quickly down into the dust.

Del hunched one shoulder almost imperceptibly—a comment; an answer to my unspoken question—and then she nodded, only once; an equally private exchange.

She turned back. Bent over the body. I saw a hand go to his throat, catch something, snap it free. And then carefully, thoroughly, with grave deliberation, she stepped outside the circle and cleaned her blade on his burnous.

She watched his companions as she did so, appraising the men who had so rudely done the same to her. Assessing expressions and intentions. She was not a mind reader but claimed an uncanny understanding of men. This understanding makes even *me* uncomfortable much of the time; I find myself carrying on conversations within my skull, answering questions and suppositions to test their validity before I give Del the chance to bestow one of her stinging rebukes.

Del straightened. "Ajani," she said quietly, into the waiting silence, ostensibly to all, but paying subtle attention to the four men now bereft of a fifth. "I want him. I will pay."

I looked at Del's face. She hoped someone would give her the information she wanted but didn't really expect it. Certainly not so openly, after what she had done. If anyone really knew Ajani's whereabouts, he was likely to keep it quiet until he could talk to Del in private. Away from the four Southroners who stared at her so malignantly.

She had silenced them all with sword-dance and invitation. But the silence lasted briefly, so briefly; before long, men were talking among themselves and trading their versions of the fight so recently witnessed. I'd seen it and heard it countless times after dances I myself had been in. But this was Del. This was a woman, a Northerner, who had so easily dispatched one of their own; who now strode calmly through the crowd into the cantina, to wait.

So much for our early start.

The crowd dispersed quickly enough. Most men went into the cantina to buy liquor, to discuss the sword-dance, to sneak glances at the Northern bascha. All of those men I did not detain, but as the dead man's companions bent to remove the body, I stopped them.

"His coin is hers," I told them. "The custom of the circle: winner takes all."

It did not sit well with them. One of them—black-eyed, pockmarked, with gray-flecked dark hair—spat at my feet. The other three were pleased by it, though none of them said a word. They didn't need to; I could see it in their eyes.

When I did nothing, the pock-marked man called me an uncomplimentary name—something to do with having an unnatural affinity for male goats—while I merely nodded affably and bent to cut the dead man's coin-pouch free with my knife. And then I straightened and invited each and every one of them into a circle.

A circle; four against one.

But they knew better. (It isn't simple arrogance; I *am* that good, because I was taught by a master, and I have worked very hard at my profession for a very long time.) They knew better, and went away as I waited for their answer.

I went in to look for Del and found her at a small table in a corner of the cantina. And not alone; it had taken less time than I had imagined to scare up the information she wanted. Also from an unexpected province: Jemina's young man of the evening before, with the stain of a newborn mustache upon his upper lip.

He wore a silken tunic, bright blue and sashed in jade-green, baggy jodhpurs of brilliant crimson, tucked into high black boots, and a plain saffron burnous hanging loosely open. He came to the table, clearly waiting, and in his hands was a clay jug. As I arrived the boy smiled, turned to set the jug down with a flourish, then swung back.

And I saw beneath the thin fabric of the burnous, tucked into the belt at the small of his back, the outline of bladed, hafted weapons I could not begin to name.

Worth watching, then, this boy.

"Aqivi," he said warmly, gesturing to the jug. "Much better than the house wine."

"Why?" Del asked flatly. "If you have information, don't waste my time with unnecessary courtesies."

It took him completely off-stride. No doubt he was accustomed to his pretty looks winning almost slavish attention from cantina girls and the like; Del's bluntness, so unexpected, was shocking. When coupled with her appearance, it is enough to strip most men of all pride entirely, reducing them to awkward silence or stammered apologies.

The boy did not stammer, nor did he apologize. He made a fluid gesture of aquiescence and sat down. On my stool, I loomed over him pointedly; finally he glanced up at me, affecting surprised innocence. And stood up again.

He was altogether shorter and slighter than I am, and certainly considerably younger. Around Del's age, I thought, which put him at twenty or so. His face was at war with manhood, still showing the undefined blandness of youth while moving inexorably toward adulthood. He was quick, lithe, supple. Possibly a thief. Certainly an opportunist; he was complimenting Del on her sword skill.

She leaned forward, resting forearms on the table. She had not put on the burnous as yet and so the arms were bare. Against the pale-gold skin, sinews twisted. The minute tensing of defined muscles was obvious, to someone who knew how to read her.

"I am a sword-dancer," she said coolly. "What I did to that man is part of my profession; I had *better* be good." Clearly, the raider's death had put her out of temper. Generally she gives the boys a bit more rope before she snugs the noose taut.

Blue eyes flickered beneath black-lashed lids. The boy smiled, nodded, moistened lips, wiped palms on scarlet jodhpurs. Then he hooked thumbs into his belt and glanced at me. I had not yet seated myself. My bulk, so close, served to intimidate him a little. Not enough, however. I judged him one of those foolish youths too full of life to be much intimidated by anything—or *anyone*—for very long.

"I heard what you said outside," he told us, "about Ajani. I might be able to help."

"Might you?" Del's tone was icy. "Where is he?"

The boy unhooked his thumbs and spread nimble hands. "I am a stranger to this land and know little of place names. But I could take you there."

"Could you?" Del's question was rhetorical. "For a price, of course."

"You did offer one." I sat down and smiled blandly, helping myself to the aqivi the boy had so thoughtfully provided.

"A small one," he answered. "I want only to accompany you on your travels."

I set the cup down, aqivi untasted. "She has a partner," I said distinctly.

"*Both* of you!" the boy amended hastily. "With the Sandtiger and his lady."

The Sandtiger and his lady. Sure enough, Del was scowling at him. But before she could say anything, I motioned the boy to sit down on the sole remaining stool. His awareness of my identity put me in a magnanimous frame of mind; as soon as I could get the wine-girl to deliver a third cup, I intended the boy to share some of the aqivi.

"You'll take us to Ajani so long as we allow you to ride with us?" I nodded thoughtfully. "Since the only way you can lead us anywhere is *to* ride with us, it seems a simple bargain."

He settled the saffron burnous as he pulled up the stool. "I mean after," he said.

"Why?" Del asked.

He shrugged, showed us both a crooked, innocent grin. "I'm a stranger here in the South . . . to the North, too, if we go there. If I'm to gain any fame at all, I need to know my way around. Riding with *you* two—"

"Fame?" I undercut his glib explanation. "You want to be a *panjandrum?*"

That earned me blank stares from both of them.

"Panjandrum," I repeated. "A man of repute."

The boy thought it over. A slow smile spread. "Panjandrum," he echoed. "I like it." He nodded, trying it on for size. "A man of *repute.*"

"That's the polite definition." I scratched the scars on my cheek. "I won't bother to give you the others since you're so taken with the word."

"Panjandrum," he murmured thoughtfully.

I sighed and sucked aqivi. Del scowled.

"Yes," he said. "Bellin the Cat, a panjandrum."

"Bellin the *Cat?*" I was startled, wondering if his foolish quest for glory and fame had led him to adopt a name similar to my own. Or, more precisely, to my animal namesake.

"Bellin." He smiled and waved a hand vaguely in a southerly direction. "I've been at sea for most of my life, sailing here and there. I thought it was time I discovered what it meant to be a landlubber."

"And you picked the *South?*" I could think of more hospitable places.

He shrugged. "Seemed likely enough."

Which meant he'd had little choice in the matter. I nodded and drank more aqivi.

"Bellin the Cat," Del said quietly. "Why do you wish to become a—" she paused, fitting the strange Southron word to her Northern tongue "—panjandrum?"

"Always have." His grin and good spirits were infectious. "A man should make his mark some way . . . insure his place among other men—and women." He shrugged again, rippling saffron silk. "I figure if I'm going to be here anyway, I may as well do what I can to make sure I'm a *somebody*."

Her tone was infinitely bland. "A humble man might prefer differently."

"A humble man would," Bellin agreed equably. "But no one of my acquaintance would ever lumber me with *that* description."

At least he was an honest blowhard. "Then why not go out and *earn* your fame?" I asked. "Why attach yourselves to us?"

He spread supple hands. "What's the sense in struggling and scraping and suffering if there's no need for it? Riding with the Sandtiger and his lady, I'm almost guaranteed to become a panjandrum long before I would otherwise." His smile was disarming. "Can you blame me for trying to take advantage of an opportunity?"

"I am not the Sandtiger's *lady*," Del said crossly. "My name is Del. I have business with Ajani. Do you know where he is?"

Bellin chose the diplomatic answer. "It should not be difficult to find him."

"Oh?" Pale brows rose. "Then I suggest you do so. *Now.*" She flicked fingers in eloquent dismissal.

"But—"

"Better go." I raised my cup in tribute. "Thanks for the aqivi."

With grave dignity the boy rose, shook out the folds of his burnous, took himself elsewhere. Again I saw the line of oddly-shaped weapons tucked into his belt.

Del centemplated me across the table. Her expression was pensive as she slowly poured herself a cup of aqivi.

"Think he knows?" I asked.

"No."

"Think we'll see him again?"

Her eyes were limpid. "If he lacks the information I want, we'd better not." She drank, made a moue of distaste. "I have no patience for fools *or* would-be panjandrums."

I laughed and poured my cup full again of the would-be panjandrum's aqivi.

Chapter 5

Without consulting me (of course), Del changed her mind. We would not leave Harquhal, she told me, until the *next* morning; she wanted to wait a night to see if anyone came forward with genuine information about Ajani.

I agreed readily enough. Del had made up her mind, and I didn't much feel like arguing it with her. For one, it was nice to sleep in a real bed again, and to drink among men in a Southron cantina, knowing with the dawn I would leave such comforts behind. For another, it wasn't difficult to look at things from Del's point of view. A band of Southron raiders had overrun her family's caravan along the border, brutally killing everyone save Del and her youngest brother. It didn't take much imagination to figure out what the raiders had done to Del *or* Jamail before she had escaped; in her place, I'd be as dedicated to revenge. She wanted Ajani, the leader, and I wasn't about to try to dissuade her.

The day was not as tedious as it might have been; Del was quiet enough, lost in private thoughts, but now that our names were known—thanks to Del's identification of me and a gregarious Bellin the Cat—men came around to ask me about my exploits. Del they pretty much ignored, being indisposed to give a woman credit for killing one of their own in a circle—which has been, heretofore, a strictly male province—but they were chatty enough with me.

Before long I was the center of attention, swilling free aqivi and explaining how it was I'd come to be the best sword-dancer in the South.

(Other Southron sword-dancers might argue the fact, but *I* wasn't about to so long as these generous individuals felt like buying me drinks. Besides, it probably *is* true, Del's skill notwithstanding; and anyway, she's a Northerner.)

Come nighttime, nothing much changed, although aqivi and wine flowed more heavily, and the stories got more convoluted even as I told them. And I was aware, very aware, of Bellin's smiling face at the edges of the crowd. He watched me, he watched the others, clearly enjoying vicariously what he wanted to badly to experience himself: fame.

I could have told him fame was *not* the name of the game. Survival is. I never knew who I might meet in the circle or when, and I *certainly* never knew what the outcome might be. I am good, very good, but I am also a realist. Any man can be defeated, depending on myriad circumstances.

Talk eventually turned to Del, in a sideways sort of way. No one wanted to say much about her, although the undertones were quite distinct. They all wanted to know how the Sandtiger had come to be riding with a Northern bascha who called herself a sword-dancer, even though such a thing was tantamount to blasphemy.

I did not tell them everything. I told them *enough*. Enough to pique their interest and cause them to wonder if indeed the Northern bascha *was* as good as she appeared. I felt it was self-evident, but no man changes his attitude overnight. Not even me. And the gods knew *I* had reason enough to know better, with Del sharing both bed and profession, not to mention lifestyle.

And so I gave them a little to chew on, knowing full well they would dream of a blonde-haired, blue-eyed woman when they crawled into bed that night. Thinking of that very thing, I wondered if perhaps it wasn't time I did a little crawling into bed myself.

With Del, of course, which was a whole lot better than being permitted only to dream about her.

Except that it appeared I might be limited to that after all; Del had disappeared. Somewhere between the first jug of aqivi and the last, my Northern bascha had vanished.

I went outside the cantina into the night. Torchlight cast eerie shadows along the wall and made black pockets out of corners, turnings, alleyways. It was not incredibly late. Passersby were frequent. In the distance I heard the watch calling out the time; the ninth hour after midday. And then I heard the step behind me.

"A full life, Sandtiger." Bellin moved to stand at my left. "Maybe someday . . ."

"Maybe someday you'll be an old man, and die in bed." I didn't smile at him, because the topic wasn't particularly amusing. "A man tells stories to please his audience, and embellishes them as he goes."

"Then none of them are true?"

"True enough." I barely glanced at him. "I don't lie, Bellin. Lies cause trouble."

Somewhat ruefully, he scratched at the smudge of mustache. "I know about that well enough." He grinned. "More aqivi?"

"No more room." I set my right shoulder against the vertical support post nearest me and leaned, squinting at him. "What do you want, Bellin the Cat?"

"I told you. To travel with you."

"Del and I ride alone."

"I wouldn't be in the way."

I grunted. "What we do isn't for fun or fame, boy. It's our profession."

"I know that. I am not without *some* intelligence." His smile took the delicate rebuke out of his words. "You could give me a chance just to see."

I sighed. "You're not from around these parts. Do you even know what a sword-dancer is?"

Bellin's white teeth flashed. "That all depends," he said lightly. "Some of them, maybe *most* of them, are honorable folk who take pride in their work. But others, I think, are no better than, say—" His smile broadened, hooked down wryly at one end "—a pirate."

I frowned. "What's a pirate?"

He blinked. Considered the best answer a moment. Then nodded slightly, lifting one shoulder in an eloquent shrug. "A man who sails the oceans and—" he paused, "—*salvages* what others neglect to adequately protect."

"Ah." I nodded. "A borjuni, we'd say, in the Punja, depending on the ferocity employed. Up here, so close to the border, the best word might be *thief.*"

Bellin laughed. "Might be," he conceded, not in the least nonplussed by my frankness.

"Sword-dancing is a *bit* different," I pointed out. "We're not exactly out to steal an opponent's wealth."

"No. Just his life." Bellin sighed and gazed upward at the moon, a blade-sharp crescent setting the walls aglow. "I'm not a pirate anymore."

"But still a thief."

He blinked at me, all innocence. "I'd rather be a panjandrum."

I couldn't help myself; I laughed. Bellin the Cat was about the most engaging and unaffected individual I'd ever met, especially considering what he chased invited affectation. I looked at him sidelong. Young, ages younger than myself, but then I felt downright elderly at times, with Del around.

And that reminded me: she wasn't.

Bellin saw my frowning search of the immediate area. "She said she'd be back soon."

That snapped my head around. "What?"

Obligingly, he repeated the statement.

I scowled. "She told *you* that?"

He scratched his chin. "You weren't listening."

"That's a load of—" But I broke it off, because basically it was true.

"She said she'd go back to the inn, stable the horses, then come after you."

Come after me. Come *after* me, like a mother sending her tardy child home.

Balefully, I scowled at him. A very cool young man, was Bellin, so blithe with his information. "*Do* you know anything about Ajani?"

He was busy rearranging the folds of his saffron robe; delaying tactics.

"Ajani," I said gently.

"The name *is* familiar."

"Remember what I said about lies, boy. How in the end they can trip you up."

"Only if you're clumsy." He grinned, reached beneath the robe to the small of his back, took from his belt three oddly shaped hand axes, or something like. I'd never seen such things before.

Casually, effortlessly, Bellin the Cat began to toss them into the air, end over end, from one hand to the other, until the weapons were little more than a blur of wood and leather and steel. "On board ship," he told me, "we often get very restless. This is one way to pass the time."

From the other side of the post, having dodged there somewhat more quickly than I intended—and paying the price with my aqivi-addled head—I watched the flying axes. Up. Down. Around. Closer to his head than I liked. And all the movement was beginning to make me dizzy.

Bellin's hands were supple and exceedingly quick. Undoubtedly he was a marvelous pickpocket or cutpurse, except his mastery of the axes indicated action of a higher level altogether.

He caught them one, two, three, stopped throwing. And handed one to me.

I examined it in silence. About a foot and a half in length, altogether, but oddly constructed. One side of the haft boasted a flattened steel blade, quite sharp, much like that of a normal single-bitted hand ax. But the other side was a rounded knob of metal. The wooden haft was leather-wrapped for a truer grip; for me, the balance was off, but obviously it suited Bellin perfectly.

"Give it a try," he suggested.

"And do *what* with it? Chop down this post?" I looked at said post. "Right now I think I need it."

"No. No—here. Watch." And threw an ax across the street into a wooden mounting block, where it stuck.

I squinted across the distance and looked at the ax-bedecked block a long moment. Then at the ax in my hand. Lastly, at Bellin himself. "There are people," I told him distinctly, "in the street."

Well, there *had* been. Most of them had panicked and quitted the street as soon as they figured out what Bellin was throwing. Or fell down to lie in the dirt, cursing him elaborately.

"I know," he said brightly, nodding agreement. "Part of the trick is in the timing, of course; it's the real challenge." His smile was eloquently innocent. "Once, I even missed."

"Uh-*huh*." I gave him back his ax as Del approached from the left, and prepared to step out and meet her. "Maybe we'll talk again some day."

"Do you think there's any chance I might join up with you you?" Bellin asked, following.

I felt the weight of Theron's sword across my shoulders. "Where we're going," I told him, "there isn't room for three. And it's personal."

Bellin stopped. Sighed. Nodded. And sank two more axes into the mounting block, ignoring renewed—and louder—curses.

Del's brows were raised as I fell into step beside her. Reading her face, I shrugged an answer. "Passing time." I stumbled over a shadow, which elicited a brief breathy snort of amusement from her. "He really wants to join us."

"No."

We turned a corner and were tunneled into a tighter, deserted street. "So I told him." We bumped elbows twice as we strolled, and I heard Del sigh. Well, I'd had a lot of aqivi. "I told him—"

I was unable to tell her what I'd told *him* because four shapes detached themselves from the shadows and came at us.

"Ah, hoolies," I muttered, unsheathing Theron's sword, "couldn't they have done this when I was *sober*?"

It was, of course, a rhetorical question, and Del did not waste time on an answer. (Although undoubtedly she had one.) I heard the whine of Boreal as Del loosed her from the sheath. I also heard a snatch of song, and knew Del wasn't going to waste much unaugmented effort on the Punja-mites. She was keying the sword, which meant they stood less of a chance than ever.

The light was bad, but only for a moment. Del's blade burned salmon-silver in the darkness, and I saw four dark Southron faces suddenly thrown into relief: all planes and hollows and black blots for eyes and mouths. They squinted, swore, then advanced with appreciable determination.

Two of them came at me, two at Del. At least they had learned that much by watching her fight.

They wore baggy robes over equally baggy jodhpurs and tunics. All the excess material makes it more difficult to separate flesh from fabric and stab the part that counts before it can stab back. I shredded one robe, sliced through a silken sash, caught a rib, but little more. He was very fast, or else I had gotten slower. (Possible, in view of the aqivi sloshing in belly and head.)

Something stung my left wrist. Providentially, as it turned out. The pain nagged me right out of my liquor haze and made me considerably more accurate; I spitted one man through the belly, sliced open the other lower still, so that he dropped his sword altogether and concentrated on keeping his entrails from spilling out to soil his silks.

I caught my balance, turned, saw Del kill one of her assailants. And then, as she spun to dispatch the fourth, we discovered there was no need. The pock-faced Southroner was engaged in falling flat on his face, quite startled to discover himself dead, and landed with nary a protest.

Protruding from his spine was one of Bellin's axes.

Del and I stared at the ax a moment, then looked up. The would-be panjandrum approached quietly, bent over the body, jerked the ax free. The sound was different than that made by a sword withdrawn; I decided the latter was less troubling to a man who had partaken too freely of aqivi.

Bellin inspected the blade, cleaned it on the dead man's robe, looked at us. "Missed the post again."

I sighed. "You still can't come."

He thought it over, nodded, turned on his heel and marched away. Juggling his three deadly axes.

"Well," Del remarked, "at least the boy's accurate."

"Boy?" I scowled at her. "He's your age, at least."

She looked after Bellin. Then back at me. "Well," she said again, "I guess he looks so young to me because I've been riding with you."

I did not dignify it with an answer.

Del grinned and raised pale brows. "Now, what was it you were telling him?" She cleaned Boreal and slid her home again. "What was it you were saying before we were interrupted?"

I grunted, doing my own clean-up duties. "That life was too short for him to waste it tagging along with us."

"Is that why *you're* coming with *me?*"

"You know why I'm coming."

"No," she said as we headed down the street again, "you never told me. You just caught up to me that day, and you've been with me ever since."

"*And* I suppose you're sorry."

She slanted me an eloquent sidelong glance, examining me at great length. "Have you ever given me *reason* to be sorry?"

I scratched ferociously at an itching armpit and tried to recapture a belch. "Not me, bascha. You *need* me."

Del did not answer, which I took to be answer enough. The woman can be tricky, but not incomprehensible.

"Here," she said. "The inn."

"Watch the step," I warned.

Del said nothing. She just went inside and let the curtain slap me in the face.

Again.

Later, much later, I snapped out of sleep into wakefulness, fully alert, as Del slipped out of bed. Sword-dancers who desire to stay alive in the midst of enemies learn very quickly how to snatch sleep whenever possible; how also to wake with alacrity, with nothing lost in the transition.

I thought, at first, she meant to relieve herself in the nightpot left for that purpose. But instead she retrieved her sword from the floor next to mine, unsheathed it, took two steps to the middle of the room. And there she knelt down, naked, with pale hair atumble around her breasts and the sword blade pressed between them.

There was no lamp, but the crescent moon slanted dim illumination through lath-slatted windows. The woman knelt on the floor, wrapped in shadows and silver moonlight. And I heard her begin to sing.

It was such a little song. Barely more than a whisper of sound, threaded through with a hiss of withheld volume. She meant not to waken me, then, although Del knew my sleeping habits, now, as well as her own.

I have a tin ear. To me, music is little more than noise; loud, soft, pitched high or low. I have heard her sing before, preparing to enter the circle, but it had meant nothing to me. Just—*noise.* Some personal petition to her gods or to her sword. Lifesong, deathsong; one and the same, to me. Little more than a Northern idiosyncracy. Theron had done it also.

But still Del sang, and the sword came alive in her hands.

At first, I did not believe it. Moonlight is often fickle; clouds, I thought, moving across the crescent to alter the intensity of its light. But if anything, the moon paid homage to the sword. Its light was clearly diluted by the luminance of the blade.

It started at the tip. First, the merest speck of light. A spark, steadfast and unflagging, welling like a drop of blood on a thorn-pricked fingertip. It *pulsed,* as if it lived, as if it *breathed.* And then it crept ever upward, finger by finger, bead by bead, slowly, like a necklet of Punja crystals. Frowning, I watched one become some become many, until the double-edged blade was ablaze with light, sparks joining to form a whole.

Pulsing. Bright—brighter—*brilliant* . . . then dimming nearly to absence, until it renewed itself.

Del sang on, and the blade burst into flame.

"Hoolies, Del—" I was upright, awkward in my haste, meaning to knock the sword from her hands and succeeding only in nearly falling flat on my face. Tangled in bedclothes (and fuddled by too much aqivi), I staggered; in the flames, her face was stark.

I fully expected to see her hair catch fire, but it did not. Neither did the flames touch her flesh. They clung to the blade, infatuated with the double edges, flirting coyly with the runes. And then died, snuffed out, as her song wavered; her eyes were fixed on the runes.

I reached out, but something in her face kept me from touching the sword. I knew I could, with impunity, because knowing the *jivatma's* name allowed me some degree of familiarity: an ability to touch a portion of the power that Del knew in full measure. Once, in ignorance, before I had known the name, I grasped the silvered hilt with its everchanging shapes and lost layers of skin off my palm. I had been ice-marked for weeks. Now, the brand was gone but not the feelings it had engendered.

Because of them, and Del's eyes, I forbore to touch the sword.

The last of the sparks winked out. The pulsing was vanquished by moonlight. The sword was a sword again, with nothing of magic divulged.

I drew in a breath and wet my lips. "I've never seen it do *that* before."

"I took care to make sure you did not." The blade, quiescent, was obscured by the twin falls of pale hair, hanging over her shoulders.

I sighed, aware that too much aqivi had dulled my senses. The first startled response had faded, leaving me tasting the sourness of reaction and sensing the first twinges of a headache. "What in hoolies were you doing?"

"Asking advice." Del rose, took the sheath I retrieved for her, slid Boreal home. "I am—twisted."

"Twisted?" I raised brows. Her limbs were straight as ever.

She frowned, shrugging one shoulder. "Twisted . . . bound up . . . divided—" She stopped, sensing her words altered intended meaning. Though she speaks Southron well, if curiously accented, there are times our decidedly diverse heritage makes communication difficult, if not downright impossible.

"Mixed-up," I translated. "Confused."

"Confused," she echoed. "Yes." She put the sheathed sword back on the floor next to mine, so close to the bed, then climbed onto the cot and dragged the bedclothes around her shoulders. "What am I to do?"

It is not often Del offers me the chance to even *suggest* what she might do. But an outright question underscored the magnitude of the confusion she now admitted.

I sat down on the edge of the cot. "Has this anything to do with the man you killed tonight?" I looked at the moon. "*Last* night?"

Del sighed. Her expression was pensive. "Nothing and everything, and all at once."

"He *was* one of the raiders—"

"Oh, yes. I recall him. I recall them all." She shook her head in negligent dismissal. "At first I thought not, because I could not believe it . . . but I could not forget their faces if I *wished* to . . . too often I see them in my sleep."

"Yes, well, even dogs dream."

A poor attempt at offhanded empathy; she didn't even smile. "I don't wish, Tiger. I wish never to forget them, until the blood-debt is collected."

"Even then, you may not forget them."

One slender arm departed the protection of the bedclothes. She smoothed folds rucked up over knees doubled beneath her chin. After a moment, in an oddly vulnerable appeal, she touched my shoulder, found an old scar, traced it. Over and over.

"It felt good to kill him," she said.

Her tone belied the words. "But not good enough."

The fingers halted a moment, then resumed their idle movement. "I am sworn."

"I know. To many things, bascha . . . and that is why you're twisted." I caught her hand and stilled it. "What did you ask the sword?"

"Which risk I should assume."

I frowned. "*What* risk?"

Del hooked her hair behind her left ear. "If I put myself on Ajani's trail, the searching may take weeks. Months. Even *years.*" Her mouth twisted. "Longer than the time I have left before my sentence is levied."

"And yet if you go North to face the judgment of your peers

and teachers, you may lose Ajani's trail." I nodded. "Not an easy choice."

"Oh, it is. *Too* easy." She took her hand away and reached both up behind her neck. Unclasped something. Held it out into the moonlight. A string of lumpy amber, red-brown in the slanted light. "I made this," she said quietly. "Ten years ago, I made this, as a birth-gift for my mother."

I recalled how she had taken something from the neck of the Southroner she had killed. How she had knotted it up in one fist without saying a word about it.

"Risk," I said quietly. "Hunt Ajani—yesterday, today, tomorrow— while others are hunting you."

Her hand shut away the necklet. "I owe my *an-kaidin* so much."

"And so you asked him his advice." I heard her song again, in the confines of my head; saw again the flaming sword. "What did he say, bascha?"

"Nothing," Delilah whispered at last, and a tear ran down her cheek.

We have been companions. Swordmates. Bedmates. But in many things we are strangers to one another, afraid to trespass where emotions may not be wanted. Having been locked so long in service to oneself, each of us, it is difficult to turn the key and *un*-lock ourselves, saying the things we desire to say, to share the things that should be shared. And so the Northern woman and the Southron man, born of violence, shaped by an angry determination to overcome those who had beaten us, had learned to say nothing of fears, knowing the admission might make those fears come true.

Del crying was enough to clear my head of aqivi befuddlement for good. And to know myself plunged into a divisive confusion; did I offer comfort? Or did I retreat to give her the privacy she demanded from me so often?

Hoolies, how did other men deal with this?

Well . . . women had cried in front of me before. But they were Southron women, with completely different outlooks and intentions. I had learned to take tears as a warning sign of an involvement no longer beneficial to my lifestyle.

But this was Del. This was a woman who demanded equality, requiring and desiring no particular favors or consideration because of her sex.

At least she didn't sob. Neither did she hastily wipe away the tears as another woman might—and had; a woman apparently afraid I might discover that somehow, beneath all the mess, she had become another person entirely, and not worthy of my interest.

Del just—*cried.* Silently. Without fuss. She simply sat and let the tears run down her face.

Oh, hoolies . . . *why me?*

Well, there was one thing . . .

She stirred as I touched her, showing her the best way I knew how that, regardless of her circumstances—and tears—I still wanted her. But, apparently, it wasn't what *she* wanted.

"Not now," she said crossly, shifting away.

"I just thought—"

"I *know* what you thought." Her face was wet, but no more tears wound their way down her cheeks. Instead, she scowled at me. That expression I understood well enough. "*That* isn't always the answer, Tiger . . . though it may be hard for you—or any other man—to understand."

I'll give her this much, she knows how and where to hit. And my pride, as always, smarted. My sense of helplessness increased in direct proportion to the sudden shrinkage of desire.

"Hoolies, Del, what do you want from me? I try to help you out—"

"Help *me?* Help yourself, you mean." She got up, ripping the thin blanked from the bed to wind around her body; paced to the lath-slatted window and glared out.

I was left with no blanket and very little patience. I plumped the single lumpy pillow across my lap, glad of *some* coverage, and did my own share of glaring. "What in hoolies is a man supposed to *do,* Del? Guess? Especially with *you.* You're so prickly, I never know when you plan to stick me."

"I never *plan* it," she said. "It just happens. You ask for it, sometimes."

"Like now?" I nodded. "Fine. Next time I'll leave you alone."

She sighed heavily. "Sometimes a woman just wants to be held."

"And sometimes a man is more than willing *just* to hold," I threw back, "but you've got to give him some sort of clue."

She said nothing.

"Especially you," I pointed out. "I never know if I'm in bed with the sword-dancer or the woman. Good as you are in the circle, Del, you're more male than female. I know it has to be that way, and I know why. But in bed I want *you,* not the *an-ishtoya.*"

She closed her eyes for a long moment. When she opened them she was dry-eyed, but curiously wounded. "You've had more of me than any other man," she said softly, "except for Ajani."

I could not look away. After a moment I rose, tossed aside the pillow, crossed the room to the woman. Remembered that the self-possessed *an-ishtoya,* the deadly Northern sword-dancer, had had her girlhood stolen from her.

And so I held her, only held her, and it was enough for us both.

Chapter 6

*S*and gave way to dirt, scrub grass to thick-meshed turf, creosote to spearlike trees and spreading shrubs I couldn't
name. Even the *smell* altered; I sniffed, disliking it, tasting it on my
tongue, and realized it came from the trees. A pungent, clinging
odor, not so different from huva weed, though lacking the same
results.

The land itself changed also. The scattered hills of Harquhal
merged here to form a family, touching hands and heads and
shoulders. And promising more to come; in the distance I could see
mountains rearing skyward out of the earth.

We beat our way northward, following the Traders' Road out of
Harquhal. With each stride the stud took me farther away from the
South, farther from what I knew, thrusting me into a foreign land
like a sword through a man's belly. I didn't much like the picture,
but I didn't say so to Del.

Well, I doubt she would have paid much attention anyway. She
was locked up in silence, unusually quiet even for her. And yet I
sensed expectancy, an anticipation that had nothing to do with fear
or trepidation, or the discomfort I was feeling. Del was locked
away, but not because she retreated. Because what she felt was intensely private: Delilah was coming home.

I knew it at once, though she herself said nothing. It was a change in posture. A subtle straightening of backbone, a squaring of the shoulders, a lifting of the chin. And a slow, glorious smile that set her face alight.

It was a remarkable transformation, but it only made me surly.

Del stopped her speckledy gelding by a small stone cairn. She swung a leg over and slid off, burnous tangling briefly on the stirrup. She jerked it free absently and walked away from the horse, ignoring him as he tried to follow. After a moment he quit and turned away, dropping his head to forage in hummocky, turfy grass. Del paid no mind. She merely climbed up past the cairn and drew Boreal from her sheath.

She faced north. Behind and below her, I could see nothing but Del's back, all swathed in creamy silk. She lifted the *jivatma*, held it crosswise to the sun so that light danced off the blade, then brought it down and kissed the steel once, twice, thrice, in a gesture of homage and dedication.

"*Sulhaya,*" she said aloud, thanking her Northern gods.

I shivered. In the sun, it was warm, but I was cold to the bone. And then it passed and I was warm again, left with a nagging memory of something I could not explain.

Sunlight glinted off Boreal's naked blade. Del had not keyed the *jivatma*, and yet I saw the palest bloom of salmon-silver. As if the sword as well as Del knew she had come home at last.

Uneasily, I shifted my rump in the saddle. "Bascha—"

Del turned. Her face and posture were transfigured. I did not speak again.

She slid the sword home. The moment had passed; she was Del again, but with a new smile on her lips. A smile I had never seen, and wished it was meant for me.

"So," she said, "I am home. Now it is your decision."

"My decision?"

She gestured at the cairn. "There lies the border."

I had figured as much. But I glared at the cairn anyway; it represented a vast unknown. A place where sandtigers never roamed.

Her voice was very quiet. "I would understand."

I looked at her. I saw comprehension and compassion in her

eyes. She was not quite twenty-one, significantly younger than I in years, far older than I in insight. Sometimes, I hated her for it; now I hated myself. "*Would* you?"

Judiciously, after a moment, she suggested, "Perhaps not."

Hoolies. Yes she did. As much as I myself did.

And so, perversely, if only to prove her wrong, I rode across the border.

And wished at once I hadn't; there was something *wrong* here.

Del, apparently oblivious, walked down to catch her grazing gelding. She turned him, led him up to the stud, mounted silently. And then she looked at me and thanked me, using the Northern word.

"What?" I was distracted.

"Thank you," she repeated, this time in Southron.

Something clammy ran down my spine. "You don't need me." Born of belligerence and discomfort, it came out rather more curtly than I'd intended. (Sometimes the truth, all tangled in unnamed feelings, makes me a tad bit sullen.) "You don't *need* me. Not really. We both know that. You don't need anyone. Not while you carry that sword."

Del frowned a little. And then a corner of her mouth twitched. "In your own special way, you are as invaluable as my sword."

"Uh-huh." I kneed the stud into a walk. "Tell me another one, bascha."

"No," she answered readily. "Because you are fishing, Tiger, and we are nowhere near a lake."

"Doing *what?*"

She opened her mouth, shut it, considered me a moment, then opened her mouth again, and told me what fishing was. And what fish were, for that matter.

"You *eat* them?" I was aghast; fish sounded like revolting creatures, all scales and fins and gills.

A line drew her brows together. "In all your travels from Harquhal to Julah, surely you must have tasted fish. Julah, I think, is not so far from the ocean . . . and Harquhal is not so far from the North. Don't men go fishing?"

I scowled. "I've never spent much time in Harquhal . . . and as for Julah, how should I know how close it is to an ocean? I've never gone past the mountains."

Astonishment parted pale brows and sent them arching toward her hairline. "Have you never looked at maps?"

"Of *course* I've looked at maps. I know the Punja, don't I? I know where all the domains are, don't I?—and the permanent villages, and all the waterholes. I know—"

Del raised a hand. "Yes. I see. Indeed, forgive me; I do not doubt your wisdom." So bland her tone, so serene her expression. Which meant she didn't mean any of what she said, and said it merely for effect. (Or to shut me up.) "I only meant it seemed odd you are so uncertain of the borders and what lies beyond them."

"And I suppose you *are* certain."

"I was taught," she said calmly. "It was a part of my apprenticeship, to know the land I meant to traverse. I have put it all up here." She tapped her head. "In addition to learning the sword-dance, we must also learn mathematics, languages and geography."

Well, it explained why Del and one or two other Northern sword-dancers I'd met spoke my language so well. Southron is easy to learn, but Desert—the idiom of the Punja—is not. Del had required me to translate. She knew a little now, having picked it up from me, but mostly we conversed in Southron. It had seemed natural enough to me.

As for mathematics and geography, the words were completely foreign, nothing more than sounds. My apprenticeship had been given over to the sword-dance only, to the physical forms and rituals that made sword-dancing so complete. I had spent my years learning how to move, how to fight, how to kill; there had been room for nothing else.

I shrugged. "We're different people, bascha . . . born of different customs."

After a moment, she nodded pensively. "Sometimes, I forget. There is always the circle for us, and the dance . . . it is difficult to recall there is more to us than swords and circles and dancing. In those ways, we are so alike . . . in others, so very different."

Downright voluble, was Del. Crossing the border into the North apparently unlocked a lot of the privacy she hoarded so carefully, freeing her to speak of things we neither of us usually brought up.

"Yes, well, you're a woman and I'm a man," I pointed out affably. "There are bound to be differences."

Del's face was expressionless. "Bound to be," she agreed, "even when there should be none."

"Oh, Del—now, let's not start that. You know I'm the first one to give you credit for what you've accomplished. Hoolies, bascha, I'm the one who spars with you, remember? I know what you're capable of. Do I hold back? Do I give way? Do I treat you differently because you're a woman?"

She considered it a moment. "Not as much as you used to."

"*Sulhaya,*" I said sourly, and subsided into silence.

Del didn't say much, either, the rest of the day. She seemed to cherish every step of the gelding that took her farther away from the South, while I caught myself, every now and then, looking back over my shoulder. Soon, too soon, the vastness of the desert was replaced with the immediacy of the North; there was no longer anything I could claim familiarity with. I was truly a stranger, cut off from the things I knew.

I hunched on the stud and lost myself to thought, so accustomed to his rhythms that I could ignore him with impunity, except when he chose otherwise. For the moment, he didn't; he plodded onward, upward, ears flicking in all directions, brass bridle ornamentation jangling with every bob of his head.

All around us the ground swelled like boils on a butt. Above us crouched the mountains, waiting to hem us in.

I shivered once. Shifted in the saddle. Shifted again, scowling northward toward the mountains. Opened my mouth to say something to Del but shut it again, with a snap, and disliked myself intensely for nearly speaking aloud.

But something here was *wrong.*

It lifted the hairs on my body. Something stirred against my scalp. It itched in response and I scratched viciously, knowing perfectly well it wasn't a nagging pest but something unknown. Something undefinable. And something that might, in Del's eyes, make me an utter fool.

I drew in a deep breath, trying to shake off the increasing sensation of wrongness. I meant only to blow air out again, but words spilled free instead. "I just don't *like* it."

It surprised even me, slipping out that way, so clipped and definitive. Del snapped her head around and stared at me, upper body moving with the subtle rhythms of her mount. "Don't like what?"

I scowled down at the clipped mane of the stud. My fingers, of their own volition, picked at the loose weave of braided cotton reins. I saw wide fingernails, some curiously ridged, others squashed, and scarred, ore-pocked knuckles. The weight I'd lost in captivity had returned with a decent diet, but the scars were reminders of a more permanent sort. It hadn't been all that long since Del and I had escaped the tanzeer Aladar's imprisonment: me, from his gold mine; Del from unwanted attentions. A matter of months, only.

"Tiger—what don't you like?"

There it was again. And I had no better answer. "I don't know," I said grudgingly. *"It."*

"It," she echoed blankly, after a startled consideration.

I lifted shoulders and rolled them, testing the fit of the harness and the weight of my sword. No, not mine; Theron's. "Bascha—don't you *feel* something?"

"Oh, yes," she answered readily.

It relieved me immeasurably. "There. See? I'm not crazy. There *is* something odd . . . something uncanny—"

"Odd?" she asked. "I think not. What I feel is *home.*"

Yes, well, she would. But me, I didn't. I felt decidedly discomfited. "Del—"

She halted her speckledy gelding. Accordingly, the stud also stopped. Del set the flat of her hands against the low pommel of her saddle and leaned forward on stiffened arms, shifting weight from rump to wrists. "What you feel," she said, "is frightened."

"Fri—"

"Frightened," she repeated, overriding my startled protest. "You have never been out of the South before. You have never left home before."

"Del, I'm not a *child*—"

"Children adapt to change more easily than adults." Her face was serious. "I know what you feel. I felt it myself, when I went south to find Jamail. Once I crossed the border from my land into yours, I knew I could not go back again until the job was finished. I knew myself cut off, denied my former life; that what I had to do was more important than anything else in my life—"

"But I don't *have* a job." Rudely, I interrupted. "I'm just here because I felt like coming along."

Del sighed and tucked a fallen lock of hair behind an ear.

I set my teeth and tried to be patient. "There's something else," I told her. "Something *more*. Tell me I'm crazy if you want, but I feel it. I *know* it's here."

Del looked around. Each step took us a little higher, rising steadily out of the vast flatness of the South. Here, spangled with hills and rises and hollows, it was hard to believe the Punja even existed. "It might rain," she offered at last. "Perhaps that's what you feel."

"Hoolies, bascha, we're not talking *rain*, here—we're talking something else entirely, something *serious*." I glared at her. "And if you don't feel it, you're deaf, dumb and blind."

Her jaw tautened. "Am I?"

I drew in a deep breath. Shoved silken sleeve to elbow and bared a muscled forearm. Sure enough, the dark hairs were standing on end. "Well?" I asked.

Del looked at my arm. Looked at me. Something was in her face, some form of inner turmoil that she fought to keep from showing itself too freely. I watched how carefully she considered the words she intended to use, and I saw her decide on them. "I think perhaps you have *convinced* yourself there is something odd—"

"Convinced myself?" I didn't let her finish. "Oh, no, bascha, this took no convincing. This is *real*. I'm not imagining anything."

Del sighed a little. "You yourself have told me you don't believe in magic, that for you, it doesn't exist—"

"What I've told you is that I don't *like* it," I said clearly. "Oh, it exists, all right. How, why or in what forms, I can't explain. All I know is that most people don't understand how to use it, and so they use it wrong." I shook my head, glancing around uneasily. "There is something about the North—"

"There is *nothing* about the North," she interrupted curtly. "It is about you. About the Sandtiger, who puts no stock in what others may believe, ridiculing their emotions. And now he can't deal with his own." She unhooked a foot and threw a leg over the saddle, sliding down to wait for me on the ground. "Come down, Tiger, and I will show you what you feel are superstitions."

"What?"

She stared up at me. "We will settle this, Tiger, once and for all, so I don't have to listen to your muttering." She stabbed a finger at the ground. "Come down here."

I considered pointing out that her tone left something to be desired—she might have *asked*, instead of commanding—but I decided arguing wasn't worth it. So I stepped off the stud and waited.

Del walked away from the horses and gestured for me to follow. I did, grudgingly, and halted as she did, in a hollow between two hummocky little mounds.

"Well?" I asked.

"Unsheathe the sword and plant it in the ground." She didn't smile. "Pretend it's a man's belly."

I looked warily at the ground, then at her. "What's supposed to happen?"

"Nothing," Del said, between set teeth. "Nothing *at all* will happen, and then you'll see you're spouting nonsense."

I sighed. "Fine. Just fine, bascha . . . take a man at his word."

"I'll take the sword's word."

I scowled at her. She was being purposely obscure simply to irritate me. (It nearly always does, too.) But this time I refused to let Del win; I unsheathed Theron's dead sword and plunged the blade into the earth.

Nothing happened.

"There," Del said, "you see—"

Indeed, I *did* see, for as long as I was able. And then the ground around us exploded.

For a single insane moment, I wanted to laugh out loud. I wanted to rub her face in it, to shout aloud that I was *right.*

But I didn't. I was too busy trying to breathe.

Eventually, my eyes stopped tearing, my ears ceased ringing, my chest halted its heaving. I sat up. Spat out dirt. Sneezed. Picked grass out of my hair. Peered through the acrid smoke and saw Del doing much the same. She was all right, then; it meant I could gloat with impunity.

Except I wasn't so sure I *wanted* to, anymore.

The sword stood upright between us, untouched by the blast that had thrown us both to the ground. The earth around it was scorched, but the blade was clean of ash or charring. It glowed a pale, luminescent purple.

I stood up slowly and slapped dirt and ash from my burnous. "Well," I said lightly, "time to get a new sword."

Del remained seated. She contemplated the glowing blade. I saw astonishment and disbelief. Careful consideration. The line deepened between her brows as she scowled at Theron's sword. To herself, she said, "It isn't supposed to do that. Theron is *dead.*"

"*Now* do you believe me?"

She didn't even glance up. "Touch it, Tiger."

I nearly gaped. "Touch it? Touch *that?* After what it did before? You're sandsick, bascha. We're leaving that thing stuck here in the ground for the next fool who comes along, and welcome *to* it!"

She shook her head. "We can't. It's a *jivatma*—made for a particular person. It would dishonor the sword to leave it. We should take it to Staal-Ysta, for proper burial at Staal-Kithra."

She was rattling off strange names, but I was too upset to ask her about either of them. "Hoolies, Del, it might have killed us both."

"No," she said calmly, "I don't think so." She chewed her bottom lip and looked from the sword to me. Twice, then once more. Thoughtfully. Deeply. As if she considered something new and wholly unexpected. And then she smiled slowly, so slowly, as if she realized something, and she laughed, as if what she considered was also an answer to a question. "The child goes where the man may not . . ." The phrase trailed off, but the light in her eyes did not. "Perhaps, after all, I *can* win."

"Del—"

But she thrust herself up from the ground abruptly, ignoring the beginnings of my question. She pointed to the sword. "I swear, you can touch it. You can use it. It's nothing but a sword."

Wariness made me curt. "You said that once before."

She pursed her lips and nodded. "Yes. I did. It was. And it is again; I promise."

"Then why is it *glowing?*"

"Because, somehow, you keyed it. Not properly—you don't know the rituals—but somehow you touched the soul within the blade." Del shrugged. "There is too much I cannot tell you, because you are not *ishtoya*. There are secrets, Tiger, that only the *an-kaidin* know."

"*You* know."

"Yes," she said, "I know. But I am sword-dancer, not *an-kaidin;* it is not for me to tell you."

"Then *you* pull it out of the ground."

Del sighed. "I can't. You've *keyed* it, Tiger. Only a little—not enough to make it serve you as it served Theron—but enough to make it aware of the differences between us." She tilted her head left, toward the hilt of Boreal. "Before you knew her name, you couldn't touch my sword without feeling her warding power. Well, I can't touch Theron's sword."

"Then neither can I. I don't know that thrice-cursed blade's name any more than *you* do."

Blandly, Del smiled. "Apparently, he or she doesn't care."

" 'He or she,' " I muttered blackly, and turned my back on them both.

Del waited until I had caught the stud, who had retreated from the explosion, and was in the saddle again. "You are the Sandtiger," she said calmly. "How will you live without a sword?"

She knew, did Delilah, so very well how to appeal to pride in addition to masculinity. But I decided it wouldn't work. "I'll get another sword."

"Where?" With eloquent exaggeration, Del spread empty hands and looked around. "Is there a tree of them nearby? Are they sown and reaped like crops?"

I set my teeth and forced a benign smile. "I can buy one in the next village."

"And if we are accosted before we reach one, what will you do then?"

My smile died; the question made sense. "I *can* go back to Harquhal, where there are swords aplenty."

Del's hands slapped down. "Then do it," she said curtly. "And why not stay there, too?"

I smiled smugly, certain of my victory. "Because you don't want me to."

I had expected a reaction, but not the one I got. At my words she looked at Theron's sword, still planted in the ground. Then switched her gaze to me. Considered something briefly; didn't like the result. She opened her mouth, clamped it shut, muttered something to herself as she scowled toward the mountains, as if they were to blame.

"I am enough," she said in a grim determination. "I *will* be enough, no matter what they say." And then she subsided once more into bitter silence, and shut me out again.

Not at all what I'd expected. Something was bothering her, and it was serious. Certainly more than I thought our squabbling was worth, considering it was mostly an excuse to work off tension.

She made up her mind. In silence I watched Del catch and mount her gelding. She pulled his questing nose away from the stud's curling lip and aimed him northward, planting sandaled heels against the flesh of his flanks. Naturally the stud tried to follow, to regain the lead and put the gelding in his place, but I held him back. He snorted, stomped, jerked at tautened reins. Noisily swished his tail and tried to sidle his way of the hill, as if I might not notice.

I noticed. I let him sidle. Over to the sword, still stuck in the ground. I scowled down at it, hating the pale purple glow. It reminded me of Theron, who had painted the night alive with the sword during our final dance. Now it was only the merest shadow of its former self, but that shadow was more than I wished to acknowledge.

Del's gelding snorted. I glanced after her and saw she was not waiting. She rode steadily north, steadily upward, intent on her destination. Willing to leave me behind.

Ah, hoolies.

I sighed. Glanced around. No, swords do not grow on trees, nor like crops are sown and reaped. And only the gods knew when I'd be able to get another.

Hoolies. I hate it when Del is right.

I leaned down and grabbed the hilt, noting absently that the hairs were stilled on my body and the itching had gone away. The feeling of wrongness abated, leaving me in relief, as if I had punctured the boil.

Gritting my teeth, I jerked. The glow dimmed, then died. The blade slid free of the earth. It was only a sword again.

And I was a fool. Again.

Chapter 7

At sunset we turned off the road and made camp against the shoulder of a hill, avoiding established campsites, in a wind-smoothed hollow carved out of thick turf. We settled in like ticks into a dog, staking out the horses, laying a fire, dragging dinner from saddle-pouches: dried cumfa, sticky dates, a loaf of pressed bread, a bota of sour wine. None of it was particularly appetizing, but it served. And it was *Southron;* I felt a strange urgency to keep myself to what I knew for as long as I possibly could. Soon, too soon, I would know nothing at all.

I ate, drank, sat huddled on my blanket as the last shred of sunlight faded out of the sky. Decided to make conversation; it was better than Northern silence. "A bumpy place, the North."

Del stopped squirting wine into her mouth. She frowned, bemused. "Bumpy?"

I lifted a single shoulder. "Bumpy. Hilly." I made an undulating gesture with one hand. "No level ground."

"Here, no," she agreed. "We are in the foothills, the downlands. Soon we will be in the uplands . . . after that, the mountains. But there are meadows, and valleys . . . enough level ground on which to build and dwell." She wiped a trickle from her chin, sighing, straying from me even as she spoke, though physically she went nowhere. "To see the forests again, and the grass, and know the whiteness of the snow—"

"Snow?" I turned my head to look at her. "We're going into snow?"

"Yes, of course . . . we are bound for the mountains beyond Reiver's Pass."

She was incredibly matter-of-fact. Uplands, downlands, mountains and Reiver's Pass . . . I debated pointing out to her that I knew nothing of her Northern geography, nor of Northern snow.

I took the bota as she handed it over, sucked down wine, handed it back. Del accepted it but did nothing with it, watching me instead. "You're still upset, aren't you?"

Upset. Well, that was one way of putting it. All I knew was that something yet again was causing my hairs to stand on end.

I sighed in annoyance and stabbed a foot at turf, thrusting sandal into soil. "I swear, there's something *here*."

"I thought you were feeling better."

"I was. It's come back." It had, about the time we'd spread our blankets. Unease built steadily. I'd tried to shake it off, but all it did was intensify. "Look, Del, I know how it sounds—how do you think *I* like it?—but I don't know what to tell you. I just sense something, *feel* something . . ." I shook my head, breaking it off. "It's like being in the circle with a dangerous opponent. You don't know *what* he'll do, but you know he's going to do it."

"Superstitious Southroner." Del grinned and shook her head. "I don't mean to make fun of you, Tiger—not really. But you have said much the same to me a time or two, when I have spoken of something I can't properly explain. You used to call me witch, remember? Northern sorceress." She tilted her head a little. "But what am I to call you?"

"A fool," I said irritably. "Why not? I begin to think I *am* one."

"Not a fool," Del mused. "No, something more, I think. Something entirely different."

I snapped my head around. "What?"

She shrugged a little, plugging and unplugging the bota. "What you did with Theron's sword . . ." Her voice trailed off.

"Well?" I sat upright. "Yes?"

Del was frowning again. "I could lie, and say it was nothing. But it *was* something, Tiger."

I swore with distinct succinctness. "And do you plan on telling me what it was?"

She shook her head. "I can't. I don't know myself. Just that— well . . . you say you *feel* something here, and obviously you tapped it."

"Tapped it." I nodded. "I see—I tapped it. With that sword."

"I don't know how—"

"Hoolies, Del, seems like there's a *lot* you don't know." I flopped down on my blanket.

She sighed. "Always, it comes to stories . . . tales of this and that. Who knows what is truth or falsehood, or if there is a difference?"

I scowled. "Stories have their uses. Just look at that boy, Bellin, wanting to travel with us . . . and who are *you* to deny their effectiveness? I don't doubt men are always talking about the blonde, blue-eyed bascha who wields a sword like a man."

"I wield it *because* of a man." Del stared down at the bota, hunching one shoulder. "By now, probably—had the raiders never found us—I would be married, bearing babies, tending a household, tending a man . . . doing all the things a woman usually does." She raised her head and stared across the fire into the blackness beyond. "But who is to say I would be happier in that life, instead of the one I have?"

"But *this* life was born of tragedy."

"Yes. And if giving up this life was a way to bring all my kinfolk back, I would. Like *this*." She snapped her fingers. "But it would not; I am what I am and have what I have. There is no turning back."

I propped myself up on one elbow. "What if there *is*, Del? What if your blood-guilt is pardoned? You left Jamail behind. There is no more kin-debt facing you. What would you do then?"

Her face was hidden by hair. "I am a sword-dancer, Tiger. It is my life; I chose it."

"For a purpose," I said quietly, "and that purpose is nearly over."

She turned her head to look at me. "And if I said the same to you?"

I shook my head. "It doesn't apply, Del. *I* became a sword-dancer—"

"—out of a desire for revenge," she finished evenly. "Don't lie to yourself, Tiger, any more than to me. You are what you are because you hated enough to survive, to acknowledge that hatred, and to use it." She frowned intently, trying to find the words. "What the raiders did to me was not so different from what slavery did to you. It broke us, warped us, remade us, shaping dedication out of destruction . . . defiance out of despair." She drew in a breath, released it. "I thought I would never say this—it is not a thing of which to be proud, in the face of kin-blood spilled—but I will say it plainly, to you, who should understand: I am the *better* for it, regardless of the cause."

I thought, briefly, of all the years of slavery. It was so easily done. I had been free longer, now, than I had ever been a slave, but the memories remained. I would never forget them.

I am whatever I am, I said. *I am what I have made me, regardless of the reasons.*

But I could not say it to her.

I rose, rearranged the fit of my burnous, snicked the sword against its sheath. "Think I'll take a look around."

Del looked after me but made no move to follow. I turned and started the climb to the top of the hill.

The downlands, she had called them. Mere *foothills*, insignificant in comparison to the mountains. But already I was aware of an oppression bearing down upon my spirit. I was accustomed to the vast reaches of the Southron desert, the wasteland of sand and sun. Here there was vegetation in abundance, rich, aromatic earth that sang with the promise of a life I'd never known, even air that smelled and tasted different. All around me the downlands rose in perverse opposition to their name.

I looked out across the distances, disliking the thickness of the night. In the South, even full dark seems bright enough. It is because the moon, spilling illumination across the miles of flattened sand, knows no obstacles. Light, unhindered, runs forever along the ground. But here, where there are hills and mountains and trees, the moonlight contests for dominance, and nearly always loses.

I shivered. "I don't like it," I said quietly. "And yes, I have a reason . . . I just don't know it, yet."

Below me, the stud whickered. Talking to me, or to the gelding, or maybe to himself. The sound carried clearly, sounding closer than it was. Looking down, I could see the fire, and the black blot of Del's silhouette, hunched contentedly before the flames.

Well, she *would* be content. She was, at last, home, after too many years.

Something goosed me in the spine. I swore. Swung around. Lost myself in the sudden shadows and stumbled over a stone. Swore again against the pain in my big toe. The stone rolled, clacked, stopped against another. There it rested. I saw it clearly, cheek-by-jowl with the second. And a third, and a fourth . . . I stopped counting at twenty-seven.

Rocks. Just *rocks*. But oddly rounded, smooth, as if they had been shaped and carefully polished. One after another poured out in a long curving line, like a necklet of Punja crystals. Black in the light of a waning moon; by daylight, by sunlight, perhaps a different color. I followed them around until the last met the first—or would have, had I not knocked it out of its bed.

The symmetry was pleasing. I was a sword-dancer, born of a Southron circle, and here I faced another. Northern instead of Southron, made of rocks instead of a line drawn in the sand, but nonetheless a circle. It made me feel better. Considerably better.

It made me feel intensely *good*.

Grinning, I bent and scooped up the displaced stone. It was cool, silky, soothing, nestled into the palm of my hand. Its touch sucked away the last residue of unease and put pleasure in its place, an intense, abiding pleasure that made me fondle the stone. Reluctantly, I bent and put it back into the nakedness of the pocket I had uncovered. Satisfied, I nodded; the symmetry was repaired.

A surge of well-being filled me. No longer was I oppressed or *de*pressed but filled with a virulent satisfaction.

And a need for sharing it.

I straightened. "Hey, Del!" Echoes abounded. "Feel like sparring? There's just enough light to make it interesting—and someone kindly left us a circle." I entered, stepping over the stone I had handled, and unsheathed Theron's sword. The pale purple glow was gone, but the moonlight set the silver afire. In the glint I saw the runes etched into the blade and sensed again a strangeness working. But the discomfort was gone entirely; what I felt was complacent joy, an anticipation of true pleasure. It was almost sexual. "Come on, Del . . . you could use the exercise!"

She topped the hill slowly, a shadow amid other shadows. "Why are you shouting?" she asked crossly. "I was enjoying the peace of the night, and you are destroying it with your noise."

I gestured. "See the circle? I thought we could spar a little."

Del frowned. "*What* circle—" And then she shut up, abruptly, biting off the inflection of her question. "Come out," she said plainly. "Come out of there *now!*"

"What in hoolies for?"

She ignored my question entirely. "Did you touch anything? Anything in or of the circle?"

"I moved a rock back after I accidentally kicked it aside. Why?"

Del swore. Pale hair was aglow in the wan moonlight. Her eyes were hidden in pockets of shadow. "It's a loki ring, Tiger. I can't come in, not now—but you can still come out. Do it *now*, before they are awakened."

"Bascha, you're being ridiculous. There's nothing here—"

There was *now*. And I felt it coming.

Something jerked me to my knees. The sword fell out of my hands as I flopped forward, splaying fingers against the turf. Something *had* me, and yet I could feel nothing at all. No fingers, no ropes, no traps. Merely a *power*, and that power was dragging me down into an obscene intercourse with the earth.

I lay flat, stretched out, belly-down, and pinned. My face, turned sideways, ground into the turf and through it, into dirt, into a cold, clammy darkness that invaded eyes and nose and mouth.

I meant to cry out, but all I did was swallow dirt and turf.

Writhing, I tried to pull free. Tried to wrench myself from the grip that held me with unrelenting strength. Dimly I heard Del shouting, but her words made no sense. My ears were stopped up with turf.

I hacked and coughed, trying to breathe, trying to spit out choking dirt and dampness. I was aware of an almost obscene urgency in my body, a need to release myself into the earth, like a man into a woman. It made me want to vomit.

The turf was *alive*. It made way for my body, then linked roots and blades with hair, fingers, toes. It tickled mouth and nostrils, tried to invade my eyes as it wove itself into my lashes. I squeezed lids shut and tried to shout again, but the opened mouth merely made way for encroaching grass. I gagged as coy blades caressed the back of my throat.

Hoolies, bascha, *do* something!

She did. She snatched off the necklet she wore and threw it into the circle. "Take that instead!" she shouted. "Take it and leave me the man!"

I was, I knew, little more than a man-shaped mound against the earth, half consumed by soil and turf. A moment longer, there would be nothing left of me at all. But something contemplated the choice. Considered Del's words. Assessed the gift she offered.

And accepted.

I wrenched free in a gout of dirt and turf, hearing the protests of ripping roots and shredded grass. I staggered, fell, thrust myself up again, trying to throw myself over the ring of rocks.

"The sword," Del shouted. "Don't leave them a *jivatma!*"

Somehow I caught it, clutched it, carried it out of the circle, where Del grabbed my wrist. I was weak and disoriented, woolwitted; she began to haul me away.

"Bascha—"

"We must repack and resaddle as quickly as we can, and *pray* the necklet will be enough for now," she said firmly. "Later, I can speak to the gods and ask their intervention."

I dropped the sword, which I hadn't managed to put back into the sheath, bent to pick it up. "Del—"

"There's no time to waste, Tiger. The loki are capricious as well as insatiable."

"But what *are* they?" I tried to shake off the aftereffects, couldn't. Rage and horror made me want to empty my belly entirely. "What in hoolies *had* me?"

She let go of me as we reached camp and began stuffing objects back into the saddlepouches. "I'll explain later." And when I did not move quickly enough to suit her, she straightened and fixed me with an angry, unblinking glare. "In the South, I was expected to do whatever you said *when* you said it, because you knew the land better than I. This is now the North—will you not do the same for me?"

Point well taken. I nodded woozily and went off to ready the horses.

At least, I *tried* to ready the horses. The stud, perverse animal that he is, decided he had done his work for the day and now was the time to rest. I couldn't really blame him; like me, he had eaten, drunk, relaxed—he was ready to contemplate whatever it is horses contemplate when they have nothing better to do. And now I was interrupting.

My mind was on Del's urgency and whatever additional threat the now-awakened loki ring presented. I was unwilling to fuss with the stud, even though he was more than willing to fuss with me.

"Tiger—are you coming?"

I slapped the pad and blanket on the stud's back, saw both start to slip as he sashayed sideways, caught them, held them, deftly avoided a head butt, grabbed the saddle, swung it up and over. The stud, well-versed in this sort of dance, tried to sidestep the descending saddle. I persevered, plopped it down, dodged a tentative hoof. "Not now," I suggested firmly; to the stud, not to Del, who was too busy to hear me anyway.

He stomped, snorted, caught an elbow with the hard bone of his face, and shoved. With equine emphasis.

"Tiger—" Anxious and impatient.

"Del, I'm *coming*—" I swore, stuffed an elbow into his ribs, shoved back. Then repeated the move as the head swung around to protest.

Nose met elbow. Elbow won.

"This is not a game, Tiger."

"No, it certainly *isn't*—" I snugged girth with malicious dedication and buckled buckles, then swung around to bridle him, "—but sometimes I have to convince *him* of that."

She sounded distracted, urgent, impatient. "Convince him another time."

A hoof came down on my foot. I wear sandals; it hurt. "You *son* of a—" But I stopped speaking abruptly as the crest of the hill caught fire. "What in hoolies is *that?*"

"The loki still want us," Del said grimly. "The necklet wasn't enough."

One bright-glazed rock tumbled over the crest of the hill. In its wake was flame.

"Hoolies—" But I never finished it. Del's giddy gelding decided to cut and run.

Picket stake parted company with the ground. Now free, though dragging rope and stake, the speckled horse stampeded by the stud and headed down the hillside at a plunging run.

My horse, being a competitive sort, decided to go with him. And would have, somewhat abruptly, had I not snatched Del's blanket from the ground and flung it over his head.

Blinded, he stopped his flight and stood there, quivering, snorting, sweating.

"Not now," I reminded him, and swung myself up into the saddle. "Del, if you're coming, come *on.*"

She came, dragging a saddle-pouch behind her. She handed it up as best she could without excess dramatics, but the stud, feeling the unexpected scrape of leather against his shoulders as I draped pouches in front of the pommel, lunged sideways. The blanket slid off his head; the glare of burning rocks was reflected in bulging eyes.

I swore, hauled in reins and pouches, sorted them out, spun

him around to face Del. Behind her reared the hillside with its unearthly crown of flames.

"He's going to run," I warned. "Be ready to jump—I'll swing
you up behind—"

The stud fought me, I fought *him;* Del waited on the ground. I
spun him, spun him again, setting him back on his hocks. And
then, as I let him run, I leaned down to thrust out an arm.

Del braced, reached, stretched; I caught, swung her up at a run;
she slung a leg up and over, clamping onto the stud with legs and
me with both her arms.

I shouted, and we were running.

One glance back showed me runnels of melting stone dripping
over the crest of the hill. Which crept, with alarming accuracy, toward the tumbled remains of our campsite.

Del was pressed against my spine. "Don't stop, Tiger. Don't
even *think* about stopping."

I didn't, because I *couldn't;* the stud had the bit in his teeth.

Chapter 8

I was not happy. With each plunging stride, the stud—
heading across, over, down and around hills I could
barely see—humped and hopped, ducking his head in eloquent
promise of his intent to shed both riders. The only thing that kept
him from thrusting head between knees and *really* working at it
was the terrain; he could see no better than we, and—thank valhail—
wasn't much interested in trying anything too hazardous in the
darkness.

But I still wasn't happy. Because each leap and lunge either
sucked the saddle out from under me entirely (not a nice sensation), or thrust it skyward awkwardly, bashing thighs and buttocks
and other more tender portions of my anatomy.

Hoolies, I'd be lucky if I could speak at all by the time he was
done, let alone in a tone approaching masculinity.

Del clung to me with both arms locked around my midsection.
The ride for her must have been even more precarious; she lacked
stirrups, pommel, cantle—anything even remotely resembling a
seat—and was reduced to bouncing up and down on the stud's
solid rump. He is slick and she wore silk; I knew she was in danger
with every stride he took.

"Don't stop!" she repeated. "Not for anything!"

"Hoolies, bascha, I can't just let him *run!* He's liable to trip and break a leg, or his neck, or *ours*—" I broke off, swore, tried to recover my breath as the saddle slammed against netherparts.

She clutched more tightly. "If the loki catch us, we'll wish our necks *were* broken. Don't stop, Tiger. Not yet."

For the moment, the stud decided it for us. The bit was firmly gripped in large, strong teeth, and until I could wrench it back down into the tender, toothless bars of his mouth, my control was negligible. All I could do was try to aim him away from the worst terrain.

Down and down we went, heading south. Maybe the stud realized it and intended to go home. The thought crossed my mind that maybe I could sort of encourage him to continue his runaway all the way back across the border, but I knew it wouldn't be fair. (To the stud, that is; undoubtedly Del would complain, but mostly I was concerned with my horse's welfare.)

And then, abruptly, he veered, turning west. No more a straight shot home, but a diagonal slash across the foothills Del called downlands. He slowed, breathing hard, trying to negotiate treacherous ups and downs. I took the opportunity to pop the bit free of teeth and began to apply my will, which was to stop entirely.

"Tiger—"

"I don't want to *kill* him, Del! Whatever those loki-things are, I'll deal with them if I have to . . . right now, I need to rest this horse."

"All I meant—"

"Later." I said it more sharply than I'd intended, too tied up with the stud to moderate my tone. I felt her stiffen against my back, but couldn't spare the time to placate bruised feelings. "Easy, old man . . . go easy . . . give it a rest, now, all right? Easy, now— *easy* . . . let's keep all four legs in one piece—I think we'll need them later."

He slowed, blowing hard. In the poor moonlight I saw sweat on neck and shoulders. Grimly I shook my head; he was too good a horse to burn out in futile flights.

Del dropped off as the pace was eased. I walked the stud out, circled back, saw her standing in moonglow. Boreal was in her hands.

"You going to cut me, or the stud?"

"Neither," she said, "for the moment." Her face was grim. "What I was *trying* to tell you was to stop . . . there is something I must do."

I snorted inelegantly. "Fight invisible beings?"

"Not yet," she said coolly. "First I will try other methods."

I circled the stud around her. "Do what you want, bascha—I've got a horse to tend."

"I don't need *you* for this." Pointedly. "The ritual requires things you cannot offer, being a Southroner ignorant of such things, and wholly unblooded, lacking even a sword of your own." Moonlight glinted off her rune-worked blade. "Forgive my bluntness, Tiger, but you are not a man who would find much favor with the gods. They prefer believers, not skeptics."

"I'm skeptical for a reason." I stopped the stud, slid off, undid buckles and stripped him clean of everything save bridle. I checked legs and hooves. "As I have said before, religion is a crutch. It's used by people who don't know how to take responsibility for their own lives, and *abused* by those who have a perverse need to enforce their wills upon the weak." I braced myself as the stud pressed his head against my shoulder and began to rub violently, soaking through my burnous to dampen bare skin. "Hoolies, Del—don't you think I did my own share of talking to the gods when I was a slave with the Salset? You think I didn't ask for my freedom?"

"And you got it, Tiger."

"Because I made it happen *myself*, not through any appeal to capricious gods."

She sighed, shrugged, shook her head. "For now, this must wait. But I promise you, whatever you may have known in the South is different in the North. You will face power you have never dreamed of, even in the depths of aqivi fog. I *promise*, Tiger, that here you will see unbelievable things. Things that may even prove fatal."

"Uh-huh. Like these loki-creatures."

Del shook her head. "Have you forgotten what nearly happened to you? How the loki sought to take you?"

"I've forgotten nothing," I threw back. "I don't know what exactly happened back there, Del, but I *do* know it had nothing to do with creatures. What I sensed was sorcery."

She sighed. "Tend your horse, Tiger. I will tend our futures."

I soothed and settled the stud as he steamed in the coolness of the night. Under a blanket I walked him out, around and around, doing my best to avoid the playful head threatening to knock me down. He was tired, but not exhausted; too often he sought out the little ways of making my life miserable.

Del walked away from us, climbed a swell of turf-cloaked hill to pause at the jagged crest. Boreal was a slash of silver in her hands, throwing back the moonglow. And then, as I circled with the stud plodding along behind me, I saw her slowly sheathe the upright sword in the flesh of the earth, and kneel.

Softly, Del began to sing.

I had heard it before in the room in Harquhal. I had *seen* it before, as well; slowly, bead by bead, droplet by droplet, the blade began to bleed luminescence, flooding the hilltop with a salmon-silver glow.

It ran *up* the sword, not down. Filled the runes, jumped along double edges, reached up to caress hilt and cross-pieces. Twisted, writhed, pulsed, changed shape against the shadows.

I drew in a breath that jumped in my chest. I thought again of the circle of stones, called a loki ring, where grass had come alive and tried to swallow a man. The memory made me shudder, which in turn made me angry; abruptly irritable, I shook it off. Northern sorcery, I knew, no more. Not power of itself, undirected and free. What I'd felt required a man to use it, or a woman, in order to make it work. Power required a source, and someone to control it.

I looked at Del, singing to her sword. And what, I wondered, was the difference? Here there was a sword set afire by a song, by a woman. There, I had touched a rock, walked into a circle, had nearly been consumed.

Was there really a difference?

Uneasily, I looked at Del. She was silhouetted against the blade-glow, still singing her soft little song. So easily she keyed the sword and summoned forth the power.

Power. Just as she had promised.

"Hoolies," I muttered aloud. "What am I doing here?"

The stud whickered, walked on, nudged my right shoulder as I circled him back again.

Del came down from the hill a little later. The stud was dry, quiet, contentedly foraging at the end of his picket line, seemingly unconcerned that his equine partner was missing. For that matter, maybe he was *glad;* Del's silly gelding had continually indicated amorous interest in the stud, who had not returned the favor. All he had returned was an occasional nip or kick; I'd forcibly prevented anything worse.

I sat hunched on a blanket with a bota of wine, waiting for her to explain the who, the how, the why.

"How is the stud?"

"Fine. He'll probably be a bit sore in the morning, but nothing much to worry about." I looked up at her. "I didn't lay a fire because I thought we might be running again."

She sighed and dropped into a squat. "Not yet. Not for now. Maybe later."

"Then we can go back in the morning and pick up the rest of our things."

"No." She shook her head. "Too large a risk, and there will be nothing left anyway. Nothing worth salvaging. The loki are—destructive."

I sighed. "Burning rocks and illusion don't seem to pose *that* much of a threat." I shrugged, scratching scars and rattling the string of claws around my neck. "Not if you can run fast."

"Illusion?"

"What I felt," I answered. "You know as well as I do none of it was real."

Del snagged the bota from me and drank. "You are a fool," she said pleasantly when she had finished swallowing. "How often did you warn me against the dangers of the South, saying I should never trust to what I did not know, nor make of myself a target?" Her gaze was level as she tossed the bota back. "I give you warning of similar things here, in the North, *my home,* and you will not give me—or the dangers—credence." She tilted her head. "Why, I wonder? Because I am a woman?"

I sprawled back and plopped the bota across my ribs, staring up at the star-pocked heavens. "Why do you always reduce it to *gender,* Del? I admit that Southron women aren't accorded the same respect as men—I *admit* it!—but must we always lay the blame for everything in this world on what shape our bodies are? Hoolies, bascha, there *are* other things to worry about!"

"Then perhaps you will listen to me as I tell you what they are."

I rolled my head and looked at her. She was serious. "Such as burning rocks and illusion."

"It was not illusion," she said coolly. "What happened, happened. The loki are powerful and tenacious, working in ways no one may fully understand. Using the soil and turf against you was merely a facet of their power. A *game,* Tiger; the loki enjoy such things."

I nodded sagely, humoring her. "So, you're saying they're real beings, these loki. Not merely a manifestation of some sorcerer's power."

"They are spirits, demons, devils . . . apply whatever term you like. They are *evil,* Tiger, and their only goal in life is to drive mortals into death—or insanity . . . sometimes, the latter precedes the former."

"Why?"

"Why?" I stopped her dead. She stared at me, plainly baffled. *"Why?"*

"Why?" I shrugged. "Don't they have a reason?"

"Do demons *need* a reason?"

I spread my hands. "Something I've always wondered about. Here all these stories abound about evil taking on human form to niggle at mortal people—and yet no one ever seems to know why. These beings just seem to exist for no particular reason . . . which makes me wonder if they aren't simply little pieces of a storyteller's tale that have somehow escaped the magical words: *'the end.'* " I smiled. "You called me a skeptic earlier. Well, I won't deny it. I'm not certain I believe in your evil demons any more than I believe in your Northern gods."

Del nearly gaped. "Tiger, that was *you* up there! That was *you* the loki so nearly took! How can you be so stupid?"

I recalled the things I'd felt while pinned against the earth. But admitting it was *real*—no, I couldn't do it. Call it safety in ignorance if you like, but I was convinced that so long as I refused to believe in such things as loki, they'd hold no power over me. "I'm not stupid. I'm just not the kind of man overwhelmed by tricks and illusion." I sighed as she shook her head in disbelief. "Did you ever stop and think that just because we can't explain things doesn't mean there isn't an explanation? A reason other than magic or gods or evil?" I patted the bota. "I don't know where wine comes from, bascha, but there must be an explanation. I don't think wine is *magic*."

Her tone was peculiar. "Wine is from *grapes*, Tiger. Didn't you know that?"

I shrugged, unconcerned. "There are many things I don't know, Del. Call me ignorant, stupid, crazy . . . I just figure there are more important things to think about, like how to stay alive."

"Yes," she agreed. "And it might be just as well, in the face of awakened loki." She sighed, dropped out of her squat, hugged drawn-up knees. "I swear, Tiger, loki are real. And *I swear*, they can be dangerous."

"So you threw your mother's necklace into the circle of stones in order to appease them, and then sang through your sword to your gods." I nodded. "Sounds fair enough."

"The necklace was of heartwood blood, Tiger . . . blood that flows from a wounded tree and, later, hardens. Heartwood possesses power; the man or woman who possesses the stone formed of its blood shares in that power, that protection. I gave it to the loki as a bribe. Surely you have done the same with men and women."

I grunted.

"It might be enough," she said, "but maybe not. The loki don't play fair. So I petitioned the gods to intervene on our behalf, to convince the loki to return to their circle."

I frowned, diverted, and chewed thoughtfully at my bottom lip. "In the South, a circle represents power. That's why a sword-dance always takes place in one."

"There *is* power in a circle; it is the line that knows no ending, only continuance. It is life, Tiger . . . the cycle personified." She lay back on the ground as I did, crossing ankles casually and threading fingers across her flat belly. "I have always found it odd that the sword-dance, which brings death to many, is played out in a circle."

"Because while one dies, the other lives." I shrugged. "I don't know, bascha . . . I never thought about it." I rolled over, reached out, caught a wrist. "And I can think of other things that might prove more diverting."

The wrist remained limp in my hand. "Not so close to the loki."

I froze. *"What?"*

She rolled her head and looked at me earnestly. "Loki are attracted to strong emotions, like flies to rotting meat. Coupling is the strongest emotion of all . . . it is well known that a man and woman, in congress, draw the loki near. They invite the loki to take possession of them." She shook her head. "Better to avoid the risk."

I recalled the urgency I had felt, the need to find release, as if the earth had been a woman. Loki? No. I thrust it firmly aside; how could manifestations of evil have influences over such an incredibly *human* drive? "Are you telling me that we can't—"

"Not tonight," she said. "Maybe next week."

"Next *week*—"

"Loki like to lie with men and woman," Del told me plainly, "for the emotions they can experience through flesh instead of vicariously. Often, they trick you into it. It is the easiest way to gain control, to gain a human body—"

"*I'd* like to gain a human body . . ." I glared. "Hoolies, Del, you're human and *I'm* human, and—so far as I can tell—there aren't any loki around. So why don't we just forget about them and think about *us*."

"I *am* thinking about us, Tiger." She sounded infinitely patient, as if I were a child. "I'm thinking about us staying alive—and sane—so that when the time is right we *can* enjoy being bedmates again, without concern for loki."

I thrust myself off the ground, hooking the bota beneath one arm. "Hoolies, woman . . . you're sandsick."

Del levered herself up on one elbow. "Where are you going?"

"To sit with the stud. I think *he'll* be better company."

"Or the loki will."

"Loki, shmoki," I muttered. "Right now, just about anything would be welcome. Even an amorous female loki . . . at least I'd be getting *something* out of it."

"Maybe the last thing you'd *ever* get, Tiger."

I hadn't thought she could hear me. "Yes, well . . . I've always thought it might be an interesting way to die. If I had to, I mean."

"You'd have to," she called. "That's the way it works with loki."

I sighed. "Great." I stopped, patted the stud, sat down, shoved away a curious nose as I unplugged the bota. "Well, old man, how's it going with *you?*"

Del, rudely, laughed.

Chapter 9

I woke up at sunrise, because I was cold. No, not cold—*freezing;* somehow, during the night, I'd lost my blanket to Del, who now slept wrapped in two. The theft was nothing particularly new, although familiarity did not make me any happier. Ordinarily I'd have simply retrieved my blanket and tried to go back to sleep, but the rising sun prevented me.

It didn't really *do* anything, the sun, but I couldn't ignore it anyway, not even to recapture a stolen blanket. Its passage into the sky was something to behold, so I beheld it. Shivering, freezing, all abump from morning chill, I watched it climb above the horizon and set the world afire.

And what a world it was . . . all uplands and downlands and everything in between, high and low, sloped and flat, aslant from grassy floor to distant sawtoothed mountaintops. In the South, the colors are predominantly browns and golds and oranges; here it was blue and gray and lavender, gilded with silver and gold. Del and I, thanks to the stud, were cradled in a soft bowl of a valley, crushed green velvet, all aglow from morning light. We were, however briefly, swathed in Southron silks begemmed with Northern dew.

I have seen dew once or twice, in the borderlands by Harquhal. But I'd told Del the truth; my experience did not extend so far north as the border town or anything beyond. The Punja was my domain, and all the encampments, oases and walled city-states that made up the puddle of sand that had birthed me. To sit and watch while the sun climbed into the sky above *Northern* mountains was nothing short of amazing.

Or discomfiting.

I looked at Del. She was the meat in a sausage-casing of woven goathair blankets, corners sucked down somewhere beneath determined hips and shoulders. Pale hair straggled free, hiding much of her face, but I saw the cut of her browbone above closed eyes, the sunbleached, feathery brows, the tiny tracery of sunlines at the corners of blue-veined lids. In the South, women go veiled for vanity as well as modesty; Del, so free and easy, subjected herself to the same sort of damage Southron men did, and suffered for it more than any of us could. Northern flesh does not thrive beneath our angry sun.

Except it was no longer Southron sun and Northern flesh, but the other way around. We had changed places, Del and I, and now *I* suffered for it, shivering in the chill.

I rose, swore softly; cracked, rolled and popped stiffened joints and sinews. It is a hazard of any professional sword-dancer—bones do take a beating, and after awhile they protest with great regularity—but I'd never experienced quite the same degree of stiffness. It made me feel downright *old.*

I scowled down at Del, still sleeping. Then I leaned over to scoop up harness and sword.

Just as well I *did*—with a bloodcurdling scream that echoed all over the valley, a noisy group of riders came pouring over the nearest hill.

Bent on murder, certainly. All their swords were out.

It was a bizarre beginning to the morning. Here was I, here was Del (she awakens quickly, thank valhail, when our lives are on the line), spine to spine, swords drawn, feet spread, teasing the air with blade tips, and all the while trying to figure out what was going on, and why. We were afoot and outnumbered—it was four to two—but we'd fought worse odds and won, and under worse conditions, too.

But they did not, at first, attack. They came running and yelling, all swathed in bright silks and shiny brass ornamentation, blades bared and glinting, but they did not move to kill us. Instead, they circled, hemming us in, tying us up in a living knot of horseflesh. And then they slowed. And stopped.

Dark Southron faces. Black hair, brown eyes, white teeth. *Lots* of white teeth; they grinned down at us from atop snorting horses, patently pleased with themselves.

Borjuni, pure and simple, lacking a conscience of any sort. Why they were north of the border I didn't know, but I had a feeling they'd tell me.

Hoolies, I said to myself, they'll want to play with us first.

Del began to tremble. It was not fear, I knew, but an emotion far more powerful than that. "They are," she whispered. "Oh, yes, they *are* . . . I remember their ugly faces."

The only way to win this game was to take it away from them. But I couldn't if Del's desire for revenge got in the way. "Bascha," I said, "wait. Please be patient; I promise, you will have your chance."

"Tiger—"

"Just wait." But *I* didn't. Instead, I smiled up at the Southron scavengers in a friendly fashion. "Out of Harquhal?" I asked casually. "Hunting anyone in particular?"

One of them nodded. He had a mashed nose and a scar across one cheek. "The female killed a comrade."

"In the street, or in the circle?"

He twisted his head, spat.

My turn to nod. "In the circle," I said lightly. "Sits in your throat, doesn't it—that a woman could beat a man? That *this* woman defeated your friend?"

"Tiger—"

"Wait, Del. For the moment, this is between Southron men." I felt her stiffen, but she held her silence. I smiled back at the mash-nosed spokesman. "Well? Are you here on business? Or personal pleasure?"

Four men exchanged glances.

"More to the point," I said, "did Ajani send you?"

The scar-faced borjuni leader spat again. "Ajani need not trouble himself with a son of a goat like you. *We* will take care of you."

"Think again," I suggested. "Would Ajani thank you for stealing a fight from the Sandtiger?"

This time they exchanged longer, startled glances. All four began to frown. I had touched borjuni pride, which might be my only weapon.

I tilted my head in Del's direction. "It was a fair dance, in the circle, between your friend and this woman. He knew it, I knew it, and so did everyone else. She is a sword-dancer, as am I; our dances are always fair."

They were displeased. Dark faces scowled down at us. Horses stomped and fidgeted, clattering bright brasses.

"Isn't Ajani a fair man?" I heard Del's gasp of outrage. "Doesn't he savor an honorable fight?" I knew as long as I kept them talking, any action would be delayed. I wanted to catch them offstride so we would stand a better chance. "I have heard he admires courage no matter what form it takes."

They could hardly disagree. Flattery has its uses.

Scowls deepened. The leader muttered something to the others, then kneed his mount forward a single step. "Ajani *is* fair. Ajani *is* courageous. He likes nothing better than an honorable fight—"

"Even between men and women?"

He glared at Del. "Ajani does not fight women—"

"No . . . he only *steals* them." I smiled, tapping a signaling heel against Del's foot. "So much for Ajani's honor."

"Ajani's *honor* is no better now than it was six years ago," Del said curtly, on cue, "nor is any of yours." She took a single step forward, away from me, and glared at them over her blade. "Don't you remember the young girl who got away almost six years ago? The innocent Northern bascha Ajani selected for himself, and later lost because he grew complacent, thinking she was cowed?"

They said nothing, staring. I could see their memories working.

"You *should.*" Her voice was thick with hatred. "You fought over me, each one of you, after the others were dead, until Ajani overruled you and kept me for himself." Del's turn to spit; in the South, a decided insult. "Because of you, I am here. Because of *you*, your friend is dead. Lay no blame for his death—or your own—on anyone but yourselves."

In five years, a girl becomes a woman. She changes mightily. Del too had altered, of course, but in ways beyond those of a normal woman, forced to it by adversity, shaped by determination. By rage and hatred. As well as by memory.

Now that memory had stepped forward and slapped her in the face. Slapped *them* in the face, as well; to a man, they knew her.

The years spilled away.

"Where is Ajani?" she asked softly. "*He* is the one I want. You are goat dung to me."

Faces darkened. Eyes flashed. Southron insults spilled from lips. But when they did not answer, as I did not expect them to, Del began to sing.

A small song, a soft song; a deadly, crooning song, full of significance. I had heard it before, in dreams and not-dreams, knowing it for what it was. Deathsong. Lifesong. The promise of beginning and ending, all at once, for the one who faced the woman.

She sang, and they moved, as she intended them to. But they were slow. *Too* slow. Boreal was alive in Del's hands, and it was too late for men with normal swords. For men with normal hatreds. Much too late for men who had never faced a *jivatma*.

Too late, even, for me. Because Del and her sword set fire to the valley and split the air apart, calling down a raging banshee-storm from out of deadly Northern heights where winter holds dominance.

—cold—

No, Del, I said, not me. I am not enemy.

But if she heard me, if she *knew* me, she gave no indication. Her world was Boreal.

My world was pain. Pain and stiffness, and fire in the bones, running through all my joints and every muscle, even rigid flesh. I was so hot I shook, and shivered, and spasmed, biting through bottom lip to teeth, not caring that blood spilled into mouth, down my chin, dripped against my neck. It was hot, the blood, so *hot*—

"Tiger."

I jerked. Bones rattled, teeth clenched, blood spilled afresh.

"Tiger, please . . . it's over. I'm finished. I *promise.*"

Familiar voice. Familiar hand on my brow, pushing back hair, wiping away sweat, smoothing out deep-carved lines. A second hand, touching mine, touching both of them; working the skin to relax upstanding tendons and rigid flesh. Soothing, smoothing, sending the spasms away, gentling the unpredictability of my fingers, locked so tightly around the hilt of Theron's sword.

"Let it go," she said. "They are dead. There is no more need. You may release the sword."

Not yet.

"Tiger—" She stopped. Tried again. "It was my fault. I forgot— forgot everything but what they had done to my kinfolk, those men; seeing only the deaths, the rapes, the mutilations—" She stopped again. And began, again. "I thought of my kin, and of me, and of them. I did not think of you."

I was so *hot*—

"Tiger, I swear, I did not mean to harm *you* . . . not with her. You know that. You *know* I would never use Boreal against you. Not intentionally."

I cracked burning eyelids. "I don't much care if you kill me in-tentionally or *un*intentionally. The end result is the same."

She leaned down to brush lips against my forehead. "*Sulhaya,*" she said, but she said it to someone else.

Hair tickled my nose. I shivered from head to toe, and finally let go of the sword. "What in hoolies happened?"

Del sighed and sat upright again, hooking hair behind her ears. "I keyed the sword. Completely. I held nothing back, allowing Bo-real her freedom, the chance to show her true power. And she did. She killed them all, and nearly you."

"Why is it so hot?"

"It's not. You're *cold* . . . it's part of the *jivatma's* power."

"To freeze people?"

"To use all the power at her disposal." Del's face showed strain; so, she *had* been worried. "There are many things I can't tell you about my blooding-blade; too many things are sacred, all part of the rituals and training, but you know each one taps a very specific power. Boreal is—special. The rituals were demanding and difficult— I might have failed at any time, and died. But I didn't fail, and she didn't break, and when the blooding was done, Boreal was whole. She was *awake* . . ." Her voice trailed off. She shrugged. "She is of the North, my *jivatma*. More so than I am, or any other human. She *is* the North, Tiger . . . and she can use any facet of her strength at my bidding."

"Your bidding." I didn't try to move, other than to work fingers still cramped from gripping the hilt. "*Your* bidding, bascha."

"Yes. Of course. She will do the bidding of no other."

"But I know her name."

Del nodded. "It is something. A little. More than any other knows. But you do not know *her*." She frowned, trying to find the words. "It matters, the knowing. It does matter, Tiger."

"I guess so." I wiped my chin and lip gently with the back of one hand, tasting blood. "Don't ever introduce me, bascha. Not formally. I don't think we'd get along, your angry sword and I."

Del's expression was troubled. "Now is not the time, perhaps . . . it could be better, I think, at another, but I can't set it aside any longer . . . not when you deserve better, as you do, for all you have done . . . and *will* do, I hope."

An odd, twisty little speech, and mostly incomprehensible. I frowned. "What?"

Del sucked in a deep breath, held it, let it out all at once. "Will you come with me?"

I blinked. "I thought I was sort of doing that already."

"I mean—come *with* me. To the far North. To the uplands, and beyond . . . all the way to the roof of the world. Where it is very cold, and very dangerous."

"It's already cold, and already dangerous." I scrubbed at a sore face. "What in hoolies did you *do* to me?"

Del looked away. "Nearly killed you. The same way I killed the others."

I tried to sit up, decided lying still was just as good an option. Maybe even better. I stifled a groan and settled down again. "Am I in one piece?"

"Yes. But—" She shut up.

I didn't much like that. "But? You said 'but'? But *what*, Del?"

"The stud ran away."

I sat upright, wished I hadn't. Swore softly. Stared out at where the stud had been staked.

She was right. He was gone.

So were the borjuni.

Well, no. They weren't *gone*, precisely. Not altogether. Parts of them remained. Maybe all of them, for that matter, but Del and Boreal had done a decisive job in dividing them up. I didn't bother to count the limbs or try to put them back with the proper heads and torsos. It would have taken too much time. All of the parts were frozen solid, rimed with glittering ice. The ground was white with frost, though it had begun to melt in the sun.

Del had moved me or made me move myself apart from the bits and pieces. All I could see were lumps in the distance. "What happened to *their* mounts?"

"They ran off."

I lay back down again and thought about what I'd seen.

"Tiger—I'm sorry about the stud."

But was she sorry about the men? Probably not; I wasn't sure *I* was, either. "Tell me that again after we've been walking a few days."

"I know he meant a lot to you—"

"Mashed toes, bitten fingers, bashed head, bumps, bruises." I shrugged. "I can survive quite nicely without any of those."

"But—"

"Forget it, Del. He's gone. At least, for *now*. Who's to say he won't show up again later? He's done it before."

She nodded, but didn't look particularly happy. "I must have an answer, Tiger. Before we go any farther, I must know."

"Know if I'll go with you to the roof of the world?"

"Yes. To be my sponsor."

I frowned. "What for?"

"I must face my accusers and be judged. If I have a sponsor, someone who speaks on my behalf, it might help. And someone of the *Sandtiger's* stature—"

"Save it, Del. Empty flattery isn't your style, and up here I doubt they even know my name." I winced. "Why am I so stiff?"

"Because you were very nearly frozen," she snapped impatiently. "It *was* a storm I called, and a bad one. A banshee-storm . . . Tiger—will you come?"

"Right now I'm not going anywhere."

"Tiger—"

I sighed. "Yes. Yes. I'll come. If it makes you happy. Hoolies, I haven't anything better to do."

"I *need* you, Tiger."

She was oddly intent. I glared. "I just *said* I'd come. Did you freeze your ears in addition to me?"

"There are—things you will have to do."

The latter portion of her sentence came out very fast, as if she were afraid I might undeclare myself if she said them plainly. But at the moment all I wanted to do was sleep, not debate where I was going, who with, and why.

Still, something nagged at me. And I'd learned to pay attention to that kind of nagging, particularly when Del was involved. "Bascha—"

"If I take no one with me, no one to speak for me, they will not favor my explanation," she said quietly, face averted. "I killed an honored and honorable man, a man well-loved by every student and teacher, regardless of status. I *deserve* to be executed . . . but I would prefer to live." She drew in a harsh breath through a constricted throat, no longer avoiding my gaze. "Am I wrong to want that, Tiger? Wrong to ask your help?"

She never had before. By that alone, I knew how serious it was.

"I'll go," I agreed. "I'll do whatever they want me to do. But not yet. Not now. Not today. In the *morning*." I yawned. "All right, bascha?"

She touched my forehead and stroked back a lock of dark hair. "*Sulhaya*, Sandtiger. You are a worthy sword-mate."

I grunted. "But not a worthy *bedmate*. At least—not while there are loki lurking."

Del sighed. "It's only a week, Tiger. Can't you wait that long?"

"A week here, a week there . . . pretty soon you're celibate and I'm frustrated." I cracked one lid. "Think it can't happen? Just think back on that journey across the Punja, while hunting for Jamail."

"I hired a *guide*, not a bedmate."

"And promised the bedding in order to get me in the circle," I retorted, "after your bout with sandsickness. *I* remember, Del, even if you don't . . . or *say* you don't. Typical woman, bascha—promising whatever you have to in order to make a man dance to your tune."

"And you danced quite nicely, as I recall—" there was laughter in her tone "—in the *circle*."

I opened both eyes. "What about now?" I asked. "Am I dancing again if I go with you? Are you singing a song for *me* in addition to your sword?"

Color spilled out of her face. And then flowed back again, angrily. "I do what I have to do," she snapped, "and so, by the gods, do *you*."

I shut my eyes again. "Already, I think I regret this."

Del got up and strode away. "Regret whatever you like."

But she came back to put a folded blanket under my head and spread the other one over my body.

Women: they tend you or terrorize you.

Chapter 10

iger," she said, "it's time to go.

Maybe so, but I wasn't ready to. I stayed right where I was.

Del turned back a flap of blanket. "We *have* to go," she told me solemnly. "They're all starting to thaw."

I frowned beneath the blanket. "*Who's* starting—oh." I flipped back the blanket, sat up, glowered out at the afternoon. Purposely, I did not look at the borjuni remains.

"If you're hungry, we can eat on the way," Del said. "I don't want to stay here any longer."

Something in her voice got my attention fast. Del had killed before, and often, and undoubtedly would kill again. She had learned to deal with it, as a sword-dancer must, taking no joy, no satisfaction, no abnormal pleasure in the death. She was matter-of-fact and wholly professional, keeping private what she felt, yet now she sounded odd. Odd and strangely shaken.

I looked at my competent swordmate and saw she was afraid.

"Del." I pushed up onto knees and toes. "Bascha, what is it?"

She rose even as I moved, stepping away from me. The set of her shoulders was different, sort of sucked in, rolled forward, as if she were feeling intensely vulnerable. Del is not incapable of normal emotions—I have seen her frightened, angry, pleased, and wholly exhilarated—but generally she locks away the deepest feelings, for fear of sharing too much. She carries a shield, does Del, and employs it even with me.

Now the shield was down. Del was clearly spooked.

She moved away again as I rose to stand. Boreal was in one hand. "We have to go," she said.

"Hoolies, Del, what's wrong?"

"This *place!*" she cried suddenly, and the echoes reverberated. "It was here . . . it was *here*—"

She was incapable of continuing. But even as I moved to touch her, Del turned away, turning her back on me. She walked away across the tuff, bypassing frozen borjuni, and stopped on the other side of the tiny valley. Hugging the sword, she stopped, and fell down upon her knees.

"Here—" she said, "—it was *here*—"

I could hardly hear her. Slowly I approached, not wanting to disturb her, yet knowing it might be for the best. Del had lost control.

Back and forth, she rocked, hugging the naked blade. She pressed the hilt against her mouth, winding fingers around the crosspieces. She clutched Boreal to her, as if the sword could offer comfort.

Well, it had before. While exacting a terrible retribution.

"I didn't know," she whispered. "I didn't *know* it—I didn't recognize it. I went to relieve myself, and then I knew it again." She sucked in an unsteady breath. "How could I not have known?"

I glanced around the flattened cleft between the foothills. Ocher-gold and lavender, sunlight glittering off swordborn frost and dampness. Such a pretty little valley, with such an ugly history. "Easy enough to forget, I think, considering what happened."

"What happened," she echoed faintly. "Do you know what happened?"

I did not, specifically. Del had never told me.

"So many of them," she said, "all aswirl in Southron silks . . . shouting and yelling and laughing . . . daring us to defy them—" She wavered, clutched the blade more tightly; breath hissed against the hilt. "We would have given them welcome, not knowing what they intended. But they took it, they *took* it and reviled us for our courtesy, not caring whom they killed, or how." Her eyes were tightly shut. "The infants they killed outright, not wishing to deal with them . . . the men they hacked to pieces . . . the women they kept for themselves and used them until they died. Those of us who were left—those of us not too young or too old—they intended for the slaveblock."

"Del."

"There were only *two* of us left . . . Jamail and myself. The others were all dead."

"*Del.*"

"He was male, and so they watched him. But I was female, and I was Ajani's. His concern, once he had made me so." Her eyes were open again, staring at nothingness. "But Ajani grew careless . . . and so I was able to flee. To leave my brother behind."

"Bascha—"

"I *left* him!" she cried. "And you saw what he became—what he was *made* to be!"

It was not a shout of fear or pain, but of rage and realization. An angry, throttled shout that rose to a wailing cry of blind self-hatred. She was beyond herself, was Del; she had stepped outside herself.

And I had an idea why.

I reached down, caught her shoulders, dragged her up from the ground. I ignored the blade in her hands, even as it fell to thud on bumpy, hummocky turf. I caught her and I held her and I made her look at me. "Don't *ever* blame yourself!"

"I *left* him—"

"—because you had to. Because there was no choice. Because you intended to help him escape as well, once you could find a way."

"They took him South—"

"—and they sold him, as they intended to do with you." I wanted to shake her; all I did was grip her arms. "You have done more to yourself in the name of kinship and duty than anyone I know. But it *ends,* Del—it has to! You can't gut yourself with it forever. Haven't you suffered enough?"

Her voice was toneless. "Not as much as Jamail."

"He is what he is!" I hissed. "Mute. Castrated. No more the boy you knew. But he never *can* be, Del . . . he never will be, now—and you have to realize it."

"He was *ten*—"

"—and you were fifteen. *You* lost as much as he did, if in a different way." I sucked in an uneven breath. "Oh, bascha, bascha, do you think I don't know? I *sleep* with you, remember? I know your dreams are troubled."

She was shaking in my hands. "I want him," she said, "I want Ajani."

"I know. I know, Del. But you've already made your decision."

"Have I?" Her tone was bitter.

"Well, you certainly gave a good imitation of it earlier—asking me to sponsor you and speak for you and do whatever else I have to do to convince them you should live." I let her go. "If you'd rather go after Ajani—"

"It isn't *fair,* Tiger!"

"Tell me something new." I reached down, retrieved Boreal—I could do that, now—and handed her to Del. "You'd better decide now, bascha. If we're going after Ajani, our best bet is to head back to Harquhal and see if we can scare up anyone who knows where he is. Obviously, he may soon know where *we* are; he seems to have loyal men."

"And dead ones," she said flatly.

"And how many does that leave?"

Del shrugged. "Ten. Fifteen. There were twenty or so. I couldn't count them all . . . I wasn't conscious all of the time." She shrugged again, more violently, as if to ward off additional recollections. "I have killed five, but that is not enough. Not till I have Ajani."

"Your decision, Del."

She looked at me in raw appeal. "What would *you* do, Tiger?"

"Your decision, bascha."

"But don't you have an opinion? You *always* have an opinion."

"I have one, yes. I know better than to state it." I smiled crookedly. "If I told you what *I'd* do, and you decided to do it, too, you might decide later that it wasn't a good idea. And then I'd get the blame for suggesting it in the first place."

She opened her mouth to disagree, reconsidered, shut it. Glumly, she nodded.

"You can go after him now," I said quietly. "You can track him, catch him, kill him. It's what you want to do. But it might take more than two months—by then *you* would be fair game as well . . . as much as Ajani is."

Del stared at her sword.

"Or you can go home and face your accusers, accept whatever punishment they levy—and *then* go after Ajani."

"If they let me live."

"If they let *both* of us live." I smiled as she looked at me in shock. "You got me this far, Del. I'll see it through."

"But if they sentence me to death, as is their right—"

"Right schmight," I retorted. "If they're stupid enough to try it, they'll have to fight both of us."

Del continued to stare. And then she smiled a little, laughed a little, nodded. "Wouldn't *that* be a tale to tell."

"No doubt Bellin would enjoy it." I turned to head back toward the blankets. "Let's go, bascha. We've got a long walk ahead of us no matter which way we go."

The sunlight beat down upon us, sucking us dry of fluids. My lungs were empty of breath, stripped by heat of moisture, so that I rasped and rattled as I walked. Scorched within and without, I knew only that if we did not find a cistern soon, we would die, as the Hanjii intended us to die, the violent tribe that had left us in the Punja. No horses, no water, only weapons, because we were a sacrifice to the Sun. A hungry deity.

"Tiger?"

The flesh peeled back from Del's bones, exposing muscle and viscera. Gone was the Northern bascha, banished by Southron sun. And now, it was my turn.

"Tiger."

I flinched away from her touch. It hurt too much. Her flesh would debride my own.

"Tiger—stop."

I stopped. Blinked. Stared. And recalled we were North, not South . . . there was no desert here.

It was a soft day and softer afternoon, full of misting rain and bits of fog, damp enough to drown me. The road was muddy because of it, and the turf exceedingly slippery. No matter which way I went, I found myself laboring.

And cursing the missing stud, absent three days now.

I'll admit it, I'm fond of the fellow. We'd been together seven years . . . and over those years had come to a companionable, armed truce. He was tough, strong, resilient—as well as mean-tempered and sly. But we'd learned one another's habits and got along tolerably well, especially in tough situations.

And now I was without him.

Men say horses are stupid. *I* say they've just figured out a way of making men believe the lie so their kind can get the upper hand when a body climbs into the saddle.

Or tries to climb into the saddle.

"Tiger," she said, "are you all right?"

"Rest," I mumbled and dropped my bundle down. I bent over, bracing hands on knees, and tried to clear my chest. My head felt full of cloth. My eyes were dry and gritty, then teared as I blinked.

"Water?" she asked quietly, reaching for the bota slung diagonally across her chest.

I shook my head. Coughed. Wished my headache would go away. Coughed again; my chest was tight and painful.

Del frowned. "Are you lightheaded? Sometimes it takes people that way when they first begin to climb."

"Not lightheaded. Rock-headed . . ." I sneezed, and wished I hadn't. "Hoolies, I feel terrible."

The frown deepened. "Why do you feel wrong-headed?"

"Not 'wrong'—*rock*," I reached up to tap my head with a sore knuckle. "My head feels like a rock."

She sighed, brow furrowed in concern. "I think you have caught cold."

Caught cold. A moment before, lost in memories of the South, I'd been scorched by *heat.*

I stood upright, trying to clear my lungs. Something wailed deep in my chest every time I drew in a breath or moved. "What exactly is that?"

Del blinked. "A cold?" She paused. "Don't you know?"

"Some sort of disease?"

"Not—*disease.*" Clearly, she was taken aback by my ignorance, which didn't please me much. "Sickness, yes . . . have you never heard of it?"

With infinite patience, I asked, "How can a man 'catch cold' when he lives in a blazing desert?"

She shrugged. "People do. North, South—it doesn't matter. Have you never been sick before?" Del paused. "*Sick* sick, not hung over from too much aqivi. That I've seen myself."

I scowled, shook my head. "Wound fever a few times. Nothing else." I sniffed and felt it reverberate inside my skull. "Did catching cold—or whatever—have anything to do with that sword? With that storm?" I frowned. "It was cold as hoolies in the middle of that mess . . . did *you* make me get sick?" Balefully, I glared. "Is this *your* fault, bascha?"

She raised a defiant chin. "If you had put on the leathers like I told you, and the furs—"

I shook my head. "Too much weight."

"Then when you freeze your *gehetties* off, don't complain to me." Crossly, she gestured toward my bundle on the ground. "Come on, then . . . we're wasting time."

I looked back the way we had come, toward the way we would go. "Where are we, bascha? I've lost track."

"Still on the Traders' Road. We have a long way to go." She paused. "You've slowed us down."

"Sorry." But I wasn't. I coughed and peered through cloying mist. "Does it ever get *dry* here?"

"Midwinter rains," she answered. "It will get worse, not better, at least until we reach the uplands. Then we'll be in snow."

I shivered as a breath of wind caressed my flesh. Silk was plastered against my body. "Hoolies, bascha—I wish you were a Southroner."

"I don't." Emphatically. "I'm not about to give up my freedom."

I sighed. "I only meant then we could be doing this where it's *warm*."

Del's mouth twisted wryly. "We'll go a little farther, Tiger. There is bound to be a roadhouse soon. We can eat there, and change into dry clothing—*warmer* clothing—and wait until morning to go on."

I bent and pulled my bundle from the ground. "I hate rain." I said it with profound clarity, just to make sure she knew.

Apparently, she did. She turned her back and began to climb.

We did not find a roadhouse. We found a worsening rainstorm, which beat me down into a large lump of sodden silk and misery. I plodded through mud, slipped on wet turf, wheezed, coughed, sniffed and labored my way up one hill and down another, knowing better than to complain and give Del fodder. I fixed my attention on taking one step after another, and managed to accomplish it.

Right into the tip of a sword.

I realized, dimly, that Del had been shouting at me to stop. I hadn't heard her. Or else her noise had joined the racket in my chest, merging sniffs and coughs and rumbles one into the other, until all I'd heard was my own wheezes, ignoring everything else. Including whatever warning might have been given.

It didn't please me at all. But I was too tired to care.

I peered down at the sword tip. It rested against my wet, silk-swathed belly. And it trembled, the sword, because the hands that held it were too small, too scared, lacking skill.

He was, I thought, maybe ten.

"Stop," he said fiercely.

"Yes," I agreed, "I have."

"Don't move." A new voice. Female. Young. Equally fierce and adamant.

I frowned. Shifted my gaze from the boy to the girl, who stood three paces behind the boy and held a pale white staff at the ready position, though I doubted she had the training to wield it properly. It takes years to master a quarterstaff, even for a man, and she, most clearly, was female, if still girl rather than woman.

Del had put down the saddle pouches. Her hands hung at her sides. She made no attempt to unsheathe her sword, or to knock away the girl's staff.

I blinked. Tried to clear my vision. For the moment, the rain had let up. But the day was gray, blue and gray, shadowed with slate and steel.

Beyond the girl and boy stood a wagon, halfway off the road and leaning away from the hillside. An elderly piebald mare drooped dispiritedly between the shafts, ears flopped, neck low, head hanging between her knees. The wagon, I thought, was as old, as well as incapacitated. One rear wheel, the right, lay flat in the mud. The tilt of the wagon would make it almost impossible for anyone other than a strong man to lift it; two children could not, nor could the woman who stood by it, wrapped in an oiled blanket. Clearly she was apprehensive, staring fearfully at Del and me and the children, and I realized they were her own.

Such brave souls, the children. And very fortunate. Del and I were friendly; anyone else could have killed them outright for their folly. Easily. Without a second thought.

I sighed; it wailed deep in my chest. "No harm," I told them. "We're travelers, like you."

"So *they* said!" the girl snapped. "We gave them welcome, and they robbed us."

"Anyone hurt?" I asked mildly.

"Only our pride," the woman answered stiffly. "We trusted too easily. But we learned. Now we do not trust."

I gestured toward the wagon. "You'll have to trust someone, eventually. I don't think you can repair that, otherwise."

"We will do it ourselves!" A fierce, proud young lady. Fifteen or sixteen, I thought. Blonde, like Del. Blue-eyed. And, like Del, determined to prove she was as good as any man.

I almost smiled. But I didn't, because I thought she was worth better.

Del was staring at the boy. Her face was pale. She drew in a noisy breath, released it, spoke softly. "There's no need for the sword," she said, "or the staff. We'll help you with the wagon."

The girl jerked the staff northward. "Just go on," she said strongly. "Just go on your way and leave us."

"And let someone else come along behind us . . . someone not so friendly as us?" I shook my head. "To prove our good faith let us shed our harnesses. Unarmed, what threat could we offer?"

"Just go on," the girl repeated.

"Cipriana." The woman's voice was gently reproving.

"How do we *know* they wouldn't cut our throats?" the daughter demanded. "What makes them better than the others?"

"You are wise," Del said, "to be careful. I respect your determination. But Tiger is right: unarmed, we could help you."

The sword wavered against my belly. "Cipriana?" The boy was clearly the shier of the two and well accustomed to deferring to his older sister.

She shrugged, jaw tight. And then, abruptly, she jerked the staff away. "I am not stupid," she said fiercely, eyes filled with angry tears. "I know if you want to harm us, you can. What good are Massou and I against you?"

"Good enough," Del said gently. "And before we are done, I will teach you to be better."

The woman came down from the wagon, clutching closed the folds of her blanket. She was neither young nor in middle years, being somewhere in between; a tall, handsome woman with red hair, firm jaw, green eyes. The dampness caused loosened strands of hair to curl; the rest was fastened to her head in a thick, coiled rope deepened to bronze by the rain.

She stopped by the girl, touching her shoulder gently. "Cipriana, Massou, you have done well. I am proud. But now, let these people have their freedom again. They have offered us help; the least we can do is accept it with good grace."

The boy relaxed his grip on the sword too abruptly; overbalanced, it fell out of his hand and thudded against the turf. He stared up at me in anguished shame.

"Massou?" I asked. He nodded. "One day, I promise, you will be big enough to carry your father's sword. For now, you might do better with a knife."

"Like this one?" The woman showed me the blade she had hidden in the blanket. At my blink of surprise, she smiled. "Do you think I will stand by and let my children do my fighting for me?"

"Or a man; we make do on our own." The girl flicked a glance at Del. "Does he do the fighting for *you?*"

Del smiled slowly. "Little *ishtoya*," she said, "your courage is laudable. But first you must learn better manners."

Color flared in the girl's face, then spilled away. Ashamed, she bowed her head. She had a slender, childish neck. "I'm sorry," she said quietly. "But without my father . . ." Her voice trailed off. She looked at the boy, at her mother, then lifted her head and squared shoulders. "There is no one left to do a man's work for us, and so—"

"—and so it falls to you." Del nodded. "I know. Better than you think." She looked across at the wagon. "We will repair it, if we can. If not, perhaps I might ride ahead to a roadhouse and see if a new wheel can be bought, if I can have the loan of your mare."

Instantly suspicion flashed in the girl's eyes. And then died. "Will he stay with us?" She looked directly at me.

I sneezed, and regretted it at once.

"Have you caught cold?" the woman asked. "Poor man, and here we stand in this wet, nattering on about wheels and wagons." She cast a glance at Del. "We are grateful for whatever help you can give us. But what can we do for you?"

Noisily, I sniffed. "Make it warm again."

Chapter 11

*T*he woman's name was Adara. Massou was ten. Cipriana
fifteen. They were Borderers, Adara said, who had left the
tiny settlement but a day's ride from Harquhal to go north.
Adara's husband had been a Northerner, though she herself was
half Southron—a typical Borderer, with a language born of both
cultures—and he had wanted the children reared as he had been
reared, knowing something solid of heritage as opposed to a Borderer's piecemeal lifestyle. Unfortunately, he would now never see
it: the journey this far had been fraught with difficulties and he had
died but a week before. Of the strain, Adara said quietly; his heart
had given out.

We huddled around a tiny fire beneath the rainbreak Adara
stretched out from the end of the wagon and staked, sipping gritty
effang tea and getting to know one another before the repair work
was begun. (Effang is not one of my favorite drinks, but they didn't
have any aqivi and beggars can't be choosers. Our wine was nearly
gone. And at least effang is Southron.) Massou and Cipriana sat
with their mother between them, clearly protecting her as much as
she protected them. Del and I gave them room, not wanting to trespass any more than was necessary.

"A week?" I was surprised they had continued on so soon after
the man's death. Also that they had continued at all.

Adara drew in a deep breath. "We considered turning back, of course. But Kesar had worked so hard to bring us this far that we couldn't dishonor him so."

I looked at the girl, at the boy, at the woman. "It isn't an easy journey," I said quietly, "not for anyone. Even Del and I recognize the risks."

"And we don't?" Adara was not a meek-tongued woman, though her tone was unrelentingly courteous. "We have been robbed twice, Sandtiger—once unknowing, at night, the other in full daylight. Our food supplies dwindle daily, our mare is old and tired, our wagon now lacks a wheel. Do you think we're blind to these risks?"

"No," Del said quietly. "What he means is, there are those who are more able to accept the risks than others."

Cipriana scraped fair hair back from her face. "Just because *I* don't wear a sword doesn't mean I can't do my part."

Del didn't smile. "Then why did you leave it to Massou?"

Cipriana opened her mouth, clamped it shut. It was Adara who answered for her. "I made her give it to him," she said calmly. "A sword is a man's weapon."

Her children looked at Del, hilt poking over a shoulder, who merely sighed a little and nodded. "Southron, without a doubt, regardless of Border habits. Well, I compliment Kesar on desiring freedom of choice for his children."

Color flared in Adara's face. "You have accepted our hospitality—"

"—and I am grateful, but it doesn't mean I have to believe as you believe." Del spoke gently. "Woman, tend your children as you see fit; they are yours, not mine. But you should know that when a woman undertakes to do things a man ordinarily does, she should be prepared to act as a man when she must." Del looked at the girl. "Cipriana, you have courage and spirit. But if you mean to use the staff, you had best learn how to do it."

Next she looked at the mother. "You, Adara, should hide a knife in your boot as well as behind your blanket; men expect panic from a woman, not forethought. As for Massou and the sword—" she shook her head, "—a boy would do better with a sling. He can hide, and strike in secret; a much more effective defense."

They stared at her, all three of them, struck dumb by her quiet and competent summation. I sipped effang, coughed, turned aside to sneeze. Tears ran down my face.

Adara, diverted, smiled. "Poor Tiger," she said. "You are in misery."

"And will be, until I'm South again." I scowled at Del. "The sun'll be down behind the mountains soon, bascha. If we're going to see to this wagon, let's get at it before I start feeling worse."

"Thanks to me."

"Thanks to you." I rose, stretched, cursed inwardly as all my joints protested.

Massou's curiosity asserted itself. "Why is *she* to blame?"

"Because it was her fault." I scowled at the unblemished serenity of Del's expression. Thought about explaining *how* she had made me catch cold, knowing how it would sound. "Never mind, Massou . . . let's just go fix the wagon."

The problem was simple enough to repair. It was a matter of fashioning a new linchpin, lifting the wagon high enough to slip the wheel back on, then driving the linchpin through the wooden axle and pegging it in place. Unfortunately, I was the one who got to do most of the heavy work; even with leverage, numbers and willingness, most of the operation called for brute strength.

Which *naturally* meant me, according to Del; the sardonic observation made Cipriana and Adara laugh, while Massou merely looked at me in perplexity.

I sighed. "Look at your hands and feet, boy. One day you'll be as big as I am, and then they'll call *you* brute."

Grinning at Massou's immediate inspection of hands and feet, Del examined the mare. Gently she checked legs, hooves—fingering splints and bog spavins, setting fingernails between cracks in the hoof walls, ticking off infirmities—yet speaking softly all the while. The mare nosed Del's hair briefly, then returned to her stupor between the shafts.

Del turned to Adara, brows pulling downward. "How far are you bound?"

"To Kisiri," the woman answered. "My husband's kin are there."

Del tilted her head in consideration, mouth twisted doubtfully. "Too far, I think, for this mare. All the way over Reiver's Pass." She shook her head, patting the mare's shoulder. Even a passing glance at the animal underscored Del's concern; in addition to the weaknesses Del had found, she was swaybacked, knock-kneed, too thin—clearly worn down from a journey still in its infancy. "The Heights will suck the wind out of her and leave her with nothing to breathe."

"She *has* to last the journey! How else are we to go?" Adara moved rapidly to the mare's head, neatly forcing Del to step away. The woman stroked the age-faded piebald face and whispered words of encouragement. "She is tired, that is all. In the morning she will be better."

"In the morning she might be dead."

Adara turned to Del. "Have you no kind words in your mouth? Must you strip away our hope?" She flicked a glance at Cipriana and her brother, both white-faced and wide-eyed with a sudden comprehension of the possibility of failure, and what it might mean for them. "Do you forget I have children to tend?"

Del's tone was gentle, but underneath lay the subtle edge of true-honed steel. "Hiding the truth from them helps no one. Suckle them on dreams and falsehood to the exclusion of reality and they'll be unprepared for life."

Adara's green eyes narrowed. She was a tall, strong woman, more substantial than Del, and with as much determination. Beneath wool skirts and long belted tunic was a firm body accustomed to hardship. It was hardship of a different sort than Del's, but equally valid.

Uneasily, I looked from one to the other. I hate it when women fight . . . unless, as has occasionally happened, they're two cantina girls fighting over me. This, however, was different.

Adara opened her mouth to answer sharply, paused, glanced

briefly at me. Reconsidered her words. She modified her tone, but the intent remained quite clear. "Cipriana will one day be a wife, not a warrior. And the man *she* tends will be her husband, a settled man, who has no need of a sword, nor of a wife who wears one."

"Hoolies." I muttered wearily. I found a stump—wet, of course—and sat on it, shivering in the dampness. The rain had faded to mist, but the sun had yet to shine. Everything was soot-gray and slate-blue; even the turf, ordinarily a rich, lively green, was dull and blotchy, channeled by runnels pouring off mounds and hummocks and terraces.

Obscurely, Del asked, "How old were you when she was born?"

Adara stared. And then answered politely enough, "Fifteen, even as Cipriana herself is now." She glanced at the girl, a mother's quiet pride evident in her smile and the softening of her face. "I had been wed but a nine-month, so clearly the gods blessed the union."

"Fifteen." Del's expression was masked, but I knew her too well to miss the odd note in her voice. One of weariness and recollection. "At fifteen, I too dreamed of a husband and daughter . . . and a softer sort of life." Her eyes flicked a glance at me, at Cipriana, at the woman. Her tone hardened. "But the gods saw fit to give me a different road."

The Border woman was neither vindictive nor cruel, and did not, thank valhail, display the quick-striking dagger of a jealous female's tongue. Plainly she heard the peculiar note in Del's tone, and it touched her. Hostility spilled away; her question was very soft. "Is it too late to take another?"

In a clipped, harsh tone, Del answered. "Much later than you know." And then, abruptly, as if she regretted saying anything at all, she was asking questions about the remaining food supplies.

Adara sighed. Lines crept back into her face, aging her beyond her thirty years. "We have what the thieves left us: a little flour, dates, dried meat, grain for the mare in case foraging isn't enough . . . some tea and water . . ." Her head dipped briefly, then snapped back up. The Border woman would not acknowledge how bad the telling sounded. "We had a nanny in kid, and another just weaned—"

"—and two hens," Cipriana said hollowly, "with a rooster. In crates." Her face was solemn. "They took them all except the mare; they said she wasn't worth it."

As one, we looked at the mare. No, to thieves, she was not. Unless they meant to eat her, but she was too old and too thin to offer much other than tasteless sinew and bone.

Del nodded. "Have you coin?"

Even Massou, young as he was, understood the possibilities in the question. And misunderstood, even as his sister and mother did. I didn't really blame them; they had been hard-used by thieves. There was no reason to trust anyone else until we gave it to them.

"Nothing *left*," Adara said sharply. "Will you take the mare, now?"

Del's tone didn't change, only the end of the question did. "Have you coin to buy supplies when you reach a settlement?"

The Borderer's color deepened. Ashamed, she looked at me, still sitting huddled on the stump. "No," she said very softly. "I thought to sell the mare."

Del shook her head. "She will bring nothing; would a man pay coin for a horse no one else will steal?" She didn't wait for a protest. "For now, what you need is fresh meat. It won't last, but it will fill the belly tonight and tomorrow morning." She looked at Massou. "Do you know how to set a snare?"

His pinched face brightened. "Oh, yes! My father taught me." The brightness fell out of his face as memory replaced it. Grief renewed, he stared hard at the ground.

Del's tone was brusquely sympathetic. "Fetch the makings, then, and you and I will snare us a meal." She paused. "If your mother doesn't mind."

That Adara wanted to was plain. But she made no protest, being a realistic woman: food had to come from somewhere and someone; Kesar was cold in the ground. Instead, she merely nodded.

Massou stared at Del. "But—you're a *woman*. Shouldn't *he* set the snares?" A finger jutted in my direction.

Del's expression didn't change. "Tiger is ill and needs to rest."

"Will you take me as well?" Cipriana asked eagerly, and then shot a stricken glance at her mother. "May I?"

The corner of Del's mouth twitched.

Adara's firm jaw was tight, stretching flesh over bone. I knew what she would say, and why; she would not lose son *and* daughter to Del. "It would be best if you stayed here, Cipriana. A woman *prepares* the meal." Swiftly, before Cipriana could express disappointment, Adara added, "Perhaps you might ask Tiger to tell you about the Punja and all of the places he has seen."

"But what'about *me?*" Massou demanded promptly, "*I* want to listen, too."

Del's tone was dry. "Don't fret, Massou. He has stories enough for us all, and for all the days of forever. And he's a hero in every one."

I sniffed pointedly. "Not much of one at the moment."

Adara smiled; Cipriana giggled. Massou looked merely confused.

I nodded thoughtfully. "Now, there *was* a time . . ."

Del turned on her heel and left.

Adara prevailed upon me to change clothes, since what I wore was thoroughly soaked. She unwrapped the remaining bundle I had lugged up and down Del's "foothills" and handed me various pieces of alien clothing, then quietly took herself and her daughter around the side of the wagon while I shinnied out of wet silk, dhoti and harness.

Unfortunately, cold as I was, I couldn't replace wet clothes with new immediately. There was the problem of figuring out how to put them on.

Eventually, muttering violent but indecipherable curses through chattering teeth (and coughing), I did sort things out, thanks to Adara's quiet explanations from the other side of the wagon.

Of something called wool, there were baggy trews that reached to ankles; gaiters cross-gartered with leather thongs stretching from knee to ankle; a long-sleeved undertunic. The sleeveless *over*tunic was of leather decorated with silver-tipped fringe. Low boots replaced my sandals.

The woolens were blue, every last bit, though none was the *same* blue, but a tangle of brights and darks. The leather was a uniform bloody brown. I felt like a patchwork man.

I looked down at the pile of sodden silk and damp dhoti. On top of both lay my sword and harness. I scooped if up and realized that for the first time in many years, the harness leather would no longer come in contact with my flesh. The Northern clothes were too confining.

Del, I recalled, wore her harness strapped over her leather tunic. Time for me to do the same.

Undoing buckles, I came out from behind the wagon. Cipriana peeped around the corner, saw I was clothed, giggled and said something to her mother mostly in Northern. Color stood high in her cheeks.

Adara did not look at me, but at the massive sword hilt jutting from the sheath. "Is that a *jivatma?*" she asked.

I stopped undoing and moving buckles. Her face was pale. Even Cipriana was taken aback, looking from my face to the sword and back.

"What do you know of *jivatmas?*" I shifted buckles again, deftly lengthening straps. The sword-weighted sheath swung.

"I—my husband was Northern. He told me a little about the swords, and the people who wield them." She touched her throat in a betraying gesture of vulnerability. "*Is* that a bloodingblade?"

I settled buckles into new places, snapped the straps, hooked arms through, head and neck, adjusted the fit with a rolling motion of both shoulders. "For another man, it was a *jivatma,*" I said quietly. "For me, it's merely a sword. And only temporarily, until I can get another."

Adara did not move her head. I saw the pulsebeat in her throat. "Then—you are not a sword-dancer?"

A tug here, pull there . . . it would take time for the leather to settle, and for me to adjust to it over layers of fabric instead of flesh. "I am a sword-dancer," I said, "but a Southron one. There is a difference. I don't know what your husband told you, but in the

South a man with a sword is a man with a *sword,* not some sorcerer who claims a blade that comes to life when you sing a song."

"Sword-singer," Cipriana said clearly, with more than a little awe.

I frowned. "Well, I suppose the term applies, in a way—at least, when it comes to a *jivatma.*" I shrugged, dismissing it; reached over my left shoulder to snick the blade in its sheath. "But Del and I are sword-*dancers.*"

There was a moment of icy silence. "Del, *too?*" Adara was clearly shocked.

Slowly, I smiled. "What did you think she was? A woman who plays with a sword merely for effect?"

It was a question Del had asked me once, when I was still blithely convinced she wasn't what she claimed, but merely a foolish woman on a foolish, futile mission to find a young brother stolen by Southron raiders and sold to Southron slavers.

Of course, I had come to know better.

Eventually.

Though she might argue otherwise.

Adara shook her head slowly. "I thought—I thought—" She broke off. "I don't know what I thought." So numbly. "But I know what sword-dancers are, what they *do* . . ." Her green eyes were dilated dark. "Do you mean to say she has *killed* people?"

It would do no good to deny it. "In the circle and out of it."

"And you?"

"And me."

Even her lips were white. Dazedly, she asked, "What have I brought among us?"

I sneezed. Sneezed again. Pressed the heel of a hand against my heavy head. "For the moment," I mumbled thickly, "nothing more than a miserable excuse for a man." I sniffed loudly and lengthily. "Gods—if you exist—could you just send me a *little* sun—?"

It made Cipriana smile.

The girl's mother did not.

Chapter 12

dara swung around stiffly and marched across the muddy
little campsite to where I'd left dhoti and burnous piled on
the ground. She picked them up, folded them neatly even though
they were wet, and brought them back to me.

Her tone was awkwardly proper. "We are grateful for the help
you've given us with the wagon. But I must ask you to go."

"Go?"

"Go," she repeated firmly. "I will not have my children witnessing violence and murder."

Oh, hoolies. "Adara—"

"Just go." Her face—and mind—were closed.

I sighed, knowing argument and explanation would accomplish
nothing. I'd met her kind before. "Do you mind if I wait for Del?"

She heard the dryness in my voice, but kept herself from responding in kind. "Until then, yes." Her own words were clipped.

"You should let them stay until morning." Cipriana's quiet suggestion startled us both. "They have helped with the wagon, and
Del is bringing food. The least we can do is let them share our fire
for the night."

The girl's mother stared at her. Convictions warred with courtesy. Abruptly, she thrust the clothing into my hands. "Cipriana—
you don't know what they are."

"Sword-dancers." The girl was matter-of-fact. "I'm not blind or deaf, and we are Borderers. We've all been to Harquhal. I've seen sword-dancers before, and so has Massou." She shrugged. "I've even seen a sword-dance."

"Cipriana!"

"I *have*." Her eyes were steady. "It wasn't so bad."

I smiled. "Most of the time, it isn't. Not much more than an exhibition."

Cipriana nodded. "They were good, those men. Father even said they were, but not good enough to be *ishtoya* or *an-ishtoya*." Pale brows interlocked. "What do the words mean? I asked, but he never told me."

I looked at Adara, expecting her to cut off the conversation. But she said nothing at all, merely turned away with a rigid spine and knelt down to tend the fire. Loosened hair, red as copper, fell forward to hide her face. Impatiently she thrust it back, mouth set in a thin, hard line.

Cipriana waited. Her face was solemn, yet expectant, similar in bone and expression to Del's. Both were blonde, blue-eyed, fair-skinned. But there was innocence in the younger girl's eyes, even as there was experience in Del's.

I bent down and tucked dhoti and burnous into the bundle and rolled it up again. "They are Northern words," I said, tying thongs. "Both mean the same thing, basically, which is 'student'—but *an-ishtoya* is of a higher level than *ishtoya*."

A lock of loose, pale hair, fine as floss, fell forward over a shoulder. Cipriana hooked it behind one ear in a gesture habitual to Del. "What are *you?*" she asked.

"Me? I'm Southron." I grinned as I rose. "In the South, things are done differently."

"And Del?"

"Del is—Del." I shrugged. "It's for her to say."

"*Kaidin*, is she not?" Adara's voice was muffled. "She carries a *jivatma*."

I let that sink in a moment. "For a woman so opposed to sword-dancers," I said lightly, "you sure know a lot about us."

She cast me a sharp, bright look of resentment, as if I'd offended her by doubting her intelligence. "I'm a Borderer," she said curtly. "We learn many things out of necessity."

"And survival is one of them." I ducked beneath the rainbreak, squatting by the fire. "And have you also learned—"

But I was never able to finish my question because Massou came running down the nearest slope with something clutched in his hands. Adara rose and turned at once, slipping out from under ropes and rainbreak to tend her son.

"Look!" he cried. "*Look!* See what nearly got me?" Stretched between both hands was a thick, dark rope of a snake. It was a pearly, indigo color, slicked with grayish speckles. "It tried to bite me, tried to *kill* me, but Del took out her sword and cut its head right off!" He displayed the headless end enthusiastically, oblivious to the gore. "It tried to bite me on the arm as I bent to lay a snare, but *she* cut the head off even as it struck!"

The *she* he indicated came quietly down the slope behind him, empty-handed. Boreal was in her sheath. "The snares are set. By morning, we should have meat."

"She says we can eat *this*." Diffidently, Massou held the bluish body out to his mother. But Adara ignored him—and the snake—altogether; instead, she stared at the woman who had saved the life of her son.

"Bluesnake." Del said briefly. "Better by far than cumfa." She ducked beneath the rainbreak, squatted to pour tea, glanced at me over the rim. Her brows climbed slowly up. "A Northerner has joined us."

I sighed. "Yes, well, everything else was wet."

"It's why I bought them," Del agreed blandly. "The farther north we go, the colder it gets. You'll be glad of the furs, too, once we reach Reiver's Pass."

Massou was still full to bubbling over of his experience, wanting to share it with everyone, but particularly with his mother. "You should have *seen* me!" he exclaimed. "I was all bent down to set the snare—just like this—" He bent, flopping the dead snake in the mud "—and there it *was*, just waiting, all coiled up and reared back. It would've bit me, too, but Del saw it and *zlipp!*—cut its head right off!"

Cipriana, having inspected the kill, made a face of bored distaste.

"You didn't look beforehand, Massou." Del was quietly reproving. "The world is treacherous if you don't pay attention."

Briefly chastened, he nodded, though deaf to the nuances in her tone. And he was too excited to pay mind to the words for long. Clearly he no longer judged Del unfit to set snares or anything else that was ordinarily a man's concern; in his eyes, she had earned her place in a masculine world. "After it was dead, Del said we could eat it. I wanted to keep the head, but she said it wasn't a trophy. She said a man should never be proud of his failures." Blue eyes were fixed on me. "She said *you* wear a string of claws around your neck, but it's a proper keepsake because you saved your people from a sandtiger who was eating all the children."

I looked at Del. Her expression was sanguine. "Well, yes—so I did." I reached beneath all the leather and wool and pulled the string of claws free, hearing the familiar click and rattle. Somehow, before the boy's disconcertingly direct gaze, I couldn't embellish the story. But neither could I entirely ignore an opportunity. "*Someone* had to do it, and there I was."

"Was it hard?"

I tapped my cheek. "Hard enough, *and* dangerous. See these scars?"

"The sandtiger did that?"

"It's where I got my name." Said casually enough, and regretted almost immediately.

"Got your name?" Cipriana frowned. "Didn't you have a name?"

I glanced at Del, who clearly was sorry she'd said anything at all. We'd both been alone too long, or only with one another; we had forgotten how direct children can be. How demanding—and deserving—of simple honesty.

I drew in a breath. "You're a Borderer," I said evenly. "What do you call slaves?"

"Chula," she answered promptly. And then covered her mouth with her hand.

Massou's blue eyes were huge. "*You* were a slave once?"

Even Adara waited. Del sipped tea.

"Once," I answered quietly, "a very long time ago."

They stared, all three of them. Just *stared.* I found it discomfiting and otherwise irritating, although I knew they didn't do it to offend me. And I suppose I even understood it: here I was, professional sword-dancer, freely admitting I had been a chula. In the South, slaves are less than chattel, less than human, and to illustrate it slaves are never named. So, when I had killed the cat, I'd taken on *his* name, to illustrate my new-found and hard-won freedom.

Adara's green eyes had the unfocused look of someone lost in recollections. Then, slowly, she turned from me to Del. "And you?" she asked. "Were you also a—"

"—chula?" Del shook her head. "Northerners don't keep slaves."

"Then . . ." Adara's glance flicked down to the fire and held. "I should not ask."

"No, you shouldn't." Del's tone was quiet. "But you have, and so I will tell you this much: I chose my life just as you chose yours . . . and I make no judgments when others take a different road than mine."

Adara's head snapped up. "I have children to protect!"

A muscle ticked in Del's left cheek. "Yes. Of course."

"If *you* had children—"

Del overrode her smoothly. "If I had children," she said with quiet clarity, "I would teach them to think for themselves."

White-faced, Adara looked at her children. First at Cipriana, clothed in gray wool, no longer a girl but not quite a woman; at Massou, a boy, in brown, still clutching his thick-bodied snake. Towheaded, blue-eyed children, showing their father's heritage. I knew she balanced Del's words against her own convictions, weighing past behaviors, past pronouncements. Of her children, neither said a word, not unaware of the tension singing between the two women, but also not knowing how to respond.

And then the tension faded out of Adara, replaced with resignation. "I will prepare the snake."

"I can do it." Del's offer was meant to help settle ruffled feathers.

Adara understood. She smiled crookedly. "No. Your task was to *catch* the meal; mine is to prepare it." There was dryness in the Border woman's tone, as if she regretted the ordering of the tasks, but no hostility. She took the snake from her son. "Cipriana, will you help me?"

The girl opened her mouth, clearly torn; there were things she wanted to ask the two strangers with swords on their backs. But she said nothing at all to either of us, merely nodded and went to her mother.

Adara did not turn away at once. Obscurely, she asked, "Do you understand?"

"Yes," Del said, "but *you* should understand that we are not the enemy."

Adara shoved fallen hair away from her face with the back of a callused right hand. "Sometimes," she said softly, "it's so very hard to tell."

We ate Massou's snake, talked a little, went to bed. Adara and the children slept in the little wagon, while Del and I bedded down outside, a little apart from the wagon. The night air made me cough; I buried my head in goathair and tried to still my lungs.

Del stirred against me. "Your cough is getting worse."

I freed my mouth from goathair. "Am I keeping you awake?"

"Well, I'm not asleep . . . what do *you* think?" And then she sighed, heavily, and hitched a hip higher on my thigh, pressing her spine against my belly. "No. It isn't you. It's me. I'm doing something I swore I'd never do."

I waited. She didn't answer at once. Eventually, I gave in and asked what it was.

Pale hair was silver in the darkness. I could see little of her face. "I'm thinking," she said wearily. "Thinking about—"

"—how things might have been," I finished. "Wondering what kind of person you would be, and what you might be doing."

She was silent a moment. Then, "Don't you?"

"Wonder about you, or me?"

"Both."

I smiled into her hair. "Never."

Del stiffened, then thrust herself up and over, settling back down beneath blankets to face me this time. Blue eyes bored into mine. "Never?"

"I *know* what I'd be, bascha. A chula, or maybe dead. Probably dead; I'd have killed someone for my freedom, and the Salset would have killed me."

"If they'd caught you."

"They might have. Although Sula probably would have given me food and water and helped me to escape . . . and paid for it eventually, if they'd found out."

Del sighed. "A strong woman, Sula. She would have risked her life for you."

Sula. I hadn't thought of her in months, although it had been only six or so since I'd seen her. Del and I had been left for dead in the Punja, intended as Sun Sacrifices, but the Salset had rescued us. An odd thing, that; half a lifetime before they had tried to kill me. But then I'd been a chula, and unworthy of a name.

Except Sula had given me one. She had given me dignity.

Old memories hurt. I shoved them away and resorted to my customary tone. "I inspire that kind of loyalty. Look at you, Delilah."

Del said something obscene. I laughed, then had to stifle another round of coughing.

Her fingers were cool on my wrist. "Am I wrong to do what I do?"

"Just because Adara thinks you are doesn't *mean* you are."

"I'm not asking Adara. I know what she thinks. I'm asking the Sandtiger."

I snorted. "I'm a fine one to ask. We share a profession, bascha . . . and other things as well." I paused significantly. "Sometimes, that is. When loki aren't around."

Del sighed and shut her eyes. "Can't you ever be serious?"

"I'm serious most of the time. As for you—"

"What do you want in a woman, Tiger?"

I froze. *"What?"*

"What do you want in a woman?" She hitched herself up on an elbow. "A soft, helpless thing, requiring your protection? Or a woman like Elamain was, hungry for constant bedding?" She sighed a little, looking over my shoulder toward the wagon. "Do you want a woman who cooks for you, cleans for you, bears you countless children . . . do you want a woman like Adara?"

"Yes," I answered promptly.

Her eyes came back to me. "Which? Like Adara?" Surprise flickered in her tone.

"No. Like *all* of them."

Del's mouth twisted. "You want three women. Why am I not surprised?"

I grinned. "You don't understand men, bascha."

"No," she agreed dryly. "I have met few examples worth the trouble of learning."

I ignored that. "There are times when softness in a woman appeals to me. There are times when an appetite like Elamain's rouses me. There are times when I think about raising a family. And there you are, bascha—all three women, but preferably in one body. I really don't want a harem . . . too much trouble when you move."

She was not in the mood for flippancy. "Have you any children?"

"Probably somewhere; I haven't been celibate. But none that I'm certain about."

"And does it bother you, that you may have sired sons and daughters but don't know who—or what—they are?"

I groaned and rolled onto my back, scratching at my forehead. "I don't *know,* Del. I never think about it."

Her voice was soft. "Never?"

I scowled into the darkness. "If I worried about all the children I may or may not have sired, I'd have time for nothing else."

"But if you died, Tiger . . . if you died with no son or daughter, there would be no one left to sing the songs of you."

"Songs?" I cast her a suspicious scowl. "What songs, bascha?"

Del tightened the blankets around her shoulders. "In the North, it is family custom to sing songs of those who have gone before. When an old one dies—or even a newborn baby—kinfolk gather to honor that person with songs and feasting."

I frowned. "You sure sing a lot in the North. Sing to your sword, sing to your dead . . ." I shook my head and stared up at the stars. "I'm a Southroner, Del. There is no one to sing for me."

"Yet," she said distinctly, as if it made a difference.

I smiled, laughed, gave in. "Yet," I agreed. "Now may I go to sleep?"

Chapter 13

I felt it before I knew it. An itch and tickle all over my body, teasing arms and legs, my scalp, even across my belly. I sat up, swearing, and tore the blankets off.

"Tiger—?" Del, blurry-toned; I was on my feet.

"I don't know," I said. "I don't *know*—"

And then, abruptly, I did. I recalled the sensation too well.

I scooped up my sword and drew it, scraping it out of the sheath.

Del knew better than to question me again. She was on her feet, like me; wide awake, like me, unsheathing her own blade.

I pointed toward the saddle slung between two slanting hills. The track was hard to see. "There," I said clearly.

"I see nothing, Tiger."

"It's there. It's *there*." And it was; I could feel it. Creeping relentlessly over the saddle. Dribbling down the track, heading unerringly for the wagon. "Wake them up," I told her, "but have them stay in the wagon. I want them in one place, not scattered to the winds."

The old piebald mare nickered uneasily, testing the weight of her line. I recalled the flight of Del's speckled gelding and the loss of my own stud.

Del went to the wagon in silence, parted the woven hangings, said something quietly. I heard Adara's stifled outcry, Cipriana's rising tone, Massou's excited voice. And then I was by the wagon, near the shafts, waiting for the arrival.

Something fluttered deep in my belly. Fear, a little, but mostly an odd, frustrated anger, that something could offer such threat and I didn't know what it was.

I could see nothing at all, save the silhouette of the saddle. Beyond it lay the sky and stars, and blacker shadows yet. "Hoolies . . ." I muttered uneasily, "I wish we were in the desert."

"They'll stay." Del slipped into place beside me. "What can you tell me, Tiger?"

"Don't you feel it, bascha?"

"No. Nothing."

It made me feel even worse. How could something so strong go unmarked by Del?

"Right *there*," I said sharply, and suddenly there it was.

There *they* were: four men on horseback, riding down the track. Little more than shapeless shadows, blackest black, shrouded in cloaks or burnouses. The horses they rode were soundless.

"I don't like it, bascha."

"Tiger—*look!*"

I squinted, even as she did, using a hand to shield my eyes, for the sudden firelight was blinding. It exploded behind each of the riders, crowning the saddleback, and made them silhouettes instead of men.

"Ah, hoolies," I growled, disgusted, as each of them bared a sword.

Horses are afraid of fire. It makes them crazy. It makes them stupid. It makes them do silly things. But these four horses were untouched by the blaze behind them or the flames dancing on each of the blades held so precariously near their heads. They just kept coming, in an eerie, uncanny silence.

And then they began to run.

"Del," I said lightly, "now might be a good time for you to start singing. We'll need every advantage we can get."

Del sang, and the horses came on, exhaling smoke. Swords blazed like brands in the night.

The riders split up, driving in four directions. Two dropped back, outflanked the others, circled the wagon. The swords were torches in their hands, lighting four familiar faces.

Four *dead* faces; we had already killed them once. But somehow they lived again.

Del's song wavered. Breath caught in her throat, then ran raggedly out of her mouth. "Tiger—do you *see*—?"

"I see, bascha. Keep singing."

She didn't. "How is it possible?"

"It's not. At least, not without using magic." I swallowed heavily. "You beat them once, Del. I know you can do it again."

"But I cut them to *pieces*, Tiger! These are whole men!"

Whole men, each of them, coming down from the Northern sky. Swathed again in Southron silks, baring blazing Southron blades, mouthing Southron words. But everything was soundless.

How is it possible?

"Never mind," I said grimly. "The trick is to win again."

"Loki," Del breathed. "It has to be the loki. They are powerful enough."

"To stitch them together again?" I drew in a deep breath. "Then let's take them apart—again."

"Last time they were *men*."

This time they were not.

"Sing," I said fervently. "Sing for all you're worth."

Loki, men, whatever, they knew how to handle swords. And did so very well, whipping in, whipping out, playing with us on the run. Del and I were forced back against the wagon, then cut away from it, herded like mindless sheep. But we fought back with all our skill, tantalizing the mounted men, until their game became less than a game and more like an execution.

I heard the old mare scream. I snatched a glance out of the corner of my eye and saw a flaming sword cut her rope. She spun awkwardly, staggered two steps, went down heavily. She did not move again.

My world was little more than noise and flame. I smelled fire and the stink of decaying flesh, the tang of sweat-soaked wool, the salt of sweat-caked leather. Blades rang on blades, filling the air with swordsong; the sweetest sound I know, and by far the deadliest.

I gasped, sucked air, wheezed, coughed, spat mucus out of my mouth. Tried to turn back the two swords that came at me time and time again. Looked for Del, saw her engaging two flaming swords, and knew that no matter who—or what—our opponents were, living or resurrected, they also were more than a little deadly.

I never touched flesh with my sword. Not even horseflesh. I couldn't get close enough, beat off by blazing steel. And then one of them made a mistake; he came a little too close. I swung, cut, tore through, and the horse disappeared into smoke.

"Del!" I cried. "They're not real!"

"—real enough," she panted.

"Duck the swords and go for the horses. None of the mounts are real, just specters made out of smoke."

I'll give the girl this much, she does know how to listen. In a moment another was unhorsed, left to ride nothing but smoke, which left *us* with two still mounted. The men on foot approached, but now they were vulnerable.

More than that, in the end; the men on foot were falling apart.

Piece by piece, things dropped away. An arm, a head, a hand. The stink of them nearly choked me.

Two were whole, and mounted. One came for me, the other targeted Del. Whatever else they were, they weren't fazed by the behavior of their comrades. Their minds were fixed on us.

One came riding. I ducked, spun, swung back, trying to notch a hock. But the rider set the horse back on his heels and rolled left, swinging his flaming sword. I ducked, but not enough; something bathed my left arm in pain.

I don't know what I shouted. Undoubtedly something obscene. But for the moment I was one-armed, handling the sword with only one hand as well. It was made for a two-handed grip and that's what I'm accustomed to. The balance was off, *I* was off, my arm was nearly off.

I heard Del's grunt of effort, followed by an outcry. I tried to look, could not; the rider was on me again.

I slipped. Went to one knee. Tried to scrabble up, to lurch aside, but the footing was treacherous. I saw the blade swing down at my head, tried to block it with my useless left arm, heard someone scream behind me.

Hoolies, bascha, not you—

Not Del. Cipriana.

I flattened, rolled, came up in time to see her jam the end of her quarterstaff into the horse's chest, then brace the butt against the wagon to support the staff as well as she could. The horse spitted himself, bled smoke instead of blood. Then wisped into nothingness.

The rider landed, grinned, fell down, broke into pieces on the ground. The sword no longer blazed, but was dead, cold steel.

Four feet away, Del severed the last horse's throat. And then we were alone, waving off smoke, except for Cipriana.

She sucked in harsh, gasping breaths. There was blood spattered on her face, but none of it was hers. What she wore was mine.

"Cipriana." I grunted, heaved myself up, staggered over to her. "Cipriana, it's over. *Over.*" I wrenched the staff out of rigid hands. "No more need for this."

Empty hands clawed for the staff, found air, then masked her face from me. In the wagon, I heard sobbing. Not Massou's: Adara's.

It made me oddly angry. The woman cried for a daughter who had acquitted herself quite well. Better than crying, she might come outside instead and see what that daughter had done.

"Tiger." It was Del, at my side, touching a charred sleeve. "Tiger, let me see."

"What? That?" I tried to shrug the arm away, hissed and wished I hadn't. "Hoolies, bascha, what are you doing?"

"Looking," she said firmly. "Hold still—" She tore wool; her face was grim. "Well, one thing for burning swords—the wound is cauterized. About all we need to do is clean it, bandage it . . . it ought to heal well enough."

My mind was on Cipriana, still hidden behind her hands. "Cipriana, you did well. You saved my life. No sense in shutting it out."

"She'll be fine," Del said flatly. "Can we get this taken care of?"

"*I'll* be fine." I touched Cipriana's shoulder. "Bascha, it's all right—" And then I stopped short, because Del had gone quite still.

Oh, hoolies, why the slip of the tongue?

I started to say something, anything, but coughing got in the way. I bent over, braced myself against the wagon, brought up gouts of mucus. My chest was tearing apart.

Through the hacking and retching, I heard Massou say the mare was dead. Somehow it didn't surprise me. And I hurt too much to care.

"Adara," Del said quietly, "can you make him tea?"

I stopped coughing. Whispered. "No more of that stuff. I'd rather have aqivi."

Del put a hand on my brow. "You're hot."

"Best put him in the wagon." Adara's voice. "He'll be warmer in there."

"Don't need *warmth*," protested in a croak. "Bascha, can you whistle up a storm? One of those Northern snowstorms?"

"No," Del said firmly, and steered me toward the back of the wagon.

"Is he all right?" Cipriana asked, forgetting her own ordeal.

"He will be," Del remarked, "once he's had some sleep. First the cold and now a wound . . . even sandtigers need time to recover."

"Hoolies, Del—I'm *fine*."

"Your lungs roar like a bellows, you croak like you've eaten steel, your arm was carved open and burned. You are *not* fine, Tiger . . . and you'll thank us in the morning."

I knew better. But I also knew that I hurt inside and out. Shutting my teeth on curses, I crawled into the wagon and stretched out my bulk on the pallet. The interior was hardly large enough for all of me; I wondered how in hoolies Adara *and* her children managed to get any sleep.

Painfully, I turned over onto my back. Blinked dazedly at the opening with its woven cloth curtain pulled back. I saw blonde hair, blue eyes, concern. "Bascha—?"

"Maybe," Del said dryly. "Which one of us did you want?"

Silence, I decided hastily, was the better part of valor.

Chapter 14

I was in the Punja. In a hyort. Bathed in heat and sweat and stink.
I stirred. Tried to talk. A cool, callused hand touched my mouth gently, quieting my mumbles, and I subsided into silence.

I knew I had killed the sandtiger. But he had also nearly killed me. My face was alive with pain; venom ran through my veins and set my flesh afire.

But I was still alive. And now I was free as well.

I stirred. Surely the shukar would see his way clear to giving me freedom now. How could he deny it? I had killed the beast that had killed so many of us—no, not us; I am not a Salset, being merely chula—and now the tribe would have to reward me for it. They would have to, and the reward I craved was freedom.

The reward I demanded was freedom.

Gods of valhail, hounds of hoolies—would they give it to me at last?

My lips were parched; I licked them. Tried to wet them and found my mouth too dry. All of me was too dry, until a cool hand with a dampened cloth bathed my face, my neck, my chest, dipped to belly and paused. I heard an indrawn breath.

Sula?

Through closed eyes, I summoned her before me. A young Salset woman with characteristic coloring: lustrous black hair, golden skin, liquid, dark brown eyes. Sula was still unmarried but of an age to take a husband; that she hadn't yet was attributable to me. And a definite breach of custom. I was a chula, she was not; yet another reason the shukar hated me. He might have taken her for himself, although Sula herself would have denied him.

The vision-Sula wavered, faded, renewed itself. Only this time it wasn't the Sula who had given me manhood and dignity; who had argued for my freedom; who had told me to go when I had fairly won it. This time it was the Sula who had rescued Del and me from the Punja and brought us back among the living. An older, fatter Sula: broad of face, graying of hair, now a widow. But still a woman of enduring strength and courage.

Del.

And I realized I was dreaming.

"Bascha?" It came out on a broken croak.

The hand with the damp cloth spasmed against my flesh, withdrew itself hastily. "No," she said, "it's Adara."

Adara. I opened my eyes. And realized how far I'd gone in my dreams.

I was in the wagon, the little horseless wagon, stuffed full of Borderer belongings. Adara knelt next to me, though there was hardly room, and held a dampened cloth in both hands. Fingers twisted and knotted it, then smoothed it out to begin again. Bits of red hair straggled down the sides of her neck, caught in sweat against flesh. Her face was sheened with it. She wiped her brow with the back of an arm.

A handsome woman, Adara. And strong, in her own way, though a bit blind about swords and dancing. "Here," she said, "I have water."

It was tepid, tasting of goatskin bota. But I sucked it down, savoring the wetness, and felt my throat come alive again. I thanked her and pushed it away.

"I have apologies to make," she said quietly.

I raised both brows.

"I have been too harsh with the children. I have been rude to you and Del."

I drew in a deep breath. "I just figured you had your reasons."

"I do. I *did*." She sighed and shredded the cloth again. "My husband was a sword-dancer."

Part of me was surprised. Part of me wasn't at all.

Adara, avoiding my eyes, stared at rigid hands. "He came down from the North to the border, to our settlement; a strong blond giant, and my heart was lost at once. I was barely fifteen—he was older by twenty years, but somehow that didn't matter. I wanted him for my husband. But he was a man who lived by the sword, and I feared he would die by it also." Her mouth was thin and flattened, hardening the set of her jaw. "I made him give it up."

"How?"

"By giving him a choice: the woman or the circle. Kesar chose the woman."

"And you've raised your children accordingly."

"Yes." Her gaze, now raised, was unflinching. Green as my own; as a sandtiger's. "I wanted Cipriana to have a softer life than I, and I wanted Massou never to take up the sword."

"Want*ed*," I said clearly. "Now you've changed your mind?"

Adara drew in a deep, noisy breath. "What Del has said is true. I can't hide my children from life, and life is rarely kind. So I've told Massou *and* Cipriana, if she wants, to learn what they can from you and Del, because one day they may need it."

And maybe sooner than she'd like. But at least she'd give them a chance. "Water," I croaked.

Adara passed me the bota. "Your fever has broken. With sleep and food and rest, you should recover soon."

I grunted, handing back the bota. "I'll be up in the morning."

"No, probably not." Adara tucked the bota away. Her manner was oddly hesitant, yet also distinctly determined. "You and Del are—bonded?"

"Not formally." Bonding was a Border marriage custom. "Not even *in*formally, really . . . we just ride together."

"And—sleep together."

"Well, yes. *Usually*." I sighed and scratched my scars, thinking about my arm, which felt strangely numb. "At the moment, it might be difficult . . . and Del's afraid of loki."

"I am not," Adara said. Clearly and distinctly.

Thoughtfully, I looked at her. Didn't say a word.

She lifted her chin and met my gaze. "My husband was often unable, once his heart weakened. So—it has been a long time."

I knew what it had taken her to say the words. In the South, women never initiate such things; it's for the man to do. Adara was a Borderer and therefore somewhat freer, and undoubtedly a Northern husband had also contributed, but all the same it was an interesting—and courageous—proposition.

And one I didn't particularly desire, Del being more than enough.

But how in hoolies do you tell a woman no?

In the end, I didn't have to. Adara knew it instinctively. For a moment she shut her eyes, then opened them again. Color bathed her cheeks, but she wasn't humiliated. "I know," she said quietly, without excess emotion. "I am only a Borderer. A woman who bears and raises children and lives in a single place. The sun has sucked the softness from my flesh and puts spots on my face. I have no gift with weapons, and I cry when I should fight back, and I couldn't wield a sword if my life depended on it. I'm not the woman for you."

"You were the woman for Kesar."

"But I made him *change*." She hated herself for it, now.

I thought about what Del had said. How she had wondered if I wanted a softer woman, a woman with different appetites, with different needs in life. A woman like Adara. And now another woman asked the same question, although the words—and who said them—were different.

I wondered if every woman alive wanted the life she didn't live.

The life she *couldn't* live.

Hoolies, what a curse.

"I'll get Del," Adara said, and slipped quietly out of the wagon.

Del came. She leaned against the wagon and peered in at me, hair hooked behind her ears. She was beginning to lose her tan, turning creamy pale again. "So," she said, "it lives."

"More or less." My throat hurt, and my chest, but at least my head was clearing. "How long have I been asleep?"

"Off and on, for four days."

"Four days!" I frowned. "It was only a little cut, and burned closed, like you said."

"Was," she agreed. "But those were loki-touched swords, and the wound turned bad. I opened it and drained it."

I twisted my head and inspected the arm, pressing chin into shoulder. It was all wrapped up in cloth, but smelled clean enough. "Four more days lost, then."

Del shrugged. "Four more, six more . . . what does it matter? If I count each day as a notch on my funeral stick, I'll die of senseless worry."

She sounded calm enough. "But, bascha—time is running out."

"Time does that." Del leaned in, snagged the bota, unplugged it and drank deeply. "When you're fit, we'll have to portion out the food and necessary belongings, then go ahead on foot."

"Belongings?" I frowned. "We've been lugging ours along well enough. Why change now?"

"Not ours. Theirs." She shrugged. "They no longer have a horse."

I blinked. "You mean—you want the five of us to travel together?"

Del tossed the bota back. "It's been nearly six years since I came down the Traders' Road. Roadhouses and settlements move even as we move; I don't know them anymore. But I do know if we leave the Borderers here without protection, telling them help lies over the hill, they could all wind up dead."

I suppose I'd known that ever since we'd met up with them. But somehow I'd assumed we'd go on after helping them with the wagon. Now that help was pointless; without a horse to pull it, they couldn't take the wagon.

"I told them to pack up what they need, once you're out of the way," Del said. "I told them they can buy a horse at the next settlement, and another wagon, but to consider this one gone." She stroked the wooden frame. "And it will be, by the time they have another. Thieves will strip this one clean, like carrion, and use the wood for burning."

"They don't have money for a horse and wagon."

"We do." Her tone was level. "I took the coin off the borjuni."

I contemplated her expression. I knew Massou reminded her of her brother, just as Cipriana reminded me of a younger, more innocent Del. And I suppose, in the back of my mind, I hadn't ever really considered leaving them behind . . . at least, not seriously.

"What's the matter, Del?"

Her face was stark. "*I* brought them, Tiger. The loki. When I got so upset in the valley . . . remembering my family—" She shrugged, oddly vulnerable. "It's what draws them: strong emotion. If I hadn't lost control—"

"It doesn't matter," I told her. "We defeated them, didn't we? We drove the loki away."

"Maybe." She didn't sound convinced.

"And now we must deal with the Borderers." I nodded. "More delay, bascha."

"Yes," Del agreed, "but what else can we do?"

Which had also been my answer, the times *I'd* thought about it.

*F*irst, there is the circle." Del pointed at the curving line drawn
 so carefully in the turf. "And then there is the sword." She
unsheathed Boreal. "Lastly, there is the dancer." She stepped over
the line and into the circle, to stand in the very center. "This is the
sword-dancer's world."

I looked at two fierce, solemn faces. Northern faces, both,
cream-fair and smooth, unmarred by a Southron sun. They'd left
before it could bake them.

Massou and Cipriana had taken to Del's lessons with a
vengeance, sucking up everything she told them and locking it
away. For a purpose, too; Del had a habit of asking them, always
when least expected, to repeat what she had taught them. Willingly
they would: Massou so quick and eager, Cipriana more reserved.
But she remembered everything, while Massou sometimes forgot.

We had left the wagon behind and headed north on foot. My
fever was gone, my head unstuffed, most of the coughing abated,
but I felt the stiffness in my bones. Surrounded by four who were
younger than I, unappreciative of the weather, I was feeling distinctly old and generally abused.

In five days, we had developed a routine. Everyone carried his
share without complaint, up the hills and down them, winding
around the track, quietly accepting the burdens of the journey no

matter how much he wanted to speak. Adara was accustomed to hardship and adapted very well; her children, though used to having a father do things for them, nonetheless were young enough to look on it as an adventure. Massou had the boundless energy and enthusiasm of all boys his age. His sister wanted to please the adults, needing our approval.

In late afternoons, we halted, and then the lessons began.

Adara said nothing as, day by day, her children learned the arts of the dance. Much of it was ritual, not an exercise of death; Del was careful in her phrasing and cut short Massou's occasional lapses into bloodthirsty discussions. She was honest with them, answering all their questions, but she taught them to honor the dance and not glory in violence.

They had only their father's sword, and so they took turns. Del could not loan them Boreal, and I didn't extend them the opportunity to try Theron's sword. Ever since I'd stuck it in the ground, only to have that ground explode, I'd been careful to keep it away from everyone. Del had said it wasn't truly keyed, not like Boreal, but I didn't want to take a chance on injuring boy or girl.

One by one, they had their lesson. And then Massou, stepping out of the circle, looked with bright eyes to me. "Why don't *you* dance with Del?"

I was sitting on a hump of ground, observing their education. "I dance all the time with Del."

Cipriana's smile was sly. "We mean—with a *sword*."

I slanted her a baleful glance. She reddened, giggled, then drew herself up straight. Fifteen years old, was Cipriana; not a girl, but neither a woman. Caught somewhere in between, yet fighting the constraints.

Hoolies, that's *all* I needed.

Del's smile was hooked down one corner of her mouth. "Why don't you, Tiger? You could use the conditioning."

Yes, well, I could. The cold and arm wound had laid me low and I hadn't danced in too long. It was past time I put in some practice, no matter how good I was. So I sighed, heaved myself up, and pulled Theron's sword out of the sheath.

Massou's grin split his face as he spoke the traditional invitation. "Step into the circle."

"I'm going, I'm going." I went, stepping over the curving line, and saw Del's peculiar expression. "Bascha?"

It faded almost at once. "Nothing," she said, "are you ready?"

Probably not. I wore too many clothes and my joints were too stiff. The day was damp, though not rainy, but I'd found it didn't matter. My bones hated the North.

"Spar or dance?" I asked. There is a decided difference.

"Spar," she said. "I don't think you're up to dancing."

The turf was damp but not slick, knotted with sprigs and tufts that offered better footing. Northern boots helped; I'd have slipped easily in my sandals. "Then let's get to it, bascha."

I'll admit it, I was lazy. Lazy and out of shape. Sword-dancing requires daily physical and mental work, and I'd done neither lately. So when Del came at me, supple and strong, I wasn't ready for her.

Two quick engagements, and she'd forced me out of the circle.

Massou's eyes were huge. "Oh, *Tiger!*"

Hoolies, you'd think he'd bet money on me! Cipriana said nothing at all.

"We're sparring," I pointed out. "Practice isn't for real."

Del was instantly ablaze with indignation. "Have you heard nothing I've said?" she asked. "Have you sat here for five days listening to me tell my *ishtoya* how to honor the rituals of the circle, and then ignore them yourself?"

I cleared my throat. "Del—"

"How can you claim yourself a sword-dancer if you don't take it seriously?" Her hostility was inspiring. "How can you dishonor your *an-kaidin* so easily?"

"Shodo," I said coolly. "In the South, the master's a shodo."

"Shodo, *kaidin, an-kaidin*—do you think I care for names?" She stepped to the edge of the circle. "I care about living and dying, Tiger, and how to uphold the honor of my *an-kaidin*."

"The same *an-kaidin* you killed."

It stopped her cold, of course; I'd expected it to. Color washed out of her face so fast I thought she might faint. But she held her ground, staring rigidly, though I think she was blind to me.

Massou was open-mouthed, Cipriana pale. Neither said a word.

"Yes," she said finally, "but at least he was worth the dance."

That did it. With pointed deliberation, I stepped over the muddy line and back into the circle. "Fine," I said, "let's do it."

No more sparring. We danced, Delilah and I. On a damp, turf-soaked hillside in the downlands of the North. I forgot the children watched. I forgot Adara watched. I forgot I was out of shape. I remembered only the habits I'd been taught so long ago.

Swordsong filled the campsite, the clash and clangor of mag-icked steel. Del didn't key and I couldn't, so the blades remained unlit, but silver was more than enough. It threw up a blinding curtain in the setting of the sun.

Beneath the noise of the swords was a contrapuntal sound. I wheezed a little, sucking in air, and Del muttered to herself. It was a constant racket from both: gasps, grunts, in- and exhalations, the low-voiced undertone of the woman.

As the dance progressed, Del's noise gained volume. And I realized she wasn't really muttering, instead she was *instructing*. She was commenting on my style, on my techniques, grudgingly approving or broadly disapproving.

"What in hoolies—" I gasped, "—are you doing?"

"You're slow . . . you're *slow* . . . your style is too sluggish—"

"Hoolies, woman—I've been *sick*—"

"And you could be *dead*—"

Step, skip, jump.

"—I thought this was only *practice*—"

"—it is—"

"—I thought we were only sparring—"

"—we are—"

Feint, slash, withdraw.

"—you never did this before—"

"—you never needed it, Tiger—"

"—and now I do?—"

"—you do. You've gotten sloppy, Tiger."

Sloppy. *Sloppy.*

Take *this* for sloppy, bascha.

"—better, Tiger—better—"

And this, *too.*

"—*much* better, Tiger. Don't stop now—"

Hoolies, the woman would kill me. And it would have nothing to do with her sword.

"—if you hadn't unleashed that banshee-storm, I'd never have *gotten* sick—"

Duck, skip, twist.

"—oh, I see—we're going to blame *me* for this—"

"—if it weren't so thrice-cursed *cold*—"

"—this is not cold, Tiger—"

Boreal kissed my throat.

"—hoolies, Del, that's *close*—"

"—and I shouldn't have gotten through . . . blame only yourself, Tiger—"

Blame *this*, bascha.

Except I missed. And Del, as usual, didn't.

Ah, hoolies . . . it hurt.

"Tiger?" Del knelt in boot-torn turf as I slowly sat up. "Tiger—is it bad?"

Carefully, I felt the slice on my jaw. Not a lot of blood. Mostly injured pride. "My arm hurts worse." Grudgingly admitting I was fine.

Del's brow smoothed. "I *said* you were too slow."

"Too slow, too stiff, too old." I turned my head, spat; the dance had dug deep in my chest.

Something flickered in blue eyes. Something akin to realization and apprehension. "Do you want to go back, then?"

"Yes." It *was* apprehension; I saw it. "But not until we're done."

Her tone was uneven. "Done with what?"

"With whatever you have to do."

Relief was a tangible thing, though she fought hard to hide it. "I'm sorry. I was angry. I forgot about your arm."

I stood up slowly, feeling my chest. "Maybe it's what I needed."

Del stood too, turning to face her students. "I was wrong," she told them plainly. "I was angry. Anger is bad in the circle."

Massou's face was pale. "Could you have killed him?"

"Yes," Del answered honestly, "or Tiger could have killed me."

Well, it was nice of her to say so.

"Could you?" Cipriana obviously missed nothing.

I bent down and retrieved the sword. "Not today," I told her. "Probably not tomorrow. But maybe the day after that . . . if I live long enough."

Within two days, I'd joined the lessons as well. I felt the better for it, even if Del did occasionally forget that I pretty much knew everything she was teaching. Admittedly our styles are very different, having come from different cultures, but there isn't a whole lot she knows that I don't. (Or, to be fair, the other way around.) At any rate, it was good conditioning and I needed it.

Adara did not trouble me again with any manner of pursuit. I was a little surprised; didn't she think I was worth it? And didn't a woman expect a man to pursue *her* even if at first she says no?

Except when I thought about it, I realized it might be a bit difficult. Loki or no loki, Del was always present. It would make any sort of assignation downright impossible.

Although, I reflected, once I'd have tried it regardless.

Just for the hoolies of it.

Cipriana came around more and more. Quietly, she asked me to tell her stories. Real stories, she said, tales of victories in the circle. And so, in the evenings, as we sat around the fire, I fell into the habit of reciting things that had happened before, being very careful not to elaborate. Embellishment has its place, as Bellin the Cat would surely agree, but I felt it best not to make me sound *too* invincible; Massou and Cipriana might believe me and try to equal my feats.

And, eventually, I worked my way around to Del. Who looked back at me gravely and did nothing at all to help out.

"These are *your* stories, too," I pointed out. "Don't you tell tales in the North?"

"The trueborn *skjald* is most honored among our people."

"Then—?"

"I am not a *skjald*."

I scratched my claw-marked cheek in a bid for patience. "No, maybe not, but you can at least hold up your end of the history."

"Now you're speaking of *skjelps*."

"What?"

She didn't smile. "*Skjelps* are historians. *Skjalds* are storytellers."

Hoolies, here we go. "And there's a difference."

"Much like there's a difference between loki and afreet."

"Loki?" Massou, of course, perked up. "What about loki?"

"What about afreets?" Cipriana asked.

Del grinned pointedly at me.

I sighed. "Afreets are Southron demons. Playful demons. They can't really hurt you, they just bother you."

"Loki can." Massou was solemn, but curiosity lighted his eyes. "Loki can *kill* people."

Cipriana nodded. "Loki are evil demons."

Adara, silent up till now, added her encouraging comment. "Kesar used to speak of how, in the far north, loki would prey on entire settlements."

And here I'd expected her to admonish her children for speaking nonsense. "Huh." Disgusted, I had nothing else to offer.

"It was loki who put those chopped up raiders back together." Massou's description, I thought, was just a tad bit too happily gruesome, if eloquently accurate.

"And loki who made horses out of smoke." Cipriana's eyes were black in the light of the fire. She had said nothing of her feat with the quarterstaff, locking it all away. "I know how they gain possession."

"Cipriana." Her mother, quietly.

"Well, I do. I've heard all the stories." Pale hair tumbled over her shoulders. In poor light, she was Del; or Del an older Cipriana. "They bed with men and women."

Massou made a garbled sound of disgust and disbelief.

"They *do*," his sister insisted. "They make more loki that way."

Adara's voice sharpened. "Cipriana, enough. You'll give your brother nightmares."

I didn't think so. Neither did he.

Massou's eyes were huge. "You mean—like puppies and kittens?"

I had an odd, brief vision: a river of demon puppies and devil kittens. I had to smother a laugh. Massou was serious; too often we laugh at children.

"Loki exist," Del said quietly. "But if we're careful, they won't hurt us."

"And anyway, you can beat them." Massou's faith was matter-of-fact. "Didn't you beat them before?"

"I *helped*," his sister said.

Adara rose. "Time for bed."

Naturally, they protested. And naturally, she won. Massou and Cipriana retired to dream their dreams of loki, while Del sent me a level look across the fire as Adara went into the shadows to tend to personal needs.

"You are a fool," she said.

I rose, popping knotted muscles. "So you've said before." I stretched luxuriously, making appropriate sounds. "*I* think it's just a handy excuse to keep me out of your bed."

Del smiled blandly. "I'm sure Adara would be happy to let you in hers."

Hoolies. Can't keep anything from women.

I fingered the scabbed sword cut on my jaw. "I'm going to bed," I remarked, "with you or without you."

"Without," she said succinctly.

I paused. "You all right?"

"Just thinking, Tiger."

"Then you're *not* all right." A heavy-handed attempt at humor. Even I thought it was poor.

"Go to bed," Del suggested.

I did, and dreamed of loki.

Chapter 16

Having displayed intense interest in the circle and in sword-dancing for well over a week, Massou and Cipriana now lost it entirely. And almost overnight; both adamantly refused to enter the circle.

We couldn't exactly *make* them. It was their free choice, and now they exercised it. But it did seem odd, until Del suggested an explanation. "They've all caught your cold. They don't feel like doing *anything*."

We sat facing one another on a goathair blanket, cleaning and honing our blades. The chore was second nature and one we both enjoyed. It was early evening and, of course, cool; Del and I both wore wool and soft leather.

"What do you mean?" I glanced over Del's left shoulder toward Adara and her children, who spoke quietly among themselves.

"They've been sniffing for two days, and just now are beginning to cough."

It was true. All three of them had been very quiet lately, if not downright depressed. If they were feeling anything like *I* had, I didn't blame them a bit for refusing to step into the circle.

"Well, then forget about the lessons. They don't really need them anyway; neither will be a sword-dancer."

It didn't sit well with Del. I doubted she had sincerely believed either of them would want to seriously apprentice, to assume the life she led, but I knew it was difficult for her to lose her two *ish-toya*. The lessons had taken her mind off the time she could not afford to lose, yet continued passing too swiftly.

Her voice was soft. "Massou could be good."

Mine was not. "Massou is too young to know *what* he wants, bascha. He just reminds you of Jamail."

Del continued to clean her blade, but I could see the tension in her shoulders. "And what about Cipriana?"

"What *about* Cipriana?"

"You refused the mother. Are you waiting for the daughter?"

I didn't even smile. "No. I'm waiting for you."

She looked up from the weapon. "I've *told* you—"

"You've told me about the loki," I said quietly. "I don't know that I *dis*believe you, after all that's happened, but I think you're going too far. It's been three weeks since I broke the circle—two since we fought those resurrected raiders. Do you plan to stay celibate forever, just in case?"

"You don't know what they can do—"

"I know what they *have* done."

Del's face was tight. "Then get it somewhere else!" She fought to keep her voice from carrying to the others. "Adara would take you. So would Cipriana."

Something occurred to me. "Are you jealous?"

"No. Why would I be?" Her voice now was cool and steady; Del had recovered herself. "We've made no vows to bind us. And even if we did, you'd do what you wanted to do. Vows would never stop you."

I stopped inspecting my Northern sword. "Are you saying I'd be unfaithful?"

Pale brows arched. "Well? Wouldn't you?"

Would I? Could I? Oh, hoolies, it wasn't worth contemplating. "Maybe if a woman didn't invent so many excuses not to sleep with a man, he wouldn't look for other bedmates."

Del's tone was decidedly frigid. "That isn't the issue, Tiger."

Well, no, but I wished it was. It was easier than the other. "I don't want to sleep with Adara, and Cipriana's too young."

"She's the same age I was when Ajani took me. The same age as her mother when Adara bore a daughter." Del tossed hair behind shoulders. "Don't disregard affection because the giver seems too young."

"Bascha—"

Del didn't avoid my gaze. "She reminds me of me. She reminds *you* of me . . . or maybe the me I'd be if Ajani had never happened."

It was true there were similarities. It was true they were much alike in body as well as in spirit. But I had never quite made the connection.

Thoughtfully, I tapped a nail on the edge of Theron's blade. "Maybe we're both fools, Del . . . looking for something that isn't there."

"Me for my brother—"

"—and me for an unspoiled Del?"

She nodded, looking away. "I know he's not Jamail, but it's hard not to pretend."

"But I don't think you're *spoiled*."

"No. Maybe not. But don't you ever wonder what I'd be like without this sword?"

Del without that sword was like the South without the sun. "No," I said truthfully. "Because if you didn't have it, I'd be dead ten times over."

Slowly, Del smiled, though it was crooked on her face. "Typical Tiger," she remarked, "thinking of his neck."

"And other portions of my body."

"As well as portions of *mine*."

Well, yes. Of course. Why should I deny it?

Del sheathed Boreal, shutting away the sheen of rune-worked steel. "Since I have lost the others, will you be my *ishtoya*?"

It *would* pass the time. "So long as you remember who I am."

She snorted indelicately. "How could I ever forget?"

I decided it might be best if I said nothing at all.

*   *   *

Next day, thank valhail, thick clouds parted and sunlight slanted through, setting the world ablaze: gold and silver-gilt. Dew burned off, mist shredded, dampness trickled away.

I hadn't seen normal light for days and was irritable because of it. It just isn't natural to be so hemmed in by mountains and trees, not to mention oppressed by clouds so arrogant they clutter the mountaintops. I was sick of turf and sedge; blush-pink flowers and purple heather; gray-smudged, slate-blue days. I wanted sun and sand, and the heat of a Southron desert.

We climbed down out of the clouds into a lush, rich valley thick with grass and vegetation. It was a small place rimmed with up-thrust mountains all tumbled together like oracle bones. At the far end lay a twisting defile, bluish black in raisin purple: narrow entryway from the north. Through the center of the valley cut Traders' Road, winding down from where we were.

Massou and Cipriana, shouting aloud, hurried down the track. They were oblivious to twisting turns and wagon ruts, too excited to slow their headlong pace. Adara started to call them back but in the end didn't, as if she as well as her children wanted company. It had been a long two weeks with only the five of us.

The encampment was large and sprawling, spreading from cradling mountainsides to the center of the valley where it huddled in clusters along the road. But it wasn't a permanent settlement, looking more like a caravan camp.

Del agreed with me. "They're uplanders," she explained, "come down from the Heights for a while. They do it twice a year, once in fall and once in spring." Her face and eyes were alight and a spring had entered her step. "They're good people, Tiger . . . generous and friendly. It will be good to see them again."

"Do you know them?"

"Not all of them, no . . . maybe none of them. But that seems unlikely. Everybody gathers. In Northern, it's called a *kymri*."

"*Every* uplander comes down?"

"No, not every. Mostly just those who are *landlopers*."

This was getting to be too much. "Who?"

"*Landlopers.* Wanderers. Those who put down no roots."

"Oh. Nomads."

Adara nodded. "Kesar told me about them. He was an uplander himself, though not a *landloper.* He always said I would enjoy attending a *kymri.*" Her face was solemn. "Now we have come to one, and Kesar isn't here." She watched her children run out onto the floor of the little valley. Already others were coming out from wagons to greet the newcomers. Her eyes were strangely blank. "Kesar isn't here."

Down below, Cipriana and Massou were swallowed by gathering *landlopers.*

Del sighed happily. "They'll have food and drink in abundance."

I brightened. "Aqivi?"

She grinned. "No. Something called *amnit.*"

"*Amnit?*"

"Even the Sandtiger might find it too strong."

"Hunh. The liquor too strong for the Sandtiger hasn't been made yet."

"Maybe." Del just kept on grinning.

It was good to see her happy. "Willing to wager on it?"

"Save your coin, Tiger. You'll need it for other things."

I sighed in resignation. "More clothing, I suppose."

"No. Supplies, yes, such as food and drink and horses, but also *other* things." Her eyes were filled with anticipation. "Many other wagers."

"Oh?"

"Oh, yes. Uplanders love to wager. Uplanders love the sword-dance." She cast me a bright-eyed glance. "Here they admire a woman with courage; we can't trick them into wagering everything on only you as we have in the past with Southroners. Here the dances will be clean, and so will the wagers."

I thought back on all the circles we had entered on our way to this little valley. "Is this why you've been hammering at me so much? All this 'be a sword, become a sword' nonsense, as if I were Massou or Cipriana?" My tone was dry. "I *do* know how to dance, Del . . . it wasn't necessary."

All the animation spilled away. The light was gone from her eyes. "I wish it hadn't been."

"You will leave us here." Adara said flatly.

Both of us looked at her. Since catching my cold she had been listless and withdrawn, although she hadn't been as sick. Nor had Massou and Cipriana. They coughed and sneezed a couple of days, slept poorly, but by and large they got off considerably easier than I.

(Just goes to show you how much *all* of me hates the North.)

Del isn't the most tactful person I've ever met. "Yes," she said. "You knew that. We agreed to bring you to help. The *landlopers* will have horses and wagons for sale—here, *everything* is for sale—and you can go on your way again." Perhaps she realized how brusque her words sounded, for she softened her tone a little. "There is no need to worry about repayment, or how you will afford so much. Tiger and I have coin, and what we spend on you can be won back in the circle."

Adara shivered. "Circle," she said dully. "The *world* is a circle, and we are trapped in it."

Del and I exchanged glances. We had been delayed long enough traveling with the Borderers, and could spare no more time. We had no choice but to buy mounts and supplies and head into the uplands as quickly as possible, regardless of what Adara or her children might prefer. Del's time was running out.

"We'll help you all we can," I told her lamely, and was rewarded with a blank stare.

It didn't take me long to discover I was at a distinct disadvantage. We had left the South and the border behind, entering another world entirely, where people spoke purer Northern without the influence of Southron words. I'd learned a lot from Del over the months and being around the Borderers had expanded my grasp of phrases, but here it was different. Here I was a stranger who spoke only bastard Northern.

I was astonished at the mass of yellow heads. Not everyone was blond, but neither was anyone really dark, except for me. With my brown hair and dark skin, not to mention green eyes in place of blue, I stuck out like a broken toe.

Del was in her element. As they had with Massou and Cipriana, people came out to greet us. Children chattered, men called greetings, women asked questions of us. Except I didn't know what they said or what they asked, being deaf to the twisty tongue.

All was mass confusion. Wagons clustered together or straggled away, horses were staked out or contained in makeshift pens, dogs ran free throughout the encampment and so did unpenned fowl. Men sat around fires and drank and talked, or huddled over wagers, or displayed wrestling and fighting skills. Women gathered at wagons to chatter and cook and sew, or watched their men showing off. The children were never still.

Del strode easily through the throng. "There will be many *kymri*-bonds."

"What?"

She smiled. "In the uplands, *landlopers* don't generally gather together very much except for a *kymri*. All the boys who long for girls and the girls who long for boys often have no one—or few— to choose from. And so *kymris* are always welcome, and the children who come from them."

I grimaced. "That explains why there are so many of them, I suppose."

She laughed aloud. "Do you dislike children, Tiger?"

"No. I was one myself, once. But I prefer them in small amounts."

Adara's hair was falling down. It straggled around neck and shoulders, spilling into her eyes. She shifted her bundle from arm to arm. "When can we stop? I need rest, food, water."

Del glanced around, then nodded, turning off the track. "Here," she said, halting by a wagon where others gathered as well. "Cheese, *amnit*, bread . . . later we can buy meat."

The man at the tailgate said something about food in Northern. I gathered it was his wagon, the contents his to sell. He was tall, fair-haired, blue-eyed; typical Northerner.

Adara dropped her bundle and scooped ruddy hair out of her weary face. "I must find my children."

"They'll be fine," Del said firmly. "Here there is no danger—

landlopers are friendly people. Let Massou and Cipriana make friends . . . they have been too long without them." She accepted a bota from the man, pressed it into Adara's hands. "Drink. Rest. You have done well without your husband; you should be proud of yourself."

Adara clutched the bota. "I am so alone . . . and so very tired."

Del's face softened. "Go and sit down," she said. "You have earned your rest."

The Borderer, still clutching her goatskin bota, gathered up her bundle once more and made her way out of the crowd. Men watched her as she went. I thought, watching them, she would not be long alone if she wanted company.

"Here." Del slapped a bota against my chest. "*Amnit*, Tiger— enough to quench your craving."

I sniffed the stopper. The aroma was very pungent. "Where do you want us, then? Any particular place?"

Del's smile was for herself. "I think I'll be able to find you. You sort of stick out here."

So I did. Glumly, I made my way back through the people and found Adara off to the side, hunched on the grass by her bundle. She still hadn't touched the water. Tears stood in her eyes.

I dumped my burden, sat down, leaned against it with a grunt of satisfaction. Unstoppered the bota and sucked in my first taste of Northern *amnit*.

My throat shut, my eyes watered, coughs exploded from my mouth. Del came by and smiled, munching on some cheese. "Welcome to the *kymri*."

I recovered as best I could, sucked in another squirt. This one went down better, and I was able to smile right back.

And then I stopped smiling, because I heard a sound I knew. An angry, high-pitched screaming that cut right through the crowd.

But it wasn't a human screaming. It came from a horse's mouth.

"Hoolies," I said, "it's the stud."

Chapter 17

el frowned. "Are you sure?"

"Do you think I don't know my own horse?" I was up before she could answer, following the sound.

In the end, it wasn't hard to find him. He was surrounded by a large circle of men, all gathered to view the storm. I heard the sound of coin exchanging hands, snatches of Northern I knew—all dealing with wagering—and the raised voice of a man calling for volunteers to try a ride. For a price, of course.

So, the old man was being difficult.

And there might be profit in it.

He stood in the center of the human circle, much as I did each time I entered the circle to dance. He was angry but unharmed, apparently in good health and none the worse for his disappearance. His legs looked sound, his weight was normal, his conditioning apparently unaffected. The shouting man held the reins to a headstall I didn't recognize, and the saddle was strange as well, but that was because, in fleeing Del's banshee-storm, the stud had also fled his tack. We had left it behind because we didn't want to carry it on foot.

The stud's latest victim was getting up from the ground. Blood flowed from a split lip and broken nose. He wobbled a little when he walked.

Can't say as I was displeased.

I threaded my way through the gathered men until I stood on the edges of the circle, not so far from the stud. His ears were pinned back in warning and he promised violence with back hooves. His handler, I saw, stood close enough to his head to keep him contained, but far enough to avoid a slashing foreleg.

Del slipped in next to me. "Well," she said dryly. "I see he's up to his old tricks."

I elbowed her in warning, then bent my head casually as she glared. Softly, I suggested, "Let's be quiet a moment, shall we?"

"Tiger—"

I laughed as if she had said something funny, then added quietly, "Let's just see how far this goes . . . and how much money is wagered."

Del shut her eyes. "I should have known."

I bent a little closer to her ear, watching those around us to make certain no one could hear. "He's not hurt. And he's *winning* . . . there's nothing wrong with a little educated entertainment."

Del smiled sweetly, muttering sardonically through clenched teeth as she looked at me in feigned amusement. "Besides, it's not like we haven't done similar things before. *Is* it?"

A shout went up. Another mark had fallen for the bait. Big, tall, blond man, looking much like all the others. He stepped forward, grinned and made comments to his noisy friends, swaggered into the circle, and said something about being willing to tame the horse.

Tame the horse. Fat chance.

The stud's handler rattled off a few things in Northern, which prompted me to ask Del for a translation.

"He says the rider has to put up a share toward the purse. If he rides the stud, he gets it all. If not, he forfeits the entry fee."

"Seems simple enough . . . unless you know the stud."

Del slanted me a glance. "If anyone here tumbles to the knowledge that you know this horse so well, I can't answer for the reaction. And I can't promise you'll survive the drubbing."

I shrugged, grinning. "That's the risk in any scam, bascha. And besides, we've faced it before."

"That was in the South."

"Oh, I see. In the North you want *them* to win."

"Let's just say I don't want to see you get your *gehetties* ripped off by an angry Northerner."

"Not a chance, bascha."

Del grunted. I watched the Northerner attempt to mount the stud.

He was, of course, doing it all wrong. Having witnessed the other disasters, he was taking his time. He grasped the reins in one hand. Put foot in stirrup, then rose. Hung there a long moment with all his substantial weight slung on one side, waiting for the stud to explode; when he didn't, the Northerner swung his right leg over the saddle and plopped himself down on top of the stud. He was big and ungainly, and supremely blind to the intelligence of the animal he bestrode.

Not to mention the determination.

"Maybe three hops," Del predicted.

"Not even two, bascha."

It took all of half a hop.

The stud is not a particularly large horse. Neither is he a particularly *attractive* horse, being a typical desert mount: medium-sized, medium-boned, heavy of head and deep of chest. His eyes are spaced too wide for good looks, but it's because there's a brain in there. He's compact, not leggy or long-bodied; he wasn't born to race. He's not muscle-bound, but what's there is tightly coiled, explosive in strength and style. He's plain old medium brown with smudgy dark points on all four legs and a straggly black tail. His mane I always clipped; now it stood straight up in spikes as high as the span of a man's hand. And his coat, ordinarily smooth and sleek, was putting on length and volume.

I frowned. "He's all fuzzy."

Del nodded. "He's growing winter hair."

"He never did before."

"Down South, who needs to? But he's North, now, Tiger. You wear wool and leather, he'll grow hair."

Yet another reason, I thought glumly, to go home as soon as we could.

The handler was shouting again. I asked for another translation.

"He says the horse is getting tired."

"No, he's not. He's hardly even winded."

Del sighed. "Do you want me to translate, or not?"

I bit back a retort. "Go on."

"He says that because the horse is getting tired, he'll only accept one more rider. But that if he wins, he wins it all—he'll also win the stud."

"What?"

"The stud is part of the winnings."

Suddenly I became less interested in seeing some stupid lug of a Northerner get dumped on his head than in claiming my horse. "Put some money on me, Del. Let's clean everybody's pockets."

"Tiger—"

But it was too late. I stripped off my harness, handed it to Del, went to stand in the center of the circle while announcing I wanted to ride.

The stud rolled a dark eye in my direction. Stared at me a long moment, during which he flicked black-tipped ears up and down. Then he pinned them again. Bared large, yellowed teeth. Cocked a powerful hind leg and begged me to come close enough.

I just smiled.

The handler was a middle-aged blond man who showed years of experience with horses in old bite scars on bare forearms. His legs were bowed—one was decidedly crooked—and he wasn't much intimidated by the stud's bad manners. He just stood there and held the headstall, absently avoiding a nip, and asked if I was sure I wanted to risk my Southron neck.

I told him yes, in Northern, then asked him why he was willing to put up the horse as a prize in addition to the purse, of which he would get a cut.

He jabbed the stud's reaching lip with a practiced finger. "Too much trouble," he said in accented Borderer speech, mixing Northern and Southron easily. "I'm horse-master, not *beast*-master—I want to sell clean, unbitten horseflesh. This one has tried to mount every mare in my string, broke the left leg of my best horseboy,

nearly crippled the stud I *do* like." He grinned, assessing me to see
if he thought I could ride the stud. "I want to be rid of this one, but
only at a profit."

"Why did you buy him, then?"

"Didn't. This one came down out of the hills and right into
my camp. Looking for mares, I'd bet. Doesn't seem to mind a bit
and bridle, but won't let anyone on his back for more than a
jump or two."

I nodded, showing the stud false respect for the Northerner's
benefit. "How long does a man have to stay on in order to win?"

The horse-master jabbed a thumb toward a boy standing
nearby. "See the sandglass in his hands? When you mount, he'll
turn it upside down. Ride till the sand's run out, and the horse—
and the purse—is yours." His tone belied a decided lack of confidence in my abilities.

"And if I come off before the sand's run out?" With the stud, it
was always possible; I am not a fool to swear I can win every time.

The Northerner shrugged. "This one's no good to me the way
he is, and no one will buy a horse that can't be ridden. He's too
small for Northern tastes, so no one'd want to use him for stud."
He shrugged again. "Doesn't leave much, so I'll give him to the
landlopers."

I frowned. "But you just said no one wants him."

The horse-master grinned. "In the South, you eat goat and
sheep and dog. Here, *landlopers* like the taste of horseflesh. I'd hate
to see this one butchered, but if he can't fill my purse at least he'll
fill a few bellies."

It took all I had not to plant a fist in his face where he stood.
"I'll win," I said flatly. "If I don't, you can butcher *me.*"

The Northerner told me the price of the ride, took it as I handed
it over, gave me the reins. "I like my meat rare. Your hide's too
charred for me."

I heard him calling out the stakes as I turned my attention to
the stud. The bay horse was staring back at me in plain, pointed
challenge. He had just spent part of the day dumping men off his
back, and that the next one was *me* appeared to make no differ-

ence to him. He knew what was expected of him and intended to deliver.

Del's warning rang true in my ears. If all the bettors *did* tumble to the truth about my relationship with the stud, they'd be in their rights to beat the hoolies out of me. So it was important that I not treat the stud any differently, or try to suborn him into complaisance.

Therefore, all I had to do was make him do his best to throw me, then manage to stay on.

"Hoolies," I muttered, "I wish this were a sword-dance." The stud flickered an ear.

I sucked in a deep breath, caught a handful of reins and mane, swung myself aboard without benefit of the stirrup. It placed me square in the saddle before the stud could blink, feet hooked into stirrups. I took as deep a seat as I could.

Now, it was *possible* he might decide his fighting days were over, at least for the moment. It was possible he might recall precisely who I was and surprise me by accepting me easily. In which case the game was decidedly up and they'd probably butcher *me* in addition to the stud.

So I planted booted heels deep into his flanks and dug in for all I was worth.

The stud blew up like a deadly simoom, all hooves and teeth and noise.

Well, the first part of my plan was working. Now all I had to do was stay aboard while the sand ran out of the glass.

I was dimly aware of shouting and laughing. Dimly aware of staring eyes and open mouths. Even more dimly aware of the human circle falling back, back, away . . . giving the stud room to work. But I was *quite* aware of the immediacy of the threat; the stud was doing his best to unhorse me as violently as possible.

"—stupid son of a Salset goat—"

—hop—hop—leap—

"—do you *want* to be butchered—?"

—plunge—buck—twist—

"—do you want to remove any chance I might ever sire a child—?"

—lunge—buck—stomp—
"—ought to make *you* a gelding—"
spin—spin—twist—
"—you arrogant son of a—"
—BUCK—

I was, of course, tossed forward. Collided with his head. Got smashed back into the saddle, where I was whipped from side to side. All I wanted was to get *off*—

So the stud helped me out.

When you're thrown from the back of a horse, sometimes you don't know which end is up. All you know is somehow you have become separated from your mount, through misfortune or violence, and are now hanging, however briefly, somewhere in the air. Right side up, upside down—you never really *know*.

That is, until you land.

I landed.

Thinking, *—stupid son of a Salset goat, now they're going to* eat *you—*

And then I stopped thinking entirely, because the stud was standing by my head nosing my blood-smeared face.

Hoolies, all it would take is one stomp of an iron-shod hoof, and my dancing days were done.

Any days were done.

Nostrils bloomed large in my face. Hot horse breath crusted the film of blood by my nose. He sucked air, then snorted noisily, spraying dampness all over my face.

I sat upright, cursing, trying to wipe blood and mucus from my face. In the end someone handed me a damp rag, which helped. The horse-master caught the stud and led him over to me as I climbed all the way up to my feet.

I looked at the innocent dark eyes and the quivering of whiskers. "Let me buy him from you," I said. "He may have won the battle, but I'd hate to see him butchered."

The Northerner grinned as I mopped my face. "Now, if I was a dishonest man, I'd agree and take your money. But I'm not." He handed over the reins. "He may have tossed you off, but he did it *after* the sand ran out." I stood there with the reins in right hand as the horse-master plopped a leather pouch into the left. "I've taken my share out," he said. "The rest of it is yours." He eyed the stud askance. "He'll kill you before winter's done."

"Or we'll kill each other." I turned, made my way through the crowd of onlookers, now clamoring for wagers won or lost, took the stud to Del.

She stood cradling harness and sword. Nodded a little. Took the rag from my hand and reached up to wipe away blood. "Not too bad," she said, "but you cut it a little close. One hop earlier and you'd have lost him *and* the purse."

"Earlier, later . . . didn't matter, bascha. He wasn't paying attention to anything I said or did."

Del patted the stud's big jaw. "Not a bad day's work. You won a purse and won a horse . . . now we only need to buy a mount for me."

And a belligerent voice asked, "What about for *me?*"

Del swung around. "Massou," she said, surprised. Then, with infinite gentleness, "Massou, you'll go on with Cipriana and your mother."

His face was defiant. "I want to go with *you.*"

"You can't," she told him. "Tiger and I must go on into the uplands, far beyond Reiver's Pass. You'll go on to Kisiri with your mother and sister."

"I don't want to."

"Massou—"

"I don't *want* to."

The stud reached out and bit him.

Chapter 18

*I*t wasn't really *bad*. Not much more than a nip. The stud simply reached out, caught the top of Massou's right shoulder and bit.

Del shouted. I swore. Massou screamed. And then punched the stud as hard as he could smack on the end of his nose.

This reaction, of course, didn't particularly please the stud, who—understandably startled—shied back violently and snapped reins taut; this reaction subsequently snapped my *arm* taut. (Hoolies, the impact nearly dislocated my elbow.) I stumbled back as the stud retreated, caught my balance with awkward effort, hung on to the reins and cursed him all the while.

The Northern horse-master, passing by, thought it was very funny.

Del, meanwhile, was trying to examine Massou's shoulder, but Massou wasn't having any of it. He cried, but silently, and the tears were from anger, not from pain or fright. His face was blotchy red. Blue eyes blazed with rage. Both hands were clenched in fists as he pulled away from Del, advancing on the stud.

Who, of course, retreated. Since he was attached to me by virtue of the reins (and I had no intention of letting go), I also retreated. It didn't much please me to be caught in the middle of an argument between an animal who outweighed me considerably and a boy who barely came up to my waist. It was, I felt, lacking in dignity.

"Enough," I said testily. "I know he bit you, Massou, and I'm sorry, but if you try to punch him again you might get hurt worse."

Massou spat out something angrily in indecipherable Northern, then turned on his heel and ran. Which left me facing Del.

Warily, I waited.

"I suppose it is too much," she began very quietly, "to expect the horse to have manners better than the man's."

Hoolies. She *was* blaming me. "Oh, Del—come on . . . how was I to know he'd take such a disliking to the boy? He never warns me about these things. He just *does* them."

Because she was so calm, the anger was emphasized. "Perhaps we might have been better off if you had *lost* the contest."

"Oh, no," I answered instantly. "If I'd *lost*, the stud would be someone's dinner."

Arched brows and pursed mouth told me that was precisely what she'd meant.

I scowled back as the stud pushed muzzle against spine. "Come *on*, Del—"

She cut me off easily. "I'm going to go see how Massou is. I don't think the bite was bad, but still—"

I waved a hand. "I know," I said, "I *know*. No need to say it, bascha."

"*Somebody* has to." She dumped harness and sheathed sword into my arms and slanted a black look at the stud. "Just keep an eye on your horse."

I sighed deeply as I watched her walk away, pushing the stud's nibbling lips away from a harness strap. "*Now* you've gone and done it."

The stud chose not to answer.

Someone stopped beside me. "I'd rather keep an eye on *her*."

It took me a moment to realize he was responding to Del's parting comment. Which meant he'd overheard. But since we hadn't been speaking loudly, it meant he'd done more than merely overhear. It meant he'd been *listening*.

I looked. He was young, male, arrogant, sure of his strength and appeal. The kind of man I hate for a variety of reasons.

He cast me a slanting sideways glance out of pale blue eyes, waiting for my response. Instead, I stared him down.

It amused him. He smiled. The smile was for himself, but directed squarely at me. "Ah," he said with irony, "the Southroner doesn't speak Northern."

He used Borderer speech, not the pure upland dialect, which meant he intended me to understand him. Which meant he was *looking* for trouble.

Inwardly I sighed (I wasn't really in the mood), then mimicked his own smile pleasantly, complete with curled lip. "Only when I choose to . . . or when the company's worth it."

The Northerner's smile froze, flickered, then stretched wide, as pale eyes narrowed appraisingly. I've seen the look before; he wanted to judge my worth before initiating hostilities. "Southron—"

"Save it," I said briefly. "If you want to fight, we'll fight, but we'll do it in a circle instead of here with words. Insults waste my time, and you're too young to be any good."

He stared back in shock. He was fairer even than Del, which made his hair almost white, and his eyes were the palest, iciest blue I had ever seen, fringed with equally frosty lashes. On one hand, it was incongruous; it gave him the look of youth as yet untested, when obviously he had been. On the other hand, it lent him a transparency that was almost other-worldly.

Of course, the jagged scar across his upper lip did diminish the innocence of his features. It looked like a knife had cut it, and done a long time ago.

He looked at the tangle of leather in my hands. He looked at the sheath and hilt. White brows lifted. "Sword-dancer?"

"Sword-dancer," I agreed. "Do you wish to enter a circle?"

Lids flickered. Pale lashes screened pale eyes. After a moment he spread his hands, smiling to show innocent intent. "I have no sword. My weapon is the knife."

I shrugged, clicking my tongue. "Well, that is too bad. I guess we'll have to be friends."

He ignored that altogether, jerking his chin in Del's direction. "Is the woman yours?"

It would have been so simple to answer yes, to stake a claim to Del and warn him away to another. But I had learned, thanks to Del, that a woman couldn't be claimed; that a woman couldn't be owned, and where she went was of her own free choice, not dependent upon a man.

It would have been so simple. But it would have been a lie.

"Ask *her*," I suggested, "but you might not like the answer. She's a sword-dancer, too."

Pale brows rose consideringly. He stared after Del, though she was gone, then narrowed icy eyes and glanced again at me. What he thought was plain: my disclaimer made me a fool.

The stud nuzzled my shoulder. Remembering Massou's experience, I shoved mouth away from flesh.

It made the Northerner smile. "I won coin on you."

I blinked. "You bet on me to win?"

"I know horses." The smile was secretive. "Perhaps better than the horse-master who was so willing to give this one up. It is my trade, if after a different fashion." The smile widened a little and twisted the upper lip. The scar didn't entirely ruin his looks, but did draw attention. And I think it pleased him instead of warping his nature. (I know a little about scars.) "I would have tried him myself, but you spoke before I could."

"That doesn't tell me why you bet on me."

He rubbed an idle forefinger across the twisted lip. "The horse knew you," he said finally. "There is a language private to horses, but I know how to speak it." He shrugged. "Not in words or thoughts, but in feelings. This one knew you well, so I knew you would win the contest."

I grunted. "You might have told me first and saved me a bloody nose."

He grinned, which stripped away the arrogance and replaced it with genuine amusement. "But I wanted to *win*. The odds were in my favor, because everyone else bet against you."

I appraised him much as he had appraised me. Tall, but lacking bulk, though not as tall as me. Graceful even in stillness; the boy knew how to move. He wore wool and leather as I did, cross-tied at calves and forearms, but his pale hair was very long and divided into two braids, one for either shoulder. He knotted them with leather thongs adangle with beads of blue and silver. They rattled when he moved.

"Then I think you owe me a drink."

He blinked. Then smiled. "Are we to be friends, then? Or enemies over the woman?"

"Oh, we can be either; that depends on you. But if you're still here when Del comes around, you'll see it doesn't matter."

He laughed. Inclined his head. And, in fluent Southron, invited me to his camp.

I agreed. Drinking a man's liquor is better than fighting him.

Unless you can do both.

He spoke Southron as well as other languages, although mostly he kept to the Borderer mix even I could understand. His name, he said, was Garrod, and he was a horse-speaker. When I asked the difference between horse-speaker and horse-*master*, he said the second was a misnomer, that no man could master a horse. I thought one name as good as another, and told him so.

Garrod sat on the ground on a blue-and-gray woven blanket, leaning against a convenient tree stump. It was a tiny little one-man camp, consisting of a fire circle filled with ash, a jumble of leather tack, and five magnificent horses.

He tilted his head a little. Braid beads rattled. "As much difference," he said quietly, "as between stallion and mare."

I snorted my response, enjoying the pleasant glow of Northern liquor as I sat on Garrod's blanket and drank Garrod's *amnit*. "You came to sell your horses, didn't you? It sounds the same to me."

"Horses, to *me*, are more than things to be sold. More than merely animals who have been trained to carry or pull." His icy eyes were oddly unfocused as he looked at his string of five, staked out in lush green grass. "Horses are my magic."

I was his guest, and there are rules; I refrained from laughing outright. Instead, I held out the bota. "Have another drink."

Solemnly he took it, drank, smiled companionably back at me. "I could have ridden your horse. I could have made him mine."

"By *talking* to him, I gather."

He gazed at me thoughtfully. His expression told me nothing, other than he appraised. And then Garrod smiled, twisting the scarred upper lip. "It would have saved you a bloody nose."

I took the bota back. "I need to buy a horse."

"For the woman, or for yourself?"

"For her. For Del. Depending, of course, on price."

Garrod shrugged indifferently. "I would need to see her. To let *them* see her."

"Who? The horses?" Incredulously, I stared at the five grazing mounts. "Do you mean to tell me you ask them their *opinion?*"

His tone was one of infinite patience; he'd met disbelief before. "Men choose horses for wrong reasons. They think of themselves, not of the animal. They buy or trade stupidly, and often the horse suffers for it." He smiled. "Or the rider does."

"You mean me."

"I mean you." Garrod sat upright, shifted his position, leaned back again, tugging left braid from under an armpit. "You and your horse could be better friends if the partnership was equal. You spend too much time telling him you are the master, while he tells you the same thing." He shrugged a little, rattling beads in thick pale plaits. "He is happy enough, and so are you, but you both could be happier."

I've heard of strange things before, but never of a man who could talk to horses. Or of horses who would listen. "Garrod—"

"Let them see her," he said. "I will sell you the one who is best for her."

I thought about Del's response. "She might not like any of *them*."

Garrod smiled. "She's Northern, isn't she?"

"Del? Hoolies yes . . . nearly as fair as you."

"Then she will understand."

Garrod and I shared the rest of the bota, trading stories full of truths and falsehoods, and generally enjoyed a pleasant afternoon. Once I'd had to tie up the stud again, since he'd pulled free of the treelimb I'd tethered him to, but I caught him before he could do any damage to Garrod's horses and made sure my knot was tight.

Since then he'd done little more than stare morosely at the others, or shred thick-woven turf and spit out globs of muddy roots.

Garrod looked up at the sky. "Sun's going down."

About this time Del arrived. "I've been looking all over for you."

I shrugged, content on Garrod's blanket. "You said it wouldn't be hard to find me."

"I thought not," she agreed, "but then I foolishly neglected to remember that you'd most likely drink yourself into a stupor."

I raised my brows. "Had a bad afternoon, did we?"

Garrod smiled and tossed her the bota. "We saved a swallow or two for you."

Del caught the bota but did not drink, appraising each of us in silence. Her gaze stayed on Garrod longer, giving nothing away; even *I* couldn't tell what she thought. But I didn't think she was pleased.

"Massou is all right," she said finally. "The bite will bruise, but nothing more."

"Could have told you that." I gestured toward my host. "Name's Garrod. Horse-speaker, he says."

"Horse-*speaker?*" Del frowned, looking more closely at the young man I judged her own age. "You are young for it."

"True talent doesn't wait on age," Garrod answered. "But I could say the same of you, couldn't I? He says you are a sword-dancer." He paused pointedly a moment. "Not to mention you're a *woman*."

Uh-oh. Not a good beginning.

Del stared him down. Then dismissed him with surpassing speed, turning to look at me. "We have made a camp, and Adara has cooked a meal."

I sighed, recalling Massou's temper and Adara's weary depression. "How much longer are we to nursemaid them?"

A fleeting expression told me she was as weary of it, though she said nothing to give the thought away. "One more night," she answered quietly. "We'll buy them a horse and wagon in the morning, and then we are free to go."

Clearly, she was ready; I saw the subtle signs of tension in her face.

Garrod shifted against his stump, rubbing at his knife-scarred lip. "He says you need a horse."

Del's face masked itself. "And you have one to sell."

He waved a negligent hand over his shoulder. "I have *five* to sell."

Del looked at the horses. Quietly they grazed, staked out like dogs on a lead. Big, sturdy horses, fuzzy from winter hair. Two bays, two sorrels, a gray. They looked content enough with their lot; considerably more so than the stud. But then that wasn't saying much.

She flicked a glance at me. I shrugged a very little, lifting one shoulder almost imperceptibly. She was asking me what I thought of Garrod and his claim of equine magic; frankly, I didn't know *what* I thought.

Del's mouth tightened, twisted faintly, loosened. "I think not," she said, "for now. Perhaps in the morning."

Garrod's smile was slow. "By morning they may not be here."

Horse-speaker or not, this language even *I* understood very well. Horse trading and haggling are as old as time itself.

"By morning," Del suggested, "you may want a lower price."

The Northerner grinned. "By morning they may cost *more*."

"All right, all right." I was tired of the game. "Let's go get some food, bascha—we'll hunt a horse in the morning."

She cast Garrod a sideways glance of cool dismissal and turned on her heel to leave. Loose blonde hair swung against her back, hiding much of the harness and sheath. But it didn't block the silver hilt, which rose above her left shoulder.

Garrod looked up at me as I got to my feet. "A word of advice, friend Tiger: never trust a woman with a sword. Her tongue is bad enough."

I laughed. Then stopped as Del swung back. Showed her an expression of innocence, then shot a grin at Garrod. He raised his bota in salute.

"Men," Del remarked, as if it said everything.

And I suppose, sometimes, it does.

Chapter 19

el and I threaded our way back through men, women, children, dogs, horses and other assorted livestock, winding around wagons, cookfires and open camps, ducking and dodging various games as we went. The sun decidedly *was* going down; it tipped the mountains with gilt and bronze and deepened the purples to black.

"Kind of rude to Garrod, weren't you?" Del is very tall; our steps were evenly matched, particularly as I was leading the stud.

"I don't like him."

I grunted. "I sort of gathered that much. *Why,* is the question. Or maybe, why not?"

She shrugged. "I just don't."

I suppose I should have been glad. Scarred lip and all, Garrod was a good looking young buck, and considerably closer to Del's age than I am. But because we'd shared a bota and swapped lots of stories, I felt I knew him well enough not to feel threatened by youth or good looks, which I'd lost some time ago (although *some* women might argue otherwise; I'm not completely hopeless.) So I could afford to be offended by Del's somewhat illogical dismissal of Garrod.

"You don't even know him. How can you judge him so quickly?"

"The same way you judge an opponent when you step into the circle," she said dryly. "It doesn't *take* a lot of time."

The stud tried to walk over the top of me; I elbowed him back. "But you didn't like *me* when we met."

Del looked thoughtful. "True," she admitted, nodding. "You were a lot like Garrod, then: smug, arrogant, dominating, convinced of a nonexistent superiority . . ." She shrugged. "But you settled down a lot once I beat you in the circle."

"You *never* beat me in the circle."

"Oh? What about the time we danced in front of the Hanjii and their painted women? I seem to remember you taking leave of your meal."

"And *I* seem to remember you jammed a knee into—"

"—your brains?" Del smiled blandly. "A man's eternal vulnerability."

I forbore to answer that, preferring to forget our initial sworddance, which had been a travesty. "Nothing's ever really been settled between us," I reminded her. "We've danced, yes, but mostly it's just been sparring. We've never done it for real, to establish who's the best."

"I have a good idea."

"So do I, and it isn't you."

Del sighed and flopped an arm in an easterly direction. "Camp's over this way . . . Tiger, I don't mean to make you angry, but you should know by now that—"

"—what? You're better? No, I don't know . . . because it isn't true." A rag ball rolled out of play into our path. The stud stopped short; so did I. He breathed noisily, ears touching at tips, and eyed the ball uneasily. I told him he was a coward, bent and scooped up the ball, tossed it back to the waiting boy. "I'm bigger, stronger, more powerful—"

"And I'm considerably swifter, and much more subtle with my strokes." Del thrust out a wrist and flexed it. "When it comes to using patterns—"

"But that's the *Northern* style. I'm a Southroner."

She swung to face me. "But we're North, now, Tiger. You've got to use *my* style."

"Why?" I asked flatly. "I'm very good at my own."

"Because—" Abruptly, the urgency spilled out of her tone. Briefly, she closed her eyes, then looked at me once more. "Because a good *ishtoya* is always prepared to learn."

I kept my voice very steady. "I am a seventh-level sword-dancer," I said clearly. "Not first, not third, not fifth. *Seventh*, Del. There aren't very many of those."

Del wet her lips, fingered hair out of her face, seemed oddly apprehensive. "Southron," she said, "*Southron*. This is the North, Tiger . . . we must adhere to Northern customs."

"*You* must adhere to Northern customs. I'm just me."

"Tiger—"

"This isn't doing us any good," I said curtly. "You can't make me something I'm not, anymore than I can make you something *you're* not. Would you have me demand you put down your sword for good and keep house for me all hidden behind Southron veils?"

Del's face was stiff. "There's a difference between sword-dancing and keeping *house*."

"Is there? One is a man's work, the other a woman's." I paused. "Usually."

"You don't understand."

A woman's eternal defense, although I didn't tell her that. "Probably not," I agreed. "All I know is, you've been acting funny ever since we crossed the border."

Her face was grim, which was a shame; Del's features demand better treatment. "I have responsibilities."

"So do we all, Del."

"And as for acting funny, so have you. Especially lately."

I scratched my scars. "Yes, well . . . things haven't felt right, lately. I don't know what's wrong, but I'm getting the same prickles I got before."

Del's brows shot up. "Prickles?"

I sighed. "I don't know how to explain it. Things just don't feel *right*." I gestured. "Shall we go find the camp?"

She hesitated a moment longer, then turned abruptly and marched off. I followed more sedately, slowed by a distracted horse.

* * *

Camp indeed, such as it was. There was the familiar rainbreak, though no wagon to hook it to, as well as spread blankets and a fire. Adara squatted by the stone ring, stirring a pot of something that smelled a lot like stew. Cipriana helped her mother by pouring cups of tea. Massou, bowl in hand, sat on a blanket and glowered at the stud.

The little campsite wasn't exactly private, being wedged in between the road and numerous scattered wagons with adjacent open camps. But it would do, and certainly until the morning. I took the restive stud aside, not wanting to trouble the boy, and staked him out by a plot of turf as yet untrampled by wheels and boots and hooves.

Del followed me over. "*Kymri* are cause for celebration. Tonight there will be singing and dancing." It was, I thought, an apology of sorts.

I slapped the stud on the shoulder. "I'm all for celebration, but I can't do either one."

"You dance in the circle."

"That's different."

"And I've never heard you sing. You might be very good."

I grinned at her. "Bascha, have you heard a danjac bray?"

She looked blank. "A who?"

"A what: a danjac. Beast of burden, down south." I smiled. "Not much known for their voice."

"No, I've never heard one."

"*And* you don't want to hear me."

She frowned a little. "Don't you *ever* sing?"

"Never ever, bascha."

Del shook her head. "A sword-dancer should sing."

"Waste of breath, bascha."

"Not when you want to win."

"Yes, well, I seem to do fine without making any noise." I removed my boot from the the patch of turf the stud wanted to plunder and turned back toward the camp. "Just because *you* sing—"

She caught my arm. "Tiger—*look*—"

I looked. Didn't see much of anything out of the ordinary, just three men riding down the road, while a fourth walked out to meet them. A pale-haired man with braids.

"Garrod," I said, "so? He's here to sell his horses."

Del's fingers bit into my forearm. "Those men . . . Tiger, I *know* them. They are Ajani's men."

I hauled her back before she could take more than a single step. "Del—wait."

"I *know* them, Tiger."

"Are you sure?"

"*Yes.*"

"And what do you want to do, storm out there and challenge them to a sword-dance?"

She tried to break free by twisting her arm. I hung on. "Tiger—you don't understand—"

"Yes I do. I also understand that right now probably isn't a good time to challenge them."

She stopped struggling. Color stood high in her face. "And when *is* a good time?"

"Probably in the morning, if you insist. We've spent the last two weeks tromping all over these hills, bascha—why not at least get a good night's sleep? They'll be here. And so will Garrod. If he knows *them*, he might just know Ajani. Or *not*; they may simply want his horses."

"They *have* horses, Tiger."

"The least we can do is *ask* him before we spit him on your sword."

"Then let's ask him right now."

"Let's not." I hauled her back again. "Del, I'll even help you, but let's wait till morning."

"We have to leave in the morning."

"*And* find a horse and wagon for these people." I tilted my head in the direction of Adara and her children. "It's our last night to-gether, bascha . . . don't you think they might want to spend it without witnessing bloodshed in the circle?"

She gritted teeth. "You are a sentimental fool."

I gripped her arm more firmly. "Better than *just* a fool, which is what you're being at the moment."

"Those men owe me blood-debt," she hissed angrily. "Each and every one of them owes me blood-debt ten times over, for what was done to my family. And if you think I can let them ride through this *kymri* without calling them into the circle, *you* are the fool!"

"And if they refuse?" I released her and saw the reddening handprint on her arm. "They probably will, Del. They're Southroners, after all. They won't take the invitation seriously. What they *will* do, however, is cut you to pieces when you're not looking, because that is how they live. They have no honor, Del. And you'll die because of it."

"Not till I find Ajani."

Something inside of me squeezed. "I don't want you to die at *all*."

The sun was nearly gone. Fading light softened the lines of Del's face and altered her expression into something more sanguine than former anger. She looked back at me blankly a moment, then drew in a deep breath. "No. Neither do I."

"Then let's make sure you don't." The men were gone, Garrod with them. "And let's have something to eat."

In an oddly private silence, Del went to the fire.

The stew was very good, although I might have preferred better company. Adara remained locked in depression, only rarely breaking her silence, and Massou continued his sulk. Del tried to draw him out and he responded a little, but sullenly, as if he blamed me for the stud's hostility.

Well, maybe whatever *I* felt also affected the stud.

Cipriana, on the other hand, had a strange bright glint in her eyes, smiling to herself, occasionally touching the neckline of her tunic. She served me in place of her mother, tending my cup until I told her to stop, and filled my bowl to brimming three times running.

Del, of course, saw it, smiled wryly, said nothing. On one hand, it was nice not to suffer the sulks of a jealous woman; on the other, it might have been nice to know she cared. Del did not appear to— or else she dismissed Cipriana as not worthy of consideration as real competition.

It became patently clear, however, that Cipriana did.

After dinner I went back to the stud, who was making a lot of noise. He stomped, pawed, dug holes, snorted, peeled back lips to show yellowed teeth. I thought maybe there was a mare in heat close by; it doesn't take much to set him off.

I soothed him as best I could, but he wasn't particularly interested in anything I had to say, nor did a pat or two still his restiveness. I tried scratching the firm layers of muscle lying between the long bones of his under jaw, which usually resulted in a silly half-lidded expression of contentment. This time all it resulted in was a wet, messy snort of abject contempt.

"Fine," I told him, "stay out here and sulk. I'm not taking you to any mare no matter *how* much you beg."

Cipriana came up to me, melting out of the fireglow. It was dark now, and the entire *kymri* was shrouded in smoke and glare, smelling of food and liquor. "Tiger?"

The stud bared teeth; I slapped his nose away from the girl. "Yes?"

"Could you—" She broke off, gathered her courage, asked it. "Would you walk with me?"

Hoolies. Oh, *hoolies*.

"Not far," she said. "Just—out there." A wave of her hand indicated somewhere beyond the stud.

She is a *girl*, I told myself. What are you afraid of?

Well, nothing. Nothing, *really*. Other than being wary of what she wanted, while having a feeling I knew. Part of me suggested I say no and go back to the fire, avoiding the situation; another part jeered for being such a coward.

But I had no experience with fifteen-year-old girls. I like my women older.

Still, there was no dignified way of refusing. So I didn't even try.

We left the stud behind, viciously digging holes in the turf. Side by side we walked out of the light from our fire into the glow cast from other campsites. In the distance I could hear the ringing of tambors, the clatter of rattle-bones, the trilling hoot of wooden pipes. I thought Cipriana deserved to go dancing instead of walking with me, and said so.

She shrugged. "I wanted to be with you."

Hoolies. "You've been with all of us the past two weeks."

She walked with arms folded across her chest, head bowed. Pale hair fell forward to obscure her face. "Because I wanted to be with *you*."

I sighed. "Cipriana—"

She stopped and raised her head, snapping hair out of her face with a deft twist of her head. "I'm confused," she said. "Things happened today that I don't understand, and I need to ask someone." She shrugged again, hugging herself. "My father is dead and Massou is too young. There is no one else but you."

Oh, *hoolies.*

I drew in a deep breath, trying to buy time. Trying to come up with an answer. "I think—"

"Men *looked* at me today," she said. "Men looked at me, and followed me with their eyes . . . some *men* even followed me. And they said things, some of them . . ." She didn't look away, plainly waiting for an explanation.

"Maybe it would be better if you talked this over with your mother." A safe answer, I thought.

Cipriana shook her head. "She's too tired. She won't listen."

"Well—what about Del?"

Blue eyes widened. "*Del* wouldn't understand!"

I frowned. "Why not? She's a woman. She knows about these things."

Cipriana was momentarily at a loss for words, searching for the right ones. "Because," she said finally, "because all *she* cares about is her sword, and the sword-dance."

I am not entirely stupid when it comes to women, even young ones. I know jealousy when I hear it. I can *smell* it.

"Cipriana," I said firmly, "when you have survived the hardships Del has, and have learned how to live freely in a man's world no matter what the stakes, you can say something like that. But you are too young and too innocent to understand what Del's life has been like, so I suggest you make no judgments."

The girl was undeterred. "They *looked* at me," she said. "One even gave me this."

I watched as she tugged something from beneath her woolen tunic. Some sort of necklet; beads strung on leather, or stones. They were dark and lumpy, lacking symmetry. The thong tied at the back of her neck.

"And you *took* it?" I was more than a little amazed.

She shrugged, clearly confused. "He said I should have it. That I was pretty enough for it . . ." She smiled a little, eyes bright. "Am I pretty, Tiger?"

Hoolies, hoolies, *hoolies.*

"You will be," I told her, floundering, "but I think maybe you shouldn't accept presents from strange men."

"I would from you." She stepped close. "Even *you* watch me, Tiger. I've seen you do it. I've seen you follow me with your eyes, and then you look at Del. You look at her, as if comparing us: hard-edged woman and soft young girl." She smelled of musk and lavender, swaying closer yet, whispering, "I'm softer and younger than Del . . . and *I've never killed a man.*"

The stud squealed. Hands reached up to lock in my hair. I took two steps back, caught her wrists; discovered soft young Cipriana had the strength of a full-grown woman who most distinctly wants a man.

"Cipriana—*no*—" I jerked her hands away, set her aside more roughly than I intended, realized the tingle was back in my bones. "Something's wrong," I said sharply. The hair stood up on my flesh. "Something is *wrong.*"

All around us the music played. People laughed, shouted, sang.

"Tiger—"

I shivered. "Hoolies—what *is* it—?" Of its own accord, my hand went to my sword hilt and jerked the blade out of its sheath. Cipriana fell back a step, gripping her lumpy necklet.

The stud squealed again. I heard him stomping in the turf, digging deeper holes. Whatever it was, he felt it as strongly as I.

Firelight glinted off my bared blade. Night-blackened runes knotted and broke as I shifted my weight, turning from side to side.

Cipriana put out a hand and touched the naked blade.

"Don't," I said sharply. "You know better."

"Do I?" Fingers curled around the edges. "This is a sword of power."

"Once," I agreed, distracted. "Not anymore. The man who blooded it is dead."

"*You* killed him."

"Yes." I was curt, too curt, but my bones itched inside my flesh. "Hoolies, I can *feel* it—"

"So can I," she said. "It's here, in the sword. Wanting to break free—"

Carefully I moved the blade away from her hand. "Theron is dead and buried in Southron sand. The Punja has scoured the flesh from his bones. There's no life left in this sword." I moved away from her, trying to locate the source of my unease. It was growing stronger, *too* strong; I felt vaguely sick. "It's everywhere," I said, moving in a circle around the campsite. "It's coming from every direction. Can't you feel it?" I turned as she followed. "Go back to the fire, Cipriana. Go back."

"I want to come with—"

"*Go back.*" My palms were wet against the hilt. I let go long enough with one hand to shove Cipriana toward the fire. "Del!" I shouted.

She came. Her blade was bare in her hands.

"Something is wrong," I told her. "Something *bad.*"

Her sword flashed in the fireglow. The feeling of wrongness intensified with that flash, making me queasy and a little disoriented. I felt hatred. Hostility. A burning dedication coming steadily forward to surround us in the darkness.

"Something—" I said again.

The fire was at her back. I could see nothing of her face. "What do you think—"

But she never got a chance to finish, because people began to scream.

Chapter 20

*I*t stinks," I said.

Del cast me a glance combining disbelief with impatience. "*Now* is not the time to worry about what offends your nose."

"It *stinks*." I repeated. "Can't you smell it? It's magic. Del . . . and not meant to be kind to us."

The *kymri* was in a shambles. No more piping, no more singing, no more dancing. Everyone was in flight.

The enemy was as yet unseen. But that one existed was plain. I felt it, I *smelled* it, and knew it was powerful enough to destroy any number of people. The hundreds gathered here would never stop it. Never even slow it.

Del and I are canny fighters. We know very well when the odds make victory impossible, and we're prepared to retreat without concern for how others may view the flight. We were prepared to fight *or* run now, but not knowing who, what or where the enemy was made it impossible to do either. All we could do was remain with Adara and her children at the campfire, while all around us *landlopers* panicked and fled into the darkness beyond the smudgy fireglow.

Fled, and died.

By the screams we were able to tell from which direction the enemy approached. The knowledge didn't please us; the *kymri* was surrounded. From the hills and mountains flowed a river of hostility, slipping like wraiths through the darkness, devouring anything in its path.

"Eyes," Del said tersely. "Look at all the *eyes* . . . human? Or animal?"

"Too low to the ground for human, unless they're crawling on hands and knees." Which was a possibility. "I think they're animals."

Del was frowning. "Too many for wolves. They're *everywhere*."

We stood on either side of the fire, our backs to one another with the Borderers in between, huddled around the ring. Campfires still burned by other wagons, but all were unattended. People fled or climbed into and under wagons, calling on various Northern gods.

"Dogs?" I said. "Dogs go mad sometimes."

"I don't think so. The *kymri* dogs are silent."

They were, which disturbed me. The stud stomped and pawed and generally made his uneasiness known, as did other horses tied at neighboring camps, but the dogs were oddly silent, all of them, as if they understood the enemy far better than any of us, and accepted the role of submission without a single show of reluctance.

The river flowed closer. The eyes were all around us, fixed and eerily feral. Slanted, slitted eyes, with the shine of ice in the darkness.

There was no doubt in my mind that we stood a better chance mounted. But we had only one horse for five.

That is, until Garrod arrived. He rode the gray, leading the bays and sorrels. All were bridled, but he'd had no time at all for saddles.

"Waste no time," he said tersely, "the beasts are all around us. There are enough to pull down the horses, but if we run we stand a better chance of breaking through the ranks."

Del and I sheathed our swords and took the reins he tossed us. "Adara, up," I said.

"Massou and Cipriana—"

"—will be fine. Come here." She came; I tried to give her a

boost up, but the sorrel shied away. I pulled Adara aside, scowling up at Garrod.

He was frowning. "They shouldn't—" But he broke it off, saying something about beasts, and began speaking to the horses.

It was in a Northern dialect I didn't know, but I heard nuances of peacemaking and placation, a song of soothing promises and endless empathy. All of the horses settled almost at once.

"Adara," I said, lifted her up, made certain she was settled firmly on the sorrel's back. Then I turned to take another horse from Garrod, one of the bays. "Cipriana."

She was there instantly, saying nothing as I made a step with locked hands and tossed her up. She landed awkwardly in a tangle of woolen skirts, belly-down across the horse's shoulders, but twisted around and yanked skirts out of the way as she pulled herself into position.

"They are good horses," Garrod said, watching. "The best. But none of them is gentle."

Cipriana gathered reins, grim-faced. "I can ride," she said firmly. "I will stay aboard."

I saw a brief glint of appreciation in Garrod's pale eyes, and then he was twisting his neck to look back at Del, making certain Massou was safely settled on the other bay. It left the remaining sorrel for Del. She swung up lightly, making an easier job of it than Cipriana because she was, as always, skirtless, wearing gartered trews, gaiters and high-wrapped boots very like my own.

It left only me. I went to the stud and pulled the stake. I'd left him bridled, which is not uncommon, tied to the earth by means of a halter, rope and picket stake. Now I looped one rope and reins and brought him closer to the fire.

"Did you know?" I asked Garrod plainly. "I smelled the stink, horse-speaker—did you *know* they were coming?"

He shook his head. Pale braids twisted against shoulders, rattling beads that glinted in the light. "Not until the horses told me. By then, it was nearly too late. I had time only to come for all of you."

I caught a handful of spiky mane, leaned back, swung a leg up toward the stud's rump. Up and over, settled, hauling in reins and rope. Bareback, he was slippery; I clamped buttocks and legs against his flesh, feeling the play of muscles. "*All* of us? But you knew only Del and me . . . why did you think of *all* of us?"

"Because I saw you," he said quietly, "when I came down to talk to Ajani's men."

I looked at Del. I knew we were thinking identical thoughts: Ajani's men stole people to sell them into slavery. Were we making it easy for them?

"Come *on*," Garrod said sharply. "Do you want to let them eat you?"

Given a choice, I'd rather fight men than beasts. We turned the mounts loose and ran.

Garrod took us toward the end of the little valley. There was no question he knew his business; I fully expected the spirited horses to prove difficult, but Garrod apparently had "spoken" to them. They were swift and alert and responsive, but they didn't panic. They didn't lose their riders.

The stud, meanwhile, wasn't particularly pleased with the direction of the flight, since he'd wanted to go the other way. I fought him with hands and heels, keeping him tightly reined as I muscled him through the *kymri*. Garrod led, while Del and I hung back to herd Adara and her children after him. All around us were abandoned fires, blocky Northern wagons, huddled humans and frightened livestock.

And *eyes*.

We ran, and they ran with us. I began to see shapes, little more than snatches of shadows as I fought to stay aboard the slick-backed stud. I saw low-slung heads, gaping jaws, tongues lolling out of mouths. Saw the hard shine of eyes and teeth. Heard the whine and whistle of panting breaths. They were four-footed creatures with brushy tails, and a mane across hunched shoulders. Smudgy gray, but dappled silver. Not wolves. Not dogs. Not foxes. Something in between.

"Hounds of hoolies," I muttered.

Del's horse was next to me. "What did you say?" she asked.

"—bedtime story in the South." It was hard to talk over pounding hooves and the noisy breathing of running horses. "Supposedly they're the familiars of Dybbuk himself."

"Who?"

"The lord of hoolies, which is undoubtedly the place I'm bound for, if we keep going the way we're going."

"Oh." Her sorrel stumbled. Del snugged reins, drew up the gelding's white-splashed head, set him to running again.

"For what it's worth," I said, "I don't think Garrod's turning us over to slavers."

Del tilted her head in consideration. "Maybe not at the moment. But once we're free of the valley, who's to say *what* he'll do?"

I grinned. "A pair of sword-dancers, maybe."

"Tiger—watch out!"

Something snapped at the stud's hocks. Swearing, I saw the flash of teeth and the shine of pale, slanting eyes. The river had reached us at last.

"Keep going!" Garrod called, twisting to shout over one shoulder. Pale braids whipped. "If we slow, they'll pull us down. Just hold on and let the horses go!"

Massou and Cipriana were hunched forward, clutching reins and flying manes. They made themselves very small, pulling knees and ankles upward to present smaller targets to the leaping "hounds." Massou certainly was small enough to succeed, clinging to his bay like a tick to a dog. Cipriana and Adara, longer-legged, had more trouble, but managed, just as Del did. I was bigger than any of them and on a less predictable mount; inwardly I swore and reached to jerk Theron's sword from the sheath slung across my back.

"Bascha—let's cull the pack, shall we?"

Del glanced over, saw the metallic glint, smiled. And freed her own blooding-blade.

Answering immediately, the beasts began to bay.

"Through the canyon!" Garrod called. "The opening's just ahead."

We went into the canyon, all six of us, cutting a path through blood and bone. Del and I flanked the others, swept around the edges, closed in. The hounds snapped and howled and yipped, trying to pull down the horses, but they were no match for slashing blades or crushing hooves. We cut them down, smashed them down, broke through their vicious ranks. And left them for their brothers.

Blood sprayed up. Del and I were liberally splattered. But it was nothing we didn't know.

The river continued to flow. The hounds didn't slacken pace, somehow keeping up with the horses. Garrod led us through the canyon and out of the *kymri* valley onto an open plain that stretched on into forever. It provided better footing, spread the river into a flood, allowed us to judge the numbers better.

"Hoolies," I said curtly. "How many of them *are* there?"

"Too many." Del was snappish in frustration. "Why do they keep coming? Why don't they turn back?" A glance at her face showed me anger and an unrelenting grimness. "If it's only a meal they want, there are plenty of dead back in the valley."

"So they're after something more." I leaned down to the right, unleashed my sword in a vicious swipe, took off the head of one of the hounds. "I told you it's sorcery, Del. They're not doing this on their own. Someone with power *sent* them."

"You're sandsick." She used my own expression. "There's no reason for anyone to kill everyone at a *kyrmi*." Del shook her head, sword flashing in her hand. "There are fights, yes, sometimes, and men do die, but there's no reason for this. Why kill everyone?"

I swore as the stud jumped over a shadow, caught my balance, gripped harder with knees and ankles. "Not everyone is *at* the *kymri* anymore. Six of us are out here, and the hounds are following."

"Not *all* of them . . . are they?" Del twisted to look back the way we'd come. "Oh, *Tiger*—"

"I know. That's what I meant. One of us is the target."

"Or maybe all of us."

"Not all of us are in danger of being proscribed for killing a Northern *an-kaidin*."

"You think it's *me?*"

I shrugged. "It's a thought."

Del swung her sword. I heard a hound yelp. "No, Tiger—*no*. It doesn't work that way. They would send men, not beasts. And they'd never kill the innocent."

"I said it was just a thought."

"Keep that one to yourself."

The flood rolled out across the plain, flanking six fleeing riders. No longer were the hounds leaping at us, trying to catch flesh and tear. Now they appeared to be herding us, running us straight toward the edge of the plain.

It was, I thought, past time to take the initiative.

Garrod still rode ahead, but just barely; Del and I galloped abreast to break a way through the flood. But the flood was beside us now, giving us acres of plain before.

I crowded his gray, still holding my bloodied sword. "Turn," I urged. "Swing left. Cut through the flank. Let's get off this plain."

He nodded and suited actions to my suggestion. Del and I dropped back to play outriders to Adara and her children, knowing they might be too tired or too slow to heed the change in direction. As it was Del and I squeezed them in between us, knees banging, legs caught between quivering horseflesh, hunching forward to guide the horses.

"They can't run forever!" Adara cried. Her hair had come loose and streamed in the wind like a ruddy pennon. "If one of them goes down, the rider will be killed . . . or one of us could fall—"

All true. But we had no other choice.

"Just hang on," I told her above the beat of pounding hooves. "Stay with the horse; he'll follow Garrod. Del and I will hold off the hounds. Just *ride*."

"I have children—"

"—as well as yourself." I bent across, lowered my sword in a flat-bladed slap across her sorrel's rump. "Massou and Cipriana are doing fine. Del and I are watching." I pointed at Garrod, whose fair-haired braids flapped behind him. "Stay *with* him . . . don't fall behind!"

Adara looked over one shoulder at the running hounds. "They haven't come for *us*."

It was distinctly unappreciated in light of the risk Del and I were taking for the Borderers; without them, we stood a better chance of escape. "Well, then," I said rudely, "why don't you just *stop?* If there's no need for you to run, don't waste the horses."

Adara flicked a glance at me and shook her head in denial.

"Then *run*, woman! Do what I tell you to do!"

It was, I admit, a bit on the heavy-handed side, but it had the desired effect. Adara ran.

The stud, I knew, was tiring. He was tough, he was game, he had heart, but even tremendous stamina gives out when tested too far. I couldn't begin to say how shredded his legs might be from repeated attacks, or his belly, or how much longer he could run before he stumbled, falling, to tumble me onto the plain into the river of beasts.

Not a happy thought. So I made myself stop thinking it and begged the stud for all the heart he had to give.

The hounds started to fall behind. Their yapping faded, the eyes winked out, the flood began to abate. I didn't for one minute think the distance would be enough—they'd proved to have a single-minded devotion to their task—and I knew they wouldn't stop. Fall behind, yes; stop completely, no. They had settled on their prey.

Garrod reached the edge of the plain and took his gray northwest, skirting the shadowed drop. Moonlight was helpful, but it didn't really give us much to go on. We all swung left as he did, saw the flood spread out behind us, and knew without speaking we'd have to find another course.

Del sheathed her sword and thrust out a splayed hand. "Wait," she said, "there may be a way."

We slowed as she did, hideously conscious of the hounds. Intently Del searched the edge, and then stabbed a hand at it. "Earthfall," she said. "Follow me down." And plunged off the edge of the plain.

The earthfall was soft and deep, swallowing legs past the fetlocks, teasing at hocks and knees, threatening heaving bellies. But it slid easily aside as the horses floundered, plowing through; breaking way soundlessly to carry us down from the plain. The stud snorted and quivered, disliking the shifting earth, but he obeyed a firm hand on the reins—the other clutched his mane—and didn't try to leap away.

Four pale heads bobbed on rigid necks. Then ruddy-haired Adara, leaning back against downward momentum. And me, the Sandtiger—brown-haired, brown-skinned, green-eyed—bringing up the rear: Southron sword-dancer on Southron stud. Somehow, I didn't fit.

Was it me they might be after?

I shook it off; maybe. And if I was? So what. I'd handle it, as always.

"Hounds of hoolies," I muttered.

The stud was sweating. Dampness soaked through my woolen trews. Salt and horsehair made me itch, but at least it was easier to stay astride a wet horse than a dry. I hugged him with legs and leaned back, staying off his withers. A misstep could render me temporarily uninterested in women—or, rather, incapable—for at least a day or two; I sort of wanted to spare myself unnecessary discomfort.

Down and down we went, sliding through soft earth. And then we hit bottom, firm bottom, and stopped long enough to stare back up at the edge of the plain. It was black against the sky, nothing more than a silhouette. For the moment, it was empty, but we knew it wouldn't last.

"Where are we?" Massou asked, gasping.

The earthfall had funneled us down into a rocky canyon. To the left—the south—stretched a wide, dry riverbed, fouled with sand and boulders. To the left the riverbed narrowed significantly, turning into little more than a crack between the plainside cliffs and another mottled wall.

Garrod shook his head. "Let's just keep riding. We don't dare stop now, not with those beasts on our trail . . . maybe at sunrise."

"Sunrise!" Adara blurted it. "You can't expect us *or* the horses to go on throughout the night."

"If we have to, we will." Cipriana surprised us all with her vehemence.

Garrod's brows went up. He tilted his head thoughtfully and grinned. "We do," he said, "and we will."

"Let's go," Del said abruptly, jerking her chin north. "Let's try this way . . . the riverbed is too open. We'll just follow the canyon and see where it goes. It's better than being up there with those hounds."

"Besides," Garrod said, "we can't let the horses stand." He turned his gray and headed north, patting the lathered right shoulder. Talking to him, maybe?

"Go," I told Adara. "Del and I ride behind just in case they follow."

"They will," Massou declared.

I frowned. "Why do you say that?"

"I just know." He glared back, still sulking over the bite.

I flapped a hand at him. "Go."

He went. Cipriana fell in behind him. Del and I brought up the rear.

"They *will* follow," Del said quietly.

"Yes. I think so."

"If they corner us—"

"I know. Let's just pray this isn't a trap-canyon."

Del drew in a deep, slow breath. "I have always known I might die," she said quietly, "but never like *this*."

"We're a long way from dying, Del."

She turned her head sharply and looked at me, very deliberately, for a long, arrested moment. And then she smiled a little. "You told me that once before, when the Hanjii left us to die in the Punja."

"And I was right."

She nodded, lost in the memory. "But there are no Salset here to rescue us."

"Maybe we'll rescue ourselves." I smiled at her and shrugged. "It's not impossible."

Del sighed. "Maybe not."

"Have faith, bascha."

Pale brows rose. "In what, Tiger? I thought you didn't believe in things like gods and divine deliverance."

"I don't. I believe in myself."

"Oh, *good.*" Her face was perfectly blank. "Now I can relax."

I grunted. Grimaced. Glared. "*Now* you can make your horse stop rubbing his head—and his teeth—against my knee."

Del looked. Laughed. Pulled aside her horse . . . *after* he bit my knee.

Such a helpful girl.

Chapter 21

Our flight ended as abruptly as it had begun. There, suddenly, was Garrod, reining in his gray before it could run smack into a cliff of looming stone. There too was Adara, white-faced, hissing something bitterly in vicious Borderer. And also her son and daughter, drooping on their horses, turning back to look at Del and me hopefully as we stopped our weary mounts.

"Trap-canyon," I said briefly. "All we can do is turn around."

"Turn *around!* and go back?" Adara stared at me in shock, face half-curtained in tangled hair. "You mean, we've come all this way—"

"We had no choice," Garrod told her, quietly interrupting. "At least it bought us a little time."

"Time," she said bitterly. "Time to die here instead of *there?*"

I looked at her children. Massou was mostly asleep on his horse, all hunched up and stiff as if he'd locked his joints hours before. His head bobbed a little and eyelids drifted closed, no matter how hard he tried to keep them open. Cipriana wasn't much different, although her lids were more cooperative. Legs hung slackly against her mount, mostly bared by rucked up skirts to show woolen leggings. Blonde hair straggled limply; she shoved it back with effort.

"What do we do?" she asked.

I looked around at the place that now entombed us. We'd made our way through a narrow, winding conduit cutting through plain-side cliffs and freeside rocks, all knuckled from wind and water. The ground itself was solid rock with only a thin crusting of dirt, and in some places it was nothing at all but naked stone. After a while, in darkness, the canyon had blurred into nothingness, defined only by looming walls and a trace of diluted moonlight.

But now dawn replaced the darkness. And in the distance I heard a howl.

The hounds would, I knew, follow very soon. At this very moment they were probably at the edge of the plains, eyeing the earthfall into the narrow canyon. Maybe they were even over the edge already, pouring down in a white-eyed river.

I looked at Del, who sat quietly on one of Garrod's sorrels. "We could go back to the narrowest part of the canyon and block them, you and I. Turn them back. Keep them from getting through."

It was, I knew, only a temporary device; it seemed likely the hounds, with their vastly superior numbers, would eventually kill us both and continue on to catch the others.

Unless, of course, *we* were the ones they wanted. In which case, maybe they'd leave the others alone.

Del unsheathed her sword. "I have a better idea."

I looked at Boreal. It occurred to me to wonder why Del hadn't used her before now. "Bascha—"

"You saw what happened before." She knew perfectly well what I meant. "You *felt* what happened before. Loosed like that—uncontrolled, un*directed*—she can injure the innocent as well as destroy the enemy . . . on the plain I didn't dare."

I glanced around. Dawn was filling the tiny trap-canyon with a weak, pinkish light, divulging countless holes and crevices cut into the walls themselves. And it occurred to me that Boreal's backlash might be redoubled here.

"Del—"

She thrust out a rigid hand. "Do you see the throat? I'll use it to direct the power, and let the walls protect all of you."

Throat. As good as another word, I guess. At the mouth of

the trap-canyon was a bulging of wind-sculpted stone that forced a narrower entryway. A natural shield, of sorts, swelling from either side—a throat of solid stone—barely wide enough to offer admittance to a horse, though it had swallowed six of them.

"What are you going to do?" Massou demanded sharply.

Del glanced back at him. As always, with him, her expression softened. Massou was Jamail to her. "I'm going to try and turn back the beasts."

Blue eyes widened. "How?"

Del was never one to lie, or even to blunt the truth. Not for anyone's sake. "With magic," she said evenly.

Cipriana urged her bay closer to Del's white-faced sorrel. "Magic," she said. "*Magic?* How? What will you do?"

Adara shoved tangled hair out of a tired face. Something glinted in her eyes: an odd, bright awareness. "She's going to use her *jivatma*."

Four pairs of eyes fixed themselves on the sword. I didn't bother, having seen Boreal before; instead, I looked at them. At Garrod, clearly startled, who only now realized Del was precisely what she claimed; and at Adara and her children, staring avidly at the blade. As if they were dying of thirst and knew it would succor them.

Lastly, at Del, who was sliding off her horse. "You would do well," she suggested, "to find places in which to hide. That way if I fail, perhaps you'll still escape the beasts."

Places in which to hide. Were there any? The trap-canyon was little more than a pen of rock, and we the gathered livestock.

Garrod tipped his head back, looking up. Beaded braids dangled, sweeping against his mount's gray rump. "There are holes," he said. "Ledges and shelves and holes."

So there were. The walls, curving around to trap us within something akin to a semicircle, were freely pocked with hollows and holes. It was possible the walls that trapped us might also provide a means of escape from the hounds.

In the distance I heard the yapping of the beasts, threading down through the narrow canyon. I jumped off the stud and went over to the nearest lobe of cliff. The morning light was very thin, but growing stronger by the moment. Shadows slid down mottled rock onto a stone floor stair-stepped by a now-banished river, losing themselves in smudgy darkness. "Any holes large enough? Any we can reach?" Methodically I checked for cubbies we could use. "Massou—over here."

He came at once, peering up at the hole I'd found. "Too high," he said.

"The whole point," I agreed. "Here—I'll give you a boost. Come on."

Garrod dismounted and conducted his own search, motioning Cipriana and her mother to dismount and join him. It didn't take long for him to discover a ledge just large enough for two. He boosted the girl up, then Adara, and told them both to stay put.

"What about you?" Cipriana asked. Her voice echoed in the canyon.

He was clearly pleased, though he answered calmly enough. "I will stay down with the horses."

"But—if those *things* break through—"

"I will stay with the horses," he repeated, with a strange dignity. "They will be frightened also. I can make them feel better."

I shot him a sardonic glance as I led the stud to the wall and looped his reins over an outcrop. "By talking to them, Garrod?"

He was unoffended. "I've heard you talk to your stud."

"That's different," I pointed out. "That's just talking. He doesn't really understand me."

Garrod grunted, "Do you want me to find out?"

I thought about it. If he *could* talk to the stud—no, never mind. "Nah," I told him. "He and I do fine."

Del stood by her "throat." She frowned a little, intently studying the interior of the canyon, the narrow entranceway, the bulging lobes of stone on either side. And then abruptly made a decision; she turned and walked swiftly straight to Garrod, who stood talking quietly to his horses.

"I need one," she said.

Interrupted, he looked at her with an oddly unfocused stare. "What?"

"I need one." Del repeated, gesturing to his horses. *"Now."*

Garrod frowned. "Why? Do you mean to ride back? I thought Tiger said this was the best place to turn them."

"It is," she agreed evenly, "but we need something to block the entrance, like a stopper in a bottle."

I understood instantly, admiring her plan, as well as her courage in asking Garrod to make such a sacrifice. Watching the interplay, I scratched thoughtfully at my scars; Garrod wouldn't like it at all, once he understood exactly what she meant.

For now, he didn't. Braid beads rattled as he shook his head. "When the beasts come, the horse will never stand. He'll try to run, and you'll lose your stopper."

"Not if he *can't* run." Del's hand was more imperative. "Give me a horse, Garrod. I can ride double with Tiger."

Abruptly, he understood. Pale eyes widened in astonished disbelief, then narrowed angrily. I don't know exactly what he said, since he said it in uplander dialect, but clearly it wasn't polite. It also wasn't agreement.

The yapping intensified. Del ignored Garrod's diatribe and reached out to catch the reins to the nearest horse. It was the sorrel she had ridden.

He is fast, the Northerner. He had his knife out before I could reach him, but I swept aside the angry attempt and carried him back against the wall.

"No," I said calmly, squeezing the knife from his hand.

He didn't even glance at me, though I held him pressed against the cliff. Instead he stared past me at Del, who led the sorrel to the opening. His fair-skinned face was blotched with anger. "She can't kill him—she *can't* kill him—"

"She can," I said quietly. "It's to save our lives, Garrod."

"How can she kill a *horse?*"

Del positioned the sorrel so that he stood sideways in the throat, blocking the opening.

Garrod lunged off the wall, set me back two steps, tried to twist free. He nearly did it, too; I only just managed to swing him back around and smash him against the wall. "We don't have time for this, Garrod—"

He swore viciously, cutting me off, and spat out something in uplander slang. Something, I think, about an old man and a nanny goat.

I leaned on him a little, smiling. "If you like, we can use *you* to block the gate."

Garrod struggled fruitlessly. "You don't understand—"

"All I need to understand is that when it comes down to it, *our* survival is more important than that of any horse. You'd agree, if you had any brains."

"I'm a *horse-speaker*, you fool! Don't you know what that means? Don't you understand?" He strained against me. "I feel what they feel—sense what they sense—"

In the canyon, coming closer, I heard the howling of the hounds. "Right now I don't care if it means you're ready to drop a foal yourself," I told him. "Del's trying to save our lives."

He spat out another angry oath in Northern. This time Del was the target.

I sighed and forcibly shut his mouth. "Any time, bascha."

Garrod mumbled urgently against my hand, then went perfectly rigid. I didn't watch Del dispatch the horse, since my attention was on Garrod, but I heard the familiar wailing whistle of an unkeyed *jivatma* in use. The horse fell heavily; Garrod's eyes squeezed shut. Then he sagged against the cliff.

Del swung stiffly from the dead horse. Her face was oddly tight. "When you have seen Ajani kill your family, killing a horse is nothing."

Garrod's eyes snapped open.

Del's tone didn't waver. "When we are free of here, I have questions to ask of you. Questions about Ajani."

Garrod said nothing at all, still struck dumb by the death of his horse. Del turned away.

After a moment, certain Garrod now would do nothing, I went over to her. "I'll be with you, bascha."

Her voice was slightly unsteady. "You might do well to get up high."

"I might," I agreed, "but I have no intention of hiding."

Lashes flickered minutely. "Because Garrod's staying down?"

I didn't feel like biting. "Because I want to stay here with you."

Her eyes searched my own. Wavered. Then lips tightened slightly. "I don't need company to die."

"Neither do I, Del. But I have no intention of dying." I glanced through the throat and to the cut beyond. Heard the yapping of the approaching flood. Took my place behind her. If they got past Boreal, they'd still have an enemy. "The hounds are coming, bascha. You'd better sing your song."

Del turned. She positioned herself just behind the dead horse, warded by towering stone. Such a fragile, delicate gate, made of flesh and bone. But I thought it might be enough, because she also was Boreal.

Del lifted the sword and held her angled from shoulder to hip. I knew, underneath the soft-combed wool cross-wrapped from wrist to elbow, Del's arms were flexed and firm. Her legs were spread and set, knees only slightly bent. She held her stance and waited.

She is tall. She is strong. She is completely unrelenting. Not a soft woman, as Cipriana had needlessly pointed out; what Del was, I *knew:* a dedicated soldier in the service of her oath.

My sword hissed as I unsheathed it. But the music of the steel was lost in the song of Delilah's making.

The canyon disgorged six hounds. The vanguard had arrived.

Hoolies, bascha, *do it—*

Chapter 22

Something flickered at the corner of my eye. Something high, up in the cliff wall, and not where Garrod and I had cached any of the others. Which meant maybe the hounds had found another way in, and the vanguard was only a decoy.

Quickly I glanced at Del, who began to sing her sword alive. She was, for the moment, untroubled by the hounds, who merely crouched against the canyon floor, creeping forward to show her their teeth. I glanced up at the wall again, saw the blob of a face in one of the holes, knew it was man instead of beast.

I sheathed, crossed the trap-canyon in two leaps, caught the convenient handholes. Toeholes as well; I clambered up easily, chinned myself on the ledge some forty feet above the floor, pulled myself up with caution. I wasn't much interested in having my eyes poked out.

No danger of that. The hole was empty, but it wasn't entirely a *hole*. It was a tunnel in the rock, smoothed by wind, water and time. Feeble light blushed it pink and apricot, which meant the tunnel gave out beyond the trap-canyon, providing a means of escape.

"Garrod!" I shouted. "Garrod, get the others down. Bring them over here. I've found a way out." I swung myself down, around, clung a moment to the lip of the ledge, caught toes in convenient holes, began the awkward descent.

I was down, jumping the last five feet, as Garrod helped the women down from their ledge. I retrieved Massou and steered him to the crude ladder in the wall. I'd found the hand- and toeholes spaced ridiculously close together, carved more for a boy of Massou's size than a man's. But there was no time to wonder about it; it simply meant Massou would find the going easy. He was quick and agile, and more than willing.

Adara, however, was not. "Up there?" she asked, aghast.

"Straight up," I agreed. "There's a solid ledge, once you get up, and a tunnel."

"But you don't know where it goes!"

"Out of here," I said firmly, and caught her around the waist. "Hike up those skirts and climb."

"But—"

"*Climb, woman!* Or would you rather be eaten?"

Hastily she gathered skirts, kilted them up into her tunic belt to display blue woolen leggings, turned to face the wall. I boosted. Awkwardly she thrust hands and feet into holes.

Beyond Del's throat and the dead horse gate, more hounds gathered. Ugly hounds they were, dappled silver against dull gray, with low-slung heads and prominent jaws, displaying awesome teeth. They had raggedy, wolfish ears, except the ears lacked hair, being leathery, grayish things that now stood firmly upright, fixed upon the song. Hindquarters were slight in comparison to heavy shoulders made heavier by tangled manes. Brushy tails hugged genitals, curled tightly against lean bellies.

In the faint glow of dawn, slanting eyes were colorless. By night, I knew, they were white, throwing back the light.

Del sang. I felt the temperature drop. Down and down, until my breath plumed the air. I knew it was only backlash; the winding conduit in front of Del would suffer the worst of the storm. But it still made me shiver, although I wasn't certain if the response was born of cold or superstition.

The hounds, too, felt it; felt *something*. As Del loosed the sword, each of them tilted back an ugly head and howled to the skies.

I shook my head, staring. It resembled nothing so much as

some uncanny form of obeisance. To Del? Or to the sword? Or maybe to the magic?

Hoolies, I hate magic. There's nothing *clean* about it.

"Come on," I told Cipriana brusquely as her mother reached halfway. "Your turn."

Her skirts were already kilted. She turned to face the wall, then abruptly swung back. She caught my neck, hugged hard, kissed me before I could say a word. And was climbing the ladder of holes, laughing to herself.

Oh, *hoolies*. What possesses some women?

Massou's expression was one of embarrassed disgust. Garrod's one of startled speculation. Then he frowned. "Do you have a *harem*, Southron?"

"She's young," I muttered, reaching to scoop up Massou. "She doesn't know what she wants." I put the boy against the wall, steadied him, sent him up behind his sister. As I'd expected, he took to the climb with ease.

Garrod's breath wreathed his face. "What about the horses? Do we take them back through the canyon?"

I sighed. "You don't learn too quickly, do you? No, Garrod, we don't take them back through the canyon. We leave them here."

"*Leave* them—" He stopped short. "You hope the beasts will be satisfied with them instead of with us."

"I'm not counting on it." I jerked a thumb upward. "Your turn, horse-speaker."

"What of your stud?"

It took all I had to shrug unconcernedly. "He doesn't have wings, does he? So I guess he stays with your horses."

Garrod glanced back. Four Northern horses stood huddled together against the far wall; the fifth lay dead in the entrance to the canyon. I saw his face go stiff, and then he was climbing the ladder.

It left me. And Del.

Del's song faltered. Then stopped. I might have told her to keep singing in order to hold the hounds, but clearly Boreal's power was not what kept them from attacking. Maybe some form of geas?

It didn't sit well. I was not at all fond of the idea that the beasts were more than predators, but under a kind of guidance.

Del voiced similar thoughts. "They're creeping closer," she said as I joined her. "See? Right now they're watching me, judging me . . . they're thinking out the attack." She shivered slightly. "They have *intelligence*, Tiger. As much as you or I."

I looked out at the hounds. Dozens of them crouched down in front of the dead horse, tongues lolling in apparent idleness, but it was belied by the alertness in pale eyes. Del was right; they *were* judging her.

I wet my lips. "It may not be intelligence," I said. "It may only be direction."

"What do you mean?"

"They cut us out of the *kymri* and herded us out onto the plain. They lost us briefly in the canyon, but now they've got us pinned. And yet they don't attack." I shrugged. "I still think it's sorcery . . . and I think they've been bewitched."

"If that's true—"

"It doesn't matter," I interrupted. "There's a way out, Del. The others are free—it leaves only us." I gestured. "There, bascha—up the wall and out. There's a tunnel."

Del stared at the ladder of holes. The swordsong had taken all of her concentration, making her deaf and blind to the rest of us. I saw her surprise transform itself into relief, and then she frowned, glancing at the horses.

"The stud . . ." She let it trail off, looking at my face. "Oh, Tiger—"

"Climb," I said evenly. "I can be as hardhearted as you."

I'd meant it as a joke. It came out otherwise. But it was too late to apologize; Del was heading for the cliff.

The hounds moved to follow.

Oh, hoolies. It *was* Del they wanted.

"Up!" I shouted. "Get *up!*"

She turned back, saw the hounds coming over the horse.

"Climb!" I shouted, unsheathing. "It's you they want, bascha. Get up that wall—get above them—get out of their reach."

"Tiger—"

"Just *do it*, bascha—I can hold them off."

Well, I could *try*.

Del was halfway up the wall as the hounds poured over the horse into the trap-canyon, making it their own. I felt their hot breaths, the scrape of claws on leather boots, the thrust of shoulders and chests against my legs. I stood knee-deep in a river of beasts.

They snapped, slashed, clawed, tried to thrust me aside. Most bit only halfheartedly, out of reflex. It wasn't me they wanted, but if I got in the way they'd take pains to put me out of it.

Well, I intended to get in the way. And let them know it, leveling my sword like a scythe. I took heads, severed spines, opened gaping holes in chests and ribs. I made myself soundly disliked.

Del was gone. Accordingly, they turned from the wall to me, pressing me back, forcing me across the canyon. Behind me, Garrod's horses were restless; the stud stomped uneasily.

The stud. Hoolies. Why do this on foot?

I pulled free of the spangled river, caught the stud, swung up onto his back. "Well, old son, let's say we try this one together." I gathered reins in one hand, hefted the sword with the other. "Let's stomp some dogs, old man."

Most of the hounds seemed distracted by Del's disappearance. Others melted back, licking at the ones I'd killed or wounded. But a few came for us. They snapped at pasterns, hocks, knees. Slashed at belly, genitals, flanks. Tried to pull him down, to shred him, to turn him back from flight. But the stud was angry and frightened, doing his best to run, and when a horse as single-minded as my old man decides he wants to run, *nothing* gets in his way.

Not even the man on his back.

There is something exhilarating about fighting the odds while astride a very good horse. Some elemental emotion that strips bare the so-called civilization we've undergone in order to live in settlements and cities, or to travel the sands in a caravan. Somehow I was not just a man anymore, but a man in tandem with the horse. It made me strong and proud and oddly content, all at once, with a powerful surge of emotion that translated itself into an intensity that, to my altered perceptions, slowed the attacking beasts to a crawl. And it made it easy to kill them.

It was a strange detachment. I felt the bunching of the stud's muscles beneath my buttocks, sensed the powerful anger, heard the snorts and squeals of rage. He struck unerringly with iron-shod hooves; together, we were invincible.

I smelled blood and urine and excrement. The stink of fresh-spilled entrails. Mostly, I smelled power, and the stench of sorcery.

"Sorry," I said aloud, "but I am not impressed."

I knew better than to give the hounds a chance to pull us down. They still outnumbered us badly, and the stud and I couldn't hold them off forever. I waited until the flood paused to reconsider, jammed heels into the stud's heaving sides, took him through the snarling hounds.

There was, I knew, a chance he might refuse to jump the dead horse. In which case we were fairly trapped, because he couldn't hold out much longer. On foot, I stood little chance. So I aimed him at the opening, fed him rein, slapped the flat of my borrowed blade across his blood-flecked rump.

He jumped, my game old man, and cleared the body easily, landing with a clatter of iron on stone beyond. And, since he had momentum in his favor, I didn't bother trying to stop him. I merely gave him a second slap and bent down over his spike-maned neck.

"Now's your chance!" I shouted.

Obligingly, the stud ran away with me.

Chapter 23

We were noisy, the stud and I. Hooves clopped and clattered against hard stone, scraping grit, crushing small rocks, scattering bits and pieces against the looming walls. It was easier to see now that the sun was up, but I was still a stranger to the canyon even though I'd ridden through it only the night before.

At a dead run and bareback, the stud was hard to stay aboard. I hugged him with all the strength in thighs and calves, locking my left hand in the stiff upstanding hair of his unclipped mane. My other hand was full of sword, which I did not, at this speed, dare to put away. I'd probably cut off my left arm.

We threaded our way through the canyon, dodging overhanging cliffs and jumping ribs of rock. At times the cliffs loomed perilously near my head, threatening to scrape off my ears, but I bent low and tried to stay as unobstructive as possible. At this particular moment the stud didn't need my help; he seemed to know what he was doing. But then again, during a runaway, the stud usually does.

At last we reached the earthfall. I knew better than to try riding up it to the plain; the footing was impossible, too soft for stud or man. And so I went straight, leaving the narrow canyon behind, and entered the riverbed instead, the wide floodplain of vanished water. A canyon remained, but here the walls parted, taking leave of one another. To my left reared the plainside cliffs, to my right the low, ridged line of reddish wall, reminding me of the tunnel I'd sent the others into.

The others. I cursed, twisting on the stud, to look back the way we'd come. The canyon vanished into little more than a thready black line, made invisible by distance.

Hoolies, where was Del?

Where, for that matter, were the hounds?

Was it possible—? No, probably not. And yet it wasn't *me* they'd been after, but Del. And Del had walked up walls, disappearing into nothingness. I had no idea how well the hounds took a scent, but it was possible they'd lose her entirely. It was even possible, I hoped, they'd give up chasing me.

Briefly, I patted the stud. "Bet *you'd* like that, old man."

He labored beneath me. I didn't like the sound of his breathing. If he ran much longer at this speed, he could break his wind. Or throw shin splints. Or even break his legs. All of which would render him useless to me or to anyone else. And a horse no longer useful . . . I swore violently. No. He deserved better than that.

I twisted to look back again. No hounds, though I could hear howling in the distance. I sucked in a deep breath, considered things a brief moment, made my decision. Carefully I eased the stud's headlong gallop, slowing him to a lope, then to a jagged trot. And, at long last, into a stumbling walk.

I hooked my leg over and slid off the right side instead of the left in order to keep the sword clear of the stud, who stumbled and weaved so badly I was afraid he might swing his head and smack into the blade itself. I caught up the reins and led him, searching for a break in the low canyon wall. I wanted to get out of the riverbed, wide as it was, and find higher ground, a place where I could keep an eye out for hounds while I gave the stud—and myself—a rest.

Something caught my eye. A notch in the ridged wall. It was possible . . . yes; not only possible, but definite. The notch was a jagged break that cut through the line of wall clear to the riverbed. A rough, treacherous stairway up to level ground.

Rain had smoothed the stone, wearing down jagged edges. There were hollows where puddles gathered, shoulders curved like a woman's, crannies wide enough for booted feet and shod hooves. It was not, thank the gods of valhail, incredibly steep, but it would still be a tough climb for the stud. He was horse, not mountain goat.

Tough climb for me, too. I didn't dare lead him up because once he'd gathered his willingness he'd also gather speed. Horses, when left to themselves, climb such things in leaps and bounds; I'd end up splattered all over the rock. And I couldn't *ride* him up; it was too steep, too treacherous to burden him with my weight, and— without a saddle—I'd probably come off. But I doubted he'd go up it alone without some sort of encouragement, so I stuffed his head into the break, tugged the bit forward, stepped aside quickly as I slapped him once again with the flat of Theron's sword.

Maybe he *was* a mountain goat after all . . . three lunging strides took him halfway up, where he slipped, slid, scrabbled, then caught himself and lunged upward again, until he cleared the top.

"Wait for me," I said lamely, and sheathed my sword at last.

He did wait, being too exhausted to go on without me. Upon topping the break myself, I found the stud engaged in standing still, head drooping in weariness. Lather flecked chest, shoulders, flanks; sweat ran down between his ears to drip off the end of his nose. He was breathing like a bellows.

"Sorry, old man . . . nothing else we could do." I caught a rein and examined him quickly, gritting teeth as I noted the damage. Red flecks stained salty white lather. Blood ran from chest, flanks, hocks, ankles. The hounds had stripped hair and flesh away in their bid to pull him down. He needed rest, attention, food and water. And I could give him none of it; the hounds were far too close.

I shivered. Glanced skyward. It was early yet, but again clouds snuffed out the sun and gave me gray light instead of yellow, softening the hard edge of the day into one of dampness, of muted sounds and colors. When the rain began to fall, I was unsurprised, and equally unhappy.

It was little more than a heavy mist. But I was miserable

nonetheless, longing for my desert. I wanted warmth. I wanted sunlight. I wanted sand beneath my feet, instead of turf and leaves.

And now that I had the stud again, I also wanted Del.

"Hoolies, you're sandsick." I said it aloud, and emphatically, generally disgusted by the intensity of my longing. "You spent thirty-some-odd years without anyone, and now you're bleating like a newborn danjac begging for his mother." I scratched the stud's wet face. "First of all, you'll undoubtedly find her soon enough—they're not *that* far from here; second of all, even if you don't, it means you can go *home* again. To the South, where it's warm and bright and mostly free of this thrice-cursed rain. Where cantina girls sit on your knee and men buy you aqivi, counting it a privilege, telling stories later of how they spent time with the Sandtiger. Where the circle is drawn in *sand*, not mud; where opponents don't mutter of Northern patterns and Northern *an-kaidin;* where the tanzeers know your name and offer gold if you'll do them a service. And *where,* for that matter, you don't have to worry if the Northern bascha might get herself killed in the circle, leaving you alone in the world again—"

I stopped. The exhausted stud stared back at me with an abiding disinterest.

"Oh, hoolies . . . I am sandsick." I turned the stud north and walked. Hunting the Northern bascha.

The hunt took until late afternoon, and when it ended I was the hunt*ed,* not the hunter, because it was Del who found me instead of the other way around.

I was relieving myself when she melted out of the mist, damp hair straggling down her back. She saw the stud, not me; I'd left him in the open while I sought the trees. I considered calling to her, then discarded it. The reunion could wait until I'd finished.

Del went directly to the stud, speaking to him quietly. He whickered a little, nosed her, rubbed his head on her shoulder as she stepped close to stroke his neck. I finished, took two steps, stopped. Said nothing. Instead, I listened to her, and looked.

"Poor boy," she said softly. "Poor brave boy, so torn by teeth and claws . . . you've been badly used, haven't you? Asked to run and fight and run some more . . . and given no chance to rest." She smiled a little as he butted against her and rubbed harder, relieving the unpleasantness of damp hair against equally damp wool. "Poor Southron-bred boy, so tired of all the cold and rain and damp . . . as much as your rider himself, my poor beleaguered Sandtiger, so far from what he knows."

Del glanced around, still rubbing the stud's head. She'd scraped wet hair back from her face, which sharpened the angles of her features and robbed them of feminine softness. I realized, looking at her anew, she'd lost weight, and tension had tautened the flesh at the corners of her eyes and mouth. It aged her, made her look more determined than ever; stole away the lightheartedness of youth to show instead the burden of responsibilities no one should ever have to know, regardless of gender.

My poor brave Delilah, so driven by the dual needs for forgiveness and retribution.

I stepped out of the trees and went down to her, watching the alteration in her eyes as she saw me; the brief glow of relief that said, *"he is alive, he is whole, he is still the Sandtiger."*

In which case, I had an image to live up to.

"Well," I said lightly, "took you long enough."

Del smiled, showing teeth. "We *did* consider leaving you."

"So why didn't you?"

"We needed the horse."

So we did, since five of them were dead. "How are the others?"

"Adara is tired and letting everyone know about it. Garrod is still upset over the loss of his horses; he's a horse-speaker, after all. Massou considers it all an adventure, and Cipriana—well—" Del shrugged. "She wanted to come along, but Adara made her stay behind."

I scrubbed a hand over my face. "Hoolies, Del, what am I to do with her? She's just a *girl*—"

"And if she were older?" Del smiled again, arching suggestive brows. "She's not really all *that* young, Tiger. I'm only five years older."

"I know, I know . . . don't remind me." I sighed. "Sometimes I think *you're* too young for me."

"Me, too." Heartlessly. "Someone like Garrod, now . . ." Her expression was elaborately thoughtful.

"No," I said flatly, "not Garrod. Not for you. Not a man who might have taken part in the murder of your kinfolk."

It effectively robbed the moment of humor. The ice was back in her eyes. "Garrod did not," she said coolly, "but plainly he knows about it. He would have to; he has ridden with Ajani."

"Ridden *with* him?" I frowned. "Knowing him is one thing; riding with him is another."

"He knows him. He said so. He's ridden with him, too. But not lately, he says, and never to murder people." Del's tone was so flat it underscored her anger more than shouting could have. "There is a distinction somewhere, but I have yet to see it."

Garrod's habits were worth discussing, I thought, in view of his link to Ajani, but there were more pressing matters. Like the hounds. And I said so.

Del shook her head. "For the moment, they've disappeared. But I think they'll be back." She braced as the stud rubbed against her again. "You may be right, Tiger. I think they're after someone—or *something*—in particular . . . and I think they're conjured beasts. They aren't natural. Otherwise they wouldn't be so selective, so single-minded. And they'd never have let you and the stud break free."

"I sort of wondered about that myself." I gathered dangling reins. "He's too tired to carry double, bascha. We'll have to walk, if you'll lead the way."

She gestured in a northerly direction. "Back that way a couple of miles. In a canyon . . ." She smiled oddly a moment. "A very remarkable canyon."

"Not another trap-canyon." I started walking, leading the stud.

"No. Oh, no. And there is no danger of the beasts attacking there. The magic is too strong."

"Magic." I stopped walking. "Magic?"

Del nodded. "A very powerful magic, like nothing you've ever seen."

I grunted. "I've seen a little in my lifetime, bascha, and I haven't liked any of it. The hounds *themselves* are magic—even you admit it."

"Even I admit it," she agreed patiently. "Yes, the hounds are born of magic; and yes, a malignant magic . . . but the Cantéada aren't."

"The what?"

"Not what: *who*. The Cantéada." Del sighed, looking uncharacteristically fatuous. "Oh, Tiger, if only you could understand . . ."

"I'll try," I said dryly. "Explain it to me."

Del shook her head. "Explaining won't help. You wouldn't understand. I don't think you *can* understand; not you."

I wasn't particularly pleased by her conviction. "How do you know that? I'm not entirely blind—"

"Not blind," she said, interrupting, "deaf. At least deaf to music."

"Music." I sighed, scrubbing my face again. "Bascha, can't you be a bit more specific? All this jabber about music and magic—"

"All this 'jabber,' as you put it, is as specific as it gets." Del pointed north, suggesting we continue our journey.

I urged the stud forward again. "You're telling me these Cantéada people are musicians."

"No," she said softly, "I'm telling you the Cantéada are *music*."

I grunted. "Same difference."

"You *are* surly, aren't you?" Del shook her head. "I said you wouldn't understand."

"What I understand," I told her plainly, "is that we've been singled out by a sorcerer who's set the hounds of hoolies on us for no particular reason, as far as I can see, except maybe for some sort of peculiar entertainment. And I don't much like it." I scowled at her. "I don't like *it*, I don't like *this*, I don't even like this *country*." I sucked in a deep breath, stopped walking again, continued unabated, since she was listening, "I've been wet since we got here, half-frozen by your sword; attacked by loki, live *and* dead bodies; savaged by conjured hounds, made to suffer the amorous advances of mother *and* daughter, all the while being turned neatly away by you. Do you blame me for being surly?"

Del gazed at me thoughtfully. "You're tired," she said finally. "You'll feel better when you've eaten."

"Eaten, schmeaten," I snapped. "I'll feel better when we're done with whatever it is you need to do and we can go back South again, where it's warm and bright and *dry*."

Del took the reins from me. "And if we don't start moving, Tiger, we'll never go anywhere."

Surliness, like the rain, was completely unabated; I turned on my heel and moved.

Chapter 24

To our right cut the narrow canyon the stud and I had traveled twice, once in, once out. To our left jutted a damp, rocky wall rising well above our heads. Its face was gray and blue, slick and sleek with rain as it drizzled out of the sky. The cliff wall looked like someone had hewn it out of the earth with a giant ax, leaving it choppy and sharp and striated. But the jagged, angry face was softened by moss and fallen leaves, littered green and gold and carnelian, with a touch of faded plum.

"The colors are different here," I said, rustling through rain-washed leaves.

Del glanced at me, then looked at the craggy cliff face, at bare-branched trees, at leaf-softened, otter brown ground. After a moment, she nodded. "They are deeper, richer, older . . . not impermanent like the South."

"Impermanent." It sounded odd.

"Oh, yes. In the South the colors are subtler, more subject to whims of weather. To simooms, blowing sand across the miles. To lack of water, sucking moisture and color out of trees and vegetation. And to the sun, stealing the life from everything, man and animal alike."

I frowned. "You told me once you liked the South."

"I respect it. I admire its strength, its fierce beauty, its determination to survive. But this—*this*—" One arm encompassed cliff, canyon, forest, "—is what I have known since birth. These colors are my own; even the *smell* of the North, the taste of rain-soaked ground. This is what has shaped me."

Something blossomed inside me. Such a tiny little bud, threatening to unfold. "You sound like you mean to *stay* here."

Del looked at me sharply. And then glanced away.

The bud became a bloom and showed me the colors of my fear. "Bascha—when this is all done, we're going South again. At least, *I* am. Aren't you?"

She still didn't look at me. "I haven't decided yet."

Women are spontaneous creatures. They don't generally think things through on a logical level, relying mostly on emotion. They tend to make snap judgments and stick by them stubbornly merely for the sake of appearances, to save face and salve pride, even if you show them they're utterly wrong. Rarely do they look at all the angles, seeing only what they desire. They see, they want, they take, or find a man to get it for them.

They talk off the top of their heads, regretting it later, always, then denying they ever said it.

Women are *fickle* creatures.

And not so different from men. Which meant I knew what Del's evasiveness indicated, regardless of what she said.

She *said* she hadn't decided, which meant, of course, she had.

I stopped walking abruptly, which stopped the stud. "Do you mean to tell me you've dragged me all the way up here on some thrice-cursed mission of forgiveness, yet you have no intention of going home?"

She didn't answer at once. Then, softly, she said, "I *am* home, Tiger."

Hoolies. So she was.

My tone was curt. "Del—"

"I said I hadn't decided."

"And when *will* you decide?"

She shrugged. "When I do."

That was helpful. I scratched at my scars, dragging broken nails across the distinctive claw marks. I hadn't been able to shave for a couple of days and the stubble was driving me crazy. "And when, do you think, might that be?"

"I don't know!" Her shout echoed in the canyon, climbed the cliff wall, lost itself in trees. The stud flicked his ears.

"Ah," I said, "I see."

Del's face bloomed angrily. "How am I to know?" she asked tightly. "How am I to know if I will even have a life to live until I have faced the *ishtoya* and *an-ishtoya*, the *kaidin* and *an-kaidin?* I must go before them and abase myself, ask their forgiveness, their judgment, their penance. How can I say what I will do with my life when they may not let me *keep* it?"

"Oh. I think they'll let you keep—"

"You don't *know* that, Tiger!"

Clearly I had upset her. "Now, Del—"

"Don't!" she said furiously. "Don't patronize me. Don't dismiss my fear as if it has no validity. Don't pat me on the head and say you'll make it better. Don't promise to chase away the shadows because you *don't know what they are.*"

Well, no, I couldn't. Unless she told me, which she hadn't.

"I don't want to lose you," I said. Then regretted it instantly.

Luckily, Del only bristled. "You don't *have* me, Tiger."

"No," I agreed, "not lately. You and your loki obsession—"

She said something nasty about the loki in succinct, scatalogical Southron.

"I imagine they'd like that," I pointed out. "After all, you're the one who explained it to me . . . how they're attracted to men and women 'in congress,' as you put it."

"They are." Only her lips moved; her teeth were tightly locked.

"Well, then, *we* don't have anything to worry about," I smiled sweetly. "*Do* we?"

Del swung around and walked.

It was the stud who warned us. Maybe by then Del and I both were sick of walking, saying nothing but thinking a lot; we simply didn't notice. But the stud did, luckily.

Ears snapped forward. He inhaled deeply, then exhaled noisily, as horses do when they're unsure. And then he stopped dead in his tracks, popping the reins taut in my hand.

I smelled them before I saw them. I remembered the smell well—the putrid, musky stench of death—from brief captivity in the canyon. "I thought you said the hounds were gone."

"They were." Steel sang as Del unsheathed her sword. "They went back through the canyon after you, then simply disappeared."

"Well, they're back now."

We weren't following a path, exactly, just making our way on the strip of ground between canyon and cliff wall. Trees hedged both sides thickly, close-grown or more widely scattered, while rain dripped from bare branches. There was little coverage, but the hounds knew how to use what of it there was.

Wet leaves don't make as much noise as dry ones. Water muffles sound, glues them together, provides a soggy carpet. But they aren't soundless, either, and I heard the hounds around us. Front and sides and back.

No trap-canyon, this time. This time they didn't need it.

It was, as always—at least to me—a day of grays: ash, iron, olive. And now the hounds as well, dull slate and dappled silver, at one with the rain and at one with the cliff, paying mind to neither. In silence they slipped through the trees, heads dipped low, tails tucked, manes flopping on big shoulders.

One-handed, I drew my sword. "What in hoolies do they *want?*"

"Us," she said.

"You."

Del glanced at me sharply. "You don't mean—"

"I do. You went up that trap-canyon wall and they came in after you. It wasn't me they wanted. They only chased me because you were already gone. Even then, they were rather halfhearted about it. What are there—thirty? Forty? Fifty? More than enough to pull the stud down, and yet they really did nothing at all."

"Nothing," she echoed. "I've seen the stud, Tiger, and I've seen *you*. That's not all horse blood on your clothing."

Well, no, but I hadn't really taken the time to inspect it. I was stiff and sore and maybe a bit ragged around the edges, but I was well enough.

"I'll say it again; it's you," I told her. "If they could speak, I'd ask them."

Del said nothing, watching as the hounds spilled out to encircle us. They kept their distance, giving us plenty of room, yet I had the feeling that if we moved, they'd go right along with us. Once again, they worked us, like a dog set on Southron goats.

"It doesn't make any sense," she said. "The *voca* would never rescind my year of response."

"Who?"

"*Voca.* Those who gather in judgment."

"Theron came after you."

"Theron applied to collect the blood-debt. By *voca* law, he was required to give me the choice between entering the circle or going home to accept the judgment of my peers and teachers." Her face was stark. "As you know, he chose to dance against me. He lost, because of you. It means no other may challenge me, until the year is up."

"We're awfully close, bascha. With all the delays we've had, it's only a matter of weeks."

"Yes, Tiger. I know. But they would never have sent the beasts. It isn't the *voca's* way." Her expression was grim. "They would send men, Tiger, and maybe women. All carefully trained sword-dancers."

"Then why do these hounds want you?"

"Maybe it isn't me."

I frowned. "I *know* it's not me, Del."

"Not you, not me." She lifted the sword a little. "Maybe they want *this.*"

I shook my head. "What would a pack of hounds want with a sword, Del? They can't exactly use it."

"They've been herding us from the beginning."

"Well, yes—"

"They've never really attacked us, mostly driving us toward the north."

"Well, yes, it does seem—"

"She didn't hold them, Tiger. When I sang. They seemed to *relish* the power, instead of fearing it."

I thought it over. They had. "Still, Del, I wonder—"

"They're escorting us to someone. Someone who wants this sword."

I sighed. "Seems a bit farfetched to me, Del. Why send a pack of nightmare hounds when a man—or men—could do as well, if not better? After all, hounds don't have hands to carry a sword."

"They don't need hands. They've got us."

I glanced out through the drizzle. Gray on gray, perfectly still, in a perfect perimeter. Staring at Del and her sword. "It just doesn't make sense, bascha."

"Evil rarely does."

I glanced at her sharply. "What do you mean, 'evil'?"

"It depends on your definition," she said, "but evil is usually bad."

The stud still stood and stared, watching the beasts rigidly. Hot breath warmed my shoulder. "Then you're saying there *is* a sorcerer—"

"Or loki," she said calmly. "Loki require power. And power lives in this sword."

I recalled how she'd yelled at me not to use my borrowed sword in the loki ring. Could they have siphoned off whatever power remained and used it for themselves?

And now they required more.

"Loki," I said in disgust.

"A sword is a sword," Del said. "A *jivatma* is more than a sword. If I key her fully, her power can be used against us."

"Well, then, let's not go keying her, shall we?"

Del smiled a little, wryly. "How many do you think we can kill before they kill us?"

"You just said they don't mean to kill us."

"Probably not, if we cooperate. But I don't intend to go with them."

There comes a time when talk is exhausted and earns you nothing. There comes a time when action is the only answer, regardless of the odds. Del and I had known for some time that it would come to this; we'd put it off because no one wants to admit his powerlessness over something that can kill him. It's a way of cheating death.

But it all runs out eventually, and what you want is blood.

I gave the stud his freedom as well as a pat on the neck. "Well, then, bascha—looks like we have a fight on our hands."

Del sucked in a deep breath. "Let's take it *to* them, Tiger."

Oddly lighthearted, I grinned. "Is there any other way?"

Chapter 25

rouble was, we never got to take it to anybody. Because even as we moved, ready to commit carnage, something stopped the hounds. Something stopped *us*.

A sound. A high-pitched, whistling sound that dipped and rose, floated, wound its way around trees, slid down trunks to splash against the ground, spreading out to entrap our feet.

The stud, wandering off, stopped. Shook his head violently, flopping ears. Then pinned them back flat and curled his upper lip, displaying impressive teeth.

The hounds, gray on gray, melted back into the trees, rumps dropped low, leathery ears pinned, manes bristling. Beasts they might be, and conjured by sorcery, but they responded like whipped dogs, running for a bolt hole.

Del and I weren't much better off, until the sound altered. No more the whistle designed to pierce fragile ears, but a flirtatious, fluting song, wreathing branches and clinging, running and humming amid cracks in the craggy cliff face, echoing out of the canyon. And then even that died, leaving us in silence.

Del sighed. "Cantéada."

"What?"

"Cantéada," she repeated. "I think you're about to meet one."

"One of these music people?"

"You heard him, didn't you?"

I frowned. "You mean it was *music* that sent the hounds away?"

"Music. Magic. One and the same with the Cantéada." Del put away her sword, smiling. "Look, Tiger. Do you see him?"

I looked. No, I didn't; I saw no one.

And then I did, and stared. "Hoolies, Del! What *is* that?"

"That is a *he*," she said. "Cantéada, and songmaster. Tanzeer, you might call him; he's the authority in the clan."

He. It, more likely; he was like nothing I'd ever seen. Not even in my dreams.

He was smaller than Massou, yet something spoke of greater age. Coming out of rain it was difficult to see him because his coloring was similar. Pale, translucent flesh, oddly opalescent. And he was ugly. He was *ugly*. There was no other word for it.

But he made me forget it when he spoke, because when he spoke he sang.

Came you here to kill?

All I could do was stare.

Came you here to kill?

He was looking at me, not at Del. Slowly I shook my head, not knowing what else to do.

A delicate, blue-nailed finger lifted gently toward my sword. *Steelsong kills.*

A polite way of calling me a liar. "Del—"

"Your sword is naked," she told me quietly. "Sheathe it; he might accept your denial. Right now he won't."

I sheathed. "What *is* that thing?" I whispered. "Not human. Not animal."

"Cantéada," she said softly. "As children we are taught they brought music to the world. But I never thought I'd ever see one, until this morning. I wasn't even sure they were real."

I looked at the little man. He reached my waist, barely, barrel-chested with spindly limbs, and long, eloquent fingers. He wore only a leather kilt. His eyes were palest purple, a bit like Theron's blade. The pupils were weirdly catlike.

Steelsong kills, he repeated.

Del drew in a deep breath. "Steelsong kills," she agreed. "But so do beasts like those."

The Cantéada tilted his head. *Sendsong halts/Steelsong no longer needed.*

I frowned. "What's he saying?"

Del smiled a little. "Don't you wish now you understood music better? He's saying we don't need our swords anymore. The hounds have been sent away."

"How do we *know* that?"

"Cantéada never lie."

"Oh, right. You yourself just told me you thought they lived only in stories. Now you expect me to believe this little man is some magical creature who sings instead of talks, and won't ever lie to us?"

"He has no reason to lie."

"Hunh."

Arguesong discordant.

Del promptly laughed.

I sighed. Looked at the Cantéada. Such a strange little man, with his prominent jaw and mobile mouth, and a throat that swelled when he talked, very much like a frog's.

"We'd prefer not to kill them," I said politely, "so long as they don't kill us. If, as you say, your song has sent the hounds away, will it be for good?"

Birdlike, he tilted his head again. His ears, too, were over-large, vaguely pointed, with the slightest suggestion of mobility. His hair, thin and silver-gray, rose from a peak at the top of his forehead and ran in a crest down the back of his neck, feather-ing out on either side. It was more like down than hair, I thought. And, like hackles, the crest could rise, speaking a lan-guage of its own.

Distance diminishes/Diminishment obscures.

"What?"

Del sighed. "I think he means if we get too far, the song dimin-ishes and the spell stops working." She frowned. "Can't you un-derstand anything?"

"I know he's singing, bascha—I can hear a few of the words—but noise is *noise* to me." I paused. "What do you hear, Del?"

She smiled with a startling serenity. "Everything. All the tones, all the inflections, all the subtleties. It's clearer even than our speech, because it expresses the emotions."

I was skeptical. "And this is the man—the thing—that rescued you this morning?"

"When we climbed out of the tunnel, he was waiting. The threat of death drew him, and some of the others. Cantéada despise death."

"Don't *they* die?"

"I should have said, Cantéada despise murder. No matter what the victim."

I sighed and went over to catch the stud's dangling reins. "I'm not too fond of it myself, particularly when I'm the target. Well, what do we do now? Will he take us to the others?"

"I think it's what he came to do."

"So what are we waiting for?"

Del sighed. "Maybe a little courtesy."

"Courtesy has its place," I agreed, "but right now so does promptness. I'd sort of like to gather together *our* little clan, take stock of things, then get the hoolies out of here before we lose more time." I stopped. "So should *you*, Del. It's your skin the *voci* want, not mine."

"*Voca*," she corrected.

"*Voci*, loki, whatever. Let's just get moving, bascha."

The Cantéada, listening, seemed to understand before Del said a word. He turned, leaped up a tree, flung himself through branches. From tree to tree he sped, agile as a monkey. In his wake floated a fragile, fluting whistle.

"Followsong," Del explained. "Well? *You* were the one in a hurry."

I clicked to the stud and walked.

The rain worsened before it got better. Del and I were both soaked to the skin. Rivulets ran down my back, tickled buttocks, squelched inside my boots. Hair was plastered against my head, spilling droplets whenever I moved. I was wet and cold and miserable, like a cat caught in a downpour.

Well, so I was; cat and caught.

I blew out an impatient breath. It plumed in the air much as the stud's did, wreathing his nostrils in transient steam. Dark brown ordinarily, he was nearly blackened by the rain. Wet tail slapped at hocks and stuck, briefly, before freed again by the motion of his walking.

"Hoolies, I hate the wet. What I'd give for a little sun and warmth. . . ."

Del didn't smile. "What *would* you give?"

"What?" I frowned, not following. "Oh. Hoolies, I don't know. It was only a manner of speech."

"If you really want the sun, they can probably get it for you."

"Who can?" I followed her gesture. "Him? You're saying that little man can control the weather?"

"I think the Cantéada can do anything."

"They're *men,* Del . . . or something thereabouts. Just because he can scare away beasts doesn't mean he can actually change the weather."

"Of course not." She was strangely solemn. "No more than I can with my *jivatma.*"

So much for a fair fight. "I don't understand your sword anymore than the Cantéada, bascha, but I'm not certain even their magic can change the weather." I peered up at thick dark clouds caught on the cliff to our left, rolling up to spill over its edge like bolts of crumpled, pearlescent silk. "If they could control it, wouldn't they? Why live in rain and cold?"

"To maintain the balance," she answered, ducking a hanging limb. "Here in the North, we believe there is a balance struck between heat and cold, good and bad, men and women. Opposites all, but important to one another. Without one, the other would fail."

"Oh, I don't know. Sometimes I think men would be better off without women."

Her mouth twisted a little. "For a while, probably. Of course, men don't live forever. Too stubborn. Too violent." Her expression was innocent. "Once you'd killed one another off, what would be left? A world without men *or* women."

"He's stopping," I said suddenly.

Del glanced around, then nodded. "We're very near their canyon. This way, Tiger."

The trees were very thick, branches so tangled I couldn't tell one from another. Trunks were striped from rain, gathering in crotches and broken knots until it spilled over edges. Mud and leaves balled on the soles of my boots. I followed in silence, still leading the stud, and hoped the homes of the Cantéada were big enough to house me.

We came, quite unexpectedly, face to face with the edge of the world. Out of trees into nothingness; the ground was no more than a sword blade, and I balanced on its edge, close to falling, until Del caught my arm and pulled me back.

"I forgot," she said.

"Forgot *what?*" I cried, stumbling back. "Forgot the world stopped just as I walked off the edge?"

Del sighed. "It wasn't *that* bad, Tiger."

"Hoolies, woman—if I didn't know better I'd say you were trying to get me killed." I paused. "Maybe I *don't* know better; were you?"

"Hardly." Her tone was dry, but she didn't look at me. Then the tone changed into wistful admiration. "Oh, Tiger, isn't it beautiful?"

To her, undoubtedly; Del was raised on uplands, downlands, heights and sharp-carved canyons. She had suckled on wind and rain.

But not me. Not me. I looked out into nothingness and saw only an emptiness filled with clouds.

The world *had* ended. What lay before us was a canyon cut out of rock, but filled to choking on clouds. I could see little but the layers, cluttering up the other side as well as the distant bottom.

Beautiful. Maybe. But I wanted a little *sun.*

"How in hoolies do we get down from here?"

"Follow him down, Tiger. The songmaster's waiting for us."

So he was. Against the clouds, against the rain, he was nearly invisible. He flicked a hand and was gone, but I heard the thread of a whistle.

"Followsong, again?"

"You're catching on, Southron."

I went after the little man, wary of the hidden canyon. It would be incredibly easy to miss a step simply because clouds blurred the edge, creeping insidiously across the ground to merge earth and sky with themselves. They clung to trunks and earth, filling the spaces in between and lingering in the treetops.

"Gods," Del whispered behind me, "I'd forgotten *how* beautiful."

"He's gone again, bascha."

"That's what the followsong's for."

"I don't *like* it, Del."

"You don't like anything."

Hoolies. There was no sense in talking to her. She was sandsick, or maybe cloudsick; her loyalties had changed.

I kept walking, leading the stud, not looking at the cloudbank. It rolled and wisped and caressed, reaching out to touch my face. It made me want to shudder, but I didn't do it in front of Del.

Not that she could have seen; the clouds were like a shroud.

Even I'll admit it, the Cantéada's followsong was incredibly compelling. I marched along, resolutely avoiding the edge of the canyon, and felt myself locked in place. As if I knew the way as well as I knew myself, which struck me as odd; who really knows himself? At any rate, I was caught. Which probably was just as well; when the ground suddenly sloped downward without warning, I didn't panic. I didn't even hesitate. I just kept on walking.

"Magic, huh, Del?" The ground continued to drop.

"He's taking us into the canyon."

"Is this the way you came out?"

"Yes. Only then there were no clouds; I could see the way easily."

I glanced back over my shoulder. Del was mostly blocked by the stud, who ambled between us, but I could see her walking steadfastly through the shreds. It looked like fog to me.

She smiled. Damp hair swung forward, slapping against her shoulders. She was as wet as I, but obviously less bothered. Her gait was smooth and unforced, conspicuously free of tension. She even hummed a little, echoing the lilting tune. Her face was alight with contentment.

Hoolies. I'm going to lose her.

Chapter 26

I could see next to nothing except my boots and maybe a
foot in front of them. Everything else was fog or clouds or
some other conjured stuff.

"This is ridiculous," I muttered. "Here I am in a place I have no
business being, following a little spit-colored man with blue fingernails who *sings* to show us the way." I let that sink in a minute. It
didn't make any more sense aloud than it did in my mind.
"Hoolies, I must be sandsick."

As if on cue, the clouds lifted entirely and we were done with
climbing down, having reached the bottom at last.

I stopped so short the stud walked into me and banged his
nose against my shoulder. But I didn't pay any attention, I didn't
even move—except to turn my head—as Del caught up and
slipped by me.

"What *is* this place?" I asked, though it was mostly of myself.

"The home of the Cantéada."

She had stopped not far from me, turning to watch my astonishment. She was smiling, if only a little, pleased to see my
reaction.

Well, it was an honest one. Now that the clouds had lifted I
could see the canyon clearly, and what I saw was amazing.

The walls were very sheer, jutting straight up from the canyon floor. The stone was mostly gray, flecked with chips of black and white, but richer colors cascaded from top to bottom. The walls were sharply cut and pocked by massive natural shelves, as canyons often are, each hollowed shelf packed with moss and grass and dirt. But this canyon differed. Each shelf spilled a fall of flowers and vines, all tangled against the stone. Reds and blues and purples, dappled canary and copper and lime.

I looked up at the sky. Cloud/fog still blocked the sun, but had lifted out of the canyon, clogging higher ground. I couldn't see the top, where I had nearly walked off the edge of the world.

"Nice coverage," I remarked. "No wonder no one believes they really exist; they hide themselves down here."

"They have reason," Del said. "If they didn't, men would try to steal their magic, or make them use it for selfish reasons."

The canyon itself was fairly small. It was a trap-canyon much as the other had been, although larger, and as pocked with hollows and holes, including the flower-box shelves.

I glanced back up the path we'd come down. Was glad I hadn't seen it, buffered by fog and cloud. It was a narrow, switch-backed trail not much wider than a horse.

The followsong had stopped. The songmaster, or whatever he was, had disappeared. But I was still aware of a quiet humming, a thread of a sound that was unobtrusive but still evident, like the buzz of bees on a summer day, though considerably more melodic.

"What's that noise?" I asked.

"Wardsong," Del told me. "Keeping the hounds at bay."

Someone shouted my name. I turned, frowning, and saw Cipriana popping free of a hole in the canyon wall like a stopper from a bottle. The hole also disgorged Massou, Adara and, eventually, Garrod.

Cipriana ran right up to me, making indications she wanted to hug me; I sort of slid out of it by pretending the stud was fractious and turned her enthusiasm aside. Del stood there smiling, half-amused, half-resigned, and didn't move to help, being disposed merely to watch.

Luckily, the stud picked that moment to *be* fractious, so my make-believe wasn't make-believe anymore, and I had to tend him closely to keep him under control.

Massou said something nasty, rubbing the place on his shoulder where the stud had bitten him.

"Then stay back," I told him, half-distracted by the stud but also annoyed by the boy's continuing bad humor. "It's sort of obvious he doesn't like you; you may as well just accept that fact and leave him alone. Egging him on won't help."

Garrod stood behind Adara's left shoulder, pale braids hanging to his waist. His fair-skinned face was pinched as he watched me with the stud, and I recalled he had lost all of his mounts. I couldn't really blame him for resenting me for keeping mine.

The stud bared teeth, raised a threatening hind hoof, pinned tipped ears flat back. Brown eyes rolled; he was glaring at Adara.

I sighed, thumbing the lip away from my ear. "Look—let me get *him* settled and then we can talk. We have to decide what we're going to do."

"Go north," Cipriana said promptly. "Aren't you taking us to Kisiri?"

I shot a quick glance at Del. She masked her face as the girl spoke, but I saw the tension in her mouth. More delay, I knew, would not be tolerated.

"Like I said, let me get him settled. Is there a place I can put him?"

Massou shrugged. "The Cantéada don't have horses."

"Well, then, I'll just stake him out. There's plenty of grazing here." I knew better than to ask Massou to find a good spot; the stud, provoked, would probably try to bite again.

"Let me." It was Garrod, moving out from behind Adara. "He's upset, and you are adding to the problem."

"Am I really? I think I know my own horse."

"Sometimes yes, sometimes no." Garrod put out a hand.

I considered it. Wondered if Garrod was the type of man who, having lost something, wanted others to lose it as well. He had ridden with Ajani; he might be a vengeful man.

"Tell you what," I said lightly, "let's both go."

Del pointed across the canyon to the hole. "We'll be there."

I nodded, turning to lead the stud away. Garrod followed, watching the stud move with an attentive eye. I heard him click tongue against teeth in dismay as he saw the tears and teethmarks in hocks and flanks, the wounds on shoulders and belly.

"Hard-used," he muttered.

"No choice," I told him flatly. "If I'd stopped, they would have had him."

"As they had *my* horses." His tone hardened. "Except for the one *she* killed."

I stopped, unlooped the stake and picket rope, bent to push the stake into the ground. Stepped on it to anchor it. "She did it to try and save our lives," I said evenly, examining my weary horse. "And it did slow them. Maybe just enough to let Del get up the wall . . . but I guess you'd prefer that she had died."

Garrod's tone was bitter. "She accuses me of murder. Of killing families."

"You rode with Ajani."

"I sold *horses* to Ajani! Who is to say that's wrong? I am trying to make a living."

"So is Del," I said. "What's left of her life, that is."

Garrod watched me in strained silence as I bent, lifted a fore-leg, used my knife to carefully cut away mud, inspected hoof and shoe. Braid beads rattled; he was shredding bits of hair.

"She says Ajani killed her kin."

"He did. He and his men."

"I was not there."

"But you do know Ajani." I set the hoof down, moved to the other foreleg.

"I have traded with him, yes. I don't kill people."

"But you provide horses to those who do." I cleaned the hoof, pried a stone loose. "And do you also buy from Ajani the horses he steals from families?"

Garrod was conspicuously silent.

I lowered the hoof, straightened, looked at him across the stud's back. "I think she is well within her rights to distrust *and* dislike you. You and men like you make Ajani's trade possible."

"And you?" he accused. "Are you better, either one of you? Hiring out your swords to whomever has money to buy you?" He spat at the ground. "How many men have you killed in the circle? How many men have given up their lives to you in the ritual of the dance? Does it make it pretty? Does it make it right? Does it make you feel powerful?" Pale eyes were angry, hard and cold as ice. "I have killed men in my life, men who have sought to cheat me or steal from me or have forced me into a fight. I am not Ajani; I don't kill or steal families. But neither am I *you;* I don't step into a circle and hold myself above the rights of other men, justified by a *jivatma.*"

I had not for some time thought about my life. It was what I was and did: sword-dancer for hire. If you think about what you do and question why you do it, it gets in the way of things. It makes you wonder why you bother to live at all. And that's deadly in my profession.

I shook my head. "I'm sorry about your horses, but provoking me won't bring them back."

His face was tight. "I'm a horse-speaker; it matters. But that's not why I say this now. I say this now because I am accused of doing things I have never done, nor have a wish to do. I am not a murderer."

"She has reason," I repeated.

"To her way of thinking, no doubt; it's easy to justify. But I think she is warped. I think she is twisted and warped and mis-shapen, all bound up by a need for revenge that eats at her soul like a canker."

"Just because you two don't get along—"

He shook his head so violently the braids flopped against his chest. "I'm speaking of other things. I'm a horse-speaker: I know things of the emotions. Things of men's and women's emotions, which are not so different from horses, when reduced to needs such as the one driving her." He paused, took a steadying breath, put out a hand and touched the stud. "I dismiss none of Ajani's actions; he is a ruthless, cold-hearted bastard. But she should look at her *own* actions. Is she so very different?"

I felt a flicker of anger. "If you'd survived the sort of hoolies she did—if you'd lived through what she did—"

"—undoubtedly I would be warped as well." Garrod nodded. "But she *did* survive; she lived through Ajani's raid. Why let him triumph now by shaping her into a woman who has no kindness, no mercy; a blade without a name?"

I frowned. "What?"

"Blade without a name," he repeated. "A thing of Staal-Ysta." His mouth twisted a little. "Ask her," he said. "Ask her if she's a blade without a name. Ask her if her song has an ending."

I shook my head. "You're not making any sense."

"No? Ask *her.* Ask her what I have said. And tell her—" He paused. "Tell her even an upland horse-speaker has heard of Staal-Ysta, and the honor codes of the *voca.*"

I sighed. "Garrod—"

He cut me off with a shake of his head. "No more of this, sword-dancer. Go and see your woman. Let me tend your horse. It is something I can do."

Eventually, I let him, and went to see my woman.

No, not *mine;* I went to see Delilah.

Chapter 27

In the South, I'm used to ducking down to enter low doors because I'm taller than most Southroners. In the North, where men are routinely as tall as I am, I don't have to do it as much. This time, though, I did. I nearly had to crawl.

The canyon walls, I discovered, were honeycombed with holes. The largest ones were at the very bottom, half-buried in the ground to form an arched opening. This, in turn, formed half-tunnels into the rock, which led into bigger caves. It was a unique way of living, but I wasn't thrilled by it.

I bent down outside the hole. "Del?" It echoed into darkness.

I waited. No answer. So, sighing, I bent down very low and ducked into the opening.

Not a lot better here. I couldn't stand up straight. "Hoolies, I feel like an old man."

The tunnel extended farther on. I pushed my way through, bumping head and scraping shoulders, twisted sideways, pulled free, discovered the tunnel ceiling was higher here. But the side walls were hardly wider than my shoulders.

It hit me then. Sweat broke out, and trembling, and I tasted the metallic flavor of fear in my mouth.

The walls closed in, and suddenly I was back in Aladar's mine.

No chains weighed me down, but recollections did. And they were all incredibly clear.

The tanzeer had robbed me of months. The months had robbed me of *me*.

Oh, hoolies, will I never forget?

Forcibly, I collected myself. Looked ahead at the tunnel, knowing Del was not so far. And managed to go on.

"Little men," I muttered. "Little men build little homes."

I walked on carefully in muted illumination that filtered in from the canyon behind me. The walls were gray but glittery, catching some of the light. The passage itself was short, for which I was thankful, and opened rather abruptly into another archway. Beyond, the light was quite good.

Shadows stroked the archway. Del's head appeared. "This way," she said. "Watch out for your head."

I grunted, bent, climbed through. And stopped to gawk, for the cave was more like a cavern.

Candlelight. Lanterns. Bright bits of glass and polished metal. I saw beakers, amphorae, cups, bowls, platters, all made of polished metal. Not silver, not copper, not gold. Not anything I'd seen.

I squinted. The motion of my entrance caused the candleflames to gutter, throwing back glints of light. "Some house, bascha."

"This is the songmaster's home," Del said. "He's hosting us for the night."

I glanced around. There were rugs and blankets, leather furniture, wooden flutes and pipes, other things made of reeds or carved from gourds. Even some made of mud with finger holes carved in hollow bellies, or small drums with heads stretched tight.

I spread inquisitive hands. "Well—where is he? I haven't seen any of these Cantéada since I reached the bottom."

"Songcircle," Del answered. "Everyone meets to discuss things; I think they're discussing us."

"Private, I take it."

"Very."

I had not expected privacy in the cave, much as I wanted it, which was just as well. Already Adara and Cipriana were rising to make me welcome. The ceiling arched high overhead, swept down to meet the floor. Someone had painted the walls with muted pigments: melon, magenta and teal, offset with a trace of lilac. The patterns flowed together like the runes on Del's sword, line after fluid line, knot after tangled knot. Enough to confuse the eye.

Del saw my frown of incomprehension. "Music," she said, smiling. "I can tell you more later; right now we should discuss what lies ahead."

Cipriana stood very close to me. "We'll go on, won't we?" she asked. "Go on to Kisiri?"

"No horses," Massou said, staying behind in a tangle of blankets.

His sister shrugged and tossed back loose blonde hair. "Garrod can get us horses."

"Maybe," I said, "maybe not. Things are different, now."

In the glow of candles and lanterns, Adara's hair was bronze. "How different?" she asked. "Will you forsake us after this?"

Oh, hoolies. Now we were *forsaking*.

Del's tone was carefully neutral. "Tiger and I must go on."

"No!" It was Massou, tearing free of his blankets to run and catch Del's hand. "You can't leave us behind!"

She didn't try to disengage, but I saw the tension in her stance. "We have to go on," she repeated. "Time is running out. Tiger and I must take a shorter route through the Heights. Kisiri will be out of our way." The cave squashed voices and flattened tones. It made her sound harsher than ever.

"You're just jealous," Cipriana accused. "You're just afraid he'll decide he wants me instead of you."

Visibly, Del collected her patience. "No man owns a woman; no woman owns a man. Tiger does as he pleases."

Cipriana was adamant. "And if it pleased him to take *me?*"

Oh, *hoolies*. Gods keep me from jealous women!

Still, I felt a flicker of deep-seated pleasure. Del, Cipriana, Adara. Three women for one man, and all of them willing women.

Then again, maybe *two*. Del was still loki-spooked.

Which, rather abruptly, made me testy. "Enough," I said

shortly. "Sit down and we'll hash this out." They sat, even Del, taking places on pelts and rugs. I remained standing, avoiding commitment entirely. "We are guests for the night of these people. Come morning we'll leave the canyon." I thought briefly of the hounds, clustering in clouds to wait at the edge of the world. "We have one horse: mine; Del and I will ride him."

"What about us?" Massou asked, staring steadfastly at Del.

She, in turn, looked straight at Adara. "Your mother should have told you. Your mother should have made it clear. You three are bound for Kisiri. Tiger and I are not."

"But you can't *leave* us!" That from Cipriana. "How can you leave us? How can you desert us? What are we to do?"

This was not the girl who had proved such a staunch foe against the loki. This was an entirely different girl. I didn't like this one.

"You'll do what you intended to do even after you buried your father," I said firmly. "You'll go on."

"Alone!" Tears glittered in her eyes. "Two women and a boy, without a wagon, without a horse . . . without even supplies!"

"Del and I will talk with the Cantéada. They may know a solution." I turned toward the tunnel, thrusting out a delaying hand. "We'll go talk to them now. You stay here."

I ducked out before Cipriana could raise another objection. I felt Del coming behind me, locked in silence. It wasn't until we were completely out of the tunnels that I felt free again, sucking in lungfuls of cool, damp air. The day hadn't known much sun, but it was setting nonetheless. Shadows were deepening.

"She's frightened," Del said simply.

I grunted. "She's a pain in the rump."

"They're all frightened, Tiger. Even little Massou."

" 'Little Massou,' as you say, is as bad as his sister. In her own way, so is Adara." I scratched at stubbled scars. "I'll be glad to be rid of them."

"It's so easy for you, then? To turn your back on responsibility?"

I stared. "Hoolies, bascha, it's for *your* sake we have to leave them. Time is running out."

She turned away, waving a hand. "Never mind. Never mind. I shouldn't have said it. I'm just—oh, hoolies, I don't know. I'm just all twisted up." She leaned back against the canyon wall, next to the tunnel entrance.

I'd grinned as she used the Southron term. But it faded when I thought about Garrod's words. Warped, he'd said. Twisted and misshapen. And a canker eating her soul.

"Del—"

"Listen," she whispered. "Hear it?"

I blinked, cut off in mid-stride. Shut my mouth and listened. Frowned a little, then laughed. "It's Garrod," I said. "He's muttering to the stud."

"No, no—not Garrod. Listen to the *song*."

Song. All I heard was the same little humming melody Del had labeled a wardsong sung to keep the hounds away. "I don't hear—"

"*Listen*, Tiger! Can't you hear anything?"

I sighed. "I've told you before, it's all noise to me. Yes, I hear something. Someone's out there tootling on a pipe. Maybe two pipes. Maybe ten. What does it matter, Del?"

Del lifted both hands and pressed the heels against her eyes, threading rigid fingers into hair. "I *despair* of you, Tiger! Gods, how I despair. What am I going to do? How can you be what you must? How can I go before the *voca* confident they'll accept my blood-gift?" She drew in a noisy breath, let it out; half sigh, half groan. "*What am I going to do?*"

Hoolies. I'd never heard her like this.

"Del. Bascha." I reached out to pull away her hands. "What are you talking about?"

Her fingers were limp in mine. Strain carved lines in her face. "I can't tell you."

"If you *don't*—"

"I can't."

"Del—"

"I can't."

It took all I had to stop asking. Instead, I turned the topic. "We *could* just light out of here on the stud come morning and head back down South. We *could* just forget all about this *voca*-thing and this blood-debt and blood-gift and all those other things that are driving you half loki." I smiled, liking the phrase, although all Del did was scowl. "We *could* just go back to being sword-dancers, knowing the freedom of the circle."

Del took her hands out of mine. "There is no freedom now. There are things I have to do."

Something welled up inside me, of realization and frustration, then abruptly burst free. "I think Garrod's *right!* I think Garrod understands you perfectly, maybe better than I do." I glared. "Hoolies, Del—do you ever stop to think about anything else? Any*one* else? Do you ever stop to think there are other things in the world besides revenge and retribution?" Her face was still and white. "Do you even know what you're going to do once this *voca*-thing is over? Have you thought past anything but the trial?" I shook my head. "No. You're so locked into your course you give yourself no freedom to even think about anything else. You're like a horse who's been reined in so tightly all his life that even once he's given his head, he keeps his neck bowed snug. Partly because he's scared. But mostly because he can't make himself relax and become a horse again."

I have never seen such a mixture of emotions in a woman's face and eyes. Hoolies, even in a man's. There was shock, pain and anger, disbelief, resentment, realization, and an odd, renewed resolve. I saw Delilah build a wall right in front of me, brick by brick by brick. Then she slapped the mortar in the cracks to make sure *nothing* could get through.

Once the wall was built, she reached for her deadliest weapon. "You love me," she said.

For a moment the words meant nothing. All I heard was the tone, made up of strange and confusing subtleties. She was angry, was Delilah, but it was a deadly, calm anger shaped of ice instead of heat, and an odd accusation.

I felt a little sick. Deep-in-the-gut sick.

Is this how it ends?

I drew in a slow, deep breath. "I ask you *why*—now, at this point, having done so much to make yourself a *person* instead of a woman—do you turn to a woman's weapon?"

It cracked the ice a little. Clearly I'd surprised her. "Weapon—"

"Weapon," I said firmly. "Now that it's out in the open, am I supposed to tuck my tail between my legs? Am I supposed to roll over in submission and bare my belly to you? Or is it meant mostly to castrate me, so I'll still be occasionally useful?"

Even her lips were bloodless. "Is that what you think it means?"

"I think that's what *you* think it means."

Del's breath was ragged. She covered her mouth with one hand. The other clutched the front of her wool tunic. "Tiger—" she said "—help me—"

Slowly I shook my head. "If you want me to hold you now, as if nothing has happened—no. Because something has happened. If you want me to reassure you and tell you everything's fine, everything's forgotten—no. Because everything is *not* fine. You have to learn that not everyone can afford to be as single-minded as you. Not everyone can hack off bits of himself because it makes the life he chose easier." I wanted to touch her; didn't. "Not everyone," I said quietly, "can force *her*self to be someone she isn't, even when her conscience tells her not to."

"Conscience—?"

"I've seen you with Massou. I've seen you with other children. Only with him and only with them have I seen the other Del."

"Other Del," she said bitterly. "That soft, kind-hearted fool . . . the sweet, gentle soul so many men desire their women to be."

"Some, yes. Maybe a lot. Down South, yes. And there are times when I wonder what life would be like if you were another kind of woman." I shrugged. "But I don't want to change you, Del. Not completely. Maybe just a little . . . maybe just enough so that horse can unbow his neck and be a horse again." Now I did touch her. I reached out and put a hand on her right shoulder, closing my fingers on the too-rigid tendons beneath her clothes. "I don't want you *soft*. But I don't want you this hard. It's tearing you apart."

Del was shaking, a little. "You don't know—you don't

understand—you *can't* know what it's like—" She checked, shut her eyes a moment, dismissed the incoherence. "No man, especially a Southroner, can know how hard it is."

"No."

"No man can understand what it is to be a woman who doesn't belong because of her sex, and yet belongs because of her skill."

"No, bascha. He can't."

"*No* man can know what it's like to watch mother, father, uncles, aunts, sisters and brothers killed . . . and then be raped and humiliated, made to feel like a *thing*, stripped of name, of soul, of *self*—" She checked again, still shaking. "You don't understand what it is," she said, "to know almost every man who sees you *wants* you—not you, not really *you*, just that body, because it pleases him . . . you don't *know*, Tiger, what it is to have men rape you with their eyes when they can't do it with their bodies . . . and then you go away and vomit."

It took all I had to speak. "No," I said, "I can't. But what I *do* know is that if you carry that guilt and grief forever, it'll make you into a monster. It'll strip you of humanity. You'll become Ajani's triumph."

Del's smile returned. "But I won't," she said in amusement. "I won't carry it forever. Only until I kill him. Until Ajani's dead."

In silence, not daring to speak, I stroked back a strand of pale hair. Thinking to myself: *Oh, my poor Delilah . . . you have so much to learn.*

Chapter 28

I heard Garrod before I saw him because his braid beads rattled as he approached. I turned from Del, frowned a little,
saw his expression matched mine.

"Your horse is upset," Garrod said.

I scratched stubble. "He *told* you that, I suppose."

"Not in so many words, no." Garrod was unamused, distracted
by something else. "But he is bothered by something here."

Del shook her head. "Tiger's stud is always bothered. It's part of
his—" she paused, "—charm."

Garrod shrugged. "I can't say what he's like the rest of the time,
but something has made him uneasy for now. He wants to leave
this place."

"Oh, I see." I nodded sagely. "What *I* don't understand is, if he
tells you this much, why doesn't he tell you why?"

The horse-speaker sighed. "It would be easier if you respected
my profession as much as I respect yours."

"Horse stealing is not necessarily the sort of profession anyone
respects," I retorted.

"I'm not a—"

"Are you not?" Del interrupted. "No, perhaps not—you only
accept the horses *other* people steal."

Garrod answered her in a dialect I didn't know at all. But whatever he said went home, because I saw Del's color go bad again. She answered sharply, and her fingers twitched as if she meant to draw her sword.

"Now, wait—" I began, and then suddenly the others were among us.

Adara's green eyes glinted. "Are they going to fight?"

"No," I told her flatly.

"Are *you* going to fight?"

"*None* of us is going to fight, and I thought I told all of you to wait in the cave while Del and I talk to the Cantéada."

Cipriana shrugged ingenuously. "We heard you arguing."

Massou's blue eyes were wide beneath a shock of ragged blond hair. "We had to come out," he said.

Del's patience quite clearly was at an end. "This is private," she snapped. "This is *private*, and requires none of your attention. Has no one taught you manners? Has no one taught you respect?"

Massou's fingers plucked at her arm. "Are you going to invite the horse-speaker into a circle?"

Bloodthirsty little brat. "No," I said, "she's not. But even if she were, it's none of your concern."

Massou glared at me. "I was asking *her*."

Rude little brat, too. "I think it would be best—"

In the distance, the stud nickered uneasily.

"See?" Garrod asked.

Massou gazed at Del. "I think you should fight him."

"I don't." Her tone was very clipped. "I think we should recall where we are. I think we should mend our manners. I think—" She broke it off. "It doesn't matter what I think." Abruptly, she turned and left.

"Angry," Adara said.

Cipriana nodded. "Lately, Del is always angry. Angry deep inside."

"And frightened," agreed Massou. "I can feel her fear."

It was, I thought, an altogether unnecessary conversation, and quickly going nowhere. "What Del is, is tired of playing herd dog to your flock of sheep," I told them bluntly. "We have business of our own, serious business, and you've slowed us down. We're running out of time; Del has that to think of."

"What about us?" Massou demanded. "Are you just going to leave us here?"

"No." I gritted it out between my teeth. "I wouldn't do that to the Cantéada."

Garrod laughed softly, said something in uplander, then bent down and entered the tunnel. Leaving us to our argument.

I tried to step around them all, but Cipriana was in the way. "Are you going after her?"

"Cip—"

"Are you?" She moved closer. "Do you always trail after her like a dog who's been abused, but comes back begging for more?" Closer yet. "*You* shouldn't. You *shouldn't*. You don't need her, Tiger. You don't need a woman like that; a woman hard and harsh and unfeeling, who'd just as soon stick you with her sword as give you a kind word. You don't need—"

"What I need is some time to myself," I told her, setting her firmly out of the way. "What I *need* is a little peace of mind, so I have a chance to think."

"Tiger—"

I looked over the daughter's head to the mother. "Isn't it time you took a hand in this? Your daughter has been running after me like a bitch in heat. You're her mother—*do* something!"

Adara's ruddy hair still lay tangled on her shoulders. "What am I *to* do? She is grown, she is a woman; it's her choice to make."

"Just as you made yours—and Kesar's for him." I nodded. "Well, then, perhaps you should both know that I'm not about to give up sword-dancing just for the sake of a woman. Not for *any* woman."

Massou's eyes were oddly bright. "Not even for Del?" he asked.

Hoolies, spare me the questions of little boys . . . and the attentions of sisters and mothers.

"I'm going to speak to the Cantéada," I said firmly. "Stay here. *Stay here*. Do you understand?"

Cipriana folded her arms. "There you go, chasing . . . but it's all right when *you* do it."

"That all depends," I said, "on whether the other person *desires* your company."

Adara's tone was quiet. "Is that why Del won't share your bed?"

Oh, hoolies—

I turned and stalked away.

Del stood in the shadows with the little Cantéada, the one she'd called a songmaster. I marveled all over again at the pale, translucent skin, the feathery cap of down with its eloquently mobile crest, the fragile limbs and heavy chest. His throat, at rest, appeared normal, but when speaking—no, *singing*—it blew in and out like a frog's.

Her face was very solemn. "They are concerned," she told me. "He says there is discord here, grave discord, and it's affecting the lifesong."

"The what?"

"Lifesong," she repeated. "The way they conduct their lives."

I sighed wearily. "Song this, song that . . ." I saw her face. "All right, Del, no more jokes. Does he say why there is discord?"

She looked troubled. "We are alien to them, like dissonance in pure melody. We kill living beings. It causes disharmony."

I smiled. "One way of putting it. But the only thing we've killed lately are those hounds."

She shook her head, shaking loose hair as well; it had dried in waves. "Doesn't matter. To the Cantéada, all living things are deserving of honor and respect. *All* living things, Tiger. It's why they only eat what they grow, not kill, or what the land provides. It's the lifesong, Tiger . . . an endless cycle of living in harmony with the world."

"They *never* kill?" It seemed impossible to imagine. "They go through their entire lives without killing *anything?*"

Del nodded. "Cantéada have great reverence for life. Any life. Even that of a biting gnat."

"Those hounds aren't exactly *gnats*—"

"No. And the songmaster understands that, which is why he shaped the wardsong and gave it to others to sing. But he insists that while we remain here, we kill or injure nothing."

"Not even a gnat."

"Not even a gnat."

"What about a—"

"Nothing *at all*, Tiger."

I grunted. "What if we were attacked? We'd have to defend ourselves."

Del smiled. "Nothing will harm us here. This is a place of peace."

"Peace, schmeace," I said. "I respect their customs, but I don't believe in all this wardsong stuff. If any of those hounds come down from the trees, I'll be doing my best to stop them."

"This is also a place of power," she warned. "Don't discount these people."

I was tired. "No. All right. I won't. Now can we get a little rest? Maybe something to eat?"

Del bowed to the little man. "*Sulhaya*, songmaster. We accept your hospitality."

His throat inflated. *Dreamsong offers rest/Healsong offers renewal.*

I looked at Del. "What?"

"They'll sing you to sleep, Tiger. They'll sing us all to sleep." Del touched my arm. "Come on, let's go back. We *all* need food and rest."

We turned even as the little Cantéada melted away, but I was brought up short. I'd expected the canyon to be little more than a pocket of darkness now that the sun was gone, but I'd reckoned without the efficiency of the people who lived in it. Every entrance, chimney, crack and airhole was bright with candlelight, which lent the canyon a smoky, muted luminescence. Stone walls glowed like a Southron funeral circle, where sword-dancers with candles gather to give the greatest of the shodos passage to valhail.

I looked around. I could still hear the lilting tone that kept the hounds away. "Don't they ever get tired of singing?"

"Do you get tired of breathing?"

"There's a difference, bascha. I *have* to breathe."

"As much as they have to sing." I felt cool fingers slide through mine. "When I was little, my mother used to sing me to sleep. And then Jamail, when he was born; probably my brothers before me.

And my father would hum when he honed the swords." She sighed, looking at the lights that danced in walls. "I can't remember the first time I heard about the Cantéada. I just seemed always to know, like everyone else. But the story goes that before the gods made the Cantéada, there was no music in the world. And people were sad, not knowing what they lacked, but knowing they weren't whole." Her fingers tightened slightly. "And so the gods made the Cantéada, and the Cantéada made music."

I let it sink in; there'd been no singing in my family, because I'd had no family. Only a bed with the goats. "Nice story," I said finally, "if a little hard to believe."

"Let's walk." Del tugged on my fingers. "Do you remember all those patterns on the walls of the song-master's cave? All those lines and knots?"

"I remember." We walked in candleglow. It was cool but not cold, although without my Northern wools and leathers I might feel differently. I was beginning to appreciate them.

"Well, those knots are notes. The line patterns are the flow of the song. Together it makes music."

I grunted. "Seems awfully complicated."

"It can be. But you don't have to read it, unless you mean to sing or play what's been sung or played before. You *can* just make it up as you go, or put it away in your head for singing another time." She smiled a little. "It's one of the things an *ishtoya* is required to learn."

"Along with languages, mathematics and geography."

"Yes. And, of course, the dance."

Ah, yes, the dance. The thing we both lived for. "I think I prefer it less complicated. No song required."

Her fingers stiffened a little. "But in the North it *is* required."

I lifted one shoulder. "Fine for you, bascha. But *I* don't have to worry about it; all *I* have to do is dance."

"But *listen* to it, Tiger . . . listen to the song. . . ."

I listened to the song. Heard the rise and fall of the melody, the mingling of many voices. Or whatever the Cantéada used to make their music.

"Nice enough," I said grudgingly, "if a little monotonous after a while."

"It's a wardsong, Tiger . . . shaped to keep out hounds, not entertain human ears."

I grunted. "It would take something to entertain *my* ears."

Del sighed. We walked side by side, fingers laced, but only slackly, insisting on nothing. Neither of us is much for pronounced displays of affection, mostly because it's a very private thing. But also because I think both of us are reluctant to use the silent language of bedmates, for fear of giving away too much. Of ourselves as well as to others.

"Do you ever just get tired?"

Her tone was odd. I glanced at her curiously. "Tired? —Well, yes . . . just like anyone else."

"No. I mean *tired*. Tired of who you are . . . tired of what you do."

I didn't answer at once. We continued walking, going nowhere in particular, just meandering through the canyon's candleglow. Ahead, the stud whickered; we were near the songmaster's cave.

Finally, I answered. "I think they're one and the same."

Del glanced at me sharply.

I shrugged, made uncomfortable by the turn of the conversation. "I mean—sword-dancing is what I do, but it's also what I am." I spread my free hand. "Sword-dancing is more than a job. It's also a way of life."

"Not for everyone," she said. "Not for Alric, with his wife and two little girls." She paused, smiling. "Maybe three by now, or even a little boy; Lena was overdue."

I hadn't thought of Alric in months. The big Northerner had proved helpful to us both down South, although at first I'd distrusted him. He was a sword-dancer, Northern-trained, but didn't claim Del's skill or rank. Nor did he have a *jivatma*, using a Southron blade instead.

I shook my head. "It's not the sort of life a man should have if he keeps a woman."

Del smiled. "I suppose you'd rather stay at home while she tends you, the cookfire and babies . . . or maybe you'd rather be in bed trying to *make* those babies."

"Maybe," I agreed. "It's better than celibacy." I cast her a meaningful glance. "Well, then? What about you? Fair is fair, bascha . . . what happens a year or two from now? Do *you* start making babies?"

Del's smile faded. Her expression turned pensive. "You said a man shouldn't be a sword-dancer if he has a woman. Perhaps you're right; it would be difficult for the woman to know how much her man risks each time he steps into the circle." She sighed, stroking back pale hair. "And so I ask myself: What sort of parent would *I* be? What sort of mother would I be if I risked myself in the circle?"

"But you have a choice," I told her. "You don't have to be a sword-dancer . . . once you start having babies, there'll be other things to do. The children will keep you busy."

Del's mouth hooked down. "And there it is, Tiger . . . a man does what he wants, even after siring children. A woman must be a *mother*."

I frowned, puzzled. "Isn't it what you'd want?"

Del looked straight at me. "Not every woman wants children."

"But it seems a natural thing—"

"Does it?" Her tone was inflexible. "Is that why *your* mother left you in the desert?"

Something pinched deep in my belly. I felt a little sick.

Del's fingers tightened. "Maybe she had no choice. Maybe she was ill. Maybe *you* were ill, and she thought you'd already died. Maybe—"

"Maybe not," I said dully. "Maybe it's like you said: she simply didn't want me."

Del stopped walking abruptly and raised my hand to her lips. "*I* want you," she said.

Chapter 29

*I*t was the stud who warned us, although we weren't paying much attention, being rather engrossed in something
other than listening to horses. And then, suddenly, they were *here*,
and we were no longer alone.

Adara's hand was on my shoulder, pulling me away even as
Massou slipped between Del and I. "So long—" she said. *"So long—"*

"Now, wait just a—"

Cipriana grasped my right arm. "You don't know how it is. You
don't know how it *is*."

I heard Del say something to Massou in a questioning tone, although the words themselves were lost beneath Adara and Cipriana. Massou didn't answer. He just hung on to both her wrists.

"What in hoolies—?" I tried to twist free of them, found I
couldn't. Found they weren't about to let me.

"So long—" Adara whispered.

"Me first," her daughter said.

"Power," Adara hissed. "Power in flesh, power in steel—"

"Get *off*—" But they weren't about to.

"Tiger!" It was Del, sounding uncommonly afraid. "Oh, Tiger—
loki—"

No. It couldn't be possible. Loki? Adara and Cipriana? Especially Massou; it was impossible.

But it wasn't. And I knew it; it all came together.

"Hoolies—"

I tried ripping away, shouting at Del to do the same. I couldn't see much, being engulfed by two determined loki masquerading as women, and poor light to boot. All I knew was they were both incredibly strong, both incredibly forceful, and if I wasn't careful they'd have me spread-eagled on the ground before I could say my name.

"Del—?" I wrenched my head around, trying to see her. Saw Massou pushing her back, *pushing* her back, until she smacked against the wall so hard her head rapped rock. I heard the scrape of her sword hilt. And then I saw Massou, who was no longer Massou.

"Tiger—*Tiger*—"

Hoolies, I've never heard her sound so frightened. I tried again to wrench free, but Adara and Cipriana were too much for me. I felt hands digging into belly, into abdomen; lower, between my thighs.

Adara: "—power in flesh—"

Cipriana: "—power in steel—"

Hoolies, they were undoing the tie-string of my trews!

Del began to scream.

I thought: *If I can get my sword free*— But knew I couldn't. I was flat on my back on my sheath; the sword was lost to me.

Cipriana bent down, tongued my cheek, traced out the scars. Something rattled against my teeth: the necklet of lumpy stones.

And then I recognized it. Reddish, irregular stones strung on a thin leather thong. She had shown it to me once before, no doubt flaunting it in challenge, and I hadn't recognized it. Now I did. Now I knew it was the necklet Del had made for her mother years before, thrown into the circle of stones as an offering to the loki in hopes it would be enough.

Obviously, it hadn't.

They weren't women. Not exactly. More. Demons in women's bodies, using a woman's wiles and a demon's strength. One was more than enough. Two would be my death.

Or whatever was left over when they were done with me.

Del still screamed. Massou, who wasn't Massou, had forced her to the ground. I writhed, twisted, rolled; saw only snatches, because the women were too strong. Del, like me, was on her back, spitting and kicking and clawing and screaming, but clearly losing the battle. Massou, who wasn't Massou, was dragging her legs apart.

But he's a boy, I said inwardly, even though he was not. There was no boy left, only a *thing* flowing out of mouth and nose and ears. Something much bigger than a boy. Bigger even than me.

There was nothing left to fight. Del's enemy had changed, but was using a man's tactics. The ones a conqueror always uses to subdue a proud woman.

Hoolies, not *again*—

I tried spitting: Cipriana laughed. I tried biting: Adara smiled. I tried kicking and clawing, too, but nothing had any effect.

Del was sobbing now.

Adara's hand was where it shouldn't be. Cipriana licked my face, thrusting her tongue into my mouth. I felt the pinching in my belly and the acrid tang of bile climbing into the back of my throat.

Hoolies, not like *this*—

No. Not like this. Because something was happening.

A sound. A thin thread of a sound. Not a sword, not a knife, but a needle, thrust into an ear. I felt nothing, but something was there. Something *inside* my head, piercing into my brain.

Vision flickered. I smelled something foul. Tasted it, too, though I had swallowed nothing. My hearing wavered, then intensified, even as the shrill sound did.

And then I knew what it was.

Gods bless the Cantéada.

Hands fell away from me. Bodies retreated, driven back by the song, and so did the demons, trapped in human, alien flesh.

I sat up. Adara, Cipriana and Massou stood stock still, hands clapped over their ears. Their faces were formed of pain.

"Del." I crawled to her, put a hand on her, felt her flesh contract. She lay face down in the dirt. *"Del—"*

And then, awkwardly, she was up. Up and scrambling away, scraping on buttocks and hands, thrusting herself away. She scrabbled across the dirt until she backed herself up against the stone wall, and there she sat, all jammed up against the stone as if she wanted to crawl inside it.

"Del," I said. *"Bascha—"* But I broke it off because clearly she wasn't listening.

Hoolies, but it is a frightening thing to look into the face of madness.

Oh, bascha, not you.

Behind me, the loki stood trapped while the Cantéada sang.

Oh, bascha, look at *me,* not at them.

She had driven fingers into the stone. She keeps her nails filed short, but one by one I saw them break, snapping against the rock.

I knew better than to touch her.

Behind me, the loki whimpered.

"Delilah." I said it quietly, with as much command as I could muster.

She looked at me. Blankly, but *at* me, which was a distinct improvement.

"Delilah," I said again.

Lips moved. Bitten, bloodied lips, already swelling. Shaping something I couldn't hear.

Very gently, a third time: *"Delilah."*

She stared back at me. She *saw* me. Sense came back into eyes, looseness to her limbs, purpose to her movements.

Del was Del again, but now she was *angry.*

Dirt coated her face. I saw spittle on her chin, and blood. Hair straggled into her eyes, stuck itself in sweat and tears and blood. She shook so hard she could barely stand, yet she did, and managed to draw the sword.

Given time, even in her condition, she would have killed the bodies, the shells that housed the loki. But she was not given time because the Cantéada took it. They took it, remade it, gave it back, in a song of surpassing strength.

It completely swallowed the thread of Del's wailing chant, the warchant, the deathsong, the sound that promised an ending. Swallowed it, chewed it, spat it out upon the ground. Seeing it, Del broke off, beginning to tremble again.

I wanted to touch her but didn't, knowing she wasn't ready. Knowing the woman before me was not the Del I knew, but Delilah, the girl Ajani had nearly destroyed on the threshold of her life. She had crossed that threshold eventually, but it was warped, planed of hatred and vengeance. She might have died—women did—but didn't, being Del, who gave no man a victory he hadn't fairly earned. Ajani hadn't earned it. He'd only stolen it briefly, and then she had won it back.

Del stared at Massou, Cipriana, Adara. At the loki in human form, who had somehow replaced human mind with loki guile, human desires with loki needs. At the woman, the girl, the boy, who had, somewhere on the journey, lost the battle to three loki I had unknowingly freed.

Doors and cracks and chimneys glowed, painted with firelight. Beyond the loki, in the darkness, I saw shadows moving. Small, pale shadows, singing the binding song.

They came from everywhere, the Cantéada. Out of and down the walls, carrying candles, creeping forward to form a circle. Even behind Del and me, coming forward, moving us inward, to be clustered within the circle.

The loki made sounds of distress.

It was cold. In darkness blushed with candleflame, I saw my breath plume forth. But the shiver that racked my body came from within, not without.

The loki in human form were more than merely human. I saw madness in their faces, and desperation, and despair. Bound by the song, all they could do was suffer. As much, maybe, as the human hosts had suffered.

The circle closed. There was flame and song and faces, uncanny, inhuman faces. Feathery crests stood up from brow to neck, rippling, tinged with firelight, speaking a language all its own. I'd seen only the songmaster. Now I saw the others. Now I heard them sing.

I am not a man much touched by music, being deaf to its intricacies. I've said it before: it's *noise,* no matter the intent. But this time, *this* time, it was far more than noise. Far more than song. The sound I heard was *power.*

Legs gave out; I sat. Even as others sat; as Del collapsed beside me, loose-limbed, rubbery, dropping the sword beside her, awkward in the sudden loss of muscular control. The loki also; I saw them, one by one, turned into lumps of flesh like clay, waiting to be formed. Waiting to be shaped.

I opened my mouth to speak. To say something to Del; to ask her what it meant, what they would do, what they wanted of us. She was Northern; surely she knew. But I asked nothing because I couldn't. Because the song had become my world.

Flame melted, ran together, made the circle whole. I saw light, only light, and then even that was too much to bear. There was only one thing to do, and I did it. I ran away from it.

Trouble was, it came with me. Just like the song.

*Birthsong?** someone asked.

Birthsong. Birthsong? Blankly, I stared into the light.

A pause. *Birthname?**

Birth*name.* The meaning was different. Shaped to make sense to me.

I frowned. Thought about it. Realized I had no answer.

A mother or father names a child. I'd known neither one. Which meant I had no birthname.

Barely, I shook my head.

The song changed a little. *Birthname,** it insisted.

The songmaster? I wondered. Again, I shook my head.

The song grew insistent. It was unbearable. I felt pressure inside my skull.

And then, suddenly, a cessation of discomfort. I felt a trace of surprise that had nothing to do with me.

*Callname?** it asked gently.

That one I could answer. "Sandtiger," I said.

The song lingered in my head. Searched for truth or falsehood. Found the answer, then told me to withdraw.

Withdraw. I frowned. Stared into flame. Then knew I was meant to walk through it.

I stood up. Drew in a breath. Walked slowly out of the circle.

I sagged against the canyon wall, conscious only of exhaustion in mind and body. No longer did I doubt what Del had said about the magic in their music. It had gone into my soul, and now I understood it.

I turned. Beyond the light sat Del, staring, as I had, into the ring of flame. The light was stark on her face, and harsh, limning lines of exhaustion and tension. I saw blood and bruises and dirt, and an endurance almost destroyed. Del was close to breaking.

I wanted to go to her. I wanted to go back into the circle and touch her and lead her out through the flame, through the song, through the circle of Cantéada. But I knew better. This time, I knew better than to ignore the existence of power.

Now it was Del's turn.

Birthname? the songmaster asked.

She stared into the flame.

More gently, it was repeated.

"Del," the sword-dancer answered.

Birthname, he insisted.

"Delilah," the woman whispered.

I waited until she was free of the circle, blinded by light and tears, and then I took her hand, led her forth, brought her to stand with me. Saying nothing, asking nothing, merely being there. Hoping it was enough.

The song swelled. I heard dissonance in it, and harshness. An underlying demand. The songmaster was inflexible as he asked birthnames of the others.

One by one, he asked them. Adara. Cipriana. Massou.

One by one, they lied.

The song intensified. I saw dozens of throats swelling forth, threatening to burst. I heard the high melodic wailing, the deep thrumming hum, the mid-range staccato whirring. I heard the power in the song, and knew the loki could never withstand it.

Nothing could withstand it.

Massou broke first. *"Shedu!"* he screamed. "Shedu, Shedu, Shedu!" The songmaster asked again.

"Shedu!" he screamed, in a voice too deep for his throat.

I looked at the boy, Massou. Who wasn't Massou any longer. Whose name was Shedu instead.

Adara's turn. As had Shedu/Massou, she broke beneath the song. "Daeva," the woman whispered. I saw anger in her eyes, and helplessness and despair. "Daeva," she said again, grinding teeth into lips. Blood flowed down her chin. *"Daeva!"* she cried, and it echoed in the canyon.

Lastly, I looked at Cipriana. Slender, upright Cipriana: flirtatious, demanding Cipriana, who had reminded me of Del. Who had done her best to seduce me. Who now repulsed the song with every ounce of her strength.

The question was asked.

"Cipriana," she answered.

The question was asked again.

"Cipriana!" she snapped.

Yet a third time it was asked.

Pale hair stood up from her head. Rigid arms thrust into the air. *"Cipriana!"* she cried.

I took a step forward. Del held me back. In silence, she shook her head.

I waited. The song didn't waver, didn't break. The songmaster asked again.

The air crackled within the circle. I saw frenzy in her eyes, and hatred and anger and fear. *"Cip—Cip—Cip—"* She stopped. Renewed her attack upon the name. I saw her features writhe. Heard the song intensify.

Birthname, came the command.

Lips peeled back from her teeth. The name was expelled from her mouth, hissing as it left. "Rakshasa," she said, sounding more snake than human. "Rakshasa—*Rakshasa*—" Almost as soon as she said it, the crackle died out of the air. Hair settled back against shoulders, hands flopped down at her sides. "Rakshasa," she said, but it was a final defiance.

Shedu. Daeva. Rakshasa. I didn't know the names, but Del clearly did.

"Bind them," she said, "*bind* them. Set the stones around them. Sing them into a captivity no one can ever break."

Inwardly, I winced, recalling how I'd freed them.

"Sing it," Del said, "*sing* it—" She broke off, pressed a hand over her mouth, bit into her hand.

The song altered. I heard the change, subtle as it was, and knew Del had her wish. Especially as each Cantéada forming the circle bent slowly, placed an object against the ground, straightened again. Still holding the candles. Still singing the song.

The objects were stones. Round, smooth stones, carved in runic patterns like the ones I'd seen on the songmaster's walls. Ward-stones, then, like the ones I'd seen on the hilltop. Like the one I'd kicked aside, breaking open the circle. Setting the loki free.

Something thumped me in the gut. From inside, not out; I recalled, suddenly, the day Massou and Cipriana had given up their lessons. The day each of them had declared they had no more interest in the sword-dance. No interest in the *circle*.

Now they were trapped in one, as they'd been before.

"Del," I said, "what about the others? What about Adara and the children? Are they dead?"

Behind sweat-dried hair, pale brows meshed. "I don't know," she answered, troubled. "Their bodies live, but the loki inhabit them. You can't have one without the other."

"Can't the loki be driven out? They didn't have bodies before."

Slowly, she shook her head. "I just don't know."

I looked at the loki. No, I looked at the woman and her children. And I knew beyond a doubt the Borderers still lived. Somewhere inside where the loki couldn't reach them lived the spirits that had made a widow and her children continue an impossible journey without the aid of a man.

"Let's see," I suggested, and we went to the songmaster. He wasn't part of the circle. He wasn't singing the song. He had shaped it; his task was to give it to others.

"Songmaster," I said, "there is something left to be done. Those names you heard before—those are the names of real people. Those are the names of a woman and her children. Names that deserve to survive."

His crest trembled, stilled. *Bindsong binds.*

"Yes," Del said, "we know. But the loki have named their true names, reclaiming them; they have freed the other names. The power has been dispersed. Can't the woman and her children reclaim *their* names?"

The Cantéada frowned.

I wet dry lips. "You are the songmaster," I said. "Surely you can shape a song that will give them back their freedom."

His expression was troubled. *Dreamsong powerful.*

I looked at familiar faces that had loki living behind them. "I think it's worth the risk."

Like me, he looked at them. And then he fluttered delicate fingers, indicating the entrance to his cave. There was command in the gesture that I didn't dare deny.

"Bascha," I said, "let's go."

She was already running.

Chapter 30

*G*arrod stood before the entrance tunnel to the song-master's cave. I saw his expression of baffled curiosity as well as stunned incomprehension. Del brushed by him quickly, hardly noticing him, and ducked into the arched doorway. Garrod moved aside, then swung back to face me.

"I heard screaming," he said. "Screaming—and *singing*—"

"Not now," I said curtly, waving his words away. Like Del, I brushed by him, but this time he followed us in.

The tunnel was incredibly confining. I wanted nothing more than to be free of the weight of stone and out in the open again, in the desert, beneath the Southron sky. But I knew, deep in my gut, now was the time for hiding.

Free of the tunnel at last, I entered the songmaster's cave. I was dazzled once again by the brillance of light glinting off metal and glass, the lush richness of rugs. Painted knots and patterns made the walls into more than stone.

"Del—" But there was nothing left to say. I saw her face as she sat huddled against the wall, taut-wrapped in a blue-gray blanket. I saw the dirt and blood and tension, but mostly I saw the fear.

So did Garrod. "What *is* it?" he asked sharply, but by then it was too late for either of us to answer because the Cantéada sang.

It staggered me. Physically, it *staggered* me, sending me reeling against the wall. Left shoulder met it, scraped wool and leather, rang sword hilt against the stone. I hung there a moment, in shock, then slid down upon my knees.

Not knowing music, nor paying much attention, I'd never understood what harmony was. But now, hearing the full-throated singing of the Cantéada, I understood.

All the voices blended together, swooped upward, downward, tangled, drew apart; slurred through incredible ranges of notes, high and low and in between, blurring the sounds, but delicately, so that the ear heard the differences but couldn't really identify any of them.

Hoolies, what glorious sound!

And then it altered. No longer was it sound, but much more. It wasn't even a song. It was the music of memories, dragged angrily out of the soul. Music that slid into the cracks of my life and rediscovered all the nightmares I'd tried to forget.

Some of them, I had. But now I remembered them all.

—*a boy, maybe six, green-eyed and brown-haired, sprawling facedown with a mouth full of sand. Trying not to cry as the shukar applies the lash in punishment for heresy: I'd said there were no gods, because why else would I be a slave?*

Such questions are not tolerated any more than heresy is.

—*now twelve, being beaten yet again, this time by a father for looking too long and longingly at his daughter. The girl has teased him into it, but now claims innocence, tears streaming down her face. But behind the tears she smiles.*

Behind the blood, he doesn't.

—*now a young man at fifteen, larger on the outside than most of the men but made tiny inside by ridicule and humiliation. Hands and feet promise further physical growth; Salset treatment promises continued spiritual shrinkage.*

Until he makes hatred his god.

—*sixteen, now become a man in the eyes and hyorts of the women, who have the right to use him as they might use hide to soften their beds. And it is in their hyorts, in their beds, that he learns he has some value; that he learns he can, however briefly, be more than a slave in a woman's arms.*

And it is in the arms of one particular woman that he concocts a plan to escape.

The plan that nearly kills him.

In the cave, still bound by song, my hand strayed to my face. Fingers sought, found, traced out the curving scars cut so deeply into my cheek that stubble doesn't grow through them. The sandtiger had marked me well, but he had also given me freedom. Even as I'd stolen his in a slow river of warm, bright blood.

Mine as well as his.

—final memory of chula made man in place of slave. No more the nameless thing, but a free man to name himself. A man who has killed the cat who has eaten Salset men and children, ignoring the shukar's magic. What I've done is a powerful thing. I deserve a powerful name.

And so I pay honorable tribute to the cat who provided the means to escape.

Sandtigers born of the Punja are not owned by any one. Not by man. By woman. Nor god.

My fingers still touch the scars, but now there are also tears.

And the Cantéada sing on.

Drained, I let the wall hold me up. I had no strength to move or even to blink my eyes. So I let them shut, shut tightly, and tried to master myself.

The dreamsong was finished. Now all I heard, distantly, was the faint glory of the wardsong keeping the hounds at bay.

I looked at Del. Still she sat wrapped in the blanket, pulled in tightly against her neck to keep herself safe from harm. But the wool couldn't have done it; only deafness might. And I doubted even that would suffice in the face of such powerful magic.

Hoolies, I hate magic. You just can't *trust* it.

I heard movement. Not Del. Garrod. I'd forgotten all about him. And realized, looking at his face, he'd been as trapped as Del and I, maybe more so; he'd expected nothing. Del and I had at least been partly prepared. The horse-speaker had known nothing.

Like me, like Del, he sat huddled on the floor of the song-master's cave. But he moved, a little, wrapping hands around long pale braids. Wrapping, locking, *tugging,* as if he meant to rip out his hair by the roots.

Dimly, I realized he might.

I stirred. Crawled. Reached Garrod, caught a wrist, held it. "No," I said gently.

Lips were peeled back from teeth. He stared at me out of white-lashed, ice-water eyes. "What I have done," he said. "What I have done in this world."

"No," I said again.

"What I have *done* in this world!"

"I know," I told him evenly. "Do you think I'm less guilty than you? Cleaner of blood than you?" I let go of his wrist and showed him my palm. "No bloodstains," I said, "but I've spilled more than my share in this world."

He still clutched the braids, but no longer tugged them taut. "Horse-speaker," he said. "I *am* a horse-speaker, which is a true gift, a magic of its own, here in the North, and yet I have made myself no better than the whores, selling themselves to the man who will pay her price. I am the whore, *I* am the whore, trading in thievery and trickery, turning my back on what they have done if only to make a profit. To profit even from *murder.*" His eyes were fixed on my face. "I am an unworthy man. I have besmirched my gift."

Wearily, I sighed. "Sword-dancer, horse-speaker . . . do you think it really matters? Neither of us is clean."

Garrod stared at me blankly, lost within his own thoughts. And then, without warning, he pushed me aside, went to Del, knelt in front of her.

"I have never killed a man who did not first intend to kill me, and no man fully innocent. Never a woman or child. I have taken horses from Ajani to sell. I have sold him horses in return. I have taken his stolen money and I have made profit from it, counting myself clever. But I am a horse-speaker. *Horse-speaker.* Not murderer. Not raider. *Not* Ajani's man."

His braids dragged on the rugs. He waited for her answer.

Del gazed back at him. "Does it matter what I think?"

Garrod bowed his head.

Her smile was very faint. "You need it as much as I do." Then, very gently, she touched the crown of his head. I don't know what more she said because she said it in upland Northern, but Garrod seemed content. He rose and went out of the cave.

I still felt shaky, too shaky to stand. The dreamsong, as we'd been warned, had been incredibly painful. Not physically, but emotionally; sometimes the worst kind of pain, though men only rarely acknowledge it. Emotions belong to women.

I sat hunched on the rugs and looked at Del. Then, slowly, I made my way over to her, turning to rest my spine against the wall. To sit next to her in silence, offering and taking nothing. Being together was enough.

After a moment, she stirred. Pulled the blanket away from her body and offered a corner of it to me. I took it. Shifted closer, so that hips and shoulders touched. Settled the weight across legs and lap. In silence we shared the violence of our songs, knowing no words were necessary.

Eventually, Del tipped her head to the side and rested it against my shoulder. The weight was negligible, but the trust in the gesture immense. It touched the edges of raw emotions and made them quiver in response.

Quietly, she said: "I thought it would be Ajani. I thought it would be the deaths."

I frowned; so had I. Both had shaped the woman from girl into sword-dancer. "What, then, bascha?"

"When I killed my *an-kaidin*."

So. There was more to Del's scars. Deeper than even I'd thought.

"That song—" I began, but Del's tone cut me off.

"It was easy," she said. "*Easy.* I thought it would be hard. I thought it *should* be hard . . . but it was easy, Tiger."

After a moment, I nodded. "The mechanics of death aren't so difficult when you've been properly trained. You were. So I think—"

Del's head rolled slightly against my shoulder. "I don't mean the *mechanics* of death. I mean the death itself. When I took the *an-

kaidin's life. When I took him into my sword." She paused. "When Boreal became mine, truly mine, as a *jivatma* must become . . . a blood-thirsty, blooded *jivatma*."

I could see little of her face. Mostly tangled hair. But her tone said more than enough. "Bascha—"

Yet again, she cut me off. She sat up, throwing off the blanket from us both, then lurched upward to her knees. A quick glance slanted my way told me to be still; I was. And Del drew the sword.

In the cave, it rang. It *sang*, as much as a Cantéada. And I realized, in that moment, that the world was made of music. Lifesong, deathsong, dreamsong. The cycle personified.

"Sword-singer," I said.

Del twitched, holding the sword. Turned her head to look at me over a shoulder.

"Sword-singer," I repeated. "The dance requires a song."

Delilah began to smile.

"It's what you do, isn't it?" I asked. "Sing. To your sword. Your opponent. Your gods. To pay tribute to the world." I nodded slowly. "I remember the old man's words . . . the old Northerner in Harquhal, who sold you the leathers and furs and wool." Again, I nodded. "He told you to sing well."

Del dragged in a breath. "No dance is danced in silence."

"And it's how you key the sword."

"Part of it," she agreed. "There is more to it than that, but yes . . . the true name, the song—all is required."

"And I suppose the song must be special, like the name? A personal song? Something no one else can know?" I frowned. "But that doesn't make sense, bascha. If someone hears you sing, the song is no longer secret."

Del turned, still holding the sword. Still on her knees. And then she tucked heels beneath buttocks and sat, laying the *jivatma* across her thighs. One hand on the hilt. One hand on the blade. With infinite gentleness.

"You make a new one," she said, "each time. You touch yourself—what you are, what you were, what you can be—and shape it into a song. It's as much you as your hand on the hilt, but drawn from a deeper level. From the you no one else may know." Behind dirt and blood and tangled hair, the flawless face was somber. "You sing yourself into the sword, so the sword becomes part of you."

"Then why bother to blood it?" I asked. "Why all this non-sense about blooding it by taking the life of an honored enemy?" I straightened a little, frowning. "What happens if the enemy isn't honored? What happens if you have to kill before you're ready?"

Del's tone was steady. "A sword requires blood. First blood is part of the ritual; it is a rite of passage." Gently, she fingered the blade. "A boy becomes a man. A girl becomes a woman. A sword becomes a *jivatma*. Until then, it isn't whole."

"You didn't kill an enemy. You killed a friend instead."

She didn't so much as twitch. But then I saw blood on her fingers. Blood running into the runes.

"In the name of my need, I killed," she said. "I killed my honored *an-kaidin*, and took him into my sword."

"And are you content with it?"

Steadfastly, she stared at the blade. "It was what I had to do."

"And are you content with it?"

Her hand tightened on the hilt. Tendons stood up in the flesh. "There are times I hate this sword. There are times I hate myself."

"Do you regret what you have done?"

Del looked straight at me. "No," she said, "I don't. And that is what frightens me."

We stood beside the loki ring at dawn: Del, myself, Garrod, and the Borderers. Fog gathered above us, skirting the top of the canyon. Below, mist clung to us, dampening our hair. My nose and ears were cold.

Massou tore free of his mother and ran to Del. "I'm sorry!" he cried. "I'm sorry!"

I saw her flinch. I saw her recoil. I saw her fight back the re-sponse that might have destroyed him, in his frenzy to make things right.

"I'm sorry!" the boy cried, clinging to Del's waist. "It wasn't me,

I swear . . . it wasn't . . . *it wasn't!*" Sobs broke up additional words, rendering them incoherent.

It was plain all of them knew. And all of them remembered. Cipriana's face flamed red. She refused to look at me. Adara was less humiliated, but I saw how hard it was even for her to meet my eyes. She clutched her skirts in fists.

I cast a glance around the canyon. Once again the other Cantéada were hidden, leaving the songmaster to represent them. But I recalled them, the night before. Recalled them with candles and wardstones, melting out of the darkness to sing the Borderers free. To imprison the loki in a ring I wouldn't break.

Such a delicate thing, the ring. So transient on the surface. Smooth, rounded stones placed in a careful circle in the center of the canyon, not far from the songmaster's cave. In it resided loki. Daeva. Shedu. Rakshasa. The demons of childhood's dreams.

"We have to go," I said. "We can't stay here. This is a place of peace, and we have warped the song."

I felt Del's glance. Well, I was just as surprised. But I knew what I said was true.

"What about us?" Adara asked softly. "I know you must go on, but what are we to do? As you say, we can't stay here."

Garrod stood just behind Del, whose face was freshly scrubbed but still showed bluish bruising. His lids were lowered, hiding pale eyes. But they lifted, flickered, raised; he looked at the Borderers. "I'll take you," he said.

Cipriana's head came around. She stared at him in surprise.

Massou still clung to Del. "Can't you take us with you?"

I saw plainly she was uncomfortable, recalling the loki-Massou. With effort she kept her tone steady and didn't draw away. "No," she said quietly, touching the tousled blond hair. "No. I must go on. There is a thing I have to do."

Adara was looking at Garrod. There was hope in her green eyes, but also a trace of confusion. And I recalled that Garrod was mostly a stranger to them, since he had known only the loki within them.

The horse-speaker looked at me. "I'll take responsibility."

I raised brows. "Can you?"

The scarred lip twisted a little. "After the dreamsong, yes. And I think it's time I did."

Adara smoothed her skirts. "We're going to Kisiri."

Garrod smiled a little, flicking a glance at Cipriana. "Kisiri is a long way upland, but the uplands are my home. I will take you there safely."

I'll admit it, I was relieved. Del and I simply couldn't afford the time to escort the Borderers, but neither could we leave them behind without worrying about their welfare. Now Garrod could do it for us; it would be good for us all.

Cipriana looked back at him. "We haven't any horses."

Braid beads rattled as the horse-speaker laughed. "Leave that to me. I know ways of getting horses."

"Through trickery?" I asked. "The Cantéada don't ride; there are no horses to steal."

Ice-water eyes appraised and found me lacking. But the smile appeared again. "The songmaster told me last night there is a settlement half a day south. I plan to *buy* the horses, Southron . . . with the money you will lend us."

"*Lend* you—"

"Or give," Adara said softly. "You did promise to buy us a horse and wagon to replace the ones we lost."

"Yes," Del said, "you did."

I scowled at her. Dug down to drag free my coin pouch. Counted out coin, passed it over to Garrod.

Adara's hand flashed out. "*I* will tend the money."

The horse-speaker looked like he'd swallowed something sour. Grudgingly, he handed Adara the coin. She tied it into her tunic as Del nodded approval.

Trust a woman to want the money. It's the woman who always spends it.

"I'll go get the stud," I said, hearing him nickering in the distance.

He was happy to see me, I think. Certainly pleased to stick his nose into my neck and blow mucus all over me. I swore, shoved the nose away, tugged the stake from the ground. Turned and saw Cipriana.

Color stood high in her face. She hugged ribs and stared at the ground, wanting to speak but clearly unable.

The stud reached out the ever-questing nose. Touched her face. Nuzzled. Then snorted all over her.

Cipriana was less than pleased, wiping a forearm across her face. I pushed the stud away, then abruptly knew what was wrong.

No. What was *right*.

"All that time," I said in discovery. "All that time . . . *he* knew something was wrong. Remember?"

Cipriana just stared, still scrubbing at her face.

"He bit Massou," I said, "and was always restive around you. The stud knew something was wrong. Garrod even said so. He just couldn't say what or why."

As if to prove me right, the stud sidled casually toward Cipriana. The girl sidled closer to me, then caught herself and lunged back. Color flamed in her face.

I whacked the stud on the nose, but only halfheartedly. "It's all right," I told her. "I don't blame you—it wasn't your fault. You had nothing to do with it."

"But—all those things I said." The girl could barely speak. "Those things I said and did—"

"It wasn't you," I repeated. "Not you, not your mother, not Massou."

"But—I *liked* you. I did." She sounded surprised, which was a bit disgruntling. "And then I acted like such a fool, saying and doing those things . . . trying to make you—*want* me." The color stained her throat; I saw a film of shame-sweat on her face. "I acted like a Harquhal cantina girl, selling herself for coin."

"You acted like a woman who wanted a man," I told her bluntly. "Cipriana, you're young, but not that young. You have nothing to be ashamed of. There will come a day soon—" abruptly, I thought of Garrod "—maybe sooner than you think, when a man will return that favor—" now I thought of her mother, "—after you are married."

Shyly, Cipriana smiled a little. "That's what my mother said."

"Then maybe you should listen to her. She hasn't done so

badly." I turned, headed slowly back toward Del. "Never blame yourself, Cipriana. Not for honest feelings. It's better to say them out loud."

Coyly, she lifted one brow. "And do you say them to Del?"

Resignedly, I sighed. "Probably not enough." She matched my pace. Then held something out. "I don't want this," she said. "It was Rakshasa's, never mine."

I took it. Looked at it: a string of lumpy stones, red-brown against my palm. Rubbed smooth from years of wear.

In my mind, I saw Del's throat. Saw myself putting it on her, as she had put it on her mother.

Cipriana smiled. Then ran ahead to *her* mother.

Chapter 31

The hounds were arrayed around us. I'd forgotten how ugly they were.

The stud, naturally, was less than happy with the standoff. He recalled all too clearly the bites and nips and clawings he'd received from them before. He stomped and pawed and snorted, trying to warn them away.

"Hoolies," I said, "*now* what?"

Del sat behind me on the stud, hands locked into leather. Thinking only about the journey, we'd left the canyon far below us, as well as the wardsong, forgetting it was the only thing that had kept the hounds at bay.

"This," she answered quietly, fumbling at her woolen tunic.

I didn't turn to look, not wanting to take my attention from the hounds. So I couldn't see what she did. All I knew was, one minute we were surrounded by white-eyed beasts, the next moment they were gone. Fleeing like beaten dogs.

Now I twisted a little. "All right, bascha . . . what'd you do?"

She looped something over her head, held it out to me. I took it: a thin leather thong and a tiny metallic tube, glinting silver in faint foggy sunlight.

"This?" I asked suspiciously. "What in hoolies is this?"

"Something from the Cantéada." She kicked the stud, urging

him forward, even though she was *behind* the saddle; it made me sit up and take notice.

"Hey—" I reined him out of a hop, skip and jump into a more decorous pace, still studying the thing on its thong. It was hollow. One end was open. There was also a hole in one side. "A whistle?"

"The songmaster said it would keep the hounds at a distance."

"But not send them away."

"No. They appear to be under a geas, or some other sort of binding. They'll probably follow along, but at least we won't have to worry about them keeping so close."

"I don't like it," I said.

Del sighed. "Is there anything you *do* like?"

I answered promptly. "A sword, a circle, a good woman. A *Southron* sword that is—I could do without this one."

"And a Southron woman?"

I guided the stud through the trees, slipping the whistle thong over my head. I've never been one to ignore an advantage, regardless of origins. "Southron women," I said calmly, "have certain points in their favor. They're more biddable, for one; you don't much have to worry about them getting all uppity if you ask them to do something. And they're definitely good at domestic things, like cooking and cleaning and tending a man's gear. And they know how to please a man, in bed and out, being brought up to know who's in charge."

Del was silent a long, thoughtful moment. I grinned at the stud's ears, waiting for her response.

"If Southron women are so wonderful," she said at last, "why is it Southron men are so quick to steal *Northern* women?"

My grin went away. Finally, I said, "Probably because they're different. In coloring, customs, personality."

"Which *could* mean Southron men actually prefer women with more independence and spirit."

"Could," I agreed cautiously, "but never once have I heard a Southron man expressing a desire for a contentious woman."

"There is a distinct difference," Del said, "between a contentious woman and an independent one."

"Only women who are truly unhappy will seek out that sort of independence," I countered. "I'll bet if you asked most Southron women which kind of lifestyle they prefer, they'd take Southron over Northern."

"Maybe," she agreed coolly, "at first, because they know it . . . but only until they had a chance to experience our freedom."

"Not if it cost them their men."

"A *true* man wouldn't be threatened by an independent woman."

"How do *you* know what a true man is or isn't threatened by?" I demanded in disgust. "With you sitting so close against my back, there's no *way* I'd mistake you for a man. Which means you can't know."

Del scooched back a little, which wasn't what I'd intended. "I can know," she answered readily, "and I can prove it by asking a simple question: are you threatened by me?"

Oh, *hoolies.* She's so good at laying traps.

"Well?" Del, again.

"A lot of men would be—"

"Are *you?*"

"—and probably with reason. You're a man's fantasy, maybe, but not the sort of woman—" I broke off there because the hole was getting deeper.

"Tiger, answer the question. Are *you* threatened by me?"

"If I said yes, I'd be lying. But if I said no, I'd sound like an arrogant fool."

"That never stopped you before."

So nice, was Del. "No, I'm not threatened by you."

"Which means that a *true* man can accept independence in a woman."

I chewed on that a little. I'm not so stupid around women as to believe all their flattery, backhanded or not.

"Now," she said, "what kind of woman am I not?"

Hoolies. She'd noticed.

I sighed. "Not the kind of woman Southroners marry."

"Only the kind they dream about . . . if they have room for imagination along with ignorance."

"Now, Del," I sighed again, giving it up; it wasn't worth arguing. "Of course Southroners dream. *All* men dream. And I'd be willing to bet that Northern men dream about Southron women."

"I have no argument with dreams," she said tartly. "It's when men oppress women in *reality* that I become concerned."

"The North and South are two different places, Del . . . with different people, different customs, different gods. One isn't better than the other . . . it's just *different*." I paused. "And anyway, where'd you become so vocal about women's independence?"

She didn't answer at once. When she did, her tone was odd. "Mostly, from my family," Del said softly. "My mother was a strong, strong-minded woman who raised her sons to respect her gender and taught her husband to, as well. I was her only daughter . . . I grew up doing all of the things my brothers and uncles and father did, even to learning the knife and sword, and how to fight like a man. But it was in Staal-Ysta where I learned to be myself. Where I learned to be a *person* instead of male or female."

Staal-Ysta. I recalled the name from something Garrod had said. Ask her, he had told me. Ask her of Staal-Ysta.

So I did.

Del didn't answer at once. And, sitting squarely in front of her, I couldn't see her expression. All I had to go by to judge her reaction was the tension in her body, by necessity close to mine.

Eventually, I asked again.

"Place of Swords," she said finally. "That's what the words mean."

Poetic enough, I thought. Appealing, too; being a sword-dancer, I kind of liked the picture the words painted.

But Garrod hadn't meant to ask her merely about the name. "What does the phrase *'a blade without a name'* mean?"

Behind me, Del stiffened. Only slightly, but I found it remarkable nonetheless. "Where did you hear that?"

I might have lied. But I didn't. It seemed a fair enough question. "Garrod. He was angry . . . upset about the horses. He said something—" I paused, frowning, "—something about you being a blade without a name." I shrugged, guiding the stud. "He said it was a thing of Staal-Ysta."

"So it is." Her tone was cool.

"Something secret, I take it."

"A blade without a name translates to outcast, outlaw, wolf's-head," she explained precisely. "It indicates someone outside the honor codes of the *voca*."

"By choice."

"By choice," Del agreed. "Someone who *can't* learn the codes, or can't finish the training, is merely told to go home. But an *an-ishtoya* who refuses the final training that would make him a *kaidin*, yet uses his sword skills for harm, is considered a blade without a name."

"*You* didn't become a *kaidin*."

"No. But I chose to become a sword-dancer, which is open to students as well. And I live within the codes."

Something tickled me in the belly. "How close are you, Del? How close to breaking the codes?"

"A matter of weeks," she said without hesitation. "If I fail to reach Staal-Ysta within three weeks, to stand trial before the *voca*, I will be declared a blade without a name and subject to execution by any who wish to try."

I'd known that. Just not the language. "One more thing," I said. "Does your song have an ending?"

She said nothing at all at first. And then: "Stop this horse."

At first, I didn't. "Del—"

"Stop this horse."

I'm not deaf; she was upset. She didn't yell, but then Del doesn't need to. She knows how to use her tone. Accordingly, I stopped the horse. Looked around as Del slid off to stand in damp leaves. Saw the ice in her eyes, but also the blaze behind it.

Hoolies. Now I'd done it.

"Del—"

"Come down," she said.

"Come *up*," I countered. "You yourself said there are only three weeks left before the *voca* can make you an outlaw. Shouldn't we be going?"

Del drew her sword. "Come down," she said. In the distance, hounds bayed.

I scratched stubble. Considered entering into argument. Decided against it; that look in her eyes told me to take her seriously and not waste any more time.

I swung a leg over and slid off the stud, retaining my hold on the reins. It wouldn't do to lose him now, after going afoot before.

Del thrust the blade into the ground. It sank halfway in the damp, decaying layers of rain-soaked leaves, then slid into mud and held. She took her hands from the hilt.

"I can't give you the oaths," she said, "because they are private things. But I swore them on the souls of murdered kin, wrote them in my own blood, told them to the runemaster who set them into the blade." Fingers indicated the alien glyphs running from hilt to tip, though half-buried in the ground. "To abdicate those oaths dishonors my sword, my training, my kin. Do you think I could do that?"

"I only asked—"

"You asked if my song had an ending."

"Well, yes—"

"Without knowing what it means."

"Well . . . yes—"

"Without knowing what you asked."

And again yes. "Garrod said I should ask you."

Her tone was bitter. "And do you always do what young Northern strangers ask you to do? Especially one whose own personal honor is highly questionable?"

I ignored her questions. "Maybe Garrod was right to do it."

It took her off guard. "What?"

"He said even an upland horse-speaker knows about Staal-Ysta and the honor codes of the *voca*. It seemed to make a difference. But I, being a Southroner, know nothing about the place. Nothing about the customs." I looked at Boreal, then over to Del. "Does your song have an ending?"

Her face was white. "You ask that, not knowing what you ask?"

"Maybe I would if I had an answer."

Del stared at her sword. It was plain I'd put her in turmoil, though the indications were subtle. Del masks her face well, but I've learned to read the signs. She stared at her sword as if hoping—or honestly expecting—it would tell her what to do, but in the end she decided all by herself.

"He'll have to know," she said obscurely, "one way or another."

Not what I call encouraging. "Del—"

"I swore oaths," she said, "as I told you. But these are oaths of a different nature than the kind ordinarily sworn. They have to do with Staal-Ysta, and what it makes you; what you become to name a *jivatma*." Her gaze was on Boreal. "I have no doubts you have sworn oaths in your life, Tiger, and they are as binding as you make them . . . but in the North, it's different. In Staal-Ysta, more different yet; the binding is permanent, made of blood and steel and magic and the blessings of the gods."

"Now, Del—"

She lifted a silencing hand. "I am giving you an answer to your question. Never say I didn't warn you; it's more than most people get."

Part of me wanted to break it off; obscurity irritates me. But Del was clearly serious, and it wouldn't hurt to listen.

At least, I didn't think so. "All right, bascha . . . go on."

"When you set yourself a task, you make yourself a song. And go on singing it until the task is completed."

I frowned. "I don't understand."

Del's face was expressionless. "My first task was to find Jamail and bring him home. As you know, I couldn't do it; that part of the song was destroyed. But there still remains another. A bloodsong, Tiger—a *death*song. My task is to kill Ajani and the men who accompanied him. Until that is accomplished, my song can never end. And a song without an end is not a true song at all, but merely meaningless noise."

In the distance, hounds yapped and howled. I glanced around, then back at Del. "Something like that," I said.

"Yes," she said, "but forever. Noise without purpose or ending."

I nodded. "What it means is a sword-dancer out of control. One without purpose or honor."

"I am hard," Del said. "Hard and cold and cruel. But my song has an ending. My blade has a name."

"For how much longer?" I asked. "If the *voca* finds you guilty and orders your execution, your task will remain undone. Your song will never end. Your oaths will all be broken."

"No," she said, "they won't. I made a pact with the gods."

I wanted to laugh, but didn't. Del was too serious.

I pointed at the sword. "Clean that thing and let's go."

Chapter 32

I woke up because I was cold, and because someone was spitting on my face. Not a good way to start the day.

I swore beneath heavy blankets, heaved myself up, realized the *sky* was doing the spitting; wet, cold things were falling out of it. Not rain; I know rain. Something like sticky ice.

"Del!"

She woke up. Peered at me sleepily. "You're letting in the cold."

So I was. I lay down again, but stiffly, blankets hooded around my head. "Del—what *is* this?"

"Snow." She hitched herself closer, hair catching on my stubble. "Why—what did you think it was?" When I didn't answer, Del pushed herself up on one elbow and looked at me more closely. And then she began to laugh.

"Not funny," I muttered. "How was I supposed to know?"

Del was stretched against me, feet intertwined with mine. I felt the trembling of her laughter; heard the giggles she tried to suppress.

I turned over onto my side, facing her beneath blankets. Cold snuck into the folds and chilled exposed flesh, turning it rose-red along the angles of Northern cheekbones. I reached out and smoothed back hair. It was good to hear her laugh, even at my expense.

I pushed the blanket off her head. Snow stuck on hair and lashes, turning to droplets on her face. Barehanded, I touched her cheek. "How long has it been since you laughed? Like this, I mean; really *laughed?*"

Slowly, the smile fell away. Tears of merriment dried in her eyes. She said nothing at all in answer, too startled by my question. There was wariness in her expression as well as bafflement.

Her tone was odd. "I don't know."

I traced the thin lace of a silvery scar threading the flesh of one cheek. "A week ago you stood before your sword and named yourself hard and cold and cruel, sworn to avenge your family. I won't disagree; sometimes you are. But you can also be other things. A woman of passion and laughter."

She shrugged. "Maybe once."

I grunted. "More than once, bascha. I'll swear to that. I share your bed, remember?"

Del sighed. We are not a man and woman for soft words between us, being too ruled by other things; locked too tightly into our roles and allowing no latitude. But I would be a liar to say I didn't think them. To say I didn't feel them. And I think Del would, too.

It was a soft and silent dawn, except for the stream nearby, and filled by falling snow. It was cold, but we were not, for the moment warmed by new thoughts and feelings, not thinking about the weather. And then she lowered snow-frosted lids and shuttered her thoughts from me, turning away a little.

"Don't," was all she said.

"Del, I don't mean to hurt you. I only mean that if you push yourself any harder, wind yourself any tighter, something is going to break."

Tautly: "There are things I have to do."

"Not at the risk of destroying yourself."

"Ajani did that a long time ago."

Inwardly, I swore. Outwardly, I shook my head, "And so you have reshaped the real Delilah into someone she is not."

"Am not," she said softly. After a moment, she shook her head.

"I don't know what I'm not. I don't know what I *am*, other than what I have to be." Del resettled the blankets. "Not so different from you."

I rose, took up harness and sword, stood up to meet the dawn even as it fell down to meet me. Such a soft, gentle thing, sneaking up like a woman's caress. Flakes fell out of the sky and took roost on any part of me they could touch, melting or sticking together. The world itself was blurred, softened by falling snow. I couldn't hear anything but my own breathing as I exhaled a cloud of steam.

"I'm a killer," I said. "Strip away the pretty words and the real ones come to the surface. Men hire me to kill; it is what I do."

She twisted to stare at me. Her face was pallid with shock.

"Not always," I said. "Sometimes the job has nothing to do with killing. But I am effective because I *can* kill, and people know I will do it. It frightens them into docility, into payment . . . into doing whatever I tell them, being hired to tell them things. I don't take sides—or very rarely. Mostly, I just take money. I take money to dance." I slid the sword from its sheath. "I'm a whore in my own way, ruled by greed, not retribution. But I think I'm happier than you."

Del folded back the blankets and sat up. Snow gathered on head and shoulders, clinging to her hair. "Why are you telling me this? What point are you trying to make?"

"No point. I just want you to realize that it's an ugly sort of life you've portioned out for yourself, in the name of retribution."

Del's mouth nearly dropped open in amazement. "You don't think I should hunt Ajani down? After what he *did?*"

"I didn't say that, now, did I?" I turned from her, found a tree limb, began to draw a circle. Snow would eventually hide most of the line, but it really wouldn't matter. We'd know where it was. In our hearts, if nowhere else. "I just meant you ought to give yourself room to be Delilah along with the sword-dancer known as Del."

Damp hair straggled on either side of her face. She gazed at me blindly, locked away in her head.

I straightened, tossed the limb aside. "I have hated as well or better than anyone, in my life, maybe even you. Because much of it wasn't a life. I never had anything—or any*one*—to lose, except myself. I don't doubt that if I'd had kin stripped from me as you did, as well as innocence, I'd be angry, too. I'd want revenge, too. But destroying myself in the process isn't a choice I'd make."

Del's stare sharpened. She frowned a little, thinking about my words, then stood up and brushed off snow. "A woman is required to be stronger," she said quietly. "Even in the North, even in Staal-Ysta. Tougher. Stronger. *Better*—if she is to be judged worthy at all. And so there are sacrifices—"

I didn't let her finish. "Did they demand those sacrifices? Or did you simply offer them, determining them yourself?"

Del stood very still. "I don't know," she said numbly. "I can't remember, now."

It made me angry, that she could be so focused on hatred and revenge that she could forget herself. I stalked back through the snow to face her squarely. "Be you," I told her curtly. "Just *you*, whoever that may be . . . that's what *I* want from you. And if it means traipsing across two countries to find the man who killed your kin, so be it; I don't much like him, either. If it means going into sleet and snow and banshee-storms, I'll do it willingly. Not happily, but I'll do it; there's enough between us for that, even if you won't admit it. But if it means warping yourself into a travesty of Delilah because it's the only way, I say it isn't worth it. You deserve better than that."

Softly, she said: "I'm afraid."

"I know you are, bascha. I've known it all along. But it doesn't make you a bad person." I smiled, reached behind her left shoulder, drew her Northern sword. "Step into the circle, Del. Let's do what we do best."

Good idea, bad execution. I'm not used to snow. And so I performed badly, giving Del an easy match, but in the end it served its purpose. She was thinking about the dance, not about herself, and it burned the tension out.

"No, *no*," she blurted, as I let one of her subtle wrist patterns break through my haphazard guard. "If you do that in Staal-Ysta, you'll impress *no* one."

I grunted, moving away again. "I didn't know I'd *have* to impress anyone. We're going there for you, remember? Not for me."

Her mouth was flat and grim. "You are the Sandtiger. One of the greatest sword-dancers in the South. If you think you can go to Staal-Ysta and *not* be called upon to dance, you are sandsick."

One of the greatest, not *the* greatest . . . as usual, she knew how to provoke me. I beat her blade back, then followed it up with a slashing blow that, had it connected, would have severed an arm at the shoulder.

"Better," she said grudgingly, skipping out of the way.

Better, schmetter. I was the *best*. "How long is this trial supposed to take? I mean, we *will* be done before spring, won't we? We won't have to winter here?"

Del moved warily, testing my intentions. Snow still fell, but softly, clearly not bothering her. But *I* could do without it. I don't like footwork fouled by slush.

"Maybe," she said quietly, mostly under her breath.

"Maybe? *Maybe?* You mean—this thing could last for months?" I dropped my guard completely, calling off the dance. "Just what will you have to do?"

"I don't know. Tiger, don't stop. You need to learn how to move. Snow, mud and slush can be difficult to dance in."

"I'm not dancing!" I shouted. "I'm coming along for the ride, and that's *it*. I suppose if someone invited me to participate in a friendly little wager revolving around a dance, I'd do it, but that's as far as it goes. I'm not a performing dog."

"No, but you are my sponsor."

Dimly I recalled having agreed to some such title. "I said I'd back you at the trial."

"And if the trial is a dance?" Del had stopped moving, too. We faced each other across the circle, fogging the air with our breath. "Here in the North, such things are often decided by combat. It seems the fairest thing."

"Wait a minute. Do you mean to tell me that you've dragged

me all the way up here to do your fighting *for* you?" I stared at her in astonishment. "Hoolies, Del, *you're* sandsick! For as long as I've known you, all you've done is fill my ears with all this noise about you being as good a sword-dancer as any man—including me—and *now* you tell me I might have to dance in your place?" I shook my head. "What kind of a deal is that?"

Del nodded grimly. "Not much of one, is it? But it may be the *only* deal. Who can say what the *voca* will do?"

"You," I accused. "I've seen that look in your eye . . . you've got a good idea."

"No," she demurred calmly. "Now, about your footwork—"

"To hoolies with footwork, bascha . . . I want to know what I face!"

Del glared across the circle. "I don't *know!*" she shouted. Then, more quietly, "But you just said again you'd go with me, so I guess we'll find out together."

I said something very rude in Desert dialect, because Del didn't know it, and because I didn't really want to call her names, but felt I had to do *something.* So, all that being said, I continued to scowl at her. "Sometimes," I said, *"sometimes."*

Del waited, brows arched.

"Sometimes," I muttered again, stepping out of the circle.

"Where are you going, Tiger?"

"To wash my face," I answered. "Maybe the cold will shock me awake, and I'll know this is all a dream."

I tromped down to the rushing stream, sheathing my sword, and knelt down on the snowy crust at the edge of the water. I had every intention of thrusting my face into the water, but something kept me from it. Something told me it would be terribly, horribly cold; *too* cold, even, for anger. I paused, considering it, and then felt the familiar warning tingle in my bones.

"Magic," I blurted, disbelieving, then spun in place to warn Del.

Unfortunately, the magic came from behind. From the water. It reached up and dragged me down.

The stream was no deeper than possibly two feet, no wider

than maybe three. But suddenly it felt like a river in full spate, sucking me into the depths.

I was, of course, cold, being soaked through in an instant. I was also frightened and angry; what in hoolies had me? And what could I do about it?

I gurgled Del's name. Knew she'd never hear that, but surely she'd hear my splashing. I was kicking like a danjac, trying to thrust my head above water so I could breathe again.

Hands were on me. For just a moment I thought they belonged to Del, coming to my rescue, and then I realized the hands were on my front, not my back, and were dragging me farther *down*.

Can't be real, I thought. The stream isn't deep enough.

Hands dragged me down.

Hoolies, not like this . . . I'm a *desert* man—

And then I realized the water was warm. Incredibly warm. So were the hands, tangling in my hair. Threading fingers through my beard. Pulling my face toward hers . . .

Hers?

Hoolies, I've gone sandsick. Or have I? There's a *woman* staring at me . . . a gray-haired, gray-eyed woman, young, not old, but all gray, gray and pallid white, but the lips are carmine red.

Hoolies, I *am* sandsick!

And then, abruptly, something grabbed me by the hair and yanked me up out of the water.

It hurt. I yelled, struggled, splashed, was rewarded by yet another yank on the hair.

"Get out!" Del shouted. "Get out of the water *now!*"

Well, I was trying. But so was the other woman, who reached up to catch my hands.

Hoolies, *two women?*

"It's an undine!" Del shouted. "Tiger—fight her off! She'll drown you if you give in!"

Red lips smiled at me. Gray eyes beseeched my own. Wet hair tied itself in knots around my wrists.

Del yanked harder yet. "Get *out* of there!" she yelled.

Hoolies, one woman wanted to drown me, the other to pluck me bald.

The hair was like wire around my wrists. I tried to twist loose, failed; lunged toward the side even as Del took a harder grip. I landed face down in the snow with half of me still in the water.

One hand was free. "Knife," I croaked, and felt Del press hers into my hand. Quickly, I cut the hair that bound my right wrist and felt the tension slacken.

"Get up," Del said, "get away. She can still reach you from here."

I pushed to my knees, to my feet, staggered two steps, stumbled, got up and ran again. Fell down again in exhaustion.

"Far enough," Del said. "Give me the hair, Tiger."

It was all I could do to breathe. I held up my arm, felt her strip the hair from my wrist. Watched, hacking loudly, as she threw it on the fire.

I thought the water would quench the flame. But for a moment it burned very brightly, red as blood, and then the hair ashed away into nothing, leaving behind an acrid stink.

I sucked in a wheezing breath. "What in hoolies *was* that?"

"Undine," she told me. "She wanted you for her own; unfortunately, she would have drowned you. It's the only way she could have kept you."

"Kept me for *what?*"

Del shrugged. "What most lonely women desire . . . she wanted a man of her own."

Coughing interrupted my outraged expression of horror. I was wet and cold and shivering; if I wasn't careful, I'd freeze. "That— *thing*—wanted to keep me?"

"Legend says undines—always female—can gain a human soul if they conceive by a human man." She shrugged. "I guess she wanted a soul."

I peered at her out of stinging eyes. "*You're* awfully calm about it."

"She didn't want *me*."

I tried to sit up and failed. "First the loki, now this. Is this how the North *is?* Filled with frustrated female spirits?"

Del laughed aloud, then smothered it, but the amusement remained in her eyes. "Here," she said gently, "I'll build up the fire. You strip down and get under the blankets; I'll come in beside you."

"At least you're *human*," I croaked. "Hoolies, I *hate this place*."

But at least the snow had stopped.

Chapter 33

*D*ays passed. So did the storm, but another followed on its
heels. Just like the hounds on ours.

They were always out there somewhere, slinking through the
trees. The ward-whistle kept them at a distance but didn't drive
them away. It made us irritable, snappish, because we weren't sure
what they'd do, other than drive us north. It was where we wanted
to go, but we wanted to do it without escort.

Del hunched down in the snow, carefully nursing a tiny fire in
an attempt to keep it burning. But wind made it difficult; wind and
snow and damp wood. I did what I could to form a shield, holding
up a large blanket, but knew the effort was futile.

"Hoolies," I said, "I'm sick of this! What I'd give for a little *warmth!*"

Del hunched over the flickering flames. "What *would* you
give?" she asked.

"My beard?" I suggested hopefully.

She grinned, casting me a glance as she made a windbreak with
her hands. "How many times must I tell you?—you'll do better
with a beard. It's a form of winter hair, just like the stud wears."

"He's a *horse,* Del; I'm a man. And I prefer bare skin to a pelt,
especially on my face."

She laughed a little, nodding. "As much hair as you've grown
lately, I begin to think you're half bear."

Well, I was. The Cantéada had given us blankets for bedding, but lately we'd taken to using them as cloaks against the increasing cold. I hadn't cut my hair or shaved in weeks; not much of my face showed, except for my nose, the bare patches beneath my eyes, and the sandtiger scars on my cheek. Everything else was covered by hair, wool and leather.

Del, of course, didn't have the advantage of a beard, which meant she spent most of her time wrapped to the eyes in her blankets. Now she had set them aside; wind chafed her face rose-red and stung tears out of her eyes.

"How much farther?" I asked.

She glanced northward, frowning. The trees were naked save for frost, and the snow caught in crotches. The storm had begun the night before and showed no signs of letting up.

Del sighed, shrugging a little. "In good weather, a week. But with the snow, maybe two."

"Too long," I said.

She hunched again over the fire. "I know, Tiger. I know."

"Won't they give you extra time? I mean, what with all this snow . . ." I let it trail off; Del was shaking her head.

"Unlikely," she told me. "A year is more than enough time. They would merely say I left it till too late."

"But you're making every effort, bascha. Won't they give you credit for that?"

Snow slapped her in the face, crusted in her hair. "I don't think so, Tiger. If I'm late, I'm late."

The wind shifted. So did I, trying to block its strength so Del could coax the fire to life. "How long do you think this will last?"

She muttered something in Northern, cursing the failed fire, then lurched up from her kneeling posture. "I don't know!" she cried. "Do you think I know everything?" And then she covered her face with her hands. "Gods, oh, *gods*, what is happening to me? Why am I always so *angry?*"

"You're tired," I told her flatly. "Tired and worn to the bone." I shoved my way through calf-deep snow, hating the heaviness, draped the blanket around her shoulders and snugged the ends together. "When you came South, all you had to worry about was Ja-mail. Now there is much more: time, Ajani, the *voca*, the hounds, even bad weather. What did you expect?"

The brief anger had spent itself. Now she was merely tired. "I don't know what I expected. At first, I was happy just to be home. But now—now there are other concerns. The ones you've made me think about, like what I will do when the trial is over."

"Good."

"*If* they let me live."

"There's no question of that." I plowed my way through snow to the stud, tied to a tree. He had turned his rump to the wind, head hanging down; I pushed off the blanket of snow that turned him from bay to gray. "After all, with the Sandtiger as your sponsor—"

"Tiger—*look out*—"

I swung instantly, reaching for my sword, but the beast was al-ready on me. I felt jaws closing on my left wrist, trying to gnaw through wool and leather; smelled the musky stink; heard the snarling deep in his throat. Caught completely by surprise—and cursing myself for it—I went down on one knee; felt the jaws com-press my wrist.

Hoolies, the thing was strong!

I felt the stud behind me, trying to snap his rope. Heard his frantic squealing. Fell backward against his forelegs and felt him quivering, trying to avoid me. A horse hates to step on a man, but will if there's no other choice.

Beyond the beast, I saw Del, Boreal raised to strike. But I also saw anguish and indecision; in her haste she might strike me. In delay, the beast might kill me.

Some choice, bascha.

She shifted her stance. Dropped to one knee. Altered her grip on the sword and used it like a pike, thrusting into the underbelly. I was grateful she missed mine.

Blood rained down, hot and acrid. The beast howled, writhed, released his grip on my arm to snap at the blade. His entrails were hanging out; Del had done more than thrust. She'd ripped the guts from his belly.

I pulled away, staggered up, ran three steps past the stud simply in reaction. Swung around and looked back, panting steam-clouds in exertion.

Through the snowfall, I saw her face. Pink from exposure, but also stained with blood. She put up one gloved hand to touch her cheek, smeared blood, took it away again. Her eyes were on the beast, now lying dead in the snow.

I caught the stud's picket line. "Easy," I told him, "easy." I untied him, led him three trees away, tied him up again. He was still frightened by the beast, but I dared not tie him farther. Where there was one there were probably more.

I trudged back through snow, marking the crimson bloodstains. Was glad it wasn't mine.

Del rose slowly. "Wolf," was all she said.

I frowned. I'd expected to see a hound, and so I had. But closer inspection proved her right. The beast was wolf, not hound.

"The whistle," I began, puzzled. "Shouldn't it keep wolves away as well?"

"The Cantéada made it for beasts shaped by sorcery. This wolf was merely a wolf, doing what wolves do in winter: feeding a family."

I cast her a sour glance. "Don't sound so regretful, Del; *I* might have been the dinner."

She shrugged one shoulder, sword dripping blood to stain the snow. "He probably wanted the stud. You just got in the way." She looked from the wolf to me. "Only rarely do they attack men, preferring other prey. But in winter, when game is scarce; when there are hungry cubs in the den, sometimes they turn to men. Or anything they can find."

She was, like many women, an easy mark for animals, particularly the young. I recalled her defiance of Southron custom by briefly adopting two sandtiger cubs, even knowing how deadly they'd be once poisonous claws broke free of buds and fangs replaced their milk-teeth. Luckily, we'd gotten rid of them before they could mature.

"No," I said flatly.

Del frowned at me. "What do you mean, 'no'?"

"I know what you're thinking, bascha. You're thinking about two or three wolflings holed up in a den nearby. Well, I say no. They've probably got a mother."

"You don't know that, Tiger."

"What I *do* know is, we can't waste even an hour hunting them; we've got no time to spare."

Del looked down at the butchered male. "No," she said, "we don't." And turned her back on the wolf as she went to clean her sword.

I followed a moment later. "We'll have to break camp now. Likely the body'll bring down other beasts. I'd rather not risk it, Del, especially so close to dark."

She cleaned the blade, slid it home again. "Let me see your wrist."

I twitched a shoulder briefly. "It's sore, but it'll do. He didn't break the skin."

"Let me see, Tiger. We don't move until I do."

I swore, muttered, stuck out my left arm. Del peeled back the layers. "See?" I said. "No blood. Just a little swelling."

She touched it. I winced, "Umm hmmm," she murmured, "I see. Swollen, as you say . . ." Her voice trailed off.

I looked down on her bowed head. "If I didn't know better, I'd say something—or someone—was out to get me."

Del didn't answer at once, deftly inspecting my wrist. Eventually she asked why.

"Well, first there were the loki . . . then those hounds of hoolies . . . that water witch—and now the wolf."

"The North is a naturally dangerous place," she said patiently, "like the South. There is no one trying to *get* you."

"How do you know? You haven't been the target."

She glanced up sharply. "No? Do you want to split up to prove it? I'll wager the hounds follow me. Me *and* my sword."

I thought about it. "No, let's not split up—*ouch!*"

"It will likely bruise by morning." Smiling sweetly, she worked the hand and wrist before I could flex it stiff. "Maybe sprained,

Tiger, but then that will never bother a big, strong man like you."
She yanked the layers of leather and wool back down, rose, slapped
me on the shoulder. "Get the stud and let's go."

So much for sympathy. Glumly, I went for the horse.

Two days later, the track took us above the timberline, into the
snowy mountains. Del called them the Heights.

"This is Reiver's Pass," she said. "From here, Staal-Ysta is maybe
a week. We might make it yet."

We stood on a treeless escarpment: Del, the stud, and I. Behind
us tumbled the uplands, farther yet the downlands, below that the
borderlands and the plateaus close to Harquhal. The snowstorm
had finally died, but the cold was colder yet. I shivered inside my
woolen blankets, wishing I *was* a bear. Because then I'd be hiber-
nating, oblivious to the cold.

There were mountains yet before us, blasted by wind and
filmed with ice. They glittered in meager sunlight like sand crystals
in the Punja. My eyes were dazzled by the light; I put up a hand to
block it.

"A good day," Del said. "The clouds are thin, and the sun shines
through. See the ring around it? It's widening, not contracting; it
means the weather will be good. The blessing of the gods."

"Hunh." I wasn't so sure. "How do you *live* up here? How do
you survive the winters?"

"*You're* surviving one." Del grinned at me, scraping back wind-
tangled hair. "Man adapts, Tiger . . . even a man like you. Once
you've adjusted—"

"Adjusted, *nothing*," I said rudely. "Once you're done with this
trial, I'm heading South again."

Too quickly, Del looked away. "We should go on, Tiger. I want
to avoid another storm."

"You just said the weather would be good."

"Maybe I lied."

I sighed. Glanced back the way we had come. "I don't see the
hounds."

Del turned. "The ward-whistle's still working."

"Then why don't they just give up?"

She shook her head. "I don't know, Tiger. Maybe they're like me . . . maybe their song hasn't ended yet."

I glanced at her sharply. Being cryptic, again; as always, it annoyed me. "I hardly think *beasts—*"

"I would," she interrupted, "if someone has given them one to sing."

"Oh, Del, come on."

She thrust out a pointing hand that indicated the treeline far below our tracks against the snow. "Someone set them on us, Tiger . . . someone told them to stay with us. The ward-whistle keeps them at bay, but it doesn't send them away. Have you any other explanation?"

"Maybe they're just hungry."

She cast me a withering glance.

I turned to the stud and swung up, suppressing a wince of pain. The wrist was still very sore, but I wouldn't tell her that. She'd only use it to claim some sort of odd, obscure victory of woman over man.

"Are you coming?" I asked.

Del grabbed my wrist, which hurt, and swung up, settling onto a furry rump. The stud had lost weight since we'd first picked up our shadows, particularly carrying two, but he was tough and stubborn and valiant and I knew he'd never give up.

Nor more than Delilah would.

Chapter 34

el leaned sideways and forward, all at once, to press against
my back. One arm curved around me, pointing. "There,"
she said. "Staal-Ysta."

I stared. I *gaped;* what she pointed at was a lake, a cold, glass-
black lake, huddled amidst the mountains. In its center swam an island. "That?" I asked succinctly.

"That," she agreed. "There's a pathway down to the shoreline."

So there was, winding down; I wasn't sure I wanted to take it.
The lake looked bottomless, and I can't swim. "Bascha—"

But Del was off the stud, striding forward to pause at the head
of the path. Here the wind blew constantly, though not at gale
force; it did, however, strip the ground we stood on free of snow,
baring dark earth and darker rubble. She stood there, hair blowing
back from her face, and stared down at the Place of Swords. What
she saw I couldn't say, except to see what it did to her.

I slid off the stud and let him graze; the tough, fibrous turf
growing in swollen patches here and there would keep him from
wandering. I stepped in behind Del and put my hands on her
shoulders. Strands of hair caught in my beard, blonde on brown;
smiling wryly, I pulled them away.

Del drew in a breath. "Nearly six years ago I came here, alone,
because it was a thing I had to do. There was no other to avenge

my family's murder; no son, no brother, no *cousin*. Only me, a fifteen-year-old girl who knew enough of the sword to know it could be her deliverance, and her brother's, if she chose to take it up." Her tone hardened. "I chose. Then, *I* chose. But now I am back, with my song unfinished, to have my choice made *for* me: do I live? Or do I die?"

I stared out at the flanks of snowy mountains, ranked in rows around the lake. The island in the center was scalloped at the edges, like lace, thorny with bare-limbed trees, veiled in bluish vegetation impervious to the cold. The colors were smudgy and dull, like the winterscape: smoke blue, steel gray, indigo black, all swathed in the pristine white of mourning. From here the island looked quite small. But from there, so did we. If they could see us at all.

I squeezed her shoulders briefly. "Let's go down, Delilah. You've waited long enough."

Down. We walked, leading the stud, because the way was steep and he was weary of carrying two. Del preceded me, I him; he seemed grateful, bobbing his head with the downward motion.

Down and down and down, until we reached the bottom, and the shoreline curved before us, left and right, butting up against treeless mountain slopes, wearing only snow.

I frowned. "What are all these lumps?"

Del didn't answer at once. Wrapped in her borrowed blankets, she walked forward, toward the shoreline, oblivious to the lumps.

The turf was winter-brown, but thriving. It crawled from the shoreline to the path we'd just descended, even over the oblong lumps, like a cloak. It softened all the edges; velvet over stone.

Halfway to the shoreline, Del stopped. Turned back to look at me. "Not lumps," she said, "barrows. See the stones? Cairns and dolmens, marking the passage graves."

I stopped so short the stud walked into me. He snorted, shook his head, nudged my elbow.

Hoolies. *Graves.*

I drew in a breath. The lumps—*barrows*—closest to me had no stones, being merely turf-covered, oblong mounds. But those closer to Del, closer to the lake, boasted conical piles of weathered dark stone, or large, flat rock caps, some standing on end, others resting across them like a table top. There were, I saw, runes, carved into the standing stones.

"Staal-Kithra," Del said quietly. "Place of Spirits."

I shivered. "How do we get to the island? There's no boat. And I don't plan on swimming—particularly as I can't."

"There will be a boat." Del stared out at the island. "There's something I must do, first. And then we will see if we're given leave to go to Staal-Ysta, or if it is too late."

In the distance, I heard the whinnying of a horse. So did the stud; he lifted his head and answered, pealing the sound through clear winter air.

"Someone's coming," I said.

She shook her head. "Not yet. Someone will come for the stud, yes, but not until it's time." She nodded her head eastward, along the shoreline. "The horses are kept over there, a mile, maybe two, at the settlement. They're tended by the children, who take turns. It's a way of teaching them responsibility. But there are adults, as well; families of the *ishtoya* and *an-ishtoya*. Those of higher rank may keep their families on the island."

"Why so far? Why not here?"

"Staal-Kithra," Del said simply. "Only the dead live here."

The stud whinnied again, smelling mares; other stallions. I gathered slack rein and kept him close even as he protested, not wanting to lose him now. I might need him again. And soon.

"What are you going to do?" I asked.

"Tell the *voca* I am here." Del peeled back her blankets, slipped them, folded them carefully and placed them on the ground. Wind rippled the wool of her tunic and gaitered trews, plucking at leather fringe and knots. "It shouldn't take long, Tiger."

Standing amidst the barrows and cairns and dolmens of Staal-Kithra, Place of Spirits, Del drew Boreal from her sheath and held up the *jivatma* as she had done before, on the border between North and South, balancing hilt and blade on the open palms of both hands, offering Boreal to the skies, to the gods, to her kin. Maybe to the spirits.

Or maybe to the *voca* who waited to pass judgment.

Then, without speaking, she shifted her stance. Brought the sword down, altered her grip, plunged the blade into the ground so the hilt stood boldly upright.

Del knelt and began to sing.

Across the water, awareness stirred. It lifted the hairs on the back of my neck.

Behind me, the stud blew noisily. Uneasily. I felt his intensity, his arrested attention, torn from mares and stallions to focus on Del and her sword. And her song.

She sang until the boat bumped into the shoreline. And then she stopped and waited, leaving, for the moment, Boreal sheathed in living earth.

A man. A Northerner. Blond. Young. Not much older than Del herself. Blue-eyed, as I expected, and spectacularly good looking. He moved with grace and economy, a mixture not trained but born, and he had it in abundance.

Like Garrod, he wore braids. But his were wrapped with gray fur from top to bottom, laced with black cord. His clothing, too, was black; plain, unadorned black, except for the leather harness. He'd studded it with silver to match the hilt of his sword, worn in harness behind his right shoulder.

Left-handed, then.

"Bron," Del said. No more than that, but I heard surprise, pleasure and thankfulness in her tone. Saw the slight lessening of rigidity in the line of her shoulders as she knelt.

"Delilah." He stopped before her, looking briefly past her to me. His expression was stern, austere, too stark for a face such as his, made for laughter and lightheartedness. But there was nothing of it in his tone. *"An-ishtoya,"* he amended, lids flickering only minutely.

"Sword-dancer," she told him quietly, speaking Borderer. "Give me no rank, Bron; you know why."

Again he looked to me. Said something to her in a dialect I didn't know.

Del answered him in the same, tilting her head slightly in my direction, and I heard the word for Southroner.

It mattered. His mouth tightened. His expression grew more severe. He spoke in accented Borderer, welcoming me, clearly preferring the pure uplander dialect but speaking instead a tongue I knew. I could not be kept in ignorance. I was the *an-ishtoya's* sponsor.

Or would be, eventually, when Bron gave us leave to go.

But he didn't.

"The year is done," he told her, "by three days. I am sent to tell the blade she no longer has a name, and to invite her to step into the circle. Here. Now. In Staal-Kithra, as is fitting, with the spirits of others as witnesses, before the blade without a name can profane the Place of Swords."

Jerkily, Del stood up. She pulled the blade from the ground. "I have a name," she said firmly.

"For three days past, you have not."

"*I have a name,*" she said.

Slowly, he shook his head.

"Bron—" But she cut it off. Swung to face me. "Sandtiger," she said evenly, "will you honor us by drawing the circle?"

I looked at Bron. He was fair, as are all Northerners, but having ridden with Del, I knew the signs. He had placed himself under rigid self-control; he liked it no more than she. But he was as bound by the honor codes as the woman who would face him.

I unlooped the stud's picket rope and peg, pushing it into the soft turf easily with a single thrust of one foot. Stepped away, unsheathed my sword.

No. Not mine. Theron's. And Bron knew it.

Very cool, he was. But I've learned to judge the eyes, the flesh, the tautness of tiny muscles. One ticked by his left eye.

They waited in silence, Del and Bron, as I drew the circle. Turf gave way easily beneath honed steel, parting to show damp earth. Their footwork might obscure it, altering the line, but I knew they would not require me as arbiter, to warn them if they moved too close. Clearly, Bron and Del knew one another well.

I stepped away. Cleaned my blade. Sent it hissing home into its sheath. Waited as they stripped off harness, gloves, placed them outside the circle, placed blades in the center, then took their positions on opposite sides, outside, waiting for my word to begin the dance.

For the first time in my life, I changed the ritual. "Three days," I said, "is nothing. She is here. She is prepared to face the *voca*, to accept their decision. Isn't this a bit unnecessary?"

Bron was shocked. He stared at me, speechless, then sent a furious look at Del, as if to blame her for my behavior.

"Or is it that you *want* to die?" I asked. "Because you will. She's that good, Bron. But then, you know that. You've danced with her before." I folded my arms. "Why not call this off and let the *voca* decide instead? There's no need for bloodshed—" I paused "—yet."

He said something to Del in fast, pure uplander. I understood nothing of it, save the anger in his tone. His control was beginning to slip, but only a little. Not enough.

Del shook her head. Taut-faced, she looked at me. "Tiger, please . . . begin the dance."

"Why?" I shrugged. "Neither one of you wants to dance. I can see it. Can't you?" I paused. "Yes. You can. Though neither wants to admit it." I shrugged again, casually. "Well then, why not simply get in that boat, row to the island and take this up with the *voca*? Don't they have the authority? Aren't *they* the arbiters?"

Bron snapped something curtly. It flushed her face with color. "Don't dishonor me," she said; not begging, asking. "Don't dishonor the circle."

I looked at Bron. At Del. Inclined my head and unfolded my arms. "Prepare."

Northerners both, they sang. Soft little songs of death in a language I didn't know. Nor did I care to know it.

"*Dance,*" I told them curtly.

Chapter 35

*I*n my life, I have seen many sword-dances. Most I haven't
actually *witnessed*, being part of the dances themselves, but
I knew, watching Del and Bron, I was seeing the purest form of the
dance. The magic of trueborn talent.

Here the style was different from the one I'd been taught in
the South. Instead of brute strength, there was finesse; in place of
power, dexterity. And speed, and incredible reflexes. I am big and
strong and powerful, difficult to bring down. But Del is quickness
personified, subtle and calculating, trained to wear down stamina
and to *irritate,* to frustrate with sheer skill, which, in the long run,
can destroy an opponent mentally. He will make mistakes. She
will not.

We have sparred many times, Del and I. We've even danced for
real, though only in exhibition. But now, against Bron, in a Northern circle and facing a Northern opponent, Del's skills unveiled
themselves entirely, and showed me a new kind of brilliance.

One of Del's peculiar gifts is the ability to *force* mistakes, to cre-
ate instability on the part of her opponent. She'd done it with me.
And now she tried to do it with Bron.

But Bron was also good, as good as any I've ever seen, and he
wasn't about to fall victim to her tricks.

The swords had been keyed by the songs. Del's was salmon-silver, Bron's copper-gold. Together they reclaimed winter and made it spring again, setting the smudgy gray sky alight with illumination born of Northern stars and nightskies.

They were perfectly matched. The dance was magnificent. But I knew one of them had to die.

Sword-dancers. Sword-*singers*. Each beautifully trained. And each one clearly focused on the need to kill the other.

Blades clashed, whined, scraped free. Spat sparks in the blue light of winter. Alien runes tied alien knots, then unwound and started all over again, with more determination.

I saw the patterns begin to form in the air between them. They built a lattice, each of them; wove a living tapestry of subtle, significant strokes, reflecting their signatures. The Northern style is one of wristwork, like a painter at a canvas. Dab here, swirl there, complex curlicue *here*. Except their brushes were made of steel, and the paint they spilled was blood.

Sweat sheened both faces. Exhalations plumed the air. Bron's expression was one of tense expectancy, a careful calculation of her movements. But I saw him begin to relax, to loosen, shedding the tension in his muscles and allowing them to flow. He was incredibly graceful, particularly for a man; he was deer to my bear. Fur-sheathed blond braids swung free as he moved smoothly, easily, clearly accustomed to the lumpiness of the turf. He was untroubled by its texture, as Del had suggested *I* become, and hadn't.

Del inhabits a different world when she dances, rising above normal physicalities and their limitations. It's almost as if she *becomes* the sword she wields, employing all the knowledge of her slain *an-kaidin*.

But I knew she would tire faster than Bron, no matter how good her skills, because she'd been too long below the border; her breath would run out before his, leaving her dizzy and fighting for air. It had to be finished quickly.

But I didn't see how it would be. I didn't see how it *could* be.

The blades were blurs of light, setting the day afire. Patterns dripped in the air like honey from a hive, running out of a spoon.

Against the backdrop of lake and island, they knit themselves new colors and overwhelmed the gray of the day.

Hoolies, let it be ended. Before I dishonor the dance.

Del cried out. In strength expended, power expelled, in utter extremity. She cried out something in Northern, then braced herself for the blow.

It came swiftly, scything through the air. Bron severed all his remaining patterns with the boldness of his stroke, and tried to run her through the belly.

Boreal flicked. Met his blade, held firm. Turned the force of the blow aside, if not the blow itself, and screeched in discordant protest as Bron's blade slid across runes.

I saw the fabric of Del's tunic separate. I saw pale flesh beneath. I waited for the blood, but nothing showed itself.

Hilts hooked. Then Del snatched hers back, reclaiming the blade; leaned away quickly, came back, with a twist of determined wrists.

Bron's blade had missed. Boreal did not.

She took him through the belly. It was a clean, simple thrust, missing bones that might turn the blade, allowing it lethal freedom instead. Her *an-kaidin* would have been proud; the death was worthy of her.

Bron fell, pulling free of the sword. His own blade swung wildly, then tumbled out of his hand to lie unattended just out of the circle. He remained within.

He gazed up at her in surprise, then said something in uplander. Del answered in the same tongue, kneeling down by his side. She was clearly exhausted, winded by exertion. Her hand shook as she touched his.

I don't know what more he said. I don't speak uplander, and his life was nearly spent. But it meant something to Del; she bent forward and kissed his brow. When she straightened, he was dead.

Del sat very still for a very long time. Slowly her breathing stilled, ran smooth. I saw the expressions in her face: grief, guilt, regret, a hardening of resolve. But the latter was most extreme; it changed her face from flesh to marble and stripped it of humanity.

Carefully, Del cleaned her sword. Rose. Stepped out of the circle. Sheathed her sword and put on the harness, then bent to collect his things, including the now-dull *jivatma*.

She gazed past me to the east. "They're coming for the stud."

I turned. Saw two children, a girl and a boy; the girl was maybe twelve, the boy a year or two younger. Tow-headed like them all.

"What did he say?" I asked.

Del stared at me. A new and frosty austerity was in her eyes, as much as had been in Bron's. "That I was to honor my *an-kaidin*."

I frowned. "That's all?"

"All that was necessary." She looked down at the harness and sword, briefly caressing silver studs. "Bron and I were swordmates for as long as I was here. His *an-kaidin* was mine; we were his favorite *an-ishtoya*."

Privacy has its place, but her manner was too rigid. "What else, bascha?"

Del looked at me. "He told me the name of his sword."

"*Told* you—" I stared. "But I thought you said a Northerner never does that . . . that it destroys all the magic—lessens the power, or something."

"It was a gift to me," she said bleakly, "to mark the things we once shared as *ishtoya* and *an-ishtoya*. And so they would know he forgave me the blood-debt; one is enough, he said."

"Del," I said, "I'm sorry."

After a moment, she nodded. "*Sulhaya*, Sandtiger. I know what you tried to do . . . how you tried to stop the dance." She shrugged a little, stark-faced. "But if you break one ritual, one oath, the others become as worthless. The bindings come undone."

The children had finally reached us. I pulled the peg, looped the rope so the stud wouldn't trip, handed the rein to the boy, who reminded me of Massou. Who reminded Del of Jamail.

I turned back to her. "What about the body?"

The impersonality of it rocked her. "*Bron—*" But she stopped; hardened her tone, said the *voca* would send someone to give him burial in Staal-Kithra.

I nodded. Looked at the island, floating on winter water. "I don't know how to row."

"That's all right. I do." Resolutely, Del turned toward the lake.

Staal-Ysta. A stark, bleak place, afloat in the center of a glass-black lake: a deep-cut cauldron filled with too dark wine, all hedged with white-flanked mountains. Born of the desert, such an abundance of water was incomprehensible to me. But here it was, everywhere: the lake, the snow, even the touch of the air. Everything was *wet*, in an odd, indefinable way.

I looked at Del's face as she rowed. She had masked herself to me, but I had learned to peel it back and discover what lay beneath. The tension of arrival at last at the place of her training had taken its own toll. Bron's death—and the manner of it—made it even worse.

She had built her wall again, the old familiar wall employed as a shield before, when we'd first met, made of harshness, coldness, ruthlessness. The angles of her face were sharp as glass; I expected the cheekbones to cut through flesh.

I am not a man for leaving a thing unsaid if I want to say it, no matter what the situation. But this time, under these circumstances, seeing her face, I held my silence. Del was somewhere else. When she wanted me, when she *needed* me, I'd be available.

She brought the boat in deftly, snugging it up into the cove out into the edge of the island itself. Holding the rope as well as Bron's harness and sheathed sword, she jumped out onto the shore, setting the boat to trembling and grating against the bottom, and waited for me to join her. She said nothing.

I rose carefully, made my way forward, judiciously selected the best place to land, and leaped. I landed in mushy, lake-wet turf and mud, slipped to one knee, got up with a muttered curse. Del anchored the rope beneath a stone, then swung around and headed inland.

There was, I saw, a pathway cut through the trees. Feeble sunlight caught on naked branches and wet dark trunks, playing vague shadows against snow and bare brown turf. Mine, blurred, walked with me, stretched taller by elongation. A bearded, bearlike man made of wool and leather and hair, with a sword strapped to his back.

The trees gave way abruptly to a large oblong field, cleared of stumps and vegetation, where wooden lodges skirted edges in curving symmetry. Smoke threaded the air from each, gray on gray, and bluish. Long, rectangular lodges, cracks stuffed with turf and mud and bits of wood to keep out the winter cold.

Gathered outside of the lodges, bared blades glinting dully in the dull light of a blue-gray day, were more than a hundred Northern warriors, and a handful of equally fair-haired women. All with swords. All in silence. All watching as we approached.

Del wore her own *jivatma*, snugged home in its leather sheath slung in a slant across her back. In her hands she carried Bron's, harness straps wrapped like swaddling around the sheath. She carried it like a woman would a baby, with care and pride and honor.

I let her go before me, taking precedence over the man. In the South, when required—and it had been, all too often—she had done the same for me.

Del walked directly to the end of the oblong circle, paying no mind to those who watched. And when she reached the end, facing the ten men who waited before it, she paid no homage to anyone but stood straight and tall and proud. Delilah to the bone.

"He died well," she told them, in clear Borderer for my benefit. "He honored his *an-kaidin*."

Ten men. The *voca*, I knew. Strong men all, of all sizes, some gray, others blond, one even with light brown hair. They were scarred, hard men, accustomed to hard lives, and unlikely to be softened by her sex. If anything, made tougher; I could see it in their eyes.

One of them said something in pure uplander. He looked past her to me, undoubtedly questioning my presence.

Again in Borderer, Del told him I was her sponsor.

He changed languages adroitly. The oldest of them all, I thought, with snowy braids and wind-reddened skin. But he was at least as tall as I, and nothing about him spoke of weakness. "A blade without a name is due no trial, and therefore due no sponsor."

Del's tone was stiffly formal. "Three days," she said. "I have known such trials to take three *weeks,* when left to the *voca.* Am I not due consideration for the weather? For hardships? For sorcery leveled against us?"

That sharpened ten pairs of eyes, all shades of blue and gray. A pale race, the Northerners; I felt sun-charred by comparison, copper-brown with bronze-streaked hair.

"What manner of sorcery?" the old man asked.

Del shrugged. "Hounds. Beasts. Even now they wait across the water . . . unless they know how to swim."

Lids flickered. He started to glance at the others, changed his mind. Clearly it was something to be considered. And since Del hadn't told them about the ward-whistle, I wasn't about to, either. It's nice to have an advantage.

"Trial," he said at last. "Beginning at dawn tomorrow."

Another of them spoke. "You know the rituals, the constraints. You are not to go out of Staal-Ysta. Not to bare your *jivatma.* Not to invoke its power. You are to remain closeted until the trial. Not a guest, but neither a prisoner; nor will your sponsor be dishonored, so long as he honors the customs of Staal-Ysta." He was younger than the others; brown-haired, gray-eyed. Something softened the line of his mouth. "Kalle is there," he told her, and nodded toward a lodge.

Del looked down at the harness and sword in her hands. For a long moment she didn't move. And then, slowly, she knelt. Placed Bron's *jivatma* on the boot-trampled ground. One hand touched the hilt. She looked up at the watching *voca.*

"It was enough to send Bron," she said tightly. "More than enough. You could give me no punishment as hard or harder than that, even naming my execution."

The old man's expression didn't change. "It was why we sent him."

Del rose. Turned on her heel and marched away. Heading straight for the lodge the younger man had indicated.

Those in front of it parted, let her through, said nothing as she opened the wooden door. I saw hard features and harder eyes. I saw anger, grief and resentment. But I also saw respect.

The door scraped against dirt. Del forced it, went inside. I pulled it closed and latched it.

The interior of the lodge was mostly dark, lighted only by vents and the smoke hole, as well as a single lantern depending from the roof beam. The lodge was wide, squat, divided down the center by two rows of posts, evenly spaced to provide a corridor without walls. On either side of the post rows were compartments, something like large box stalls. In them I saw women and children, as well as dogs and cats. The earthen floor was hardpacked and covered with straw for warmth. It was like nothing I was accustomed to.

More than ever I missed the South.

"Kalle," Del said quietly.

No one answered. No one moved. And then one of the women bent, whispered something to a small girl, sent her forward to greet Del.

Sent her forward to meet her mother.

A single glance told me. There was no need for an explanation. And Del offered me none. She simply turned the girl to face me, turned to face me herself, let flesh and bones tell the story.

"Kalle," she said simply. "The result of Ajani's lust."

Oh. Hoolies. Bascha.

"Well," I said inanely, "at least she takes after her mother."

Slowly, Del shook her head. "Mother *and* father. Ajani's a Northerner."

Chapter 36

S he was five years old, and magnificent. Small, delicate, shyly beautiful, like a fragile, pristine blossom. But she was also clearly a child: active, awkward, blunt. Plainly she stated her preference, which was to be with her *mother*, not Del.

Del let her go, binding her to nothing. She made no claims on the girl's loyalty, since there was no foundation for it. She made no claims on courtesy, either, understanding a child's thinking. She simply let Kalle go outside with the woman she knew as her mother, in name if not in blood, and sat down in a corner compartment the rest left conspicuously empty for the blade without a name.

She knelt. Unbuckled harness and *jivatma*, set both aside in silence. Then pulled a blue-speckled pelt over her legs and looked up at me, still standing, too full of thinking to sit.

Del pulled up legs, clasped her arms around pelted knees, sighed a little, wearily. "When I escaped from Ajani and his men, I had nowhere to go. *All* of my kin were dead, except for Jamail, and him they took south almost at once. I knew better than to try and rescue him without weapons, without proper training . . . I'd have failed. He'd have been sold anyway, and probably me as well . . . so I went north. North to the Place of Swords."

"A difficult journey, alone."

Del scooped tangled hair back from her face. "By the time I arrived, I was heavily pregnant. But I had made up my mind, and nothing would turn me from my course. I didn't want the child, I couldn't *love* the child; it was nothing more than the result of casual seed spilled by a wolf's-head Northerner . . . why should I want his byblow?"

Why, indeed; the question made sense. Yet it sounded so horribly cold.

"The *voca* refused to turn me away, offering succor to someone in need, but neither would they admit me as *ishtoya*. It was only once I swore to prove myself after the birth of the child that they agreed to even consider admitting me as a probationer. And so I bore Kalle in the dead of winter, and when I was physically able I showed the *voca* I knew how to handle a sword." She sighed. "Not as well as I needed to, for my purposes, but enough to convince them of my worth. And so they admitted me."

Del and I had been together nearly a year. Prior to that she'd been in Staal-Ysta for five. But she'd also borne a child; it meant she'd had, at most, four and a half years of training.

I sat down across from her, leaning against the divider. "So very good," I said quietly, "in so very short a time."

She didn't avoid my gaze. "I had a need," she said. "A great and terrible need. You have seen the result."

"Revenge."

"Rescue," she countered, "that first, always. Revenge later, yes. I want to collect the blood-debt Ajani owes me."

"As the *voca* wants to collect the one you owe Staal-Ysta."

"Once again, a choice," Del said. "In killing Theron, you gave me the rest of the year to live in freedom from the blood-guilt. Even then, I might have ignored the summons and remained in the South, free of the *voca*, declared a blade without a name." Fingers smoothed the pelts stretched over her knees. "But I *have* a name, a true name, and I won't let them strip it from me."

"And if *death* strips it from you?"

Slowly, she shook her head. "I will be buried in Staal-Kithra, with Bron and others like him. An honorable death; my name will be carved into the dolmens and sung in all the songs."

My mouth twisted wryly. "Immortality, such as it is."

Del sighed. "A Southroner wouldn't understand—"

"I understand death," curtly, I interrupted. "I understand permanence. Your name might live on forever, but I'd rather you did, too."

Too abruptly, she changed the subject. "There is *amnit*," she said, "if you want it. And food. We're not prisoners, as Stigand said; we have the freedom to do and say what we want, so long as it is in here."

"Stigand being the old man?"

"Yes. The other, the youngest, was Telek." She smiled, but only briefly, as if too weary to hold it. "When I left, he was but newly made *an-kaidin*. At least it hasn't ruined him; he always was a fair man."

"And Stigand isn't?"

"Not *un*fair. Just hard. Demanding. Difficult to know. He is of the old school, as Baldur was . . . and Baldur's best friend." She sighed. "It was Stigand himself who gave me the choice between being sword-dancer or *kaidin* . . . I insulted him when I left Staal-Ysta. He expected me to stay. And then, of course, I killed Baldur. He has hated me for that."

I could see why. But I didn't say it to her. "Telek seemed reasonable."

"Telek is a good man. He and his woman took Kalle as their own and have given her a fine home."

"But she isn't their own," I said. "Kalle is *your* daughter."

Del's expression wasn't one, being masked again. This time I couldn't read it. "I may not live beyond tomorrow, depending on the verdict. What good would it do Kalle to lose a mother she doesn't know? A mother she never had?"

I had no answer for her, because she wasn't arguing with me. She was arguing with herself.

Lines dented her brow. "Why should a child be taken from the only parents she has known, given to a stranger, and told to love her as a mother?"

Still I made no answer.

Del threaded fingers through hair, scraping it back from a haggard face. "Why," she began raggedly, "am I expected to *want* the girl? I'm not fit to be a mother."

Delilah was, I thought, more fit than many women. I've seen her with children before.

But I was afraid of this one. Of who and what she was; of what she represented. Of the threat she distinctly provided.

"About this trial," I said. "Just exactly what will it be?"

"Exactly? I don't know." Del shrugged, slumping down against the wall. "We'll find out in the morning."

"I'd rather know now."

"You'll have to be patient, Tiger. We're to stay in here until we're sent for."

I frowned. "And not go out at *all?* But what about—"

She waved. "The nightpot's over there."

It was, I thought, sufficient to end the conversation. And so I bundled myself up in one of the pelts, stretched out, slept—

—and dreamed of dozens of blonde little girls clinging to Del's sword. Preventing her from using it even to save my life.

I woke up later, long enough to eat and drink what we were brought, then went back to sleep again. The trip north had taken its toll, and I was incredibly tired. I didn't think Del would mind; she was asleep herself.

I hoped her dreams were better than mine.

I slept heavily, woke up in the dead of night. Sleep was completely banished; I'd done my catching up. I got up, used the pot, looked around the lodge.

The light was bad, but I had marked where the door was. Quietly I grabbed Theron's sword, made my way down the corridor between the parade of posts, unlatched the door, slipped out. Didn't make a sound.

The night was cold. The mud and turf underneath my feet had frozen into hardness. Light was negligible, but reflection off the mountains lent enough to see by. I sucked in frigid air, wishing I'd brought a pelt.

The hand came down on my shoulder. I twitched, swung, lifted the sword, saw Telek's face in the dim light. We were of a like size and build, though there the resemblance stopped. He was fair to my dark and probably a year or two older. Young compared to the rest.

He'd untied and loosened his braids. Light brown hair flowed around his shoulders. But that was the only difference from the man he'd been before.

In fluent Borderer, he reminded me I should remain inside.

"I know that," I agreed. "But when I'm told for no particular reason that I shouldn't do a thing, I generally try to do it. It's my way of fighting injustice."

He took his hand from my shoulder. "You think we're being unjust when we expect you to honor the customs of Staal-Ysta?"

"I want to see Stigand."

Telek drew in a breath. "Now? Why? What business have you with him?"

"Private business, Telek. Will you take me to him?"

Grimly he shook his head. "At dawn the trial begins."

"Which is why I want to talk with him *now*. He won't have time, later."

"Custom requires—"

"I don't give a danjac's rump *what* your custom requires," I snapped. "This has to do with that woman in there, the one you've all declared a blade without a name, when she has a greater sense of honor than any of us on this island." I jerked my head toward the door. "I've spent almost a year with her, Telek . . . I will swear on anything you name that what she did was out of need, not desire; out of conviction, not caprice. And I will swear also that she bears the guilt with honor, as a true *an-ishtoya* should, paying respect to her training, her sword, her *an-kaidin*. She does not dishonor you, or anyone in this place. She does not dishonor Staal-Ysta."

The dim light hid much of his face in shadow. "And if I require you to swear the oath you offered?"

"Do it," I said curtly.

His mouth curved a little. "Then I will," he said smoothly. "I require you to swear by the life of Delilah's daughter that you will not interfere with the trial, but will accept its requisites. No matter what they are."

My blurted response was automatic. "But Kalle is *your* daughter."

Telek's gaze didn't waver. "Yes," he agreed tautly, "and that is what you will say if Del asks you for advice concerning Kalle's future."

It was, I thought, an ironic, if interesting, pact. I was afraid Del would decide to stay here, to keep the girl, forsaking the life we'd shared. Telek was, too—if for different reasons.

It was an easy oath. But it made me feel dirty.

Telek latched the door. "I'll take you to Stigand's lodge."

The old man was distinctly displeased to see me. He spoke in rapid staccato uplander to Telek, who answered calmly, quietly, reasonably. And eventually Stigand agreed to listen.

We hunkered down in his compartment within the rectangular lodge. His woman was rolled up in pelts, sleeping soundly. Snores issued from other compartments, and the noises of coupling. A baby squalled briefly, stopped. One of the dogs yipped in dreams. I would have preferred more privacy, but short of going outside it seemed none existed.

Telek took his leave. Stigand waited in silence after waving me to begin.

He was old. Older by night, with his braids shaken loose and a pelt wrapped around his shoulders. I saw the seams of scars in his face, the crookedness of his nose, the line of a jaw that lost more teeth each year. Outside, facing Del, he had been a strong, if aging man. Now he was simply an old one.

I drew in a deep breath. "Friendship is an honorable thing," I said quietly. "The bond forged between childhood companions, swordmates, fellow *ishtoya, kaidin,* and *an-kaidin,* is something to be cherished. Something to be respected. A thing of deep and abiding honor."

Pale blue eyes stared back. He didn't even blink. He was going to be very tough.

"Men who grow old together in adversity and mutual admiration are closer even than babies born at one birth. But one must die first. One always dies first, leaving the other to grieve."

Still the old man said nothing.

"His death was hard enough," I said, "but does it deserve another? Is that what Baldur would want?"

Stigand's lips worked briefly. "It might be what *I* want," he said.

After a moment, I nodded. "But it's also what *she* wants, Stigand. To avenge the death of her kin. The slavery of her brother. The loss of innocence at the hands of a Northerner who cast off his honor long ago, replacing it with brutality."

"We gave her a place," he said. "We gave her skills and a trade. We even gave her honor, offering her a thing no other woman has ever been offered."

"You didn't *give* her honor. What Del has, she earns."

"She repudiated Staal-Ysta."

"She had other responsibilities."

"She blooded her sword in one of *us*—"

"And now Baldur will never die."

It startled him. He gaped.

I nodded. "You may have buried his body in Staal-Kithra, but his spirit survives in her sword. His *teaching* survives in her sword; Baldur's wisdom is undiminished. His skills are not forgotten. He teaches her every day."

"*You* say, Southroner—"

"I have seen her dance."

"You don't understand our customs—"

"I have danced against her."

Stigand glared. "Does that make you any judge? What do I know of you?"

"Probably nothing," I admitted. "In the South, I am known, and well . . . but this is the North. This is Staal-Ysta. I am most likely an empty name. But it might mean something to you if I say I defeated Theron."

Wrinkled lids twitched. Now he was paying attention. "He was sent to give her the choice."

"And he did, but badly. He wanted to dance against her." I shrugged. "Del accommodated. But I was the one who killed him."

"Have you proof?"

I put the sword into the dim light. "I don't know its name," I told him, "but this is Theron's *jivatma*. Would I have it if he lived? Would it be a powerless blade?"

The old man looked down at the sword set across my lap. I rested my hands upon hilt and blade, letting him see what I did. Letting him see I survived; once, I wouldn't have.

Stigand put out a gnarled hand. I saw blotches on it, twisted sinews, swollen knuckles. He touched fingers to the runes.

"It must be painful for you," I told him quietly, "to look at the woman who took the life of your friend. If you give me the chance, I will take her away from here."

It startled him. He jerked back his hand and stared. "Take her out of Staal-Ysta?"

"Provided she's *alive*."

Slowly, he shook his head. "I am not the sole judge. The *voca* is made of ten men."

"But you hold the power here. Traditionally, they defer to you; I can see it in Telek. You could sway the decision."

Stigand hissed something angrily in uplander. "Do you know," he choked, once he had recovered his Borderer, "do you know I could have you killed for this? For asking such a thing?"

"I'm asking out of need."

"*What* need?" he demanded. "What is the woman to a man like you, a *Southroner,* to whom women are merely things?"

I fought to remain calm. "Everything Baldur was to you. I honor her as much as you honored him."

Stigand spat by my knee. "You know nothing of honor. If you did, you wouldn't be here like this, trying to twist me this way and that. Trying to shape justice to your liking. What do *you* know of honor?"

"I know the circle," I told him, "the sword-dance. If you like, I'll swear by that, so you'll know I mean what I say."

Tears glittered in rheumy eyes. "He was my *friend*."

With difficulty, I swallowed. "We have a saying, in the South, about cats. A desert cat, born of the Punja, an animal worth avoiding. We say: *'the sandtiger walks alone'*."

Stigand stared; I went on.

"But this one has tired of that. The Sandtiger has chosen a mate . . . swordmate, bedmate, lifemate. Yet now you place her at risk; do you think I will let you do it?" I leaned forward, over the sword. "Old man, I will honor your customs to a point, because they are worth it—*to a point*. But if you sentence that woman to death, I'll exact my own revenge. A sandtiger's revenge."

His chin trembled. "You threaten an old man."

"No." I shook my head. "I address a warrior, Stigand. I address an *an-kaidin*. I address a man I respect, because, in my tongue, you are a shodo. Sword-master. One who teaches others the circle, and the beauty of the dance."

Stigand looked at the sword. "That is not yours."

I took it out of my lap and set it on the rugs. "Then I gladly give it up. It belongs in Staal-Kithra."

The old man frowned. Worked his tongue against his teeth. Glanced briefly at the woman still sleeping in her pelts.

Heavily, he sighed. "It is hard to lose a friend."

"Even harder to lose a mate."

"Go," Stigand said.

I started to rise, held back. "May I have an answer?"

"In the morning," he answered gruffly.

Alarm flickered dully. There were nine other men involved. Without assurances from this one . . . "Shodo—"

"*An-kaidin*," he corrected. "I have told you to go."

Hoolies. There was nothing left to do.

I rose. Looked down at the *jivatma* I'd carried so long. Then bid it a silent farewell, turning to walk away.

"Southroner." I swung back. Stigand's expression was enigmatic. "How many years have you?"

It caught me off guard. "Altogether?—I don't know. Thirty-four, maybe thirty-five . . . I grew up without mother or father."

"How long a sword-dancer?"

I shrugged. "Eighteen years, give or take a day. Without knowing my age, it's difficult to say."

His gaze held my own. "Baldur and I were born on the same day in the same village, seventy-two years ago. From birth we were companions. It was a strong bond, and one we greatly honored."

Silently, I nodded.

"My woman and I have been together more than fifty years. *That* bond I also honor."

Baffled, I frowned.

Stigand's tone was rough. "That is my answer. Now go."

Silently, I went. Wishing I knew what he meant.

I made my way back toward the compartment Del and I shared in Telek's lodge. But I stopped short before reaching it, pausing to look down on Telek himself, asleep in a corner with his woman and the daughter Del had borne.

Mostly they were lumps beneath pelts, huddled together against the cold. The girl slept between them, snugged up for body warmth, but one arm was free of pelts and blankets. One small, slender arm, with delicate hand and even more delicate fingers. And I wondered, looking at it, if that hand would ever hold a sword, as her mother's did. If the girl would ever step into a circle.

Fine pale hair spilled out into the fur of pelt-swathed pallets. Most of her face was hidden, but I saw the mouth—Del's mouth . . . the subtle cleft in her chin—Ajani's, I wondered? The curve of one cheek. And lashes curled against it.

I turned. Moved to rejoin Del in our compartment. Found her eyes open, looking at me; saw the shine of tears in them. Saw the desperate tension in the line of her mouth as she fought to keep from giving herself away.

I wanted to tell her it didn't matter, that I understood. That I comprehended the incredible tension she had been under, knowing she had left a child behind; I even recalled our brief discussion of mothers and fathers, and children born to sword-dancers; Del's pensive melancholy, the undertone of despair. I wanted to tell her it all made sense now, that I *understood,* and didn't blame her for it.

But as I lay down beside her, Del turned from me toward the wooden wall and shut me out decisively.

I spent the remainder of the night wide awake. So, I knew, did Del.

Chapter 37

*J*ust before dawn, Del and I were separated. I wasn't happy about it, being more than a bit concerned for her state of mind, but Telek assured me it was customary. His woman, Hana—with Kalle as a helper—took Del into a compartment at the far end of the lodge. Telek himself took me into the one he shared with his family and presented me with fresh clothing.

"Northern garb, not Southron," he apologized courteously. "But we are of a like size, and there is none here other than our own."

I shrugged. "If I'd come north with only a dhoti, burnous and sandals, I'd have frozen my *gehetties* off long ago—or so Del repeatedly told me." I smiled even as Telek did. "I've gotten used to the weight."

He cast a glance down the way at Hana, busily aiding Del. "I won't ask what passed between you and Stigand last night—it's your business—but I will ask you to recall the agreement you made with me."

I was stripping out of garters, gaiters, boots. "Yes. I remember. I will abide by the requirements of the trial." I tugged the tunic over my head. "I don't suppose you could give me an idea what to expect?"

Telek shook his head. "I am only one man. The *voca* is ruled by a majority. Even if I told you the sentence *I* might prefer, others may desire otherwise."

I scratched my chest, loosening hair bound up by close confinement. Hoolies, but what I wouldn't give to wear the silks and gauzes of the South again, unfettered by scratchy wool, heavy furs, stiff leather!

"And what *you* want, Telek, is to see Del gone from Staal-Ysta." Stigand as well, though I didn't say it; I figured the trial's results would speak for themselves.

Telek's face was grim, eyes oddly hostile. "I am afraid," he said quietly. "Afraid she will grow too attached, if she stays, and will lay claim to Kalle."

I lowered my voice, not wanting Del—*or* Kalle—to hear. "But she *gave* her to you, didn't she? Asked you to raise her daughter?"

Briefly, he nodded. "The day after Kalle's birth, she was given into our care. We named her, not Del. I had been *kaidin* to Del's *ish-toya* before she was elevated to *an-ishtoya* and became Baldur's—she knew me, respected me, honored me . . . and it was a joy to accept the girl. Hana is—barren." He flicked a glance down the post-lined corridor; everyone else save Hana, the girl and Del was gone, including the dogs and cats. "It was a gift of the gods. But now—"

"Now you're afraid the gift will be rescinded." Grimly, I nodded, tugging on fresh woolen trews. "No more than I am, Telek. I think we have much in common."

He frowned, passing me the brushed wool undertunic. "What would *you* have to fear, Southroner? What is Kalle to you?"

"Change," I declared succinctly. "I happen to like my life. I like the freedom, the challenge, the risks. And I like sharing it with Del . . . unencumbered, you might say, by anything as significant as a child."

"Significant," he echoed. "Indeed, a child *has* significance. And the man or woman who can't see that is without honor."

Honor, again. A familiar refrain. "It's not that I don't like children, or that I think Kalle isn't a beautiful little girl—"

"—but you don't want the responsibility." Telek nodded. "Once, I felt the same. But then *once* I swore never to take a woman to wife, preferring the ease of uncomplicated relationships." His smile was wry. "We all change, Southroner. Sooner or later. Some of us more than others." His gaze was on Del's distant head bobbing above the privacy divider.

It sobered me. Too often I didn't bother to think about what would happen when I got old—well, old*er*, maybe not old—and was unable to earn my living as a sworddancer. There weren't a whole lot of old *or* older sword-dancers around; age takes its toll, and we tend to kill ourselves off.

So I don't think about it much. I decided not to think about it now.

I finished dressing in silence. The borrowed clothing was of good wool dyed a deep blue-black: long-sleeved tunic with fringe depending from the neck, ornamented with silver beads that clattered as they collided; soft-combed trews, silver-tipped fur gaiters cross-wrapped from ankles to knees; heavy leather bracers stretching from wrists to mid-forearm, weighted with round silver bosses.

Hoolies, such vanity!

More *yet:* a matching belt so wide it guarded nearly my entire midsection, also elaborately bossed, and finally a heavy wool cloak dyed a rich, bright indigo-teal, to set off the darker color of tunic and trews.

Telek twisted it from shoulder to shoulder, folding it back, then pinned it in place with massive silver brooches, one on each shoulder. The weight of the cloak spilled down my back, reaching to my boots.

I rolled shoulders unaccustomed to such weight. "If I fell into the lake, I'd *drown* in all this finery."

"You'd drown anyway; Del says you can't swim." Telek grinned. "Except for the sun-coppered skin and brown hair, you could be one of us."

"No thanks," I said politely. "Too many traditions attached . . . I'd rather just be a Southron sword-dancer, whose only obligation is to survival in the circle."

"A worthy ambition," Telek said quietly, then nodded his head in Del's direction. "The *an-ishtoya*, Southroner—Baldur's greatest student . . . and his greatest failure."

I turned. For a moment all I could do was stare at Del—white-faced, stark-faced Del—who wore the same color Bron had, in the circle: somber, unrelieved black, as well as fur-sheathed, cord-wrapped braids. As I did, she wore bracers on her forearms, but in place of leather they were silver. At her left shoulder rode the *ji-vatma* named Boreal.

She was magnificent. She was also hard and cold as death, whose color she wore so well.

Her expression was implacable. "They are calling for us."

Telek nodded, preceded us out of the long lodge. His light brown hair had been freshly braided and wrapped by Hana, and he wore subdued brown. The cloak was warm sienna, reminding me of the South.

As we passed, Hana reached out and caught Kalle by one shoulder, pulling her out of the way. Del paused, abruptly knelt, brushed back the girl's fine hair. "I will make you proud of me today."

I saw the blossom of fear in Hana's face, though Kalle merely smiled, not comprehending the undercurrents of the moment.

I looked at Telek. His face was grim and hard, though I saw something else in his eyes. Apprehension, impatience, a tremendous tension struggling to show itself in spite of the iron grip he had on his emotions. He saw me looking at him, abruptly pushed open the door. "The circle awaits, Del."

She rose. Fingertips lingered briefly in Kalle's hair. Then she walked resolutely away from the girl.

As we stepped out, I was grateful for the voluminous cloak. Pinned back for effect and ease of movement, it lacked the freedom I needed for total warmth, but at least there was a little. The air was crisp and clear and cold; snow and turf crunched under my boots.

The light, as yet, was newborn, filtering through bare-branched trees to paint faint striped patterns on the ground. It lent everything an ethereal, blue-gray tint, polishing the silver of the sword hilts strapped to so many backs. Everyone was gathered, even the smallest of children.

In the center of the clearing stood nine men, among them Stigand. Each of them bore a sword. Telek gestured me to stand aside, away from the center, though separate from the audience. Del he took to the very center, before the *voca*, and commanded her to stand before those who would judge her.

She took her place. She was in profile to me, sharp as glass, rigidly correct. Whatever sentence they would declare, she was ready for it.

Telek went first. He drew his sword, stepped close to Del, set its tip into the ground. And pressed, thrusting it down, until the hilt and half the blade stood upright in the dawn.

Nine men followed suit, until she was caged by a circle of swords. Her own she wore on her back.

Stigand stood in the middle of the line of men, side by side, framed by those who were younger and stronger than he. But none, I knew, with his power; I hoped it would be enough.

For the sake of the *an-ishtoya's* sponsor, he spoke in Borderer, "Declare yourself before us."

"Delilah," she answered quietly, "daughter of Staal-Ysta."

"Why are you come before us?"

"To stand trial for the death of the *an-kaidin* Baldur, whose life I took last year." Del drew in a breath. "To expiate the blood-guilt and to pay *swordgild* for his loss."

The silence was heavy. Unobtrusively I glanced around, trying to judge the others. I saw stiff Northern faces; heard crisp Northern comments in the tongue I didn't know. They were not disposed to give her leniency for the death of the old *an-kaidin*.

"Tell us why," Stigand said.

"I needed to blood my *jivatma*."

"But why blood it in Baldur? He was not an honored enemy— he was an honored *friend!*"

Oh, hoolies. Now Stigand was angry.

"I needed him," Del said. "I needed him in my sword."

Stigand's voice shook. "Tell us why, then. Tell us why it was worth his life."

Del told him. She spoke to Stigand, not to the others, though they could hear as well. So could everyone else. Quietly, unemotionally, she related what had happened to her family. How Ajani

and the raiders had destroyed everything she knew. The dry factu-
ality of her report stripped the impact completely from it, and made
me fear for the result.

At last she finished her explanation. It wasn't really a defense,
being little more than a tale related, and I was afraid the icy control she exerted over herself would prejudice them against her.

Now it was my turn.

Stigand's eyes were sharp. "Will the *an-ishtoya's* sponsor step
forward and declare himself?"

It wasn't really a question, though he phrased it as one. I
stepped forward a little, heard murmured comments, tried to catch
Del's eyes and failed. Her gaze was locked on the *voca*.

"I am the Sandtiger," I said. "Born of the South, born of the
Punja . . . I'm a sword-dancer, seventh-level."

The declaration produced silence.

After a moment, Stigand nodded. "This man is known to me.
He is indeed the Sandtiger, bearing the scars of the cat he killed to
gain a name, won in honor and dignity."

Well, there hadn't been much dignity about it, really. The cat
had nearly killed *me*. It had been sheer good fortune that I'd dodged
the worst of his paw-swipes while managing to pin him against the
rocks with my crude spear, until I pierced his vitals.

Honor? Maybe. I'd just wanted my freedom; it had seemed the
only way.

Stigand droned on. "You have come to Staal-Ysta as sponsor to
the *an-ishtoya*."

I said I had.

"Knowing what the responsibility entails."

Well, more or less; I'd support Del's story and tell them I
thought her actions had merit. I said so.

"Willing to accept that responsibility in whatever form it takes."

Inwardly, I sighed. Told him I'd agreed. Wished they'd hurry up.

"How well do you know the *an-ishtoya*?"

Hoolies, at this rate it would take all day just to establish my
credentials!

Briefly, I told the *voca* I'd spent the last ten months riding with

Del, and that I probably knew her as well or better than anyone, since we'd been bedmates as well as swordmates, and had sparred with her in the circle as well as dancing in exhibitions, *and* had accompanied her on missions of employment, easily verifiable if they wanted to take the time to track down our Southron employers.

I thought that might shut him up; it would take a very long time.

Stigand's expression was fierce. "And do you support everything the *an-ishtoya* has said? Do you support her reasons for killing Baldur?"

It was a true test, and tricky. I'd have to choose my answer carefully.

Cursing my lack of fluency in Borderer, I nonetheless embarked on what I hoped was an eloquent, impassioned defense of Del's actions. But halfway through I ran out of eloquence entirely, stopped, took another step forward.

"It doesn't matter," I told them. "What matters is the *voca's* interpretation of her actions, not a decision based on wrongness or rightness. We all have been faced with doing things we'd rather not do. I doubt any of us *enjoys* killing people, but we do it when we have to. I say that *have to* is determined by the strength of the circumstances." I drew in a breath. "Del swore an oath on the souls of her murdered kin as well as her *jivatma* that she would avenge their deaths. That in itself has honor, as taught here at Staal-Ysta. But she knew her chances of succeeding were slight; a woman alone, no matter how good with a sword, can't overcome twenty or thirty men." I gestured briefly in Del's direction, indicating the sword. "She could count on no one but herself—collecting a blood-debt is a thing left to kin, and she had none left—so she called upon the only man she knew capable of giving her the strength, support and power she required—she called on her *an-kaidin.*"

"She *killed* her *an-kaidin!*"

Stigand's impassioned cry hung in the morning air. And I thought, looking at him, I'd been a fool to hope he would suggest as a just sentence anything but her death.

I wet my lips. "But Baldur isn't dead. He lives on in her *jivatma.*"

"Not possible," Telek declared.

I disagreed. "Don't Northerners believe that by blooding a *jivatma* in the body of an honored person, enemy or otherwise, that the sword takes on the attributes of that person?"

Telek gestured. "There is more to it than that."

"Broken down," I said distinctly, "that's basically what it means. And maybe what it is; I've seen *jivatmas* 'die,' when deprived of the sword-dancer's life. First Theron's sword, then Bron's . . . they became merely swords instead of remaining *jivatmas*."

The *voca* exchanged glances. Clearly I'd unveiled nothing new, but maybe they'd hoped I wouldn't know so much about their customs.

"So," I said quietly, "Del called on Baldur to help, and Baldur did. He stepped into the circle. He danced with his best *an-ishtoya*. And he died, so that Del's *jivatma* could live. So that she could collect the blood-debt, in true Northern style. With true Northern *honor*."

The old man stared at me. I saw grief, anger, acknowledgment. But he said nothing. He merely swung around and walked away, while the other nine followed him.

Hoolies, I hate waiting. But waiting is what we did, Del and I. While all the others stood and watched, waiting as much as we did.

Eventually, Stigand came marching back with the *voca*. Took his place again before Del's cage of swords. Said nothing as the others fell in to flank him; Telek avoided my eyes, as did Stigand.

Not a good sign.

The old man looked straight at Del. "You have killed one of our number. That is unforgivable. But so are the deaths of others."

Del didn't even blink.

"You have agreed to pay *swordgild* to Baldur's kin; he has none. You will pay it instead to Staal-Ysta, to help in times of need."

Del nodded once.

"As to the sentence for the murder of your *an-kaidin*, we will be lenient. We offer you a *choice:* death, or life. Exile yourself and go, or stay here and be executed."

Instantly there was an outbreak of conversation among all

those watching. Some clearly felt the sentence was just, others argued against it.

I looked at Stigand. So. The old man had upheld his end of the deal. I looked at Telek. His face was stony, but I saw satisfaction in his eyes. The honor of Staal-Ysta was upheld, Del was punished, they both got what they wanted: Staal-Ysta empty of painful reminders of deaths *and* births.

I released a sigh of relief. Now we could go South. Now we could go home.

"How long," Del asked, "is the exile?"

"Forever," Stigand told her.

Unsurprised, Del nodded. "I'd like to buy back a year."

It stopped all the clamor dead. Everyone stared; some gaped.

Stigand was clearly puzzled. "Buy back a year?"

Del's voice rang out clearly, carrying through the cold air. "I want the first day of my exile moved back twelve months. I will pay for it."

"Why?" Stigand demanded.

"I have a child." Del looked straight back at him. "I'd like to be a mother, if for only a year."

Telek shut his eyes.

Stigand was shaking his head. "This isn't acceptable. You gave the girl up—"

"—because I had no other choice." Her voice was quiet, but the underlying passion carried as clearly as a shout. "What manner of mother would I be without honor? What life could I offer a child? None. And so I swore my oaths and gave her up so I could collect the blood-debt to regain my family's honor . . . to give *Kalle* some honor." She looked squarely at Telek. "I don't mean to take her from you. I mean only to *share* her for a year—and then she will be yours forever, undivided, while I spend my life in other lands." Bitterness crept in. "Is that so much to ask? One year in exchange for a lifetime?"

Oh, hoolies, bascha. This wasn't part of the deal.

Stigand didn't look worried, though Telek's face was gray. The old man merely smiled. "You said you would buy back the year.

With what? You must pay *swordgild* to Staal-Ysta . . . what is left to spend?"

"Blood-gift," she said steadily, "for the space of that year."

Stigand's voice was gentle; he was certain of the outcome. "I say again: what? Do you mean to give up your *jivatma?*"

"No," Del answered quietly. "I give you a new *an-ishtoya.* I give you the Sandtiger."

Chapter 38

oise. Everyone was talking to me, talking *at* me: Stigand, Telek, other members of the *voca,* other Northerners. But it was all just noise, *all* of it; I walked away from it easily, pushing through the throng, and finally reached Del.

I reached out, caught one arm above the elbow, pulled her close. "We have to have a talk."

The *voca* had uncaged her, each man pulling his sword from the ground and sheathing it, denoting acceptance of her proposition. All but *two,* that is; neither Stigand nor Telek had been satisfied, but they were soundly defeated by a distinct majority, and so eventually they had plucked their swords from the ground. Del had purchased her year.

She tried once to disengage her arm from my hand, failed, gave in. Allowed me to physically escort her away from the commotion, back through the trees to the shore to where the boat was anchored.

I released her arm, knowing I'd undoubtedly left red finger-marks in her flesh that would by morning turn blue; Del is that fair.

She stood stiffly, almost awkwardly, staring resolutely across the lake to where mountains bumped the sky. Water carries sound; I heard horses in the distance. I thought I heard the stud.

Slowly I pointed to the boat. "What," I began quietly, "prevents me from getting in that boat and leaving?"

Del's tone was flat. "You don't know how to row."

"Oh, I learn pretty fast . . . and you have given me *more* than enough provocation to get in there now and do it."

"Then go," she said tonelessly.

I caught her arm again, swung her around to face me. "You know perfectly well I *can't!* You saw to that, didn't you? You knew once I agreed to abide by the *voca's* sentence I'd be trapped by my own words, and you could do whatever you felt like doing, regardless of what I wanted."

"You have a choice," she said curtly. "You aren't a prisoner. You're a student, just like all the others . . . no one will keep you here against your will. No one will chain you up or lock you into a lodge. At worst they'll give you a *jivatma!*"

"I don't *want* one!" I shouted. "What I want is to get in that boat—*with you*—and go back across the lake, where we can collect the stud and get the hoolies *out* of here, right now!"

"I have a year," she said grimly. "Duly purchased and paid for."

"With *my freedom,* Del!" I stared at her, astonished at the depth of her resolution; her lack of compassion for me, whom she had dispensed with so readily. "You didn't even *ask* me!"

She swung to face me squarely. "And if I had come to you and said, so prettily: 'Please, Tiger, will you do this for me; Tiger, will you give me a year of your life?' " She shook her head. "Why should I waste my breath? I knew what you would have said."

"No you don't. You haven't the faintest idea. Because you're so wrapped up in yourself and your own needs right now, you're totally blind to mine."

"Not blind!" she cried. "I see you! But I also see Kalle. I also see *my daughter*—"

"—whom you gave up the day after she was born."

"Because I *had* to—"

"Don't give me that goat dung, Del. You didn't *have* to do anything of the sort. No one forced you to. No one snatched that child away from you and said you couldn't see her again until you'd avenged your family. That was *you*. That was you—"

"What do you know about it?" she cried. "What do *you* know

about love and honor within a family . . . what do *you* know about responsibility to one's kin . . . you've never accepted any responsibility in your entire life!"

It hurt. "And how responsible were you to *Kalle* when you gave her up? Were you satisfying *her* needs, or your own?"

Del's eyes were blazing. "It was something—"

"—you had to do, I know." I shook my head. "You have every right to make harsh decisions for yourself, Del, even wrong ones, but you have no right at all to decide how others will live their lives."

"Kalle is mine."

"You gave up your rights to her."

"No."

"Yes." I sighed heavily and scratched at the clawmarks in my beard, trying to maintain patience and temper, and being hard-pressed. "She has a good life with Telek and Hana—you said so yourself—why destroy it now?"

"I'm destroying nothing. I'm *sharing* her for a year."

"And how do you think Kalle will view that? Are you a temporary mother, coming to see her at *your* convenience, expecting her to give you the same love and affection she gives to Hana?" I shook my head. "How will it be for her, Del?"

Del wrenched her head around to stare angrily at the lake. I saw tears glisten in her eyes. "It's a year against a lifetime."

"And how will it be for you when that year is up, and you have to leave her forever? Do you think it will be easy? Do you think you can simply walk away, saying your time is done?"

"I'd rather go knowing I *had* a year with her, than go now having had nothing."

It was incredibly frustrating. "But you gave her up the day after she was born, Del! You've spent the last five years apart from her—why be so demanding now?"

"Because I was wrong." Del turned to face me again. "I was *wrong*, Tiger." She held herself so rigidly I was afraid she'd break. "I was so angry when I came here I could see nothing else but the revenge I'd exact from Ajani and his men. It was what *fueled* me,

Tiger, during the journey here. Knowing I carried his child. Knowing that once I'd learned the sword, once I'd earned my *jivatma,* I could do what I wanted to do. I'd have the skills and strengths to do it."

More quietly, I said, "I understand revenge. I understand hatred. But you can't live a normal life by depending only on those emotions."

Del's mouth was flat. "I lived for five years on those emotions, Tiger. Don't tell me it can't be done."

"I said *normal life,* Del. Your life isn't normal. It isn't even close."

"Maybe not," she agreed. "But maybe spending a year here with Kalle will give me the balance I need."

I spread my hands. "What about Kalle? How will *she* feel?"

Del shook her head so determinedly her braids swung against her shoulders. "Tiger, you don't understand. You have no idea—"

"—how Kalle might feel?" I finished. "Think again, Del."

She put the palms of her hands flat against her temples. "You don't *understand,*" she repeated. "How could you? You yourself admitted you don't know if you've sired any children—maybe you have, maybe you haven't. You're sublimely indifferent to the possibility there might be sons and daughters of your blood scattered throughout the South." She pulled her hands away, slapping them against her thighs. "Yet you stand here and tell me you know how my daughter will feel?"

"Yes," I told her flatly. "More than *you* can know."

Impatiently, "Oh, Tiger—"

"*I know,*" I told her, tapping fingers against my chest. "I know— deep inside, deep in *here*—what it's like to be deserted. What it's like to grow up knowing no one claims you . . . what it's like having no one at all but yourself . . . what it's *like* knowing the woman who bore you dropped you into the sand like a load of stinking dung, then left you there to rot." I stepped closer to her, very close. "*I know,* Del. I know very well."

She stared at me, white-faced. I'd shocked her with my passion, but I hadn't changed her feelings. Too easily she dismissed mine. "It's not the same, Tiger. I'm not *deserting* Kalle—"

"She won't know the difference," I said bluntly. "Oh, yes, you and Hana and Telek will try to explain it to her, but she won't understand. All she will know is that you've left. That you've left *her* . . . it's the only thing that matters. She won't understand all the reasons behind your departure. She'll only know you've *gone*."

"When she's older—"

"How much older?" I asked. "It takes years, Del. Many, many years until you come to terms with it . . . and even then you never really do. You understand it a little better, but the hurt's still there inside." I drew in a breath. "Your own sentence is harsh. Permanent exile from Staal-Ysta, from your daughter . . . but have you thought about what your purchased year will do to *her?*"

Woodenly, "Give her time with her mother."

After a moment, I shook my head. "Hana is her mother."

"You *don't understand!*" she shouted. "How can you understand? You're so ruled by your own lusts and selfishness that all you can see is the threat she provides to the life you and I have shared. Well, *it's finished!* What is there left of it?"

"One year," I said grimly. "You made sure of that, didn't you? Way back when you first started talking about dancing styles and the customs of Staal-Ysta . . . way back when you first started instructing me as if you were the *kaidin* and I the *an-ishtoya*." I nodded as she stared. "I should have seen it then. All this blather about the North . . . I should have seen it then. You knew there was a chance you could buy your way out of an execution by offering a blood-gift to the *voca*—and that gift, you decided, was me."

Del's tone was flat. "Yes."

Anger, oddly, diminished with her admission. I sighed heavily. Turned from her, faced the lake and mountains, folded my arms across my chest. "I suppose I don't really blame you. And I think that's what makes me the angriest—I *do* understand what you've done."

"And *why?*"

I shrugged. "Enough of the why, I guess. Mostly, I just feel empty. Tired, numb, empty . . . I feel like I've been *used*."

Stark-faced, Del said nothing.

Idly I rolled a stone out of its pocket in the ground. Bent, picked it up, tossed it out into the lake. Watched it fall, heard its splash. Saw the rings ripple out from its passage. "I can't stay here."

She drew in a deep, uneven breath. "There may be an honorable way yet. I think if you spoke to Telek, or maybe even Stigand, they could find a way to release you from the year."

It brought a blossom of hope. Then it faded. "A way for *me* to buy myself out of my sentence?" I smiled and laughed a little. "But what have I to sell? What have I to trade?"

Del turned from me abruptly. Stared blindly out at the water, then just as abruptly swung back. "I want that year with Kalle. But I also want it with you."

Well, I suppose that's something.

But I'm not sure, *now,* it's enough.

Chapter 39

*I*t was sundown. In the North, the colors are different. Here the sun moves behind snow-flanked mountains and sucks the daylight with it. But because much of the day is gray and blue and ivory, the colors of sunset are muted. It simply fades to deeper blues and bleaker grays, until the sun is replaced by moonlight, holding luminous court against pallid black.

We gathered near a dolmen on the island: Stigand, myself, Telek. For questions and explanations, hoping for solutions. None of us was happy.

Stigand was wrapped up in a warm green cloak, white braids corded with gold. He'd shrugged the folds up near his head, warding his neck against drafts. Gloomily, he stared past me to the dolmen, sucking the teeth he had left.

Telek was little better. He still wore deep brown and warm sienna. His mood was decidedly darker.

"She won't be moved," I said. "She has made up her mind."

Telek's mouth twitched in wry displeasure. "Del always was stubborn."

Stigand's tone was querulous. "She has no respect for our customs."

"*That's* not true," I retorted. "And you know it, old man."

We had gone beyond the sometimes troublesome courtesies of

strangers, being faced with the same unhappy reality we each had hoped to avoid. It cut through the need for banalities like a shearing knife, showing us the brighter colors of need in place of duller conversation. We wasted no time now.

Stigand sighed, snugged his cloak closer. "The others are adamant. She has bought her year, they say, with her gift of the Sandtiger. A worthy addition, they say, to the ranks of *an-ishtoya*."

I scratched through beard to chin. "I might have thought I'd at *least* be a *kaidin*."

Telek smothered a brief laugh. "Yes, well—undoubtedly. It was not intended as an insult. But you have no knowledge of our styles, other than what Del has taught you, and that in itself is what gives you the *an-* honorific rather than making you merely *ishtoya*. It is something, Southron; be thankful."

I looked at him squarely. "No. What I *am* is disgusted." I pulled the borrowed cloak around me, swathing myself like a Southron sandbat. "I don't belong here. I don't want to *be* here. What I want is to go back across that lake and get my horse, so I can go home again. Down South, where I belong. In the Punja, where it's *warm*."

"Would that I could send you," Stigand muttered.

"You will be here a year," Telek told me patiently, ignoring the petulant comment. "There will be much to do. I doubt you will remain a mere *an-ishtoya* for long—with your Southron skills already in place, you will surely be elevated more quickly than most to the rank of *kaidin*—and then you may teach worthy students."

I grunted. "I don't want to teach. I'm a sword-dancer; I dance."

Stigand worked something out of his teeth, spat it onto the ground. "It is a waste of time—ours *and* theirs—when students choose sword-dancing over the more honorable rank of *kaidin*."

Telek sighed. "Sword-dancing is also an honorable profession," he said patiently. "Your own son chose sword-dancing over the rank of *kaidin*, Stigand . . . don't let your prejudice get in the way."

The old man spat again. "My own son was a fool," he said curtly. He looked at me searchingly a moment, then his face twisted in uncertainty. "Do you know?"

I frowned. "Know what?"

"That Theron was my son."

It rocked me. All I could do was stare in shock at the old man, whose son I had killed in the circle to keep him from killing Del. Theron, who had come South to find the *an-ishtoya* and give her the choice of meeting him in the circle, or going North to face the *voca*.

Whose dead *jivatma* I had presented to his father.

"No," Telek said, "why should you? Unless Del told you, which seems unlikely; Del says very little very much of the time."

I reflected aloud there were times Del said entirely *too* much altogether.

Stigand grunted. Telek smiled.

"I'm sorry," I told the old man. "Had I known—"

Stigand didn't let me finish. "Did he die honorably?"

The dance was fresh in my mind. No, Theron had not died honorably because he had cheated. He had requenched, as Del called it, making his *jivatma* doubly dangerous. Doubly powerful.

"Yes," I lied, "he did. It was a good dance."

Stigand sighed deeply. "Theron always was a stubbornly headstrong boy . . . much worse than all the others."

I glanced at Telek, raising brows in a silent question.

"Stigand has—*had*—eight sons," he said quietly.

Well, that was *something*. At least I hadn't killed the only one.

Telek's smile was very bland. "And I'm one of them."

Hoolies! Here I was standing alone in the trees in the dark with the father and brother of a man I'd killed. Not something to make a man feel particularly welcome.

Uneasily, I stirred. "I didn't have much choice, you know. It was a dance to the death."

Telek nodded. "Theron knew that when he left here looking for Del."

Stigand's tone was glum. "She always was better than Theron."

Telek nodded. "And he always resented it."

I cleared my throat. "About our problem with me leaving Staal-Ysta . . . ?"

Father and son wore identical expressions of annoyance.

"There must be a way," I said flatly, equally annoyed. "Find me a way."

Telek glanced briefly at Stigand, who said nothing; looking gloomy. "Del promised you to us for twelve months, and the *voca* accepted."

It was all I could do not to shout at them. "Look. I'm a Southroner, not Northerner . . . I can't be bound by your *voca* or your customs if they interfere with my personal lifestyle. Del didn't warn me about what she intended to do, so I was never given a chance to refuse." I shook my head. "This is not my place. I don't intend to stay here."

Telek's expression was grim. "You agreed to abide by the results of the trial."

I nodded vigorously. "Yes—before I had any idea Del intended to sell me back into slavery—" I broke it off before my desperation could begin to show. "There must be some way, Telek. An honorable, Northern way to set this Southron sword-dancer free."

After a moment, Telek looked at his father. Stigand looked no more pleased. "You're asking for a special dispensation," he growled.

"I don't care what you call it. I just want to get out of here."

Telek scratched his jaw. "Perhaps there is a way. Even so, have you thought of the consequences?"

I frowned. "What consequences?"

Telek didn't mince any words. "It means leaving Del behind."

I looked directly at Stigand. "Talk to the *voca*," I said. "Find me a way to leave."

The old man sucked a tooth and spat.

Waiting drives me sandsick. So does inactivity. Generally, when faced with the former, I turn to banishing the latter with as much force as I can muster, seeking out opponents to meet me in the circle. Only this time, I couldn't. I had no sword.

I asked, of course. I thought surely *someone* could give me the loan of a sword. But no one would. I was told—politely, of course—that only the *an-kaidin* could choose a sword for me. When I protested that I had to have *something,* if only to keep in shape, the declaration was repeated. Students were incapable of selecting the right sword for themselves; the task fell to the *kaidin* or *an-kaidin.* Since I had none yet officially assigned, I'd have to wait.

Waiting, again.

I could make no headway no matter how much I protested, so at last I demanded someone to row me across the lake to the other side, where I could at least ride the stud. This was agreeable. And so they gave me Del.

Silence is an odd thing. It can be uncomfortable or relaxing. Peaceful or disturbing. Companionable or hostile. But the silence that reigned as Del rowed me across was none of those things, being composed of an absolute absence of communication. I thought of all the things I wanted to say, yet said none of them. I hadn't sorted them out.

I jumped out as the boat was grounded. Two of the settlement children had brought the stud and another mount, a gray—signals from the island negated the need for hiking down the lakeshore to the corrals—and I took his reins immediately, not bothering to see what Del was doing. Anchoring the boat, most likely . . . but I didn't wait. I strode through the barrows and dolmens of Staal-Kithra, leading my horse, and climbed the steep path overlooking the lake.

The stud was snorty and inquisitive, shoving a demanding muzzle beneath my arm and nibbling. Absently I scratched the underside of his jaw, not really giving him the attention he craved. Instead I looked down at Staal-Kithra, watching the woman accept the reins to her borrowed mount. She peered up at me, shading her eyes; I gave her nothing in return.

Del came up, of course. As I had, half-climbing, half-scrambling, trying to stay out of the way of a horse in a hurry to reach the top.

The gray was a gelding, a dark steel-colored horse with a frosting of darker dapples, pale mane and tail, smudgy muzzle. Like the stud, he wore winter hair, made oddly shapeless beneath the weight. Del brought him over, gave him rein, let him graze as she moved to stand beside me.

For the first time since I've known her, I didn't want her there.

The day was bright, clear, cold. Wind ruffled my hair, stripping it out of my eyes and giving me an unobstructed view of the island in the water.

"I don't belong there," I said.

Del's tone was quiet, inoffensive. Yet the words offended me. "You belong wherever you want to."

"I don't *want* to belong down there," I told her curtly. "It isn't my place. I'm an old horse, Del. You can't take me to water and expect me to drink every time, just because you say so, especially if I know the water is tainted."

She looked at me sharply, braids swinging. "Tainted! Staal-Ysta isn't—"

"It is," I said firmly, "for me. It's not what I want, Del. It's what you want, maybe what you *need*, but it isn't what I desire. I'm a Southroner. I have no intention of changing myself just to fit into your world. Down South I have *my* world, and that's where I'm going."

Wind put color back into her face. "Then—you've spoken to Telek and Stigand."

"Yes."

"Have they found you a way to be excused from the year?"

"Not yet."

She nodded. "What happens if they don't? Will you go anyway?"

I turned abruptly, shutting off the conversation. Led the stud away from the overlook. "I came up here to ride, Del, not to talk. If you want to ride, fine . . . if not, just wait for me down below." I swung up. "Unless, of course, you'd rather make me swim."

Del held the gray back as he tried to follow the stud. I saw the conflict in her face: surprise, anger, guilt . . . then all poured swiftly away. Her flesh was hard as stone. "I did the right thing."

"Right for whom, Del? Yourself? Maybe. Kalle? No. Me? Most definitely not. But then, you weren't thinking of me. You weren't even thinking of Kalle. You were thinking of Del."

"Don't you think I *should?*" Her shout rang across the mountains. "Don't you think it's time I stopped thinking only of my murdered family and thought of myself instead?"

"Maybe," I agreed, "but maybe you should think of me, too, before you sell me back into slavery." The stud was filled to bursting with energy. It was all I could do to rein him in. He crowhopped, pawed, sidled, gnawed the bit in his mouth. Letting me know how he felt. "Del, I don't doubt it's easier for you simply to ignore my feelings by saying you've done it all for Kalle; maybe you did, in some weird, twisted way. But it doesn't change the fact you've made me a prisoner of a lifestyle I don't want."

"It's only for a *year!*"

"Too long," I flung back. "Sixteen years a slave with the Salset was too long for me. Four months a slave in Aladar's mine was too long for me. *This* is slavery, too, Del, because you gave me no choice. You just decided this was what you would do, without even bothering to ask me."

"I had no choice!"

"That's goat dung, Del, and you know it." Bitterly, I paused. "Well, bascha, you made your choice—and now you have to live with it. But *I* sure as hoolies don't."

"Tiger—"

"No." I reined in the fractious stud. "One moment more arguing this with you is entirely too long, too . . . so I propose we end it."

"Tiger—*wait!*"

I reined back, swung the stud, looked down at her. Waited, as she'd asked.

"Tiger—" Del came across wind-wracked turf, leading the gray. She came up to the stud, to the stirrup, put a hand on my leg. "Tiger, I swear . . . *I swear* I didn't plan it. It's not why I rode with you, *slept* with you—I've used you, yes, and I don't blame you for being angry . . . but I swear I did none of those other things simply to buy myself time with Kalle. But when I saw her, saw what she could be even without me, I couldn't bear it anymore. I had to do something to find a way to buy some time with my daughter."

I shook my head. "But you did know, Del. Maybe not what seeing Kalle would do to you, but you knew there was a chance you could buy your way back into the *voca's* graces by offering them a new *an-ishtoya*." The Northern term came out bitterly. "You asked me to come, to be your sponsor . . . and you did it knowing full well I might wind up in exactly these circumstances."

Del's face was ravaged. "Tiger, *please*—"

I shook my head. "You told me once I loved you. Maybe so. Maybe I do. But right now, with all of this, I find it very hard even to *like* you."

Del, too shocked, said nothing. I turned the stud loose and rode.

Chapter 40

We met again at the dolmen, again after sundown. Stigand looked gloomier than ever, and Telek, who had spent most of the day with the *voca*, looked decidedly weary. Also disgusted, which didn't augur well for the results of the meeting.

I folded my arms beneath the borrowed cloak. "The others said no, I take it, to a special dispensation."

In uplander, Stigand muttered something beneath his breath. Then he muttered more loudly, this time in Borderer. "Fools, all of them. Why should they care about one Southron sword-dancer, who has no respect for our ways?"

It stung me more than I'd expected. "I have respect for your ways," I told him defensively. Then I thought about my situation. "At least—those I *can* respect."

Telek's expression was serious. "Will you listen to what I must say?"

His tone chilled me. "Yes."

He turned slightly, staring at the dolmen. "Prospective students come to Staal-Ysta from all over the North. Most are turned away following a period of probation because they do not measure up." He flicked a glance at Stigand, sucking teeth sourly. "Those who do pass probation are admitted to the rank of *ishtoya*. After that, providing they prove themselves worthy, they become *an-ishtoya*."

He paused. I told him I understood, wishing he'd get on with it.

Telek continued as laboriously as before. "Once the *an-ishtoya* is judged worthy by his or her *an-kaidin*, he or she is given a *jivatma* and gains the rank of *kaidin*. This may take as many as ten years, perhaps even longer. Many students give up. Many fail to complete the training. Some decide to become sword-dancers, like Del, like Theron, therefore depleting the *kaidin* ranks even more."

I frowned. "What are you trying to say?"

Stigand glared at me. "Staal-Ysta survives for teaching. Without students, there is no reason for being."

Telek's tone was solemn. "Of late, fewer and fewer students are worthy enough . . . fewer and fewer of them make rank past *an-ishtoya*. We need good students. We need those who will make good teachers."

I nodded, comprehending all too well. "And so the *voca* doesn't want to lose a single student, not even a Southroner made one against his will."

Telek's tone was smooth. "You would bring honor to Staal-Ysta."

I wanted to say something rude. Instead I shook my head, scowling out at the dolmen. An alien sense of futility and despair welled up inside me. What in hoolies was I doing here? Why didn't I just *leave?* They couldn't keep me here. Not against my will. *Del* had pledged me; I'd commited myself to nothing.

As if reading my feelings, Telek turned to his father. "Stigand— it's late, and growing colder. It does old bones no good to stay out here when it's unnecessary. Why not go to bed and let the Southroner and me discuss this more fully?"

Stigand smiled slowly. " 'Said the fox to the hound of the hare.' Very well, I'll go . . . just remember yourself, Telek. Yourself *and* your kin."

The old man faded into the darkness quickly, more easily than I'd have imagined for a man of his age, and with that obscure quote. I looked at Telek, frowning my question.

He smiled, pulled his own cloak more closely, nodded. "Indeed, now we may talk openly. Stigand is the oldest of the *voca;* he carries the most responsibility, and appearances are important. I am the youngest and carry the least. But if it can be made to appear as though Stigand knew nothing of my plan, his power may have more value than ever. And he will approve."

"What plan?"

Telek shrugged. "Even though you are judged worthy of the *an*-honorific due to your Southron ranking, it's mostly out of courtesy. For anything more, you'd have to prove yourself, just like all the others." He sighed. "This *is* the North, after all; we're not anxious to *give* a Southroner the rank Northerners must earn."

My frown deepened. "No. Of course not."

"How good are you?" he asked. "I mean no disrespect, but the Southron style is not well known here. When you say seventh-level, it has no meaning as we judge things. But Stigand has heard of you because Stigand hears of everyone, and Del has spoken for you."

Ordinarily I'm quick to claim my superiority in the circle. But Telek was so serious and the question sounded like there was more to it than just what showed on the surface.

"I'm good," I said. "Very good. And if it's any help, Del and I have yet to prove which of us is better."

"And you did beat Theron." Telek's smile was thin, sharp as a knife.

"Why?" I asked. "Why is it so important?"

He looked directly at me. "For you, what would be the easiest way to earn your freedom?"

"In the circle," I answered promptly. "Just tell me when and where."

Telek laughed, teeth gleaming in the moonlight. "I thought so. Well, perhaps we have found the simplest solution of all. Southron . . . if I can get the *voca* to agree to a dance."

I shrugged. "Easy enough. Appeal to their pride. Appeal to their honor. Make it Southroner against Northerner . . . style against style . . . technique against technique." I smiled. "Make the stakes high enough."

"I thought to," he agreed. "Perhaps something that makes it *worth* dancing for." He rubbed his bottom lip thoughtfully. "Something simple . . . something elegant . . . something *obvious*. We could make the *voca* as thirsty for it as a drunkard for wine."

A man after my own heart. "Have you any suggestions?"

Telek nodded. "Let me be very plain: if you were a *kaidin*, the *voca* would no longer have any say about your dispensation. Del couldn't offer you against her year with Kalle. You would be a man who had earned rank as we do, following our customs, and the *voca* would be made helpless by their own adherence to custom. They would *have* to give you that dispensation."

"Fine," I agreed dryly. "How do I get to be a *kaidin* without spending five or ten years here?"

Telek didn't flick an eyelash. "By beating a chosen champion in the circle."

I stared. Then I laughed. "If it's *that* simple, why haven't other students tried the same shortcut?"

"Others have. All have failed."

I nodded thoughtfully. "That's the trick, then? Defeating a champion selected by the *voca*?"

Telek's expression gave nothing away. "But not just any champion. One who well understands your position . . . one willing to lose a little face in the short run if only to *save* some in the long one."

Hoolies, he wanted to throw the dance. "Not exactly the *honorable* thing to do, is it, Telek?"

Quite abruptly, he was angry. "She threatens my family, Southron . . . she offends my lodge and my woman. *That* is the dishonor; this is the means to expunge the taint."

The change in him shocked me. But only because I'd been blind. Telek was every bit as dedicated to Kalle's welfare as Del, and maybe with more right. I should have seen it sooner; he *would* help me get free, but only if I in turn helped him.

After a moment, I nodded. "So *Del* is the issue."

His voice was clipped. "Del is your price. Do you think I can't see it? You were made for one another, you and the *an-ishtoya* . . . you are blades of the same temper, the same edge, quenched in the same blood, regardless of where it was spilled. And if I have to bring dishonor on myself to rid Staal-Ysta of her, I will do it; it will be worth it. As for you? Take her with you. You want her. *Take* her. Win the dance and *take* her—as *an-kaidin,* I can nominate you for ritual elevation gained through a sword-dance. One *I* will challenge you to; I understand the situation better than any, do I not? I comprehend the need for defeat. I will *give* you this victory, here and now, beforehand, if you will rid me of Delilah."

"What I understand," I said softly, after a moment, "is that I killed your brother."

Telek's head came up sharply. "Do you think I want revenge for *that?*"

I laughed, though it held no humor. "It is a possibility. You trick me into a circle on the pretext of winning my freedom, and you kill me. Honorably. All in Theron's name."

Telek's voice hissed. "This is not because I want revenge—that is *Del's* personal song." He shook his head, speaking more quietly, clamping down on his emotions. "No. I want her gone. This is not a dance to the death, merely until one of us yields. The loser, of course, will be me; if losing to you in the circle guarantees she'll go from here, I'd do it a thousand times."

"So," I said, "if I win—*when* I win—I become a *kaidin* on the spot and am therefore free to go where I wish, with no obligation to Staal-Ysta."

"And you take Del with you," Telek agreed. "Don't you see? With you elevated to *kaidin,* you are no longer a bargaining stone. Del has nothing with which to buy her year; the *voca* will deny her the year with Kalle."

Quietly, I said, "And then, of course, they reinstate her immediate exile."

Telek's eyes didn't waver. "Isn't that what you want? Isn't that your price?"

"Maybe," I said, "maybe. And maybe I don't have one."

The Northerner laughed. "You are a Southroner. A sword-for-hire. You sell your soul to the highest bidder. In this case, the bidder is me . . . and my coin is the *an-ishtoya.*"

I took a deep breath to calm myself, found it difficult. "So much offered for honor," I said. "And yet I think you've thoroughly compromised your own."

It struck home. "What of you?" Telek demanded angrily. "What does it say of *your* honor when you accept the terms?"

And I would. I wanted out of here that badly. Del wouldn't thank me, I knew, but I hoped one day she'd understand. And I'd tell her the truth, too: I believed it would be better for Kalle. As I believed it would be better for Del, no matter what *she* felt.

Besides, she'd used *me* for coin before; two can play her game. And I'm a fast learner.

"When and where?" I asked curtly.

Telek's smile was delicately contemptuous. "First, there is the matter of a sword."

"I'm listening."

"Are you? Then listen well: I have a *jivatma*."

In my head, a tocsin rang. "I don't want a *jivatma*," I said pointedly. "I want a sword, just a sword—a hilt with a blade attached. Can that be arranged? Can you just loan me a *sword?*"

Telek's smile was slow. "Go and see Kem."

A ripple ran down my back. "I don't want a *jivatma*."

Telek nodded, still smiling. "Go and see Kem. Tell him what you need."

Chapter 41

He looked me dead in the eye, saying nothing. He read me, I knew, with a look—and then peeled back all the layers and looked deeper, *deeper*, until I shifted uncomfortably.

He didn't smile. "Let me see your hands."

Sighing, I held them out, palm down, showing him the sunburned backs all pitted with ore flecks and other assorted scars, courtesy of slavery.

He caught them before I could protest. His own were huge, but his grasp was gentle. He did nothing other than hold them. Oddly, it was as if he weighed me as a man by their feel.

"Over," he said, loosening his grip.

Accordingly, I turned them. The palms were tough, callused, more like hide than hands. Once again he held them, studying them, and then once again looked me dead in the eyes.

"You should believe," he told me flatly. "You of all people. Haven't you felt the essence ever since you crossed the border? Haven't you *smelled* it?"

I blinked. "What?"

"The essence," he repeated. "Magic has a smell, a taste, a *feel* all its own. Some of us feel it more than others. Some of us are more deeply troubled." Slowly, he nodded. "I think you are one of them."

I started to protest, to ask him what in hoolies he was talking about, but he ignored me altogether, releasing my hands and moving on to another subject.

"I can give you a sword," he said, " *'just'* a sword, as you want . . . but it won't stay that way. None of them do. But this one, matched to you . . ." he shrugged. "You will have to learn quickly, if you are to control it."

I looked at him through a gauze of acrid coalsmoke. "Telek said—"

He didn't let me finish. "Telek told you to come to me for a *jivatma*." He nodded. "That's what I do: make *jivatmas*. At least, I do the Shaping—you will do the Making, the Binding, the Naming . . . all the rituals."

It all sounded very confusing. "All I need is a sword. A plain sword, nothing more; don't you make any of those?"

He shook his head. "I make new blades, *unnamed* blades, but full of raw potential. Once blooded, they are *jivatmas*."

My disbelief was rude, but I couldn't hide it. "Are you telling me *every* sword in Staal-Ysta is a blooding-blade?"

Patiently, he explained. "No sword is 'normal' here, merely potential as yet untapped. My purpose is to find and shape the potential, matching it to the warrior. All come to me for that purpose; it's what I was born to do."

I sighed, too tired to argue. "I need a sword. Just give me a sword. I'll take what I can get."

He dipped his head. "Then I will make you a sword."

Kem was, of course, a Northerner, and—like all of them— tall, broad, well-built, very blond and very strong. But he was not *ishtoya* or *an-ishtoya*, *kaidin* or *an-kaidin*. He was the swordsmith, the man who probably received greater respect than anyone in Staal-Ysta.

And now here I was in his smithy looking at lumps of iron.

His Borderer was curt. "Don't look: *touch*."

Twelve lumpy bundles, now bare of wrappings. I saw grayish, pitted metal, like bread dough only half-kneaded. Kem had lined them up in double rows of six, waiting for me to *touch* them.

The smithy was small in comparison to the lodges, though mostly dwarfed by the equipment stuffed into it. Anvils, bellows, tongs, tubs and hammers and grinding stones, and countless other things, all jammed in corners and against the walls as well as hanging from rafters.

Kem waited. His face was broad and pitted as the iron, seamed and pocked with scars. His blond hair was dulling to gray, pulled back in a single braid. He wore only a thin wool shirt, trews, boots and leather bracers.

Kem smiled, showing crooked teeth. Idly he crossed his big arms and waited, patience personified.

I knelt. Touched the lumps, one by one, humoring the man. Until I reached the eighth.

Kem saw my face. Smiled. Nodded. Then lifted the lump from the hardpacked floor. "So," he said lightly, "now I am neither a fool nor a liar, but a man who knows his trade." He set the eighth lump onto his largest anvil and left it there, then one by one wrapped up the other eleven and put them away in a trunk.

"It was warm," I said in surprise. "The others all were cold."

"Warm, cold; it makes no difference. The iron knew your touch."

"But I'm a *Southroner!*"

Kem shrugged big shoulders. "Do you think it cares *where* you were born? You touched it, and it knows. Just like the magic knows your name, your presence—your *own* essence."

"It's only a *lump of iron.*"

"Much more than that, Southron . . . it's sky-born, from the gods, and full of wild magic." Kem's tone was stolid. "Once we're done, it'll be far more than a lump, and the magic will be harnessed. It'll be a blooding-blade."

I watched him kneel at the edge of a shallow pit. It was filled with glowing red coals dusted by fine gray ash. Carefully he raked them, teasing them hotter yet.

Suspiciously, I asked, "What do you want *me* to do?"

"Hold that lump of iron. Cherish it like a woman. Caress it with your breath."

"*What?*"

"You heard me, Southron. Do it."

I had some knowledge of how swords were made, and this wasn't part of it. But Kem didn't seem the type to tease for the hoolies of it, having no sense of humor, and so I picked up the lump of iron and cradled it against my abdomen.

"Is that how you fondle a woman?" Kem still knelt by his pit. "You don't *really*—"

"I do. Breathe on it, like I said. Put your mark on it, like a cat."

I looked at him suspiciously, searching for a jibe at my expense, but saw nothing in his blue eyes except utter peace and endless patience. Scowling, I stared down at the pitted, knurled lump of metal in my hands. Then lifted it to my mouth and fogged it with my breath, feeling more than a little ridiculous. It was warm in my hands, much more than cold metal, with a silky texture that belied its pitted appearance. I found myself searching for flaws, as if I really could find them before the blade was made.

In disgust, I made myself stop. But my skin was somehow attuned to it, wanting to touch it more. Uneasily, I wondered if it had anything to do with Kem's mutterings about *essence*.

"Bring it here," he said. I carried it over, then put it into the coals as he indicated. He raked it covered, then sat back. "What do you want in a sword?"

I shrugged, thinking it obvious. "True temper. Proper balance. A keen, sharp edge that holds."

Kem's eyes didn't waver. "What do you want in a sword?"

His tone stopped me cold. He wasn't being facetious. He really wanted to know. I thought it was some sort of test, maybe, and I wanted badly to pass.

"All the things a good sword *should* have," I told him. "I want a sword I can trust, of course—one with a strong but flexible blade, cutting cleanly every time without snagging or turning on bone. One that *knows* its master, unceasingly seeking to please." I shrugged, not knowing how to explain it. "One that is *mine* in my hand, unlike any other, with a personality much like my own." I smiled wryly. "I've handled many swords; they all have certain tricks. I want one that understands mine."

After a moment, Kem smiled. "Maybe you *are* a sword-dancer."

"Just give me a sword," I suggested cheerfully. "A sword, a circle, an opponent . . . that is my world, smith. And now you're a part of it."

Kem nodded thoughtfully. "This may work after all."

When the lump was hot enough, he lifted it from the pit with tongs and placed it on the anvil. Then he took up his hammer. "*You* may hold it," he said. "It's your job as much as mine."

I held the tongs while Kem worked the iron. We fell into a ringing rhythmn: hold, hammer, reheat; hold, hammer again. It was important, Kem explained, that the temperature remain fairly constant, not too hot and not too cool, or the soul of the metal would be ruined.

The noise was deafening. And then, slowly, I became accustomed, beginning to like the sound, which had a song all its own. I thought of the Cantéada. Heard the echo of their music. Knew it was in Kem. Knew it was in the sword.

Maybe, even, in me?

I thought abruptly of Del's singing, to key her blooding-blade.

A shiver ran down my spine. "Can you leave out the magic?" I asked.

Kem nearly missed his stroke. The rhythm returned again, but I saw the furrow in his brow as he stared at me over the hot lump of iron, sweat-faced, flushed red from reflected heat. "When we are done with this, it will be much more than a sword. And you will be much more than a sword-dancer."

The hairs on the back of my neck rose. "A *kaidin*, yes, I know . . . but only if I quench it."

Kem waved me away and returned the lump to the coals. "You are a fool," he said. "And I am a fool as well, for wasting my time on a man who doesn't appreciate what Northern sword-magic is . . . or what he himself can be."

It was the end of whatever rapport we might have built. Over the next two days I watched Kem hammer the lump into a bar, then begin to fold it. He took thin iron rods and twisted them around the bar, then hammered them all together, then twisted and hammered again. I lost track of how many times, though I'm sure Kem knew. He was a man who knew his art.

The hammering continued. But now the lump was more than a bar, and the bar was more than itself. There was a *shape* in the iron, though it lacked its final form.

"Do you see it?" Kem asked.

"Point, tang—yes."

He grunted, still hammering. The rods were no longer visible, having been worked into the bar. The blade was a solid thing, showing no signs of its lumpy, gnarled origins or its slender, twisted cousins.

He let it cool, stopped hammering. Then picked it up and gave it to me. "Take it to bed with you. Every night until it's done."

"Do *what?*"

"To bed," he said, "each night. It's part of the Binding ritual; the sword must know its master."

The unfinished blade was warm in my hands. "Am I supposed to *couple* with it, too?"

Kem didn't crack a smile. "Just bring it back each morning."

I took it to bed with me. I brought it back each morning. The ritual was carried out, even though I felt like a fool.

The balance was magnificent, even without hilt, grip, pommel. Unwhetted, it still lacked edges, but the promise was inherent. The thing was alive in my hands, smooth and warm and *alive.* I stared at the blade in amazement.

"So," Kem remarked, "the skeptic begins to believe."

I shivered, wanting to wipe hands on woolen trews. But not daring to before him. "In your skill, absolutely. In other things, I'm not sure."

He took the blade away. "It's time we made it steel."

Once again he heated the blade, this time until it blazed white-hot. Kem covered it with coals, left it alone, manned the bellows when I didn't. "Almost a sword," he crooned. "Not so long, now."

*　　*　　*

It was night, and very late. I heard the whir and wheeze of the bellows, Kem's droning uplander mumble. Dragged myself out of sleep and stood up from my place by the door. "How long *now?*"

"Not so long, now." He took it out of the coals, set it on the anvil, began to hammer the edges, packing them to hold. And then he put it back in the coals and covered it one last time. "When it comes out, it'll be done. And then I will give the blade to you, and you will take it to the lake, and you will quench it in the water."

Flesh prickled. "*How* quenched, Kem?"

He laughed silently, showing crooked teeth. "Not that kind, Southroner. This is the gentle quenching. A baby's first bath. Not the true quenching, or blooding yet; there will be time for that later."

I was immensely relieved, but too embarrassed to show it. "Easy enough just to dip it in the lake."

Kem's gaze didn't so much as waver. "And while it is being quenched, you will ask the Blessing."

That I knew something of; even my Southron sword, Single-stroke, had been blessed during its making. But it hadn't been asked by me. The shodo had simply done it.

"I don't understand."

"The Blessing," he repeated. "You will ask it of the gods while the blade is in the water. It must be quickly done; if you leave it in too long, the blade will cool too much."

I sighed, humoring him. "What happens if the gods *don't* bless it, Kem?"

He shrugged. "Then the steel will be flawed. The sword will fail you . . . probably when you most need it."

I scratched through beard to chin. "I don't believe in gods."

The Northerner just nodded. "Tell them that," he suggested. "I'm sure it will amuse them."

In the end, I took the hot blade to the lake, dipped it into the water, squinted against the steam as I held onto the tongs. Black water roiled and bubbled, sucking the heat away.

Ask the Blessing, Kem had said.

Well, I owed the man that much.

"Gods," I said aloud, "I don't know what to say. I don't know what to *ask*, other than this Blessing. So why not give it to me, if only to please Kem?"

It was, I thought, enough; I lifted the blade from the water. The steel glowed wine-red. It smoked in cold air.

I took it back to Kem.

He nodded, pleased. "Now," he said, "into that trough; the water isn't so cold."

I saw the trough he indicated, a long iron pan filled with water. I set the bar into it, let it rest, handed the tongs to Kem. "What now?"

"We wait," he said succinctly.

We waited. And then at last Kem stirred and used the tongs, plucking the blade from the trough. "Done," he said, "for now. All that's left is the Shaping . . . the Whetting . . . First Keying when you blood it."

"First Keying," I echoed. "What is that?"

He looked down at the blade. "You quench your *jivatma* in flesh and blood . . . that is the true quenching, the first blooding, when the magic is first *roused*, first acknowledged and harnessed. But it's in the *sword*, not in you—you need a way to tap it . . . a way to focus yourself. That's what the singing is for—to focus you as you tap the power. You *key* the sword to tap it, or else the magic goes wild."

I wanted to scratch the back of my prickling neck. "But if you don't sing, it's just a sword . . . right?"

He sighed. "They have taught you nothing."

"I'm a *Southroner*, remember?"

Kem picked his teeth. "You can't key it until it's truly blooded in living flesh. Quenching rouses the power, *keying* it controls it. But if you want only a whisper of power, not much more than simple sword skill, you don't bother to sing."

I thought back to all the times Del and I had sparred in practice circles. Never had she keyed the sword, not even a little; I couldn't remember her singing. Only against the enemy. Only when she needed the power.

I remembered the question he hadn't answered. "What is First Keying?"

Kem bit off a nail. "You can't key until it's blooded; it doesn't know you till then, not as it needs to know you. So the magic is wild. But the first song you sing thereafter becomes the focus for First Keying; after that the power is yours."

My interest rose considerably. "So, if I don't sing—even if I kill someone in the circle—the sword never becomes a true _jivatma?_"

Kem spat out the nail. His tone was very gentle, as if he spoke to a child. "You may pink someone in the circle, and the sword will remain unblooded. You may even cut him severely; the sword will remain unblooded. But if you kill anyone, _anyone at all,_ you have quenched the sword, and the sword becomes a _jivatma,_ with the dead man's skills and attributes; a piece of the dead man's soul." He shrugged. "If later you sing to key it, that soul is yours to tap . . . that and the Northern magic."

It seemed clear enough. So long as I could get South and sell it without having to kill anyone, I could keep the sword a _sword._ And even if something came up and I _did_ have to kill someone, I'd never, ever sing while doing it. The _jivatma_ would never be keyed.

I peered suspiciously at the blade. It was steel, no longer iron. With a bright, shining skin like nothing else in the world. The edges were blunt as yet, but visible, waiting for the rest.

"Take it," Kem said.

Warily, I took it. No tongs, just the blade. It was cool from the water, but I felt the deeper warmth, like blood running through veins. I swear, there was _life_ in this sword—

Sweating, I rang it down on the anvil. "I don't want this thing."

Kem's face didn't change. "You have made it yours."

I felt distinctly queasy. "I don't want it. It's not a sword—it's _more_ than a sword . . . have you lied to me? Is that thing already a _jivatma?_"

Slowly he shook his head. "It's not a *jivatma* yet. It's hardly begun to live . . . but what life is there is yours."

I badly wanted to back away but refused to show so much. "A sword is a weapon, a killing instrument, a tool designed to take life. Not to live on its own. It's simply a piece of metal—"

"And so it is," Kem agreed. "This sword is only half-made. You needn't fear it yet."

"I don't want to fear it at all!"

He stood bathed in the dim red light of coals, and the glow from a single lantern set high in a corner. "It's too late to turn away now. It would be like killing a child who's only begun to live."

"It's a *sword*—"

"—in need of a name," Kem finished quietly. "It doesn't know itself yet. It only knows what you've given it: a taste of what life is."

I felt the prickle on neck and arms. "Something's wrong," I said sharply. "There's sorcery in the air!"

He looked at me piercingly, not even asking how I knew. Only, "Where?"

"—something *wrong*—"

In the distance, I heard screams. Faint, small screams, warped by water and echo.

Kem heard them, too. "The settlement!" he cried.

Chapter 42

I was out of the smithy and running, heading through trees to the lakeshore, where boats bobbed on the water. The screaming was clearer now, and the squealing of frightened horses.

I was not alone for long. Kem was there, and others, pushing off in boats. I waited, looking for Del; saw only Telek.

"Where is she?" I asked.

"With Kalle." He bent to free the rope.

I blinked. "Why? It's not like Del to ignore someone's need for help."

Telek straightened, holding the rope. His gray eyes were almost feral; his tone precisely even. "I told her not to leave the island. That if she wants to stay with Kalle so much, she should *stay* with Kalle."

I shook my head. "That's not fair. No matter how you feel about her, you're still depriving Staal-Ysta and the settlement of a good sword."

"Get in the boat," Telek repeated. "There is no more time to waste."

He was right, much as I wanted to argue. I clambered into the boat, sat down, watched grimly as Telek pushed off and jumped in. He settled the oars and began to row, heading us diagonally across the lake toward the shrieks and screams.

By the time we reached the settlement, there was nothing left to fight. People clustered in groups, talking about the attack. Some carried wounded into lodges for tending. Others gathered together the bodies, preparing for funeral rites. I saw the marks on the bodies. I knew what had done this.

"Hounds," I told Telek on the way to the corrals. "Beasts, I call them the hounds of hoolies—I don't know what they are. But they've followed Del and me for weeks."

His face was stark. "After they left *us*."

I glanced at him sharply. "*These* hounds? Are you certain?"

His expression was bleak. "We've said nothing, because up till now we've been safe. The beasts can't swim, so Staal-Ysta has been a haven. And they left us weeks ago, trailing other prey . . . we believed them gone for good." He shook his head and frowned, looking around at the carnage. "They ignored the settlement before, watching Staal-Ysta only, as if there is something there . . . something that draws them. They want something *specific*—"

I nodded. "I think they want her sword."

It stunned him. "Her *jivatma?* Why? What use would *hounds* have for it?"

"I think they've been sent by someone." Briefly, I told him how they had dogged our trail, herding us, driving us toward the North. And how they had responded to Del's sword when she'd keyed it in the canyon.

When I was finished, Telek nodded. "You may be right," he agreed. "If indeed there is someone behind the hounds—someone who has sent them for whatever purpose—" He started to shake his head, then snapped it around to stare at me in shock. "It *is* her sword! It *must* be! Because up until tonight, none have been here at the settlement."

I frowned. "I don't understand."

He was impatient with my ignorance. "We elevated two *an-ishtoya* to *kaidin* only three days before you and Del arrived. Their swords were not yet blooded . . . they were preparing to ride out with their sponsors to blood them in the circle; this was their last night here. They came to spend it with their families—*off* the island: here." His face was intent. "But maybe it isn't just *Del's* sword. Maybe it's any *jivatma* at all—and that's what drew the beasts tonight."

I shook my head. "But if the swords haven't been blooded yet—"

"The magic is still in them," he snapped, distracted. "Just not roused, not harnessed by blooding . . . a sorcerer, knowing *jivatmas*, would also know that. It wouldn't stop him from sending the beasts—*if* that's what he's after."

I could be as terse. "Then I suggest you find those new-made *kaidin* as soon as you can. See if they're here. See if their *swords* are here."

Telek looked at me in dawning shock. And then he turned on his heel and ran.

We'd reached the corrals. Some of them had been broken down and emptied as the horses panicked and ran, but others remained standing, poles and brush left intact. In one of them was the stud.

I felt the knot in my belly loosen. "So, old man, you survived . . . still too tough to kill."

I unlatched the gate, slipped in, slapped milling horses out of my way, let the stud come up to me.

I scratched the stud's jaw, glad to touch him again; it gave me an unexpected peace. "They want something," I mused aloud; he flicked black-tipped ears. "Those hounds of hoolies *want* something. They've been very patient, but I think they're tired of waiting." I patted his hairy neck. "Yes, I think they'll be back . . . there are more *jivatmas* here, and one due to leave very soon."

Telek was back, and panting; his breath was white in the air. "They're gone," gasped, "both of them. Them *and* their swords."

I reached to my neck and slipped the thong over my head, handing him the ward-whistle. "Give this to someone here who is responsible. It will keep the hounds away; it's what allowed Del and me to get through. I'll need it again soon, but for now it should keep the settlement safe."

Telek frowned, looking at the whistle. "What do you intend to do?"

I tugged the stud's ears; smiled as he pulled away. "I intend to beat you in the circle, Northerner, and then leave Staal-Ysta." I shrugged. "Maybe get in a little hunting."

There was a new respect in Telek's eyes. "You will leave with your own *jivatma*. If that really *is* what is drawing the beasts—"

"—then I can draw them away." I smiled. "I guess you can say it's my way of making up for a dance that isn't a dance; I want to buy my deliverance somehow. *Honorably.* This is one way to do it." I shrugged. "Besides, I figure it's one way of helping a lot of people I know: you, Del, Kalle . . . a Borderer woman and her children . . . even a horse-speaker from the uplands." Again, I shrugged. "Something to do to pass the time."

Slowly, he shook his head. "I didn't expect it of you."

"No, probably not." I grinned. "Of course, people have been misjudging me for *years.*"

But Telek didn't laugh. He didn't even smile.

One night later, I faced Kem in the smithy. Faced him *and* my sword.

"It will cut water," Kem said. "Cut it cleanly, like flesh or silk, and make it bleed; even water."

He had fit blade and hilt together, melding them into one, so that the sword was a single unit. All was washed with silver, though steel underneath: hilts, grip, pommel; a twisted rope of silk somehow turned into metal. Its color was moonlight and ice.

In my hand, it was an extension of myself. The balance was as pure as any I've ever known, so fine and clean it carried me instead of the other way around. And it was warm in my hand, like flesh.

Del's sword, to me, was cold, but she'd said to her it was warm. I wondered if this was the same: hoarfrost to everyone else, sunlight only to me.

"Of course," Kem said pointedly, "it isn't ready yet."

I looked at him over the blade. "What do you mean, 'isn't ready'?"

He tapped his anvil. "Lay it here. This will take only a moment."

Suspicion flared instantly. "What do you mean to do?"

"There is the Naming, yet. Right now, it's an unnamed blade. Left so, it's not worth its Making. Here." He tapped the anvil again.

Slowly I set down the sword, oddly reluctant to take my hand from it. Then Kem drew his knife, motioned me forward, took hold of my left hand and turned it over, palm up.

"Wait," I blurted.

"This isn't the true blooding," Kem said patiently. "I've explained all that, remember? This is part of the Naming."

I held my silence as he nicked deeply into the fleshy part of the heel between thumb and wrist. When blood flowed freely, he nodded, then guided the hand to the sword. Carefully he held the sword in place, then slid my hand the length of the blade, smearing it with blood.

And again, when he turned it over. The steel shone bloody and dull, moonsilver sheen now obscured.

He grunted, gave me a rag. "Blank." Graying brows knitted a moment. Then he heaved a weary sigh, as if I'd disappointed him. "Well, it comes of being matched with a man who doesn't believe."

I frowned down at the sword, stopping the nick in my hand with the rag. "What's it *supposed* to do?"

"Once Made, once Bound, once Blessed, there is a heart in every blade . . . a soul known only to it. And it shows itself in the runes."

I recalled the alien, twisted shapes carved into Del's blade. The runes were alive to me, never the same; everchanging. But my blade was blank as blood.

"Does it have a name, now?"

Kem looked straight at me. "If it does, you'd know. Since you don't, it doesn't."

"Will it *ever* have a name?"

"Probably once it's blooded. Or maybe when you finally come to believe; the sword will tell you, then." He shrugged; his tone was one of delicate contempt. "But you don't want to blood it. You don't want to believe. You'd rather leave it unnamed, and only half alive."

I felt a twinge in my belly: guilt, resentment, acknowledgment.

"So long as it serves me in the circle, that's all I require," I told him flatly. "Down South, skill is the only magic. We don't depend on other things."

Kem put hands on hips. "I don't care what customs are down South. This is a Northern sword." He gestured sharply. "Take it to the lake. Wash it free of blood. My work is done; from now on it's in your care, inadequate as that may be."

Not a courteous man, Kem. But then, I hadn't expected it. I was a stranger to him, and Southron, and yet I bore the rank of *an-ishtoya*. Accustomed to Northern students come begging for a *ji-vatma*, my indifference to the magic was startling as well as disturbing.

And it probably bruised his ego.

I lifted the sword yet again; yet again marveling at the silken texture of steel, the uncannily perfect balance, the life that cried out in the blade. Singlestroke, too, had been made for me, to precise specifications, but even that noteworthy sword felt as dross to gold compared to Kem's masterwork.

As if reading me, he shook his head. "I was the Maker, yes; the rest is all from you. The Binding, the Blessing . . . whatever else you choose to do. This sword will be whatever you wish it to be. It will be *you*, growing out of whatever things have shaped you over the years. No other may use it once it's blooded, because it will guard itself against them, turning only to you."

"*If* it becomes a *jivatma*."

Slowly, Kem shook his head. "You dishonor this sword, Southron. Pray gods it doesn't dishonor you."

Disagreements aside, he'd made a marvelous sword. Not knowing what else to do, I asked him his price for the work, knowing full well I couldn't pay it. But he said he would take nothing; that his magic was from the gods and they repaid him well. His life was here on Staal-Ysta; all his wants were attended to. He needed nothing from me save respect for the weapon I carried.

I thanked him, left him, went down to the lake in darkness to wash the blade free of blood.

And there Delilah found me.

"So," she said, "it's done."

Still I knelt by the water. "No. Not all of it. I have no intention of blooding it. All I want is a sword."

"It's far more than that."

I dried the steel carefully with the cloth Kem had given me for my hand. "Only if I let it."

"Tiger—" Del knelt beside me, clenching hands against wool-clad knees. "You must understand what you've done . . . what manner of responsibility you've accepted. I know you don't *intend* to ever name this blade, or make it into a true *jivatma*, but you may have no choice. You may be *forced*—and the results could be disastrous."

I shook my head. "I'm going to use this sword in the circle here to prove my worthiness to be named *kaidin*. And then I will go home." I didn't look at her, tending carefully to the drying. "*South*, Del, where I intend to sell this—or trade it—and get me a Southron sword."

After a taut moment of shock, Del shook her head. "The sword will never allow it."

"Oh, hoolies, Del—are you sandsick? This is a *sword*, not a person! Not something that dictates my life!" I turned on my heel, still kneeling, and looked at her in frustration and exasperation. "It's a piece of steel, no more."

My protests made no dent in her wall of superstitions. "You should know it's unlikely you will reach the South without having blooded this blade. And if that's so, you may have no choice in the instrument of its naming—Tiger, don't you see? We are taught to choose an enemy carefully, because the blade, once blooded, assumes the characteristics and attributes of that enemy."

"Then how in hoolies does everyone manage to blood their swords in the *proper* enemies?" I demanded. "What happens if they kill the wrong person? What if they kill an unskilled laborer? Wouldn't it weaken the sword?" I shook my head. "All this superstitious nonsense . . . what keeps an enemy, knowing about these magical swords, from sending out a halfwit to throw himself on the sword, thereby rendering it nearly useless?"

Del's jaw was tight. "When a newly made *kaidin* goes out on his blooding journey, a sponsor goes with him. If there is killing to be done, he takes care of it. Until the new sword is blooded."

Well, it did make sense. And took all the angry bluster right out of me. I rose, stroked the cloth across the blade once again, felt the fabric separate neatly against the edge. Like silk. Like water. Like flesh.

"Of course, *you* didn't need a sponsor. You'd already blooded your sword." I looked at her. "And you keyed it as well; how else would you get his power? How else would you gain his skills?"

White-faced, Del thrust herself up from the ground. *"Listen to me,* Tiger . . . if you go out there tomorrow and kill a *squirrel,* that is a true blooding, and your sword will take on whatever habits that squirrel possesses. Do you see?" Her expression was earnest and intent. "What kind of a legend would the Sandtiger be if he took a *squirrel* into his sword?"

I don't know why it struck me so funny, but it did. I started laughing, and I couldn't stop. It echoed out over the water.

Del spat out a concise comment in uplander, probably something to do with disrespect, noise and idiocy, but by then I didn't care. I just laughed, nodded, turned back toward the lodges.

"You thrice-cursed son of a Salset goat!" she cried. "Can't you see I'm trying to help you?"

I swung back and stood very still. All the laughter was banished. "If that were true," I told her, "you'd come with me now. *Tonight.* You'd leave this place behind."

Her posture was awkwardly tense, lacking characteristic grace. "I have given you my reasons again and again. It is your choice to disagree. But it is *my* choice to make. No one can make it for me, unless he wears my boots. And you decidedly don't; maybe you never will."

It was, I knew, a jab at my profound lack of interest in fatherhood. Well, I'd give it to her; I *wasn't* wearing her boots.

"You know," I said lightly, "I wonder if anyone has asked Kalle what *she* thinks of this."

The moonlight was harsh on the marks of tension graven into Del's face. "Kalle is five years old."

I shrugged. "I remember when *I* was five. Very clearly; what about you?"

Del didn't answer. Del swung around and departed.

I looked after her into the darkness. "Ask her sometime," I said. But nothing answered me.

I walked back alone to Telek's lodge, having introduced myself to my sword. There was nothing of ritual or magic about it, being little more than some time spent learning the steel. I'd found it ridiculously easy to do so, almost *too* easy; the sword was clearly mine. And clearly, it knew it, too.

My harness was in the lodge, in the compartment I shared with Del. I intended to go in, sheathe it, then go to sleep. But voices distracted me. I paused before the door, heard men talking quietly in the trees directly to the right of the wooden lodge.

It wasn't my business. I might have ignored it. But the voices belonged to Telek and Stigand, and my name was in their mouths.

Silently I moved into the trees, hiding myself in shadow. I couldn't see them, but I didn't need to; all I wanted was to hear them.

Telek's tone was strained. "—wins the dance, he'll go. And he'll take Del with him. It's easiest this way."

Stigand was obdurate. There was nothing old about the way he sounded. "He killed Theron. Dishonor enough, don't you think? Shall we allow him to heap more on us?"

"But a dance to the death serves nothing. If he loses, *our* cause is lost, because he can't take her with him, and she stays."

Stigand made a sound of derision. "Are you a fool? Are you blind? If he loses, he *dies* . . . Theron's death is therefore avenged, *and* the *an-ishtoya* loses her bargaining stone. There is nothing left with which to buy her year. The *voca* will exile her immediately." The tone was thick with satisfaction. "It's already been decided, Telek, as of this morning. The dance will be to the death."

So, Theron's death *did* rankle. There would be no simple exhibition in the circle, no clearcut pitting of Southron against Northern to see if I was worthy of elevation. No, nothing so simple as that. It was to be vengeance after all, and a chance to send Del away in dishonor, a blade without a name.

And a mother without a child.

I gripped the newborn sword. I felt its warmth, its strength; felt the promise of power unkeyed, untapped, straining to break free. Wild magic, indeed; it needed harnessing. Demanded a proper song.

And suddenly I was frightened, because I knew what I could do. It would be the ultimate victory. The ultimate revenge.

Del had done it once. Why not do it again? He was not my *an-kaidin,* but most distinctly an enemy. If not precisely honored.

Something deep inside told me it was an ironic sort of justice.

I smiled down at the sword. Thinking: Telek will be shocked.

Chapter 43

I basin-bathed in icy water, then put on the clothing borrowed, ironically, from Telek: blue-black tunic and trews,
silver-tipped fur gaiters, silver-bossed bracers and belt. All I left off
was cloak and brooches, putting them aside for later. *After* the
dance was won.

I buckled on my harness with its weight of Northern steel. Before, with Singlestroke, I'd worn the straps and sheath without
even thinking, because it was second nature. Then, once I'd been
left with broken steel, I'd carried Theron's dead *jivatma* because I
needed a sword, chafing at the need.

But now the weight was different. Much less, because, oddly, it
felt a part of me. And much more, because I knew the truth of the
sword; that—blooded, keyed, *invoked*—it could prove—*would*
prove—the most devastating weapon a man could hope to own.

Or hope *not* to own.

Skepticism is healthy. It keeps you from growing vulnerable to
words of manipulation. Disbelief, in its place, is also occasionally
healthy, because the proper amount keeps you honest. But when I
put my hands on the twisted-silk hilt and felt the growing impatience in the sword, the power and strength and life suppressed
only by my denial, I knew there was no more room for disbelief.

It's difficult admitting you're wrong. Even more difficult admitting it when you have scoffed and otherwise ridiculed the truth with blind, unremitting determination, so blithely confident of your own infallibility. But then one day—or one night—the truth is put into your hands, and you realize those stories and songs and legends told by Northern strangers are truths after all, and that no one has lied to you.

Not even the Northern bascha, who has lied about so many things for so many different reasons.

No. Not so many. Two.

One: fear of execution; facing such a verdict from such men as Staal-Ysta's unpredictable—and bloodthirsty—*voca,* I too would have used whatever was at hand—even, I thought, Del.

Maybe.

Maybe?

Hoolies, I don't know.

And *two:* fear of losing Kalle; fear which was, perhaps, misplaced, since she'd voluntarily "lost" Kalle long ago, but maybe not, because the very existence of the child now promised endless possibilities.

The possibilities that now drove Telek to dance to the death with me; that, and his father's desire for vengeance.

My hands lingered on harness straps, fingertips caressing the supple leather. Telek came quietly to stand beside me.

"It's time," he said softly.

I turned. Looked directly into his eyes. They gave nothing away. I hoped mine didn't, either.

"Tiger." At the end of the post-lined corridor, by the door, waited Del. Black-clad, braid-wrapped Delilah, wearing a deadly *jivatma.*

Deadlier than mine, since the soul—the pure power—in my sword was as yet untapped by blood and song.

But for how long?

It is intoxicating: *power.* In and of itself, but also the knowledge that it lies so closely to hand.

All it requires is death, blood, a *song.*

Hoolies, I want to go home. Back where I belong; where I understand how things work, things without much magic other than simple tricks and sleight of hand; back where swords are *swords*, clean and bright and deadly, with no recourse to such power as Boreal, who summons, at Del's whim, all the terrible, awesome strength of a Northern banshee-storm.

I'm a *Southroner.* What do I want with banshee-storms?

What do I want with this dance?

A chance to go home again. A chance to be *warm* again.

And now a new and frightening desire: A chance to blood my sword.

I walked out with Del. It seemed a fitting thing.

Stigand himself drew the circle in the turf, cutting through winter-brown grass to hard dark soil beneath. It was in the very center of the oblong field where Del had faced the *voca* before, surrounded by the lodges, where all the others had gathered to watch: men, women, children; some warriors, some not, but all witnesses. Just as they gathered now.

The old man finished. Nodded. Gestured for me to put my sword in the very center of the circle.

I stripped out of harness and unsheathed the new-made sword. In morning light it was momentarily bright white, unblemished, free of runes that marked it named and blooded. But the blinding light faded. There was no color to it other than that of newborn steel.

Shortly, there would be blood. And, maybe, runes?

I discarded the harness. Walked silently to the center, put down the unnamed sword, turned and walked away. To stand just outside the circle.

Stigand nodded briefly, then pitched his voice to carry. "We have before us the Sandtiger, Southron sword-dancer, who has been pledged to live in Staal-Ysta a year. But he contests this pledge, claiming he knew nothing of it and therefore is not bound by it. His claim has some merit." The faded eyes looked at me, showing me nothing but neutrality. "The *an-ishtoya,* known as Del, pledged the Sandtiger in order to delay for one year her permanent exile for the murder of her *an-kaidin*. In good faith, the *voca* accepted that pledge. But now the validity is called into question and must be settled in the circle."

I looked at Telek, standing with the other members of the *voca*. His sword peeped over his shoulder.

Stigand went on. "It's the decision of the *voca* that a champion shall be named to dance against the Sandtiger. It's the decision of the *voca* that this dance shall decide the following: that should the Sandtiger win, he will be elevated to the rank of *kaidin* and may leave at any time. But should the champion win, the Sandtiger agrees to abide by the original decision and remain here for one year."

At this moment, Telek expected me to be very calm, too relaxed, not anticipating the truth. Undoubtedly he intended to come at me instantly, hoping to catch me off-guard, so he could kill me easily.

No, I don't think so.

Stigand droned on again. "This champion shall represent the best we have to offer: strong, proud, determined, dedicated to upholding the honor and customs of Staal-Ysta even against a sword-dancer as devastating as the Sandtiger."

That was for my benefit; I didn't bother to smile.

"This champion shall, if need be, die in ritual combat to uphold the honor of our ancestors and the gods."

Telek's smile was wry as he listened to the pompous statement. I wondered idly: Are gods impressed with such?

"This champion shall present herself before us: the *an-ishtoya* known as Del."

*Her*self, not himself. Del. He said Del. He meant—*Del?* Had the old man gone sandsick?

No. No, of course not. He knew precisely what he was doing.

And now, so did I.

"No," I said calmly, "that wasn't the agreement."

It sent a tremor through all the spectators. Telek stepped forward quickly.

"This man came to me and asked me to purposely lose the

dance, so as to give him his elevation and free him to leave Staal-Ysta. He deliberately called the honor of Staal-Ysta into question, as well as my own." His tone was thick with contempt; he was doing it very well. "I agreed for the sake of the moment, so I could discuss it with the *voca*. It was decided to let the dance go forth, but with a new champion. One whose honor is already lost."

"Then how can she uphold the honor of Staal-Ysta?" I snapped. "If she has none, she can hardly be champion!"

Telek inclined his head. "This is a way of gaining it back. Commonly done, I believe, even in the South. A service done for someone can cancel a debt, regain employment . . . certainly regain honor."

I looked at Del for the first time. She was staring in horror at Telek.

Stigand took over again. "Let it be so, then, as decided by the *voca*: Del shall act as champion, representing the North and Staal-Ysta, the place that gave her succor in her extremity. Should she win the dance, her exile will be commuted; she will be free to come and go as she pleases."

A shiver ran down my spine. For all of that, she would do it. For honor and freedom and Kalle.

"Let it be so: Should the Sandtiger win, he gains the rank of *kaidin* and his freedom from the pledge made by the *an-ishtoya*. But if he loses, he stays."

It didn't sound so bad, when compared to what Del stood to lose. One year. That's all, out of however many I had left. It would be easy enough just to give Del the victory and *stay* the year, if only to avoid this dance.

But Del would never stand for it. And I wasn't sure Stigand would, either. I knew if Del *did* win, they'd find another way of getting rid of her, probably permanently; they had shown their true colors. They wouldn't let her stay here with Kalle. They'd contrive yet another way to rid themselves of the *an-ishtoya*. And I wouldn't be here to stop it.

Which meant I had to win so I could get her out of here.

While she tried to beat *me*.

"Del," Stigand said, "will you accept your place as champion?"

Her tone sounded merely controlled, but I knew how to read it. She was decidedly unhappy. But also just as determined to do what she had to do. "Yes. I accept."

"Then place your sword in the circle."

I watched her walk out of the people to the circle. Black clothing, blonde hair, white flesh; *too* white. All the color was gone from her face.

She stepped over the curving line, moved to the center, placed Boreal on the turf next to my unnamed blade. Mutely, she turned and walked back out, then swung just outside and faced me, taking off her harness.

Mouthing: *"Tiger, I have to."*

All I did was nod; she didn't need anything more. We knew what each of us would try to do, and using every skill we knew.

Probably even some tricks.

Del dropped the harness to the ground. Her hands were empty; her eyes were not. Blue, bleak eyes, full of realizations.

She had brought us to it. And now maybe I would end it, forcing her to yield.

"Prepare," Stigand said.

I saw her body change. I saw her manner alter. Del was a sword-dancer; no matter what she felt, the dance was most important so long as she was in the circle. There would be no weakness displayed, no matter what she thought. No matter how she *felt*, facing me for real.

It nearly made me smile. Now, maybe we'd know. Maybe once and for all. We'd find out which of us was better.

But I didn't think it was worth it.

"Dance," Stigand said.

This was what we lived for, both of us, *this*; sword-dancers and -singers born of hatred and prejudice and the desire for revenge; shaped by pride and need and a desperate determination.

Both of us.

Dance, Stigand had said.

How we danced, Del and I.

Danced.

Sweated.

Bled.

She rained blows: I turned them aside.

She painted the air with exquisite patterns: I slashed neatly through them.

We thrust and feinted and parried, each of us; searched for openings and weaknesses in a dancer who provided nothing but consummate skill, combining strength and power and speed, dexterity, wit, flexibility. And other things unnamable; the intangibles that separate the good from merely adequate, the superb from very good.

Until, eventually, it comes down to Del and me. No more than that, because no more is necessary; just Del and me; Delilah and the Sandtiger, clean and pure and proud: Southron strength against Northern quickness. Masculine power against feminine finesse. To artistry and artfulness, seeking out the chinks.

Patterns broken, blows turned aside.

Parried thrusts and lightning ripostes.

Even hacking and slashing, eventually, when it seemed the only way.

Like mine, Del's breath ran ragged. We neither of us had been North long enough to adjust, although Del was closer than I. Certainly close enough to sing; all I tried to do was breathe.

She could, I knew, sing me out of the circle. And would, if I didn't stop her; I could see the song beginning. She was turning to her *jivatma*, tapping some of the power. Not a lot, I knew—she didn't want to kill me—but drawing as much as she needed to win.

I had none to tap. My sword was screaming for blood, screaming for life, and I couldn't give in to it.

So, I was left with only one way to stop her: to blunt her personal power and replace it with my own twisted version, one built of innuendo, of lies, of suggestions, all intended to force mistakes she'd otherwise never make because Del never makes mistakes.

But now she'd have to, if I was to win this dance.

And I had to win this dance.

I watched her closely, moving all the while. We teased one another with blades, scraping, tapping, sliding, coyly promising nothing we wanted to give. With Del and me, sparring, there is always a sexual element, a vicarious intercourse, because we are so well matched, in bed and out; the dance becomes a courtship as much as ritualistic combat.

But this time it went far deeper. We each of us needed a gratification the other wouldn't, couldn't, didn't dare give.

Yet now there was something more. Something *growing*. I sensed it before I knew it, and when I knew it, it frightened me. What I felt was anger.

Not really at Del, at this moment, because this moment was only the dance. But at the stupidity that put us here, dancing against one another for the pleasure of Telek, Stigand and others, who wanted both of us gone. Who wanted both of us *dead*, and were willing to cheat to win.

Anger. Now, *at* Del, who had so determinedly ignored my personal needs to tend only to her own. Who had so easily put me back into bondage, not thinking what it might do.

Quiet, abiding anger. Until it grew. Until it passed out of me into my sword and into my dance, and reached out to touch Del.

Our patterns grew more intense. Our engagements more demanding. And anger slowly increased, robbing me of comprehension outside of the driving need to win.

How many times had Del and I met in the circle, sparring? How many times had we stepped out again, not really knowing who was better, but inwardly claiming superiority?

Hadn't Del even done it aloud at the *kymri?*

It had never been decided. Now, maybe, it would be.

Time to end this farce.

She hung back, legs spread, flexed, always moving, at least a little, never stopping at all, never giving me time to judge. Beneath the silver bracers I knew her wrists were iron, yet prepared to paint with steel.

I needed my breath to fight, but words can be just as effective. And as few as possible, designed to cut her open and destroy her personal song.

I let my anger flow into my tone. "Recognize this?" I asked. "Listen. See if you do."

Across the circle, she opened her mouth as if to sing, but I beat her to it.

"The *an-ishtoya* who wants freedom—"

Del didn't so much as flick an eyelash.

"—the *an-ishtoya* who needs to blood a *jivatma*—"

Still no response. Her expression, as always, was fierce. But this time she meant it for me.

"—who will do whatever is required—"

She darted in, tapped my blade, dodged back again.

Hoolies, I hate her speed. She leaves me in the dust.

"—to regain what was *lost*."

It got through. Something flickered in her eyes. I cut the wound deeper yet. "Sound familiar, Del? Are you seeing yourself?"

Clearly, she did. I saw the startled shock in her eyes, and dawning acknowledgment.

One final blow: "I'm taking you out of here. To the South once I'm done, where I can have it all: *jivatma*, power, Delilah." I paused for effect. "Once I've put you in your place."

It worked. She was furious, *too* furious for total control. Instantly I followed up my advantage, meaning to shatter her guard.

Trouble was, I tripped on ragged turf. It was only a slight misstep, but more than enough for her. The advantage became Del's.

She broke through, thrust, cut into me, just above the wide belt. I felt the brief tickle of cold steel separate fabric and flesh, sliding through both with ease, then catch briefly on a rib, rub by, cut deeper, pricking viscera. There was no pain at all, consumed by shock and ice, and then the cold ran through my bones and ate into every muscle.

I lunged backward, running myself off the blade. The wound itself wasn't painful, too numb to interfere, but the storm was inside my body. The blood I bled was ice.

"Yield!" she shouted. *"Yield!"* Shock and residual anger made her tone strident.

I wanted to. But I couldn't. Something was in me, in my *sword;*

something crept into blood and bones and sinew and the new, bright steel. Something that spoke of need. That spoke of ways to win. That sang of ways to *blood*—

"I'll make you," she gasped. "Somehow—" And she was coming at me, *at* me, breaking through my weakened guard and showing me three feet of deadly *jivatma*. "Yield!" she cried again.

My sword was screaming for blood.

You may be forced, she had said, *and the results could be disastrous.*

I shouted aloud, denying it. Trying to *control* it; knowing I could not. The sword was far too powerful.

So this is what it is, I thought fleetingly, to have a *jivatma*, even unnamed: power, strength, an incredible dedication.

Like Del's.

Hoolies, what would it be if I blooded it?

And that was precisely what it wanted.

Wild magic, Kem had warned. Unsung, unkeyed, unharnessed. And now I paid the price.

But not as dearly as Del.

Chapter 44

He stood at the edge of the overlook. Below him lay Staal-Kithra, lumpy with barrows, dolmens and passage graves; the glass-black lake flanked white on white, stark peaks against bleak sky. And Staal-Ysta herself, in the center, floating black on black on winter water, with rack upon rack of bare-branched trees punching wounds in the sky, like swords.

He turned, and the bright, rich cloak unfurled; furled back again to lap at the heels of his boots. He strode free, to the bay stud who waited, and patted him, rubbing the dew-speckled muzzle buried in twin spumes of steam.

And then strode away again, carrying the sword.

He took it to the edge, unsheathed and naked of runes, and set the tip to the ground, and thrust, driving it into turf, into soil, into the heart of the North.

Silently, he knelt. Slowly, stiffly, on one knee only, the right; left foot planted flat, holding himself rigidly upright. He reached out both large hands and trapped the hilt in them. The wind whipped back his cloak.

It was a cold, bitter wind, thrusting fingers into bronze-brown, too-long hair; scraping nails along the right cheek laid bare by sandtiger claws that showed even through the beard, cutting four curving lines from cheekbone to jaw.

An icy, vengeful wind, bordering on banshee.

The hilt, as always, was warm. The twisted, silk-skinned hilt, promising him power.

He listened, holding the sword. And he heard the song, if only faintly. Little more than an echo thrumming on memory. And then he knew: Cantéada. Their song was in his head.

Their song was in his sword. He had only to learn how to sing it.

The stud, bored, snorted. It roused him; he rose, pulled the sword from the ground, then stopped very short.

Runes ran down the blade. Clean, newborn runes. Telling him a name.

The color was gone from his face. He stared at the runeworked blade, gripping the twisted hilt. And then looked down at Staal-Kithra, Place of Spirits; the place of deaths and births. Mouthing the newborn name.

"Samiel," he said. "Now we're even, Del."

Carefully, he cleaned the blade on his cloak, then took it back to its sheath and harness, hanging on the saddle. He put it away, sliding it home, hiding the glory of sky-born steel.

He swung up, suppressing a groan; hooked the cloak out of the way so it wouldn't foul on gear or harness, or irritate the stud, who required no excuses.

Once more, only once, he glanced back. Then gathered reins and spun the stud, digging divots in turf and dirt. Destroying all the pawprints.

"Come on, old man," he said. "We've got the hounds of hoolies to hunt . . . and now a sword to catch them."

He turned the stud loose and went east.

Author's Note

What Comes Next?

I have, in my professional life, written books that were "easy," and books that were difficult—though of course "easy" is a matter of degree and context. Though at eight volumes the Cheysuli series was a lengthy task, it also offered escape from college classes (I was an adult student), and part-time work. I lost myself in an "alternate universe," if you will, and, being an organic writer, discovered much of the tales as I went along, just as readers did. Every free moment I had was spent creating the worlds, the characters, and stories of the Cheysuli. But in the midst of writing the series, *Sword-Dancer* appeared in my head. It arrived completely out of the blue one summer evening and more or less wrote itself in a burst of white-hot creative energy; it was what many authors call an "attack book." *Sword-Dancer* came pouring out of my typewriter over two weeks of twelve- to fifteen-hour days. Tiger had a story to tell, and I was his chosen scribe. I had so much fun I went on to write five more novels featuring Tiger and Del.

Then there was *The Golden Key*, a collaboration with Melanie Rawn and Kate Elliott. I said from the beginning that no one of us could have written that massive, complex novel. All of our brainstorming on world, customs, characters and plotlines was interconnected, and we critiqued one another's work along the way. We each of us was responsible for writing our specific sections (me, Part I; Melanie, Part II; and Kate, Part III), but they were born out of many three-party discussions via phone, e-mail, and fax machine. *The Golden Key* was a huge undertaking and an immensely challenging task, but it was also a creative "high" and made all of us better writers. To this day I am extremely proud of that novel.

Authors always have ideas bubbling away on the back-burners of the brain, and eventually there came a day when I told my agent I had an idea for an entirely new fantasy universe unrelated to the Cheysuli and *Sword-Dancer* series. By saying it, I made it real. Now I had to write it. And so in fits and starts and bumps along the way, I embarked on a new fantasy journey.

It was the first brand-new universe and cast of characters that I, as a solo author, had created since 1983, when I wrote *Sword-Dancer*. *Karavans* wasn't another volume in an existing series with people, places, and plots already in place, but a wholly new undertaking. And I knew I wasn't the same person, much less the same writer, that I was in the early to mid-'80s when the Cheysuli and *Sword-Dancer* series debuted. *Karavans* became, in fact, the most challenging fantasy novel I'd ever written. Afterall, in keeping with traditions of the time, the first several Cheysuli novels and *Sword-Dancer* arrived on the bookshelves without fanfare. I was a completely unknown author. But *Karavans* would be published *with* fanfare. I knew readers would have expectations. And I had expectations about those expectations. (Never let it be said that authors don't speculate about what their fans will think!)

I've been most fortunate to have two fantasy series, both markedly different from one another (and both published by the same publishing house), become very successful. It allowed me the luxury, with DAW's blessing, of alternating between worlds, writing styles, and plots and characters instead of living in the same universe day in and day out, something that can make an author— and her work—go quite stale.

Now, with *Karavans*, I begin all over again once more, some twenty-eight years after I began writing about a race of shapechangers and their magical animals, and twenty-six since Del walked through the door of a Southron cantina and into Tiger's heart. With those experiences behind me, I have high hopes for the new world and an eclectic slew of characters.

In the aftermath of a bitter, brutal war waged by ruthless neighboring warlord, many residents of Sancorra Province have turned refugee, fleeing the destruction of farmsteads and settlements to begin new lives in another province. But it is very late in the karavan season with the rains due any day, and the roads are made even more dangerous by opportunistic bandits and the warlord's vicious armies and patrols. Also threatening the safety of the refugees is the land called Alisanos, a living hell-on-earth that changes location at will, swallowing everything—and every*one*—in its path. Infamous as the dwelling place of demons, devils, gods and demi-gods and countless other horrors, Alisanos wreaks tragedy on entire villages or single individuals. Few humans, once taken into Alisanos, ever escape—and those who do have been terribly altered in mind and body by the poisonous magic of Alisanos, fated to be shunned by the human race they were once a part of.

I invite readers to join karavan guide Rhuan and his cousin, Brodhi, a courier, both born of a legendary race called the Shoia; Ilona, the karavan diviner who reads in the hands of others the dangers and griefs facing them, but cannot read her own; demons Darmuth and Ferize, hiding true forms and secrets; and a farmstead family desperate to reach Atalanda Province before the new baby is born, each on a perilous journey along dangerous roads much too close to the living evil threatening them all as Alisanos prepares to go active.

Karavans *will be published in hardcover by DAW Books in April 2006.*

Watch out for

KARAVANS

Jennifer Roberson's first all-new fantasy universe in twenty years

Coming in hardcover in April 2006

Read on for a special introduction to the series: the short story that debuted the world of *Karavans*

Ending and Beginning

*F*our had died. Killed ruthlessly. Uselessly. Three, because they were intended as examples to the others. The fourth, merely because he was alone, and Sancorran. The people of Sancorra province had become fair game for the brutal patrols of Hecari soldiers, men dispatched to ensure the Sancorran insurrection was thoroughly put down.

Insurrection. Ilona wished to spit. She believed it a word of far less weight than war, an insufficiency in describing the bitter realities now reshaping the province. *War* was a hard, harsh word, carrying a multiplicity of meanings. Such as death.

Four people, dead. Any one of them might have been her, had fate proved frivolous. She was a hand-reader, a diviner, a woman others sought to give them their fortunes, to tell their futures; and yet even she, remarkably gifted, had learned that fate was inseparably intertwined with caprice. She could read a hand with that hand in front of her, seeing futures, interpreting the fragments for such folk as lacked the gift. But it was also possible fate might alter its path, the track she had parsed as leading to a specific future. Ilona had not seen any such thing as her death at the hands of a Hecari patrol, but it had been possible.

Instead, she had lived. Three strangers, leaving behind a bitter past to begin a sweeter future, had not. And a man with whom she had shared a bed in warmth and affection, if not wild passion, now rode blanket-wrapped in the back of the karavan-master's wagon, cold in place of warm.

The karavan, last of the season under Jorda, her employer, straggled to the edges of the nameless settlement just after sundown. Exhausted from the lengthy journey as well as its tragedies, Ilona climbed down from her wagon, staggered forward, and began to unhitch the team. The horses, too, were tired; the karavan had withstood harrying attacks by Sancorran refugees turned bandits, had given up coin and needed supplies as "road tax" to three different sets of Hecari patrols until the fourth, the final, took payment in blood when told there was no money left with which to pay. When the third patrol had exacted the "tax," Ilona wondered if the karavan-master would suggest to the Hecari soldiers that they might do better to go after the bandits rather than harassing innocent Sancorrans fleeing the aftermath of war. But Jorda had merely clamped his red-bearded jaw closed and paid up. It did not do to suggest anything to the victorious enemy; Ilona had heard tales that they killed anyone who complained, were they not paid the "tax."

Ilona saw it for herself when the fourth patrol arrived.

Her hands went through the motions of unhitching without direction from her mind, still picturing the journey. Poor Sancorra, overrun by the foreigners called Hecari, led by a fearsome warlord, was being steadily stripped of her wealth just as the citizens were being stripped of their holdings. Women were widowed, children left fatherless, farmsteads burned, livestock rounded up and driven to Hecari encampments to feed the enemy soldiers. Karavans that did not originate in Sancorra were allowed passage through the province so long as their masters could prove they came from other provinces—and paid tribute—but that passage was nonetheless a true challenge. Jorda's two scouts early on came across the remains of several karavans that the master knew to be led by foreigners like himself; the Hecari apparently were more than capable of killing anyone they deemed Sancorran refugees, even if they manifestly were not. It was a simple matter to declare anyone an enemy of their warlord.

Ilona was not Sancorran. Neither was Jorda, nor one of the scouts. But the other guide, Tansit, was. And now his body lay in the back of a wagon, waiting for the rites that would send his spirit to the Land of the Dead.

Wearily Ilona finished unhitching the team, pulling harness from the sweat-slicked horses. Pungent, foamy lather dripped from flanks and shoulders. She swapped out headstalls for halters, then led the team along the line of wagons to Janqueril, the horse-master. The aging, balding man and his apprentices would tend the teams while everyone else made their way into the tent-city settlement, looking for release from the tension of the trip.

And, she knew, to find other diviners who might tell a different tale of the future they faced tomorrow, on the edge of unknown lands.

Ilona delivered the horses, thanked Janqueril, then pushed a fractious mass of curling dark hair out of her face. Jorda kept three diviners in his employ, to make sure his karavans got safely to their destinations and to serve any of his clients, but Tansit had always come to her. He said he trusted her to be truthful with him. Hand-readers, though not uncommon, were not native to Sancorra, and Tansit, like others, viewed her readings as more positive than those given by Jorda's other two diviners. Ilona didn't know if that were true; only that she always told her clients the good and the bad, rather than shifting the emphasis wholly to good.

She had seen danger in Tansit's callused hand. That, she had told him. And he had laughed, said the only danger facing him were the vermin holes in the prairie, waiting to trap his horse and take him down as well.

And so a vermin hole *had* trapped his horse, snapping a leg, and Tansit, walking back to the karavan well behind him, was found by the Hecari patrol that paused long enough to kill him, then continue on to richer pickings. By the time the karavan reached the scout, his features were unrecognizable; Ilona knew him by his clothing and the color of his blood-matted hair.

So Tansit had told his own fortune without her assistance, and Ilona lost a man whom she had not truly loved, but liked. Well enough to share his bed when the loneliness of her life sent her to it. Men were attracted to her, but wary of her gift. Few were willing to sleep with a woman who could tell a lover the day of his death.

At the end of journeys, Ilona's habit was to build a fire, lay a rug, set up a table, cushions, and candles, then wait quietly for custom. At the end of a journey clients wished to consult diviners for advice concerning the future in a new place. But this night, at the end of this journey, Ilona forbore. She stood at the back of her wagon, clutching one of the blue-painted spoke wheels, and stared sightlessly into the sunset.

Some little while later, a hand came down upon her shoulder. Large, wide, callused, with spatulate fingers and oft-bruised or broken nails. She smelled the musky astringency of a hard-working man in need of a bath; heard the inhaled, heavy breath; sensed, even without reading that hand, his sorrow and compassion.

"He was a good man," Jorda said.

Ilona nodded jerkily.

"We will hold the rites at dawn."

She nodded again.

"Will you wish to speak?"

She turned. Looked into his face, the broad, bearded, seamed face of the man who employed her, who was himself employed several times a season to lead karavans across the wide plains of Sancorra to the edge of other provinces, where other karavans and their masters took up the task. Jorda could be a hard man, but he was also a good man. In his green eyes she saw grief that he had lost an employee, a valued guide, but also a friend. Tansit had scouted for Jorda more years than she could count. More, certainly, than she had known either of them.

"Yes, of course," she told him.

Jorda nodded, seeking something in her eyes. But Ilona was expert at hiding her feelings. Such things, if uncontrolled, could color the readings, and she had learned long before to mask emotions. "I thank you," the master said. "It would please Tansit."

She thought a brace of tall tankards of foamy ale would please Tansit more. But words would have to do. Words for the dead.

Abruptly she said, "I have to go."

Jorda's ruddy brows ran together. "Alone? Into this place? It's but a scattering of tents, Ilona, not a true settlement. You would do better to come with me, and a few of the others. After what happened on the road, it would be safer."

Safety was not what she craved. Neither was danger, and certainly not death, but she yearned to be elsewhere than with Jorda and the others this night. How better to pay tribute to Tansit than to drink a brace of tall tankards of foamy ale in his place?

Ilona forced a smile. "I'm going to Mikal's wine-tent. He knows me. I'll be safe enough there."

Jorda's face cleared. "So you will. But ask someone to walk you back to your wagon later."

Ilona arched her brows. "It's not so often I must *ask* such a thing, Jorda! Usually they beg to do that duty."

He understood the tone, and the intent. He relaxed fractionally, then presented her with a brief flash of teeth mostly obscured by his curling beard. "Forgive me! I do know better." The grin faded. "I think many of us will buy Tansit ale tonight."

She nodded as the big man turned and faded back into the twilight, returning to such duties as were his at the end of a journey. Which left her duty to Tansit.

Ilona leaned inside her wagon and caught up a deep-dyed, blue-black shawl, swung it around her shoulders, and walked through the ankle-deep dust into the tiny tent-city.

She had seen, in her life, many deaths. It rode the hands of all humans, though few could read it, and fewer still could interpret the conflicting information. Ilona had never *not* been able to see, to read, to interpret; when her family had come to comprehend that such a gift would rule her life and thus their own, they had turned her out. She had been all of twelve summers, shocked by their actions because she had not seen it in her own hand; had she read theirs, she might have understood earlier what lay in store. In the fifteen years since they had turned out their oldest daughter, Ilona had learned to trust no one but herself—though she was given to understand that some people, such as Jorda, were less likely to send a diviner on her way if she could serve their interests. All karavans required diviners if they were to be truly successful; clients undertaking journeys went nowhere without consulting any number of diviners of all persuasions, and a karavan offering readings along the way, rather than depending on itinerant diviners drifting from settlement to settlement, stood to attract more custom. Jorda was no fool; he hired Branca and Melior, and in time he hired her.

The night was cool. Ilona tightened her shawl and ducked her head against the errant breeze teasing at her face. Mikal's wine-tent stood nearly in the center of the cluster of tents that spread like vermin across the plain near the river. A year before there had been half as many; next year, she did not doubt, the population would increase yet again. Sancorra province was in utter disarray, thanks to the depredations of the Hecari; few would wish to stay, who had the means to depart. It would provide Jorda with work as well as his hired diviners. But she wished war were not the reason.

Mikal's wine-tent was one of many, but he had arrived early when the settlement had first sprung up, a place near sweet water and good grazing, and not far from the border of the neighboring province. It was a good place for karavans to halt overnight, and within weeks it had become more than merely that. Now merchants put up tents, set down roots, and served a populace that shifted shape nightly, trading familiar faces for those of strangers. Mikal's face was one of the most familiar, and his tent a welcome distraction from the duties of the road.

Ilona took the path she knew best through the winding skeins of tracks and paused only briefly in the spill of light from the tied-back door flap of Mikal's wine-tent. She smelled the familiar odors of ale and wine, the tang of urine from men who sought relief rather too close to the tent, the thick fug of male bodies far more interested in liquor than wash water. Only rarely did women frequent Mikal's wine-tent; the female couriers, who were toughened by experience on the province roads and thus able to deal with anything, and such women as herself: unavailable for hire, but seeking the solace found in liquor-laced camaraderie. Ilona had learned early on to appreciate ale and wine, and the value of the company of others no more rooted than she was. Tansit had always spent his coin at Mikal's. Tonight, she would spend hers in Tansit's name.

Ilona entered, pushing the shawl back from her head and shoulders. As always, conversation paused as her presence was noted; then Mikal called out a cheery welcome, as did two or three others who knew her. It was enough to warn off any man who might wish to proposition her, establishing her right to remain un-molested. This night, she appreciated it more than usual.

She sought and found a small table near a back corner, arrang-ing skirts deftly as she settled upon a stool. Within a matter of mo-ments Mikal arrived, bearing a guttering candle in a pierced-tin lantern. He set it down upon the table, then waited.

Ilona drew in a breath. "Ale," she said, relieved when her voice didn't waver. "Two tankards, if it please you. Your best."

"Tansit?" he asked in his deep, slow voice.

It was not a question regarding a man's death, but his antici-pated arrival. Ilona discovered she could not, as yet, speak of the former, and thus relied upon the latter. She nodded confirmation, meeting his dark blue eyes without hesitation. Mikal nodded also, then took his bulk away to tend the order.

She found herself plaiting the fringes of her shawl, over and over again. Irritated, Ilona forcibly stopped herself from continuing the nervous habit. When Mikal brought the tankards, she lifted her own in both hands, downed several generous swallows, then care-fully fingered away the foam left to linger upon her upper lip. Two tankards upon the table. One: her own. The other was Tansit's. When done with her ale, she would leave coin enough for two tankards, but one would remain untouched. And then the truth would be known. The tale spread. But she would be required to say nothing, to no one.

Ah, but he had been a good man. She had not wished to

wed him, though he had asked; she had not expected to bury him either.

At dawn, she would attend the rites. Would speak of his life, and of his death.

Tansit had never been one known for his attention to time. But he was not a man given to passing up ale when it was waiting. Ilona drank down her tankard slowly and deliberately, avoiding the glances, the stares, and knew well enough when whispers began of Tansit's tardiness in joining her.

There were two explanations: they had quarreled, or one of them was dead. But their quarrels never accompanied them into a wine-tent.

She drank her ale, clearly not dead, while Tansit's tankard remained undrunk. Those who were not strangers understood. At tables other than hers, in the sudden, sharp silence of comprehension, fresh tankards were ordered. Were left untouched. Tribute to the man so many of them had known.

Tansit would have appreciated how many tankards were ordered. Though he also would have claimed it a waste of good ale that no one drank.

Ilona smiled, imagining his words. Seeing his expression.

She swallowed the last of her ale and rose, thinking ahead to the bed in her wagon. But then a body blocked her way, altering the fall of smoky light, and she looked into the face of a stranger.

In the ocherous illumination of Mikal's lantern, his face was ruddy-gold. "I'm told the guide is dead."

A stranger indeed, to speak so plainly to the woman who had shared the dead man's bed.

He seemed to realize it. To regret it. A grimace briefly twisted his mouth. "Forgive me. But I am badly in need of work."

Ilona gathered the folds of her shawl even as she gathered patience. "The season is ended. And I am not the one to whom you should apply. Jorda is the karavan-master."

"I'm told he is the best."

"Jorda is—Jorda." She settled the shawl over the crown of her head, shrouding untamed ringlets. "Excuse me."

He turned only slightly, giving way. "Will you speak to him for me?"

Ilona paused, then swung back. "Why? I know nothing of you."

His smile was charming, his gesture self-deprecating. "Of course. But I could acquaint you."

A foreigner, she saw. Not Sancorran, but neither was he Hercari. In candlelight his hair was a dark, oiled copper, bound back in a multiplicity of braids. She saw the glint of beads in those braids, gold and silver; heard the faint chime and clatter of ornamentation. He wore leather tunic and breeches, and from the outer seams of sleeves and leggings dangled shell- and bead-weighted fringe. Indeed, a stranger, to wear what others, in time of war, might construe as wealth.

"No need to waste your voice," she said. "Let me see your hand."

It startled him. Arched brows rose. "My hand?"

She matched his expression. "Did they not also tell you what I am?"

"The dead guide's woman."

The pain was abrupt and sharp, then faded as quickly as it had come. *The dead guide's woman.* True, that. But much more. And it might be enough to buy her release from a stranger. "Diviner," she said. "There is no need to tell me anything of yourself, when I can read it in your hand."

She sensed startlement and withdrawal, despite that the stranger remained before her, very still. His eyes were dark in the frenzied play of guttering shadows. The hand she could see, loose at his side, abruptly closed. Sealed itself against her. Refusal. Denial. Self-preservation.

"It is a requirement," she told him, "of anyone who wishes to hire on with Jorda."

His face tightened. Something flickered deep in his eyes. She thought she saw a hint of red.

"You'll understand," Ilona hid amusement behind a businesslike tone, "that Jorda must be careful. He can't afford to hire just anyone. His clients trust him to guard their safety. How is he to know what a stranger intends?"

"Rhuan," he said abruptly.

She heard it otherwise: *Ruin.* "Oh?"

"A stranger who gives his name is no longer a stranger."

"A stranger who brings ruination is an enemy."

"Ah." His grin was swift. He repeated his name more slowly, making clear what it was, and she heard the faint undertone of an accent.

She echoed it. "Rhuan."

"I need the work."

Ilona eyed him. Tall, but not a giant. Much of his strength, she thought, resided beneath his clothing, coiled quietly away. Not old, not young, but somewhere in the middle, indistinguishable. Oddly alien in the light of a dozen lanterns, for all his smooth features were arranged in a manner women undoubtedly found pleasing. On another night, *she* might; but Tansit was newly dead, and this stranger—Rhuan—kept her from her wagon, where she might grieve in private.

"Have you guided before?"

"Not here. Elsewhere."

"It is a requirement that you know the land."

"I do know it."

"Here?"

"Sancorra. I know it." He lifted one shoulder in an eloquent shrug. "On a known road, guiding is less a requirement than protection. That, I can do very well."

Something about him suggested it was less a boast than the simple truth.

"And does anyone know *you?*"

He turned slightly, glancing toward the plank set upon barrels where Mikal held sovereignty, and she saw Mikal watching them.

She saw also the slight lifting of big shoulders, a smoothing of his features into a noncommittal expression. Mikal told her silently there was nothing of the stranger he knew that meant danger, but nothing much else either.

"The season is ended," Ilona repeated. "Speak to Jorda of the next one, if you wish, but there is no work for you now."

"In the midst of war," Rhuan said, "I believe there is. Others will wish to leave. Your master would do better to extend the season."

Jorda had considered it, she knew. Tansit had spoken of it. And if the master did extend the season, he would require a second guide. Less for guiding than for protection, with Hecari patrols harrying the roads.

Four people, dead.

Ilona glanced briefly at the undrunk tankard. "Apply to Jorda," she said. "It's not for me to say." Something perverse within her flared into life, wanting to wound the man before her who was so vital and alive, when another was not. "But he *will* require you to be read. It needn't be me."

His voice chilled. "Most diviners are charlatans."

Indeed, he was a stranger; no true-born Sancorran would speak so baldly. "Some," she agreed. "There are always those who prey upon the weak of mind. But there are also those who practice an honest art."

"You?"

Ilona affected a shrug every bit as casual as his had been. "Allow me your hand, and then you'll know, won't you?"

Once again he clenched it. "No."

"Then you had best look elsewhere for employment." She had learned to use her body and used it now, sliding past him before he might block her way again. She sensed the stirring in his limbs, the desire to reach out to her, to stop her; sensed also when he decided to let her go.

It began not far from Mikal's wine-tent. Ilona had heard its like before and recognized at once what was happening. The grunt of a man taken unawares, the bitten-off inhalation, the repressed blurt of pain and shock; and the hard, tense breathing of the assailants. Such attacks were not unknown in settlements such as this, composed of strangers desperate to escape the depredations of the

Hecari. Desperate enough, some of them, to don the brutality of the enemy and wield its weapon.

Ilona stepped more deeply into shadow. She was a woman, and alone. If she interfered, she invited retribution. Jorda had told her to ask for escort on the way to the wagons. In her haste to escape the stranger in Mikal's tent, she had dismissed it from her mind.

Safety lay in secrecy. But Tansit was dead, and at dawn she would attend his rites and say the words. If she did nothing, would another woman grieve? Would another woman speak the words of the rite meant to carry the spirit to the Land of the Dead?

Then she was running toward the noise. "Stop! *Stop!*"

Movement. Men. Bodies. Ilona saw shapes break apart; saw a body fall. Heard the curses meant for her. But she was there, telling them to stop, and for a wonder they did.

And then she realized, as they faded into darkness, that she had thought too long and arrived too late. His wealth was untouched, the beading in the braids and fringe, but his life was taken. She saw the blood staining his throat, the knife standing up from his ribs. Garotte to make him helpless, knife to kill him.

He lay sprawled beneath the stars, limbs awry, eyes open and empty, the comely features slack.

She had seen death before. She recognized his.

Too late. Too late.

She should go fetch Mikal. There had been some talk of establishing a Watch, a group of men to walk the paths and keep what peace there was. Ilona didn't know if a Watch yet existed; but Mikal would come, would help her tend the dead.

A stranger in Sancorra. What rites were his?

Shaking, Ilona knelt. She did not go to fetch Mikal. Instead she sat beside a man whose name she barely knew, whose hand she hadn't read, and grieved for them both. For them all. For the men, young and old, dead in the war.

In the *insurrection*.

But there was yet a way. She had the gift. Beside him, Ilona gathered up one slack hand. His future had ended, but there was yet a past. It faded already, she knew, as the warmth of the body cooled, but if she practiced the art before he was cold, she would learn what she needed to know. And then he also would have the proper rites. She would make certain of it.

Indeed, the hand cooled. Before morning the fingers would stiffen, even as Tansit's had. The spirit, denied a living body, would attenuate, then fade.

There was little light, save for the muddy glow of lanterns within a hundred tents. Ilona would be able to see nothing of the flesh, but she had no need. Instead, she lay her fingers gently upon his palm and closed her eyes, tracing the pathways there, the lines of his life.

Maelstrom.

Gasping, Ilona fell back. His hand slid from hers. Beneath it, beneath the touch of his flesh, the fabric of her skirt took flame.

She beat it with her own hands, then clutched at and heaped powdery earth upon it. The flame quenched itself, the thread of smoke dissipated. But even as it did so, as she realized the fabric was whole, movement startled her.

The stranger's hand, that she had grasped to read, closed around the knife standing up from his ribs. She heard a sharply in-drawn breath, and something like a curse, and the faint clattered chime of the beads in his braids. He raised himself up on one elbow and stared at her.

This time, she heard the curse clearly. Recognized the grimace. Knew what he would say: *I wasn't truly dead.*

But he was. Had been.

He pulled the knife from his ribs, inspected the blade a moment, then tossed it aside with an expression of distaste. Ilona's hands, no longer occupied with putting out the flame that had come from his flesh, folded themselves against her skirts. She waited.

He saw her watching him. Assessed her expression. Tried the explanation she anticipated. "I wasn't—"

"You were."

He opened his mouth to try again. Thought better of it. Looked at her hands folded into fabric. "Are you hurt?"

"No. Are *you?*"

His smile was faint. "No."

She touched her own throat. "You're bleeding."

He sat up. Ignored both the slice encircling his neck and the wound in his ribs. His eyes on her were calm, too calm. She saw an odd serenity there, and rueful acceptance that she had seen what, obviously, he wished she hadn't seen.

"I'm Shoia," he said.

No more than that. No more was necessary.

"Those are stories," Ilona told him. "Legends."

He seemed equally amused as he was resigned. "Rooted in truth."

Skepticism showed. "A living Shoia?"

"Now," he agreed, irony in his tone. "A moment ago, dead. But you know that."

"I touched your hand, and it took fire."

His face closed up. Sealed itself against her. His mouth was a grim, unrelenting line.

"Is that a Shoia trait, to burn the flesh a diviner might otherwise read?"

The mouth parted. "It's not for you to do."

Ilona let her own measure of irony seep into her tone. "And well warded, apparently."

"They wanted my bones," he said. "It's happened before."

She understood at once. "Practitioners of the Kantica." Who burned bones for the auguries found in ash and grit. Legend held Shoia bones told truer, clearer futures than anything else. But no one she knew of used *actual* Shoia bones.

He knew what she was thinking. "There are a few of us left," he told her. "But we keep it to ourselves. We would prefer to keep our bones clothed in flesh."

"But I have heard no one murders a Shoia. That anyone foolish enough to do so inherits damnation."

"No one *knowingly* murders a Shoia," he clarified. "But as we apparently are creatures of legend, who would believe I am?"

Nor did it matter. Dead was dead, damnation or no. "These

men intended to haul you out to the anthills," Ilona said. Where the flesh would be stripped away, and the bones collected for sale to Kantic diviners. "They couldn't know you are Shoia, could they?"

He gathered braids fallen forward and swept them back. "I doubt it. But it doesn't matter. A charlatan would buy the bones and *claim* them Shoia, thus charging even more for the divinations. Clearer visions, you see."

She did see. There were indeed charlatans, false diviners who victimized the vulnerable and gullible. How better to attract trade than to boast of Shoia bones?

"Are you?" she asked. "Truly?"

Something flickered in his eyes. Flickered red. His voice hardened. "You looked into my hand."

And had seen nothing of his past nor his future save *maelstrom*.

"Madness," she said, not knowing she spoke aloud.

His smile was bitter.

Ilona looked into his eyes as she had looked into his hand. "Are you truly a guide?"

The bitterness faded. "I can be many things. Guide is one of them."

Oddly, it amused her to say it. "Dead man?"

He matched her irony. "That, too. But I would prefer not." He stood up then; somehow, he brought her up with him. She faced him there in the shadows beneath the stars. "It isn't infinite, the resurrection."

"No?"

"Seven times," he said. "The seventh is the true death."

"And how many times was this?"

The stranger showed all his fine white teeth in a wide smile. "That, we never tell."

"Ah." She understood. "Mystery is your salvation."

"Well, yes. Until the seventh time. And then we are as dead as anyone else. Bury us, burn us . . ." He shrugged. "It doesn't matter. Dead is dead. It simply comes more slowly."

Ilona shook out her skirts, shedding dust. "I know what I saw when I looked into your hand. But that was a shield, was it not? A ward against me."

"Against a true diviner, yes."

It startled her; she was accustomed to others accepting her word. "You didn't believe me?"

He said merely, "Charlatans abound."

"But you are safe from charlatans."

He stood still in the darkness and let her arrive at the conclusion.

"But not from me," she said.

"Shoia bones are worth coin to charlatans," he said. "A Kantic diviner could make his fortune by burning my bones. But a *true* Kantic diviner—"

"—could truly read your bones."

He smiled, wryly amused. "And therefore I am priceless."

Ilona considered it. "One would think you'd be more careful. Less easy to kill."

"I was distracted."

"By—?"

"You," he finished. "I came out to persuade you to take me to your master. To make the introduction."

"Ah, then *I* am being blamed for your death."

He grinned. "For this one, yes."

"And I suppose the only reparation I may pay is to introduce you to Jorda."

The grin flashed again. Were it not for the slice upon his neck and the blood staining his leather tunic, no one would suspect this man had been dead only moments before.

Ilona sighed, recalling Tansit. And his absence. "I suppose Jorda might have some use for a guide who can survive death multiple times."

"At least until the seventh," he observed dryly.

"If I read your hand, would I know how many you have left?"

He abruptly thrust both hands behind his back, looking mutinous, reminding her for all the world of a child hiding booty. Ilona laughed.

But she *had* read his hand, if only briefly. And seen in it conflagration.

Rhuan, he had said.

Ruin, she had echoed.

She wondered if she were right.